I0822290

IGNITION 2084

BY JORDAN HAMPTON

Copyright

The story and characters in this novel are purely fictitious and are entirely the fabrication of the author. Any resemblance of these characters to actual persons, living or dead, is purely coincidental. Certain long-standing institutions, agencies, and public offices are mentioned, but the characters and events involved are wholly imaginary.

theonlymrh33@gmail.com

www.authorjordanhampton.com

ISBN (Print): 979-8-9858346-0-4

ISBN (eBook): 979-8-9858346-1-1

Cover design by Jay Koala Photography and Jordan Hampton

Edited by Kenne Stu

Printed in the United States of America

Empress of the Moonlight

Black Woman,

Empress of the Moonlight,

It is your place to

Glow, to Flow,

To Slay, to Pray.

Do as you see fit when the mood strikes.

They judge what they don't understand--

And never will. The thrills you present

With the calm waving of your hand,

The chills you send down their spines

With your gentlest command

Terrifies them,

You, whose Nubian skin is to them a Thundercloud,

Whose dark eyes strike like lightning,

Whose love falls on hers like showers of fresh rain,

Whose words dance in the atmosphere like a gentle breeze.

You are a force of nature in an industrial world.

Authenticity amid preferred artificiality.

You are the *real*.

Black Woman,

Empress of the Moonlight,

Whose skin shines ebony as the sea at night,

You are the tide change,
The shift of the waves,
The salt in the air with the sweetness of a flower.
You shift and transform,
Give life and wisdom,
Strength, and knowledge,
And fury unparalleled.
Who are they to tame you?
Can a man still an earthquake,
Or quiet the fires of Nyiragongo
When they decide to spill their rage?
Life is yours, so live,
So thrive, so intoxicate
With the perfume of your existence,
Because it is your right,
And you are our privilege.

Mfalme, Kumkani, King

Mfalme, Kumkani, King,

Look at what you're worth

With the sounds of these words

And rise!

They gave you thuggery

When regality was your birthright,

Stole from you your name, your land, your pride,

But no longer.

By the changing of the tide

You rise,

Give your sons and daughters and wives

The vision of life in the form of a King.

Mfalme, Kumkani, King,

You are the payoff of every lash of the whip,

Every empty clip

Every slave that was stripped upon arrival,

Raining vengeance through your survival,

So thrive

In the face of every enemy that tries to break your will

But can't,

Never recant the victories you won

Before African blood began to run in your veins.

Mfalme, Kumkani, King,
Breathe beyond your limits--
No, break beyond your limits--
No, never set a limit for yourself,
Because limits have been set for us in the past
That were surpassed.
Loss and grief were our lot
Until our VICTORY we got up and fought for,
So fight, with everything that you have,
With everything that you are,
For everything that is you.
Mfalme, Kumkani, King,
Your world needs you most
So in the moment of despair don't vanish,
But rise,
To meet the challenge of change for the better,
To give your world an endless future,
To take back what was stolen from you
Before you were even born.
Without you, there is no direction
For the love you hope to protect,
So don't run, stand. Rage.
War for yours like a hurricane through the heavens.

Strike and flash and thunder!
Let them see the power of a King.
Mfalme, Kumkani, King,
You are defined by an irrelevant world,
Called a liar and thief, a thug, a slave
But I pray you realize that their marks have no place
On your flesh.
Rest,
In the knowledge that their fear
Gives you the adversity you needed to rise,
That their projections and misdirections
May be a loud dog barking with the voice of a train
But it's not you, for you are Mfalme, Kumkani, King.
Mfalme, Kumkani, King,
Mflame, Kumkani, King,
And what they call you doesn't matter.
What you are is whatever you deem.

Prologue

The conflict started in the year 2001, where a group of rogues attacked high priority targets in the old New York City and sent the world into a state of paranoia and mutual hostility. Even in that era of persistent (and predominantly pointless) struggle, there was a degree of peace in the day-to-day ongoings of the people. Fifteen years after that first attack and in the wake of hundreds more like it all around the country, the Dawn King rose. A master of the public eye, he preyed on the fears of the common folk to get elected to the highest office in the country, and with his questionable decisions and lack of morals he manipulated the masses to violently turn on each other.

All-out war swept the populace by 2021, and the democracy that put the tyrant in power was upended in the chaos. The United States of America, the country that this man once ruled, shattered to dust. The police and military turned on the people they swore to protect, and men and women were imprisoned for speaking out against their oppressive conditions. Riots broke out as outrage grew against a government that once boasted "for the people by the people," and before long, the first public execution in the post-Jim Crow era was broadcasted live to every home and business. Bombs were dropped in cities and neighborhoods that were suspected of opposition to the Tyrant and his forces. Martial law was enacted. Homes were raided in search of contraband or potential threats, and under the slightest suspicion of treason, parents were forced to watch as their children were brutally killed in front of them before ultimately dying themselves.

America was dead, and in its place arose a marred wasteland known as Prevalence. Here, a number of factions continue to engage in volatile confrontation. The major Territories of economic interest and tactical advantage were united under the leadership of the Tyrant's followers and reorganized as Kingdom Scarlet. The surrounding ghettos, dominated by the ruins of

American life, were occupied by the Yaiba Insurrection, the Kabuto Sanctuary, and the Yoroi Alliance, all born of the many marginalized peoples who refused to bow to the autocratic regime of the Kingdom.

****

July 19th, 2046

"Sir, we have confirmation that the terrorists are hiding out in the abandoned bunker of the old White House building," Major Simon spoke into his headset as his forces advanced on the structure. Left and right squads moved to flank the eastern and western wings of the ruins respectively with teams of three armed gunmen branching off from each one to cover the main exits. The frontmost unit, led by the Major himself, held their position. "Proceeding as instructed."

"Excellent," General Osmond responded with a smirk on his lips as he waited from the comforts of the command center. "They'll be trapped like rats, and I'm sure the King will reward us for snuffing out the biggest thorn in his side since the Charlottesville Massacre."

"Wait, Major Simon, sir, we're picking up three thermal signatures on our scanners," said Lieutenant Kluger of the right flank. His entire squad came to a halt, and through their visors they watched as the lifeless remnants of the old capitol building glowed with an almost impossible intensity.

"So what," General Osmond interjected before Simon could proceed with his orders to hold. "We've spent months compiling intel that led us to this moment, and years cutting through the Yaiba Insurrection's support systems. These cowering dogs have run out of places to hide and don't have enough men to save themselves, and you're freezing because the scanners in your visors are picking up a few heat sigs?"

“But sir—,” Kluger interjected, but was promptly cut off by his superior.

“But nothing,” yelled the General, which made the Major grimace as he cut his eyes at the headset in his ear. “We didn’t go through all of that trouble just so you and your little fears could compromise our operation. Proceed as instructed, Lieutenant, and that’s an order!” The comms channel went silent, and Major Simon couldn’t help but think of how much he hated it when alien commanders disregarded the concerns of his men.

He refocused on the field and switched on the heat vision function of his visor just in time to see three blazing humanoid figures emerge from the broken spaces in the White House walls. Each of the three took to a position that faced one of the three military units, and in their hands they held what looked like swords with heat readings much higher than what their natural bodies could produce.

“What are those?” Kluger asked through the communication channel.

“It doesn’t matter,” said the Major. “Snipers, you’re up.”

“Understood,” confirmed Sergeant Crawford from a rooftop across Executive Avenue. The spotter on his left passed him his readings, and based on the number of targets, distance, angle, and direction of the breeze, the sniper took aim at the first of his three targets. The scope of his Barrett M82 couldn’t pick up the heat signature of his targets, but the gear they wore was of special interest to him. He mused that he might pull it from the bodies after he took his shot.

****

They could hear the Scarlet Troopers from off in the distance as they approached the old presidential estate. After they had done everything they could to lay low and buy time, they were cornered yet again, but this time without the manpower or resources to carve out an escape. There were no guns on the Yaiba side of things, not since the old government confiscated the public's firearms and shut down manufacturers across the country. They reasoned that the availability of weaponry would enable rebellion. Little did they know that rebellion was coming either way, and the weapons they did have were beyond the expectations of the Scarlets and the Yaibas alike.

"Looks like it's time," came the voice of Director Ishikawa through the Yaiba headsets. "The field test of Dr. Masamune's Hanzo Gear is about to begin. Enable geo-sensors."

"Geo-sensors engaged," confirmed Carson Rouge, the team leader. "Awaiting further instructions." The director remained silent for a moment, and the footsteps of the Scarlet Troopers became a deafening induction of anxiety and apprehension. The comm came back to life.

"Three squads are advancing on your position from the north, east and west. A sniper team has taken up a post on the building to the east."

"Number of hostiles?"

"By my count, thirty-five," Ishikawa confirmed. "Prep kyoketsu-shoge for deployment, and power up repulsor boots."

"You know," interjected Dre Hamlin, the field tester poised at the northernmost wall of the White House, "if this stuff doesn't work, it'll be the end of the Yaiba Insurrection."

"We can't afford to think like that, Rairyu," replied the third member of their makeshift team, Lukas Bautista. Dre chuckled. It truly baffled him how Bautista could sound so optimistic when certain death was on its way to meet them. "There's always a chance, just as long as we—"

"What, believe in the heart of the—" Dre started to joke, but was cut off by a stern faux cough from the Director. "Apologies, Director. Awaiting your orders, sir."

"Masks up," Ishikawa commanded, "initiate heating sequence and move into position."

"Acknowledged," said Carson, who then turned his attention to his two teammates. "Rairyu, there's an addendum to your part of the mission. The sniper cell has eyes on our intended locations and is perched on a rooftop across Executive Avenue."

"You want me to find my way up to him and take him out before he has a chance to put one between your eyes, right," Dre supposed.

"It'd be a huge help, brotha," Lukas whimsically answered, already crouched behind the front door to the north side.

"Sure," Dre said with a sigh as he exited through a hole in the east side of the White House wall. "You know, I'm not sure how I like being teamed up with you guys. It seems like I'm already doing all the heavy lifting."

"Just make sure that you don't get shot yourself," Carson cracked back as he took to the west.

"Enough with the chatter," the Director ordered. "Geo-sensors are showing that the enemy has stopped. Seems like they picked up the abnormal heat signatures. Time to engage. Move into the open." The three field agents held for a moment and listened for the oncoming footsteps of the enemy, but just as their superior had said, the Scarlet Troopers held their positions.

"I guess we'll have to take the fight to them," Lukas optimistically chimed.

"Oh joy," Dre uttered with dripping sarcasm.

"From here on out I'll be directing each of you. This is gonna be tough for all of us, so you'll have to listen for my cues and follow my instructions to the letter." Ishikawa's voice gave his subordinates no room for question or comment. They all merely watched their enemies through the cracks in their sections of the wall. "Rairyu, geo-sensors are picking up minimal pulses from the treasury building to your right. The sniper team is preparing to engage. Make your way towards Executive Ave and deploy the kyoketsu-shoge to increase mobility. Boost that and your speed with short bursts from your repulsors and change directions as often as you can. The eastern squad is sure to follow you since they couldn't close you in before you noticed."

At the Director's orders, Dre made his move. He started towards the eleven troops of the eastern flank, but just before they could turn their weapons on him, he launched the bladed chains on the sleeves of his cloak at the ground. He vaulted into the air and flipped so that his feet pointed towards the west. As the troops below him took aim, Rairyu's repulsors came to life and blasted him at a diagonal towards the treasury building.

****

"What are they," asked the sniper as he did his best to track the movements of the target closest to him. His spotter called out a plethora of positions to him, but none of them lasted. The moment the sniper committed to any one placement of his weapon, his adversary dodged in seemingly impossible fashion. He fired a couple of shots, but all he managed to hit were the troops in his own platoon below. Now only six of the eleven eastern squad members remained, and this oddity of a warrior gradually advanced on his position.

"Woohoo!" The shout of his overly whimsical adversary was almost as humorous as it was aggravating. The sniper fired again, this time with the assurance that he'd nailed his opponent with that one bullet, but then the unexpected happened. The rogue whipped the sword in his hand in a diagonal motion, and the bullet melted before it ever made contact. What was worse, the rounds that should have at least found their way through his enemy's flesh merely bounced off the cloak and mask that captured his attention mere moments ago.

"Incoming," cried the spotter as he abandoned his rangefinder and sprinted for the other side of the rooftop. The sniper followed suit, and together they watched as the masked assailant drove the blade at the end of his chain clean through the sniper's Barrett. The chain pulled his body to the rooftop, and the Insurrectionist landed in a crouched position with his sword held off to the side. The sniper eyed it as he took a step back. It was a smoldering orange, as if the man had snatched it fresh from a forge before entering the fray, but it was unlike any blade he'd ever seen before. It was round, save for the tip, and from what the sniper could tell, the hilt was curved almost in the same fashion as an old pistol from the 1800s.

"Looks like you terrorists have come a long way," said the shooter, "but do you really believe that three people with some fancy toys are enough to take down a group of thirty-five trained soldiers?"

"Terrorists, he says," the assailant scoffed with a humored glance at the spotter. "You know, we weren't the ones who savagely beat the weak into submission and manipulated their fear to gain power."

"No, you're just doing everything you can to disrupt the peace of the Scarlet Kingdom," spat the spotter. The assailant glared at him and the sniper by his side carefully reached for the pistol holstered behind his back.

"I didn't come here to debate which of us is right or wrong," the attacker retorted with a sigh. "That'd be more of an uphill battle than climbing this building was. But let me just ask you, what if it were *you*?"

"What do you mean?"

"What if *you* grew up in the dimming lights of a society that already thought the worst of you because you were born dark-skinned like me? What if you watched as your loyalist parents were murdered in cold blood alongside your siblings because of the suspicion of treason? What if you had to spend every single day of your life on the run because injustice found you and you resisted?" The heart of the gunman pounded as he listened to the warrior's line of questions, and for a moment—just a moment—he thought to go against his task. The heat that radiated from the strange man's sword heightened, and the air around the sniper cell began to swelter.

"The only justice is what the Scarlet Kingdom decides!" The sniper looked to the spotter, who had brandished a pistol of his own and opened fire on his target. The mysterious Insurrectionist spun his heat-sword around his body as he seemingly danced across the platform. The heat became unbearable, to the point where the air ignited with each robust swing. All of the bullets volleyed in his direction melted, and before long so did those that rested in the chamber of the spotter's pistol. Once the threat of the firearms had been neutralized, the Yaiba operative threw out his arm and the blade that guided his multitalented chains found its way into the throat of the spotter.

"See, I don't think that's right," said the swordsman. "Justice isn't defined by a nation or an ideology. It's defined by the ability to obtain what one deserves. That's just my opinion anyway."

"I surrender," uttered the sniper with an urgency that was so uncharacteristic of a Scarlet. The remaining six members of the squad managed to reach their position from the old stairwell to the rear, and as they filed through the door, they trained the muzzles of their M16s on their enemy.

"You misunderstand," came the assailant. "I'm not here to negotiate either." Without another word, the swordsman tossed a chained blade into the heart of one of the opposing troops and drew them in closer. The other soldiers opened fire, but the body of their comrade served as protection to the Insurrectionist. He charged them boldly, and when he neared the enemy line, he tossed the corpse of his human shield onto the nearest soldier and whipped his chain back into his gauntlet, though not without a decapitation on the way. Gunshots fired as another of the troops shot at him, but he moved around the beheaded soldier in time enough to avoid the bullets.

He slashed his blazing sword and burned through the legs of the shooter as he propelled the chain on the opposite arm into another soldier's forehead. His eyes met those of the last newcomer, who stood before him atremble. The swordsman looked him over. He was a green-eyed boy of about eighteen, pale skin, shaky hands, and from the hesitation he showed, he was nothing like his fallen comrades.

"Why are you here," asked the bladeworker. The boy stuttered, and though he gave his best intimidating glare at the obvious enemy, he was little more than a mouse before a lion and he knew it. The swordsman momentarily switched off his headset. "Get out of here. Drop your headset and move southeast from here. There should be an old mall somewhere in that area. Change out of that awful blood-colored camouflage uniform and into something less conspicuous. Get out of town as soon as you can and head westward towards California. There's a man in the Yoroi Alliance territory by the name of Eric Gallion. Tell him Rairyu sent you and that you need passage to the Kabuto Sanctuary." The boy's eyes widened, and he moved to thank the swordsman for his kindness but the latter held up his hand. "Get out of here before I change my mind." The boy nodded, and in the next instance he was gone.

The Yaiba operative turned to face the lone Scarlet sniper, and lifted the burning sword as he prepared to strike.

"Wait," called the sniper, and so Rairyu complied. "Why'd you let that soldier go?"

"He was just a kid. I've fought this long because I needed to. The same rules don't apply to him," spoke the swordsman.

"That's…" the sniper was at a loss for words. He'd been taught that these Yaiba Insurrectionists were cold and ruthless, and that ideas such as mercy were beyond their reach. But the man before him, though he had cut down all of the men in the easternmost squad, spared a teenager fighting in a war in which he had no business being. "You're kinder than I expected."

"To be fair, you never expected much of us," the Insurrectionist shot back. He looked into the sniper's eyes, and he breathed a heavy sigh. "You gonna tell anyone?" The sniper shook his head and raised his hands. "Then leave. If you come looking for us again, I'll kill you before you can speak a word."

"Understood." With nothing more to be said, the sniper kept his promise and made his way back through the falling buildings of a ruined Washington, DC to the extraction point. Rairyu, however, switched his headset back on and strode back to the edge of the treasury rooftop.

"Rairyu, come in," the Director spoke. "Is everything alright?"

"Yeah," he responded. "Just had to fix a malfunction."

****

Ishikawa gave his orders with a degree of calm confidence that made the three field testers feel at ease in the midst of the hostility. Lukas, though he couldn't see into the east garden room where he knew Dre to be, glanced in that direction as if to gauge what his teammate was thinking. He had his directive, but Lukas wondered if the Lightning Dragon of the Yaiba Insurrection would be able to handle the squad and sniper team alike. The Director continued to delegate roles to the remaining teammates.

"Suiryu" he called to Carson, "occupy the attention of the enemy squad to the west. The path between the ruins of the Eisenhower Executive Offices and the west lobby wing of the White House should be sturdy enough for you to use your Hanzo Gear with the same mobility as Rairyu would on the east side. You actually have an advantage. The office building is closer to the west wing of the ruins than the treasury is to the garden room, so you have a little more to grapple onto. In the event that you need extra cover, the geo-sensors have picked up a reading of an active water main protruding from the ground just fifty feet southwest of the west wing entrance. Use your Reikiken to cut through it."

"Yes, sir," Carson acknowledged. "Moving to engage on your order."

"Oh, and one more thing," Ishikawa added. "Be careful to regulate the heat of the blade when you cut through that pipe."

****

"East Squad is almost down half its members," one of the grunts in the Scarlet command center reported to General Osmond, who slammed his fist on the monitor board in front of him.

"Is that the enemy's doing?" The General asked the question in such a draconic growl that it made the busy room of thirty men visibly tense.

"The working street cameras in the DC area show that it…" the grunt paused, much to the ire of the General.

"Spit it out," the leader barked, and to the mass of scientists and soldiers around him felt shockwaves rattle through their bodies.

"Our men were taken out by shots fired from our own sniper," the grunt stated with as much calm as he could manage. For a moment, Osmond looked as if his head would explode from the news, but to everyone's surprise he remembered that he wasn't there merely to bark orders and get angry. He was one of the Scarlet Kingdom's best tactical minds, and now was the best time for him to tap into that strategic thinking.

"I need visuals on the entire battlefield. Sergeant Williams, bring up field monitors Bravo and Charlie. Focus in on the enemy and… what is that gear?" General Osmond watched as the easternmost target vaulted into the air with chains, and evaded shots by changing his trajectory in mid-flight with what seemed like repulsors in his boots. His eyes widened when the terrorist swung what looked like a bright red sword at oncoming bullets and melted them without ever making contact. The ground troops had the man cornered on the same rooftop as the sniper, and with a breath of relief, the General ordered that focus shift to West Squad.

****

"Don't let him get away," Lieutenant Kluger ordered his subordinates as the cloaked figure with the burning sword led them southwest of the west wing's main entrance. He came to an exposed water main surrounded by damaged cars and fragments of the Vice President's Ceremonial Office. There was nowhere for him to run, and with an eerie calm, the terrorist turned to face the firing squad. "For your crimes against His Majesty the King and the esteemed Scarlet Kingdom, we hereby sentence you to immediate execution. Have you any last words?"

"What, no trial?" The hooded man's sarcasm was enough to make the Lieutenant brandish an overconfident smile. He stepped closer, moved through his ten soldiers to stand between the muzzles of their firearms, and it was then that the Insurrectionist recognized him. There was a notable change in the trapped rat's eyes that made Kluger savor the moment even more. He never did understand why the anguish of his enemies proved so potent a drug to him, but it was inconsequential. "You…" was all the man said, but the fresh anger in his tone sent a pulse of joy through Kluger's heart.

"Do I know you," the Lieutenant started, but then held up his hand before his enemy could speak further. "On second thought, I don't care. Men, take aim…" The sound of thunder pierced their eardrums, and water dropped before them. The more the rain met the heat of the Yaiba operative's unusual sword, the more the falling water turned into floating steam. The Lieutenant watched with humored grin as the trapped rat slashed the blade aimlessly through the downpour. The water vapor permeated the air, and with every spin and slash of the firesword, it grew thicker. The Scarlet soldiers were all but blinded by the fog that now surrounded them, save for the dimming glimmer of the enemy's glowing weapon.

"Lieutenant Kluger," came General Osmond's voice through his headset, "Quit wasting time and kill him. Now!" Without any further hesitation, the West Squad Captain gave the order to open fire, and a barrage of bullets pelted the direction in which the target had last been sighted.

"Hold fire!" Lieutenant Kluger moved forward to investigate the corpse, only to find that against the wall of automobiles and debris there wasn't one. Horror took his face as the air grew still. "There's nothing here! I want that terrorist found *now*!" The troops at his back were filled with dread. How could they miss? How could their quarry escape? He had cornered himself, trapped himself between the proverbial rock and hard place that limited his options to simply being smashed. The sound of silence was unbearable, and each of the ten men, planted firmly in their positions, kept a vigilant watch of all sides.

Their nervous pivots and turns generated the sound of boots to the ground that otherwise masked the terrorist's steps. He dropped the blade of his kyoketsu-shoge just enough so that the chain would dangle silently at his side. A Scarlet Trooper turned to face him, but before he could call to his comrades, the rat slit his throat with the chained blade and bisected him with one swift turning motion. His body came full circle, and he slashed the muzzle of his next enemy's firearm before he brought the fire blade back around and, ultimately, right through his opponent. There was a scream this time, and the remaining soldiers took aim and fired at the spot from which it came. The attacker had used his repulsors to vault into the air, and with his chained blade he quickly pierced the skull of one of his enemies.

Three Scarlets down, eight left before he could advance on their commanding officer with no interruptions. The master of stealth landed in the middle of the line, now, and with fiery blade swept through the midsection of one and the head of another in a single, graceful motion. Five down. The two troops on either side of the freshest kills took notice of him, but before they could even train their guns on him the silent stalker launched both of his kyoketsu-shoge into their hearts and violently ripped the blades back out. Seven down. The kill count increased, as did the rate of the neo-ninja's heart as he realized that finally, *FINALLY*, he could make Kluger suffer.

Kluger was mortified. The control that he thought he had over the situation slipped through his grasp in the blink of an eye. His men were being murdered by a man that merely gave the impression of being trapped, but the Scarlets themselves were the ones lured into the trap. Now, their enemy was cloaked and only telegraphed his position with the screams of the Lieutenant's comrades or the chilling rattle of flying chains.

"Fall back," he commanded to any troops that remained, though his voice was too shaky to warrant any notice. "Fall back! We've been lured into his trap! Escape the mist and open fire!" His three remaining subordinates did their best to adhere to the order that had been given, but two of them were pierced through the chest from up above by twin chained blades. The third had been pounced upon and split down the middle. As his halves collapsed to the ground, the merciless warrior turned his focus back to the heart of the mist, where his true enemy stood. "You're quite the monster, I hope you know. Your manner of warfare is reminiscent of the horror movies of old."

"Nah, this isn't horror," corrected the chain master. "But I'll teach it to you."

"I see now," the Lieutenant cooed. "Carson Rouge; it's been such a long time! Tell me," his voice became darker now as twisted humor seeped into his eyes. "How's the wife?" There were no words now, just gun shots and sizzling rain as the adversaries clashed. The Lieutenant rolled out of the way of an incoming blade attack, and shot the second kyoketsu-shoge off to the side. The steel of the weapon shattered under the force of the bullet, which drastically improved his chances of survival. He trained his crosshairs on his opponent and shot round after round at him, but the heatwave generated by his unusual sword distorted the bullets in mid-flight and made them far less aerodynamic. The studs fell to the ground, and the swordsman charged. He pushed off the ground with the remaining chain, and when the Lieutenant took his shot, the chain master used his repulsors to quickly change directions. He launched the serpentine weapon at his opponent's back as the Insurrectionist flew, but the Lieutenant turned and slapped the blade aside with the butt of his rifle. Two shots were fired into the air, but with another mist-generating swing of the blazing sword they melted like the others before them. Carson used the repulsors to right his position and returned to the ground. He smiled.

"That all you got?"

“No,” Kluger happily replied. “This is.” The troops from the Center Squad could be heard approaching from the north. They halted, just as the previous squad had, but the Major that commanded them wasn’t foolish enough to wander into Carson’s cloud of smoke and mist. He was cornered, outgunned, and with his best card played, he had no choice but to stay on his guard.

****

“Kazeryu, once Suiryu and Rairyu have created your opening, head south from your position to lure the northernmost enemy squad into the White Ruins. Use your kyoketsu-shoge to take a vantage point and start picking them off from the shadows.” That was the order that Director Ishikawa gave to Lukas at the start of the field test, but his attempt to lure the northern squad into the White House ruins had failed. He waited for them to enter, but they never came, and with radio silence from Dre and Carson, he knew that something had gone terribly wrong.

Lukas, who had always been the most upbeat person in the room (even on the battlefield), suddenly adopted a grave expression. He activated the communications channel to the Director. There was static at first, but eventually he got through to the other side. His heart pounded as fear swept his mind. The mission should have been over by now. The only variable was the sniper to the east that nobody had accounted for, so why was the op taking so long?

“Sir, something isn’t right here. I did as ordered and tried to lure the North Squad into the ruins but they didn’t take the bait,” Lukas reported. The director hummed as he checked the readings of the geo-scanners.

“North Squad is moving southwest on Suiryu’s position,” Ishikawa explained with an air of frustration. “A single enemy is fending off his assault. As long as this troop has him locked up, the incoming force will have an advantage.”

"You don't think that they'll kill one of their own just to take one of us down, do you?" The urgency in Lukas' voice was met with uncomfortable silence.

"The way the Scarlets operate, they'll try to exterminate us all by any means necessary. In any case they've given us a wonderful opportunity for a makeshift pincer attack. Kazeryu, exit the ruins and follow the enemy squad."

"Yes, sir." The order had been given, and with great haste, Lukas pulled himself up to the roof through the use of his kyoketsu-shoge. He landed silently at the corner of the rain-soaked platform and saw as the last three troops of the squad of eleven turned the western corner. Lukas repulsed himself from the roof and used the blade-chain to pull himself down to the ground. He quickly gave chase to the enemy squad, and did his best not to slip in the mud and grass. He turned the corner, but it was too late. The enemy surrounded Carson and carefully trained their weapons on him. The kyoketsu-shoge weren't fast or agile enough to take out twelve enemies at once, and his Reikiken wasn't suited for long-range combat.

The Lieutenant, the Major, and the remaining Scarlet soldiers drove Carson back against the wall of ruined vehicles and fractured stone structure. Lukas trembled. He had to do something. He had to move! Or else those filthy Scarlets would kill his friend and, just as bad, take the Hanzo Gear prototype back with them to the Kingdom. He looked at his friend's face, and noticed that Carson's eyes were locked on him. Carson pulled his mask down so that his lips were in clear view. Lukas watched him for a moment longer, but with tears in his eyes he turned his back on his friend.

Carson surveyed the expressions on the faces of his enemies, and as his eyes shifted from person to person he caught sight of Lukas in the distance. He glanced to his left, and noticed that the exposed water main spouted cold water back into the hole from which the pipe had come. The blade in his hand rested at

3,677°F, and was more than hot enough to melt the lead tube with little resistance. He looked back at his friend in the distance, steeled himself, and lowered his mask.

“Run, Lukas,” was all he said. When Lukas turned his back to the scene, Carson drove his Reikiken through the lead and into the water. The rapid heating of the cool water created a hydrogen explosion that was only amplified by the now-failed power cells in Carson’s repulsors.

Dre dropped to his knees amid the bodies on the treasury rooftop. The cold rain could do little to cool his rapidly heating face. Tears welled up in his eyes as he screamed profanities at the clouds and pounded his fists against the concrete beneath him. The west wing was gone, and all that remained of his friends was the crater left by the blast.

“Suiryu, Kazeryu,” he called through his headset. There was an uncharacteristic desperation in his voice, and no answer on the line. “Come in, Suiryu. What’s your status?” Still nothing. “Kazeryu,” he yelled into the microphone. It was all he could do to keep their names a secret in case he was being watched. “Kazeryu, tell me you—” he choked, and scrambled to the edge of the rooftop, “—tell me you have eyes on Suiryu.” Again he was met with silence. The only sound he heard was the steady beat of rainwater against the remnants of DC. He surveyed the White House grounds for any piece of his teammates, and then he saw just beneath the rubble a Reikiken clutched tightly in the tan hand he knew belonged to Lukas.

He deployed his weapons and launched himself from the treasury building. He kicked the air to either side as he made his descent to the patchy lawn of the once glorious presidential residence, and sprinted for the pile of fallen brick and damaged metal. He hastily started to dig into the debris, hoping against hope that there was something left of his friend to salvage.

He reached the bottom, and the way he found Lukas churned his stomach. The heavy fragments of the building beside him crushed his head flat. His left eye was open, but his right was half-shut. There was a dent in his chest that hadn't been there before, and everything below the waist had been burned up in the blast. His own repulsors were probably to blame.

"Rairyu," came the voice of Director Ishikawa, much gentler than Dre had ever heard it. "I'm sorry, but it's time to go." Without a word, Dre pried the Reikiken from his comrade's petrified grasp, and made his way for the bunker, utterly defeated in his moment of victory.

Chapter One

July 19th, 2084…

The mountain base was alive with chatter as people eagerly arrived on Training Level C. It wasn't an unusual practice, but it always did annoy John, even back when he was a trainee. He didn't see fit to challenge it, though. After all, ever since the White Ruins Miracle of 2046, everyone in the Yaiba Insurrection wanted to get a glimpse of the Hanzo Gear in action, regardless of whether or not they were warriors. This was even more true of the Insurrection's potential allies.

John heard word that some ambassador from the Yoroi Alliance would be sitting in on the day's session, though knowing why was above his paygrade… not that he was being paid in anything more than food and water. He heaved a sigh as he looked to the stands that surrounded the training floor. They were originally there so that the masters of the early days could observe and critique their students, but now they were less for instruction and more for entertainment. John was less than enthused with the eager faces that steadily strolled into the training grounds, but then he saw Bill Jerrick enter the crowd.

Bill was a tall man with alabaster skin and brown facial hair that made him look distinguished, albeit a bit older than he actually was. He was a gentle spirit, and a cunning warrior, and he was one of the oldest friends that John had. He didn't know if that was because he'd been drawn to Bill's nurturing nature, or if it was because Bill was the most extroverted person in the base, but they'd grown close, and John didn't really have a problem with that. John looked at the old analogue clock on the wall, and surmised that he had just enough time to go mess with his friend and make it back to the floor before the trainees came in.

He slipped through the growing crowd of people to make his way towards Bill's seat. Bill, who entertained conversation with a couple of his old classmates, seemed to not notice John's approach. *How careless of him*, John thought as an evil smirk crept across his face. Bryan Piccio, the man beside him with the blue eyes and blond hair, cracked one of his signature (but incredibly dated) jokes, and Bill, ever the good sport, laughed heartily along with him. John's grin grew wider as he closed in on his target. His footsteps were masked by those of the people on all sides of him, and the laughter his two friends shared negated the small rattle of the steel ball inside his whistle.

Bryan noticed when John moved in and maintained his smile, but Bill was scared half to death by the loud ring of the whistle in his ear. Bryan and John cracked up at the flustered expression on Bill's now cherry-colored face, and though Bill punched John in his shoulder the laughter only escalated.

"You know I have to get you back, don't you," Bill asked through the cackles of his friends.

"Bring it on, brother," John responded. "But you already know I'm a one-upper."

"Hamlin used taunt," Bryan chimed in, and his smile expanded as Bill's head shook in defeat. "Anyway, John, I thought you were supposed to be on the floor with the trainees. I heard there was some kind of special guest who was supposed to be watching the session. Still don't know why though." The mention of the esteemed mystery guest caused a groan to echo from John's throat.

"Yeah, something like that. I guess that's why they brought me back to work this session, even though I haven't really seen the inside of this place in a few years," John admitted. "Quiet as it's kept, though, this isn't an ordinary training session." Bill's eyes widened and ears twitched with excitement at the implication.

"Wait, you don't mean…?" he asked, and John nodded.

"Yeah, it's a graduation test. Looks like you came to spectate at just the right time, huh," the guest instructor said. He could understand the excitement, since graduations from the training program were never announced to anyone ahead of time. The trainees had to remain humble during training, and to be treated as though they were on the same level even if some were more advanced than others. It minimized dissension in the ranks and maximized teamwork (or at least the possibility of it). In a brief moment of nostalgic humor, John had to ask, "What was it you used to say during our training back in the day?"

"'I'll never be caught dead in the stands,'" Bryan teased. John snapped his fingers.

"Yep, that's it exactly."

"Well you know, people change little brother. Speaking of…" Bill's voice trailed off as he motioned to the upper rungs of the stands. There, amid the last of the attendees, stood an intimidating man of dark skin and frizzled hair. He walked with a cane, but it wasn't for support, and the only emotion that seemed to register on his face was impatient disgust.

"You've gotta be kidding me," John said as their eyes locked, and immediately the air around them thickened from the tension. "He never comes down here." Bryan averted his gaze and focused his attention on the floor as the trainees started to take their places.

"Well if he's here, it must be for something important," Bill commented, and John narrowed his eyes in suspicion. "Maybe you should talk to him."

"Nah," John replied with a sudden seriousness that chilled the core of his friends. Bryan shifted in his seat so that he faced the opposite direction of the conversation. "The trainees are here so I gotta head back to the floor." He was gone before Bill had a chance to say anything more, and though the elderly man watched him, John paid him no mind. No, now was not the time to think about *him*, it was time for him to focus on the job that he had to do. "Everyone," he called to the plentiful pack of people peering upon the pristine pupils in their presence, and quickly did they silence themselves, "if you would be so kind as to take your seats. Today's session is about to get underway." The crowd obeyed, and once everyone was seated and quiet, John turned his attention back to the three young men that stood before him.

Each of them was dressed in violet and black from head to toe. Heat-resistant masks covered the lower halves of their faces while the hoods of their black cloaks provided shadow to the upper. Their black trousers and violet tunics were fitted to their bodies, and on their sleeves, they bore the reels of titanium chains that ended in a blade of equal strength and shimmer. John, who stood ready in his own Hanzo Gear, couldn't help but smile at the trio that twitched with anticipation.

It took him a moment, but he came to recognize the Yaiba Insurrection's newest troops. The leftmost member of this makeshift cell was a tall, lean, chocolate-skinned, brown-eyed kid of about eighteen by the name of Cal Richmond. From what John had been told, Cal had always had a knack for the tech that went into the Hanzo Gear, and often got in trouble for figuring out ways to modify it.

The rightmost trainee was a little on the short side. Black hair that elevated the hood a bit too much for it to hide his dark brown eyes rested atop his head, but it wasn't that that gave him away. The tan skin of his face dripped with sweat as he laughed from the suspense he felt. This was Lukas Bautista, the son of a man who'd saved John's life more times than he could count, and if not by his heroic actions on the battlefield then by his sometimes painfully optimistic demeanor. From what he knew, Lukas inherited the name from his grandfather, a man who sacrificed himself for the survival of the Yaiba Insurrection back when the base was in the White Ruins Bunker.

Then there was the centermost. John didn't even need to try that hard when it came to him. His bushy black hair, medium-dark skin, even his semi-muscular build and composure in training mirrored his own. His hazel eyes, however, matched those of his grandfather, who undoubtedly watched with inextinguishable disgust from the stands above. Darius Hamlin, John's own son, stood proudly on the training floor, which was a bit too confident for John's taste. He was well-trained in hand-to-hand combat, and excelled in the ways of the sword, though that wasn't a surprise since his training started a lot earlier than most others'.

John chuckled, because between them the warrior, the equipment and the morale were all represented in equal measure. He wondered if they knew that, and if they did, he wondered how much trouble it would give him.

"Trainees," he called to them, and rested his arm on the hilt of the Reikiken attached to his hip, "you've been trained to use your body," he paced the ground before them, and he could feel their nerves worsening, "your swords," he continued, and gestured to his aura sword with his head, "and your wits to stay alive. Today, the three of you are going to apply the skills you've learned in a mock battle, but instead of thinking for yourself, you have to think for each other as a unit." Their eyes went wide with delight, and the trembling in their bodies dissipated. John chuckled as excitement took hold of him as well. "One more thing," he added, which gave the young upstarts apt pause. "You'll be fighting against me. Now, switch your headsets on and brace yourselves, because I have no intentions of taking it easy on you."

****

He couldn't believe it. After three years of training, Darius' father was in attendance for one of the sessions. He'd dreamed about this moment since the first time he hit the floor. When it came, though, he saw that his father wasn't in the stands like everyone else, he was to be the guest instructor for today's practice. Even so, he was more than excited to show his dad what he could do. Then he found out that his father was the obstacle for his makeshift team to overcome. Darius breathed a heavy sigh as he looked to John, who stood clad in the same purple and black garb at the other end of the training floor. Metal cylinders emerged from the floor between the two parties at staggered heights, and John's pacing came to a stop as he smiled upon his only son.

"Whenever you're ready, kids," he called to them through the metal obstructions. They didn't have this when he was first training, but John couldn't help but admire how a little salvage goes a long way.

"We need a plan," Lukas said evenly into his headset. "Darius, that's your dad, right?"

"Yeah," Darius confirmed with his eyes on his opponent. He wasn't "dad" in this moment, just the mark as defined by their mission. It wouldn't be wise to give way to sentiment in a real fight, and even though this was just practice, Darius knew that to his old man it was about as serious as it could get.

"You know anything about his battle style?" Cal asked as he carefully surveyed the spaces between the poles. There was just enough room for them to maneuver themselves, but they'd have to be smart about it. The technicians in the fight lab were generous enough to give them surfaces to grapple onto and spring from, but not so much that they'd just give them free rein to move as they saw fit.

"He's a master of the Rairyu style of swordsmanship, so he's prone to using a single-hand grip on his Reikiken. His techniques are fast and precise, and while he's at his best when he's grounded, he's managed to adapt his movements to full capacity with the Hanzo Gear," Darius supplied.

"So then we have to disarm him, right," Lukas asked with an upbeat ring in his voice, despite the serious expression that took his face. Darius shook his head.

"That wouldn't work," he admitted. "His Reikiken is fitted with a smaller hilt, and as a whole it's as balanced as the battle techs can make it. If we got in close, there's a big possibility that all three of us would get stabbed and fail the exercise."

"Hmm…" Cal hummed as he stroked the few hairs on his chin. "Then we won't take him down by conventional means."

"Not at all," Darius agreed. "Fighting him on his terms, especially as a group would be a suicide mission."

"Then you fight him by yourself," Cal suggested, and Darius cut his eyes at him.

"What do you mean," Lukas asked, and Cal merely smiled.

****

"I wonder what they're whispering about," John asked aloud as he surveyed the trio through the forest of metal. His eyes lit with intrigue, and silently he commended them for not rushing into battle without working on a strategy. As the instructor, John wasn't allowed to make the first move, even if this was supposed to be a head-to-head bout. He could only wait for the opportunity to strike, but that wasn't so bad. The principles of the Rairyu style dictated that the swordsman had to be patient for the opening to present itself, and though the students in his charge might have been familiar with his preferred battle style at a glance, they never even realized that they were playing into his hands.

John's eyes narrowed at the sound of the trainees' shifting feet in the training grounds. He watched as Cal and Lukas stood by and let Darius rush to engage. The boy darted with grace and agility through the poles, and just before he could clear the forest on his own, he used the combination of his kyoketsu-shoge and repulsor boots to vault to the ceiling of the arena. The corner of John's mouth lifted before he realized. As Darius blasted himself back to the floor, John used his own chains to push himself off the ground and out of the way. Darius now held John's former position, and John stood with his back to the emergent pikes. The crowd erupted with gasps and cheers as some slid to the edge of their seats, and Bill and Bryan could be heard cheering at the top of their lungs.

"Strong start," John complimented, "though I'm not entirely sure you grasp the concept of teamwork." Darius chuckled.

"I might understand it more than you know," he replied. John lifted his sword so that it stood perpendicular to the ground, then with an elegant spin he redirected the tip to the ground. Darius, on the other hand, hoisted his weapon over his head and angled the tip at his father. They paced the ground, eyes locked on their respective opponent, and in that moment there was no crowd, nor were there any teammates. This was a bonding moment between father and son that the both of them had looked forward to, probably since the day Darius entered the world.

John, overtaken with excitement, stepped in and attempted a strike to his son's shoulder but was knocked out of the way by Darius' instantaneous block. The boy swiveled around and copied the same opening move of his father, but when he was met with the sturdy wall of the trainer's sword, he attacked the other shoulder at heightened speed. The crowd came to life again as the rookie seemed more competent than they'd first believed. John again moved his blade to protect himself, one hand tucked behind his back as if to taunt the young upstart, and rolled his sword in an upward-swinging motion aimed at his son's midsection.

Darius was surprised at how fast the move went, and even more surprised that he'd somehow managed to parry it out of the way and track his opponent's blade back to the inside. John's midsection was exposed, or so he allowed his son to believe, and at the moment he noted confidence in his boy's expression, he spun his weapon downward in a parry of his own, the energy of which he promptly redirected into a stab at Darius' abdomen. Every heart in the audience beat ferociously as the blazing sword made its way toward the skilled trainee, but the determined youngster narrowly swatted the end of John's Reikiken out of the way, and followed the momentum into a powerful overhead attack that, John noted, was somewhat uncharacteristic of the style that Darius employed.

The combat veteran moved his displaced firesword in a circular fashion that shielded his head from the blow as he moved off the center line. He quickly straightened up, and with pristine fluidity, John fiercely swiped at both legs of his momentary enemy before the boy disengaged.

"You've gotten pretty good at the Suiryu style," John was forced to concede. "It's been a long time since anyone's been able to cross blades with me like this." Darius shrugged.

"Yeah, well, I wanted to make sure that today's training was worth the watch," he replied with laughable faux humility. John knew exactly what this was. His boy picked the one style that would be the most difficult for him to break through just on the off chance they had to fight each other. He was pleased to know that even in his time away, Darius had taken his lessons to heart and did what he could to be one step ahead of his opponent. He opened his mouth to praise his son, but the sound of rattling chains behind him sparked a tension in his muscles that unwound as he spun and shot his kyoketsu-shoge upward to knock Cal's off course.

The titanium blades clashed in the middle, and as his chain retreated to his wrist, John was greeted with a leg sweep by Lukas. *How did he manage to sneak up on me*, John asked himself as his upper body drifted sideways towards the ground. He caught himself on his free hand, and with a single-handed cartwheel he was back upright again.

"Okay, I'll admit it," he started as he looked between the three fledgling warriors, "I'm pleasantly surprised."

"Does that mean that the training session's over," Lukas asked with his signature optimism. John laughed, and then tucked his free hand behind his back as he extended his blade forward.

"Oh, on the contrary, kids," he said with a degree of excitement that put the opposing team on edge. "One decent attack formation does not solid teamwork make. I'll need to see a little more before I give you my seal of approval."

"Say less," Cal uttered as his heavy repulsor boots met the dusty ground of the training floor.

"Just don't blame us for what happens next," Darius continued, and John raised his eyebrows.

"We did give you the chance to give up," Lukas culminated, and as they all took up a fighting pose, John dropped his. The trio was confused and slightly terrified, emotions that only intensified when John used his grapple to take to the metal forest behind him. "Well, that happened."

"Cal, Lukas, you work your way around the pikes to flank him from the left and right respectively. I'll charge in straight ahead, see if I can't distract him like before."

"Roger," they said in unison. They had no problem with Darius taking charge, especially when it was his dad that they were up against. Their plan, though, was roughly the same as the one they used before, and he'd expected that trainees without actual battle experience would be limited in their scope.

"Eyes on target," Lukas informed through the headset. He jumped between pikes and used his repulsors to extend his leaps to cover distances that his legs were too weak to. He dug one of his blades into the cylinder in front of him, and as his target continued to jump and glide through the scrap-iron thicket, Lukas turned his second kyoketsu-shoge on his quarry. John crossed his legs and fired his repulsors to spiral out of the way. He grabbed hold of the nearest of the junk spires, and used another boost from his repulsors to spin back into the direction of the oncoming Lukas. The boy was caught off guard as John vaulted towards him, but before they made contact, Darius met John in the middle. Their blades clashed in midair, and sparks abounded in the battlefield.

The father and son pair had no choice but to hold as they drifted back to the earth below. The lack of ground to stand on would rob their blows of any power should they decide to strike each other, and John mentally applauded Darius for being able to discern even that much. Their feet touched down, and just as John threw himself off balance to attack his son, he felt the chain of a kyoketsu-shoge wrap around his foot.

Cal, who sat in wait through a line of the vertical cylinders, had John trapped. Darius attacked his father's head, not to deal any damage, but to limit his mobility and force him on the defensive. The cheers of the crowd became a deafening roar as John struggled to hold back his own son.

"Better than I'd imagined you'd be," John told them through gritted teeth and loud enough for all of them to hear.

"Lukas, now," Cal yelled across the battlefield.

"Already on it," Lukas called back, and before John had the slightest clue of what was going on, Lukas had flown to their positions on repulsors alone and slid against the ground with such a force that it knocked John's legs clean out from under him. In a well-timed maneuver, Cal retracted the chain and their instructor was dragged towards the incognito student. Darius and Lukas ran alongside the grounded body of the former's father as he rapidly approached their teammate. John slashed the chain, but the heat from his Reikiken was too low to melt through the titanium. He clenched his jaw, because the trap they'd set for him was more effective than he first gave them credit for.

His body came to a halt before an overly confident Cal, who lazily pointed his sword at the instructor's face. Darius and Lukas, who kept the pace with him as he was pulled against his will, followed the lead of their teammate, and John could do little more than power off his weapon. He looked between them all as he stood back to his feet.

"Much better," he commended. "I yield."

"What, really," Darius asked with more surprise than he initially intended to convey. John pulled down his mask to show his son the smile that swept his jaw.

"I mean, you really didn't give me much choice, kid," John replied. "You could've gone a little easier on me. You know I'm old."

"And old people fight dirty," the son shot back with a chuckle. John laughed along with him.

"That's my boy." There was so much pride behind those words, and as the pikes receded into the ground, John raised his voice so that everyone in the arena could hear him. "Through your victory here today, you've shown that the training you've received here has been placed in capable hands. May they guide future generations to a brighter future… as full-fledged members of the Yaiba Insurrection's Violet Shadows!" The crowd erupted with the news, and the boys by John's side stood stunned and incapable of moving. He laid a gentle hand on his boy's shoulder, and with fatherly warmth, he whispered, "I'm so proud of you."

"Thanks," Darius told him with a crack in his voice. He tried to right himself, but there was no stopping the emotion in this moment. "Dad, I—" His father shook his head as he met his son's gaze. He already knew what this meant to the boy, and how much it meant coming from him than from one of his more permanent instructors. After all, if he could've had this moment with his father back when he graduated, it would've brought him to tears. Instead, he was slammed against the wall, berated, and disowned.

John's mother tried to tell him that it was just because his father wanted a better life for him, but that wasn't good enough. And so they stopped speaking, Dre and John, and haven't spoken since John's twentieth birthday.

But now was not the time for that kind of thinking. Today, his son had become a trusted warrior of the Yaiba Insurrection, his equal in almost every way. John shook the hands of Cal and Lukas, and wrapped his arms around Darius to congratulate them all.

"I have to go," John told the boy, but with a smile he added, "make the most of this moment. We'll catch up later." He said nothing more, and left the training grounds through the back exit with his head held high, and an aura of pride that permeated the entire floor.

****

A couple of hours passed, and John barely had enough time to shower and change into a proper suit before the meeting. After a sprint through Residency Block G, he reached the power-lift that would take him up to the Conference Level. He always hated the diplomatic aspects of his position. Politicians were always so unbelievably stiff and boring. He'd rather be down on the Entertainment level celebrating his son's moment in the sun. Instead, he had orders from Director Ishikawa to show up in the last place he'd ever want to set foot in this place.

The power-lift rose from Level G to Level D, and with a brisk step he moved for the Director's personal office. John had always been impressed with the layout of the Roan Mountain base. When the Yaiba Insurrection first arrived, all that was here inside the mountain was a network of caves and the occasional unstable mining shaft. By the ten-year mark, a scavenger crew brought back enough Scarlet tech from a hidden base just outside the ruins of Johnson City to dig deeper and stabilize as they went. He grew up in these caves, but the desire to explore every inch of the Yaiba base proved as potent now as when the renovations first began. The fact that he had to go be all official only exasperated his adventurous feelings.

He restrained himself, though, as his hand met the solid metal door of the Director's office. He paused for a moment and did his best to collect himself before he had to deal with the Director and their esteemed guest. John opened the door and eased inside with confidence befitting an ace warrior. The Director's office was spacious to say the least. In lieu of a desk, a silver conference table with seven black chairs on either side occupied the floor. A number of Ukiyo-e prints covered the walls that gave the otherwise sterile room the pop of color it would have otherwise been deprived.

"Ah, John," said Director Ishikawa, "you're here. I thought we would have to start without you." Emiko Ishikawa was a thin woman with snowy skin, red cheeks, and shadow-black hair that was tied into a neat bun. She robed herself in a sleeveless top of violet silk, and a long black skirt that draped over silver heels. She had been a friend of his since childhood. Well, perhaps she was more of his big sister. That still didn't make up for the fact that she ordered him to be here. He resisted the urge to groan at her, and merely faked his best smile.

"Hm, so this is the man outdone by three whelps on the training floor," came a raspy, heavily accented voice from behind him. John abruptly turned and reached for the sword that wasn't there as he caught sight of a wrinkled, dark-skinned man with green eyes and an air of mysticism about him.

"John, this is Ambassador Ezequiel Vargas of the Yoroi Alliance," Ishikawa enlightened, and John's fake smile grew, more from irritation at the old man's comment than a desire to keep things peaceful. "Mr. Vargas, this is John Hamlin, a leading operative in our black ops division."

"It's a pleasure," John spoke as he extended a hand towards Vargas. The Ambassador merely looked down at it, and circumvented the veteran warrior to take a seat at the table. John could feel the vein in his forehead pulse as his aggravation grew, but still he said nothing.

"I came here," Ambassador Vargas began, "because the news of the White Ruins Miracle spread like a virus through all of the Territories. Flying men with blazing swords and snake-like spears subduing a Scarlet Extermination Platoon. It all sounded so… impossible—"

"And it inspired the Yoroi Alliance to try and steal the Hanzo Gear," John interrupted, to the displeasure of the dignitary and his own Director. Emiko shot him a look, and John cleared his throat. "But clearly the hostilities that our factions had toward one another have subsided."

"Not entirely," Vargas returned. "The Yoroi Council has felt for years now that this Hanzo Gear of yours puts the Yaiba Insurrection at an unfair advantage. After seeing it in person, and knowing how your ranks have expanded in the last thirty-eight years, I cannot help but agree."

"I can assure you, Ambassador, that our focus for these weapons is taking down the Scarlet Kingdom. We have no interest in going to war with the other factions, we simply want our freedom back," Ishikawa assured, and the Ambassador gave an unimpressed hum as his eyes shifted to her.

"You speak of freedom as though you were there before the dark times came upon us. You know nothing but war, my dear. Am I to believe that when the one conflict ends you won't seek out another?" John moved to stand behind the Director and watched their guest carefully. He didn't much care for the old man's tone in addressing the head of the Yaiba Insurrection, but it was not his place to call him on it.

"Mr. Vargas, the entire reason I sent my envoys to you and had this meeting arranged was to quash any bad blood between our two factions. Our numbers have increased steadily over the years with defectors from the Scarlet Kingdom and the family growth of our own people, that I cannot deny. But even still, your faction still far exceeds ours in terms of manpower and has expanded from the crags of your Grand Canyon base to cover the entire southwestern border," Emiko explained as she sat at the head of the table. The shrewd man that sat to her left lifted the corner of his mouth in moderate admiration. "In fact, the Yoroi Alliance's expansion has meant the reduction of the Kabuto Sanctuary on more than one occasion. An interesting trend, don't you think?" Vargas' expression reverted to its stern look, though his eyes seemed much more intense than before.

"Judging by the look on your face, it seems as though you didn't expect us to know much about the Yoroi," John teased, which again drew a cautious glare from his superior.

"I have no idea what you are talking about," Vargas spat in vehement denial, but the single raised hand of Director Ishikawa quieted him instantly.

"I trust you didn't come here to meet my desire to negotiate an alliance with the intention of making demands, Ambassador Vargas," the Director told him. The aged man interwove his fingers and leaned back in his chair. "After all, it would be in everyone's best interest if these talks went smoothly." Vargas took a moment to regain his composure. They knew more than they were supposed to, and if their intel was this good, then it was of high probability that they knew of a way to exploit the Yoroi's biggest weaknesses.

"I would have to agree with you," he finally said, and Emiko smiled. "What did you have in mind for this alliance?"

"You make me sound so conniving, Ambassador," she cooed, which did little to amuse her company. "But in truth all I did was see through your attempts to intimidate us. If I might be so forward, you won't get anywhere with us through intimidation tactics. The White Ruins Miracle proved that one of our operatives with Hanzo Gear is worth at least eleven troops with old world weapons. If we went to war, it'd be more to our advantage than yours." Her words incited the man to anger, just as they were intended to do.

"What makes you so sure of that," Vargas demanded of her.

"Simple. Your expansion into Kabuto territory has attracted more attention from the Scarlets than you were prepared for. You made them feel desperate, and now they've started to expand their reach as far west as the San Antonio area to apply pressure. With the Kingdom slowly getting closer and your forces spread so thin throughout the Southwestern Territory, you'd have a hard time fighting off just one enemy force, let alone take on a second." Vargas visibly ground his teeth as Emiko spoke, and John, who refused to sit at the same table as such a shifty man, couldn't help but smile with mild smugness. "Meanwhile," the Director continued, "the Yaiba Insurrection is relatively unnoticed and consolidated in or around the Roan Mountain area. We have tools that outclass even the latest technological advancements of the Scarlet Kingdom, and they're made from scrap, salvage and stolen goods."

"You underestimate our defenses," Vargas offered. John supposed that the elderly man didn't much care for being spoken to as if he barely understood the position that his group was in. "The secrecy of the Yoroi Alliance has kept us safe since the rise of the Red Regime, and our guerilla tactics have made us more than a match for our mutual foe."

"Your defense is legendary," John willingly conceded, "perhaps even as much as our own Hanzo Gear. But be realistic, Ambassador. Your cover's been blown, not just as far as we're concerned, but the Scarlets could attack you any day now. Hitting and running will only get you so far when your enemy knows your tactics as well as we do…"

"What do you mean by that, Mr. Hamlin," the irate guest uttered in a muted snarl, and John simply shrugged.

"While our envoys were meeting with your council, I led a team of Yaiba black ops to survey your territories and map out any and all known or possible ambush points and hiding spots. Whatever advantage you believe you had is out of your hands, I'm afraid." John's serious tone reverted to a state of utter disinterest. To Ambassador Vargas, he sounded as though he didn't care. To Emiko, on the other hand, he sounded as though he'd drive his head into the wall. "So, are we going to discuss terms, or are you gonna insist on your ill-advised plan A?" There was silence in the room, and tension with it. Vargas looked between his hosts, the Director whose eyes never betrayed her, and the warrior who knew more about political maneuvering than he initially let on.

"As I said before, the Yaiba Insurrection has but one enemy, and we believe that with our joint forces and pooled knowledge, we'll finally put an end to this war. To that singular goal, we merely wish to enter an agreement to cease hostility with the Yoroi Alliance and bolster our strength for the battles to come," Director Ishikawa restated in a more official tone of voice than her earlier whimsy.

"What would you be offering in exchange for our cooperation," the elder asked. Emiko folded her hands as she leaned in.

"In exchange for your cooperation, your knowledge, and your military might, we would offer you knowledge of the Hanzo Gear, as well as the proper training to use it. In addition, we would deploy a garrison of Yaiba elites to assist in day to day operations such as training, scavenging, and battle, of course," the Director explained. Vargas took his time in giving his response, but everyone in the room was more than aware that this was just for show.

"Then on behalf of the Yoroi Alliance, I hereby accept your proposal," said the Ambassador. The Director and the spy both smiled with relief, and without anything further, the meeting was done.

Finally, John thought. *I can get out of this suit.*

Chapter Two

July 25th, 2084, 3:27 a.m.,

He nestled on the rooftop, his spotter by his side, and with the same cool confidence as always, he lined up his shot on the east-standing enemy. That was the one closest to his position, and the one who had the least cover to duck behind out of the three confirmed targets that hid among the White House ruins. His spotter spoke, and he himself readily eased his trigger finger into place, but everything changed when his prey looked dead at him.

Suddenly there was nothing more than fog and darkness. There were no people, no structures, no remnants of what life used to be like before the old capitol fell, and no sounds, save for the eerie rattle of distant chains. He knew what they were, where they'd come from. They were closing in, and out of the utmost feelings of panic and desperation, the sniper ran. He was fast, and the sound of the nearing chains momentarily fell to the background again. His breath thinned, but he yet had hope that he would survive. Then his strides began to slow.

He ran as hard as he physically could have to the point where every ounce of energy drained from his body. The chains grew louder, and with a lashing sound the dark ground beneath his feet began to swallow him up. Still he pressed, still he worked himself through failing breath and stinging muscle to reach the edge of the black pool, but with a glance over his shoulder he met the glowing red eyes of his pursuer and resigned himself to his fate.

The demonic aggressor twitched a finger, and the serpentine chain wrapped itself around the sniper's throat. He watched as his enemy brandished a burning sword, the likes of which he'd only ever seen once in his life, and as the monster laughed maniacally, the chains drew its victim towards it. The creature held its sword an inch from the man's flesh and watched as the sniper winced and hissed from the heat. Its fanged smile grew all the more excited, but then the unexpected happened: the monster tossed him away into the dark abyss.

****

Alan Crawford awoke in a cold sweat, just as he always had. The feeling of terror that he felt that night thirty-eight years ago remained with him every moment of every day, and as much as he tried not to let it rule over him, he always heard that man's words in his ears. He rubbed his grizzled face and took a deep breath. It was a relief that he could, given the vividness of the nightmare. He looked to the window, and saw that night had not yet lifted.

"Babe? What's the matter? Are you alright?" Alan looked to his right as his wife stumbled out of her own sleep. He smiled at her, and the concern in her groggy voice quieted his racing heart. He rubbed her on the arm as he leaned over to place a gentle kiss on her forehead.

"Go back to sleep, Ash," he said gently. "Everything's just fine." She watched him as he sat at the edge of the bed popped his lower back. He looked distressed, but just as always, he did his best to keep her from worrying. Ashley Crawford was less than thrilled that her husband was so tight-lipped about his night terrors. He always told her that he dreamed of losing her or their sons, that the Scarlet Kingdom was destroyed or that the King called for his execution for something that was out of his control, but she was unsure of the truth in all that. What she saw in his eyes every time this happened was a kind of fear that couldn't be so easily explained away.

Alan didn't like keeping anything from Ashley, but how could he confess that he was spared by and ran away from the enemy? How could he look her in the eye and describe to her the pure, controlling terror that he felt for thirty-eight years after his one and only encounter with those Yaiba neo-ninjas? He'd been branded a hero of the Scarlet Kingdom, the legendary sniper who took out two of the super terrorists that destroyed an entire extermination squad. Fortunately for him, General Osmond lost his surveillance feed during the battle, so it was easy for him to spin that story and make a good life for himself.

A great life, in fact. He had a beautiful blonde bombshell of a wife the likes of whom would have graced the magazines of the bygone era, two sons of significant military rank and achievement, a mansion in the heart of the new capitol, and the kind of clout that was second only to the King himself. He tightened his fist. He would never betray the image he'd created for himself, because it wouldn't just mean his own personal ruin, but could potentially cost the lives of his wife and children.

Alan rose from his bedside as his wife resigned herself back to her pillow, and strolled down the stairs and into the kitchen. He took a glass from the cupboard and pulled a pitcher of water from the refrigerator when he heard a faint cough from behind him. He quickly pulled the pistol from beneath the kitchen counter as he wheeled around, and pointed it squarely at his visitor's head.

"Your reflexes aren't bad," said the effeminate figure cloaked in shadows. "At least, not for an old man." She stepped close enough to be seen, and with her hands raised she sought to show him that there was no need to be alarmed of her. Not in this context, anyway. The old man smiled.

"Serenity," he said with warmth in his voice. He stowed the gun back in its hiding place. "What brings the leader of the Scarlet Scourge to visit me so late at night?"

"Ugh," she exclaimed with a roll of her eyes, "hearing that coming from you just sounds weird."

"Well it'd be even weirder if I addressed you as if you were still the little girl from before, wouldn't it," he asked. He remembered the day he first saw her. She had tears in her little green eyes, bright red cheeks, and dark black hair tied into pigtails on either side of her head back then. Her parents were among the soldiers that died that night in the skirmish with the Yaiba Insurrection. It was his responsibility as the only survivor of the platoon to break the news to all the family, but when it came to her, it was almost too much for him to bear. "You never answered my question," Alan resumed, partially to break himself out of the tragic memories that swirled about in his head. "To what do I owe this little visit?"

"What, can't I just show up in the middle of the night to surprise the only parent I have left?"

"Serenity…" there was a sternness in Alan's voice that definitely took her back to her childhood in his house. She had the utmost respect for the man that stood across from her. He made sure that she never felt adopted, even though she frequently lashed out at him in those earlier years. It actually wasn't until Kyle was born that she knew Alan saw her as part of the family. The nurses brought her into the delivery room to see her adopted mother and the squishy little baby that cried in her arms.

"Is that him," she remembered asking with an intentional air of disinterest. Alan nodded as he placed his hand firmly but gently on her shoulder.

"It is," he told her. "That's your little brother." He'd always been conscious of her feelings and her need for inclusion, even when his own problems from work made him want to distance himself from everyone. When she was older, she joined the Scarlet Kingdom's military and learned from her commanding officers about the Battle of the Old White House. Alan was the only one left alive after an extermination mission went sideways. It explained so much about him that she never understood as a kid, and it made her respect him even more. Now, she had to face him like this, in the middle of the night with Ashley upstairs and asleep.

"Fine," she said finally. Weighing her options didn't mean a whole lot when she was under orders. "Yesterday we received word that the Yaiba Insurrection and the Yoroi Alliance are joining forces. The generals have called a war meeting at the palace tomorrow at noon. Your presence has been requested."

"Absolutely not," Alan fired before he'd even realized. His nostrils flared and his heart sped up enough that the room started spinning. He had to grip the counter to maintain his balance.

"But Alan—"

"I said, 'No,' Serenity," he interrupted with raised voice. "Do you have any idea…" he trailed off, and his daughter's eyes softened. "The nightmares," he started again. "They—they won't go away. Thirty-eight years, and the images are still with me." Serenity took a deep breath as she moved to comfort the elderly sniper before her.

"You don't have to fight," she whispered to him. "Nobody's asking you to go back to the battlefield. We just need information, is all. Our enemy is stronger now than they were before. The Yoroi Alliance has expanded, and now they've joined up with the Yaiba Insurrection, and you're the only man alive who knows what happened on that night. If there's anything you can tell us, it can only help our cause." Alan quieted down as she spoke to him in a soothing voice. He considered her words, despite the deep-seated aversion to the affairs of the military, and once the fear subsided he determined that it would probably be best to attend the meeting. At the very least, he could show them exactly why continued service should be completely out of the question.

"Very well," he agreed against his better judgment. Serenity's face brightened with joy, and while Alan lived for that expression, any feeling of happiness was overshadowed by the darkest sense of dread in his heart.

****

War meetings were a common occurrence in New York City, the new capitol of the Scarlet Kingdom. Even after the Second Civil War that divided the once proud United States of America, the city itself was a bustling hive of economic prominence, as well as a bubbling cesspool of scum and villainy. The historical buildings and multitude of skyscrapers that once stood in the great city from era to era were inevitably lost to time. What sprang in their place were noble manors, military research facilities, administrative offices, and of course, the Scarlet Palace. The institution of public school and healthcare were all but abolished. The Founders determined that such things were wasted on the general public, and that education and the general right to live were only to be granted to those who saw fit to sacrifice all for their nation. It bred dependency on the State, and served to keep in line the masses that remained under the rule of the King.

Whatever resistance there was to the new order was either executed or expelled from the Northeastern Territories, and over time the Way of the Reds became the way of the world. It seemed so normal, so *right* to Alan. He recalled that his parents voted in favor of the legendary Dawn King, the founder who instituted their present way of life. The lazy or rebellious said that they were on the wrong side of history, but history had proven them wrong when the Dawn King turned the nation on its head. But he was too young to understand the implications of their society, or the blood that it was apparently built on. *What if* you *grew up in the dimming lights of a society that already thought the worst of you because you were born dark-skinned like me?* He heard the words of his one-time attacker in his ears so clearly since the night of the mission. At first he dismissed his enemy's sentiments as the simple musings of a terrorist, but when he returned, there was an execution in the streets of New York, televised as it used to be before the old country fell. *What if you watched as your loyalist parents were murdered in cold blood alongside your siblings because of the suspicion of treason?* The question burned in his mind as he watched a line of men and women meet their end via firing squad. After his debriefing in an isolated chamber of the research facility, he entered the administrative offices with the request to see the charges. After a little bribery, he was granted access, but what he found was only further validation of what the freedom-fighter spoke. The men and women that he watched get murdered in the street, had been suspected of teaching children who were not their own, and their neighborhood was scheduled for termination in the following days.

That was the last time Alan dealt with government officials, as he waited out the remainder of his contract in anything but peace and quiet. Now, after a thirty-eight-year absence, he sat in a limousine alongside the daughter they'd sent to retrieve him.

"It's not going to be as bad as you're imagining, Alan," Serenity assured him. Alan let out a chuckle.

"God, I hope not," he muttered as he looked through the window to the gray sky. "Even still, I'm not comfortable with this at all."

"I thought you'd say that," the daughter said with a smirk.

"You did, huh," Alan asked as the car pulled to a stop, but she gave no further answer. The doors were opened for them on the outside, and the two latest arrivals for the war meeting were assisted out of the car by the public servants. Alan was old enough to remember a time when that term meant something completely different, but now it was only applied to those too poor to do anything more than offer themselves as servants for public abuse. Very rarely were they treated with any kindness. Before he could thank his help for their gesture of care, Alan noted a rather imposing figure atop the palace stairs. His arms were folded, and a bright white smile lay plastered on his sharp jaw. He was a tall man, and though his muscles were the mother of intimidation, the bright blue eyes and rosy cheeks came together in a face that was as inherently gentle as his mother's. Perhaps, Alan mused, that was why he was so good at espionage.

"Hey, Dad," he said as he offered a salute. His father returned it with a weary grin.

"Hey, Kyle," Alan said when their arms had fallen to their sides. The son moved to embrace the old sniper, and with as much pride as conflict the old man held his son close to him. "I didn't expect for you to be here."

"I didn't either," Kyle had to admit, "but apparently something big is about to happen and they need all hands on deck for this one. What about you? You're retired so what brings you to the Scarlet Palace?"

"Your sister says they need some insight from me in order to proceed. Apparently the Yaiba Insurrection and the Yoroi Alliance are getting a little too friendly with each other," Alan answered. The mention of his sister made Kyle perk up. It'd been ages since he saw her. She was special forces and he was intelligence, and while there was always the possibility that their paths would intersect in the field, it was much more likely that their specific units would never work together. Despite the fact that they weren't related by blood, in the eyes of the higher-ups they were family all the same.

"Serenity!" There was such excitement in Kyle's voice that they both forgot that she outranked him, and in lieu of the appropriate salute, the siblings opted for a brief but meaningful hug. "It seems like I haven't seen you in forever!" Serenity gave a girlish giggle for the first time in a long time, and the sound of it brought a smile to their father's face. That quickly subsided though, as it was more than apparent that the family ties that would typically be thought of as a potential risk were overlooked in the calling of this meeting.

"I think we should head in," Alan commented, much to the surprise of his children. "Kyle, is Ryan inside?" The tone of their miniature family reunion shifted to match the seriousness in Alan's face.

"Yeah," Kyle responded solemnly. He paused for a moment. "Something doesn't feel right about this." It was a feeling that the family shared, and with nothing more to say, the three soldiers moved with haste for the palace war room.

****

The Scarlet Palace, at one point known as the Empire State Building, was once home to the descendants of the Dawn King. When the Dawn King's family line died out, the leader of the Knights of O'Neill was next in line to take their place. He cemented a legacy of loyalty to the ideals that founded the new nation, and continued the work of his predecessors with astounding diligence. It was under him that the historic tower was expanded into the intricate castle that presently adorned New York City.

Kyle led Serenity and Alan along the black and white marbled floors from the lobby to the war room in the eastern hall. The three entered, and were immediately met with the holographic projection of the Southwest Territory. A number of prominent military figures and the nobles with the deepest military ties sat comfortably around the massive circular table that held the projection suspended above. Their eyes shifted to the now-open door, and while the majority of the attendees did little to hide their distaste for the Crawford family's tardiness, Ryan Crawford, an expert marksman like his father before him, came alive with joy.

"Excellent," started Marquis West of Upstate. "Now that we're all finally here, we can proceed with the matter for which you've all been summoned." Alan narrowed his eyes at the obvious jab.

"My apologies, Marquis," he spoke. "I'm mostly to blame for our tardiness." Marquis West, who boasted a nose much too large for his face and beady azure eyes, raised a brunette eyebrow at his latest arrivals.

"I suppose that it would be difficult for a man of your age to be in place on time for much," sneered the overweight noble. The room snickered at the veteran's expense, save for the now flustered but outwardly calm Crawford children. Alan shrugged.

"Only when I'm called on by the dimwitted to waste what little time I have left, my liege," Alan shot back with artificial humility and real venom.

"I was the one who requested your presence," said the noble, who apparently felt that this knowledge would inspire some sort of self-correction on the part of his clear elder.

"And I stand by what I said, though you're more than welcome to try and prove yourself intelligent enough for my attention. Who knows? You might even convince me to help you." The room fell silent at the brazen mockery as the angry noble did his best to restrain himself.

"Please, take your seats," Viscount Leyva interjected. He was a short, pointy-eared man whose family was only made nobility due to their blind loyalty and sycophantic nature towards the King. Alan never really could stand them very much. "Squabbling amongst ourselves does not serve the glorious Scarlet Kingdom. Besides, Sergeant Crawford, you're not the only person with other things they'd rather be doing."

"Then get on with it and quit wasting my time," Alan shot back, perfectly happy to lean into the role of a cranky old man. "I've been here long enough already."

"As many of you may know, the Yoroi Alliance and the Scarlet Kingdom have been mutually beneficial to one another for the last twenty-two years," West opened. He was, of course, referring to the Flagstaff Ceasefire of 2062, where after years of fruitless raids on Yoroi territory and heavy Scarlet casualties, the

Kingdom extended an olive branch. The offer was accepted, of course, and the two bitter enemies eventually grew into a more amicable working relationship. "Due to recent developments, the more or less peaceful relationship between our wonderful nation and the outlying faction has been disrupted." The room came alive with chatter. The more detached nobles contributed nothing to the conversation, but of course they ran their mouths along with everyone else if for no other reason than to give the appearance of understanding.

"Ladies and gentlemen, quiet, please," asked Viscount Leyva, who steadily showed himself to be the peacekeeper of the meeting. Once the group had ceased their murmurs, the short Viscount returned attention to the Marquis. "What exactly do you mean by that, Marquis West? And more importantly, how do we know this isn't some sort of elaborate attempt to curry favor with the King?" The atmosphere of the silent room now thickened with tension as Marquis West locked eyes with his technical inferior.

"Excuse me, Viscount," West asserted with utter disdain, "but are you trying to insinuate that I would engineer a conflict out of pure self-interest?"

"I think what the Viscount means, my lord, is that the last time we entered into conflict with the Yoroi, our forces took a massive hit, and with the Yaiba Insurrection up to King knows what, we would have to make certain that the Yoroi Alliance has truly violated our agreement." The Marquis and the Viscount glanced in the direction of Ryan Crawford, a young man with curly brown hair and green eyes. Alan looked upon his youngest child as well, proud of his ability to deescalate a conflict far above his paygrade without fail. He was the perfect combination of Alan and Ashley, and was the spitting image of the former's grandfather. It pained his heart that the boy had decided to follow his path, but at the same time filled him with a sense of joy.

"Yes, well," the Marquis continued, and called Alan's attention back to the matter at hand, "allies may very well be the wrong word to use to describe the Alliance. After we had gained their trust, they allowed a diplomat from the Scarlet Kingdom to have a seat on their council. Recently, we have lost all contact with our representative in the Yoroi Council. Our spies have suggested that she might have defected." Alan's eyes went wide, but he quickly returned to his former military bearing. The very sound of defection made him tingle with excitement and fear, and it was when Marquis West spoke the word that Alan realized how terribly sick of this place he was. He wanted out, but there was no way to get to it from here.

"So what does that matter? If our representative wishes to join the Yoroi permanently, so be it. That does not change the relationship we have with the Alliance, nor should it," came one of the more detached nobles, Baron Stalks. He was a Hispanic gentleman, brown eyes and black hair, whose presence among the nobles was less than appreciated but begrudgingly accepted. The Marquis rolled his eyes, less because Stalks was an undesired guest in this meeting and more because of the futility of his thinking.

"Alone, Felicity's defection means nothing, and would hardly warrant a second glance," West answered. "But two other factors contribute to our present urgency. First, the Yoroi Alliance has been steadily encroaching on established Kabuto land for the last year and a half. The exact scope of their acquired territory is difficult to determine without someone directly on the Council. In response, the King has ordered that troops be stationed at key points in the Western Territory, though the effectiveness of that tactic is somewhat limited."

"And the second," Serenity asked, and the Marquis flashed a self-important glare in her direction before a stern expression from Alan made him correct himself.

"Second," West went on, "the Yoroi have apparently been in contact with the Yaiba Insurrection, though the nature of their engagements have been as of yet unclear." Again, the room came alight with the noise of chatter, and again, Alan Crawford found himself thrilled beyond comprehension. He was certain of it now. If the Yoroi, who excelled in guerilla warfare, managed to obtain the same kinds of weapons and training that those three monstrous Yaiba operatives had, then there was a chance that they would be able to wipe out the Kingdom forces sent to keep them in check. Even better, they would actually stand a chance of usurping the Scarlet regime altogether! And if he betrayed them, if he just found a way to get out of dodge and cripple them without them finding out, he might just be able to see his wife and children spared by the freedom-fighters that they thought were meager terrorists. The noise of the room settled at the standing of Countess McBride, a rather stout woman with brown hair and frail composure. Her face distorted as she processed what the involvement of the Yaiba Insurrection could mean.

The Insurrection was once the biggest joke among all the factions, not just the Kingdom. They were hunted mercilessly, and rightly so, because they were the only ones so bent on being a thorn in the King's side. It was true that the Yoroi Alliance and the Kabuto Sanctuary weren't friends of their autocracy, but neither of those factions went out of their way to become express enemies. They were, at least in the eyes of the aristocrats of the Scarlet Kingdom, reasonable people who simply sought the path of least resistance to the preservation of their lives. The Yaiba, though… They were a pitifully outmatched band of scoundrels and thugs who knew neither class nor intelligence.

Ten years after the rise of the Dawn King, the military strength of the Yaiba Insurrection began to decline, though they managed to make up for their falling numbers with rising technological advances. Their geo-sensors alone gave them more than enough escape routes when the situation looked too desperate for them. But it was sixteen years later, when their military shrank to the size of a third world militia force, when things changed forever.

They were surrounded, outgunned and outmatched, and though their total elimination was nigh, they somehow managed to not only survive another day, but destroy an entire platoon of Scarlet troops, save for one man. That night turned them into the stuff of nightmares, and their disappearance into the shadows of decimated America only cemented their legend.

The Countess spread her fingers on the table before her, and with a cold expression, stared at Sergeant Crawford with an intensity that rivaled the delicacy of her body. Eyes shifted between the two, and tension rose as even the Marquis silenced himself.

"You allowed this to happen," she said, and Alan coughed out a half-laugh. "If you lot had handled those brutes thirty-eight years ago, we wouldn't be in this situation today!"

"Lady," Alan started as he matched her stare with his own, "you don't even know what you're talking about."

"He's right," Marquis West agreed, "you don't. So stay your tongue, Countess, or I will stay it for you." Countess McBride took her seat, and the Marquis continued. "Now then… if the Yoroi and the Yaiba are, in fact, on the cusp of a new partnership between them, then we must do what we can to ensure not only our survival, but our continued dominion in this land."

"I suppose that's why I'm here," Alan cut him off. "You don't know enough about the Yaiba, and you know that if they team up on us you're practically doomed so you want me to tell you everything I know."

"Correct, Sergeant Crawford," replied the Marquis, who emphasized Alan's former position as a means of making him behave. Of course, it wouldn't, and both of them knew it, but West was determined to ensure that everyone present knew that they were beneath him in his own eyes. "You were there the night that everything changed, and you were the only one to survive. Now it's time for you to put that pitiful life to good use." Kyle, Ryan and Serenity all cut their eyes at the Marquis, who felt the animosity that they projected pricking against his exposed skin. He cleared his throat, but refused to correct himself.

Alan lifted a hand as he smiled and shook his head. He walked around the table to stand before Marquis West, and for just a moment they stared each other in the eye. There was a smugness to West that Alan thought severely undeserved of someone so young. The sniper looked him up and down. West was just a couple months past 25 years old, and now that Alan saw him up close, he knew what this attitude was about. There was a fear in the boy's eyes, a need for control that most likely came from being the youngest person in the room with the highest rank. Alan's face went blank, and the noble's face took up confusion as its banner.

"What are you—" West began, but was promptly interrupted by the meeting of the Sergeant's skull with his own. The Marquis, now devoid of the respect of everyone in the room, hissed from the pain that ran through his head as he fell to his knees and writhed. Alan, whose face was still expressionless, stood high above him while his kids looked on with utter delight.

"You know," Alan started in a tone only loud enough for the Marquis to hear, "I used to see a lot of people like you back in my military days. Young, dumb, and given a little bit of power because of a fancy title. Those people always overcompensated for the fact that they were the least respectable people in the whole army, and you? You're no different from that. Scrawny kid like you throwing his weight around because of some fancy title, like it makes you better than everyone else. Fact of the matter is I saw hell on earth and survived it. You're just riding on mommy and daddy's name trying to get other people to show you what I *earned.* I'll make this real simple for you, kid. I don't give a damn about your name. I couldn't care less about you being Marquis Whoever. I'm not military anymore, but if you ever disrespect me like that in front of my kids again, I'll make sure your parents have one less. Capisce?" The Marquis hesitated. "Answer me, boy," Alan said as he raised his voice.

"I understand," West replied as his nerves got the better of him. Alan smiled, and turned his attention to the rest of the group.

"Now then," he said, "let's get down to business."

****

The nobles and military officials looked on with an even mix of horror and intrigue as Sergeant Crawford explained what he saw the night of the extermination mission. Even as he recounted the experience, he could still hear the chains and feel the heat from the Yaiba operative's red-hot sword. Alan did his best to regulate his tone, but everyone in the room could hear the fear in his voice, and as the retelling of the events progressed, they slowly came to understand why he wanted no part of the military anymore. He reached the part of the story where he and that boy were spared by the dark-skinned man beneath the hood, but the kindness of a former enemy made him keep quiet about it. He took a deep breath, and stood for a moment as he gathered his thoughts.

"That's all I got," he told them with unintentional aggression. At this point, nobody questioned him. They all reasoned that a man who had seen what Alan had would be of a different species to not walk away with any mental or emotional scars. "Well, that's all that would be useful information, at least." The room remained silent for a moment longer. "The good news is, we only have speculation. There's no confirmation that the Yoroi and Yaiba have formed an alliance."

"Yes," agreed the Marquis, this time without a hint of superiority in his voice. "For now, avoiding a direct confrontation with those groups would be best. Our best course of action at the moment is to relay this information to the research labs. It'd be foolish not to work towards countermeasures for their gear."

"While I don't dispute the logic behind that line of thinking," Alan commented, "I'm not telling that story again."

"You won't have to," Viscount Leyva assured him in his typical haughty manner. "This meeting is being recorded for just such a purpose, and with what you've given us today, I dare say that the time to adjourn this engagement is upon us."

"I second," stated the Marquis, much to the surprise of all in attendance. "We will reconvene this war council at a later date. Sergeant," he directed his gaze to the only man who had ever checked him, and rubbed his forehead in hopes to soothe the pain. "Thank you for your cooperation. You are free to leave." Alan said nothing in return, and merely took his leave of the war room. Footsteps approached from behind him as he journeyed the palace halls, and he knew them to be those of his children.

"Well," Ryan started as he caught up to his father, "that was probably the most entertaining meeting I've ever been to."

"Yeah," Kyle chimed in. "Whatever happened to, 'Always respect those higher than you,' Sergeant?" Alan laughed as he wrapped his arms around his boys' shoulders. He realized that it'd been so long since they were together like this, and was resolved to savor the moment before they had to part ways again.

"I'm no sergeant, kid," he said with a crooked smile. "I've been retired for thirty-seven years."

"Still, Alan, you could've gone easier on the nobles. You could've been executed for pulling a stunt like that," Serenity scolded, but the old sniper shrugged it off as they approached the palace entrance.

"That's not likely to happen," he assured her. "I'm a war hero, whether we like it or not. According to Scarlet law I'm immune to any punishment short of murder or rape. Honestly, we're fortunate I wasn't completely broken by my experience. Who knows what kind of mayhem I'd cause?"

"I suppose you have a point, but it wouldn't kill you to show a modicum of decorum when dealing with the nobility, would it?" Serenity rubbed her forehead in mild agitation.

"I dunno," Alan replied, "it might. And if that did happen, would you wanna see your old man go out like that?" The boys snickered at their sister's defeated glance, but then tensed when they saw Alan tense. The four of them exited the palace, and they were all more than happy to do so. The entire time they moved through the corridors for the exit, each of them could tell that they were being watched. "Do you trust them," Alan asked. His children hesitated to answer. They all knew that they could be punished for even entertaining the thought of disloyalty.

"No," Ryan admitted finally. Kyle and Serenity shot him a look, to which he threw up his hands. "Something about us all being together didn't feel right, especially since they tend to keep family members apart during military proceedings of any kind."

"It is suspicious," Kyle was forced to admit. He folded his arms as he gave way to deeper thought, but couldn't put his finger on any motive to have them all together.

"It's more than that," Alan clarified. "The way I see it there are two possibilities."

"What are you thinking," Serenity asked. She hated to entertain the thought, but knew her father better than to assume that he was simply spouting conspiracy theories. If he was on edge about something, then there was a decent possibility that his hunch was spot on.

"The first possibility is that they wanted to remind me that you kids were at their mercy. If I'd had any intentions to resist cooperation, all they'd have needed to do was point a gun at any one of you and the fight would've been knocked right out of me," Alan explained. "The second is something that I feel is a lot more likely."

“And what’s that, Dad,” Ryan inquired with a boyish tone that took Alan back to their earliest years together.

“One of you kids did something you weren’t supposed to and got caught.” The young trio stood quietly as their limousine approached. The driver stopped beside the curb and the public servants came to open the doors. Alan turned to face his eerily silent children. “So, are you gonna tell me what you’ve been up to or are we gonna have a problem?”

Chapter Three

August 10th, 2084

Bryan Piccio scrambled in the lab as the signal wavered. He was on an important conference call with a contact in Gansu about the latest shipment of tungsten when the wires to the ever-aging comms system shorted out and distorted the audio. It was a problem that only seemed to happen when he was in the middle of something important, and for that he resented the old equipment. He never even fully understood why Director Ishikawa wouldn't authorize the "retrieval" of another system. But that was inconsequential to his current mission. He felt along the tape-covered cord that slithered from the walls into the central unit, and after he pushed against the centermost part of the line, the sounds stabilized. He stood, and finished his conversation as he watched his expected guests come through the door.

"*Gǎnxiè nín yīzhí yǐlái de zhīchí. Zhídào nà shí. Zàijiàn.*" Bryan ended the transmission as soon as he spoke the last word and directed his attention to his four guests. The first was a man with whom he'd shared the battlefield. He was tall with a trim yet muscular physique and deep chocolate eyes that not only matched his skin, but allowed him to see through just about everything. He was a prodigy in warfare, and was skilled enough with the Reikiken that he was named after the style he practiced: Rairyu. To the right of his old teammate stood his spitting image and son, the boy who not even two weeks prior became a member of the Yaiba Insurrection's ranks, Darius. Bryan couldn't help but smile at the way the kid still tugged at the collar of his uniform. The new ones always had to be broken in, but he knew from his own experiences that it wouldn't take all that long. To John's left was Bryan's own son, Jaden, who in Bryan's mind had the perfect mix of his parents' qualities. The boy's hair was brown like his mother Sharon's, but it was shaped like a muffin as had Bryan's been in his youth. He had the beginnings of a scraggly beard, brown like the lively hair atop his head, and bright green eyes that were as energetic as he was when he was little.

"This facility is astounding," spoke the fourth man. Bryan's eyes narrowed on the stranger as he looked him up and down. He was young, about in his mid-twenties, and though he was dressed for diplomacy, he had the frame of a warrior. His wavy brown hair and green eyes were startlingly close to Jaden's, but something about his skin was brighter. "Given the limited resources, it's amazing that you have this much advanced technology at your disposal."

"John, who's this?" Bryan immediately dispensed with the pleasantries, as he felt that this random stranger was an unwelcome intrusion to his workspace.

"Relax, Bryan," John told him with a chortle and a friendly pat on the shoulder. "This is Johannes Thornhill, an envoy of the Yoroi Alliance." Before John or the boys could explain, the researcher rushed the newcomer and, in a matter of seconds, thrust a nearby Reikiken at the young man's neck. The blade came alive with Vulcan heat almost as soon as he'd touched it, and of the trio, only John was fast enough to deflect the attack and train his own Reikiken on his old teammate. "Hey!" John's forceful vociferation did little to relax their guest, but it did inspire hesitation on Bryan's part. "He's here on Ishikawa's orders."

"Say what," Bryan blurted out in total surprise. He looked at Johannes, who at this point had fallen to the ground, and quickly disengaged the firesword in his hands. "My apologies, then." He turned back to John. "What's he doing here, though?" Rairyu, too, stowed his blade, and moved to help the envoy off the ground. The young man shook, and his facial expression told John that they'd probably be hearing about this incident later.

"You haven't heard," Jaden asked in such a calm that it made his seniors turn a glance at him. Bryan had always thought the boy took life too lightly, but given the perpetual battles that raged on all sides of them, he was grateful that his son could be as carefree as he was. “We have a partnership with the Yoroi Alliance now.”

“That’s kinda why we brought him here, Uncle Bryan,” Darius remarked with folded arms. A huge smile was plastered to his face as he shook his head, and Bryan’s cheeks reddened in embarrassment. “Ambassador Vargas of the Yoroi wanted a show of good faith, so the Director opted to let one of their emissaries see where the magic happens.”

“Mmmm…” Bryan folded his lips inward, turned his head to the side and narrowed his eyes. “You probably shouldn’t’ve said it like that, but I guess I understand. Still kinda miffed that nobody tells me things around here, but oh well. Alright, kid, take a look around and feel free to come to me if you have any questions about any of the equipment in this place.”

“Y-yes, sir,” Johannes replied, and excitedly began to pace the floor with the younger warriors in tow. Bryan and John took a step away and went into the office of the junky workshop. John, who hadn’t been on this level since old man Masamune retired, looked through the office window and admired the pieces of scavenged metal and failed experiments that still covered the floor from one end to the other.

“You’ve still got it, I see,” he said as he took in Bryan’s fuller figure and strong arms. “Looks like you might’ve picked up a little more since the last time you were out in the field with us.”

“Alright, alright,” Bryan laughed as he waved off the comments. “I’m nowhere near as good as you are. That response time, man? Jeez. If I were a real enemy, you’d have run me straight through right off the parry.”

“Probably, yeah,” John replied with a grin. “How’s Sharon doing? I’ve been so busy helping Emiko keep the peace with the Yoroi that I haven’t been around to visit you both like I should.”

"She's good. Been a bit overworked with the Civil Center. It's hard enough directing people who are trying to take care of people. It's even harder when everyone's spread so thin." Bryan sobered a bit, but then let out a huff and changed the subject. "So, escort duty, huh?"

"Yeah," John admitted in acceptance of the topic change. "Yeah, Em thought that with that guy coming and my boy freshly graduated, it'd look cute to give us a simple mission like this one." Bryan couldn't help but smile at his old friend as he took his seat behind the desk and motioned to the chair in front of it.

"You've really gotta start calling her Director," he said, but John shook his head.

"Absolutely not. She grew up in these tunnels same as us. I'm not gonna call her by her old man's title." Bryan rolled his eyes. "Especially when she's got me babysitting our kids and their Yoroi Alliance playdate." The comment made Bryan laugh, and John couldn't help but let his lips curl up at the corners a bit. A wave of nostalgia hit Bryan, as they often did, and John could see it on his face.

"I remember when they were small and all they thought about was playing," said the researcher.

"Yeah, and we were always acting like old men back then," replied the soldier. Both of them thought back to the old days, where Kirin Squad ran roughshod over the Scarlet forces from the Roanoke Weapons Cache to the Maryland Wall. Missions like that were always fun for them, because they were often so easy. Rairyu, the Lightning Dragon often got into trouble, and it was up to the man known as Usagi no Kamikaze to bail him out. At least that's how Bryan remembered things. Neither was without regrets on the battlefield though. After the Maryland Wall, Bryan made the choice to hang up the Hanzo Gear and commit to making it instead. It afforded him more time with his wife and son, a life change he never realized the importance of until his retirement.

"Yeah," he agreed, "and now we really are old." John grunted in exhaustion.

"Bryan, you're 39. You act as if you're over 100."

"I might as well be, given all the crazy stuff we used to do back in the day," he shot back. John tipped his head and folded his arms as he shifted and let one leg hang over the arm of his chair.

"Fair enough," he said. "By the way, what was that call about? The one you were on when we came in?"

"Oh, that?" Bryan sounded less than pleased when he remembered the hassle of making his machine act right. "Just got word from our contact in Gansu, China that our latest shipment of tungsten blades is coming in the next three weeks or so."

"Huh, so it looks like someone's gonna take a trip out to Yorktown, then," John uttered with passive excitement. "Wonder who that'll be…" his voice trailed off as he looked over his shoulder to the boys on the other side of the glass.

"You almost look worried, John." Bryan's voice was somewhat teasing, and inspired the lax warrior to raise his eyebrows.

"And you're not? If I remember right, you threw a fit when your little *Hrairoo* came back with the news that he'd be joining the military," John teased back, and the red in Bryan's cheeks deepened.

"Yeah, no, that's true," he was forced to admit, "but a rendezvous with the Chinese supply ships is as easy as it comes. It's so routine that the Director pretty much only sends out the newest recruits for it."

"And you probably still want me to convince Emiko to let me tag along, too," John assumed. It was spot on, and he could see it from the look on Bryan's face.

“It’d help put Sharon’s mind at ease,” he returned, and John knew that it was only half a joke. “After what happened with Lyla you can’t really blame her.” Even now, the mere mention of the young woman’s name drove daggers into both their hearts. Before Bryan became a researcher under Masamune, he tried his hand at instructing the next generation of Yaiba warriors. One student in particular was as a daughter to him. She’d lost her own parents, and while she was under the care of the Civil Center, she never really had much luck in forming bonds with the people around her. It was almost as if she’d expected them all to die.

Bryan and Sharon, however, were able to change that. They gave her skills to survive in ways that her parents couldn’t, and more than that they filled her life with laughter and love. That is, until she accepted a mission to Gansu. John thought to ask if he’d heard anything from her, but before he could part his lips there was a knock at the door.

“So much for catching up,” John mused, and rose to get the door. It was Jaden.

“Excuse the intrusion, Captain,” spoke the boy, overjoyed that he was able to work alongside his uncle in any capacity. “Dad, Johannes has a few questions he’d like to ask you.”

“Questions, you say,” Bryan inquired in his most over the top voice. “About what, if I may ask?” Jaden raised his eyebrows, widened his eyes, and huffed as he scratched his head.

“Well, everything,” he stated bluntly. “Dude’s rattling them off so fast that Darius and I can’t keep up. We thought it’d be best if we left it up to you.”

“You mean you don’t wanna be bothered with him, so you’re pushing him off on me,” Bryan deduced.

“I will neither confirm nor deny the accusations made against me,” said the junior soldier. John’s eyes went wide with humored surprise.

"I don't think you're even old enough to get that reference," he said. The kid looked to his uncle now and folded his arms.

"Are you?" The question made them all laugh, and as he made his way back into the greater lab, Bryan was able to discern that it was this warmth that he'd been missing in his life.

****

"I see," Johannes all but whispered as he eyed the masterful craftsmanship of the Reikiken. Master Piccio had explained to him the nature of the weapon, and from start to finish it was a captivating description. The name translates to "aura sword," and after such a close brush with it, Johannes could see why. The amount of heat generated in just seconds of it being switched on was staggering, but not as much as the contents of its hilt. Master Piccio said that the Reikiken swords were designed to funnel the heat of the user's palm into an internal processor that fed into thermal amplifiers. Those amplifiers would then channel the same heat energy into the tungsten blade. What Johannes found so amazing about it was that the blade would funnel energy back into the mechanism until it reached about 4,000 degrees Fahrenheit, at which point the processor and amplifiers would automatically shut off. "So, Dr. Masamune basically created a burning sword that'll never melt itself."

"Exactly," Bryan said with a fairly unexpected degree of excitement. "That's not the only perk though. See, Dr. Masamune wanted a weapon that bridged the classical swordsmanship of Sengoku Japan with the sophistication of 21st century tech. In order to do that, the weapon itself had to come ready with the ability to handle gunfire." Johannes' jaw dropped and his eyes widened in surprise.

"Those things can deflect bullets?" The young emissary blushed when he realized he'd asked the question louder than he'd originally intended, and quickly apologized. Bryan laughed and waved it off.

"They can't deflect bullets, unfortunately," he clarified. "But, the heatwave the Reikiken gives off is hot enough to distort most materials. It tends to make the bullets less aerodynamically sound, and the distortion knocks them off their marks. As added insurance, we wear those violet and black suits your escorts are in. They look comfortable, but really their outfitted with repurposed Kevlar once used in old US military tactical gear. From the hood to the boots, everything is protected." Johannes caught Darius in the corner of his eye and looked him up and down.

The young warrior was clothed in a form-fitting body suit with a hood attached at the shoulders. Gauntlets rested on his wrists, with chains wrapped around them and held in place by the blades at the ends. The bottoms of his boots were wider than normal ones, but Johannes couldn't tell why.

"What about the chains," the visitor asked with a nod of the head to Darius' wrists. Bryan looked and smiled wider.

"Ah, you mean the kyoketsu-shoge!" There was such an excitement in his voice that Johannes couldn't help but get excited. "Those are probably the most versatile weapons we have."

"And some of the most fun," Darius spoke up. "They're grappling hooks and bladed weapons rolled into one."

"Yeah," said Jaden as he rushed across the lab to join the conversation. "The kyoketsu-shoge can be pretty useful when navigating a complicated landscape. After the Second Civil War, most of the old cities are in shambles if not completely destroyed, so having a three-dimensional mobility pattern is invaluable."

"That sounds amazing," Johannes commented. He practically salivated at the idea of trying them out for himself.

"That's not all. The kyoketsu-shoge are treated with a heat-resistant fluid that prevents them from deforming or flat-out melting under the heat of the Reikiken, so we can move around without much concern," John said. Nobody heard him come over from the office door. He just appeared, and it gave Johannes the slight impression that if John wanted to end his life rather than preserve it, there would be nothing he could do to stop him. "You know, ol' Bryan here is known by us Yaiba as Usagi no Kamikaze. Any idea what that means?" Johannes shook his head with childlike excitement as Bryan rolled his eyes and face palmed.

"John, don't—"

"It's Japanese for 'Rabbit of the Divine Wind,' right dad?" Bryan cut his eyes at his son, but couldn't resist the urge to smile. It had been a long time since someone had even called him by his old codename, and longer still since someone came along who didn't recognize him on sight. John stood by with a smirk of his own plastered across his lips as Johannes, whose dignified image had already gone out the window, stood in awe of the legendary Usagi with a childlike brightness to his eyes. John moved to stand next to his dear friend and nudged him in the side with his elbow.

"I think the kid wants to see a demonstration," the Lightning Dragon said as his own blood boiled at the idea that crept into his head. "Think you're up for a quick match?" Bryan's eyes went wide and his humored face became as serious as the weapons they discussed.

"John, I have a lot of work to do around here," Usagi told him. "I have to run a ballistics test on the latest store of battle suits, run maintenance on the Roan Security System, and take inventory of all the armaments we're sending to the Yoroi Alliance research team." There was a pause as the two men looked at each other, and with the softening of his face Bryan continued, "Of course I'm down for a fight."

****

John knew exactly what he'd done. It'd been far too long since they got to mess around on the training floor of Level C, and they'd never done so while their sons could watch. Today, all of that changed. In retrospect, John wanted it to be a little bit of friendly competition, a small amount of fun to appease their honored guest, but what it became was a fierce battle of pride. Neither man wanted for his son to see him lose, even if it was technically just a game between friends.

"Are you guys sure this is a good idea," Darius called down from the eastern stands. He held a rifle in his hands, per his father's orders, and aimed it squarely at his uncle. Jaden, who took up position at the other side, trained his own firearm on John.

"It's fine, boys," John called to them. He was happy, happier than he'd been in a long time. "This isn't our first rodeo. Just do what we told you."

"We'll be fine," Bryan added, "promise."

"Cool, cool," Jaden answered back. "What's a rodeo?" The two seasoned warriors rolled their eyes and choked back laughter. Johannes, who sat at the northern stands, steadily grew more eager to witness the clash of powerful warriors. More than the people involved, he was invested in the technology. The descriptions in the research lab were riveting to him, and even before the scheduled arms shipment arrived at Yoroi headquarters, Johannes just knew he had to get his hands on a set ahead of time. He sat already at the edge of his seat, and watched carefully for how the battlements might be applied.

It was the Lightning Dragon versus the Rabbit of the Divine Wind, two legends in their own right, and the three spectators could feel the tension in the air. Their hearts pounded almost as hard as the combatants.

"This is pretty exciting," John had to admit. His fingers twitched with the electricity that pulsed in his veins.

"Yeah, there's no denying that," Bryan agreed. "Heh, my first opponent in seven years and it's you of all people. You sure you're not doing this to bully me?" John shook his head inaudibly. There was no way that he would ever do so much as underestimate Bryan, especially not after how many missions they worked out together. The Lightning Dragon tucked his left arm behind his back as he drew his Reikiken and ignited the blade. His sword burst to life as he held it up before his face and promptly pointed it at the ground. Bryan returned the salute of his friend with one of his own. He powered on his own sword and lifted it over his head before he slammed it down before him.

This sort of contest was the kind of thing that heightened their senses. They could hear their heartbeats in their chests become more rapid. Their hands gently caressed the hilts of the blazing weaponry in their employ, and though they both donned the hooded violet and black body suits that came standard for Yaiba operatives, the heat was still as potent as ever. The pillars in the floor began to rise, and the ripples in the dirt beneath them pulsed through their feet. Jaden and Darius fired their first rounds, and at the mere sound the two seasoned combatants vanished into the metal forest.

Johannes watched with excitement as the two legends clashed in the center of the floor. The boys continued to fire at their respective targets, but that did little to disengage the battle of the fathers.

Bryan swiped his burning blade at his friend's midsection with enough force to cut through the metal beams that stood on all sides, but John parried the blade through and revolved to his attacker's back. Rairyu lunged, but was pushed aside by a rolling block and pushed on the defensive again when Bryan followed the momentum through for a downward diagonal slash.

"Not bad," John willingly admitted. "I see you've grown strong in your Tsuchiryu style." In the old days, John had always been the best swordsman in the entire Yaiba military, and though Bryan was always with him, he barely stood a chance during sparring. He'd improved tremendously, and it made John happy to see it. The downward blow meant nothing, either way, as the pristine Hamlin parried his friend's weapon away once more and tracked the blade back to its owner's hands.

"Being retired gave me a lot of time to practice," Bryan quipped as he jumped backwards. The gunfire continued on either side of them, but the power and agility of their movements created a heat-shield around them that distorted the flight paths of the projectiles. *So he wasn't lying,* Johannes thought with escalated excitement. Bryan struck at both of John's shoulders with as much speed as power, and though he was blocked, it only gave him the energy he needed to multiply that power tenfold. He transformed the energy as he jumped into the air and executed a revolving slash, the signature move of the Kiryu style known as the Falling Leaf technique. It was enough to catch John off guard, but not enough to end the battle. John pushed the oncoming firesword out of the way as he moved off of the center line, and with his free hand he projected his kyoketsu-shoge towards a metal beam.

Bryan slashed at his friend, but before he could make contact, John had slipped away into the upper atmosphere of the room and grappled from pole to pole. Bryan smirked, as did the young man Johannes in the stands, as they both realized that John had made the fatal error of taking the fight to his enemy's comfort zone.

The boys saw their opening, and one after the other they shot at their fathers without hesitation. Bryan leaped backwards and used his chains to grapple in an unpredictable and three-dimensional pattern. He was fast, and he was terrifying. John, on the other hand, slipped behind another pillar and disappeared. He waited patiently in position, and used the blade atop his weapon hand to peer in all directions that he couldn't directly see. Bryan was still a ways off. *Good,* he thought, *if I can figure out a way to...*

Bryan knew where his friend was. He'd passed his location at least twice already as he shifted between the air, ground, and the pillars in between in his efforts to evade the gunfire. It was when he was certain that the boys wouldn't be able to snipe him that he grappled the ceiling and threw his other kyoketsu-shoge directly at John.

John was impressed. The blade he used as a mirror was knocked away, and as Bryan swiftly closed the distance between them, he had no other choice but to give ground. He swung around the pillar and grappled to another one a ways away from Bryan's flight path, but what he didn't account for was the versatility of the chains. Bryan latched onto a nearby pole only long enough for him to get his footing. He then vaulted into the air and grappled onto John's kyoketsu-shoge midflight to guide his body as he swung overhead. He gave some slack to the chains, but even as his feet hit the ground, John's trajectory was slightly off.

Bryan watched as the chain came back to him and his friend intentionally spiraled in midflight to avoid crashing into the pole he sought to land on. Bryan's lips twisted, as that was the move that he'd created during their attack on the Naval Weapons Station near Yorktown. As soon as the first chain retracted, he extended the other one towards his friend, but to his surprise, John had already expelled one of his own in the final turn of his revolution. The blades locked, and with John now anchored to the roof, he pulled his friend slightly off the ground.

The sheer surprise that Bryan felt was enough to make him lose his rooted stance, and the pulling of the two chains dragged the temporary enemies towards each other in a diagonal fashion. Bryan blocked instinctively, but a hard strike from John's Reikiken knocked Bryan's away from his head. John, ever the agile fighter, pulled his sword back and thrust his knees into his friend's chest, and with a ridiculous amount of force, the two crashed unceremoniously to the ground.

John sat with a knee in Bryan's chest and a burning blade pointed at his face. Bryan rolled his eyes as a grin crept up on his face. There was no way out, so he tapped the ground with his free hand to signal defeat. John removed himself and helped his old teammate back to his feet.

"That was so cool!" Johannes' voice echoed through the emptied arena as he raced for the floor. Even Jaden and Darius were taken aback by the brief but flashy show between men twenty years their senior. They knew the stories of their parents, but never had they assumed that there might be any truth to them. With a glance to each other across the stadium and through the now recessive metal trees, Jaden and Darius resolved to live up to and surpass the legacies of their fathers.

John looked up to see that determination in his son's eyes. He was proud to be able to show off a little bit in front of him. Of course, he knew that his boy looked up to him, but he wanted to do more than just give him a legend to admire. He wanted to give him a mark to go beyond. By the look on Darius' face, it was clear that the elder Hamlin had accomplished his mission rather well. It was, on all counts, as he'd expected it to go… but what he hadn't expected to see at all, was the ever watchful—if ever disapproving—gaze of his father, Dre.

****

Every time Dre saw his son, he felt a pang in his heart. John looked so much like his mother, yet so much like him that it was scary. Maybe that was why he silently watched from the shadows as his boy trained and fought.

John, on the other hand, also felt a pang in his heart at the sight of his father, but it was too difficult to navigate whether what he felt was anger or sorrow. Every time his deep chocolate eyes met with his father's hazel ones, he could hear the argument they'd had on John's eighteenth birthday. It wasn't something he cared to revisit, but lately he couldn't seem to escape the feeling that things were about to explode just like that all over again.

No words were spoken between the two as John came up from the training grounds. He'd sent the boys back with Bryan to help outfit Johannes with the same practice gear that the initiates used while he dealt with the man who was both closer to and farther away from him than anyone else he'd ever known.

Dre took a deep breath. He saw the uncertainty in his son's eyes, all the pain that he'd caused him, and it shook him more than the many horrors of the battlefield.

"Hey, John," he finally spoke. It still sounded as scratchy as ever, but more distressed than the younger Hamlin remembered.

"Dre," John responded coldly. "I gotta say, this is uncharacteristic of you. You've sought me out twice in almost as many weeks. Something on your mind?" There was a sadness in John's voice that he tried to disguise with the sarcasm, but Dre picked up on it nonetheless.

"I just want to talk," he said with his arms spread as a sign of good intention. John couldn't believe his ears. It'd been twenty years since they last spoke peacefully. Twenty years since John made his decision to follow in his father's footsteps. Twenty years since his father disowned him in a fit of rage and cast him from their family home.

"Wait, I'm confused," said John, who rubbed his goateed chin as his eyes narrowed from a genuine mix of surprise and outrage. "What happened to never wanting to see me again? Weren't you done talking to me back in 2064 or did I just imagine the huge falling out we had that almost put Mom in the infirmary?"

"John," there was a calm sincerity to Dre's voice that was so alien to him. "I'm sorry for what I did—"

"Yeah I bet you are," John shot back before his old man could finish. There was so much bitterness and rage in that miniscule utterance that it gave Dre pause. "Look, I'm sorry, I just…" his voice trailed off as he pondered the words to say. He'd run through this exact scenario thousands of times since the day he'd been kicked out. He was certain of what he would say, how he would feel, how he would act. But in this moment, he realized just how different theory was from practice. Dre could see the conflict in his son. Twenty years of distance between them did little to dull his senses as a parent. It made him ache to know that he was the source of so much misery and division within his own family, but seeing this opportunity to interject, Dre opted to speak in an effort to soothe his son's mind.

"I know," he started. John looked at him with furrowed brow, as if asking what the hardened soldier could possibly know about him. "I wasn't fair to you back then. I—"

"Look, can we not do this right now?" John's voice rattled this time, and Dre observed as his son's nostrils flared and his eyes watered. He still cared, at least to some extent, about what his father could say to him. The issue was that he didn't want to be reached. It made Dre's heart smile to know that in all this time his beloved boy hadn't completely shut himself off from him, and that was the part that he chose to focus on. "Why are you actually here?" The shake in John's tone had vanished, and in an impressive show of military bearing he straightened up to ask the question.

Dre paused for a moment. His eyes narrowed at first as the silent stare-down with his son persisted in all awkward tension, but softened his expression as he worked up the nerve to speak what was truly on his mind. Inwardly he chuckled, because that ability to see through his niceties was a trait he'd inherited solely from his mother.

"John," he spoke with a crack, but did what he could to pull himself back together, "Your mom's…" Dre couldn't bring himself to finish the sentence. It was too painful for him, and he didn't want to cause his son anymore pain than he already had, no matter how necessary it was for him to know. The hesitation on the old man's part proved to be naught more than a nuisance to John.

"Mom's what," John asked, and Dre stammered in desperate search of the right words to say. "Tell me!" There was panic in his voice now, along with sadness, uncertainty, anger, and a slue of other things that blended so well into the mix.

"She, uh," he struggled to put the quake in his voice behind him as he tried to relay the information. He grunted to clear his throat. "A few weeks ago she said she was feeling sick. Said she was lightheaded and that it felt like she had speakers in her brain that kept pounding louder and louder. I went over to check on her, but then she stopped speaking. Half of her face just dropped. Her eyes started shifting back and forth and I didn't know what was happening." The fear returned to him long after it was over. He'd never seen anything like that, something that seemed to rip her apart from the inside out. His body began to shake from the sheer confusion of what to do, and the more John watched, the more concerned he got. "I didn't know what to do. I called for help, and the medics came and took her to the infirmary but they wouldn't let me see her until late."

"You didn't wanna tell me this sooner?" John was irate, and just as soon as he'd decided the conversation was over and moved past his father did Dre reach out his hand and grab his boy by the arm.

"Son, I tried," he insisted, but the look John shot him was rife with disbelief. "The day I came down to Level C, I planned to talk to you, but seeing you there, in uniform, laughing and joking around with your friends, I froze."

“Something horrible happened to my mother and you didn’t tell me because you saw me having a good time with the people that actually care about me?” John pulled his arm away from his father, who stood there like a scolded dog before his son. His expression was still as rough as it always was, but John was able to detect the subtle changes in his demeanor.

“It isn’t that simple,” Dre told him with raised voice, and they both thought it was for the best that Darius couldn’t see them behaving like this.

“Then by all means,” John fired back with arms wide open, “explain it to me so I can understand, Dre.”

“I didn’t feel like I had a right to disturb your happiness,” the old man yelled, and beat his fist against the nearby wall. John stood there silently, bearing still in place while his heart beat savagely against his ribs. “But the time for that is gone now, son. I don’t know how to say this so I’ll just come out and say it. Last night, your mother…” he took a deep breath and tried to stop himself from falling apart. “She’s gone, son.”

Chapter Four

August 24th, 2084

They'd been walking for hours through the great expanse once known as the Cherokee Forest, each of them in full Hanzo Gear but with an additional sack for storing found treasures. Since the Second Civil War, the roads and small industrial areas that once existed outside the realm of trees had been all but demolished, and without anyone to occupy and tend to them, the flora and fauna of the forest expanded unchecked. The threat of a storm loomed over the 4-man cell, and the frantic cries of birds in the canopy echoed in their hearing. The wind blew, and the crunchy shifting of broken concrete and earth emerged with every step. The sun steadily fell behind the treetops, so the black and violet of the bodysuits would soon blend into the night. It was a routine scavenge trip, this time in Johnson City, and the Director's shopping list was a lengthy one.

Callan Rouge led the excursion. He was a strong if not slender man of pale skin and bright blue eyes that were perfectly offset by his dark brown hair. His serious demeanor was intimidating to Cal, but to Lukas and Darius he was just another of their weird uncles. None of them could deny his record as a warrior, though. Director Ishikawa believed him to be the best choice for a mission like this. He, on the other hand, didn't think so. Callan was the kind of person who preferred the tactical excellence and waves of adrenaline that typically came with combat and espionage missions. Scouting for salvageable materials and medical supplies for the base was of little interest to him. Orders were orders, though, and with a glance back at Darius he knew that this terribly basic mission was more for the kid than it was for him.

It'd been a week since May Hamlin was laid to rest deep within the mountain. Her funeral was a difficult one for all within the community. Thousands of people knew her, were pushed by her, learned from her, and by the droves they all wept for her loss. None, however, cried more than her beloved son John, who earnestly regarded May as his only parent. Darius could still remember how shocked he was to see his old man drip from his eyes. John was known for his near-flawless military bearing, and only ever broke it to give a cocky smile to whatever adversary was dumb enough to challenge the Lightning Dragon of the Yaiba Insurrection.

Darius couldn't blame him. It was hard enough for him to get a grip on things, and he'd known May for half the time his father did. He thought about the kind of grandmother she was, sweet and gentle. She insisted that he call her "Suga Momma," which he knew was a reference to something but wasn't sure to what. He remembered that it made him feel awkward at first, but eventually he grew to call her by that name with the greatest affection. Losing her meant losing the part of his soul that told him anything was possible, and everyone knew it. That was why the Director sent the boy out with his friends and Uncle Callan.

"Time check," called the team leader to the three newest soldiers that marched behind him. Cal checked his watch.

"It's 16:30, sir," he responded nervously. Callan took notice, but decided against teasing him about it.

"We're making good time, then. We'll be there in the next hour, give or take a few minutes. Let's go over the plan again just so we're clear on how this is gonna go down." Cal, Lukas and Darius came together as their leader pulled out an electronic pad with a digital map of their destination already on the screen. "Once we make it into the city ruins, our objective is to stock up on anything we find that might be useful to the Insurrection. We'll move in Scavenge Formation Diamond so we can stay within range of each other and avoid spending too much time in each area. Once we make it to the old Veteran's Hospital and nab some medical supplies, the mission's done and we make our way back.

Keep our comms channel open and pay attention to the geo-sensors in case anything goes down."

"Yes sir," Lukas said with a fervent salute. Even in his liveliness, Callan could see that he had a question, and gave him permission to ask it. "But what do we do if something happens?" It wasn't uncommon for Lukas to ask questions that demonstrated an expectation for the worst possible scenario. Growing up in a war-torn climate will do that to a person. Nevertheless, the cheery manner in which he spoke proved to be almost contradictory to the nature of his inquisition.

"Then we hang back," Callan stated plainly. He glanced in the direction of the city, though they were still some ways off and couldn't see it in full. "We're on a scavenger mission. Our priority is to get what we need and get out. Battle in this scenario," he paused, as the words he would speak caused him a great deal of pain before they even left his lips, "is a last resort only." He observed the fading lights of the setting sun, and determined that it was time to go. "Let's move." The troops under Callan's command proceeded without protest, and advanced in small number on the city.

With the brief mission over, Darius returned to his thoughts, much to Callan's displeasure. The boy—for in Uncle Callan's eyes, he'd always be the cheery little boy from back then—should make every effort to be present in the field, both physically and mentally. But he wasn't. He wasn't alert to his surroundings, and was barely awake enough for the orders that Callan gave. The senior soldier, then, made the decision to place Richmond in the front while he took up a rear position next to his nephew.

"How are you holding up?" The question caught Darius off guard. People knew what the answer was. Even in a world where death was such a commonality that the masses—or whatever was left of them—largely didn't care, May's death seemed to rattle the foundations of the mountain in which they lived. Many of them were focused more on processing their own grief than monitoring how the youngest Hamlin dealt with his. But Callan was from a different generation. Of course, he wasn't as old as Dre or that legendary generation, but he was raised in a time where the casualties of the Yaiba Insurrection were outnumbered by the souls that filled its ranks and community. What almost startled Darius just seemed natural for Callan.

"I don't know how to answer that," admitted the boy. They walked in silence for a while, and Callan waited patiently for Darius to find the words. "I feel like I should've been left at home. My dad—"

"Your old man'll be just fine," Callan told him with such surety. "Anyone ever tell you that you focus too much on other people and not enough on yourself?"

"Yeah," Cal chimed in from a few feet away. Callan raised an eyebrow and stifled a laugh. "I keep telling mans that all the time, but does he listen to me? Nope!" His tone was playful as always, and it made Darius smile.

"Look here, Mr. Rich," Darius started in a playful tone all his own, "I don't need you speaking for me; and besides, this was a private conversation between me and the captain." Cal shrugged as he slowed his pace and took position beside Callan. He and Darius exchanged looks, and to the latter's surprise there was a sincere degree of concern in his friend's expression. It made Darius pause.

"Yeah, but how you're handling this is a pretty public concern," Cal replied.

"May was your grandmother, kid," Callan said sympathetically. "Your dad is taking this hard, that's true, but you gotta realize that what he's feeling about this doesn't negate what you're dealing with on your end."

"I know that," Darius spoke with more attitude than was appropriate. He corrected himself instantly at the stern expression of his superior, and Cal moved up ahead to cover Lukas as they advanced on the nearby ruins of Johnson City. "I know that. I just… I wanna focus on the mission. I can have feelings later." Darius moved past his uncle, who watched him with concern masked behind the seriousness he was known for.

****

They entered the city in silence as protocol dictated, but Callan understood that it was more than that. Nevertheless, he issued hand signals to mark the starting positions of the troops in his charge. The place was in shambles, and with the tallest structures of Johnson City lying in heaps of rubble, ash or some combination of the two, it was easy for Callan to maintain visual contact with his subordinates. He gave a nod, and the four soldiers spread out to four points no more than 500 feet away from their comrades.

Cal remained south and investigated an old plasma clinic while Lukas zipped to the east with his kyoketsu-shoge and repulsors. The weeks between their graduation and their first field mission had been rather unkind to his skill in using the equipment, and he almost looked as a duck with a wounded wing. Darius took to the northernmost position, and surveyed the remains of abandoned cars and busses that dotted the streets for scrap metal that the research lab could rework. Callan bolted to the western position and sifted through the remains of buildings and cars for anything he could find that might prove useful.

He remained vigilant and watched the territory for any sign of the Scarlets. He pulled a metal bar from a door, some glassware, a few reams of paper and a box of matches in surprisingly good condition. Five minutes passed, and with a signal through the comms channel to the others, they moved westward and deeper into the city.

Their positions changed now, and as the soldiers rotated in a counterclockwise pattern, Cal took to the west with more excitement than the mission required. Of course, it was less rooted in scavenging and more due to his desire to test out his latest modification to his Hanzo Gear. He looked through his visor at the cars and buildings that adorned his westward path and glowed with delight as objects of value blinked from the geo-scanner readings. With his kyoketsu-shoge and repulsor boots, the young soldier practically flew about the terrain on a hunt for anything that would curry favor with the Director and show up his teammates. He didn't think that this mod would make much difference at first, but now that he was on this type of mission it was proving to be somewhat invaluable. In fact, it almost made the tedium of his task more enjoyable.

Lukas, who held the easternmost position before, shifted southwest to continue his search. He landed at an old building that looked as if it had already been burnt out and plundered. The half-destroyed sign at its front retained the word "Brewery," clearly a mark of the past. Lukas and his generation had no idea what such a thing was, but in his optimism he inspected it. There was a stale stench to the place, sour and heavy enough to make him just a little bit dizzy. He knew that he couldn't remain there for long, so he quickly floated through the facility and grabbed all the scrap he could manage before he would inevitably drown in the haze left in the building.

Callan went north and continued to raid what cars were left in the area for cushions, metals, plastics, and recyclable papers. He was still on his guard. Something didn't feel right to him about this mission, and while it didn't seem to be out of the ordinary, he went about his collection duties with a heightened sense of precaution. He made sure to avoid open spaces if he could, and never spent more than two minutes on any vehicle or structure. For difficult items that he couldn't just strip, he used the blades of his titanium kyoketsu-shoge to cut through whatever caused the issue and quickly moved on in the event that someone other than his teammates lurked in the shadows of the decaying Johnson City.

Darius, in contrast, was less attentive to anything more than the terrain. He covered the east, so his responsibilities for the position after the initial scouting of the area were to be mindful of any suspicious activity to the rear of the formation and do a once-over of previously searched structures. He, like his uncle, kept to the shadows as much as he could, and mindlessly performed his duty in silence. He did his best to lose himself in the mundanity, but with every passing second his grandmother's face filtered into his mind. He shook it off, but she always came back.

Callan gave the signal, and the team switched places again. The four of them picked at the remains of the dead city and carefully surveyed their surroundings as they moved west towards the Veteran's hospital. The eerie silence of civilization's remnants made the group more nervous than the mission typically would have. Something wasn't right, and the entirety of their cell could feel it.

"Uncle Callan," Darius whispered on the comms.

"I know," the senior officer commented. "Lukas, what's the readout on the geo-scanners?"

"Gimme a sec," replied the subordinate. He scanned the terrain with his visor for any sort of movement or shifting of the ground. There was nothing in all directions. "No movement whatsoever, sir."

"That's a relief," Cal sighed, and wiped the sweat from his brow.

"No, it's not," Callan responded. "Since the war, areas like this with large spots of unruly vegetation and a substantial lack of people should be home to all kinds of animals. We've been here for almost an hour and haven't seen or heard any signs of wildlife." He took a moment to scan the terrain himself, but instead of movement, the team leader carefully observed for high concentrations of pressure on the surface. His eyes went wide, and his prolonged silence made the others uncomfortable. "We need to regroup. On my position."

****

It had been a month since that day in the war council at the Scarlet Palace, and the Kingdom was still formulating its plan to bring the Yoroi Alliance back under subjugation. All reason dictated that the faction was beyond total destruction, but they weren't untouchable. Now, it was up to Colonel Serenity Crawford and her Scarlet Scourge to wait for the appropriate opening to exploit.

Currently under her command was an entire troop of Scarlet Kingdom military personnel that ranged from infantry to medical support with the Scourge as a nice centerpiece. The intelligence unit, headed by Major Kyle Crawford, was sent ahead by a week to scout out the newly acquired territories of the Yoroi while Serenity and her men held at the old East Tennessee State University campus and awaited their report.

It'd been two weeks since they'd arrived, and in that time they'd managed to turn the tattered ruins of the college town into a sustainable hub for military life, even if it was a temporary base. They'd even kept up on their physical training, martial skills and target practice. Even now, the entire troop made use of the old university gym and the surrounding area for an evening workout. They were strength personified, and as Serenity caught sight of a squad out for a run, a smile crept across her face.

"Colonel." The mildly exasperated tenor of the Second Prince emerged from behind her, and immediately the look of contentment transformed into resentment. She turned her head to see the ruggedly handsome blond prince. He had entrancing stardust-gray eyes with flecks of brown and gold, pink-ivory skin, and a build that rivaled a Greek god. Serenity couldn't deny that he was pleasing to the eye, but the simple presence of this noble made her feel undermined as a military leader. "I am experiencing a rather embarrassing technological issue. If you would, please accompany me to my quarters." Serenity let out a heavy sigh, unafraid of what such a display of attitude would earn her at the hands of a royal.

"I suppose I can't refuse," she said aloud. "Fine. Gallaher, hold things down until I get back. Hopefully this doesn't take long."

"Yes ma'am," responded the subordinate. Without further delay, the colonel and the prince journeyed from the makeshift gym to the building labeled "…Jr. Hall," the only building big enough to provide modest comfort for the King's second son. Serenity looked over her shoulder, and with a great deal of excitement she realized that they were out of view of her physically active subordinates. She took the prince by his hand and led him back to his quarters with greater urgency, and he, in turn, adopted the very crooked smile that made every woman in the Kingdom buckle at first sight. They turned a corner and came to the doors of Jr. Hall, which the royal pushed open in a bid to take charge. Serenity giggled, because beneath all the celebrity cool that he presented to the people in the Kingdom, under the façade of dignity and composure, was a man just like any other but with an ego twice as fragile.

She immediately took his lips with hers as the doors drifted shut, and he ran his fingers through her shoulder-length black hair. Serenity crossed her arms around his neck as she pressed her body against his. They came up for air as she again took control, and spun away from him with his hand in hers. They went up the stairs and into a spacious room that, at one point or another, had clearly been two. The prince closed the door, and as soon as he turned around, she pounced on him again. Their lips locked, and he almost fell over from her force. He braced the door with his palm and laughed through the kiss.

"I've missed this, James," she told him, and stroked the center line of his chest with her finger. She knew that what they had was beyond forbidden and, even worse, unprofessional, but to her it didn't matter. She'd made a life of covert missions and risking her life. What was one more insurmountable obstacle? His eyebrows raised as his crooked smile now stretched to either ear.

"You called me by my name," he said. He had never heard her say it out loud before, and she said it with such a degree of tenderness and warmth that he now surprised her with a kiss. He pressed his lips against hers, then against her neck and she moaned. He relished in the fact that he could feel her quiver with delight at his every touch. He moved her over by the bed, but Serenity pushed him down onto it, and just as she removed her jacket and shirt, the alarm blared. Prince James sighed as Colonel Crawford reapplied her uniform, and with an exchange of apologetic looks, the two of them exited the room.

Serenity exited first and managed to make it back to the first level before she was noticed by any of her subordinates. She turned and walked down the hall next to the stairwell, then turned into their makeshift command center. She accessed the central console as quickly as she could, and realized that the proximity sensors had been tripped not once, not twice, but four times. At first she assumed it was because some forest fauna had broken the perimeter, but quickly dismissed the idea since she knew that the Scarlet presence in the run-down Johnson City caused any animals to keep a safe distance.

"Colonel Crawford," Gallaher called as he entered the command center. "I came as soon as I could."

"What's the situation," James spoke as he strode in after Crawford's second in command. Serenity typed away, eyes fully focused on the holographic screen before her instead of the prince she so desperately wanted another taste of.

"Working on that now," she said with a tinge of aggravation and a tilt of her head. The feed from the surveillance cams opened up on the screen. So far there was nothing, but when she input the coordinates for the triggered sensor, she saw them. "Got a group of four males, age range from 18 to roughly 40 years, and…" her voice trailed off as she zoomed in on their equipment, and noticed the unmistakable bladed gauntlets and dense metal pole at their sides. "Looks like we've got some Insurrectionists on our hands." The mere mention of the Yaiba was enough to put the gentlemen in her company on high alert.

"Not exactly the most ideal news I could've gotten this evening," remarked the prince. Serenity looked at him and noted the calm in his eyes. He was hardly a military leader by her standards. He was too calm, too open to negotiation and diplomacy. But what she hadn't realized during their six months of secret romance, is that James observed her every move, as much on the battlefield as in bed, and that was why it surprised her that he took charge here. "For now, stand by and observe. I doubt they know we're here, so this gives us the perfect chance."

"The perfect chance for what," Serenity asked from her state of shock, but when he cut his eyes at her, she remembered that her rank was substantially less than his, and quickly added a more docile, "sir?" He overlooked the unintentional disrespect and smiled as he turned his gaze back on the screen.

"Why, to capture one alive, of course."

****

There was no movement in the decrepit hospital, or at least none that Callan could make out through the readings on his visor, and for a moment he thought to drop his guard.

"So," Lukas asked with a tinge of uneasiness in his voice, "what do you think?" Callan sighed as he turned to face the subordinates at his back. They all stood only halfway facing him, and watched the surroundings carefully for the first sign of danger.

"I still don't trust it," he said frankly. "In any case, this place is the main part of our mission. Once we finish up here, we'll get out of dodge and head back to the base."

"Sounds good to me," Cal stated in his typical humorous manner. "This place gives me the creeps."

"Same here," Darius agreed, and visibly shook from the discomfort.

"You three know what to grab," Callan asserted as he gave the terrain another once over. "Head towards the center of the facility. The pharmacy somewhere around there and you might be able to find some salvageable medicines. Meanwhile, I'll take up position on the roof and keep watch over the entrances and exits until you guys are on the way out."

"Understood," said the three subordinates, but before they could propel themselves forward with their kyoketsu-shoge and repulsors, Callan placed his hands on Lukas and Cal's shoulders. The three turned to face him and saw the face of no military commander, but of a genuinely caring and concerned uncle.

"Be careful," he warned them, "and watch each other's backs." They silently nodded, and with a fleeting smirk he barreled for the east entrance of the medical building and, with a timely deployment of his kyoketsu-shoge, grappled up to the roof in record time.

"Show-off," Lukas teased under his breath. "I wanna be like that one day." The others grinned, and cautiously made their way towards the facility.

****

The Scarlet Scourge watched from the second floor above the pharmacy area waiting room. Chairs lay strewn about the floor, papers scattered among them, and with the long cracks in the stone tiles, fledgling plants began to show themselves. The glass of the skylight was broken in spots, and the falling rain splashed against the old, worn, centermost wares of the place. Quietly, the huntresses awaited the prey that perimeter surveillance showed them was in the area, and each of the team of six held a different position. Serenity glanced at her comrades, her sisters in arms, and took stock of their expressions.

Amelia Kluger, to her immediate left and the only member of the Scourge Colonel Crawford saw as her equal, stood ready with her favorite dagger drawn and clutched in a reverse grip. Amelia, along with most of the Scourge, were either the daughters or granddaughters of the men and women who'd died on the night of the White Ruins Massacre, and each had a score to settle with the Yaiba for what transpired. Amelia crouched just below the damaged railing along the second floor bannister, her golden eyes like those of a hungry tiger as she watched through strands of her fiery red hair.

Kerri Waldheim, a staggering brunette with eyes to match and twin pistols at her disposal, was more serene in her expression. She was hardly the kind of person to get riled up on a mission, even at a time like this. Of course, she wanted to exact vengeance on behalf of her family, but more than anything she wanted to do her part in helping the King extend his reach to the farthest coast of Prevalence.

Cecelia Kant, a voluptuous blonde with green eyes and full pink lips, sat with her rifle against the steps and visibly struggled with the idea of capture and not kill. She was, without a doubt, the loosest cannon on the team, but suddenly calmed down when she remembered that the prince only needed one of them alive. That meant that she could kill the others, provided that she could beat her teammates to the punch. She glanced to her sister Trisha, a thinner, more tech-inclined version of herself, who took her place on the opposite wall. Trisha, who was about as even-tempered as Kerri, worriedly eyed her sister, but relaxed when Cecelia flashed her a toothy grin.

"Picking up movement on the heat scanners," whispered Aria Black into the comms. She watched the first floor opening to the pharmacy with a muted ferocity, as though she were tired of her opponents' antics without ever having met them before. She wore black lipstick, which somehow deepened the tone of her already semi-dark skin. Her near-black eyes scanned the metal blinds that prevented them from seeing directly into the storage area, and in her head she did her best to arrive at the most likely conclusion as to what her adversaries were doing.

"Alright, everybody focus. We'll only get one shot at this and I'd prefer it go as smoothly as possible," Serenity commanded. The rusted doorknob twisted, and as the squeak of it perforated the silence of the abandoned clinic, the Scarlet Scourge readied themselves.

****

"Hostiles detected!" Darius shouted as soon as the door had opened. The team scrambled, and as Darius dove behind the nearest support pillar for the second floor platform, he noticed the dark skin of an oddly familiar woman on the upper level. Her garb was unmistakably Scarlet, but there was a familiarity about her that twisted his gut. Their comms unit buzzed.

"Tetsuryu, come in," came Callan's authoritative voice over the headset. "What's going on?" There was no answer at first. The three of them took a moment to size up the enemy, but that was easier said than done given their current position mere inches from the storage room door. Cal answered with the repetition of his callsign.

"We got surrounded," he said in a lighthearted calm. "Scarlets are here." They could all feel Callan's eyes widen on the other end.

"That's impossible," he assured them, "I would've seen a ground force move in from my position, and there's no way they could've made it here so fast unless…" he paused as panic quickly took its hold.

"There seem to be only a handful of them," Lukas told him. From behind another pillar he counted the heads he saw from the space just above him. "I count two from my end."

"One across the way from us," Darius confirmed. Shots fired from just in front of the stairs that led up to the higher platform, and Cal took cover behind the pillar nearest the front of the steps. He held up the blade of his kyoketsu-shoge to use it as a mirror, and noted the remainder of the group.

"I got eyes on three," he told their commander. "Huh. They're all women."

"Get out of there. *Now*," Callan ordered with so much force in his voice it instilled fear in the subordinates. It was clear to him exactly with whom he was dealing, and the destructive force that those six women commanded was far beyond the skill level of three rookies fresh out of training.

"On it," Darius said, and ended the transmission. The three newest soldiers of the Yaiba ranks brandished their swords and laid their bags on the ground. One by one, their Reikiken weapons came to life and escalated the temperature of the otherwise chilly room.

The Scourge smiled. This was a treat for them the likes of which they never thought they'd see. For years they'd carried out covert ops within Yoroi or Kabuto territory, sorting out things that could have turned into messy failed attempts at uprisings against the Kingdom, but deep down they all knew that it all meant nothing. The Yaiba had always been the prize.

Kerri, the stoic brunette, jumped down from the second floor and narrowly dodged a bladed chain that launched at her face. She opened fire on the position of her attacker, and though she knew she wouldn't hit him, it made him feel better.

Lukas only narrowly dodged her bullets, and sighed in relief as he listened for the irregular sound between her shots. She was walking towards his position, so he launched his chains at the ceiling and grappled up in wait of her.

Kerri emerged, the barrels of her smoking pistols aimed at the space where her enemy should've been, but he was gone. All that remained was the sweltering heat that steadily filled the entire room.

The playful warrior purposefully rattled the chains of his weapons like a ghost in the night, and pounced upon the huntress as she gave him her attention. As Lukas descended, Cal waited for the opportune time for his enemies on the stairs to cease their hail of bullets and reload. By the sound of it, the ladies at the top of the steps used M16 semiautomatic rifles. He smirked as he glanced to the ceiling and counted in his head. *One, two, three...* The huntresses kept firing, and Cal, ever the witty fighter, grappled to the ceiling and maneuvered through the air with his repulsor boots. *Thirteen,* he tracked as he continued the cycle of grapple and repulse, *fourteen, fifteen...* The shots were in perfect sync but opposite angles. Cal smiled, because he knew they were trying to narrow his range of motion. What they hadn't accounted for was his ability to maneuver in more than just a two-dimensional plane. *Eighteen, nineteen, twenty.*

The sisters, Cecelia and Trisha, marveled at his graceful movements and the sheer duration of his airborne path. They'd never had the chance to fight against an enemy with so much style before, and while Trisha was apprehensive to see more of what this foe could offer, Cecelia was alight with joy.

The last ten shots fired quickly and, in Cal's opinion, expertly, but not a one packed enough power to end his aviation. He pulled himself higher with the kyoketsu-shoge, then repulsed himself headlong into an unsuspecting Trisha. She fell unconscious from the sheer force of the assault, but the animal Cecelia relished in the surprise of the moment. She pointed her gun at him, but with a swift slice of his titanium blade the weapon split in two. He wagged a finger at her, and as she charged him to engage him unarmed, Amelia cut in and pressed her prized dagger against his throat.

The ceasing of the gunfire in the background gave Darius all the signal he needed, and with no further delay he launched himself up to the second floor. Aria watched him drag against the air on the recoiling chain and kick himself onto the platform with a blast of his repulsors. He was a strong, young, physically attractive black man that made her cheeks burn as she thought of all the possibilities. He, on the other hand, was too focused on the order his leader had given him and aimed his sword at the enemy's face. Her eyes smiled darkly before her black lips did, and as Serenity came to Aria's assistance, the latter of the femme fatales snapped her finger.

A blue pulse fired through the room, and the burning swords that the Yaiba troops brandished with such pride fell dull before their eyes. The three of them were shocked, but they quickly rebounded as they stowed their Reikiken and engaged their opponents hand to hand.

Behind the pillar on the ground level, Kerri threw Lukas off with more strength than he'd assumed she had, but as she sprang to her feet the jovial but cunning Insurrectionist kicked her first pistol from her hand and ducked as she fired with the other one. He went for a leg sweep, but she lifted her exposed leg and extended it to his face. To her surprise he was nimble enough to roll out of the way and lift up a metal trash can to block the bullet that pierced the air en route to his forehead. He threw it at her, something that she didn't expect, and though she swatted it out of the way, she failed to do the same with the follow-up kick to her ribs.

Cal pushed Amelia's knife away from his throat with the explosive force he was known for, and without letting go performed an elbow to the side of her face. She stumbled back, but Cecelia quickly stepped up to take her place. She punched at his sternum, and was quickly met with a gentle push off to the side. Cal saw the opening that he created with the move, and issued a twisting punch to her kidney that made the flesh around it swell up. Cecelia fell to one knee, and Amelia used her as a stepping stool to vault herself into the air. She poised her knife to bleed Cal dry, but the crafty neo-ninja flipped out of the way with a perfect back handspring. His feet caught her weapon hand and knocked the knife into the wall. She looked at it, then at Cal, and he couldn't help but smirk at the flustered look that took her face.

On the other side of the second floor platform Darius deflected Serenity's punches and kicks with relative ease. What he couldn't do was create an opening. He was being pressured by the flurry, and with his teammates preoccupied he was on his own. He vaulted to the rear to establish distance, but then came back at the seasoned Scarlet with a shot of his own. He drove his leg sharply forward at her chest, but she sank low and tried to sweep him. Darius knew the kind of opening the push kick would create for her, and instinctively threw his legs back over his head and landed soundly in a crouched position. From the low station, he whipped his backmost leg at her head with staggering speed, yet somehow she dodged him. The two adversaries stood, wholly focused on each other as Aria watched the chaos from the background. Darius delivered a roundhouse kick, and though it made contact, he found his leg caught between Serenity's hip and her arm. She pressed against the side of his knee and made him fall to the ground, then stomped hard on his abdomen. He coughed, and with a blank expression she pulled out a pistol from the holster at her lower back. Surely they could take one of the others. He kicked her in the back and made her stumble off of him, and groggily he returned to his feet. She pointed the gun at him now, frustrated that he'd lasted even this long when he was so clearly green.

Lukas charged his foe, careful not to give her the time to breathe. Time to breathe meant time to aim, and that would only end badly for him. He slashed the blade at the end of his chain through the air at her, but she rolled out of the way. He slashed again, but the result was the same. He didn't need to beat her, he just needed to hold her off until Callan arrived. He spun in place and extended both of his chains within a limited area, but the cunning Kerri slipped beneath the whirling blades. In an almost serpentine manner, she slithered behind her opponent and pressed her pistol to his skull.

Though Lukas was forced to hold, Cal still raged like the titanium tempest he was. He used the blades chained to his wrists as daggers of his own, and with every slash came some unorthodox flip or roll to quickly change the direction of his next attack. To his enemies, he looked as a wild man, a human storm fused with a maddened beast, and before long the versatility of his movements became too much for them. Cecelia, the staggered juggernaut, watched as one of the deadly titanium fixtures rocketed towards her face. She smirked, then took Amelia by the hand and pulled her in the way. Her shocked teammate took the blow straight through the abdomen. Cal was just as stunned as his victim, and in the moment he took to digest the situation, Cecelia rushed him and pinned him to the ground.

The doors of the main entrance opened. It was Callan. He surveyed the battle, his three charges disarmed and beaten.

"Stop!" he yelled, and with a look of indifference and her gun fixed on the intruder, Serenity pulled the trigger.

Chapter Five

The moment he heard the gunfire, Callan raised his arms and blocked his face with the titanium blades of his kyoketsu-shoge. The bullet ricocheted, and the dark-haired woman who sent it his way raised her eyebrows in intrigue when she saw it. Darius thought to move, but the second his leg twitched, Serenity's gun turned back to him. The newest Insurrectionists were not only beaten, but held captive, and their leader was powerless to help them.

"Well, well, well," came a familiar voice from the shadows of the second floor. A voluptuous figure swooped down to the ground level on the other side of the remnants of a reception desk, her back turned to him. Callan was taken by surprise at the agility of her jump and the grace of her landing. She stood slowly, cautious not to give him a reason to throw those deadly blades in her direction. The woman turned around to face him now, and as his eyes fixed on the dark hair and lipstick that adorned the otherwise delicate face of the enemy she said, "If it isn't Callan Rouge..." Callan shifted in place, and something clicked in Serenity's mind. She'd heard that name before.

"Am I supposed to know you?" But as the question entered the air, he slowly started to remember the person she used to be. "Aria..." She smiled at the mention of her name, and slowly started towards him.

"Nice to see you remember me," she taunted.

"You know this guy," Serenity cut in. She was hardly as amused as her subordinate, especially since Amelia was run through by one of these children. Aria knew that Colonel Crawford wasn't to be kept waiting in suspense.

"We go way back. I actually used to be on his field team in the Yaiba Insurrection, back when we were still looking for a permanent base of operations." She turned her attentions back to Callan, whose face distorted with disgust. "You know, I've always wondered if you guys ever found one."

"You should've stayed with us, Aria. Then you would've known firsthand." Callan was as even-toned as ever, but his heart pounded rapidly at the sight of his subordinates—his nephews—totally at the mercy of the Scarlet Scourge. He knew their reputation, the destruction they wrought in the northern territories of the Kabuto Sanctuary. They alone were the reason why the Helmets were forced underground and why they kept it that way.

"Yeah, well, living in the ruins of a dead society didn't really suit me. I mean, come on. I'm way too high class for that," Aria told him. Callan looked around at the Scourge. A brute. A boss. An unconscious wimp. A gunner. All of them wore their crimson uniforms with pride, even though it was generations of bleeding the innocent dry that gave their clothes their color.

"I don't see it," Callan admitted. "At least not from the company you keep."

"Alright, that's enough," Serenity interrupted. She was losing her patience, something that her teammates knew was something they all should fear whether friend or foe. "I'm getting bored of this little reunion. We're here on business and I'd like to get on with it. Black," her voice became ten times as commanding as it had been before. "Say your goodbyes. We're heading out." There was a panic in Callan as he saw her finger move from along the slide release to the trigger. Another member of the Scourge, the brunette with the blank expression, followed her lead and prepared to shoot.

"Wait, wait, let them go!" Callan's sudden burst of emotion pricked Serenity's ears as much as it brought a smile to Aria's twisted face.

"I'm disinclined to oblige you," the Scourge leader told him calmly. Still, her body language said that she wasn't exactly closed to the possibility of negotiation. “We’re under orders to bring one of you into custody.”

“That means that we really only need one of you alive,” spoke the brutish woman that pinned Cal to the ground. She had no weapon in her hands, which told Callan that the boy was safe, or at least safer than his comrades Lukas and Darius. He returned his focus to the leader, who watched him carefully. What he couldn’t tell was that her focus was due in part to the familiarity of that name of his. It bothered her that she couldn’t place it, and the more she dwelled on it, the more she simply wanted to move forward with the mission.

“Alright, fine,” Callan said, his voice as cold as ice. The three subordinates at his command angled their heads to listen at his position, and for but a moment they’d felt their leader had lost his faith in them. “I want to stop you, but we all know that there’s no way that I can realistically do that. What I can do, though, is propose a suitable alternative to taking one of those rookies you’ve got on your hands.” Serenity held up a hand at the suggestion, and the Scourge stood down without question. The young Insurrectionists widened their eyes as their captors turned their attention to the man at the pharmacy door.

“What exactly are you trying to do,” Serenity asked, her gun still trained on Callan’s nephew. She watched Darius through her periphery while her main focus remained at the door. There was a chill in the air that only made the Yaiba more uncomfortable by the second. The skywater that fell to the floor through what remained of the glass ceiling provided an even more dramatic flair to the scene.

“Don’t do it,” Cal called out, and was promptly kneed in the gut for his outburst by the imposing beast that spread over him. Serenity glanced across the way at Cecelia, and as though she could feel the disapproving gaze, the vicious woman bowed her head apologetically. The leader of the Scourge again observed the grounded Callan, whose weapons remained stowed as he lifted his hands.

"It's simple," Callan continued as though the boy never spoke. "A trade. I'm offering myself in exchange for the boys. Release them unharmed, and I'll willingly go wherever you need to take me." In that moment it, it seemed like all the cold air was quickly sucked from the room. No-one, from any of the factions for that matter, had ever witnessed the surrender of a Yaiba Insurrectionist. Nobody even suspected that such a thing was possible, but here it happened for all to see.

Darius glared at Serenity now. He hated her for forcing Callan's hand like this and with every fiber of his being he wanted to rip her apart with his bare hands, but the cold woman on the other end of her pistol shot him a look that begged him to try. He stood motionless, save for his increased breathing rate and the tremble that overtook his arms. Serenity looked back to Callan, who stood on the broken tiles of the ravaged floor with an unreadable expression that reminded her of the most seasoned of politicians. He was a skilled negotiator, or at least she figured. She weighed her options carefully as she looked between the captives and their obvious team leader. Still, she had no idea how valuable an asset he could prove to be, and surmised that it would be fun to test the waters a bit.

"Why exactly would I oblige your little request? What makes you more valuable than what we've already captured?" Her questions registered with Callan as playful, or at least, as playful as someone like her could get with an enemy in her sights. He knew that she must've already assumed his role in their mission, but she wanted to confirm it for herself. For a moment, he thought to provide false information, but in a situation as precarious as this, he felt—no, he knew—that the best course of action was to be forthright about his station.

"Hey, if you wanna take some grunt on a scavenging mission back to your leadership instead of a Yaiba military officer then fine. I'm just a little surprised that the legendary Scarlet Scourge would be so clumsy when given a golden opportunity." The entirety of the Scourge looked on Callan appalled, but they knew that if what he said was true, and it was, they'd end up looking like fools in front of Prince James. They had no choice but to take him at his word, and just like that, Callan was in.

"Ladies," Serenity spoke with an air of discontent, "release them." The other members of the Scarlet Scourge reluctantly let go of their captives. Cal, Darius and Lukas proceeded to the door from their respective places around the room, and as they marched so did their leader stride to meet them. The unconscious Trisha finally stirred awake, just in time to see the captives walking away. She thought to ask, but then looked at her leader, who seemed more than content with the progression of events and dismissed the idea.

The battered boys that Callan now looked at with such pride stood before him, visibly upset that their leader would even think to sacrifice himself for their sake.

"Uncle Callan," Darius began, but the firm hand that his senior placed upon his shoulder halted any inquiry or protest he thought to produce.

"Take the salvage and the medical supplies back to the base. Right now that's a lot more necessary than I am," Callan told them. Lukas opened his mouth to object since Darius could not, but a stern look from their commander shut the boy down. With nothing else to say to them, Callan pushed through their line and addressed the leader of the Scarlet Scourge. "I'm ready when you are." Serenity said nothing, but motioned for Kerri, who was already on the ground to restrain their bounty.

Kerri was obedient, and briskly stepped over the tattered tiles with some kind of reddish-pink band in hand. She forced Callan's arms behind his back and bound his hands together with the odd strap, then tugged on it to find that he was unable to break free. Serenity looked down on the prisoner with satisfaction at his obvious discomfort, and smiled as she turned away from them. The three boys that fought the Scourge and lived hurriedly reclaimed the supplies they'd come to salvage in the first place, and just as they were to flee the scene, an order was issued that stopped them in their tracks.

"Open fire."

****

They came from the shadows of the upper levels, ten soldiers in all black and weapons long outdated on the field of war. The smoke bombs dropped first and obstructed the view of the Scarlet Scourge. The leader of the notorious faction whirled around to a literal dark cloud about the pharmacy, and gritted her teeth as she instantly realized they weren't alone. The dark figures then descended in the huntress leader's view. Their own commander, who wore the crest of a golden helmet on the front of his black mask, descended last and locked eyes with an irate Serenity Crawford. The savage women muttered profanities as Serenity hurled orders left and right.

"Black, secure the prisoner! Kant, make us an exit! The rest of you open fire! We're not letting any of this scum get away." The huntresses eagerly obeyed. Aria swooped down to the floor and retrieved Callan from Kerry, who now fired straight ahead of her. Cecelia rapidly descended the staircase and placed charges against the wall just in front of her. She detonated them, and with rifle in hand she stood guard over the new exit.

The gunfire discharged by each armed member of the Scourge only contributed to the cloud of smoke that blanketed the lower levels of the pharmacy. Serenity watched carefully for the figures she knew still lurked in the darkness below her platform, desperately she hoped to hear the sound of bodies drop in the black smokescreen, and with a single call to her troops the hail of bullets relented. They waited for a moment, and watched as the rain that now poured in from above dispensed with the onyx cloud below. What they found was a stark absence of the intruders and the potential victims. The Scourge turned their attention to their leader, but hesitated to ask whether or not they should pursue.

"Come on," Serenity finally said through clenched teeth. "We'll regroup with the rest of the troop and organize a search party to pursue and execute those brats and their accomplices. The show's not over yet, ladies. The fun is only just beginning…"

****

It took them substantially less time to reach the city limits than it had for them to enter the hospital. The boys Lukas, Cal and Darius all felt lost without their leader and under the care of dark-clad soldiers. The shadows that rushed to their aid had managed to extract them from the VA medical facility without any more scratches than they'd suffered in their scrap with the Scourge, but now that they entered the abandoned plasma clinic, the boys couldn't help but wonder if they simply traded one captor for another.

The ten warriors exchanged a series of hand signs, and silently took up positions around the makeshift base. The Yaiba trio sat in the back of the clinic, just as wordless as the men that supposedly guarded them. They occasionally exchanged looks, and as the minutes ticked by, the suspense, self-pity, and anguish they felt over losing their leader grew stronger and stronger.

"Is everyone alright," asked the man with the golden insignia on his mask as he approached through the damaged corridor. The lights of the sun had already faded, and with the collapsed portion of the roof suspended by a few withering wires, any view of them was obstructed. The leader of this random crew closed the almost immovable door behind him as he entered the back room. The three young men sat there and wondered what kind of man it was that asked of their well-being. They offered no response, and so the leader let out a sigh as he sat on the floor just to the right of the door. "A little paranoid, I guess. I can't say it's completely unfounded since you pretty much discovered that you're in enemy territory. But," said the man as he removed his mask, "I can assure you we're not your enemies." What the young Yaiba saw was the face of a man as pale as a ghost with only a hint of pink in his cheeks, a diagonal scar across his face, and a passionate soul that burned in his steeled green eyes. He looked to be no older than John or Callan, and like them he'd seen his fair share of hardships in war. Unlike him, though, he didn't make it look half as good as they did. His shaggy brown hair dripped with a combination of sweat and rainwater, and though he was undoubtedly the most imposing person in the room, he offered a comforting smile.

"Thanks," Lukas spoke. Darius and Cal looked at him as if it was a cardinal sin to use his voice, but he ignored them. "For the rescue, I mean."

"Really, it's no problem at all. We have just as much to gain from taking the Scarlets down a peg as you do," said the chief. "After all, they're invading our lands quicker than we could've expected." Darius raised an eyebrow.

"And who exactly are you," asked the junior agent with a narrowed glare. "Our reports show that this area has been unoccupied for years. Even if they didn't, the only signs of life around here are the Scarlets that somehow we managed to outrun."

"Your reports don't show occupation in this area because our group only recently moved here. We lay low, and do what we can to avoid any unwanted scans or readings on our position. To answer your question, though, my name is Erik Kincaid, and as of six months ago, I'm the leader of the Kabuto Sanctuary." Each of the young scavengers adopted a look of astonishment at the revelation.

"Whoa, that's *crazy*," Cal exclaimed with a wry smile. "Weren't y'all the group of rebels that went underground back when all these conflicts first started?" Kincaid's eyes narrowed on him, and instinctively Cal reached for his Reikiken. There was still no life to it. The EMP that knocked out all functionality in it was more than a match for Yaiba tech as it was. The Kabuto leader followed the boy's hand with his eyes and calmed his expression accordingly.

"Yes, that's true," Erik admitted. "Our Elders were always… cautious, and with the Scarlets monopolizing power in Prevalence, the smartest thing appeared to be to lay low. Even now, our people live underground, but lately we've been looking to change that."

"How's that," Lukas asked, without a shred of his usual cheer in his voice. All that was left was a nervous animosity that disquieted his teammates. The Kabuto operative offered a grin.

"Well for starters, we saved you," he said, and the shrewd Darius, in the moment the spitting image of his father John, crossed his arms.

"Which does what for you, exactly?" Darius' question made Kincaid smile wider, but then his emerald eyes softened as if he got lost in memories of the distant past.

"It puts you three in our debt," he responded bluntly. *There it is*, Darius thought, and from the expression he bore, Erik figured that the boy had already determined what their momentary savior was about. "Don't worry, it's not like I'd force you to do anything unbecoming." Lukas shifted, and kept his hand near the hilt of his Reikiken just in case a fight broke out. Still, if this man was able to lead a team of ten men plus the three of them safely into hiding when their enemies pursued them, it didn't seem like a stretch to him that it would be hard to fight against someone like him. There was a sort of desperation to his actions, as if he could not afford to fail at any stage in this elaborate game that none of the Yaiba cell wished to test themselves against.

"You'll forgive me if I don't believe you," Lukas said. It was so strange to hear him sound so formal. Even he thought it went against his nature to speak as some 60-year-old man, but information was always a most valuable commodity to any who lived in Prevalence, so it made sense for him to keep as much of his true self a secret until prompted to do otherwise.

"That's fair," Erik said flatly. "Then how can I start down the path to earning your trust?" Cal shrugged with a funny expression on his face.

"I mean you could tell us what's happening right now," he suggested in a tone that matched his face. He never did do well in tense situations, and typically came with two standard reactions: fight or joke. His sword was out of commission and his inexperience was on full display, so the first option was a no.

"You can start with where your comrades went," Darius added. He had watched them exit the building just moments before their leader started towards the back room, and figured that in the event that the worst should happen, Mr. Kincaid believed himself more than able to handle three striplings with faulty weaponry. Kincaid looked Darius up and down. He knew that the kid was out of his depth, but the way that he spoke was totally calm, almost pensive as if he knew to choose his words carefully in each situation. *I'm impressed*, he was forced to admit to himself, and resolved to answer their question in full.

"Very well," Kincaid agreed. "Six members of my team have split up throughout the city to draw the enemy forces to a few decoy locations. A remaining team of three is keeping watch on our immediate surroundings while incognito. After we get the signal, we're to move into the Cherokee Forest and out of the range of any Scarlet surveillance tech in the area."

"You're really trying to help us, aren't you," Cal asked with a signature crooked smile. He relaxed his hand and took it away from his presently defunct Reikiken, and Erik shrugged in a manner that reeked of "I told you so."

"It seems like it, but why?" It was Lukas who posed the question, and Darius couldn't help but grin. "You said that it puts us in your debt, but you haven't told us exactly how you intend to collect."

"To be blunt, I need an in to the Yaiba Insurrection compound. Nobody on our side knows where you guys are even hiding, just that it's somewhere in this area." The statement stunned the room silent. Each of the young Insurrectionists glared at him now, as if put on red alert.

"Who told you that," Cal started unconvincingly. His voice was too playful, and while his usually jovial demeanor could be a great asset in the field, he neither knew how nor when to use it to his advantage.

"And more importantly," Darius inquired, "why are you trying to get into our home base?" There was a moment of silence as the Yaiba trio sized up the Kabuto leader. He was smart enough to return the favor. They were, after all, legendary for a reason, and anyone with offensive tactics like those of the Insurrection would likely try to double down with any number of different support strategies. In part, it was their warrior's spirit that Erik admired the most. But time was short, and he realized that this was going nowhere.

"About thirty-eight years ago, my father was a part of the extermination mission against the Yaiba. He was eighteen, I think, and scared out of his mind, especially when he saw some muscular black man tear apart his whole team with a sword of fire." Kincaid paused to see if there would be any comment from the proverbial children at his feet, but found that there was none. "Dad thought that the man was going to kill him, too, until he was spared. That scary figure that rained down terror on my dad's squad not only let my dad escape, but he helped him get to the Kabuto Sanctuary by way of the Yoroi Alliance."

"Good for him," Darius shrugged. "So I'm guessing that your mission is to get into the Insurrection hideout to ask for help against the Yoroi Alliance. That sound about right?"

"Not at all, actually," Erik responded with far more smugness than he intended. He corrected himself, then continued. "The Yoroi Alliance and the Kabuto Sanctuary have reached an agreement to pool our forces in an assault on the Reds. As a show of good faith, the Elders of the Sanctuary gave the Yoroi freedom to expand into our old territories." There came a look of utter confusion on the faces of the three young Yaiba. They exchanged glances, and turned their attention back to Erik.

"So the Yoroi haven't been taking over Kabuto lands?" Lukas asked the question with upbeat tone but an unreadable expression. Kincaid laughed at the sight of him, and thought that the three of them would one day make for fine soldiers if they hadn't already.

"No, not in the way that you're thinking. In the spring of last year, the Scarlet Kingdom was amid the development of a new kind of warhead. What it was for we can't say for certain, but more than likely it was designed to quickly do away with your faction," he explained, which only added to the confusion of the three.

"Why is that relevant," Cal asked, and folded his arms.

"Well obviously it was the whole reason for our agreement. See, the testing field for their new toy was Kabuto territory in the Northwest. They took out Seattle, and about a hundred of our scavengers. Imagine a group of your childhood friends and their families gone in a literal flash of light. Up until that point we'd been exclusively non-violent, but I guess His Royal Majesty would've started gunning for us at some point." Erik's tone became a bit more frantic and his hands shook as he spoke. He took a deep breath to calm down, and the three that watched him were shaken to the core. They'd heard the murmurs of their teachers during training and gleaned a few kernels from the occasional whispers from the upper echelon of the Yaiba group that something terrible had happened in a distant region of Prevalence, but to find out that it was this…

There was an explosion out in the city ruins. The ground shook beneath them almost as much as the decrepit walls that served as their makeshift base. A single pair of footsteps approached through the hall with a sense of urgency that put the inhabitants of the back room on edge. They stood up together with the boys poised to strike with the kyoketsu-shoge on their gauntlets. Erik swiftly drew the sword that was fastened to his back and angled it at the floor. He bent his knees and sunk his weight as he pressed his back to the wall. It almost looked like one of the five stances of the Rairyu form, but it seemed more secretive, more ancient. The door opened, and within seconds Erik lifted his blade to the neck of one of his masked subordinates. The newcomer quickly tapped her leader's extended arm twice with a single knuckle, and at the sign the sword was lowered.

"What's happening," Darius demanded as Kincaid reapplied his own mask. Before any of the Insurrectionist three-man cell had their answer, the lot of them were on the move. Erik glared at the paranoid young man.

"We just got the signal. We move out in two minutes. Prepare to lead the way to your compound," Kincaid spoke with increased urgency. Darius thought to dispute him, but that explosion wasn't so far off, and any moment whatever was left of the Scarlet forces would crash down on them with malicious intent. If what this Erik said was true and his allies were hiding in the city ruins, then it would be unsafe for them to seek shelter here.

"What about your people," Lukas felt compelled to ask. For someone who spoke so emotionally about the lives lost in the destruction of his former home, he seemed a little bit too eager to let the rest of his comrades die off. "You're really just going to leave them?"

"My people are holed up in an underground network beyond the reaches of the city ruins. Whatever scanning tech the Reds have, it won't pick us up. Even if we were in range, the Kabuto Cloakers have kept us perfectly incognito for years," Erik replied as he programmed something into the comms unit on his cuff. Cal's eyes went wide at the comment, but also the fascinating technology only an arm's length away. He focused.

"Wait, then why do we have to take you to our hideout?" His question wasn't an unreasonable one, though from the silence that their rescuer momentarily maintained, he wondered if it had registered as one. The Yaiba links crackled back to life as they slowly rebooted, as did their Reikiken.

"You have to ask? Another reason the Kabuto have been able to survive this long is by not trusting outsiders. Even if I were to bring you to the entrance to our hideout, my word alone wouldn't get you through. You'd need approval from the entire Council of Elders. Really we'd just be leading our enemies to my doorstep." Kincaid's tone darkened a bit at the idea, and the Yaiba knew that he had already suffered more loss than any normal man could handle. Yet still he was here, fighting against the threat of the Scarlets. For that, he had earned their respect.

"It makes sense to bring him back with us," Darius spoke. Everyone raised an eyebrow at him, and he continued. "The sun is setting, and with the cover of night only accented by the trees of the forest we can achieve a tactical advantage over our enemies should we be detected. That's the worst-case scenario. In the best case, we can throw them off our trail entirely if we can make it to the outskirts of the city ruins fast enough and use the darkness and the trees to make it back to the compound before the Scarlets even notice we're gone." Erik strode back into the hall of the abandoned clinic to assist with the perimeter surveillance with a smile on his face that the boys couldn't see.

"We should get moving," he called out behind him, and the three followed him without question. The masked subordinate from before guided his master and their current leaders to the front of the building, and drew his sword from his back as he made a swift exit. "You three lead the way. I'll cover you. Esau, Levi and Nick will create more of a diversion to slow down our enemies." The Sanctuary Commander lifted his comms unit to his mouth. "Activate the traps," he ordered, and three voices acknowledged in unison. Loud crashes and powerful booms reached their eardrums, and Erik's expression darkened. Too many traps around the city were being sprung at one time, which told him two things. First, that his foes' search party was bigger than he'd expected. Second, it told him that if they didn't leave now, the chances that they would be caught and summarily executed escalated.

Cal and Lukas looked to Darius, just as they had since their days in training. He was the de facto team leader among them, but only now when their lives actually depended on his skills did the weight of it start to get to him. Even still, he steeled himself and took command. It was what his Uncle Callan would've expected of him. He took a quick headcount. There were the three Insurrectionists, the three-man team of the Helmets, and the master of their whole organization. He took a deep breath and then got to work.

"Break off into teams of two and head southeast towards the forest. Keep off the main roads and pay attention to your surroundings." The group within earshot nodded their heads, and Erik modified the settings on his wrist-comm so that the others in their squad would be able to hear. "This would be a lot easier with everyone here, but in any case, Erik can relay the message. Cal, you're with Nick. Lukas, you've got Esau. Levi and the Commander here will be with me." With time winding down, Darius took off to the right and bolted around the corner with the Kabuto leader in tow. They sprinted down a dark street with plenty of debris to use as cover should they be spotted. Another of the hooded men swooped down beside them with comrades close at his heel. Kincaid reapplied his own mask and Darius took a look at his friends. His expression was grave, as if he attempted to order them telepathically to stay safe. He nodded, and with understanding and soft expressions, Cal and Lukas split from the main group.

****

"Got eyes on three teams heading in different directions! All units fan out! I want every last one of them brought back to me alive! I want to kill them myself…" First Lieutenant Chase Gallaher lived for these moments. His cold blue eyes widened like a vampire's at the sight of blood, and his mind raced with the possibility of being the first commander in the last thirty-eight years to lead a victory over those Yaiba dogs. He was hungry for it, the bloodshed, the glory, and wanted it so badly that he didn't even care that the fugitives in question were little more than children supposedly led by Kabuto cowards.

He took to the streets himself when his mistress, Colonel Crawford, gave the order. *All of them must die,* she had told him. *Can you make that happen for me?* His platoon of forty-five split off in pursuit of those unsightly deviants while he and a patrol of fourteen soldiers tracked the movements of the enemy's main group of three. Gallaher had heard the stories, and after the initial search party literally went up in smoke from the earlier detonation, he resolved never to let his guard down with these savages. Indeed they had proven themselves to be worthy opponents, and had to have been if they escaped the Colonel and her Scarlet Scourge.

The young Yaiba leader glanced back to see Gallaher's patrol approaching, and with a word to his allies, deployed some sort of grappling device into a nearby structure. The other two employed similar tactics, so that Gallaher's prey now ran across what was left of the city rooftops. Gallaher, who led his platoon from the front like any good First Lieutenant would, lifted his balled fist in silent command. His available troops stopped on either side of their leader in a tight formation and aimed for their quarry.

"Fire," Gallaher commanded, his voice like a crack of ominous thunder through the stormy night, and his soldiers followed their orders without delay.

****

The cold air frosted their exhausted lungs, and though it rained, dehydration took its root in the Yaiba rookie and his Kabuto companion. He was always the one to see the light, to shed the light of optimism on dire straits, but this proved almost too much. He glanced back to the ground below, and on instinct alone he blocked an oncoming bullet with the blade of his kyoketsu-shoge. Lukas couldn't hold in the aggravated grunt that seeped through his vocal cords.

"We have to get out of their line of sight," he said as they pressed onward, and realized as soon as he said it that it was easier said than done. They ran through the tattered remains of abandoned businesses and broken homes, none of which had enough stability or room for proper evasion.

"There's nowhere to go," Esau's voice called out over the continuous crack of the gunfire. Lukas briefly looked at his impromptu teammate and marveled at how easily he seemed to evade the hail. "Most of these buildings don't have enough of a rooftop for sure footing. We'll have to work something else out."

"You make it sound so easy," Lukas snarked, and he could tell that Esau was smiling beneath his face mask. "But hey, I'm game, man."

****

"Man," Cal exclaimed a bit too loudly for the cautious Nick. He glanced at his new partner, and the nasty glare of the masked man caused Cal to straighten up.

"Are you trying to get us caught?" Nick was a Helmet, so it made sense to Cal that he'd be more accustomed to stealth than any who lived amongst the Yaiba.

"Oh my bad," he offered in a less boisterous tone of voice. He couldn't help but be nervous. This was Cal's first time in the field, and Nick picked up on that very quickly. It was annoying. Soldiers passed their position and spread out through the area enough to create an opening.

"Time to move," Nick asserted, and took off without waiting for the man who was supposed to act as his guide. Cal made a face, but used his kyoketsu-shoge to grapple to higher ground and follow him. Gunfire resumed in the distance, and before Cal could make a move to check on his teammates, a trio of bullets whizzed past his head.

"Yo, man!" Cal yelled as he looked to his rear, "I'm walking here!" Nick rolled his eyes from down below, and pulled out a tear gas canister from the pouch at his hip. The other troops in the area took notice of the fugitives and fired rounds alongside their comrades. Nick pulled the pin and dropped the gas grenade, then dropped a smoke bomb as Cal rejoined him at ground level. The Scarlet troops that pursued them were overwhelmed with the sting of the tear gas shortly after their prey disappeared into the cloud of smoke. A few of them fired aimlessly in a desperate attempt to hit something even if they couldn't see.

Nick lifted his wrist-comm to his mouth, and now followed Cal's lead with a sharp change of direction. It wouldn't be long now, the forest was only just out of their reach.

****

Lukas and Esau felt the pressure of their relentless pursuers, and in mere seconds they would run out of decaying roof to run on. *The forest is just a little bit past those buildings,* Lukas thought, *if we could just make it a little further...* The two braced themselves as much as they could on the move, then vaulted over the edge. What they didn't expect, however, was the group of ten Scarlet troops that awaited them below. The patrol of Reds readied their weapons, and just like that, all the blood drained from Lukas' face. In that moment, he just knew that his life was over, and while he would have loved to have relied on that optimism that he was known for, he quietly resolved himself to his fate.

"Duck!" The voice of their momentary commander, Darius, came from somewhere nearby, and the severity of his command compelled the Yaiba/Kabuto duo to obey. Not even a second later, the rhomboid blades of Darius' kyoketsu-shoge whipped about like a tornado. The chains rattled as they swung at their master's behest and like the excess of a freshly mowed lawn, the heads of the enemy soldiers scattered about the asphalt. There was little more exchange between Darius and Lukas than a nod, and they split up once again. Nevertheless, their objective was the same.

Darius, Erik and Levi took the quickest route to the edge of town while Lukas and Esau circled another block to throw off any additional enemy units should they be found. The trees rustled just ahead of Darius' cell, but the clumsy rattle of the brush told him that it was nobody other than Cal. Darius breathed a sigh of relief, and motioned for his enlarged squad to move deeper into the forest.

Lukas and Esau followed not long after, and once they regrouped under the cover of the trees, they made haste back to their mountain.

Chapter Six

August 27th, 2084

He was spurred awake by the click of the dingy gray door to his dank and depressing cell. He was isolated from anyone that could've told him where he was, but he had enough information. Sure, the Scarlets put a black bag over his head before they brought him here, but Callan could tell from the smell of oil that the rain couldn't mask, the banging and whirring of machinery, and the occasional yell of a workman that they housed him in the same place as their vehicles. By his count, 259,207 seconds had passed since they first dragged him up the stairs and chained him to the uncomfortable metal chair.

They offered no water or food, nor anything comfortable to sleep in. Perhaps the worst thing about his current situation, though, was the fact that for three days not a soul came to speak with him. No interrogations, taunts, not even so much as a glance, though how he knew that he had no idea. Perhaps that was just mania brought on by the fumes of his unwashed flesh magnified by the bag his captors had somehow failed to remove.

But now, after three long days of isolation, now there was a visitor. As much as the smell pained him, he took a deep breath and calmed himself. *Keep your wits about you*, he told himself. *Don't let them win.* The bag slowly lifted from his face, and for the first time in days he could clearly see the sunlight through the window of what looked like an old office. Papers lay scattered on the broken desk and messy floor. Some kind of greenish mold formed on the wall by the door. Rats scurried through the walls and ceiling. It certainly wasn't his lodging in Residency Block G, but he reasoned that captives can't be choosers.

Callan, weary from a lack of rest but loath to show any signs of weakness, cracked a smile at the black-clad dark-skinned woman that he knew all too well. She had innocent-looking features: wide, chocolate eyes, a small but perfectly round nose, and smooth, near-flawless skin draped over the delicate curves of her cheeks and jawline. She was, without a doubt, so unbelievably beautiful, and the sight of her made Callan want to vomit.

"Oh great," he spoke aloud, "as if things didn't smell bad enough in here they send a human trash can to stand right under my nose." Aria gave a faint smirk as her eyes narrowed. She looked cunning, devious, and Callan knew that it was all to keep him from picking up the hurt she felt at his comments.

"Actually, I came here of my own volition," she told him threateningly. He was unimpressed.

"That's so surprising," the captured Insurrectionist replied with a wave of sarcasm. "The Legendary Gaslighter couldn't wait to jump at the chance to twist someone's mind. Really, you must be the best interrogator that they have on Team Red Dead." Her eyebrow twitched against her wishes, and though she wanted him to overlook it, the smile that slid across his face confirmed that he knew she was annoyed.

"Let's change the subject, shall we?" The smug look on Callan's face was enough to prompt the question alone, but she had more pressing matters to see to than even her own ego. "Are you doing alright? You look a little tired, Callan. Are you sleeping okay?" He openly guffawed at the question and stared at her with enough intensity that for a moment she thought he would kill her with just the look.

"I'm tied to a friggin chair," he chided, "what do you think? Honestly I'm not impressed." He leaned his head back, and his nonchalant attitude drove her crazy.

"Not impressed with what," she asked with venom in her tone. Aria never did care for Callan, even when they were on the same squad. She found him to be emotionless and demanding, the only kind of man that she couldn't manipulate.

"I'm not impressed with you," Callan stated flatly. "You do whatever you can to get a cheap rise out of people and then get mad when they don't take the bait."

"You just love to talk about me, don't you," Aria spat, as if her temper was supposed to mean something to him.

"Actually nobody in the Insurrection has talked about you in the last ten years. You're pretty irrelevant, you know." His words cut deeper than she expected them to. She thought she was over this, that she'd moved on from moving around the trash heaps and broken buildings that the Yaiba called home during her time with them.

"Still bitter about my defection, I take it?" She was smug now, and while Callan's face remained unreadable Aria knew when she touched a nerve. "Or are you mad that I chose John over you way back in our training days?" Her tone became almost seductive, teasing, as if to see if Callan had secretly missed her after all this time. The problem was, he didn't care at all. She turned his stomach, and he was more than happy to let her know. He whistled, face still to the ceiling and not a care in the world.

"Still jumping to conclusions, I see. I already told you, you're irrelevant. You choosing John over me is kind of moot at this point isn't it? I mean, before you traded us in for your new Scarlet buddies, didn't you trade him in for some old pilot's son?" Aria had forgotten all of that. She wasn't particularly proud of that moment and did everything she could to rationalize it away so that she was a good person.

"Oh you don't get to judge me—"

"But you get to judge everyone else?" Silence, and Callan sat up straight. His bright blue eyes chilled her like ice against her skin, and he reveled in her discomfort. "You know, you used to be so proud of yourself, of your heritage as the granddaughter of some of the first freedom fighters to stand up against the Dawn King's ideals. You wanted to follow in their footsteps and bring down the

Scarlet Kingdom with your own two hands, but what did you do, Aria? You joined them—"

"I was made for better than what the Yaiba could offer me! I was made for mansions and gourmet food and fine wine, not living in ruins and junkyards and fearing for my life! You'll never understand what it was like for me—"

"You think you were the only one suffering? All of us are fighting a war that we don't know if we'll walk away from and unlike you, we haven't lost sight of our mission!"

"The mission was freedom, wasn't it? To be done with oppression and nomadic tendencies? To finally come out of hiding and into glorious light? I haven't lost sight of anything, Callan, I've bought into the very thing we always talked about at our briefings in the Insurrection. I am free! I live life according to what I want when I want it."

"No, Aria, you're just another expendable pawn in the hand of your King. Let me ask you, how many people around you in this dump actually look like you? When you go out in public, do people show you respect because you're human or because you have a spot in the notorious Scarlet Scourge? You're not a real person to them and you'll never be."

"How would you know anything? You people don't have any idea of what it's like in the Kingdom!" Aria was totally beside herself now. Her nostrils flared, her eyes were bloodshot, and all in all she bore the look of one deeply unhinged.

"No, but your grandparents did," Callan retorted. "They lived in that place back when Prevalence was the United States. They grew up in times where black men were slaughtered in the streets for minding their own business, where Latinos and Latinas were detained in cages for trying to get away from the oppressive governments and volatile circumstances in their own countries."

"I don't need you to tell me what my grandparents lived through," Aria said with a disturbing calm as she straightened herself up.

"I suppose not. My bad, I mistook you for someone who cared about somebody other than herself. Won't happen again, I promise." He leaned his head back again and tried to drift to sleep when he heard her drag the metal legs of an old chair across the floor and take a seat.

"Come on, Callan, you know me better than that," she said with a degree of seriousness that made him almost think she was being sincere. "You remember our first mission together? We didn't really know each other at all back then but Old Man Ishikawa put us on the same squad and named you team leader. Said it was something about honoring your late father, right?"

"That's right," Callan admitted. He didn't look up at her, but stared at the ceiling as he suddenly saw the old picture of his father Carson as clear as day. He never got a chance to know him, not from personal experience, but everything that his Uncle Dre told him about him was warm and loving. Every time Carson was mentioned, Callan couldn't help but get swept up in the emotions that came with never knowing the father who, as he was told, loved him more than anything in the world.

"I was five years into my military career there, I think, and that mission was—"

"Recon," Callan finished, and Aria smiled at the resignation in his voice. "It was a recon mission on a Scarlet weapons factory located just outside of Danville, Virginia." She had him right where she wanted him from the beginning. In her mind, acting as the hardline interrogator was almost never effective. It was much better to allow her guests the chance to establish an emotional connection with her in all their anguish and agony. Callan chuckled as he thought back on what felt like a simpler time. "I remember we entered in from a blind spot in their surveillance equipment. Came through the Dan river."

"And five minutes after we infiltrated the building and started placing the mines, you got yourself surrounded by a group of Reds," Aria reminded him with an almost friendly smile. For a moment, Callan nearly forgot that she was an enemy now and cracked a grin himself. "You let your equipment get too wet and it took a while for you to use your Reikiken. I had to come and bail you out, remember?" Callan took a moment to recall the incident and, much to his displeasure in the moment, she was right. She came in like a burning tornado and cut down seven Scarlet troops with only a few wide swings. "That doesn't really sound like the kind of person who only cares about herself. I want to help you, Callan. I want to let you go so you can get back to whatever life you've built since I've been away. Will you let me do that?" She was good, he had to hand it to her. A decade's worth of manipulating minds for her benefit and she finally landed in a job that could make use of her evil powers of persuasion. Still though, she wasn't as good as she thought she was.

"If you want to let me out of here free of charge, then by all means," Callan said with a coy smirk. Aria's amicable expression slowly gave way to one far more terrifying, like a spoiled brat who had been told no candy before dinner.

"As if," she barked. "You know *I'm* trying to help *you*. You have the chance to get out of here free and clear, even lead your little comrades in an attack on our position from wherever you rats are hiding today. All you have to do is tell me what I want to know."

"Okay," Callan told her as he leaned forward in his chair. "Suppose I was dumb enough to trust a crap-bag like you. What would you want me to tell you? The location of the Yaiba compound?"

"No," She responded flatly, all evidence of animosity suddenly removed from her voice and her face as sober as Callan's was now. "It might come as a surprise to you but nobody on my side feels that to be necessary information. You all have a habit of coming to us, after all. Just like moths to a flame…" She adopted a smug look as the words left her, and gave more credence to the fact that she was truly an unsightly enigma. Callan, however, couldn't care less.

"And yet somehow your side hasn't been able to kill one of us in 38 years." Every ounce of smugness drained from her face when he spoke. "So," Callan continued before his interrogator could issue a comeback, "if it's not that, then what do you want to know? Depending on what that is, I might or might not answer your question."

"That's simple." She moved from the chair to sit on the desk that stood between them in the dingy office of the makeshift motor pool. Aria stroked the side of Callan's face with the back of her hand. He jerked away as his skin crawled with disgust. "Word on the street is that the Yoroi Alliance and the Insurrection have formed a gentleman's agreement. I want to know if there's any truth to that little rumor."

"And what makes you think I'd know anything about that?" Callan said it with more of a laugh than he wanted, and quickly tried to sober up. He at least wanted her to feel as though he was taking her seriously.

"You want me to believe that the inheritor of the Suiryu title doesn't know anything about a political shift inside the Insurrection," she challenged with her arms now folded over her chest.

"You want me to believe that a traitorous dog has my best interest at heart? Not that it's any of your business, but Director Ishikawa no longer keeps the Seven Dragons as an inner circle. Only one of us helps out with the business side now." Callan's arrogant tone made her wary of what he was saying. Could he really be telling her the truth? Or was this some elaborate lie to get her in trouble with her superiors? If it was the former, then she was on the cusp of becoming second in command of the Scarlet Scourge, something that no doubt every member of the team had been thinking of since the last right hand, Amelia Kluger, met her unfortunate end at the hands of the Insurrectionists. But if it was the latter, then Aria Black would meet her own demise, likely at the hands of the very commanding officer that she admired the most.

"You know who it is," she uttered with caution, with suspicion, "but you're likely not going to tell me, right?" Callan couldn't help the grin that spread across his face.

"On the contrary, I don't mind telling you all about it. See, Ishikawa's right-hand man is your ex-boyfriend, John Hamlin. You might know him as the guy whose emotions you played with while you actively cheated on him." She froze at the news. She had a feeling that John was still alive, but to know that he'd become this powerful… if she stayed on with the Yaiba, she could probably have manipulated him to overthrow the Ishikawa family and take over the entire organization. It would've been easier then to join up with the Scarlets for a better life because all of them would have had no choice but to join her.

"I don't get it. Why would you give him up like that?" Callan supposed that to her it did seem like a betrayal. What else did the traitor know besides just that? But where she struggled to make sense of what he'd done, Callan knew all too well what this really was. He was doing what he could to give Aria over into John's skillful hands.

"Well, because that young man that you and your mistress held at gunpoint is John's son, and right about now, he's probably telling his father how you threatened him with deadly force. Get ready, dearie," Callan cooed with almost savage excitement. "He'll be looking to do much worse to all of you." Aria's lips pursed for a moment as her eyebrows raised, but then relaxed her features into the look of one unbothered.

"Good," she asserted with a quiver in her tone. "Let him come."

****

August 27th, 2084,

Director Ishikawa sat across from the salvage team, unimpressed with the Kabuto men that her newest soldiers had brought with them. Guards stood with their Reikiken at the ready, and like their leader, their faces were expressionless and difficult for anyone to read, except for John, who sat at her side as a right-hand should. Even Johannes Thornhill, the emissary from the Yoroi Alliance sat off to the side, silently observant of the Yaiba proceedings. Everyone that needed to be was already in place. Everyone, that is, except Callan Rouge.

The salvage team was silent before their leader, who was in everything but name identical to a feudal lord in medieval Japan yet twice as terrifying. They'd arrived three days prior, and Erik Kincaid and his men were immediately escorted to Holding Level AA while the three junior operatives were told to rest. The next day, the supplies that they managed to procure on their mission were turned in at the Civil Center and dispersed throughout the compound. The Synthesis Department of the Medic Corps would do what they could to stretch the medicines brought back from the VA pharmacy, and Bryan Piccio and the other developers of the Engineering Corps would handle the recycling of the metal wares. Once that part of the mission was complete, Cal, Lukas and Darius were subject to mandatory counseling. That was normal for a first mission, pass or fail, and with everything that had happened in the community in the last few weeks, the supervising staff thought it to be even more necessary for this particular cell.

Now, though, with the formalities and routines taken care of, the boys and their unwelcome guests awaited the thoughts of the Director Ishikawa. Their eyes were kept low as a sign of respect, but the tremble in their bodies was the clearest signal of fear. The ambience of the audience chamber did little to help their nerves. The room was built like what could be seen on the inside of a traditional Japanese palace from the Sengoku Era. A line of pillars stood on either side made of wood painted red. Rings of gold adorned the top- and bottom-most points, but looked almost orange in the glow of the brilliant fire that offered its warmth and light from behind the two Yaiba leaders. Emiko looked at the boys, each of them, with the slightest hint of pride in her eyes.

"What do you come to report," she asked them. Her voice was as sudden thunder on a silent night to them, and it showed. "While you're at it, who are these strange soldiers you've brought into our compound?" There was silence on behalf of the three boys. Each of them had grown up around Emiko. She was, typically, a sweet, nurturing figure to the Yaiba, almost motherly in her knowledge and concern for everyone around her. Here, though, in this moment, a different aura radiated from her. This was her power, her intensity, and the severity with which she conducted the business that kept them all alive and safe.

"Director Ishikawa," Lukas slid forward, still on his knees, and kept his eyes to the ground. "The salvage mission to Johnson City was successful. The VA pharmacy was loaded with a plethora of medicines and the city was rife with useful scrap, but…" Lukas' voice trailed off. He struggled to utter the words, but couldn't. He didn't really need to. Nobody did, because everyone could tell just by looking that something happened to Callan.

"Director," Darius took his place beside Lukas with the same humble motions as his teammate. "Uncle Callan was—" his voice caught, so he cleared his throat and continued with as much boldness as he could manage in the face of his intimidating leader.

"Uncle Callan was captured by our enemies. The Scarlet Kingdom is occupying Johnson City for some reason."

"We were fighting this group called the Red Disease," came Cal, who sat in his initial spot and somehow lost his fear. Darius glared back at him and motioned for him to move up and tuck his chin to his chest as they had done. "Oh, my bad. So anyway, the Red Disease had mad guns, you know, but—"

"Do you mean the Scarlet Scourge?" The Director raised her eyebrow as she asked the question and stifled a laugh. She had to admit that in Cal's brand of humor was a welcome addition to this otherwise tense meeting, but then the weight of what he told her finally set in. Her seriousness returned in all strength as she asked, "Wait, what?" The officials in the room, Emiko, John and Johannes exchanged looks, and the delegate from the Yoroi alliance moved closer to the back of the room to join his hosts.

"You boys encountered the Scarlet Scourge, the legendary team of Kingdom spies rumored to be all women?" John's voice reeked of disbelief, but the sober expressions that each of the boys displayed checked his doubt without a word. "So the Scarlet Scourge is involved in this, then. But if they captured Callan then something's not adding up."

"If they captured him, they want information, John," Ishikawa explained, and John nodded.

"Yeah, that much is clear, but what exactly is it that they're after?" He paused for a moment. Johannes, however, kept his eyes firmly fixed on the Kabuto men that knelt behind the scavenger cell. "More than likely it's our location. The Scarlets haven't been able to get a lock on us since the Hanzo Gear field test. Our nomadic strategy worked well enough to through them off our scent and using a mountain as a base of operations helped keep them from picking it back up again."

"I don't think that's it, though," Johannes interjected. He was much calmer now than when he'd first seen the Hanzo Gear up close in the lab. John supposed that he was getting used to the Yaiba way of life.

"You don't," Emiko asked. She was neither amused nor convinced that Johannes actually had their best interest at heart. He was, after all, a representative of a faction that never really saw the benefit of sustaining allies. It was then, though, when the thought crossed her mind, that she realized, "Our alliance. The Scarlets must've been fed information about our alliance from somewhere." She turned her gaze to the delegate, full suspicion written across her face.

"Not to worry," Johannes asserted with his hands raised defensively. "I wouldn't dream of betraying your trust. Besides, if I had, why would I even suggest that the Scourge is after confirmation in the first place?"

"The obvious answer is that you're trying to shift focus somewhere else," John replied. "Let me guess, you half-expected us to turn on each other, right?"

"That's not it at all," Johannes shouted back, appalled at the accusation. "The Insurrection has shown me greater kindness than the Alliance. I would never willingly put you in a position to be taken advantage of. But you just said that the Scarlet Kingdom has no idea where you are. If that's true, wouldn't it be prudent of them to sow seeds of discord through something like this?" The room fell silent, and seeing that he had the floor, Johannes continued. "What I'm about to tell you, you can take as a gesture of good will. Part of the reason why the Yoroi Alliance has existed for so long is because of a ceasefire agreement between our faction and the Kingdom. By making the move to ally with you, Old Man Vargas and the agreeing Yoroi Council members essentially broke the pact that many in the Alliance believed kept them safe. It wouldn't be completely unimaginable for a Scarlet loyalist within the Yoroi to reach out and feed information to the enemy."

"That makes sense," Emiko admitted. "If that's true, then it also makes sense that Callan would've been captured to give confirmation. The Kingdom knows better than to haphazardly storm the Yoroi, even if it would be easiest to do it now. They'd want to check out whether or not they still stand to benefit from the situation first."

"Hmmm… but when they have their information, Callan will likely be killed," John thought aloud. Cal, Lukas and Darius could feel as their hearts dropped to the pits of their stomachs.

"We can't let that happen!" The three leaders fixed their gaze on Darius for his outburst, though not with anger. It was with sympathy. "We have to do something to help him." His voice quieted now. In this moment, he wasn't the strong soldier who fought the Scarlet Scourge on his first mission. He was a boy in pain, who had only recently lost his grandmother and was terrified to lose anyone else he loved. It hurt John to see him like this, and he understood all too well what his son was experiencing, but his hands were tied. Now was not the time for fatherly comforts. It was the time for military action.

"As much as I would like to tell you that it won't come to that, the truth is we have no way of knowing how long Callan can hold out against the enemy," Emiko informed them. "Moreover, the Scourge is notorious for killing every enemy that sees them. I don't think you realize how much of a miracle it is that you escaped with your lives. Even so, I'll put a team together for a rescue op as soon as we're done here. Hopefully we can get to him in time."

"Some of the other members of the Seven Dragons should be up to the task," John told her in a hushed tone, and as if on cue, Erik Kincaid cleared his throat.

"You have something on your mind?" Emiko's voice was as cold as anyone had ever heard it. Kincaid mused that not even the ominous fire that heated the room would be enough to wipe the chill from his spine.

“Director Emiko Ishikawa of the Yaiba Insurrection, my name is Erik Kincaid of the Kabuto Sanctuary. My father, Charles Thornhill, was a Scarlet Kingdom deserter who fled to the Sanctuary with the help of a man named Dre Hamlin.” Those words floored everyone in the room, save for the other three Helmets, but not nearly as much as what Erik said next. “My mother, however, is the granddaughter of Philip and Elizabeth Ashworth.” Emiko froze for a moment, and her face, as Cal had imagined it, looked like a glitch in a computer screen.

“You’re *their* great grandson,” was all she could manage. Everyone in the room could see the wheels in her head turn. “This is incredible. To think that I’d actually get a chance to talk to a descendant of one of the Legendary Founders…”

“Uhhh…who they?” Cal asked with his hand slightly raised. Lukas couldn’t help but laugh, but then fixed himself under John’s stern glare.

“Oh man! They were the ones who founded or co-founded the anti-Scarlet factions,” Lukas explained in his usual perky yet knowledgeable manner. “Kazuma Ishikawa and Wayne Hamlin founded the Insurrection, and the Ashworths founded the Kabuto Sanctuary. I think the Alliance was headed up by a guy named Ahmad Hassan but nothing really confirms it. He’s kinda my favorite either way, though, because he was so stoic, you know? He was also huge into hit and run tactics, which you wouldn’t expect from a man with that much broody angst.” He gave a slight chuckle. He really did enjoy diving into the depths of history. He thrived on the age-old human struggle for righteousness, and all the peace and violence that it wrought.

“They were all the students of a legendary martial artist who went by the name of Sasori. In the years that preceded the Second Civil War, they were an average martial arts group,”

Kincaid offered. It struck Emiko as unusual yet refreshing that someone understood this much of their shared history. Up until now, it was something that very few outside of the Seven Dragons and the Director herself knew, at least within the compound. Erik continued. "The Founders, all master martial artists in their own right, initially learned the way of the samurai, and then each created their own fighting styles based on how they interpreted what they learned. At first, it was all about having fun and engaging the community. But when Henry Lloyd was murdered in cold blood by the police in California, it sparked unrest and civil disobedience across the nation." He had to take a moment to gather himself. The looks on the boys' faces showed how little they understood about why things were the way that they were, so Emiko decided to take over from there.

"Henry Lloyd was a black man, and his murder was carried out for little more than twenty Old American Dollars and the color of his skin. The officer that performed the execution bound him by the hands, put him into the pavement and pressed his knee into the back of the man's neck until he died. The bystanders recorded the event and leaked it to the press, and Lloyd was just the straw that broke the camel's back."

"What do you mean?" Darius finally spoke now that the climate had become far less formal. Emiko sighed.

"You know that racism exists," she said. "You learned about it in the 'Why We Fight' briefing from the training program. What the course didn't tell you is that people like us, people of color, have always been treated like property more than people on this continent. The Scarlet Kingdom is, in large measure, resistant to any assertion that we're more than that. Hundreds of years ago, white settlers from Europe came to this continent and displaced the natives of this land. They enslaved African peoples and brought them here. Those slaves were placed in subhuman conditions, raped, murdered and abused openly in the early days of the United States, but then when they were freed, they weren't really treated with more respect than what they had as property. There was an era where black people weren't allowed to enjoy the same quality of life as their white counterparts. They weren't able to eat together or walk on the same side of the street or drink from the same water fountain, and any violation of any of the ridiculous rules could have resulted in abuse or death."

"At the time when segregation ended, this place saw more instances of quiet discrimination and police brutality, which endured from the downfall of the split society to the dawn of the Second Civil War," John added. "But the white supremacists of the old United States also placed Japanese Americans like Emiko's—I mean, like the Director's ancestors in internment camps. They deprived them of any sense of normalcy and treated them like criminals. They openly vilified Arab Americans, still very much their own people by virtue of that name, as terrorists after the bombings that ultimately gave rise to the Dawn King. They blamed the Chinese and any other people of Asian descent for the outbreak of a disease we only know as 'The Rona,' and treated them like human-shaped rats."

"Oh… That's awful," was all Darius could say. The hearts of the young soldiers beat wildly, their nostrils flared, and their eyes were only another word away from shedding tears. It was then that Erik again took the helm of the conversation.

"It really was. You probably know all about the protests against the Dawn King's autocratic tendencies and the mistreatment of minorities, but what you probably don't know is that Sasori-sensei was the driving force behind the Legendary Founders. He was the one that deployed his students around the country with plans to go underground. With the help of the Ashfords and Hamlin, all of whom had prior military service in the United States, they devised all of the protocols that keep our factions safe and active even now."

"In fact," Emiko added, "the reason why our faction names and code names are Japanese is because that was the language that the old masters decided upon. They knew that it would be better for communicating their plans and keeping their identities a secret since your average white supremacist demands that you speak their native tongue."

"Not that I don't mind a history lesson," interjected the incredibly focused Johannes, his tone was much graver than Emiko's in this moment, "but Mr. Kincaid was in the middle of telling us his business here. So?" Johannes turned his attention back to the Kabuto who rested across from them on his knees. "What is it that you're after?"

"Well, in short, I want in on the alliance between the Yoroi and Yaiba," Erik told them, much to the disbelief of the delegate and the Director. He walked them through how the Reds used Kabuto land as a testing ground for dangerous weapons, how too many men, women and children were snuffed out without warning, and how the peaceful ideals of the Kabuto died with them. "My rescuing of your scavenger team was a strategic move to get into the Insurrection's compound, yes, but I wanted more than anything to show that as the leader of the Kabuto Sanctuary, I have your best interests at heart." There was silence for a long while. The three boys dared not speak as the intensity of their superiors suffocated the room. Though Erik's expression returned to the friendly nature that he had upon his self-introduction, the slight tremble of his body and the beads of sweat that formulated on his brow showed that he was just as nervous at their quiet contemplation.

"If we were to add the Kabuto Sanctuary to our alliance, what would be our basis for doing so?" Emiko's voice was even and contemplative rather than mocking. "Surely you don't think that by virtue of our shared history you're entitled to a seat at the table."

"No, of course not," Erik assured her. "To answer your question, the Kabuto were a peaceful faction, yes, but how we maintained that pacifistic approach to life was by infiltration and sabotage. The Yaiba Insurrection excels at direct confrontation and the Yoroi Alliance is gifted at hit and run tactics as Lukas pointed out just moments ago. What we can offer you is the systematic dismantling of the Scarlet Kingdom's most valuable tools and weapons." He had their interest and he knew it. Cal's especially. Learning how to sabotage machinery meant looking at its core and figuring out how it worked. If he could learn to do that, there would be no limit to his mastery over all metal.

"It is true that we would rather dismantle our enemies over their tools, but there's no denying that taking out their fancier toys would help our cause drastically," John offered. Darius admired the calm on his father's face. It was interesting to see this side of him, the warrior genius at work. To Darius, John had only ever been loving, slightly doting but not too much. He reckoned it was because John didn't want to spoil the boy. But here he was stern and intimidating, as should be expected of the First Dragon, Rairyu. "Even still," John continued, "That by itself isn't enough to earn our trust."

"I figured you might say that," Erik shrugged. His relaxed demeanor was markedly untrustworthy, given the number of Reikiken that would cut him down should he step out of line. Still he smiled though, as if he hadn't a care in the world. "That's why I have two additional proposals for you if you're interested."

"That depends on what you're offering," Emiko informed with all shrewdness in her face. She had grown adept in her role as the political head of a major faction, and couldn't be swayed or inspired by any such baiting tactics as these. She required an honest proposal up front, and cared incredibly little for whatever suspense her potential ally believed that they were building. "The Yaiba have been holding a strong lead over the other factions for the last thirty-eight years. With the assistance of the Yoroi, our military strength has increased by nearly double. Besides your skills with sabotage, what else is there that you could give us?"

"Land," was all Kincaid said, and just like that, silence filled the room yet again.

"Come again," Johannes begged as he tilted his head to the side and furrowed his brow. "Did you just offer them land? Are you somehow not aware of where you are? Their base is in a hollowed-out mountain."

"I'm aware that the Insurrection has to scavenge for parts and medicine just to keep themselves afloat, and that it was that kind of mission that got your friend captured in the first place. If you were able to expand your reach into a territory with everything you need to sustain yourselves, you'd be able to make a greater stand against the Scarlet Kingdom," Kincaid shot back.

"Well what territory do you have in mind," Johannes asked before anyone else, albeit a bit harsh. There was something between them, a steep animosity, but none outside of the scavenge team seemed to care. Kincaid, who smiled wider out of simple spite, spread his arms wide.

"Why, Johnson City, of course."

Chapter Seven

August 30th, 2084, 11:33 p.m.,

Bill was still mad. It'd been three days since he got the news that Callan had been captured, three days since he erupted on John, who was its unfortunate carrier. He knew he needed time alone, even away from his adoptive little brother and wife, so he took the first mission that the Director offered. He took a look at the slip of paper on the nightstand as he sat at the edge of the bed, and for a brief second looked at his wife. He'd be gone for four days, and with no way of knowing what would happen on this mission, he was determined to savor her features.

Bri was his light in all this darkness. It was because of her that Bill maintained as much optimism and rationality as he did in these conditions, and being away from her like this was nothing short of flirting with danger. He reasoned, however, that perhaps it was danger that he needed. It had been some time since the last time he hit the field and put his Tsuchiryu skills to the test, and his inability to accompany the Kabuto on the rescue mission gave him plenty of rage to fuel the swings of his Reikiken.

He got up from the bed and moved across the small room to the closet. He pulled out the purple tunic and black trousers of the Hanzo Gear and got dressed as quietly as he could. Bri deserved to rest, especially given her role in the Civil Center. She had three children, two teenagers and a toddler in her case load and was determined to find good families within the Insurrection that would take them in. She was a saint, and Bill suddenly felt as though he didn't deserve her.

"Bill?" Bri was still half asleep when she heard him open the creaky bedroom door. "It's really late. Come back to bed." Her head hit the pillow again and she was out in an instant before he could say anything. Bill smiled with every ounce of love he had in him, but then moved from the doorway through the circular living room and into the armory. There, the Earth Dragon stocked up on smoke bombs, his Reikiken and the titanium kyoketsu-shoge that adorned the sleeves of his bulletproof shirt. Bill took a final look back through the doorway, but instead of a return to his bedroom, he exited his domicile on Residency Block G to the outer corridors.

"You ready," came the voice of Manuel Bautista, the Kazeryu. He walked up to Bill and pat him on the back with a friendly smile. "I brought snacks." Just like his son Lukas, Manny Bautista was the upbeat type that always tried to take care of the people that he knew. Right now, that person was the obviously and understandably upset Bill Jerrick. Bill offered no response. "It's been a while since we worked together, huh?" There was a shift, and the silence now was more nostalgic than it was awkward.

"We haven't since we were the Entry Controllers for our dorms during training," Bill answered, finally. A smile crept across his face. "Remember when John would crash on our couch?"

"Yeah man," Manny said with the same rattled laugh that Lukas often exhibited. "He always brought snacks."

"That, and we always used to have the best talks after lights out," Bill added. He chuckled as the two walked the corridor towards the power-lift. "We got in trouble a lot for that." He specifically remembered the time where there was a surprise inspection on their dorm, and while the other 57 people in their barracks were fast asleep, John was wide awake in the lobby and in deep conversation with Bill and Manny, who were supposed to be focused with their eyes on the door to prevent such an unwarranted entry.

"It was worth it, though," said Manny. "Hey, didn't he used to sleep with a big gray body pillow?" The grim expression on Bill's face subsided entirely now at the memory.

"Oh yeah! I remember that thing! I let him use it whenever he crashed with us. That couch just looked so uncomfortable for him..." Bill's determination to care about his comrades was the defining feature of his personality. Whether they were his childhood friends like Manny or Callan or John, a fresher ally like the Rabbit Bryan Piccio, the love of his life, or the students that he had been training since his promotion to Tsuchiryu, he loved fiercely across the board. That was why he couldn't help but be angry that Callan was in such a dangerous situation while he was running students through drills on the training floor. If he could've been there—

"You know it's not your fault," Manny said out loud, and placed a sympathetic hand on Bill's shoulder. "What happened to Callan, I mean."

"I know that, but…" he trailed off. It was hard for him to rationalize what it was that he felt. He was undisputedly the protector of their social cluster, and took the job more seriously than anyone expected he would. "I should at least be allowed to go on the mission to bring him back. What if he gets killed because those outsiders don't know what they're doing? We've already waited too long to take action anyway." This world they lived in, this endless string of tension and conflict, took away from Bill more of his loved ones than he could count. His parents, grandparents, and so many of his friends were gone now. These men and women that filled the ranks of the Seven Dragons and his pregnant wife that, by the grace of God, never joined the Insurrection's military force were the only family he had left.

"You're a little too heated to be on a mission like that, Bill," came Bryan from around the corner adjacent the power-lift. "You have a big heart, and sometimes that can make you act more recklessly than you intend to."

"I'm here," called Bryan's son Jaden as he emerged from the same passage as his father. He was out of breath, and placed his hands atop his knees to catch it. The brown hair that usually took the shape of a muffin now draped like curtains in front of the boy's face as he said, "I'm here. Dad, did you press the button yet? Press the button! I've already been late twice for a mission and I really don't wanna be scolded by Director Ishikawa again."

"Relax, kid, we're not that far behind schedule," Bryan consoled. Jaden breathed an audible sigh of relief as he straightened up, and it was then that he finally noticed his old teacher standing there just a few feet away.

"Jerrick-sensei!" There was that excited look in his eye. Jaden hadn't had a chance to see his old teacher in the months since he graduated the training program. Being the son of Usagi no Kamikaze came with a lot of pressure to live up to his father's astounding reputation, but the Director she sent him on mission after mission to help him establish a name for himself apart from Bryan Piccio. "How've you been, Teach?" Bill wouldn't even attempt to hide the smile on his face. He was touted by all of the graduates as the fun teacher, and the higher ups that heard about it knew that it was because of his loving dealings with his students. He was a rarity, unlike any of the other Dragons, who all but lived up to that name in their training of new recruits.

"Can't complain, kiddo," he told the boy, and noted the smile in Bryan's eyes. Everyone knew that the Rabbit wanted to spare his family as much worry as possible. After everything that happened when Lyla went missing, nobody could really blame him for being so protective, especially of his only son. "Just heading out for a boring ol' tungsten retrieval. Nothing too fancy. What's the Director shipping you out for?"

"I'm on escort duty… again!" Jaden tried not to let the irritation filter into his voice, but his most common type of mission was escorting trainees on practice runs or guiding visitors from other factions through the Yaiba compound. "Just once I'd like to go do something that means a little more to the faction, you know?"

"What you do right now is already important enough," Bryan told him, but the boy shook his head in firm opposition.

"Dad, you don't get it," Jaden started to protest, but Bryan held up a hand.

"You oversee trainees at your age and make sure that they're well-protected, AND you keep people like me from cutting down harmless visitors. That situation with Johannes would've been a lot worse if you hadn't been there," said the father.

"Yeah but it was Uncle John who stopped you from cleaving him in two," retorted the son in a way that took them all back to his childhood. He was always a pouty one, and if annoyed enough, it was easy to see that some things about Jaden just would never change. "At least this time I get to a little bit past the front door."

"Is that right," Manny asked, and Jaden noticed him for the first time. His face lit up at the sight of the uncle that secretly spoiled him the most. Manny, though incredibly upbeat, also had a catalogue of gruesome historical facts that he'd been covertly feeding to Jaden since he was born. "Well don't drink the Kool-Aid wherever you end up!" His excitement was child-like, and while Jaden flashed a grin Bryan was filled to the brim with offense.

"So it *was* you that taught him stuff like that," he complained. "Manny, how many times do I have to tell you? My boy has no business learning about that kind of darkness."

"I'm not a kid anymore, you know," Jaden shot back before Manny had the chance to. The power-lift drifted to a stop on their level, and Jaden was the first to board it. "You should know that better than anyone, dad." Bill saw the disgruntled look on his old student's face, but knew that it wasn't his place to intervene in what had now become a family matter. He did, however, realize that Jaden was a much tougher kid than his old man probably gave him credit for. He pat the boy on the shoulder upon entering the elevator, a gesture that meant more than all of Bryan's overly protective antics.

The whirring of the machine was the only sound that entered their ears aside from the occasional clang of hard metal against the stone walls of the mountain. Nobody spoke. Nobody wanted to speak. Each party only wanted to reach Deployment Level A and get out of dodge as quickly as they possibly could. The ride to the mountain's peak seemed to stretch on for hours, but it was only a few minutes. Bryan said nothing to Jaden, who still fumed over his father's treatment of him. Bill wished he could ease both their minds, since he didn't think it right for them to be in conflict. Manny gave no thought to the situation one way or the other. His mind was on his mission, as it always had been and probably would be until the day he either retired from the Yaiba military force or was taken out by an enemy. The lift came to a halt at the peak, and three of the four passengers were met with the remaining members of their teams.

For Bill and Manny, they were met with Shonda, the Hiryu, a soft-spoken but incredibly strong woman with skin the color of brown sugar, soft features, and the gleam of determination in her eyes. She was a mother of two girls, Hope and Aya, and wife to a former Yaiba enforcer named Ezekiel, all of whom supported her drive to fight for her family. She hated the harsh conditions of living in the dark depths of the mountain as much as anyone, and she made it her business to do whatever it took to make a better life for her husband and girls.

"Bout time you made it," she told her teammates. "Does everyone have what they need? We're in for a couple days' travel, and the only food out there is what you can hunt for yourself." Bill rolled his eyes.

"Yes, mom," he mocked and Manny grinned. "But thanks for checking in." Shonda shrugged.

"Don't mention it," she told them. "Come on, we gotta get to our transport and get on the road."

"Yes ma'am," Manny said excitedly, and walked with her briskly down the eastern side of the mountain. Bill caught himself in a much better mood, and realized that these guys were exactly who he needed.

****

Jaden watched as his teacher departed on his own mission, and lamented the fact that he was left there with his overprotective father. It was true, his team was there, as was the person they were assigned to escort, but even the sight of his friends wouldn't so easily subdue the feelings of humiliation and irritation that took residence in him. Bryan moved to speak, but Jaden left to join his team before he could.

"Looks like we're all here, then," said Moses, a scrawny young man with big ears, blue eyes, brown hair, and skin as pale as freshly fallen snow. He was one of the orphans that knew his parents before they died, but resolved that he would be a hero like them one day and joined the military training program anyway. Bryan couldn't help but think that Moses looked an awful lot like his *Hrairoo*, and it only made him more sympathetic to the orphan's tale.

"Finally," came Moses' brother Clay, whose skin was a bit darker but otherwise shared the same features as the others on the team. "Let's get this show on the road! I'm ready to see what the Yoroi territories are like!" The very mention of such a journey made Bryan's heart pound. He wasn't sure how he felt about his little boy making such a trip by himself, but he did know that whatever he felt wasn't good.

"There's nothing too exciting to see there, really," Johannes assured them from the middle of the group, and suddenly it all became clear. The Director assigned Bryan's son to guard that outsider. The feeling in his gut became even more unsettling, but he sucked it up and turned back to the power-lift. After all, the word of Ishikawa was absolute in the Insurrection.

****

August 30th, 2084, 6:57 a.m.,

The sun had only just begun to rise, so there were still plenty of shadows about the ruins of Johnson City. The Kabuto operatives had been deployed by their hopeful Yaiba allies only two days ago, and in that time it became clear to them all that their hasty escape from the area had incurred. Scarlet Troopers patrolled every major entrance and exit of the city. Squads of twelve patrolled the streets, and the entirety of that first day back was spent mapping out patrol routes and getting back to the Kabuto hideout.

On the second day, after Erik, Esau, Levi and Nick made sure that their home was safe, the leading Kincaid approached the Council of Elders about the deal with the Yaiba. The Council members were less than pleased, especially since it meant cohabitating with a faction that the Kabuto had long thought barbaric. However, as Erik pointed out during their meeting, the way of pacifism did nothing to stop the Reds from shamelessly bombing them out of their territory. Moreover, it would've been a complete waste for them not to take the opportunity that the six decoys from their escape died to create for them. The Elders had no retort for that argument, and reluctantly the Council resigned themselves to the inevitability of their allegiance with the brutish Insurrectionists.

Now, on the third day, Erik took his position in the command center of the Kabuto hideout while Esau, Levi and Nick made their way through the city's ruins under his command. Kincaid watched the monitors carefully.

"Esau, head south from Main Street and hold position behind the abandoned auto repair shop. You have a Red patrol coming in from the west. I'll let you know when it's clear," he warned. Erik was okay with the idea of being in a fight if there was no alternative, but really he much preferred what he did at present. It was much easier to think clearly from safety, and he didn't even feel shame for thinking, as some in the other factions might deem, so cowardly.

"Gotcha," came the methodical timbre of Esau's voice. He, along with his team of three junior agents, followed the instructions and kept a low profile. Esau Tillman was a rather short man with unimposing features from a distance, though he was reasonably fit. His alabaster skin and brown hair gave him the most inconspicuous of looks and, when matched with the all-black attire of the Helmet faction, proved to be more than helpful in hiding in the shadows.

"Nick, hold your position by the coffee shop to the north of the college campus. Wait for Esau's team to get into position," Kincaid instructed. "Esau, you're free to move; continue to head west." He analyzed the area. The scan of the city showed that a single person was being housed in the office of an abandoned gas station, someone who had the occasional visitor. The person never moved from the spot, but the visitors, likely interrogators, would pace the floor and draw nearer to them, presumably for taunts and displays of bravado.

"Yessir," Nick Resnick confirmed in his usual carefree tone. He was about as physically fit as Esau, with chocolate waves in his head and piercing green eyes. He was stealthy, if only to get out of putting forth his best efforts, but surprisingly it made him one of the most reliable officers in the entire Kabuto group. His three subordinates held fast, and together they watched as another patrol passed in front of them.

"Levi, come in," Erik called through the comms. "What's your status?"

"Don't worry, Chief, I'm here," responded Levi Taylor with his usual cool. "We ran into some trouble with a small cell of the Reds, but don't worry. We handled it." The way he said it caught Erik off guard, as if he had already grown used to fighting on such violent terms. He was, by the appearance of his milky skin, innocent green eyes, straight brown hair and scrawny physique, an unimposing teenager of a perpetually neutral disposition. Underneath that, though, was a boy who had lost his girlfriend to the warhead only a year after his parents were mauled by a bear during a scavenging assignment. He was angry, and his taste for people dwindled by the hour.

"How long before you're in position?" Kincaid awaited the answer as Levi thought.

"I'd say we're ten minutes out from the mark," he finally replied.

"Same on this end," Esau chimed in, "We should be in position shortly." Just like that, the Reds' makeshift motor pool was covered from the north, east and west.

"Get ready, boys," Erik ordered with a devious grin. "We've got a rescue to perform."

****

August 30th, 6:10 a.m.,

Six days… Callan Rouge, the Suiryu, one of the Seven Dragons of the Yaiba Insurrection, sat in his own filth tied to the same chair for six excruciatingly long days. Aria ordered the grunts at her command to blast him with an enormous water hose, but all it ever did was make the smell worse and the chaffing all the more unbearable. Aside from that, they largely left him to his own extremely limited devices. It drove him insane. He chuckled to himself, and had to admit that they knew what they were doing. The interaction a few days ago was just to bait him with a familiar face and human interaction, but when he didn't tell them what they wanted to know they left him alone in his discomfort for days.

Then there was a knock at the door. Callan donned a goading grin, fully expectant of Aria's return, but to his surprise his visitor was a rather distinguished gentleman with chestnut-colored hair and stoic stardust-gray eyes entered the room. Callan's expression sobered as he looked the man over. He dressed well:

brown fur coat draped over his shoulders, black gloves, a blood-red tie against a dark blue shirt tucked into a gray pinstriped suit that perfectly accented the muscles in his body. He was nothing if not imposing, but the sheer glory of his appearance told Callan that he wasn't here for a violent negotiation, but that he had hopes for a peaceful negotiation.

"Who are you?" The man's face distorted, undoubtedly a reaction from the putrid stench that, until now, had been confined to the room. It robbed him of his ability to answer Callan's question at first. He pulled a red handkerchief from the inner breast pocket of his suit and covered his mouth and nose with it. It bore the crest of the Scarlet Kingdom's royal family, and Callan's brow furrowed with disgust and apprehension. "Ah, you're a royal. What brings you to my humble holding cell?" It was all Callan could do not to snarl at the man, but he forced civility in the hope that he could stave off the threat of immediate death. He watched as the man gingerly came closer to where he sat, and then propped himself up on the dirty desk before him. The smell of Callan's ripe flesh and beyond soiled pants made him visibly uncomfortable, yet there he sat.

"My name is Prince James of the O'Neill Royal Family, and I simply came to check on you, is all." The admission, however true it sounded or false it was, took the weary Suiryu by surprise. It was more than what he wanted in that moment, for the simple concern of another human being, but his senses were not so far gone that he couldn't tell when he was being pumped for information.

"To check on me?" Callan's voice oozed disbelief and contempt, but he noted the seriousness in the Prince's eyes. "Your subordinates have me bound to a chair with my hands behind my back. I can't change my clothes, can't wash myself, and don't even get me started on the crap food I've been given. But you want to check on me?"

"We may be enemies, but that doesn't mean we have to be so hostile all the time," spoke the Prince. Callan blinked a few times, stunned to silence for a moment at the very idea behind what he said. "Besides, my subordinates have only done what I've instructed them to do. We want information from you, Mr. Rouge. That's all. The sooner you give us what we want, the sooner we can let you go, no strings attached."

"Typical," Callan mused and spat at James' feet. "You Scarlets live your lives inflicting the worst on people, saying it'll be better if they just don't resist and then have the nerve to say that there's no need for hostility. It's all you are!"

"Calm down, Mr. Rouge. I've already said that if you comply, we'll let you go without question," repeated the royal.

"Yeah, I heard you. You don't think I'm dumb enough to take your word for it, do you?" Callan flashed a toothy grin, and all the wrinkles in his face came to the fore. "Besides, I already told that lackey, Aria, that I don't know anything about what she asked me."

"Hmm, yes, I did read that in her initial report," James admitted, "but I find it hard to believe that someone of your rank and temperament doesn't have the information we're after. So I'll ask again: Are the Yoroi partnering with your Insurrection?" Callan rolled his eyes.

"Jeez, you're real thick in the head, you know that? I. Do. Not. Know. *Hontou ni shitte iranai. Eu não sei.* Whatever language you need it in to understand, man," Callan taunted. The Prince smiled at him through the red handkerchief as he adjusted in his makeshift seat.

"Well, so much for that plan," James told him, and visibly relaxed himself. "You know, you're a lot tougher than I imagined you would be." Callan was, once again, blindsided. He had to wonder how many sides this man had to him. "I really am sorry about all this, you know. I can't even imagine being trapped like this with no shower and only enough food and water to make sure I didn't die. Even still, you won't talk, which means you have to be telling us the truth." Callan didn't offer a response. He just watched the man before him as a starved wolf watches his prey. For all intents and purposes, he very much felt like exactly that. James nervously swallowed as his eyes diverted from the captive. "Well in any case," the Prince continued, "I think it would be prudent to keep you here for a while longer."

"So I was right," Callan shot. "You weren't going to release me at all, were you?" He jerked in the chair as he spoke, which caused the royal's fear to escalate.

"Not really, no," James admitted. "You saw right through me from the start. If I can be so candid, I like you, Mr. Rouge. You have a sharp tongue and an even sharper mind. It's not something that you see every day, especially when dealing with soldier-types who think that the quickest way to resolve an issue is with their weapon of choice."

"Careful, you almost sound like you want things to change," Callan taunted, and James stiffened. He raised an eyebrow at the captive and folded his arms with intrigue, but before he could say anything further, three explosions rocked the earth.

****

August 30th, 7:17 a.m.,

"On my count," Erik said over the comms. The gas station was in his sights from the command center, and his three most trusted agents were in position. The mark was Callan Rouge, and standing in opposition was a troop of Scarlet soldiers that they'd recently made an enemy of. It would be difficult for just the three men, each with their three subordinates, to get into the jury-rigged motor pool, but fortunately they had made preparations. "One," called Kincaid, and with a smile Levi held up the detonator in his hand and pressed the button at its top. A massive explosion to the west-most position took out Highway 321, which cut off the quickest and most efficient way out of town. Kincaid offered a smile of his own as sweet, sweet sabotage flashed across the screen. “Two,” he said, more excitedly now, and Esau pressed down on the switch in his hand. A bomb went off in the center of the old college campus that the Reds used as their base of operations.

Erik could see the brilliant blaze over the screen, and more excitingly to him, the barracks and mess hall that got caught in it.

“Nice,” Esau whispered as the sky filled with black smoke and red-orange light.

“Three,” Kincaid finished with a degree of fervor that further motivated the other saboteurs. Nick detonated his bomb, and with it the entire VA hospital that witnessed Callan’s capture in the first place. “All units, move in.” Erik looked at the screen in total satisfaction. The Scarlet troops scattered throughout the city, frantic at the sight of their resources gone up in smoke. The commanders of each platoon in this troop exuded worry, or at the very least extreme disdain at the idea that they would have to use their already limited water supply to try and save what they could.

Amid this chaos, however, the Kabuto demolitionists were able to approach the interrogation site via the rooftops with relative ease. Ten minutes was all it took, and caution was of little importance now that the bulk of scarlet troops were otherwise occupied. The twelve operatives of the Kabuto squad made their way into the building. No alarms sounded, and all was still from what they could see. The building was split into two levels with a balcony that circled out from the top of the stairs. It appeared to be empty, but gave Kincaid ample apprehension regardless.

“Be careful in there, guys,” Erik instructed as he watched them enter through the network. The floor was mostly open, save for a few cars and carriers that made the transport of goods and resources easier for the Reds. The smell of oil was strong in their nostrils, but the dim lights were easy on their eyes.

"Intruders!" The scream came from the top of the stairs, and as soon as the reverberation made its way through the building, seven more armed Reds rushed to the scene.

"Levi," Kincaid started, but the boy had already begun to move. He may not have liked Levi's propensity for violence, but in moments like this he was hard-pressed to say that it didn't come in handy. The Red Team rained down a hail of bullets, but their shots were unorganized; sloppy.

"Way ahead of you," he said with far more glee than the Kabuto Head was comfortable with, but what could he do? The rest of the Kabuto men took cover, and suddenly Levi was the sole focus of the enemy crew. He brandished a pistol in one hand and a sword in the other. His movements were irregular, and he moved about the floor of the motor pool with little effort. The sloppy shots of the enemy became even less coordinated, and before long, Levi fired three shots of his own.

The bullets launched lodged themselves in the skulls of the north-, east, and south-most assailants, and the remaining soldiers moved about the upper balcony to better surround him. Two more shots exited the chamber of his gun and found their new home in the chest and eye of another two enemy troops. Five down, two more to go.

The rest of the rescue squad watched in awe. It was true that they all received the same weapons training as a self-defense measure, but few in the Sanctuary had actually had to use it in a combat scenario. To witness such mastery was grotesque, yet captivating to the former pacifists.

Another shot. The enemy grew careless with the falling of their comrades and succumbed to emotions of rage and vengeance. When the red-faced Scarlet man approached the bannister of the upper balcony and fired aimlessly in the hope that he might hit Levi, Levi struck him with a bullet to the heart. Even Erik had to admit that his accuracy and manner of movement was scary. He wasn't particularly fast in his evasions, just erratic enough to confuse his enemies. Even so, he moved with just the right amount of stability that allowed his shots to go unwasted.

As the man crashed to the floor with a thud, the last of their enemies watched in horror as Levi calmly ascended the stairs. The silence left in the wake of the gunfire was three times as deafening, and as Levi took point the others came out from behind the Scarlet transports. Levi looked at the sole surviving troop in the motor pool, a young woman with dark brown hair and equally dark eyes, and she panicked under his gaze.

"P-please," she stuttered as she clutched her rifle to her chest. "I surrender!" Levi flicked his wrist, and in the blink of an eye he covered the distance between them. He plunged his blade into her throat and twisted as he watched with as much ice in his deceivingly innocent green eyes as in his veins.

"You'll get no mercy from me," he spat. "Human trash." He withdrew the blade, slashed it through the air to clear the blood, stowed his weapons, and walked back to the office door to stand beside his brethren. Esau stood directly before it, and with a powerful kick forced his way into the room. The putrid odor wafted through the air and watered their eyes before they could see anything, but with intensified focus they fought through it.

"We have a visual," Nick informed command with a hand over his mouth. There, across from the doorway and on the other side of the office desk, sat the man they'd come to rescue. Nick took a step forward, but the sudden light contact of a knife to his chest made him stop on a dime. He looked to his right, the direction from which the weapon came, and saw a man with stern gray eyes and regal attire.

"That's far enough, don't you think?" His question made Nick smile and roll his eyes. It was too much effort, but he supposed that since it just became a matter of life and death for him, he might as well show off a bit. He grabbed his assailant by the arm and slipped behind the stranger's back. There was a crack from the sudden jerk, and when the man cried out in pain the knife dropped. He walked the attacker, arm still forced behind his back, over to the desk and slammed his head down onto it.

Levi and Esau dispatched their teams to keep watch over the facility while they moved to untie Callan.

"You guys…" the captive spoke with some relief, "are pretty cool." The comment made Esau smile as he unbound him.

"It's only the beginning, bud. Wait until we get you out of here to start praising us," he joked, but the mix of gunfire and the screams of their underlings disrupted their lighthearted mood. "Looks like that's gonna be easier said than done. Up you go," Esau said as he helped Callan up from his chair and supported his weight as they walked.

"I guess I'll stick to the fighting then," Levi shrugged as he drew his gun and sword once again and moved toward the door. Nick chuckled as he suppressed the struggles of his would-be assailant.

"You make it sound like you're tired of it," he poked, and Levi raised his eyebrows as he turned to face his comrades again.

"Did you not see how much I had to do to take down those eight hostiles," Levi inquired in disbelief.

"Seven," Esau corrected. "The last one wasn't really a threat anymore what with the whole surrender and all. You didn't really even have to kill her."

"She still had a weapon," Nick interjected, and shifted his hostage's bent arm sharply upward to embellish the pain. "Her surrender could've been false. You know these folks don't adhere to the Geneva Conventions anymore and would do that kind of thing if it meant offing some enemies. I say Levi made the right call."

"Whether or not that's true, it doesn't really matter, does it," Callan interrupted. He was still groggy and extremely uncomfortable. "Argue later. Right now, I'd really like to leave this place behind."

"That's too bad," came the sultry yet taunting voice of Serenity Crawford from the doorway, "because you're not going anywhere." She stepped forward and reached for her pistol, but the sight of her prince in the clutches of these criminals stayed her hand. "Let him go," she demanded, but Nick hiked the Prince's arm even higher. The royal yelled, and in a quick motion, Serenity drew her pistol on her enemy. "Let him go or I'll shoot!" Her heart raced, far more than just a loyal citizen of the Scarlet Kingdom's would, and for the first time since she became a soldier, her hand trembled.

Laughter. She looked about the room for its source and came to rest her gaze upon Levi, the volatile one who knew no fear as he calmly approached the desk with his blade in plain view of her. The second she trained her gun on him was the moment he pressed the edge of his blade against the nape of Prince James' neck and fixed his gun on her as well.

"I don't think you will," he told her smugly. "You know why? It's because you're smart enough to know that before you can press down on the trigger, I'll have shot you and decapitated him." She caught sight of the silver helmet emblem on their shoulders and recognized them instantly as Kabuto agents.

"You're bluffing," she insisted, only half-confident in the stories she'd been told of their pacifism. Levi relaxed the wrist of his sword hand, and even that infinitesimal lack of support caused the blade to drift along the Prince's skin. Blood dripped onto the desk, and Serenity's eyes widened.

"Care to test that theory?" Levi was less than amused now. He hated being called a liar, even in jest, but while he knew it wouldn't take much effort to end this man's life, Levi knew that it was precisely his life that gave them leverage in this situation.

"What do you want?" Serenity's question caught James off guard.

"No, Serenity, you mustn't—" he was irate, but her voice overpowered his.

"Your Highness, I am sworn to protect you at all costs! Now," she addressed the clear intruders as James fell silent, "what do you want?" James had to admit that her military bearing was impeccable. Even under this much pressure, the only ones in the room that knew they were together were they themselves.

"We're taking Mr. Rouge back with us," Esau stated flatly as he marched with Callan up to Serenity's face. "Tell your men to stand down."

"This is absurd," James protested from his face-down position.

"Done," Serenity assured them, "though there isn't enough time for us to break the news to the entire troop. So here," she slowly reached into her back pocket and pulled out a single key drive. "That's the key to the personal transport of the Scarlet Scourge parked just out front. That should carry you to the edge of town without much notice." Callan donned a shocked expression while Nick and Levi smirked devilishly. Esau, however, maintained his stoic composure as the Scourge leader tossed the drive to him.

"Thank you, ma'am," he said. "Oh, and enjoy the rest of your day." Nick released the Prince, and just like that, three Helmets and a Blade just walked out the front door.

Chapter Eight

August 30th, 2084, 7:29 p.m.,

It took twelve hours for the fires to get under control, and even worse, the Scarlet water supply had been drained by almost three quarters of its max capacity. A number of troops were injured, but nothing too serious to rebound from, fortunately. Only a handful were killed, though none from the explosions wrought by the enemy.

Serenity was agitated beyond compare, but it wasn't clear to her what about the day's events bothered her the most. There was the fact that not once, but twice in the span of a week that the Kabuto elite had infiltrated their operation without the slightest detection. The first time was to save the Yaiba brats and the second to save the team leader. Then there was the fact that those same Helmets managed to close off the main road, deplete the water supply and nearly eradicated their food and lodging in one fell swoop. To add fuel to the flames was the matter of Prince James risking his life in an attempt to stop the Kabuto rabble from rescuing Callan Rouge, something that put her and the Scourge at a major tactical and personal disadvantage.

"Idiot," she muttered as she walked through the old college campus. James was in his chambers in the Jr. Hall with his personal physician. He, being the magnanimous royal that he was, allowed the full medic staff to assess the other personnel before they saw to his injuries by that little… she took a breath and calmed herself. She'd spent eighteen years in the Kingdom's military and very few times, if ever, had she lost herself to her emotions. She resolved that she wasn't about to start now. Even still, it was difficult. Her lover was injured in the chaotic meeting with the enemy, but not killed. In fact, there was relatively little bloodshed in the Helmets' incredibly well-executed plan, which impressed her as much as their plan itself. The fact that it did only frustrated her more.

She entered Jr. Hall, and only just then wondered what she would say to that beautiful but stupid prince of hers. At first it was her belief that she would see about his injuries, but she knew better than that. It was her nature to call out stupidity, especially when the stupid prince willingly subjected himself to her leadership and expertise. She worked through numerous insults in her head that she couldn't wait to try, and mused that she wouldn't have to go out of her way to hide her relationship with him too much.

It was in the midst of this verbally abusive brainstorming session that she entered his chambers without even the slightest bit of attention.

"Colonel," James said calmly, but it jolted her just the same. The physician, an elderly man with pale skin, liver spots, and more wrinkles than the love child between a Siamese cat and a pug carefully observed the redness in James' injured arm.

"Excuse me," Serenity addressed the doctor, who now looked at her with eyes that smiled like a loving grandfather's, "would you mind giving us a moment of privacy?"

"Not at all, my dear," he told her kindly with a gentlemanly bow. "My only request is that you treat him gently." It took her a great effort to stave off the sarcasm that threatened to spill out of her. She offered her kindest smile, which given the level of her frustration, was more of a twisted grimace than a heartfelt grin. The medic gave her a concerned look, as if at any moment he would take care to see about her afflictions. Nevertheless, he walked past the Colonel and, for the moment, took his leave. After he closed the door behind him, Serenity returned her attention and all her fury back on the Prince.

"What were you thinking," she snapped, and the monarch's eyebrows raised. "If you hadn't been in the way I would've been able to kill those helmets without a moment's hesitation."

"I'll have you know that I was already in the room when they arrived. It's not like I could've just vanished at the first sign of danger," James retorted defensively. The corners of his mouth curled into a grin as he realized how ridiculous it was for him to even react that way. He calmed himself down, which he could see only made his beloved more furious, but he didn't waver for a moment. "The only thing that would've happened if I hadn't been there to 'get in the way,' as you put it, would've been Callan's expedited escape. I'm sorry to say, but one way or another you were too late getting to the motor pool and I was too outnumbered and outmatched to be of any real help." Colonel Crawford, for in this moment Serenity was buried under tremendous mounds of boiling rage, advanced towards her Prince and took him by the collar.

"How can you be so nonchalant about this? Our only chance at confirming the rebels' plans just went up in smoke and all you have to say about it is, 'Oh, well,'?" As soon as she finished yelling, she was stunned to find that the lackadaisical heir to the Red Throne slapped her hand away from his clothes. He stood from the king-sized bed and brushed his shirt free of any wrinkles or lint.

"In war," James spoke evenly as he paced towards the window and casually parted the blinds, "there are certain outcomes that can't be avoided despite our best efforts. The loss of Mr. Rouge was just such a case of this. However, the escape of our prisoner is little more than a slight inconvenience." He turned his head just in time enough to see the angry face of the Colonel wash over with more confusion than anything, and with a genteel smirk, he crossed his arms behind his back and peered through the open blinds once more.

"What do you mean," the Scourge leader inquired skeptically as she moved closer to the Prince.

"I took a call in the command center before it was time for my physical assessment," Prince James informed her with a tinge of excitement in his tone. He turned to face her now, and the way he smiled, the way his stardust-gray eyes shimmered in the dim lights of the room made her almost forget about every annoyance she'd suffered that day. "Apparently, Major Crawford's left a platoon to guard established routes into old Yoroi territory."

"But I thought that the intel unit was supposed to scout out the old Kabuto territory that the Yoroi took hold of," Serenity spoke, and the hint of irritation returned. It was just like a little brother to get on the nerves of their older sibling, but this was a new level of disrespect. To disregard the King's orders was asinine at best.

"They were," James confirmed, "but I thought it would be in our best interest to expand our range of vision, as it were. As luck would have it, some good came of your brother being smart enough to follow my orders." Serenity was taken aback, and couldn't decide if she was enraged at the idea that her younger brother could be publicly executed or intrigued by the prospect of renewed advantage. For now, at least, she settled on anger.

"I think 'reckless' is a more appropriate word," she chided. James raised his eyebrows and smiled wider, as if he was asking for her to inquire further. She let out a sigh and folded her arms in front of her. She knew the kind of danger that Kyle was in for not following the orders assigned along with the mission, and she also knew that while James was a prince, he was no King. "Fine. What've you got?"

"I thought you'd never ask," James teased. "It would appear that we've stumbled upon a caravan at the center of the route heading west. A Yaiba caravan, and with a Yoroi emissary at its center."

****

August 30th, 2084, 7:37 p.m.,

As promised, Erik and his crew reentered the Yaiba compound to the utter halt of every passing foot or flowing breath. The Kabuto leader and Nick, his most unbothered subordinate, parted to either side and revealed a perfectly intact Callan Rouge, supported by Levi and Esau. The onlookers of the Yaiba faction erupted with cheers as the strangers led their rescued ally to the power-lift. Callan managed a smile, but the exhaustion finally took him under. Levi and Esau did what they could to brace him, and once they had him secured they piled into the lift.

"That… that felt good," Nick commented once the power-lift doors closed and the eyes of the Yaiba were no longer on them.

"This is what accomplishment looks like, bud," Esau teased, which prompted a toothy grin from Levi. Nick scowled.

"What I mean was this guy must be pretty important to these people, and not just because he's one of the Seven Dragons," Nick clarified with a pensive ring in his voice. The others grew silent, as contemplative as their comrade who, at this moment, carefully observed the dirty, unconscious man that so desperately needed their support.

****

August 31st, 2084, 7:18 a.m.,

Bill stopped the transport amid the wreckage and debris that adorned the beach-adjacent road. The sputtering halt to the engine startled Shonda and Manny out of their sleep.

"Come on," Bill directed, exhausted. Six and a half hours they'd been on the road, but he was the only one who had to sacrifice his rest. "Try not to stand out in the open too much. Last time you almost compromised the whole operation, Shonda." Shonda cut her eyes at him with a wry smile in place as the memory flooded back.

"For your information my knees got cramped from trying to walk all hunched over. Besides, it worked out okay, so I don't see what the problem was," she said with half a laugh and a lot more defense. The sky was still dark, and the air was rife with the smell of salt. Getting caught by any Scarlet patrols wasn't likely, but even after the escapades of the Dragon and Rabbit combo squad cleared most of the Red presence from the Yorktown area, it would've been unwise for the Dragons to relax their guard at all.

The three-man cell moved along Water Street as quietly as they could, and were careful to use the old, rusted cars and shambled buildings as cover. The rush of being in the field again was intoxicating to say the least. Manny had been given more administrative duties on the Medical Level of the compound, so it was difficult for him to even spend time with his wife and sons, let alone go on field missions. He grinned. It'd been five years since his last one, and he joked to himself about how rusty he must've gotten.

Shonda was in a similar case. She was a proud Insurrectionist leader, but she also took the first opening in the Education Center that opened up so she could spend more time with her girls. She wasn't as out of practice as Manny had gotten, but finding balance between work, war, and family life was a struggle, even for the mighty Hiryu. She was happy to choose her husband and girls over the field when necessary, but she was equally grateful that her family understood how important it was for her to fight for the future they deserved.

The sounds of the tide as it washed against land and the cries of hungry gulls gave Bill goosebumps. No, that wasn't it. It was the people with whom he shared this mission. These days he spent all his time on the Training Level with the new recruits, so working the field was as much to him as revisiting an old friend as it was to the old friends that sprinted through the shadows with him toward the beach. He drew energy from them, and even with the lack of conversation that typically accompanies a stealthy retrieval mission like this, he still felt like he did when Shonda first joined the team. There was a newness amid all this ancient history that invigorated him.

The three Dragons worked their way to the other side of the run-down Riverwalk, and while Manny and Shonda maneuvered their way to the treacherous rooftops of the decomposing restaurants, Bill approached the pier on foot. He felt confident here, like he used to in the old days before he became one of the Seven. He loved what he did now, the work that he put in with the young recruits, but he had a life outside of those kids once. He loved them as his own, and in a couple years' time, his own would likely follow in their father's footsteps. Nevertheless, he needed this.

For a long while, there was little more than the sounds of crashing waves and calling seagulls. The wind blew gently against his face and the water splashed the path upon which he stood. The darkness of the morning began to lift, and as the black of the sky stood pierced by the bright reddish-orange of the rising sun, a small container ship with a gray metal hull and the initials of the Transglobal Shipping Company brandished on the side approached the pier for docking. Bill whistled at the sight of the many cargo containers and wondered how many of them were filled with the tungsten rods they needed to produce more Reikiken.

As the ship pulled to a stop alongside the edge of the pier, a familiar face emerged on its deck. Bill only grinned, but inwardly he was as happy as a child opening a birthday gift. He walked to the now-lowered boarding platform when he wanted to run, stood when he wanted to jump, and calmly shook the hand of the man across from him when he really wanted to hug him.

"Well let's not stand on ceremony," said Dr. Kazuya Masamune as he spread his arms. Bill lit with childish joy and gladly hugged the old Yaiba scientist. "Easy, now! I'm not as young as I used to be, Billy Boy." Dr. Masamune audibly sighed as Bill loosened his grip a bit but still clung to him. It had been years since last they saw each other. Bill thought three, but Masamune knew it to be at least seven. It wasn't without good reason. The combined efforts of Dr. Masamune and Bryan Piccio kept the tensions with the Chinese Trade Union to a minimum and secured off-books shipments of tungsten to the Yaiba Insurrection among other things. The Union was free to enjoy commerce with the Scarlet Kingdom, and the Yaiba were able to lay waste to it however they saw fit.

"What are you talking about," Bill waved off with bright hazel eyes. "I bet you could still beat any of the new recruits if you wanted to." Masamune laughed, and they both looked him over. His beard had grown long over the years and his skin was a touch darker than it had been. There were more wrinkles now, and he knew that he wasn't for swift movement these days. Bill, however, never stopped seeing him as the warrior-scientist with the biggest heart.

"Always with the jokes," the old man said as his laugh descended to a throaty chuckle. "But let's talk about you! One of the Seven Dragons, huh? You sure have grown up on me. It seems like just yesterday that you were asking me to read you another bedtime story in the Civil Center nursery." There was a hint of emotion in his voice that matched the sudden glisten of Bill's eyes. "I'm proud of you, son."

"I think I needed to hear you say that," Bill choked, and the elderly scientist gently pat the young soldier's shoulder.

"Rough couple of years, huh?" Bill nodded, in much the same way that he had when he was a child, all alone and yearning for attention. "Well, we can talk about it after we unload your order." He offered a loving smile, and it was all Bill could do to hold back tears. They walked through the containers as Kazuya searched his clipboard for the right one. Bill on the other hand reflected on his gratefulness. Had it not been for Kazuya, he didn't know if he would've been as loved growing up. His parents died in the Destruction of Greensboro Base, along with over a hundred

Yaiba elites and 500 leaders overall. All of their efforts went into saving who they could and holding off the Scarlet raiders that sought to snuff them out. Masamune was the one who saved Bill, and ever since, the former lab tech did everything he could to ease his pain.

Now, that same little boy whose fingers were so small as they clutched to his lab coat, whose voice so strained from the smoke and the trauma, stood before him a bright, confident, and well-beloved leader in the Yaiba ranks.

They came upon a pasty blue container at the far back of the ship, and with Masamune's prompt, the younger and stronger Jerrick opened its double doors. Inside, four crates of refined tungsten rods, two crates of medical supplies, five crates of food rations that should minimize the hunting effort for at least a couple of months, and a crate of assorted materials for the tinkering of the new research division head.

"I guess we should get unpacking," Bill said with an excitement that could only be described as his. It made the old man beside him smile, and with a nod Masamune retrieved an auto-dolly from the front of the ship. He turned the power on, pulled Bill's hand in front of a small scanner, and after a moment left the Tsuchiryu to his own devices. The work wasn't hard overall, at least not insofar as the food, medical supplies and assorted materials were concerned. The auto-dolly followed him to both the shipments and the delivery transport the Dragons arrived in, and for each of those trips it was a relatively painless experience. The pain, however, came from the tungsten shipments.

Bill expected there to be some delay when dealing with such a heavy metal in such large quantities, but the leisurely walk back to the transport had become tedious. The weight of the crates proved almost too much for the auto-dolly, so after the second one, Bill had to help push the load from the ship to the transport. After the third crate, he took his time and caught his breath as Dr. Masamune laughed at him.

"I thought you were supposed to be a young man," teased the scientist. Bill cut his eyes at him but couldn't keep his lips from widening in humor.

"Hey, it's not as easy as I make it look, Doc." Bill looked into the massive shipping crate and noted the final shipment of tungsten with a mix of pain and excitement. He never was one to back down from a challenge, but that didn't mean he didn't think about it sometimes. "I guess I should get to moving that last one." There was a tinge of sadness in his voice, because he knew that once it was loaded up, Masamune would have to leave again.

"Well the good news is," Kazuya started once he heard what the boy, his boy, was thinking, "next time I don't think I'll have to carry twice the metal as I did this time. Still, it's nice to know that my Hanzo Gear and the Reikiken are earning me more notoriety." A sly smirk took to the old man's face, and Bill couldn't stop his eyes from rolling before they did. Of course he would feel a sense of pride about his innovations in war. Still, Bill got the sense that the pride the old scientist felt was more due to his achievements as a scientist rather than the lives his inventions claimed.

Bill let out a huff, then loaded the final container of tungsten onto the dolly and rolled it out onto the pier. He didn't get the fight that he wanted when he left the compound, but the smooth execution of a mission was worth far more. He smiled. By now, Callan should be back where he belongs, so the fact that this mission wrapped up so seamlessly was of great benefit.

A thunderous crack penetrated the still air and startled the gulls to flight. Bill's smiling expression shifted to a hardened scowl as he whipped out his Reikiken and whipped it through the air. The heat of the blade distorted the flight path of the bullet, but the extra hot metal of the projectile went through the flesh at the top of his shoulder. The sheer force of it took him a step back, but it wasn't enough to knock him down. Bill stooped down behind the crate, and with his free hand, he clutched the burned and bloody flesh. His vision was hazy now, but it didn't matter. He refused to go down here.

He thought to do a quick scan as more bullets hailed down against the crate and dolly but decided against it. He was on an old pier. The most he could do was use his kyoketsu-shoge to rapidly bound away, but there was no certainty that the decaying wood of the pier would hold up if he did. Worse still, he would just open himself up for more fire from his enemies on the Memorial Bridge. His best course of action was to press forward with the tungsten shipment as cover.

The gunfire roared continuously, but no bullets reached his position. For only a second did Bill think it strange, but then he remembered that his teammates were perched atop the long-defunct restaurants that stood before the pier. He looked back for the ship, for Dr. Masamune, but fortunately it had already departed. Bill allowed himself to breathe a sigh of relief, and used the distraction of his allies to move alongside the shipment. He watched Shonda and Manny go about the work of effortlessly dispatching a team of Scarlet troops that targeted the transport, and while his blood burned to take part in the battle, it was all he could do to remain conscious and move at the same time.

He was almost there, almost in the clear, almost back on the road to the Yaiba compound. But they would have to get up to that bridge before they drove off into the distance. The compound remained a secret to their enemies for so long not just because of the Yaiba's nomadic disposition, but because of their unwillingness to be followed home. At first that meant extremely attentive rear guards attached to every team deployed, but as time went on and the mountain base became more permanent, it was more prudent to simply exterminate the waves of enemies that presented themselves. Not everyone that went on a mission survived, but for every death of a Yaiba operative, roughly 30 more Scarlets went down as well.

As Shonda and Manny cut down the last of their immediate enemies and the ones on the bridge stopped to reload their guns, Bill entered the back of the transport, pulled up the ramp with one hand, and was shut in by Manny while Shonda took to the bridge. It took her all of five minutes and the agility given by the kyoketsu-shoge to climb the supports of the Memorial Bridge and rise to the top. There were over a dozen Scarlets with their weapons trained on her, but none were fast enough to land a shot.

Shonda was the Fire Dragon, the Hiryu, because of her expert mastery of the repulsor boots and her complete reliance on the Reikiken in combat. Her speed, agility and overwhelming power was enough to scorch the earth along with the bodies that met her sword, and the unfortunate souls that rose their guns to her would soon discover that for themselves.

The squad of armed Scarlets opened fire on her as she turned her back to them and descended to the cracked concrete of the bridge. Bullet after bullet was absorbed by the hooded cloak of the Hanzo Gear, and while it glowed red with life, a smile broke onto Shonda's face. After a moment, the troops that opposed her noticed the rise in temperature as the back end of her Reikiken gave off a heat almost as intense as the blade of the magnificent sword. They could feel the deep burn in their skin through their blood-red uniforms, and as the gunfire slowed for their reloading, Shonda whipped around with delight in her expression.

She noted their position as the soldiers before her scrambled to reload their guns. They stood in a messy arc, staggered so their bullets would hit their target and not each other, but what they failed to realize was that it also made them swift targets for the Hiryu.

"Oh, the arrogance," she muttered with a huff, and before the woman at the front of the formation could find her aim, Shonda's repulsors ignited. In a single fluid motion the doubly hot Reikiken burned its way through the woman's neck and retracted to its mistress' side. The commander of the group called for her execution, which did little more than make her lips twist upward into a smile.

The enemy troops opened fire only after Shonda cut down two more of their number. She was fast, but she was twice as calculating. The hail of bullets returned, and while a few struck her Hanzo Gear, they did little more than fuel the intensity of her fire as she moved gracefully through the barrage. She spun to one side and burned through the legs of one of her attackers. He screamed, but ultimately fell silent when she cut through him with a spinning jump towards her next assailant. Before the unfortunate girl could bury a bullet in Shonda's forehead, a flash of bright red split her at the waist. Shonda jumped, and used the combined power of the repulsor boots and the kyoketsu-shoge to add to her already impressive height.

The Scarlet troops closed ranks and focused their fire on Shonda as she drove the heavy blades of her kyoketsu-shoge into the pavement of the bridge. She pulled herself downward and rotated as the chains slithered back to their launching point. Her body turned with grace and poise, like a leaf dancing easily in a furious gale. Her repulsors muted the impact of her legs to the ground, though they sacrificed nothing of the rotation and speed thereof. The Reikiken in her hand fed off of the momentum generated by her body and burned at jarring speed through the clothes and flesh of three more Scarlet aggressors.

Twelve Scarlet soldiers were reduced to four in less than ten minutes. The heat from the Reikiken spread through the pavement as much as the air, and the remaining Reds felt every bit of it. Their feet felt like they were on fire in their boots, and the weight of the heatwave strained their lungs. Shonda was fine, as the Yaiba trained with these weapons in their Hanzo Gear for years before their field work ever began. She had a clear advantage, and relished the looks on her opponents' faces as they realized it too.

She ran for them, and with a Falling Leaf she cut through the first one. She jumped and twisted for a second time, though this time when she landed her blade swung outward in a horizontal slash. Her Dancing Leaf bisected another enemy, and already the sum of her remaining opponents was reduced by half. She jumped backwards with the blade of her burning sword fully extended to once again cut at the legs of an enemy. They toppled to the ground with a scream that startled the seagulls to flee. Then stood the commander, all alone and in her sights. He aimed his weapon with a tremble of the arms, and though he pulled the trigger, nothing came out. The clip was empty, and with the realization so too were his hopes of escape or entreaty. Regardless, the commander of the team of Reds charged her in one final defiant act before Shonda predictably and swiftly whipped her blade straight down through his body.

She didn't bother to see him literally fall to pieces, but instead turned from the scene and walked through the carnage towards the edge of the bridge that had served as her entry point. Between the kyoketsu-shoge and the repulsor boots, she made it back to the transport with little effort and even less wasted time.

"You're insane," Manny said as Shonda entered the passenger's seat. "What, did it take you eleven minutes to take them all out once you got up there?" Shonda shrugged, her face as still and serious as the mountain in which they lived.

"More like thirteen," she responded. She looked back to where Bill lay unconscious and noticed that the bullet wound near his collarbone was hastily patched and still red from the blood. Even still, he would be okay until they got back to the compound. "Is he gonna be alright?" She knew the answer, but asked the question anyway to steer the subject away from ending life. Manny looked back at Bill.

"Yeah, but we should probably get back ASAP." With a twist of the keys and a survey of their surroundings, they were off.

****

August 31st, 2084, 4:34 p.m.,

"Well, well," John said as he entered the classroom and spread his hands, "what do we have here?" She looked up at him, toddler in her arms, and watched as his mouth took the shape of a crooked smile. He sighed, not out of frustration or confusion, but out of pure wonder that the chocolate pools she called eyes still staggered the beat of his heart all these years later. She pushed her straightened hair to the side of her delicate face, and to him every move she made was as regal as the black empress he knew her to be.

"What," she said with a smile of her own and a roll of her eyes. John always acted this way towards her when he was home from a mission. It always felt like they met for the first time all over again. John's smile grew, and he leaned against the cold gray counter with his arms folded.

"Nothing…" he started playfully, "I just love seeing you here, at work." She approached him, and his heart started to beat again, fierce as the day they'd first locked eyes. "These kids are lucky to have someone as gentle and patient as you looking after them." Her eyes glinted in the artificial light of the classroom, and a chill went through her at the tender tone of her husband's voice.

"And what about you?" She raised an eyebrow at him as she set the little one down to go back to playing with the other kids. "What brings you down to my little corner of the world?"

"I just needed to be around you for a little while," he told her honestly. He thought back to the events of the last few weeks. The death of his mother, the conversation with his father, Callan being taken captive and the trauma it'd meant for their son. Then there was all the politics and the Director's dependence on him. The more time passed, the harder it became to keep his wits about him. "Aaliyah," he spoke her name with soft intentionality that gave her pause, "do you think we could speak privately for a moment?" Their eyes met, and with an elegant gesture she called for her co-teacher to cover for her. Aaliyah followed John back through the door and into the tunnel that was Education Level E.

"What's going on," she asked as soon as the door closed behind her. "Did something happen?" Her mind went to the worst possible scenario. "Did something happen to Darius?" John took her hands in his own and brought them to his lips.

"He's alright," he said gently and watched as the worry melted away from her. "Just a little shaken up, is all."

"What's wrong?" Her hands fell back to her sides.

"He's just had it rough. I mean first his grandmother died," the words hurt him to speak, "then he had his first real mission outside the compound a few days ago and his squad leader got captured. He blames himself for that, you know," John clarified, and Aaliyah shook her head.

"That doesn't make any sense," she said, "he just graduated a few weeks ago."

"That's what I told him," John replied, a little exasperation in his voice. "I'm just afraid that this'll scare him off and make him resign from the Violet Shadows."

"Would that really be so bad, though?" Aaliyah met John's eyes when she said it, and noted the incredulous look on his face. Even so, she stood firm. She was worried enough that John risked his life out there on the front lines, and she wanted a better future for Darius. She felt that he deserved that much.

"It wouldn't," John agreed reluctantly. It was a point of pride for him that his son followed in his footsteps, but it would be an egregious lie for him to say that he didn't want Darius safely within the walls and tunnels of the Roan compound. "But regardless of what we want or where he goes, this struggle with the Scarlets affects us all. People will die, hostages will be taken, hideouts will be crushed. It's the way things are for now, and it hurts, but the pain always passes."

"Have you tried telling him that," Aaliyah asked with a hand on her hip. John smiled subconsciously. He loved it when she did that, when she took that serious stance and looked at him so intently, no matter the reason.

"I have, but the kid is locked in his quarters right now and I know if he won't hear me out, you can get through to him. Can you check on him after you get off work?" She stepped closer to him and ran her hand over the black hooded cloak that covered his arm. It was oddly soft for bulletproof material, and almost gave her the impression that it was John's skin that lay beneath her fingertips. She met his gaze and gifted him a reassuring smile.

"You're so cute when you're worried about him, you know," she teased, "but yeah, I'll check in on him." John gave her a gentle but meaningful kiss that made her stagger a moment. She gripped the doorknob to brace herself, so dazed that the call for pertinent personnel sounded like the crackle of a flame in her ears.

"Thanks, Love," John told her as intently as he could and started to back away from her. "Looks like I have to get to Level D. We'll talk later though! See if you can get Darius out of his shell enough to come have a family dinner!" Before she could even respond, he was already down the tunnel and out of sight.

****

August 31st, 5:15 p.m.,

It had been a while since a meeting like this was called. The leaders of the Yaiba Insurrection rarely met all at once. Each one knew their role in maintaining their people's way of life, and if supplies were ever needed, the person in need would approach the Director themselves. The only time that the leaders were gathered from their respective levels and duties was if it had to do with a major political or social move that would greatly impact the entire Yaiba community.

Emiko Ishikawa looked around at the table from its head. On the immediate right of her sat Micah and Sam, the husband and wife duo that ran the Civil Center nervously avoided her gaze. They were relatively new to the leadership and showed a lot of promise, but they had heard the rumors of such meetings and even now the tension was unmistakable. To Sam's left was Bill Jerrick, the Tsuchiryu, bandaged and poorly rested from his altercation with the Scarlets earlier that day. He was holding a conversation with Shonda and Manny, who occupied the next two chairs. On the other side of the Earth, Wind, and Fire of the Seven Dragons was a slightly weary Callan Rouge, the Suiryu, who stared patiently at his hands for this to all be over.

John Hamlin, the Rairyu, sat at the other end of the table with a sympathetic hand on Callan's shoulder. To his left sat Bryan Piccio, the Rabbit of the Divine Wind. Sora Kaneuji, the other head of technical development and research, took his place beside him and prattled on about upgrades to the defense system to the Kiryu, Raven Shadid, who only pretended to care. She tossed her curly hair with her hand and secretly wondered when Kaneuji would shut up while Vanessa Duncan, the Kageryu that sat next to her, was genuinely and deeply invested. The door opened, and as Anna Dominguez, the Chief of Medicine took her seat Director Ishikawa called the room to attention.

"Good evening, everyone," she began, discomfort in her expression and tone. "As you may have already assumed, the reasons I have called you here are serious, and affect us all socially and politically." She cleared her throat and forced her hand to stop trembling.

"Director," John said, and shocked the entire room with his formal address, "is everything alright?"

"That remains to be seen," she responded honestly. "I've just received news that a group of enemy soldiers raided a Yoroi outpost nearabout Midland. 148 Yoroi operatives and their families were killed, and among them…" she struggled to keep herself under control as she locked eyes with Bryan, "among them were the three junior agents assigned to guard the Yoroi's envoy on his way home."

Chapter Nine

"What," Bryan muttered under his breath as the image of the previous morning thrashed violently to the front of his mind. He could still see his little one, his baby boy, so eager for a mission away, so excited to be like his sensei, Bill. That's right, this had to be some kind of mistake. Bill trained Jaden to be one of the best fighters in the Violet Shadows. The boy earned the black hooded cloak before he even graduated the training program. He was exceptional! How could this have happened?

"Jaden Piccio, Moses Fields and Clay Fields were all killed in the line of duty," Director Ishikawa clarified, though she knew that it would only make things worse. "The loss of such heroes is a major blow to the Yaiba Insurrection, but by every breath in my body their sacrifice won't be in vain."

"What of the envoy from the Yoroi Alliance?" John asked the question quickly to cut Bryan off before he said anything too rash. "Do we know what happened to Johannes at all?" Emiko gently rubbed her forehead before she fixed herself in her seat.

"It's believed that the Scarlets that laid waste to the outpost took him hostage, possibly in retaliation to the rescue of Callan Rouge," she said grimly. The Dragons looked at each other from around the table.

"What does this matter, exactly?" It was Micah who asked. As one of the two new leaders within the faction, he was nervous. His wife held his hand, but it was more to receive comfort than to give it. With the gravity of the conversation, though, it surprised none of the more seasoned officials that they would be a little unnerved. Emiko turned her head to see the couple. Micah was a fairly slim man of less than thirty. His brown eyes averted their gaze from the Director, and with his free hand he fondled his trimmed facial hair. Sam was a bit more composed, and while she didn't make eye contact with Emiko either, she at least moved her brown hair behind her ear to look in that direction.

"Essentially a foreign representative has gone missing on our watch," Raven spoke before Emiko had the chance. She was of a tan complexion with dark, vivacious hair that curled loosely down to the small of her back. Her green eyes fixed on the new leaders as she folded her hands together and placed her elbows on the table. "Even though we've brokered an alliance with the Yoroi, it's reasonable to think that this little mishap would make them renege on the deal."

"That's only the best-case scenario," John spoke up now. "When the deal was made, it was because we had due leverage and all but bullied the Yoroi Alliance into joining up with us."

"Now, it looks like what leverage we had doesn't even matter anymore," Shonda sighed, and John slumped in his chair like a bored child.

"This is such a pain," he complained, his hatred of political meetings on full display for everyone to see. "Shonda's right, though. What leverage we had in the beginning is null and void because we screwed up a chance to get their guy back where he belongs safely. If he tells the Scarlets why he was heading back to Yoroi lands with an armed escort of three Violet Shadows of the Yaiba Insurrection, the Yoroi would probably be forced to take up arms against us to prove they haven't turned traitor on the Reds." John's mind searched for all the possible outcomes of this scenario for some shred of light, but it was faint.

"Well there has to be something we can do to keep that from happening," Bill said as he played with the stitches in his shoulder.

"There's a chance we can, but it's still a questionable outcome," the Director explained. "When Ambassador Vargas was here, he didn't seem too convinced that he needed our help anyway. Of course at the time, he let us believe that the Kabuto territories they acquired had been taken by force, probably to give the impression that the Yoroi are stronger than they let on. In the span of the last week, however, we learned that the Kabuto hastily fled their old home and gifted the land to the Yoroi to do with as they would. That isn't to say that our friends at the Alliance are weak, but if things do get bad for them, they have the ability to go so deep underground that neither the Reds or the Yaiba will be able to find them."

"Which means that they'd be able to hit both sides with relative ease while preserving themselves," Vanessa surmised to a low hum from Manny.

"Not necessarily," he told her. "If they go underground like that then it could end up working against them if their opponents—which might include us if we can't win them back—find out how their system works."

"If they do try to strike us, they would have to go through the Texas route to get to us so we would see it coming," Dr. Dominguez thought aloud.

"Even if we didn't, my team and I have already mapped out their previously defined territory," John assured her. "Provided that nothing goes wrong with our alliance with the Kabuto, we could probably get a stream of information on what their old turf looks like all the same."

"Before we get too used to the idea of fighting," Sam asked, "shouldn't we try to smooth things over with the Yoroi?" Bryan slammed his palm against the table, and for the first time since the Director gave the room the news did anyone look in his direction.

"Smooth things over? For what? It's their fault that my son is dead, so from where I'm sitting, we're even." His face was red and his breathing was hard, but who could blame him? Every word he spoke stung in a way that most of the others couldn't understand.

“Bryan, please,” Ishikawa implored with the sort of gentle tone with which one might soothe a startled animal. “It isn’t that simple.”

“I don’t care,” Bryan retorted sharply. “The fact is my kid is dead because he was on a mission to guide that punk from the Yoroi back to where he came from and you guys are talking about how we haven’t hit our lowest point yet?” He paused and looked around at each of them as methodically as a lioness with prey in her sights, and none of the others around the table could meet his gaze. “Unbelievable.”

“We can’t bring him back,” Manny told him with a placating gesture, “but we can do what we can to bring his murderers to justice.”

“And how long will that take,” Bryan snapped, and Manny sat back in his chair. “We always talk about taking down the Scarlets and bringing the Reds to justice and living in actual houses and not in some cave in the mountainside but here we are! What progress have we made? Tell me, Em, are we winning? Because I sure as hell don’t feel like it right now.” Emiko’s eyes went sharp in an instant, and Bryan immediately remembered his place.

“Bryan, your family has suffered a monumental loss that I can’t begin to understand,” she began with a hint of venom in her gentle tone, “but it would serve you well to remember that we’re on your side here and even better to remember that I have little patience for petulant outbursts at my expense. Moreover, the time for waiting around has passed. The Scarlets have some idea of what’s happening behind the scenes, and if we wait too long we risk losing our window to strike back at them.”

“Callan, by your estimation, how long would it take for us to drive out the remaining Scarlet forces in Johnson City?” Kaneuji asked. Callan looked up at the small-framed man and noted a childlike whimsy in his dark eyes. Sora was a part of the tech and research division, but for all the seriousness and duty that Bryan and Masamune presented, this dark-haired developer seemed to have a knack for strategic destruction commonly displayed with juvenile joy.

"If we mobilize a sizeable force against them we could have it done in about half a day," Callan responded warily. He never really knew how to deal with Sora, or how the man would take his suggestions. "That probably won't be necessary, though."

"Oh, it never is, Mr. Water Dragon, sir," Sora said with a giggle, "but if we don't have the time to spare, then we need to expand our territory as quickly as possible."

"He does have a point," Raven offered. "Johnson City is nestled on one of the easiest routes to the western regions. Occupying it would delay coordination between the Scarlet capitol and any troops they have deployed in the field."

"It would also open us up to the same kind of attack that they hit the Helmets with," Vanessa warned. Sora, who hated to be contradicted, fixed his eyes on the dark-skinned woman with bounce in her hair.

"Well if we knew what kind of weapon was used I could probably figure out a way to suppress its firepower. Maybe even negate it altogether if given the proper materials," the last was a question aimed at the Director. She paused for a moment to consider what he asked. A new defense system would be beneficial, and would allow the Yaiba to establish a firm foothold on territories outside of the mountain base. It had been a long time since the children of the Insurrection regularly saw the sun.

"I'll consider it, though we'll have to coordinate with the Kabuto to bring any plans to fruition undetected," Emiko conceded, much to the delight of Sora. "Which leads us back to the Yoroi once again." Bryan grimaced at the sound of the name, but dared not speak as rashly as he had before.

"I think there might be something we can do to placate them, at least for the time being," Bill chimed in. "The three of us went on a mission to pick up the tungsten rods shipped to us from Gansu, but there were more than we'd expected. Correct me if I'm wrong, but would the extra tungsten be for the Yoroi Alliance to use and not us?"

"When we struck our deal with them, we promised to share our weaponry and instruction to properly use it," Emiko confirmed, and then smiled when she realized what Bill was getting at. "You know, that might actually work. If we carry on with that plan to offer up our Reikiken and Hanzo Gear, we might be able to keep them from turning against us out of fear of the Reds."

"If it's not guaranteed to work," Bryan spoke cautiously, "then why would we give up our best-kept secrets to a potential enemy?" He had a point. Not that long ago, all the factions in Prevalence were at odds with each other. War was threatened on every side, and for the right reasons that tension could return.

"We don't have much of a choice," Manny said frankly. "The Yoroi are a powerful ally, and if we have the chance to unite them to ourselves and the Kabuto then we have to take it."

"Or at least keep them from coming after us," John countered. "The Scarlet Kingdom and their secret weapon are already a big enough issue on their own. With the help of the Helmets, we have an army of saboteurs ready to dismantle their weapons. From what Callan and the kids told us, they're about as good at infiltration and extraction as we are, so if we cause a disturbance and ultimately engage the Scarlets in a frontal assault, they can slip behind enemy lines and do their thing."

"Going back to the matter of the Hanzo Gear, how soon can we expect to produce and send them to our would-be allies," Micah asked, a little more used to the tension in the room now. All eyes fell on Bryan and Sora, who at this moment looked more like the masks of comedy and drama than anything.

"With the large volume of tungsten and materials that have come into the lab, we could probably churn them out in about six weeks if we pushed it," Sora projected optimistically. Emiko raised an eyebrow.

"That's sooner than I was expecting. Good. Also, make sure that the colors of their Hanzo Gear differ from our violet and black. If they do decide to take our peace offering and turn it against us, it'll at least be easier to identify them," Emiko reasoned in a calculating tone that made Sora blush. She clapped her hands loudly and her expression lightened a bit. "We have our plan in place, and all the possibilities have been carefully considered. Does anyone have anything else that they want to say?" A moment of silence passed, but then Bryan stood from his chair.

"I intend to work alongside the other technicians over the next six weeks to get that shipment out as a courtesy for housing my family for as long as you have, but once this project is finished, I'm out." Bryan's words left the room stunned, and with nothing more to say, he simply left the room.

****

The pain that he felt was entirely new. It was stronger than when Bryan first found out that Jaden had joined the Violet Shadows, more poignant than his own father's death from brain cancer in his early twenties, and more pointed than any physical or mental injury sustained on the battlefield. It took everything he had to hold back the tears, and everything was not enough. He wept as he walked through the winding tunnels of the Insurrection compound and hardly cared to meet the gaze of any one of the soldiers and civilians that surrounded him. The only thing on his mind, the only thing that seemed to carry any weight for him right now, was that he wanted his baby boy back in his arms.

This feeling was amplified by the memory of the morning prior, how Jaden looked at him when he got protective. *I'm not a kid anymore, dad,* he had said. Even now, Bryan could see how his boy's face twisted in disappointment, how his energetic green eyes sharpened with a quiet intensity that resonated louder than any bell the world over. He was so adamant that he was an adult, that he didn't need Bryan's protections or parental musings, but Bryan couldn't help it. Jaden was—and always would be—his baby boy.

The Master Rabbit held the space above his heart as the emotional pain became physical. There were so many things that he had hoped to teach his boy, so much time he wanted to spend with him. He wanted to see Jaden get married and be there for the birth of his first grandchild. He wanted to fill his ears with as many "I love yous" and "I'm heres" as Jaden could handle and beyond, to see the joy and anger and frustration and sadness in those excited eyes that had grown so much over the years. Those eyes that would never open again.

"Bryan," called John. Bryan was just about to open the door to the lab and wondered how he'd gotten there so quickly. "Bryan, what was that?" His eyes narrowed on his unwelcome friend.

"What was what?" There was a pause as the sharpness of Bryan's tone cut through the air. John hesitated to answer. He knew of the predicament that Bryan was in, but he couldn't understand it. Not really.

"Did you mean what you said? About leaving the Insurrection?" The question hurt to ask, and if John was honest with himself, he didn't really want to know the answer.

"Yeah," was all Bryan offered, and the succinct nature of the response drove John mad with questions.

"Where would you go?" Bryan gave no response, and without more than a second's hesitation, John asked, "Do you have a plan?"

"Look, I don't know, alright? I need to get out of this place and figure things out for myself. If I stay—" Bryan looked at John, and in the place of his friend he saw only the training his son received, the institution he'd died for, and the futility of their mission.

"You'll just be reminded of everything you lost," John finished after a moment. "But what about Sharon?" There was another pause. Bryan closed his mouth and thought for a moment, his eyes still locked on John.

"She'll be free to do what she wants after I tell her what's happened," he finally said. John's eyes went wide with disbelief.

"So that's it then, you're just giving up on your family? Abandoning everything that your father and grandfather worked towards just like that? Letting your wife go when she's gonna need you most? I understand that this is rough on you—"

"You understand, huh," Bryan snapped, which would've intimidated the average person but did nothing more than irritate John. "Tell me just what the hell you understand about what I'm feeling right now! Your son is *alive*! He's here with you! You can walk into his living quarters right now and tell him to your heart's content that you love him and you'll be there for him! You can wrap your arms around him and hug him! So what could you possibly know about what it's like to lose your child, man?"

"Listen, I understand where you're coming from, but you'd do well to watch your tone with me," John shot back in a tone so deep and dragonic it proved him worthy of the title Rairyu. "If you remember, I was there for you when Lyla disappeared. I saw the kind of broken mess it turned you into and I helped you get through it. That's all I'm trying to do now and I'd appreciate it if you didn't bite my head off about it."

"Yeah, well, who asked you for your help, John?" Bryan's eyes were cold when he spoke, and John marveled at how deeply the words cut. "You may think I owe you some deeper insights into my life or my grief or something but I don't. Now if you don't mind, I have a lot of work to do so I'll see you around."

"Fine," John said curtly, desperate to disguise the tremble of emotion in his voice. "Then I guess I'll be on my way. Give your family my best, if you don't mind. You don't have to worry about me offering my help as freely anymore either."

****

August 31st, 7:22 p.m.,

John walked into his home emotionally wounded and angry, more than anything else. Bryan was recklessly making decisions out of emotion, and while he could empathize with his friend, he knew that emotional miscalculation wasn't a luxury that the Insurrection could afford, especially by someone so integrally involved with their technology and resources. The alternative would be to let Sora handle everything, and that would end up…bad.

"Hey," Aaliyah spoke in a hushed tone as she greeted her husband at the door. Instantly his hardened expression melted away like soft butter in the noonday sun, and he took her lips with his as passionately as he could. "Hey, cut it out," she whispered with a girlish giggle. "Darius is just in the next room."

"Don't stop on my account," the boy groaned with a grin that his parents couldn't see. "I grew up around you two, remember? I already know that my presence isn't enough to stop you from further scarring me for life." John and Aaliyah grinned.

"It's alright, kid. Actually, you're my sole focus tonight anyway," John said as he came into the main room. It was quaint, held together by a few wooden chairs and a small steel and class coffee table that was a bit too low. An armor stand for John's Hanzo Gear rested at the front of the room in clear view of the established seating arrangement, adorned with the black hooded cloak he'd only bother to wear for group training or missions. Darius sat in the chair closest to it and admired it.

He looked at his father, who smiled on him with eyes that even now only saw the beautiful little boy from years faded. "Why's that?" John's smile remained firm as he looked at the cloak, the symbol of his mission to fight for the freedom of his family, for the safety of the Yaiba, for the destruction of the Scarlet Kingdom. It was John's greatest blessing and curse.

"Well for starters, I have to apologize to you," John told him with a nonchalance that put the boy at ease. "Ever since you were little, I had such high expectations for you. I think in some ways I did more to imprint my own ideals on you than to teach you to find your own. I'm sorry about that."

"Dad, if this is about me joining the Shadows—" John placed a hand on Darius' shoulder to quiet him.

"It is and it isn't. I just know you've been under a lot of pressure from the time you joined. With my mission to the western regions I wasn't here for you during some of the hardest moments of your life. It was out of my hands, but I still blame myself for not being there for my son during the critical years," he explained with a degree of pain. He chuckled. "Even though I'm here, I get so bogged down with my duties as the right hand of the Director that I haven't really been there after your grandma passed."

"Pops," Darius interrupted again with the name he called John by when he was feeling particularly emotional. Darius' throat tightened as tears welled up in his eyes. John pat the boy on the head in a motion to soothe him, just like he did when Darius was little.

"Hold on, I'm not done apologizing yet. The hardest thing for you was when your Uncle Callan got captured by the Reds for your sake. You must've thought it was all your fault, didn't you? Always so ready to take responsibility for things out of your control," John mused wistfully. "You really are my kid, aren't you? Brilliant, strong, creative, and so unwilling to burden others with your problems that you keep things dangerously bottled up." John paused to allow Darius the chance at reply, but when the boy started to cry, John pulled him closer and wrapped him in a hug. "I'm so sorry you've had to feel alone for so long. I'm sorry for the part I played in that by not giving you the support you needed when you needed it." John pulled away for a moment and placed his hand on Darius' shoulder again. "Kid, you gotta know that I love you with everything I got."

"I know, Pops," responded the boy. "I love you too." As Darius pulled closer for another hug, Aaliyah smiled on her boys with radiant pride and hidden relief. John, however, held his boy with the fear that this time could very well be the last.

****

"No," Aaliyah gasped at the news. John made a point to tell her only after Darius had left. He'd been through enough in the last week alone, and deserved at least one night of rest. Her heart sank, as did John's when he retold it. "Is Bryan alright?"

"Would you be if it was our son that died in the line of duty?" John immediately felt her gaze sharpen. "I'm sorry. I snapped and I shouldn't have. It's been an emotional day and I'm still not very good at processing them the way I should."

"You're better than you were when I met you," she assured him dryly, and came to rest beside her husband near the armor stand. She placed her hand gently in his, and he rested his head against her shoulder. They sat in silence for a moment and thought of their friends, their home, their lives. John massaged the back of Aaliyah's hand and kissed her shoulder. She smelled of lavender perfume, and wore a mint green dress with a ring of white flowers around the waist. To him, she was beauty itself, and everything beautiful about the world merely compared to her and judged accordingly.

"He's as good as I think he's gonna get here, Love. Unfortunately he never really recovered from Lyla's disappearance. He became so tense and timid after that."

"Wouldn't you, though?" Aaliyah asked, but immediately answered her own question. "You can barely handle when Darius has one of his isolated episodes, what am I saying?"

"There's no argument there, Love," John admitted with a sigh. "That boy is so much like me it's almost painful. Actually, scratch that, it is painful. Even so, the only thing that would be more painful is losing him or his brother." For a second John thought of the possibility of losing Cal, of never hearing his tech jokes again or scolding him for making lethal modifications to his Hanzo Gear. It hurt more than he was willing to admit. Losing them both together was unthinkable.

"I couldn't imagine losing those boys," Aaliyah whispered, as if from John's own mind. "That family has been through more than we have a right to talk about."

"Maybe," John started and sat up, "but we're not too far off from where they currently stand. They adopted Lyla, we adopted Cal. They had Jaden, we had Darius."

"But they lost their kids, John, both of them," Aaliyah protested. Her tone was motherly, sympathetic in a way that only another parent could understand. Even so, John shook his head.

"When those kids chose to enter the Violet Shadows, they knew what they were getting themselves into and every risk that came along with this line of work. Their parents knew, too."

"So you're saying they shouldn't grieve their children when they die or go missing?" Aaliyah asked incredulously, and John shook his head again.

"That's not it at all. Grief is one thing, but leaving the Yaiba when the Reds would kill you on sight?" Aaliyah opened her mouth to object to the implication but found that she couldn't disagree.

"It is reckless. What does Sharon have to say about it?" John didn't say anything. "What?"

"I just want to make sure you're safe in all this. With all the political shifts on the horizon I'm not entirely certain that we should be concerned about someone else's marriage. It's that shady Ambassador Vargas that gets me. He seems like the kind of person to target what a person loves most to make them suffer for their mistakes, and undoubtedly he'll view the deaths of our men and the capture of one of his as just that." Aaliyah rubbed his arm and kissed him on his cheek, and John could feel the weight of his worry lift from his shoulders.

"You just go and be as fierce as a Lightning Dragon should. We'll be fine." She kissed him again for reassurance and took him by the hand. "I promise."

****

August 31st, 9:22 p.m.,

The makeshift command center was deserted by now with the exception of James the Scarlet Prince. He sat by himself as he eyed the clock and waited for the transmission to come through. He hated these moments, and knew that with the report filed to the capitol New York 24 hours ago, he would catch hell for everything that happened. He tapped his fingers along the edge of the holographic projection unit, irritated that another minute ticked by without so much as a ring from the other side. James let out an exasperated sigh, but silenced himself when the projection came to life. Before him, surrounded in blue light, was a man of dark hair, ruggedly sharp features, a firm build, and a similar set of stardust-gray eyes that, unlike James', pierced through to the soul. James scowled

"Good to see you too, brother," spoke the projection. "I understand it's been a difficult couple of days for you and your troops." The edge of the projection's mouth curled into an arrogant smirk, and suddenly James' face seeped with sarcastic intent.

"Well, we can't all be tucked away safe and warm in the palace, Nash," James answered. "Some of us have things to do."

"Like getting stomped by a bunch of pacifists?" The question stung, and while James wanted to respond to his older brother, his words and wit failed to filter through the open door that was his mouth. "Granted, they are only in the area because of my attack on the Helmet lands. Maybe you want me to… assist you?"

"What I want is for you to find some business of your own to monitor for once," James snapped. "I merely underestimated my opponents. That's all." Nash exhaled sharply as he eyed his brother.

"I suppose that type of blunder is only natural for someone as poorly suited for tactics as you, James." James' usually playful eyes narrowed on his brother with near-murderous intent.

"Says the man who spurred the pacifists to violence," James retaliated coolly. Nash's face contorted in a motion of genuine surprise, but he offered no response. James stood with arms folded in all smugness. "Your little weapon test took out numerous members of the Kabuto's upper echelon, not to mention the treasured family members of some of their more influential families. Our recent troubles are a direct result of your flippant behavior."

"I'll admit that's surprising, James, but the decades they've committed to weakness can't be undone in a single year. They lack the resources and the tactical knowledge to best our forces, even if they are led by you," Nash chided with a dismissive wave. James clenched his fist in anger.

"Even if they've joined forces with the Yaiba?" The words peeled the petulant grin from Nash's lips, his eyes narrowed, and he paced the floor where he was.

"I wasn't aware that they had…" his voice trailed off, but his would-be pensive look was thrown off when he caught sight of the humored expression that his brother donned.

"Well, if you took the time to read the report my men filed for more than just my mistakes, you might have actually seen that. We don't know if what they learned is from the Yaiba, and with the raid they executed on our motor pool it seems unlikely. It's more reasonable to believe that they never stopped training in the art of war for such a time as this, when you and your equally overzealous subordinates give them a reason to lash out at us." Nash once again signaled his lack of concern, and James could see exactly what his older brother thought. If the Yaiba weren't teaching the Kabuto how to fight, then the Kabuto would be a simple matter to deal with. If that were the case, the capitol would, under the instruction of the elder sibling, treat the Helmets as an afterthought.

"They're not a worthy challenge, little brother," Nash said, much to James' chagrin. "In fact, I don't see a need to waste broader Kingdom resources on dealing with them. Why don't you send in your squad of maidservants to handle it?" James blinked as if he didn't quite understand.

"I'm sorry, I don't have maidservants at my disposal right now, so I'm at a loss at trying to figure out to whom you're referring," he responded. Nash rolled his eyes, then paused for a moment as if trying to think.

"They were named after some kind of disease, I think," he responded thoughtfully. "Weird enough for a group of maids to have a team name anyway, but you know how the womenfolk get when you tell them they can't do something—"

"Ah, the Scarlet Scourge," James supplied, and Nash snapped and pointed at his brother.

"That's it! Send them in to deal with the Helmets. Aren't they usually the ones we get to do the menial tasks in the field anyway?" James shook his head at his brother, which prompted Nash to ask, "What?"

"It just surprises me how remarkably dense you can be, Nash. The Scourge is one of if not THE top squad in the entirety of the Scarlet Kingdom Armed Forces. They handle all of the serious business, and despite their assortment of ranks, they command thousands upon thousands when they have the need. If Colonel Crawford heard you minimize their importance, she'd probably snuff you out like an old-world lamp without thinking twice." James smiled as he said it, equally due to his brother's horrified expression and the simple fact that it was probably true.

"Bite your tongue, James," Nash snapped. "No subordinate of a Kingdom prince would ever raise a hand to the royal family!" James chuckled.

"Clearly you've never met Serenity Crawford. The woman cares nothing of noble titles or positions, especially when it interferes with the objectives of her precious Scarlet Scourge. She lives life according to the principle of mission success. Jeopardize that, and you die. I hardly think it matters who you are or what your rank is, because the simple fact of the matter is that if she deigns to kill you, even the King himself would simply assume that you deserved it." James' explanation did little to put his brother at ease, and the look of discomfort on Nash's face brought so much satisfaction to the field-stationed prince. James shrugged. "In any case, the way they attacked us was oddly…familiar."

"What do you mean," Nash asked, happy for the change of subject. James locked eyes with his brother.

"When they attacked, bombs went off in several different places. A string of dead bodies could be found only in one. They took out our resources, delayed our exit of the city by a few extra days, and seemingly came out of nowhere." Nash's eyes went wide as he spoke. Nash paced the floor a bit more, clearly unnerved, and neither of them knew if it was because of Serenity's nature, or the troubling implications of the Kabuto's attack and escape.

"So what, you think that they learned their tactics from the Yoroi Alliance?" The question sounded ridiculous at first, but further contemplation on the events of the last two days made it a reasonable assumption.

"Not entirely," James answered as he ran his fingers through his blond goatee. "When the Alliance employed their guerilla tactics in the past, it was more hit and run. Wild. Unpredictable. The Helmets were precise. They knew exactly when and where to hit us to ensure mission success. They outsmarted the Scourge and played all our forces from the highest ranking to the lowest for fools. Their methods remind me more of experienced saboteurs with a knack for war."

"Hmmm…" Nash grew more excited the more he heard, and James more irritated the more his brother grew excited. "It seems that I might've underestimated the little Helmet rabble."

"Join the club," James said dryly. "You know what this means, don't you?"

"What?" James exhaled sharply and folded his arms across his chest.

"It's amazing how little you're aware of the world around you. The Yaiba have an alliance with the Kabuto. That means that a powerful army has just gained the aid of incredibly proficient saboteurs if my guess is correct. To make matters worse, the Yoroi Alliance has broken the treaty with us and is in talks to join up with the Yaiba as well," James explained through teeth clenched in fear. Nash's eyes grew wide from the revelation.

“I thought that that was only a rumor,” Nash all but objected. “How do you know if they’ve broken the treaty?” James smirked devilishly, as if he’d been waiting for someone to ask him that question but nobody would oblige him. He snapped his fingers, and his attendants who stood on the other side of the door wheeled in a rather thin man with a black sack over his head.

“May I present,” James spoke up in his best showman voice as he strode towards the captive with glee. He pulled the sack from the man’s head to reveal the exhausted green eyes and disheveled brown hair of “our old friend, Johannes Thornhill, whom we…rescued from a Yaiba armed escort in Texas.” Nash was silent, Johannes breathed hard, and James stood in calm admiration of the turning of the tides.

Chapter Ten

October 3rd, 2084, 8:45 a.m.,

"Let's go!" Bryan barked orders at the junior operatives that pulled the wheeled crates of Yaiba weaponry out of the power-lift. He'd become a hard man in the last month and a half. The death of his son Jaden affected more than anyone in the Yaiba could have predicted. He shunned his friends, distanced himself from his wife, and took to his work in mind, body and soul. His only goal right now was to finish the Yoroi's order of Hanzo gear and get out as quickly as possible. Their group was already on Conference Level D, supervised by the Director and a few of the Dragons for added insurance, and they would depart as soon as they had their weaponry in hand. "Move it! The longer we take, the longer that Yoroi filth sticks around and the longer I have to be here dealing with the lot of you."

The younger Shadows had become accustomed to the verbal abuse and general unkindness that Bryan had displayed of late, but today they were especially conscious of it. They knew that he was gone as soon as this deal was done, and while it would be a blow to the Insurrection to lose such a legendary warrior, it would come to the ease of everyone's mind. The few workers pulled the crates into the foyer of the Director's personal office as Bryan moved ahead of them. He entered the room without so much as a thank you, because at this point he figured that he'd said his thanks and his goodbyes on the day he got the news.

Inside the Director's office, around the silver table, sat the delegation from the Yoroi Alliance. Bryan's face exuded visible disgust at their presence, and even the sharp glare Emiko flashed him couldn't correct him. It hurt her heart, but she realized that in his mind he'd already left the Yaiba, and so moved to make peace with that herself.

"As promised, Mr. Vargas, the fabrication of Yoroi Hanzo Gear is complete," Emiko said in a placating voice as Bryan took his seat at the table. He couldn't stand to look at her. For him, these men and women from the Yoroi that sat at this table were the reason his boy was dead, and the woman that sat at its head marched him right into his demise. There was no forgiveness for these people, only liberty for himself.

"You speak of promises," Vargas responded in a scathing tone that made Bryan's face contort in indignation, "but you failed to keep the one that mattered most, Director Ishikawa. The safety of our representative was your responsibility, and the most important show of good faith with regard to the alliance of our peoples."

"You have a lot of nerve," Bryan growled. Vargas' green eyes shifted to the engineer and, despite the scowl across his lips, smiled at him. "The Scarlets attacked your territory, killed your men in their own turf, and took my son with them. But you come into this place with the assertion that it was our fault?"

"Ah, but you see," Vargas started with a smack of the lips, "it was your transport that they were looking for. Your people interacting with ours. Your son and the ones with him got sloppy, and they led our enemies right to our front door. So yes, it was your fault, and because of your blunder our enemies know that the Yoroi have violated the Flagstaff Ceasefire." Bryan opened his mouth to argue, to yell, to put this old dust bag in his place, but Emiko shot him a look that told him if he did anything of the sort it would cost him. He begrudgingly closed his mouth as his hands balled tightly into furious fists beneath the table. The other emissaries from the Yoroi Alliance murmured to each other, half about the clear complications of the negotiations and half about Bryan's petulant outburst.

"It looks bad," John offered to a scoff from the elder ambassador, "but we can still salvage the situation. The fact that there has been no visible contact between our factions for the last six weeks might have been enough to give the Scarlets pause about making things harder for your side." Vargas shook his head, and the redheaded woman next to him folded her arms across her chest as disapproval took to her bright blue eyes.

"Their sanctions have already begun. The direct routes leading into our territories have been occupied by Kingdom forces. The trade we Yoroi used to enjoy with the other factions has been reduced to an exclusive agreement with the Scarlets, and we only get their scraps and cast-offs. Just coming here was a massive risk to our lives," Vargas' voice raised as his eyes shifted between John, Bill, Vanessa and Emiko. Their faces were hard and unresponsive, as if the weight their guest put behind his statement was of little consequence overall.

"The Hanzo Gear we've supplied you with should give you a sturdy edge in solidifying your defenses and preserving your autonomy," Bill interjected, and Vargas slammed his hand hard against the steel table.

"What will your toys do for us," he demanded through a thickened accent. There was a fire in his eyes that wasn't there before, and all the cunning that John and Emiko had observed in their prior meeting with him had completely washed away. "You offer us the firesword and the bladed whips, your fancy cloaks and combat attire but leave us to figure out how it works on our own!"

"The fact that we've supplied anything at all is more than you deserve," Bryan muttered, and Emiko threw her pen at his head. It landed in between his teeth before his mouth could close, and the exposed tip of it made his tongue bleed. His eyes widened, as did those of Vargas, his four accompanying envoys, and the three Dragons present in the room. Emiko was anything but the helpless bureaucrat many perceived her to be, and with the slightest flick of her wrist she proved that before them all.

"I think that what my subordinate means to say," Emiko said with narrowed eyes, "is that if you need a teacher, we can supply one." It was Vargas who became shrewd now, his face returned to some degree of cunning calm.

"Who would you suggest?" The question came out barbed, with the clear implication that not just anyone would do. Emiko, however, kept her calm as she clasped her hands together on the tabletop.

"The first person that comes to mind is one of the pioneers of the Hanzo Gear, Dre Hamlin. He was one of the three men chosen to take part in the field test. He's more than a valuable asset to the Yaiba, and I think he could prove to be just as beneficial to the ranks of the Yoroi," Emiko informed him. While the four men and women that sat on the Yoroi side of the table gave the obvious signs of interest, Ambassador Vargas was hardly impressed with the Director's offer. He let a moment pass as he weighed his options. If what she said was true, then they would have a legendary fighter to escort them home and give their people all the secrets of the Insurrection's Violet Shadows. That would be valuable in the fight against the Scarlet Kingdom, but could also prove useful if ever they were to engage with the Yaiba themselves. On the other hand, something about this felt wrong. It was curious to Vargas just why she tried to sell him on the point so hard.

"Correct me if I'm wrong," Vargas finally said as he stroked his beard and turned his head slightly to the side, "but this field test. It took place on the night of the White Ruins Miracle, no?" Emiko hesitated for just a second, but it was long enough for Vargas to see that he was right to question her motives.

"That's correct," the Director confirmed.

"Ah, and you how old would that make Mr. Hamlin, if you don't mind me asking?" Vargas' face was an irritating calm as he asked the question. Emiko sighed at her momentary defeat and crunched the numbers in her head.

"He'd be somewhere between 68 and 70 years old at this point," she admitted, "but he has kept himself in prime fighting condition. Anyone trained by him would probably be better than half of our forces combined."

"While I appreciate your respect of the elderly," Vargas quipped, "I was hoping for a teacher with a little less… experience." John couldn't help but smile at the idea of his father being snubbed for his age. It was something that would drive him insane, and petty though it was, John delighted in that fact unashamed.

"If you want someone without as much experience, I have a recommendation," Bryan offered. His expression was cold, just as it had been for the bulk of his time with the Yaiba following the news of Jaden's passing. He paused for dramatic buildup and carefully surveyed the expressions of those around the table. His eyes locked with Johns as he spoke the words, "Darius Hamlin, the son of the current Rairyu and grandson of the first."

"Absolutely not," John shouted, and watched as the faintest flash of a grin passed like a lightning strike on Bryan's face. "That's out of the question." A string of profanities filtered into his mind as he stared a hole in Bryan.

"I wonder if it is," Vargas chimed in with a pensive charm that was magnified by his accent. It held no sway with John, but Emiko was on the fence about it herself. John emphatically shook his head.

"He's only just graduated from the training program," John protested. He spoke as if this were a bad thing, that Darius' inexperience in the field would get someone killed or make him ill-suited to be a teacher, but Vargas' ears perked up.

"So I'm to understand that he's fresh on the material," the elder ambassador said. "That should prove to be quite useful, then."

"You're not taking my son from me," John threatened with his hand just barely over the hilt of the Reikiken at his hip.

"Ms. Ishikawa, how badly do you want this alliance," Vargas asked before anyone could say anything further. Vargas' tone was even, cool, totally unfazed by the man who so visibly and shamelessly threatened his life. He met Emiko's gaze, and for a moment nothing was said. John began to sweat from the tension, but his hand still hovered ever so slightly above his weapon. Emiko exhaled.

"It isn't a matter of wanting anything," Emiko spoke in a defeated tone that sank the heart of her second in command. "The fact of the matter is that we need to be on the same page if we're going to stand a chance against the Scarlet Kingdom. Anything that I can do to get us there, I will."

"You've gotta be out of your mind," John shouted with the thunderous boom of a true lightning dragon. The very atmosphere of the room had changed drastically, though Vargas' face would do little to show it. John's eyes darted around the table. Bill held his shoulder to keep him from making a very lethal mistake. Vanessa refused to meet his gaze. Vargas gave a pitying smile, and Emiko eyed him apologetically. Then there was Bryan, the man who suggested this egregious shift in expectation. He smiled boldly, as if he actually meant to do what was best for the Yaiba.

"Rairyu," Emiko spoke solemnly, "You will bring the boy to me for mission briefing this evening. Until then, you have the day to spend with him as you see fit. By tomorrow morning, he will meet with the Yoroi envoy to return to their territories. Am I clear?" John didn't answer. His throat tightened as if around a small fist. His eyes welled with tears. His mouth moved, but no sounds came out. Emiko cleared her throat. "Am I clear?" John, who's venomous glare fixed on Bryan, nodded in compliance. "Then meeting adjourned."

****

Crunch. That was the sound that Bryan's chest made when John kicked it square in the center. Even so, Bryan laughed as he fell to the ground.

"What the hell were you thinking," John demanded of the man he'd once called his friend. Bryan merely laughed between gasps of air, and that exasperated the raging Dragon before him. John picked him up from the ground. "Answer me you springy son of a bi—" Bryan's raucous laughter cut him off in the middle, and John punched him in the gut to shut him up. Bryan spit a little blood and smiled.

"I was only trying to help, John. I'd appreciate it if you didn't bite my head off about it," Bryan finally replied with a sadistic laugh. John released an unhinged roar in Bryan's face before he slammed the former soldier down hard on the stone floor of the tunnel. Bryan hissed from the pain that shot through his back, but somehow managed to breathe a sigh of relief. "What's the matter, John? Where'd all that understanding go?" John spat on him, then walked off. "Not so enjoyable when it's someone else in *your* business, is it," Bryan called, and when John was out of sight, he writhed for a moment in solitude.

****

October 3rd, 2084, 12:17 p.m.,

John picked the lock of Darius' residence. He knew that the boy would be angry that he'd shown up at random, but it wasn't like he had to care about that at the moment. He only had today to tell him everything that was happening, only today to ensure that Darius knew what position he was in and what was going to be done about it. Moreover, he needed to organize things with Cal but that could wait a couple of days. That sort of mission would be a tricky thing to work out, and would take a little time to manipulate.

He sat on the one cushioned chair in the common room of Darius' dwelling and waited patiently. It was hard for him to be here with the knowledge that his beloved son was about to be moved away from him so abruptly. Nevertheless, he would be the one to tell the boy of his mission, and how difficult his life would become in their time apart. He steeled himself for the ordeal, which came a lot easier to him than he'd expected it to. He just thought about kicking Bryan in the chest again, and allowed his mind to wander to greater acts of retribution against a man he could barely call a friend.

The door opened, and in came the young man that was the sum of his parents' best qualities with none of their worst. His face was closer in detail to his mother's, but his attitude, his demeanor, his physical and emotional strength, those were of his father without a doubt. Darius startled at the sight of John in his living area, and John smiled his best, hopeful that his worry and sadness wouldn't seep into it.

"Jeez, Batman," Darius joked, though they both knew he only had a minimal understanding of the archaic character. "I thought we talked about you just appearing in my place."

"I'm your father, boy," John shot back with narrowed eyes and a hint of authority in his voice, "I'll come in if I want to." Darius dared not challenge his pops, and instead sought to change the subject.

"So what brings you by?" John opened his mouth, but hesitated. It was in that instant that Darius, sharp-eyed as his old man, knew that something was wrong. "What's wrong, Pops?" As the boy's voice softened, John's face hardened.

"I'm here to give you your next mission, son," he said, and Darius' eyes lit with childlike excitement. Seeing such joy on his face made it even harder to tell him, but John was not the kind of man to back down from his objective, even if it did hurt him so.

"What's the mission," Darius asked in the playfully devious tone that usually meant he was confident. Ironically it always came before he knew what was about to happen.

"You're going to the Yoroi Alliance to train them to utilize our Hanzo Gear," John said frankly, and the excitement in his son's face slowly drained away as he realized what this meant.

"Wait, I'm…I'm leaving the Yaiba Insurrection?" There was anguish in his voice, and for a moment all John could hear was the terrified whine of the frightened boy from years long gone. John's expression softened to a more comforting one as he placed a gentle hand on his son's shoulders.

"It's going to be alright, kid," he said gently. "It'll be different, a little dangerous but welcome to our lives, am I right?" Darius furrowed his brow.

"How dangerous," he asked, and John flashed a guilty smile. It was his guess that the news of Johannes' abduction had finally made its way around to Darius, and the death of his accompanying escort with it. It seemed, however, that the identities of the Shadows tasked with the safe transportation of the emissary had been withheld from whatever report Darius had heard, so John opted to avoid mention of them as well.

"The last group of ours to head out that way bit the dust in a Scarlet raid," John confessed hastily, "but you don't have anything to worry about. You'll be taking an alternate route, and for added insurance I'll be watching your back until we break the Yoroi border." Darius thought to say something but held it back. He thought about what his father just told him, and decided that having the leader of the Seven Dragons was more than enough insurance.

"I guess that does make things a little bit better," he voiced, but noted that the unease in his father's face was still potent. "So I'm supposed to head up their training?"

"That's correct," John said with an attempted nonchalant shrug that did little to convince the boy.

"I'm sensing a 'but.'" The corner of John's mouth turned up in a barely noticeable smirk that would've gone unnoticed by anyone other than his son. "Let me guess, you're gonna tell me that the Alliance is a different climate than the Insurrection is?"

"As a matter of fact," John replied, his mouth now in a full smile, "that might've been a part of it." His expression sobered again as he ushered Darius towards the seat opposite his own. The boy sank into it carefully, as if wary of an attack, and it was then that John could see through his outwardly calm façade. "Even though you'll be going there on business, they'll probably still think of you as a child. Even though you've proven yourself to us, you haven't yet proven yourself to them, so it would be wise of you to expect a certain disrespect from their ranks."

"Hmmm…noted. I guess I'll just have to be thorough when teaching discipline in my training sessions, huh?"

"You will," John confirmed with a severity that told the junior Shadow that there was something more to be said. "Speak as little as you can. The Yoroi can be stubborn, and won't be quick to trust the word of an outsider. Stay out of their politics as much as you can. I'm serious," John said in an attempt to mask his smile. Darius had given him a look that jokingly begged the question, "However would I meddle with their daily lives," but John knew better than to trust that look. It was the same expression that the boy had since he was a toddler, the one only deployed before he did what he wanted instead of what was asked of him. "The Alliance has had limited contact with the outside world in the years since the Second Civil War. They believe that what their leaders do will bring about less harm than good, so whatever you see them doing, just go with it." Darius pouted a bit but fixed himself when his father's eyes narrowed like only a parent's could.

“Yes, sir,” he complied, and watched the challenging glare wash from John’s face. John clapped him on the shoulder.

“Good. Now I’m going to be honest with you. Part of the reason you’re going is that negotiations for our alliance with them are on the verge of a breakdown. We need to show them that we make good on our promises and that we can arm them to defend themselves better against the Scarlet Kingdom.” He inhaled deeply to calm himself. The image of Bryan’s face when he fed John’s son to the lions was still fresh in his mind, and it took every ounce of energy he had to keep from hunting the man down for it. Still, he refused to tell Darius. What would the young Shadow think if someone he loved like an uncle so easily put him in the line of fire without a second thought? “I know how it sounds, kid. This mission is gonna be a rough one, but it does come with some pretty nice perks.”

“Oh,” Darius said as he leaned back and placed his folded wrists against his hips. His tone radiated excitement and a smile crept across his still childlike face. “And what would those perks be, Father?” John rolled his eyes, but he was grateful. It’d been a few weeks since the boy smiled like this, and he wasn’t about to waste it. He wrapped his arm around Darius’ shoulders and walked him back for the door.

“Come on,” he said. “We have a few stops to make before you go.

****

October 3rd, 2084, 12:46 p.m.,

The first of those stops was on Level L, the floor of the research lab. It was dangerous business for John to be there for all the things he currently felt for Bryan, but his son, as always, was his main priority. It caught Darius by surprise when the Rairyu led him past Bryan’s workshop and down the hall towards that of Sora

Kaneuji, the more unhinged head of technology and research within the compound. His was a much busier station, too. Many of the young men and women who hadn't the knack for fighting or the stomach for blood often came to work on the lab level if they wanted to contribute to the rebellion effort. They stirred about, frantically engaged in the many projects that sat before them. Kaneuji himself, however, stood in the upper rafters above his workstation and watched his busy bees buzz. His eyes scanned happily, and when he saw the two guests make their way towards the stairs, he lit up even more.

"My, my, my, my, my," Sora cooed like a giddy child when they reached the upper level of the lab. "The Rairyu and his dragonling have come to pay me a visit! To what do I owe the pleasure?" The excitement in his tone inspired a moment of hesitation in the father-son duo, but they quickly righted themselves.

"Kid's got a mission," John told him as nonchalantly as possible. "In Yoroi turf. I thought it'd be a good idea to bring him by so you can trick his stuff out." Sora raised his eyebrows at the request as Darius handed him his Hanzo Gear, and John cracked a wily smile. "Off the books, of course." Kaneuji returned the smile and eagerly took the weapons and clothes in his hands.

"Funny that you mention it," he said to the two visitors, "but I've been working on a few redesigns to the standard HG formula and they're all amazing. Still, I have to admit that about half of them are courtesy of that Cal kid. I can see why he's always getting in trouble for tampering with the gear. He's friggin great at it."

"Figures," John said with a shake of his head, but smiled all the same. "How soon can you have him outfitted with all the new toys?"

"Three hours, tops," Sora said before John could even complete the question. "There's a less-combustible repulsor boot that we've been working on that streamlines the thermal energy going into the amplifiers in the soles that'd minimize the threat of a massive explosion if something goes wrong. There's also this awesome fixture of copper blades that attaches to the kyoketsu-shoge. Get this: it comes with a thermal-powered battery pack and runs an electrical current through the copper extensions! Oh, and the hachimaki with a protective armor plate in the front. After the Tsuchiryu came back with a bullet wound at the shoulder, I started working with Cal on a system of inner armor. That kid really has a knack for—"

"Thanks, Sora, I think we'll leave you to it," John said with more than an ounce of reservation in his tone, and walked back towards the entrance of the workshop. Kaneuji, on the other hand, still rolled through all the possibilities with arms spread wide and euphoria on his face.

"That was…" Darius started, but failed to complete the statement out of fear of being rude.

"Weird?" John supplied. Darius grinned, and so did his father.

"Yeah." Rairyu laughed at that, and pulled his son into a one-armed hug. His heart beat frantically, because he knew that it would only be a few more hours until he had to sacrifice this small show of affection for God knows how long.

"That's the general perception of that guy. Little wonder why Cal spends so much time with him, though. That kid isn't exactly what you'd call normal either," John joked, and Darius laughed.

"Yeah, but most geniuses aren't," spoke the dragonling. He was just as sad as his father, but that sorrow was dampened by the calm his old man exhibited. Even as a young boy, Darius was always aware of the subtle changes in his dad's demeanor. There was the politically active, sharp-minded, cunning warrior-hero of the Yaiba Insurrection, the man that the whole community could see and was forced to respect if not for his brain then for his sheer mastery of a battlefield. Then, there was the kind, gentle, often humorous man who loved his wife and son as if they were physically attached to him. That man never had a care in the world beyond making them feel like the most important things in it. He loved to laugh, loved to live, and though his life wasn't perfect, he was always determined to live it by any means necessary. It was hard for Darius to leave that man behind, but to get to see him like this before he left at least cushioned the blow. "So," he said after a moment as the two sauntered back to the power-lift, "where to now?" The father grinned and leaned his head against the son he still held close.

"I'm glad you asked."

****

October 3rd, 1:12 p.m.,

They found themselves in the massive audience chamber on Conference Level D. It'd been weeks since the debriefing of the scavenge mission that went awry, and because the only time Darius had ever entered it was shrouded in the fear of discipline, he couldn't shake the fear that he was in trouble for something that he'd somehow failed to do. The ambiance was just as intimidating as the last time, but now, he had no team of his peers, no visitors from a foreign land to take the heat off him. Now he only had his father, which was no small thing, but against the prime authority in the Insurrection, even John Hamlin was powerless to say or do much. Darius took a deep breath as his head touched the ground in proper homage to Director Ishikawa.

"You may rise," she said, and the boy sat up. John was motionless, back in his serious mode, which did little to comfort the dragonling at his side. The Director looked between the men before her, her eyes as cunning as a war-hardened soldier. "Darius," she spoke, as if his timidity amused her, "the code." As soon as the words left her lips, Darius knew what this was. He looked to his father, who only nodded for him to continue.

"'Refine the mind through art, history, and culture, for it is impossible to live in a world one does not understand. Protect the weak, for it is the responsibility of the strong to do so. The community is a lifeline, and is only as well off as the least of its citizens. Live in peace with allies, rain terror on enemies. Lead fearlessly. Survive at all costs,'" Darius recited nervously. Nevertheless, John sat with a satisfied smirk, as the boy made it through the code without so much as a misstep. Emiko, however, narrowed her eyes.

"Does survival come through war alone?" She asked the question as if he had offended her in some way. That, too, was merely a part of the test. Darius shook his head.

"Survival comes in many ways. The raising of children, the protection of the community, the passing of knowledge, and artful expression," he answered. Ishikawa sat in silence, looked over the boy, and inhaled deeply before she spoke again.

"Which of these is the most important?" The question caught him off-guard, but nevertheless he thought on it for a moment.

"The passing of knowledge."

"Why do you think that?"

"Through knowledge one can raise children in the way that is appropriate for them. Through knowledge, one can lead and protect a community of tens or of thousands. Through knowledge, the artistic expression of mankind is embellished. Knowledge is the root of success, a catalyst for empathy, and a worthy protector against a great many threats," the boy reasoned. The corner of Emiko's mouth twitched briefly in the manner of a smile, but she would not allow for her satisfaction to shine through just yet.

"A wise answer," she complimented, but there was a shade of inquiry in her tone that signaled the coming of another complicated question. "When does one acquire the knowledge to lead?" Darius' eyes narrowed, but a sour look from the Director returned him to his prior expressionlessness.

"The practical answer," he started after another moment's pause, "is through steady training and continuous education." Emiko raised an eyebrow.

"Oh?" she asked. "It sounds as if you've found a better answer."

"I believe so," he said respectfully. "I believe that one acquires the knowledge to lead when one has no other choice but to do so."

"Is that how you knew to lead your squad to safety after the Scarlet Scourge took your captain hostage?" The mere mention of the incident was enough to take Darius back to a situation that he was loath to revisit on his own. He remembered the smell of gun smoke in the air, the hostility that seeped from the pores of the barbaric women warriors, the threat of death that resounded with every raindrop that descended from the holes in the roof to the floor. He remembered being nearly gunned down by the Scourge and rescued by the Kabuto Sanctuary. He remembered being forced to lead them, and leaving his Uncle Callan behind at the mercy of those brutes. It took him a moment to answer, but nevertheless he steeled himself to do so.

"It wasn't my doing alone. If it wasn't for the Kabuto coming to our aid, I never would've gotten out of there alive," he admitted. It wasn't something he was proud of, but it was the truth, and telling the truth in this moment meant more than all the bravado he could muster.

"Regardless, you took charge of a team you knew and one you had never met to escape a veritable army without losing a single man. That display not only gave you the distinction of one of very few who have fought the Scourge and lived, it ultimately ended with an alliance between the Yaiba and the Kabuto, which gave us even more of an edge in our upcoming battles." There was a moment of silent deliberation before Director Ishikawa continued. "I have made my decision. Darius Michael Hamlin, you will depart on your mission to the Yoroi Alliance this evening, and will upon arrival instruct them in the usage of the Hanzo Gear…" she held for a moment and surveyed his face one final time, this time as if to savor the sheer suspense that it held, "as a Master Shadow of the Yaiba Insurrection. Represent us well." She winked at him, and with the formality done she waved him over for a hug.

John watched his little one with tears in his eyes, but wiped them away before they were discovered. He swore, after all, never to let the boy see him cry. Not even for a time as joyous as this.

****

October 3rd, 2084, 4:44 p.m.,

They were sixteen minutes early for their departure. Following Darius' promotion ceremony, Emiko christened him Hanran no Ryu, the Rebel Dragon of the Violet Shadows, for his refusal to sacrifice his men or die in the face of a Scarlet death squad. He'd proven himself worthy of the rank of Master despite his recent induction into the Yaiba military force.

John, proud of his son, was also still a worried parent above all else, and petitioned to lead the Yoroi envoy and their new teacher back into Yoroi lands. The Director begrudgingly agreed. From there, John brought his son to Aaliyah's classroom on Education Level E, where they told her both the good news and the bad. She cried openly, and hugged her baby close one more time before she had to return to her duties, and more painfully leave him to his own.

Afterward, John took Darius to reclaim his Hanzo Gear, load the newly forged shipment of Hanzo Gear and aura swords into a transport, and finally to see his uncles Callan, Manny, and

Bill, who hugged him tight and congratulated him on his recent rise through the ranks. He nearly buckled under the weight of all the affection, but held himself together if only because of pride.

"You know, your old man was also a prodigy. He was made a Master by his third mission and inherited the name 'Rairyu' from his dad," Bill told him with a wide grin. "Looks like an apple/tree situation to me, kid." Callan was, as per usual, less expressive than his counterparts, and merely pat the boy on the head.

"I'm glad that you got by on some of my old philosophical musings," Manny said with his signature chuckle as he clapped the Rebel Dragon on his shoulder. He was the first to see him as an equal, and not the little boy that he'd watched grow up right in front of him. Even though he knew that there was a certain level of danger that came with that title, Manny wasn't worried. After all, he knew what the squirt was capable of. "You know to be honest," he continued with a smirk as wide as Bill's grin, "I never expected answers like those to work on the Director. I just taught you stuff like that so you could give me a good chat every once in a while." Darius' jaw dropped and a frown took John's jaw without delay.

Now, the two of them stood at Deployment Level A in silent admiration of the distant sunset. There was a slight chill in the air, but it did little to affect either of the Masters. They were garbed in the signature black hooded cloaks, violet tunics and black trousers that made up the Hanzo Gear. Titanium blades in the shape of diamonds rested at the end of the lengthy chains wrapped around their wrists, and dark repulsor boots adorned their feet. Their Reikiken rested at their sides.

"You ready for this, kid?" John asked, his eyes firmly fixed on a pair of birds that flew just above the trees of the forest below. Darius looked at him.

"Are you?" The question was a joke, but John still wasn't sure how to answer. How does one prepare for the child they love so much to leave them behind to start a new chapter in life?

"Probably not," he said honestly and chuckled to keep from crying. "But we'll find out when I get you there safely. So, how does it feel to be escorted by the Lightning Dragon of the Yaiba Insurrection?"

"It feels like this is the least your people could do," came the unimpressed voice of Ezequiel Vargas from behind them. In an instant, John's face sobered and his eyes narrowed as if a target had just wandered into his crosshairs. "I trust that you've said all the goodbyes you needed to?" Darius nodded.

"Then we shall be off. We've already wasted enough time as it is." Vargas's lack of patience was enough to sour even the best of moods, and did little to improve the current depressive psyche of the two Hamlins. Regardless, they led their envoy to the Yoroi transport they'd arrived in, and took to the combat bikes they'd signed out for their own use.

Night approached, and the Blade and Armor Caravan was on its way.

Chapter Eleven

October 8th, 2084, 12:14 a.m.,

The journey to the Grand Canyon was a lengthy one, but it was smooth. The number of Scarlet patrols in the area was minimal, and if the alternate route was followed without deviance, it was essentially a straight shot through the area and into territory free of Red eyes. Darius' disappointment was palpable. He'd thought that at some point in the last five days that he'd get to fight someone on this mission, but it was disgustingly peaceful for the lot of them. The only source of conflict emanated from Vargas' terse comments and disagreeable attitude, and even so, that was hardly the fight the young Rebel Dragon needed to prove himself.

The caravan came to a stop just at its edge, and while the Alliance envoy stretched their legs under the Yaiba escort's supervision, Vargas pinched the collar of his vibrantly colored cape. Darius and John exchanged looks of surprise. Vargas was a cranky old man, but one that was full of life and culture if anything. The cape was colored with dark and light shades of green that were accented by the bright orange and yellow floral patterns that gave the impression of a South American jungle. It was something that they would expect a man of power to wear, one generally unconcerned with the goings on of the battlefield, but the fact that it was outfitted with communications technology made them wonder exactly who this old man was.

"Extend the ramp," he spoke in a hushed tone, and after a few moments the sound of metal upon metal filled the night air. It was a slow, almost painful sound that the foreigners could feel in their bones but that the Yoroi natives were used to. It screeched as it came to rest upon the lip of the canyon, and without further delay, the caravan loaded up and made their descent.

At first there was nothing of import to see beyond the massive gash in the planet's surface, but as the traveling party rode deeper towards the side of a massive mound of stone, something akin to a city appeared to be visible from the distance. An array of multicolored lights radiated in the darkness and twinkled like the stars in the open desert sky. The air became slightly warmer as they drew nearer, which sharply contrasted the outside chill.

"This place is incredible," Darius couldn't help but say. He'd never seen anything like it, though he'd hardly seen much beyond the tunnels of the Yaiba compound and the ruins of Johnson City. For a moment the sense of combined dread and worry that had been with him since his departure from his home faded away, and was replaced with the intoxicating thrill of adventure.

"It truly is," Vargas said through the comms, almost as if he spoke of a lover. "Pull over at the check-in. The guards will need to inspect you to ensure that you two are not a threat." John and Darius did as they were told, and after a fifteen-minute inspection of their persons and their combat bikes, there was a tense pause between the father and son.

"Hey, listen, kid," John started. There was an unfamiliar rattle to his voice that cut at Darius' soul. "I gotta head back now. You know what the Director said. But listen, I will always be there when you need me. Come here," he said, and waved his beloved son into a hug. Vargas turned his eye away from them, and John couldn't help but think that the man had some sort of moral opposition to human sentiment. It mattered little, because now John was free to tell Darius what he'd intended to without the observant eye of a man he struggled to even like, let alone trust. He hushed his tone as he spoke to his dragonling, "Listen, I don't trust that man. I've already got a team on standby waiting for your signal. If anything happens, tap frequency 22597 and they'll immediately dispatch." He pulled away, his hands on his boy's shoulders, and looked at him with a pained yet proud smile. "I didn't think it'd be this hard to leave you, kid." Darius chuckled.

"I didn't think it'd be this hard to leave home," he responded. John looked up at the darkness above him and smiled to keep back the tears. Before he had the chance to speak again, Darius hugged his father tightly.

"I love you so much, kid," John told him earnestly. He fought every instinct that told him to throw the boy on the bike and speed off.

"I love you, too, Pops," Darius replied, and wanted more than anything for his father to keep him from going. He wanted to be scolded, to be told he wasn't ready, to be hauled away at his parent's behest and be suffocated by a wave of overprotective antics. But he wasn't. John believed in him. He trusted him. And for the things he didn't trust, he'd set up plans for any contingencies. John let out a difficult huff.

"Guess I better get going." Without another word to Darius, John walked over to the Yoroi transport that held Ambassador Vargas. He knocked on the window, and the driver rolled it down. John smiled at him as he leaned in. "Mr. Vargas, I trust you'll take care of my son in my absence." Vargas blinked. He was nervous now. Something about John's tone was different, as if the Ambassador could feel the stinging cut of electricity through his entire body.

"Of course," Vargas assured him. "No harm will come to him on my watch." John pat the side of the transport in a manner that instilled a great fear in Vargas, a fear that made him question the wisdom of all the snide comments he'd made from their first meeting. Even so, the Yaiba general smiled at him.

"Good," John exclaimed, his hand now on Vargas' shoulder. "That's good, because if anything were to happen…" John's hand began to close, and to Vargas it felt as the gripping claw of a dragon as it bored into his skin, "well, I'm sure I don't have to say it." Vargas shook his head, and John smiled. He pat him on the shoulder, and Vargas winced from the pain. John gave a thoughtful look. “Huh. You should get that checked out, Ambassador.” He looked back at his son and pointed at him with a fatherly authority as he said, “Survive at all costs.” Darius smiled back at him, and allowed a single tear to fall as he moved for his combat bike.

“Survive at all costs,” he spoke under his breath. John watched his baby head into the Yoroi’s city with the cargo and their charge, and as he returned to his own transport and started home, he silently wept.

****

October 8th, 2084, 9:15 a.m.,

It was quiet, but this silence rang out like a thousand gongs in the wake of a funeral.

Sharon knew it was coming, but knowing didn’t take the pain away. She did everything that she could to keep him with her, to keep Bryan from leaving her alone. *It wouldn’t be fair of me to make you come with me*, he’d said. She spat on the memory, and snarled at her husband as she stood in the way of the door to their home. He was armed with his Hanzo Gear, ready to deploy as if on a mission, only this time there would be no return for him. There would be no restoration to their marriage, and it broke her more and more with every second that passed.

“So that’s it then? You’re just going to leave?” Her voice was hushed but indignant. Bryan wouldn’t speak. He couldn’t, or else it would turn into another argument. He moved to push her out of the way of the door and leave, but then she said, “I really have to lose you after losing both of the kids?” The words stung.

“There’s nothing left for me here,” was what he told her. It was a lie. He knew it was a lie and yet he said it anyway, because what else was he supposed to tell her? That he was too broken to go on? That the Yaiba was a constant reminder of the children he'd lost and the thought of staying there made him want to commit suicide? That he felt like he'd failed to protect the kids and failed as a husband in the process? No, he couldn't bring his mouth to even form those words. He was desolate, stripped of his last tears when his son was murdered by the Scarlets.

"You have *me*," Sharon protested, and tears took her eyes. Bryan averted his. "I don't want you to go." She wanted to scream it, but the words resonated at barely a whisper. In Sharon's mind, she saw the early days of his career when he would bring her small treasures from his missions away. She remembered the things he said to her. It was like listening to sonnets written by a master poet. The night that they danced beneath the moonlight in the forest was as clear to her now as it was when it happened. She saw the love in his eyes back then. When did they become so pained?

"It isn't about wants," Bryan told her softly. "I need to get out of here. I need to do something else besides just sit here working on weapons for war."

"Then take me with you," Sharon demanded, and Bryan released an exasperated sigh.

"Sharon, we've been over this—"

"*You've* been over this," she interjected angrily. "This is so typical of you. You figure yourself to be some great paragon of wisdom. Bryan Piccio always knows best, doesn't he? And everyone else is just expected to go along with it."

"That's not fair," Bryan challenged with a bright fire behind his emerald eyes. "You don't—"

"What?" Sharon interrupted again with boldness in her voice. "No, go ahead. What were you about to say, Bryan? That I don't understand what it's like to lose my son after losing my daughter?"

"It wasn't your path that got him killed, Sharon!" Suddenly the woman had no response or retort, just somber silence. "He joined the Shadows because of me. He put himself in danger because of me. If I'd never—"

"He made his own choices," she interrupted, though this time to keep him from going down a dangerous path of thought. Bryan was less than amused to hear those words from anyone, because he knew that his son idolized him. Jaden might have been embarrassed by Bryan's overprotective nature, but even so, he wanted nothing more than to be like the man that raised him. Bryan sighed.

"He made his own choices," he started grimly, "but we were left with the consequences." Sharon's eyes narrowed again as the tears that welled up in them streamed down her plump and rosy cheeks.

"Be careful," she warned, "you sound like you're dangerously close to getting the point."

"You think I want to leave you?" Bryan snapped now, and upon the sight of his wife in fear, he ran a hand through his unkempt hair. "You think I want to abandon the most stable home I've ever known? The home I built with you?" He spoke softer now, and for just a brief moment Sharon could hear the faintest revival of affection through all the pain. "I *want* to be with you. I want to *stay*! I wish that none of this ever happened, and that everything could just go back to normal, but it can't. Our son is dead. The Scarlet Kingdom took him from us. The Yoroi Alliance had a part to play, and the Yaiba Insurrection gave him his marching orders. I need you, Sharon. I do. But I need someone to answer for what's happened to this family."

"That is such bull," Sharon shot back. She couldn't believe what she was hearing. "How dare you use our son's death to just absolve yourself of any responsibility! You need someone to answer for what's happened to this family? How about what you're doing to it right now? You're not even trying to cope or recover from this. You're just running away and blaming everything and everyone else for the decision you're making now." There was a palpable silence between them that stretched on for a long while. Bryan looked at his Sharon now, their eyes locked in mournful observance and raw emotion.

"Maybe," Bryan admitted with a quiver in his voice. He heaved an exhausted sigh. "Maybe I don't want to get over it. Maybe I just want the rest of the world to suffer like we have for a change." With nothing else to say, Bryan finally pushed past her and left the best parts of his old left behind.

****

October 8th, 2084, 4:58 p.m.,

The trip was a quiet one, and with nobody to take his mind off of what he'd been forced to do, John cried once or twice on the way back to the compound. Everything about this situation made him sick to his stomach, but this was the way of things. He knew that at some point his son would go off on a mission to another land and he'd be powerless to stop it. Even so, it didn't hurt him any less. If anything, understanding the dangers that awaited Darius made the worry grow even fiercer. Luckily, Cal was at the main entrance of their mountain base, and where Cal was, there was humor.

"A-yerrr," Cal called excitedly as John closed the distance. John approached with a slight desperation in his step, but he caught it and corrected himself before he arrived. Cal watched his adoptive father with an exaggerated bewilderment in his expression, and just the look of it was enough to make him laugh. Cal looked from one side to the other as the Rairyu approached, and made a high-pitched "hmm" sound as he placed his wrists on his hips and leaned back. John couldn't tell if the confused expression bore any truth to it or if it was just a ploy to get him to cheer up, but for the moment he did forget the pain of leaving his other son behind, and the sudden reprieve was enough to inspire a tender hug.

Cal accepted, though he wasn't the most outwardly affectionate person. Still, he could tell that John needed it, and while he wouldn't admit it, Cal did too.

"Hey I know you just got back and all, but the Director said she needs to see you," he said as casually as he could when they stepped away from each other. John raised an eyebrow to keep the disappointment off his face, but it still registered in his voice.

"What about," he asked briskly, as if the question made his already foul mood even worse. Cal put up his hands in a placating gesture.

"Hey man, that's all I was told. If you wanna find out, go talk to her. As for me…" he trailed off at the sight of a rather voluptuous young lady in the typical violet and black of the Shadows. He watched her as she strolled off without a care in the world and a sway in her hips. He looked at John, then back at her, then back at John, and smiled like a helpless boy. John shook his head with a chuckle.

"Why don't you go talk to her? She might be willing to let you take her on a date," John said, and Cal cut his eyes at him as playfully as ever.

"Man you know I ain't gone say nothing," Cal laughed, but it was very likely true. For all his technical genius and his collected disposition on the field of battle, Cal Richmond was a little bashful when it came to expressing romantic interests with the opposite sex. What he didn't realize was that a good deal of his interests thought him attractive, and doubly so when they found out how shy he could be. From where John stood, it was the only thing that stood in the way of Cal getting a girlfriend.

“We need to talk about your confidence level, kid,” John said with a bit more sternness than the situation called for. Cal folded his arms.

“Well right now you need to go have a talk with the Director about…” Cal paused, then shook his head. “I don’t really know, but you need to go!”

“I’m on it, I’m on it,” John assured him. “Jeez, you nag me like my mom used to.” Cal shrugged.

“Just trying to keep us both out of trouble,” he reasoned. John clapped him on the shoulder, and made his way for the deeper levels of the compound.

****

October 8th, 2084, 5:30 p.m.,

“You rang,” John asked as he entered the Director’s office. He froze instantly, as he saw Erik Kincaid and three of his men seated around the table with Emiko at its head. The Director smiled, and waved him to a seat. There was a moment of tense silence, and the visitors from Kabuto could easily see that John still had some degree of difficulty accepting their help in the fight against the Reds. Even still, they smiled at the dragon, bearing no mind of his roar or fangs. John assumed that it was an attempt at a peaceful gesture, but the smile of a saboteur proved more disquieting than anything.

“I’m happy that you were able to join us on such short notice, John,” Emiko said honestly. “I can only imagine how difficult the last few days have been on you. I trust the emissaries from Yoroi are back at home safely?”

“Yeah, they’re alright,” John confirmed, “but I still have my reservations about joining up with them. The Yoroi leaders are selfish, and I feel like they'd betray us at the first opportunity if it spoke to their survival."

"I wouldn't put it past them if I'm being honest," Erik spoke with a soothing nonchalance. John's eyes shifted warily to the guest, who sat in his shadowy garb with his hands folded together in front of his face. "But at the moment we can all agree that there are bigger concerns that warrant our attention."

"Agreed," Emiko spoke grimly. "The time for these little hit-and-run games is coming to an end. The Scarlets have already started to mobilize towards the west. We know that from their occupation of Johnson City."

"Our team managed to slow them down a little bit during the rescue of Callan Rouge, but since they have an advantage when it comes to resources, I doubt it'll take them very long to overcome the obstacles we produced," Erik explained. John continued to eye him suspiciously.

"And what brings you gentlemen here," John asked with such a haughty air about him that one could easily confuse him for a prince.

"The short version? We heard the Reds took a Yoroi emissary hostage and slaughtered a few of his Yaiba escorts in the process. If that's true, then that means they no longer doubt the possibility of a pact between the Alliance and the Insurrection, which also means that it's only a matter of time before Prevalence is steeped in open warfare for the first time in 63 years." Erik's clarification wasn't enough to ease the tension, and Emiko sighed with frustration. It seemed to be her most frequented mood these days.

"So what, your Elder's Council decide that you're in over your head and you're looking for a safe place to hide out," John prodded in a tone most unimpressed. Kincaid narrowed his eyes.

"I'm assuming you arrived at that conclusion because of our lack of contact in the last month and a half. Let me be the first to assure you that we haven't just been twiddling our thumbs, hiding in some hole in fear of the enemy," Erik responded with a muted ferocity that only stoked the flames of John's foul mood. The three young warriors at Kincaid's side grew more attentive, and one of them a little more savage. A single glance at Director Ishikawa, however, cooled all of them before the tension could escalate.

"I understand that you gentlemen have something to share with us," she asked with enough sweetness to still the uneasiness but enough venom to dare the others to try her. The message was received, and at Kincaid's command, one of his subordinates pulled a drive from his pocket and plugged it into the table. The table spurted to life, and in the center of it emerged a round base from which extended a slightly smaller box that emanated a faint blue light. The light projected a three-dimensional holographic map of the entire Northeastern Region. Kincaid's face exhibited a calm grin, while John and Emiko sat arrested in shock. Emiko looked at the map, then back at the Kabuto operatives, her face still suspended in disbelief. "How did you…" she couldn't even finish the question.

"Ever since our home was bombed last spring," Kincaid began, "several of our top black-ops teams have been in rotation scouting out the enemy territory. About three weeks ago, we discovered this," he said, and his subordinate with the milky complexion and the innocent-looking green eyes—Levi Taylor, if John remembered correctly—touched a point on the map about 200+ miles west of the Scarlet capitol of New York City. The map zoomed in on the now-bright red mark left by Levi's finger, and revealed the ruins of a college remodeled into a strong military outpost with numerous hangars, workshops, motor pools, and a very curious building without any labels or identifying features. It was plain, which made it stand out more than the more noticeable landmarks around it.

"What you're looking at," started the voice of the stern but somehow deceptively non-threatening brown-haired man that sat next to Levi, "is a live 3D map of the entire Scarlet Kingdom, maintained through a camera network linked to an old Kabuto hideout from the years before the Civil War." John looked this man over. Esau—that was his name—presented a friendly disposition on the surface, but his voice betrayed him as it was rife with the kind of irritation that was synonymous with a lack of patience. John assumed that his earlier hostilities hadn't gone over well, and while he hated playing the part of the diplomat, he realized that he needed to resort to that mindset if he had any hope of salvaging the situation.

He breathed deeply, and when he was calm enough, he asked, "How'd they manage to create a system like that way back in the day? I'll be honest with you, I didn't even know it was possible to do things like this." Nick, the usually unmotivated youngster with wavy brown hair and piercing green eyes, smirked like a devious child.

"They didn't," he said with frank excitement. "In the 63 years since the war, we maintained the support system and, up until about a decade ago, updated the cameras in the field through an old contact of Sasori-sensei that lived in the Baltimore area. Until the incident last year, we hadn't had a need to keep watch over it consistently. Now we do."

"That's…" John paused as his mind raced to think of all the technological advancements the Kabuto must've facilitated over the years, "that's impressive, I have to admit." He spoke with a degree of disbelief wrapped in hesitation so that it would appear that he'd been humbled, and watched as his show visibly lifted the moods of the Kabuto men. "But what's so special about a repurposed college campus? It's hardly the first one that the Scarlets have tainted since their ban on public education."

"But it is the one that we think houses the weapon that destroyed our old home," Kincaid explained sharply, as if just the mention of the incident was enough to drive the man to rage. "Our teams surveyed a few outposts along the edge of Red territory during the first two weeks and came up with nothing, save for one group. They reported a strange energy signal from inside that unmarked building. We know that they're using a warhead of some kind, but as to how it works we have no idea. All we know is that the tech used to deploy it requires a lot of power." There was a weighted pause between all the agents in the room. Kincaid and his men sat in total calm, but Director Ishikawa and the Lightning Dragon exchanged poorly masked looks of worry.

"So what's the plan," Ishikawa asked as she clasped her hands together when they touched the top of the table. "I assume you don't want me to send my men to this outpost with you as some sort of distraction while yours slip into the holding center or something crazy like that." Kincaid laughed and waved his hand as if to brush the idea from the table itself.

"That would be irresponsible of me to even think," he said firmly, and sobered before adding, "provided that I want our alliance to work. No, what I want, Director, is to let you know exactly what we're up against as it happens. This intel meeting is a show of good faith, and more…" he pulled his hand from the table and hid it underneath, but his hosts could still see that remembering shook him. "I simply don't want anyone else to have to go through what we did."

Emiko waited a moment, her dark eyes unreadable as the man before her calmed himself. She shrugged, and said, "I appreciate your intent, and if I may say so, I find your candor to be a bit surprising for the leader of an entire faction of deceivers and saboteurs. No offense," she added as Erik's face grew a tinge more intense. He smiled.

"None taken," he told her. "I understand that our way of life, while having preserved our peace in the past, might've earned a disreputable image in the minds of those that hear of us. But, while I am here, there are some matters that need to be attended to.

For instance, have you considered how you intend to take Johnson City?" The Director hesitated at the mention and offered an almost bashful smile.

"I'll admit that in the last few weeks it hasn't crossed my mind." She leaned back in her chair, a little laxer than she typically was in these scenarios. "I haven't even bothered to send a team to scout out the territory for our assault."

"Well, the initial group of Red soldiers has moved out further west, and with the ruckus our men have caused, they now know that we both lie somewhere within the immediate area of Johnson City, or at least that's their assumption," Esau submitted to the floor.

"It is a sizeable force," Kincaid offered, "but admittedly without the Scourge to add a level of cunning to their strategies, a battle against their encampment should only last a couple of days."

"But if we engage, they could just as easily call for help in their efforts. What would we do if reinforcements arrive?" Emiko asked. She sat up again, suddenly disquieted by the thought of such danger. She knew that they endeavored to free Prevalence and unite the factions as one nation behind the fall of the Scarlet Kingdom. She knew that such a thing would only come about at this point through violence. Nevertheless, she never took joy from her assignment of missions, and loathed the idea of open warfare when the memory of their near-extinction just a mere 38 years ago was a constant fear of all those 30 and older. Her job was to go to war, yes, but it was also to do what was best for her people. Survive at all costs.

"Provided that we work together on this, the Sanctuary can do what we can to cut off all entrances and exits to the city and sever communications to the capitol," Esau extended as if he were in charge of the negotiations. Levi had already tuned out, but the anger on his face was something that tugged at John's heart. Nick, just at the mere mention of additional labor, visibly displayed his disgust. Erik looked on the three with an almost parental look, one of both pride at how far they've come, and worry for where their individual quirks might lead them. Emiko, however, was not so parental when it came to the outsiders, and while she understood some of their ways by virtue of what the Legendary Founders left behind, she was reluctant to trust the idea that they knew all of what the Yaiba stood for.

"I will say that my motivation for that kind of move is purely out of self-interest," Erik admitted with a smile and a shrug. "Having the infamous Violet Shadows as protectors would definitely come in handy. That said, occupying Johnson City comes with a reasonable advantage for the Insurrection should you elect to do it." Director Ishikawa looked to her lead general curiously.

"It does," John affirmed with his arms folded across his chair and a pensive expression on his face. "Johnson City is on the path of one of the most frequented routes to the western regions. Not only does it cut off whatever supplies the capitol might send to their deployed troops via ground travel, it would also separate the Scourge and one of the princes from their home or any reinforcements. We could overwhelm the Scourge with sheer numbers if we can get the Yoroi to commit to our agreement, take the Prince hostage in the best-case scenario, and negotiate the surrender of the Scarlets once and for all." The suggestion made the Kabuto men raise their eyebrows and drop their jaws a touch out of sheer shock.

"Well," Nick said as his lips curled into a smile and the piercing quality of his eyes gave way to a boyish twinkle, "didn't see that one coming. You almost sound like one of us." John shrugged and let a half-smile take to his jawline.

"The Insurrection doesn't shy away from open warfare, but we're not savages," he said. "There are a few things that concern me though. For instance, how are we going to prevent an airstrike from the capitol? It'd be impossible to do away with every plane at the Kingdom's disposal, even with all our men combined."

"That is a valid concern," Erik validated with a wry smile that told the Yaiba Director and Rairyu that he had something up his sleeve. "We may not be able to do away with all of their aircraft, but we might just be able to hack the system they use to control it." The Scarlet Kingdom had been the first country in the world to do away with their pilot training program in favor of a more automated approach to aerial warfare. It was part of what made the rest of the world shy away from conflict with them, and the main reason that they were so dangerous.

"This," Emiko started slowly, "this could work if we coordinate it correctly. Do you have an idea of when you'll be hitting the college outpost?"

"We'll begin preparations for it this week, and head out within the next two," Erik confirmed, and Emiko smiled.

"Then I propose we link command centers. Once we receive word from the Sanctuary that the Scarlets' secret weapon is out of commission, I can give the go-ahead for our assault on their forces in Johnson City." She shook at the thought, but whether from fear or excitement she couldn't tell. She looked between each of the faces that sat at her lengthy office table and smiled devilishly. "This will be the first strike of all-out war against the enemy."

Erik smiled back at her and said, "Then by all means, let's make this count." He signaled to his men, who each rose from the table and shook the hands of John and the Director as they made for the exit of the room. Erik shook their hands too, and before their hosts could offer an escort back through the facility, Erik told them with an unnerving level of surety, "We'll see ourselves out." They did just that, and while it was difficult to allow them to go, both of the Yaiba leaders could rest easy in the knowledge that a plan of action was finally coming together.

****

October 8th, 2084, 9:45 p.m.,

John was exhausted. Putting on the brave face and rushing into another meeting with Emiko was enough to double the stress he felt after practically giving his son away to Vargas and the Yoroi. He gave a thumbs-up to the technician in the simulation booth, and the projections came alive with images of squad after squad of Scarlet soldiers. This was his third combat sim, and though his legs were wobbly and his breath was short, he still challenged himself to breeze through the images with the weapons at his disposal. He watched as the terrain shifted. No longer was he within the mountain base of the Yaiba. Now he stood in a lush field, some undetermined location from a world long-tarnished by the unchecked dominion of the enemy.

A buzzer sounded, and just like that, the Rairyu lunged. He spun like a bladed top as the kyoketsu-shoge on his wrists extended further and further out. The blades at the ends of those chains whirred like a propeller, and in an instant the first wave of attackers lost their heads. Once the revolution was complete, John slammed the titanium blades into the ground as he jumped into the air, and used the repulsor boots to give him extra height. Airborne, he drew his Reikiken and it sparked to life without delay. The images shot at him, but with careful timing and elegant maneuvering, John evaded the shots that weren't distorted by the heat of his blade.

He landed, and with a series of elegant flicks of the wrist, his firesword melted through the enemies' weapons and burned their flesh to ash upon contact. He decapitated the first man, followed the energy through into a downward diagonal slash through the woman after him, redirected the energy into an upward rolling motion that cut down his next enemy, and manipulated the flow of his blade with so much precision and regality that an onlooker might think him painting a masterpiece with his enemies' newly ashen remains. He wasted no movement as he worked his way around the wave. Every attack was delivered with precise movements but the graceful movements between them, the wide and narrow arcs that swept the air around his body, all laced the flow together with near impenetrable defenses that distorted bullets and disrupted their trajectory.

The technician in the booth was impressed with the speed at which John picked the enemies off, even this late in the game. He only used the one hand when his sword was active, and even with three rows of enemies that ranged from ten to twenty in number, he never felt so pressured that he needed to take his left hand out from behind his back. It was akin to watching a streak of lightning tear through storm clouds. The Lightning Dragon thrust forward at the last remaining enemy in the second row, and then watched with glee as the remaining twenty converged on his location.

John wasted no time, and stabbed the man in front of him, cut through him to bisect another woman at the waist, redirected the energy in an upward cut that split a man from groin to head in a flash, stabbed to the rear to impale an oncoming enemy, sliced through three guns in a single fluid motion, cut through one leg, two arms and a head on three different enemies, slashed in a diagonal against another, kicked one in front as he stabbed one to the rear, swung out in a wide arc through the waists of four enemies and then took the top of the skull off another one. The technician was completely taken aback at just how easily John cut through fifteen armed opponents with a literal hand behind his back.

Five more remained, and though they unleashed a hail of bullets, John was less than impressed with the display. He drove a kyoketsu-shoge through the lips of the figure to his left as he brought his sword upward through the torso of the enemy to the right. He defended himself elegantly, and the shift of relentless heat in the air made the bullets all but useless. A gun popped in the hands of two of the enemies, and without much effort on John's part they were taken out of the game. One enemy remained, and though he aimed to shoot, John brought his blade down in a slash that split the weapon in two, then rolled it into a piercing lunge that drove the weapon through his enemy's sternum.

As the lights left the eyes of his foe, the lights of the simulation dulled and the steel and stone of the training level returned. There was a slow clap from behind him that made the corners of his mouth reach for his ears. He turned and saw her, the light of his life, Aaliyah seated in the otherwise empty stands.

"I had a feeling you'd be here," Aaliyah almost sang, or at least that was how it registered in John's ears. "You always push yourself in training when you've had a rough day."

"You know me so well," John replied as he sauntered towards her as though he had all the time in the world. "Although it was more like a tough week than a day. Dropping the kid off and coming right back was rough, these never-ending diplomatic meetings are annoying, and worst of all, I've had to go several days without seeing you as much as I want." She walked towards him now, and after a moment they met in the middle aisle between the seats. He held her waist as he looked lovingly into her eyes, and she gripped the sides of his black hooded cloak to pull him closer. She bit her lower lip as the artificial light danced in her eyes. He was hypnotized by her, captivated by her shape, enthralled by her expression, taunted by her lips. He leaned closer, as did she, and seconds before she could treat him to a taste of her, a raucous *boom* shook the very foundations of the mountain to pull them apart again.

"That doesn't sound good," Aaliyah said in a more serious tone. The alarm blared throughout the base, which meant that all civilians were to evacuate the first level and all able personnel were to rise to it.

“We’re under attack,” John said calmly, and Aaliyah’s heart dropped to the pit of her stomach, though her face didn’t register it. “Go back to our quarters. Your Hanzo Gear is in a locked box just above the bed in a secret wall compartment.” She raised an eyebrow at him that made him marvel at her all the more. She was so calm, even in this crisis.

“You hid it from me?” John shrugged as a sheepish smile crossed his lips.

“You’re technically not supposed to have it. I didn’t want you getting in trouble. But go,” he repeated, and when she heeded his command the composure of a loving husband washed away. John, bathed in the fury of the leader of the Seven Dragons muttered as he rekindled his aura sword, “Seems I have some work to do.”

Chapter Twelve

The base was thrown into chaos. All operational power-lifts were filled to max capacity with civilians who fled to safety beneath the Deployment Level. John walked at a hastened pace, and once he was out of sight of the frantic non-combatants, he opened a hatch in the wall of the current level and entered it. The frightened screams of the people without this wall still reached him, despite the layers of stone that now separated them. He shook his head. There was no way that he could focus on that, not right now.

As the second in command of the Insurrection compound, John's first responsibility after securing his family was to secure the Director and make sure she was safe. Of course, that would be endlessly easier if Director Ishikawa was anything like her father. Where he took to the command center on Tactical Level X, she took to the battlefield whenever the situation called. Where he would fill his days with meetings with foreign emissaries and dignitaries, she would pencil in time to train in all seven styles adapted for the Reikiken, and kept her Hanzo Gear in the inner chamber of her office for such a time as this.

John tapped the earpiece of his mask to turn it on, and came to the multilevel staircase that could take him anywhere in the base. It felt strange to have a comms unit on within the walls of his home. Stranger still was the fact that the base was under attack by outsiders. "Director," he started with more urgency than he typically displayed, and hoped that the stone wall that surrounded him didn't interfere with the signal. Static came through from the other side, followed by the last part of his name. "Director Ishikawa, can you hear me?"

"Yeah," she replied. Her breath was heavy but her voice was rather indifferent. "Where are you? We got a swarm of hostiles at the front door making their way deeper into the mountain."

"I'm on my way," John told her with gravity in his voice, "I had to make sure Aaliyah got home safely but she's secure. I'm using the hidden tunnels now to get to you faster. Where are you?" There was a feminine grunt, a few manly screams, and the sound of gunshots and rattling chains.

"Sorry about that," Emiko finally said after a moment. "I'm heading to the power-lift on Level D. Maybe I can help some of our men and women on the front line—"

"Em, you know you're better off in the command center giving us orders," John protested, but his suggestion fell on ears deafened by spontaneous gunfire.

"No can do. It'd take too long to get to Level X through the secret tunnels and by then the Reds could kill off a sizeable number of our friends and family," Emiko responded, then chuckled. "Maybe I should've made more than an hour's time for training with this stuff. You guys must be built as crap if you're lugging all this around on missions."

"Em, this isn't the time for joking around," John scolded, but then checked his tone when he heard the Director clear her throat. "I'm sorry. But you're too valuable to risk losing, so I have to insist that you get to the command center as quickly as you can." There was silence again. A few gunshots rang out, a little bit of screaming. The sound of shattered glass could be heard faintly through the comms. Then she was back again.

"Sorry, Johnny," she teased lightly, "but that's out of the question. As for orders, reach out to the other Dragons and whoever you see fit. Tell them that we're executing Defense Pattern Delta. That ought to be enough to scare these Scarlet Sissies away." John was tempted to laugh but remained silent. He didn't know if he should admire her for her lackadaisical approach to the situation or what. He did know that at the very least he shouldn't encourage her bad behavior. "While you do that, I think

I'll have a little fun with this." John rolled his eyes as a silent grin took his face. All he could do was sigh and get to work.

****

Emiko Ishikawa took a moment to catch her breath. She looked around, satisfied with the bloodied and otherwise charred remains of her fallen enemies. Her office on the Conference Level was silent now, and after she could breathe easy again, she started on her way. Her heart was aflutter with excitement and nerves as she stepped over the bodies and headed to the power-lift like she said. She hadn't been on the front lines in so long that she'd gotten rusty. Her movements with the Hanzo Gear were still as sharp as anyone else's in the Insurrection, but she could tell that she'd gotten rusty.

Nevertheless, she always wanted to do more to protect her people than just hide behind a desk and bark orders. That was the purpose for developing the Defense Patterns, to provide the Shadows a means of fighting without constant instructions from the tactical team. The fall of the second base taught everyone left alive in the Yaiba Faction that there was a chance that the tactical team might not even have a chance to get into position. Much like right now.

Emiko made her way out of her office and into the lengthy hall. There was the distinct sound of an enemy radio, and Emiko ducked into one of the more pronounced dips in the cave wall. It was wide enough for her to remain undetected, even with minimal movement. She pulled a pair of small, black smoke bombs from the utility pouch on her belt, lit them, and rolled them down the corridor. She couldn't run the risk of being detected before she had the chance to make a grand entrance to the main battlefield. Honestly, the fact that they'd managed to get to her level in the first place was more than a little irritating for her. She hated delays almost as much as she hated being cooped up in her administrative quarters for political meetings.

The smoke filled the tunnel, and the wily Director closed her eyes. The enemy was blind to her, yes, but there was a sizeable disadvantage to using smoke in a dark mountain tunnel. Her eyes would be a distraction here, and in matters of life and death, distractions would only cost her everything.

"Someone's here," came a masculine voice that reeked of twisted excitement. Emiko rolled her eyes, and dispatched a kyoketsu-shoge to deal with the speaker. The rattle of chains startled the others to life, and while they wondered what was going on, Emiko slipped closer to their position.

"Everybody stay on your guard," a woman whispered. It was loud enough for her allies to hear, but just soft enough that Emiko couldn't trace it. It blended into the smoke as well as the Director did. There was a stillness now, a silence that swept the chamber.

"Em," John whispered through the comm link, "teams are assembled and heading to their positions now. How are things on D?" Emiko offered no response. It was clear what this silence was now. It was a trap. The enemy on the other end was trying to gauge her position, which told Emiko that whatever equipment they had wasn't suited for this kind of fight. She chuckled silently. To think that all their skirmishes with the Yoroi had taught the Reds nothing. She found their arrogance disturbing, and that was something she resolved to rectify.

****

Bill took point on Training Level C, and lurked just behind the doors to the stadium that served as the primary training floor. He was beyond irritated. These filthy Reds dared defile such hallowed ground with their inefficient battle gear and their superiority complexes. The whole thing was farcical, and as such, he decided to make a game of it. When the order came through, Bill challenged two of his best former students to join him in eliminating the threat. The catch, though, was that they had to go for ten minutes without being detected.

Zayvier Peters was the first one to jump in. He was a laid-back man of caramel complexion and strangely bright blue eyes. His full lips almost always bore a smile, and personality-wise he was Bill's spitting image. He was strong, even by Yaiba standards, and though stealth wasn't exactly his forte, he couldn't resist the chance to bond with his teacher once again.

Devin Dross was the other, who had more of an explosive attitude than the other two but surprisingly excelled in stealth. He was, like Zay, on the stronger side of the spectrum, though his skin was as ivory as Bill's. His hair as golden as wheat, and his deep brown eyes swam in emotions far too complicated for anyone but him to figure out.

The floor was shaped more or less like a pitchfork. The main corridor contained the stands and the main training floor that usually facilitated the classes of the quickest teachers to arrive. Just beyond the main floor and its stands, the corridor divided into three separate paths, each with their own fixtures for the refinement of the Yaiba's Violet Shadows. Devin and Zay were as still as the stone around them, and measured their breathing so as not to be noticed in the darkness. The smoke bombs had been deployed on each path, and with Devin positioned in the rightmost, Zay in the leftmost, and Bill positioned near the floor's entrance, all they needed to do was wait.

Bill watched as the power-lift screeched to a halt and their enemies disembarked. One complained about the smoke and how it interfered with their heat vision goggles. Another told the group to be on high alert and gave them their marching orders.

Two men were to sweep the stands of the main floor while the other nine went on ahead. When those soldiers came to the split, they separated, three to a path. Bill smirked darkly as the two soldiers entered his domain. He did nothing more than watch them pass him and noted how closely they stood. He extended the blades of his kyoketsu-shoge just long enough for him to use the blades without attracting attention, and moved to strike his prey.

He covered the ground quickly, and just as he stabbed the farthest one in the base of the neck with a diamond shaped blade, he slit the throat of the man that followed. They fell together on the slightly imprecise steps between the seats, and Bill couldn't help but think of how uncomfortable it looked. He shrugged, and like the shadows and smoke around him, Bill slipped into the hall.

As his teacher moved, so did Dross. Three hostiles filtered past him, and once the last had done so, Devin threw out a kyoketsu-shoge and pulled his first victim into the darkness. The rattle of the chains alerted the other two enemies, but it was the sudden cracking of their brethren's neck that really put them on edge. With the smoke and darkness as cover, Devin slightly adjusted his position when the two remaining soldiers opened fire. He lay with his stomach to the ground now, tucked only slightly behind the fresh body that he'd just made.

He tossed out another of the chains and wrapped it around the ankle of one of his assailants. The man screamed as he was pulled into the darkness, and was silenced by a knife to the throat. Devin was concerned that Bill might take the random gunfire as a sign that he'd lost the game, but fortunately the video surveillance footage on the right side of his mask would show that his enemies hadn't technically discovered him. He hadn't been seen at the very least, as evidenced by the fact that the last Scarlet on this path frantically searched for him. Devin moved again, this time in an effort to get closer to the frightened enemy soldier. He crawled quietly along the ground until he snuck past the intruder, then turned to face him. Devin rose from the ground, and with a single fluid motion of his arm, he pulled the pristine blade of his kyoketsu-shoge from the groin of his final opponent through his skull.

****

Cal and John took to Level L to defend the research lab. Fortunately none of the enemy forces managed to get this far, but it was better to be safe than sorry. John couldn't imagine what would've happened if the enemy got their hands on Yaiba tech and weaponry. Cal couldn't imagine what he would feel should the Scarlets sabotage his innovations.

There was no conversation. Nothing through the comms. It was dead silent on this level and from where Cal sat, it sucked. Still, he dared not voice it, since John was still in a mood. It didn't seem as bad as it did before, which was nice, given the circumstances.

For John, though, this quiet was extremely uncomfortable. The Director hadn't responded to him. The upper levels of the base were being ransacked. Aaliyah was on her own, and the Dragons were all occupied with guarding high-priority checkpoints in the levels from G and below. He wondered if he'd made the right call in letting Shonda guard the homes on Level G and not taking it himself. He wondered if he was cut out for this leadership thing at all right now. He needed Emiko back in her rightful place as soon as possible.

****

Gunfire broke the silence first, and was followed by the hysterical screams of one of the enemy soldiers.

"Commander, what are you—" another questioned, but in an instant they both met their demise on the ends of the Director's blades. The other woman, their commander, smiled and fired two shots in the direction of the chains just as Emiko launched into the air and retracted the kyoketsu-shoge. The first bullet missed, but the second connected with her shoulder. It wasn't enough to pierce the armor of the Hanzo Gear, but it was more than enough to send a sting from the point of impact through to her upper arm.

Ishikawa was thrown, and she only barely caught herself as she came back to the ground. The enemy noted the thud and laughed at the lack of response afterwards. This commander was sadistic, and the way she treated her subordinates sent a chill down Emiko's spine.

"What's the matter," the haughty Commander taunted through the smoke and shadow. "There are only three of us left after your little assassination ploy. Surely you won't be outdone by the likes of us." There was something in her voice. Pride? No. Pride was too soft an emotion for this one. It was almost like a sense of misguided determination.

****

The enemy came to Residential Level G, but the first thing they saw upon their arrival was the Fire Dragon, the Hiryu, Shonda McRae. The unit commander issued a retreat order, but before the soldiers could load back up on the power-lift she had already closed the distance. There was a momentary pause, like what a gazelle might show before the lioness strikes from the tall grass of the Serengeti, and then there was a sudden crackle, like wood and tinder in a campfire. The commander's body, slightly charred, fell to pieces before his men, and the soldiers behind him screamed and scrambled for the power-lift on the feeble hope that they might be spared.

Shonda, however, was less than merciful, for these gnats wandered not only into her own home, but the home she shared with her daughters and husband. Worse, they came with the intention of causing them harm, and that was a most unforgivable sin. The bright orange glow of the tungsten blade in her hand glimmered in her eyes as she cut them down, and while their faces radiated horror as they burned away from the heat, hers was blank, as if killing them were as easy as drinking a cup of water.

****

Emiko was the picture of patience. She couldn't risk making a move yet with the injury to her shoulder and numbness in her arm. Rushing here would gain her nothing and would only work in the favor of the already overconfident enemy.

"You can't hide forever," the Commander sang, but the Director wouldn't be so easily coaxed from the cover of darkness. The enemy commander gave a frustrated sigh, then turned her attention to her two remaining troops. "Fan out and search for her." Her tone was passive, as if she'd already won the battle, and Emiko couldn't stand being underestimated. She was the Director for a reason, and she would prove that here and now.

One of the two soldiers that now searched for her drew near. She could hear his weighted footsteps against the hard floor of the tunnel. He was cautious of her, and because of his healthy fear, she decided to reward him with a quick and painless death. She silently lifted her kyoketsu-shoge and closed her eyes as he came closer still. She breathed shallowly, which took her by surprise, and slowly regulated herself with deeper, more focused breaths. The soldier had arrived, and Emiko wasted no time. He turned to see her just in time enough for her to cleave the diamond blade straight down through his head and deep into his neck. He dropped to his knees as the halves of his skull drooped left and right, and when the Commander fired shots in the direction of his lifeless thud, Emiko rolled to the other side of the cave with her leg extended for a sharp kick.

The female soldier that sought the Director's position felt the blow crash against her knee and all but shatter it. She buckled and fell to the ground, and though she pleaded for mercy, Emiko drove the kyoketsu-shoge into the woman's throat. She rolled backwards instinctively, but when the shot never came, the Director stood up and looked in the direction of the power-lift. The smoke was still potent, Emiko's shoulder was still hurt, and there was still the threat of the Commander at the other end of the cave, totally fresh and unaffected by the chaos of the raid.

****

Bill had them cornered now. Neither Devin nor Zayvier could slip into the last path without being noticed immediately. Zavier was too loud and Devin, while gifted for striking from the shadows, was ill-equipped to deal with three enemies that were already on high alert. Bill, on the other hand, had the perfect angle to take them all down.

He deployed more smoke bombs to intensify his cover, because the trick that entered his mind would definitely necessitate it. He kicked off the ground as he drove one of his kyoketsu-shoge into the ceiling of the cave. Suspended, he gauged the distance between his current position and the wall behind the final crew of three. He took a moment, and caught a brief glance at his subordinates who were already on the move to claim his kills.

The usually confident grin on Bill's face immediately fell into a frown, and without a moment's delay he flung the free chain at the wall and hoped it would stick. Much to his delight, it did, and with the release of the first, he angled his body forward, pointed one repulsor to the ground to keep himself suspended, and pointed the other straight behind him as he pulled himself towards the remaining threat.

He arrived in seconds, and just as he hit the ground he lit his Reikiken. As soon as the blade became hot enough, he burned through the skull of the first victim, retracted the blade, swept powerfully in a diagonal arc through the second, then retraced the arc as he exited the central path through a door of his final victim's ashen flesh.

"That's not fair," Devin complained, which only made Bill smile wider. "You got more kills than us."

"Of course I did," Bill teased with a twinkle in his eye. "I'm a Dragon."

"Yeah he even flies now," Zay chimed in with a bright smile under his mask. "That move was clean, teach."

"It was," Bill acknowledged, his tone appreciative. He looked towards the power-lift, and his eyes suddenly became serious. "We should get moving. The training level is clear, but that doesn't mean we can take it easy when these people are trying to burn our home to the ground." His subordinates agreed, though they offered a silent nod in lieu of verbal agreement, and like that, they were off to the next level. They were off to Level D.

****

"Who are you," Emiko called from the shadows, "and what do you want?" The Commander strode deeper into the cave toward the Director's office, as if the corpses of her comrades were tiles on the floor and she had an appointment with the Yaiba leader. Of course, in her mind, that very well could've been so, given her treatment of her men and disregard for the person that was Emiko Ishikawa.

"My, my," said the enemy commander with a giddy flair. Her footsteps came to a stop in the middle of the hall, mere inches from where Emiko crouched. "You kill all my troops and now you want to have a conversation. Am I crazy or is that a little rude?" Emiko offered no response, and the Commander shrugged. "I suppose it doesn't hurt anything to tell you. My name is Serafina Leyva, daughter of the Viscount."

"Never heard of him," Emiko chided. Serafina grinned nonetheless as she pulled a small ovular device from the utility pouch on her belt and tossed it onto the ground. It radiated a blue light, and in a matter of seconds it released a strong current of air. The cloud of smoke that provided the Insurrection leader her invisibility was pushed back to the far lining of the cave. Exposed, she stood up and faced her enemy, her hands curled lightly and ready for combat.

"It's inconsequential," Leyva said, and tilted her head girlishly so that the delicate curls of her hair draped to one side of her. "As for my reason for being here," she continued with laser focus in her eyes, "aside from following your Dragon to the door, it's pretty simple. I'm here to kill you."

****

The enemy made their way down to Level L as expected, which was both a blessing and a curse for John. He'd only managed to rest for about an hour during the time it took to mount a counterattack against the Reds. He was drained physically from his journey and his training. He was drained emotionally from the experience of leaving his son in unfamiliar territory. Now his mind was overrun with thoughts and ideas as it ran through numerous scenarios, both good and bad. The arrival of the Scarlets meant an interruption of those thoughts, as well as an intrusion on his coordination efforts.

John and Cal grappled up to the rafters. The lower level of the lab had been blanketed by the black smoke since the first signs of the power-lift's emergence, and the upper level only just began to hide beneath the dark veil as well. The enemies that made it this far underground were few, which told John that their numbers had been thinned significantly on the upper floors of the base. These few were likely all that remained of the Reds' attack force, and they would suffer John's wrath, though Cal's was probably more of a threat in this place.

Metal crashed on the floor below, and glass broke shortly after. Cal was indignant, and bounded from one of the steel beams to another as he overlooked the floor. He couldn't make out the exact details of the figures that trudged their centuries' bloodied boots through his technological haven, but he could at least see their shapes. There were four, which meant two for him and two for the old man on the other side of the ceiling. He looked at John after the pained screeching sound of an undiscernible machine. John's face was beyond stern as it typically was on matters of combat and training. It was arctic cold, unconcerned with humanity or what humanity wrought, and it terrified Cal to see him like this.

"Something," came the nervous tenor of one of the men that walked the floor, "something doesn't feel right…" Cal looked at John more intently as the thugs made their way deeper into the young Shadow's second home. It physically pained him to hear these barbarians sully his second home without regard to the amount of care pored over the gadgets they wrecked, so when John finally nodded his approval, Cal was the first to get to work.

He watched his first target delicately advance into the workshop, careful to abstain from the further disturbance of its wares. There was the distinct rattle of chains from just above him, and when he looked to investigate it was then that the diamond-shaped titanium blade of Cal's kyoketsu-shoge pierced his forehead. Cal retracted it with a splatter of blood, and the already tense enemy troops became slightly more frantic in their patrol.

John, however, was less violent to begin with. When his first target was in his sights, he used the kyoketsu-shoge to grapple the ceiling and swing to the ground below. He timed it well enough so that his knees collided with the shoulders of the target rather than the floor of the lab, and with a swift and elegant slice of his free blade, the only sound the man beneath him could make was of gurgled blood as it pooled around him from his throat and mouth.

"What was that," called a voice from the other side. John smiled as he grappled back into the upper steel beams of the workshop. The man's voice was aggressive, but not out of authority. It was out of pure, unmitigated fear.

"I don't know," called the second of the two remaining troops, "but I don't think we should be—" the other man screamed. "What happened?"

"We got a man down! Stay on your guard, someone's here!" He shouted out of fear, and with the aura sword lit, Cal descended behind him and ran the brute through. He screamed as the bright burning blade pierced his torso and burned the surrounding flesh to ash in a painful, brutal way. The other soldier turned to run towards his comrade, now even more terrified than before. John kicked off the metal beam, his own sword bright and hot and hungry for its latest victim. His repulsors rocketed him through the air, and the way his black cloak billowed behind him from the oncoming gust of air made him look like a man-sized bat.

He neared the enemy that neared his adopted son, and with a swift, extremely precise motion, John's Reikiken burned its way from one side of the man's neck clean through to the other. Decapitated, the last remaining enemy on Level L fell to the ground mere inches away from Cal. Cal whistled as he stowed his blade in the heat-resistant scabbard at his side.

"Darius was right," he said with his usual charming grin. "You a bat-man." John rolled his eyes, but just before he could say anything, Sora Kaneuji burst through his office doors on the top floor of the workshop and fired a machine gun frantically as he screamed profanities. The two soldiers took cover and waited, unsure if they should laugh or yell back that the threat was neutralized. Cal tried to get his mentor's attention but failed. Sora was more than a little disoriented, as many combatants typically were when danger appeared at their doorstep. When his voice failed to reach the wily scientist, Cal looked at John, who quickly grappled up to the level and, from the side, held the blade of his kyoketsu-shoge to Kaneuji's throat.

"Threat's over," he said when Sora carelessly dropped the weapon. "You can calm down now." Kaneuji scratched his head as his pale cheeks flushed red.

"Oh…"

****

Emiko wasted no time. She stood to her feet, walked to the center of the breeze-made circle, and after a moment of sizing up her opponent, she took a sharp swing at her face. The limber Serafina ducked just as swiftly and swept Emiko's now extended front leg. Emiko, however, wasn't impressed. She performed a back handspring as she felt her front foot slide along the cave floor and landed before Leyva made the full revolution. By the time she did, Emiko had bridged the gap that her acrobatics had created and threw her knee at the lovely caramel face of the enemy commander.

Serafina dropped her back to the floor as her legs pushed against Emiko's knee and ankle from either side. She buckled from the scissor takedown, but as she fell, cushioned herself and rolled through to her feet on the opposite end of the makeshift ring. Leyva kipped up from the ground and gave an approving smirk.

"This is gonna be fun," she giggled in that same girlish manner with which she had flipped her hair earlier. Something was off about her, but that was none of Emiko's concern. The only thing that was on Director Ishikawa's mind was taking this woman out and restoring safety and order for her people.

Before too long they were back at it, and a series of punches and kicks, elbows and knees, flurried back and forth between the two. Emiko blocked a knee with her hand, then quickly turned in such a way that she drove her elbow into Serafina's jaw. The first hit. Leyva spat a little blood, but her face was all joy as she paced the circle like a hungry lioness.

"That was good," she said, and cracked her knuckles. "But that's the only hit you're gonna land on me today. I guarantee you that." She dove back in, but her speed and power seemed to multiply. Before Emiko could even put up her arms to block the hit, it connected. She felt three more mad knee strikes to the gut before she rolled backwards to establish distance, but the brutal Scarlet fighter charged in yet again.

Emiko deployed her first kyoketsu-shoge in a sweeping motion at Leyva's legs, but it failed to connect. The enemy commander donned the look of pride in her own abilities, a mocking grin that told Emiko, *I dodged your desperate attack, you fool.* What the cherub-faced nutjob failed to see was that as soon as she vaulted into the air to avoid the sweep, the second blade was launched. It struck through her shoulder, and when the Director pulled it back, it jerked the enemy along with it. Emiko, who lost speed from the vicious assault earlier, saw this as an opportunity to deal a decisive blow. She spun out of the way of the chain and, with that momentum, drove her elbow as hard as she could into the side of Serafina's head. The intruder hit the ground with a horrible thud. Emiko stood there for a moment and watched her. The blade was still lodged in her shoulder, the chain still dangled from Ishikawa's arm, but the enemy seemed unconscious, and Emiko was thankful for the break.

She coughed up blood. It hadn't occurred to her just how hard she'd been hit. Paired with the pain in her shoulder from before, she was in a truly bad way. In the silence, for just a faint second, the Director thought to respect this agent of the Reds as a formidable opponent. Then she spoke, and startled Emiko enough to jump back again.

"I'm impressed," said Serafina as she pressed a hand to her head. She hissed as she pulled the diamond-shaped blade from the wound, but never once did she take her eyes off of Emiko. "You managed to get two more hits. Even took out my arm. I guess I have no choice but to take you seriously now." Emiko was startled by the suggestion.

"You still intend to fight me," she asked in disbelief, and before she could laugh, Serafina was back to her feet. "With only one arm?" Commander Leyva shrugged.

"You might've tagged me well enough, but even on my worst day I only need one arm to beat you." Emiko knew what she was trying to do. Using taunts as a means of disrupting an enemy's battle flow was an age-old tactic. Even still, she was unnerved by the show of bravado on Serafina's part.

The Director blinked, and when she opened her eyes the strong Scarlet noblewoman punched at her, but it was a feint. The follow-up attack struck Emiko hard against the ear and caused her to stumble. Serafina gave her no time to regroup, though, as she dove for her knees first and nailed the Director in the chest. Ishikawa rolled along the ground, hard of breath, unable to hear clearly, and in a panic she launched her kyoketsu-shoge at the enemy again. She was stunned when Serafina dodged its blade and grabbed the chain.

"Nice try," she taunted in a sultry voice. It was in this moment, where Serafina wrapped the chain around her hand and pulled the Director off her feet, that Emiko knew what she was. She was a monster, and so much more so than the average Red was. Emiko flew towards her and was met with a stiff bicep to the throat. Emiko hit the ground hard, and all the air in her lungs left her in an instant. Leyva loosened the chains from around her working hand and reached for the sheath at the Director's side.

There was a brief moment of awe as the heat from her hand funneled into the weapon and spurred it to life.

Emiko shakily activated the comms device in her ear. She tried to call for help, but strained coughs took the place of words. Serafina pressed the live Reikiken into Emiko's chest, and though the Hanzo Gear she wore was heat-resistant, it was only finitely so. She stood there over her fallen opponent and calmly eyed her as the heat became more intense by the second. Before long, the heat limit was reached, and the exposed skin of Emiko's upper face started to burn.

Another moment passed, and with a sick smile, Commander Leyva listened to the forced screams of her enemy with the full knowledge that anyone on her frequency would hear the same. Another moment, and the Reikiken now burned through Emiko's chest with her eyes open, frozen in the pleading expression that she couldn't help but don in those waning moments of life. In another moment, the Scarlet forces both inside and out were gone.

****

October 12th, 2084, 5:45 p.m.,

It took all day on the 9th to clear the base of the bodies. Allies and enemies alike fell in the attack, and the attack itself left the remaining Insurrectionists stunned and appalled. Even though peace was restored for a moment, it would take a long time before anything about their lives felt normal again.

On the 10th, they held Emiko's funeral. Nobody from the oldest man to the youngest child could hold back the tears. She had given her life in service to those she swore to protect. In life, she nurtured them, taught them, and did all that she could to ensure the survival of every single one of their number. Her loss was felt deeply by all of them, recognized by Director Ishikawa as her own family, but it resonated with the Dragons above all others. Vanessa and Raven were on Medical Level I, and were too far away to rush to her aid. Manny was on the Education Level defending the school on the floor just below hers, and hated himself a little more by the second for being outnumbered and so ineffective. Shonda was on G, and begged her childhood friend Emiko to forgive her for not being there for her when she needed it. Callan, who took to A as soon as he could manage, questioned why he hadn't been there on Level D with Emiko. But Bill and John had the worst of it.

Bill was the one who discovered her body, and kicked himself for making a game of the invasion that claimed his friend's life. If he'd just killed those intruders, he could've made it in time to save her. Bri held him tightly afterward, but the guilt still ate at him.

John knew. He knew that she was reckless and worked outside protocol. He should've forced her down to Level X, where she was supposed to be. It would've caused him some serious trouble, but he should've insisted that she go for her own safety. He'd already lost too much. They all had. And now this…

On the 11th, nobody spoke or worked or left their residences, save for the technical crew responsible for repairing the damage that the Reds had done to the entrance. No, this was a day for mourning their fallen leader, and for savoring every second they could with their families.

Now, though, on the 12th of October in the year 2084, the Seven Dragons met with the supplemental leaders of the Yaiba Insurrection on Conference Level D. Only a few additional parties were allowed entry, but the small audience was welcome, as none in the room or in the Insurrection at large felt like abiding the company of too many others.

A vote was taken to appoint the new head of the Yaiba, the new Director, and it came as a shock to no-one that the person selected was the second in command, John Hamlin. He hated the idea of playing politics, being stuck behind a desk, and being responsible for such a large body but he accepted, as this was something that Emiko would've wanted.

"My first order as Director of the Yaiba Insurrection," John said to the Dragons and dignitaries. He paused, hurt by the memory of his old friend and the idea that he could replace her, but steeled himself to continue. "My first order as Director… is to declare all-out war on the Scarlet Kingdom." He exited immediately, and those left in his wake came alive with a war cry.

Chapter Thirteen

October 15th, 2084, 7:20 a.m.,

She'd been back in New York for a week now, seven days since she'd cut off the Yaiba's head, and only now had she been brought before the King's Court in the Palace. She was as smug now as she had been after she watched the lights leave Emiko's eyes, and to her delight, nobody was able to solicit an account of her deeds from her or her remaining troops in the days since. She would be the one to tell the story, and relish in the deed once again. She stood before the court with a confident calm as she glanced between their faces.

Before her sat her father, the ever-patriotic Viscount Ronaldo Leyva, the short, pointy-eared man of Hispanic origin whose presence in the King's Court was more of a safety measure than a recognition of his worth. Serafina was especially conscious of this fact, and was ready to revel in the implications of her accomplishments and the undisputed fact that she, a Leyva, a Hispanic woman pledged to serve the Scarlet Kingdom, had managed to accomplish a greater feat than any of their alabaster comrades.

She caught sight of Marquis Harold West of Upstate, with his beady blue eyes, chestnut brown hair with strands of gray, and that titanic nose of his. He scowled at her as if to project inferiority onto Commander Leyva, but the deliberate smile and smugness in her eyes told him that she knew nothing of her place.

It was true, she was defiant and always had been. Had it not been for her need to challenge the orders of her superiors, she might've advanced much farther in her career as a soldier in the Scarlet military. Even with her rebellious nature, Countess Miranda McBride, the stout brunette woman with a frail composure, always admired her for having the boldness that she so clearly lacked.

Not everyone felt this way, however, namely the pearl-faced menfolk that supposed it was their right to lead and the responsibility of women, more so women of darker complexions and savage heritage, to follow orders as given and service their betters without question. Baron Arthur Stalks, though a Hispanic gentleman like Viscount Leyva, was a vehement supporter of this notion if for no other reason than a shameless attempt at getting the other nobles to warm up to him.

Lord Phineas Blackwell, the King's righthand man, was a borderline skeletal figure whose skin and hair were twice as white. He merely watched as Serafina avoided his neutral gaze, and allowed his thin lips to curl with delight at the realization that he made her uncomfortable.

Instead, she looked at Prince Nash, and though she wanted to smile, his stardust-gray eyes pierced her very soul and froze her where she stood. She couldn't help but admire how his dark hair contrasted those wonderful orbs, or how the right amount of grizzle adorned his cut jawline, or how his body, much like his brother's, looked as if it had been carved by the deified artisans of centuries gone by. She wanted him, and it was a thing as primal as her bloodlust in battle.

In the center of the Court, between Stalks and McBride, sat an empty chair fit for a king, a pair of scarlet cushions surrounded by handcrafted gold with lion's feet on the legs and its vicious head at its top. A door opened from the back of the room, beyond the semicircular table at which the Court sat, and in came the King.

Shane O'Neill, the King of the Reds, was an imposing man whose gray hair, scarred face and crushing gray eyes added such a gravity to the room that the entire court stiffened at his mere presence. King Shane had been a warrior in his younger years, and was one of the few men alive to have had the experience of fighting the Yaiba Insurrection before the advent of their precious Hanzo Gear. It was under his leadership as a general that the Yaiba almost died, but even for all his accolades in war, he'd never managed to kill the leader of any major faction. Not like Serafina.

"Do you know why I've brought you here," asked the King as he took his seat. He was still strong, still able to fight if he was forced, and he had a reputation for personally handling any trouble within the borders of New York. Serafina hesitated to answer, but the narrowing of his eyes compelled her to nod.

"The King has summoned me before the Court to give my report of my attack on the Yaiba Insurrection," she said as humbly as she could, and while her father the Viscount looked pleased by her display, the others at the table looked at the girl in shock.

"Out with it then," said Lord Blackwell, who was the first to regain his senses. The way he spoke was exactly as she imagined, with the eeriness of death hidden behind an elderly fatigue.

"Yes, of course," she obliged, and cleared her throat as she bowed her head. Such was the formality but given that it allowed her to more blatantly avoid eye contact with Blackwell without reprimand, she was relieved to do so. "On October 8th, 2084, my company received word from Major Crawford's intelligence unit about a single transport leaving Yoroi territory. Our orders were to track it to its destination, but when we discovered the location of the Yaiba base, we coordinated an assault." Leyva twitched with discomfort at the realization that his daughter had been in the lion's den. Everyone else, however, took in this revelation as the latest manifestation of Serafina's rebellious nature.

"So," spoke Leyva before the others had the chance to light into his daughter, "you once again disobeyed your orders. Haven't you suffered enough demotion in your career, *mi hija*? Once again you disgrace our family, and in the presence of the King no less!" A serpentine expression traversed Serafina's face as she picked her head up, and the smile that twisted her lips provoked the stern looks of the entire court.

"Disgrace?" She started with a ring in her voice. "Forgive me, ladies and gentlemen of the Court, for believing that taking the life of Emiko Ishikawa, Director of the Yaiba Insurrection, would bring honor to us all, most of all my family." She said nothing further. She allowed their uncertainty and awe to fill the room and strangle any obstinance she might face in getting what she wanted most.

"Director Ishikawa..." Countess McBride started shakily as her eyes darted around frantically, as if mentioning the Ishikawa in the King's presence would incite wrath beyond mortal comprehension.

"Is dead," Serafina reiterated. "By my own hand, no less. The initial explosion at their front door took out a sizeable chunk of their defensive forces as well. I dispatched teams into the lower levels of the Roan Mountain, by the way."

"To what end," Baron Stalks inquired, his hand cupped around his chin. Commander Leyva smiled mockingly in his direction.

"Why, Baron Stalks, you didn't expect me to defy orders without yielding results, did you? Before my teams were dispatched by the Dragons and their subordinates, my troops managed to scan a few of the more prominent levels of their facilities. Civilian housing, medical stations, laboratories, training centers, and a conference level that was home to the office of our dearly departed Director." She spoke with such a chill that it made Lord Blackwell shiver. That, she did catch out of the corner of her eye.

"Where are those scans now," Prince Nash asked in the tone of an arrogant brat, though Serafina was certain that that was just how pampered princes sounded.

"I sent a copy to each member of the Court and military generals in need of that kind of intel," she responded with an indifferent whimsy in her voice that excited the prince, but showed her lack of discipline to the others.

"This is more information on the Yaiba than even the intelligence unit could muster," said the King. "But be honest, child. An Ishikawa wouldn't fall to someone like you, now would they?" The arrogant smirk that taunted the Court had fallen to a frown, and with a shake of his head, the King said, "I thought not—"

"You thought wrong," Serafina cut him off with an indignant tone that chaffed at the heart of the other nobles. The King's eyes hardened on her as her father's denoted a fresh hopelessness as if they both knew in their mind that she'd earned her own execution. Just as King Shane parted his lips to pronounce it, she pressed a button on the collar of her red, skin-tight uniform to reveal a recording.

The King and those by his side sat in silence as they watched Serafina drive the Reikiken into Emiko's chest. They heard the screams as the bright orange blade burned its way through the heat-resistant Yaiba armor, and then the silent crackle of her heat-charred flesh. "The Dawn King thought that body cameras were a slap in the face of hard-working American law enforcement. He called them an 'unpatriotic and divisive tactic of the far left," and so our society phased them out along with racial sensitivity training. Even though they can get in the way of us doing what needs to be done, you can see here that they have their uses." The room was silent. Not even the King could find the right words at first.

"You've…" he tried, but was still at a loss. His eyes burned with jealousy and rage, neither of which he'd felt since the decades of his youth, but he stilled himself as he tried to formulate a coherent thought. "You've done well, Commander," he finally told her, and the Viscount breathed an audible sigh of relief. "Is there anything you would like in return for services rendered?"

Just like that, the devilish smirk was back, and Serafina said simply, “I want in on the Scourge.”

****

October 15th, 2084, 8:20 a.m.,

The main compound of the Yoroi territory was divided into three city-like structures, and each structure had their own training areas fit for a slue of different weapons. The eateries were abundant, the schools were spacious and surprisingly well-equipped, and everything from the governmental buildings to the housing units was kept clean and radiant. The attitudes of the Yoroi citizens, however, did little to imitate this beauty.

Darius had been among them for a week now, and though they toured him through the different facets of the triad compound, it was done in such a manner that made it clear, they only needed him there to do his duty and avoid trouble. This was no vacation for him, and how could it have been? He was hundreds of miles away from his family and friends and had no way to contact them for updates without being immediately noticed. The Yoroi watched him like wolves in the thick of a forest and waited for the slightest reason to strike at him.

Today, though, was different. It was his first day on the job, the first day that he could assert himself as the master and earn the respect of the Alliance's warriors. Each day up until this point he'd been nervous of them, terrified, borderline consumed with the uncertainty of his new position in life and the distance from everything he'd ever known. Today, though, he had the chance to take his mind off of everything else and focus on the job.

He paced the orange stone floor of the Yoroi training grounds and marveled at the fact that the space before him held a scattered pattern of orange and brown pillars cut from the same rock as everything within the base. The space behind him, however, was smooth and flat, as if it was made for holding a demonstration or a brief of some kind. All in all, it wasn't the same as the adaptable terrain that the Yaiba trained on, but Darius supposed that it would suffice. The rugged nature of the pillars would act as its own reward/punishment system, as the trainees would soon find out.

The door to the facility slid open, and with a turn of his head, Darius was met with the image of his first three students. The first was a woman of a youthful glow, though it was still clear to him that she was his senior. She was full-figured, the whole of her body perfectly balanced and, if the boy was honest, inviting to the senses. She bore honey-brown hair with eyes that matched, and had a cinnamon complexion that soothed him in a similar fashion to his mother's. She gave him a look that radiated welcome, but hid an air of uncertainty as if she hoped he might impress her. The man beside her looked, not unimpressed, but surprisingly neutral, as if he was unfazed by life in general. He had pitch black hair and dark brown eyes, milky skin, and a beard that gave him both a sense of brutal potential and gentlemanly distinction. The third person, of androgynous quality, had short black hair, dark skin, and golden eyes that looked around at the training facility with a childlike wonder. Of the three, this person was closest to Darius in age, and when their eyes fell on the Hanran no Ryu, they gave a startlingly girlish smirk that made something in the boy jump.

It was in that moment, as other students began to file into the facility, that he questioned which of his instructors he would channel. Did he want to be like his Uncle Bill and strive for excellence with gentle nudges and playful disposition? Would he take on the neutral approach of his Uncle Callan and let the facts of the Hanzo Gear make or break his students? Would he be like Uncle Manny who exuded optimism, even in the face of the most helpless of students? He dismissed each one as too complicated for the mission at hand. He was in a foreign land where he had no respect, despite the title he'd been hastily given before he left home. He was the master, and if they were to acknowledge him as such, he couldn't afford to coddle them or make them feel like they had a choice in the matter.

The last two students trickled into the room, and Darius gave a quick headcount. There were easily fifteen, an assortment of men, women and others, all dressed in and armed with their own Hanzo Gear. "Good morning," Darius started with his best attempt at a relaxed but authoritative voice. It made him feel silly, because the voice he used was the same one that John used when Darius had found his way into trouble. "As you may or may not be aware," he continued with his father's disciplinary disposition as he paced the stone beneath his feet, "your home is on the radar of the Reds. The Yaiba Insurrection's alliance with the Yoroi and the Yoroi's northward expansion are believed to be the motive for a recent attack on a Yoroi outpost in Texas. Does anyone know what this means?" The eyes of his students, many of them older than he, were knowing enough. Their overall expressions, however, feigned ignorance. Darius disregarded it as best he could. "It means that at any given point, the Reds will be on you like heat on the Southwest Territory."

"Why should we care," one of the male students, a blond man with razor sharp blue eyes and a muscular build asked loud enough for Darius to hear. "Our whole territory is surrounded by bombs, mines and traps. We've survived so long because we take a lot of precaution."

"That would mean something," Darius returned dryly, "if your people hadn't entered a ceasefire agreement with the Kingdom years ago and divulged your free paths to them in the interest of good faith. Even if you didn't, do you honestly think that the Scarlets care how many lives they have to throw away to get to you?" The young man opened his mouth to retort, but no words could escape. "The fact that you're here for training tells me that you realized it too. Your best bet is to fall in line and let me do my job. If you don't, then your friends, your families, your significant others, will all be victimized while you wonder why you and your defenses fell short." The students came alive with concerned whispers that became indignant cries on all sides. Their offense was palpable, and though the raucous culmination of their voices disquieted the young dragonling, he showed no evidence of it on his face. Instead, he allowed the corner of his mouth to curl into a dark smirk. He folded his arms across his chest and waited for the commotion to calm. As expected, the muted change of his position was the very catalyst for their return to passivity.

"How old are you, anyway?" shouted the indignant blond man from before, his sharp eyes now alight with a fire that Darius knew would serve him in battle. "You look like a kid. Do they really expect us to listen to someone who just figured out how to tie his shoelaces?" The room got quiet, and all eyes fell on Darius to see what he would do. The grin grew wider.

Darius calmly motioned for the man to come forward, and when he did he noticed that this student was much bigger than he'd realized. He was strong, and the way he put his feet to the ground showed that he was the sort that knew very well how little others could move him. Darius looked around, and noticed that his other students had all moved about the room to get a better view of the undoubted fight that would happen between this foreign "teacher" and the student.

"Tell me," Darius asked, "are you the toughest man here?" There was silence when the young blond nodded with a cocky grin. "Excellent. You may use any weapons on your person." The blond man's eyes went wide.

"What are you saying," he asked with a low, suspicious growl. Darius flashed an overconfident smile.

"I'm saying that if you can touch me once, I'll step down as your teacher and none of you will be obligated to listen to me." The crowd came alive with chatter at that, and Darius took in their excited gasps. "If I win, however, you'll do what I say when I say it, no questions asked. Deal?" The big blond man nodded, and without the need for further invitation, the brutish student unsheathed his Reikiken and brought it to life in the palm of his hand. He slashed directly in front of him, and in his mind it was certain that at this range his teacher had no other choice but to be smashed and burned for his arrogance. To his surprise, though, Darius pulled his blade from its home on his hip and pushed his enemy's Reikiken through in an elegant parry.

The brute used the energy of the parry to whip it back around to the other side, but Darius was both fast and strong enough to block the attack with only a single-handed maneuver. The tough guy aimed for the Rebel Dragon's exposed leg, but another parry moved him further out of the way.

"You're strong," Darius commented loudly enough for everyone else to hear, "but sloppy." A downward chop by the brute left him open for another parry, and when Darius did, the strongman disconnected the blades and went for the hip of his otherwise unbothered teacher. "You're creative," Darius continued coolly as he pushed the blade through again and followed his opponent's movements to keep the fireswords connected, "but your excessive emotion and your need to be the best rob you of effectiveness." The beastly student's eyes widened and the crowd around them donned expressions that mirrored that same awe as the teacher moved his blade according to the energy of his opponent, as if nothing his opponent did was outside of his calculations. The student became frustrated, but the teacher smiled as he toyed with him. "You're angry. You thought you had control here. You thought that because they fear you, I would too. But now the reality is setting in. *I* have control, and the more you try to resist, the more you embarrass yourself." Hanran no Ryu stepped in just as the blond man tried to bat his sword away. Darius connected his bright orange Reikiken with the pant leg of his opponent, all from a perfect block. "My point. Now, everybody fall in line. We have work to do."

****

October 15th, 2084, 12:32 p.m.,

Prince James watched the area through the monitors surrounded by Major Kyle Crawford, Colonel Serenity Crawford, and a small combination of elite intelligence operatives and the members of the Scarlet Scourge. They observed thermal readings of the area first, but the Arizona heat was too much, even in October. It was almost as if the archaic notion of climate change was credible, but it was beyond the understanding of the Scarlet Kingdom and nobody cared to change it. What they did have mind to change, however, was their methods of surveillance.

The thermal scans were replaced with the less informative but still somewhat effective direct surveillance. Either way, the monitors didn't show anything out of the ordinary in the Yoroi Territory, but the presence of the Yaiba at the Midland outpost had confirmed that the two factions worked together. Aria Black led the interrogation efforts on Johannes, but in the month and change that they'd had him, they found the emissary tougher to crack than they'd hoped.

The Prince was aware that Thornhill was necessary, and so the threat of death was not effective. The fact that the captive knew this himself rendered such a threat even less so. For all their additional means of making him talk, Johannes Thornhill was surprisingly tight-lipped. Apparently he had been trained to endure torture, but it was only a matter of time before he cracked. Even the strongest will had its breaking point, after all.

It was his obstinance, however, and more specifically the longevity of it, that brought the Prince and his beloved Serenity together with Major Crawford and the intelligence unit. They'd been watching for days now, and the most interesting thing they'd seen was the lone Yaiba transport that'd driven so boldly back east. Since then, the Yoroi territory was silent.

"This is unusual for them," Kyle commented with a gravity in his voice. His bright blue eyes reflected the sheen of the monitors before him and his rosy cheeks flushed a deeper red, as if the silence of a potential enemy force unnerved him. "The Yoroi were in the middle of expanding to the Northwest Territory but then all of their movements just stopped."

"It makes sense. The attack on their Texas outpost and the slaughter of their forces couldn't have been received well," Serenity told him, and gave a sisterly pat to his shoulder. "It was an excessive show of force that took out the Insurrectionists and every Yoroi soldier at the base, plus civilians. It would make sense that they would respond with fear." Serenity was proud of that, overjoyed at the prospect of potential rebels bowing out of terror, even though it was only really "terror" if it attacked the Scarlet way of life. She relished the act of turning their tactics against them and cementing the Reds as the true superior force.

"But is it fear that they respond with," James asked, his voice as grave as her brother's, "or caution? Their silence could be just as threatening as it could be comforting."

"That's what I'm afraid of," Kyle told him. "Fear's always how it starts, but what they do with that fear always has an implication for trouble." James immediately thought of the bombing of the Northwest. The Kabuto didn't even show fear when they stormed their motor pool and liberated their Insurrectionist hostage. His hand shook, and as he balled it into a firm fist the prince decided that he would learn from his brother's mistakes and avoid leaving the enemy unattended.

"Regardless of the trouble, Major," Prince James assured him, "we'll be watching, and we'll be ready."

****

October 15th, 2084, 5:40 p.m.

Darkness slowly encroached on the landscape, and the covert Kabuto forces that moved swiftly and silently through the thicket of trees came into view of the old Penn State campus. The whole thing was surrounded by a sturdy wall with only a couple of direct and scantily guarded points of entry. Erik Kincaid stood at the head, tired from the long journey but pressed for time, and through a pair of old binoculars he watched the pair of guards in the distance.

He was happy that when John took over the Yaiba Insurrection he saw no need to change the plan that they'd come up with only hours before… He shook his head in frustration. He was in such a rush to get back to his people that he not only missed the arrival of the Scarlet raiding party, but failed to lend support to a fresh ally that he thought was rather charming to say the least.

The guards moved, and he signaled his men. They watched the shift change, fully aware of the long gap between the first crew's dismissal and the second's arrival. With these facilities positioned in the heart of Scarlet Kingdom territory, the presence of guards at all was more of a formality than the result of any healthy respect of their enemies. The Yaiba Insurrection had only just lost their leader, and as far as the Helmets could tell, the Scarlets thought that whatever remained of the Kabuto were naught more than a ragtag group of rebel scum bent on exacting revenge. The Reds were far from threatened, and their arrogance provided the perfect opportunity for the savvy saboteurs.

Kincaid waved his hand, and with the wordless order his forces dispersed to their positions. Four teams of saboteurs were assigned to this mission and numbered twelve men each. Kincaid manned Alpha Team, which operated on his order to act as the distraction. They knew that there were hundreds of Reds in the base, and while Erik trusted his men to infiltrate without being discovered, it was only prudent to make the job as easy as possible to ensure mission success. Beta Team, the first team over the wall and now on the way to the old water treatment lab, was headed by

Esau Tillman. His stoic nature made him the perfect choice to be second in command on this mission, though the competition was fierce. Levi Taylor was a master of both stealth and open war, and could certainly handle himself well enough if they'd been discovered should things go south or the distraction fail. His Gamma Team would certainly benefit from having such a leader, and their target of the high pressure combustion lab was a fitting choice.

Of course, that is not to discount the young Nick Resnick, who was captain of Delta Team. He was the least engaged of all the Helmet ranks, but he was indisputably effective at accomplishing whatever task was set before him. Whatever the mission objective was, it was almost always replaced with his personal mission of getting back to free time as quickly as possible. Everything that Erik had him do only ever served as an obstacle between him and his natural laziness. Erik shrugged indifferently with a grin plastered to his face as he realized that as long as he continued to produce results, there really was no reason for him to care how lazy the boy was.

He let out a sigh and stepped out of the trees directly in front of the checkpoint. One of the guards yelled at Erik and trained his firearm on its target, but the sudden emergence of the other Kabuto that hid in the dark prompted the poor man to frantically change from one target to the next. The Helmets were perfectly calm, albeit somewhat amused at the startled demeanor of the Scarlet guard. Erik lifted his hands.

“I assure you that there's no need for hostility,” he told them in a soothing voice so smooth it caught the enemy off guard.

“Why are you here?” demanded the confused troop with authority in his voice. His comrade came over, weapon drawn, and together they waved their muzzles around at the twelve Kabuto men and women that, as of yet, posed them no threat.

"We're here," Kincaid clarified, "because we've obtained intel on the alliance brewing between the Yaiba and Yoroi."

"The Scarlet Kingdom is already aware of that," said the second guard, a little man with a weaselly voice and trigger-happy disposition. For a second, Erik couldn't help but wonder if this was what it was like in the America of old, where civilians had to fear being shot by frightened policemen who were supposedly well-trained. He narrowed his eyes.

"But are you aware of the attack they're mounting on the capitol?" The Helmet leader's words gave the soldiers plenty of reason to hesitate. The first one kept his eyes and muzzle pointed at the crowd while his friend spoke into his comms unit to some superior officer. There was a few moments' wait, but Erik didn't mind. It was honestly his pleasure to stand here, hands raised without a single weapon in them, full of the knowledge that just his smug expression was enough to unnerve a pair of hardened Red soldiers.

Another word came through the comms, and the soldiers straightened up. They accepted whatever orders they received, though their hostility ceased to fade and their guns remained pointed. Erik offered no change in expression, even when he let out a tired yawn. For him it was always the same. These super soldier types, ever loyal to their damned Scarlet Kingdom, could only contemplate orders. Even if they were suspicious, it was always easy to mislead them about the true intentions of the Kabuto. The superiors, however, would be trickier.

Within moments, a swarm of Reds approached the gate. A core group of thirteen separated from the rest of the crowd, obviously led by the overseer of this operation. These thirteen were the ones that would handle his squad, Erik assumed. That meant that the others came to watch whatever was about to happen with the intruders. The overseer stopped a couple of feet away from Erik. He was a dark-skinned man with a trimmed goatee and brown eyes that looked black in the night. Judging from his muscular physique, Erik assumed that the man could crush his skull with nothing more than a tight grip. It was almost enough to make him nervous.

"My subordinates tell me that you know something that we don't," said the overseer. "I feel it necessary to point out that that's the only reason you're still alive right now."

"Well, I do appreciate the courtesy, Mr…." Erik trailed off so as to ask for his name without asking. His tone was so genuinely gentlemanly that the Scarlets, who long thought themselves to be the only sophisticated life on this continent, marveled at such a minor display of grace and dignity.

"General Barkley," he filled in, and Erik nodded with a gracious smile. The time was near and by now, most of the attention of this base should be on the southwest gate. Teams Beta, Gamma and Delta were now free to pursue their courses without interruption.

"General Barkley," he corrected. "It has come to our knowledge that now that the Yaiba and Yoroi have joined forces, they intend to attack the heart of Scarlet territory. I thought it prudent to come and warn you so that you can alert your King." Barkley raised an eyebrow.

"And just how do you know that," asked the General with folded arms and unshakeable stance. "Moreover, why should I trust you? You're a Helmet; you've survived for years lying and cheating just to avoid coming to a head."

"And what good has that gotten us," Erik barked, the sting of their attack still fresh in his mind. He straightened himself. He was better than this situation, better than the anger that gnawed at him every day, and better than this inferior general. He needn't give them more than was necessary to get them to lower their guard. His face softened, and he spoke again, "We've come a long way. Our home was hit by whatever bomb you were testing last spring and our forces were depleted. What you see before you are as many as are able to move around freely. If the Yaiba and Yoroi are standing together, then it's in both our interests to cut them off at the head."

General Barkley mulled it over for a moment. His eyes remained locked onto the fierce emeralds that sparkled even in the dark. What the intruder said made sense. The union of two factions was enough to even stir the dilapidated souls of the jaded noble class, so banding together against them was a smart move. However, it was more than above his paygrade to make those kinds of decisions on his own. He needed to relay the intel to his superiors. After he verified it to ensure its accuracy, of course. He eyed the squad of Helmets suspiciously, but waved for his men to approach them.

"We'll be taking you in for questioning," he informed them. "Of course, you'll have to hand over any weapons you brought with you." One of the Kabuto subordinates lurched forward at the thought, but the raised fist of Erik Kincaid was enough to stay him in his position.

"Do what you will," Erik complied with a calm smile. "We don't want any trouble." The General approached Kincaid specifically and stripped him of his utility belt and sword. He ogled the archaic armaments and noted their slight contemporary appeal, as if they were more than just relics of a long-gone age. The other twelve soldiers that accompanied General Barkley followed suit and stripped Alpha Team of their weapons and gadgets.

"Bring them in," the General ordered, and as his subordinates surrounded the Kabuto crew, Kincaid raised a hand gingerly so as to gently grasp Barkley's attention.

"That won't be necessary," he said plainly. "We'll be taking it from here."

"What," Berkley asked.

"What?" Kincaid mocked, then spoke loudly for everyone to hear, "Code 1642 engage." A surge of electricity flowed through each of the soldiers that surrounded the southwest gate. They hummed for a bit, and the look of superiority in Barkley's expression was immediately replaced with one of pain and deep hatred. He would lose consciousness soon, so Kincaid opted to tell him quickly that, "This whole area was mined days ago with our Shock Pads. We needed a distraction, but in the event that I got a bad feeling, I wanted a quick and easy way to incapacitate a lot of you guys at once." He looked to the Scarlet soldiers behind him, and unsurprisingly they jolted from the shock as well. "Our weapons are also fitted with a smaller but equally effective model. Nice of you to liberate us of our tools, gentlemen."

After another ten seconds, the sum of Scarlet solders smoldered in the soil. Alpha Team reclaimed their wares, and without delay they strolled through the front gate as though it was their own base. An explosion in the distance to the northwest of their position told Erik that the water treatment lab was finished. Another to the southeast meant that the high pressure combustion lab had been taken out as well. The farthest target was all that remained, the repurposed chemical ecology lab to the north, and it would be up in smoke soon enough. Erik signaled to his Alpha Team.

"Fan out," he ordered as he frisked the unconscious General for his badge and keycard, "and find me an access point. It's time to have a little fun."

Chapter Fourteen

October 24th, 2084, 3:04 a.m.,

John sat in the trees of the overgrown Cherokee Forest and watched the parade of Scarlet Troopers march about Johnson City with a confidence born of ignorance. The poor fools didn't yet realize how helpless they were, but they would in a matter of moments when three days' worth of coordination rained down upon them.

"Is everyone in position," he asked through the comms unit in his mask. He received a hasty confirmation from the other Dragons, Devin Dross, Zavier Peters, and Cal, then proceeded to give instruction. "Western Company, on my order you'll close off the 321. There won't be much cover on that highway, which is why you've been outfitted with ballistic energy shields. It'll be hard, but stand your ground and keep the enemy locked inside Johnson City."

"Yes, sir," Callan confirmed. It was weird for him to say, but not that much weirder than ascribing honorifics to Emiko when she was… in charge. He trembled slightly, beneath the notice of everyone else in his company. It hadn't been all that long ago that he was a captive here. Now he was one of the driving forces that would bring the enemy to their knees. He smirked, and switched to the 7708 channel designated specifically for the Western Company. "All WC forces enact Attack Pattern Epsilon. Wait for my order."

A force of 200 Yaiba subordinates fell to the sides of the road, nestled behind and inside the damaged buildings and the unkempt trees that obscured any possibility of detection. Callan, along with two of his subordinates, took to the center of the road, their Reikiken drawn.

"Eastern Company," John continued through the main channel, "Same orders. Close off the 321 on your end but split focus between the city and the open road. Nobody in or out of the city that isn't wearing Hanzo Gear."

"Understood," replied Raven Shahid and Vanessa Duncan. They preferred to work together, and as the Hikariryu and Kageryu respectively, they were as natural on the battlefield as the light and dark from which their names derived.

"I'll man the city," Raven volunteered, and moved 99 others into Spear Formation. She smiled. It'd been a couple of weeks since the Reds attacked their home and took their leader, and Raven was more than a little excited to make them regret it all. Vanessa, who watched as the Light Dragon arranged her half of the Western Company, smirked with a shrug of the shoulders and got her own crew in order.

"Guess that leaves us with watching for reinforcements," she called loud enough for the men and women at her command to hear. "Fall in! Counter Spear Formation!" The remainder of the Western Company arranged themselves in staggered formation, blades drawn and angled forward, ready to strike down any unfortunate souls that dared charge in.

"Northwest and Northeast Companies," John advised, and he surveyed the map projection from his gauntlet. "You'll be blocking off I-26 and the old Route 19W respectively."

"Yes sir," Manny almost sang, though John could tell that the optimism in his voice was particularly hollow. It was hard for him to lose the people that he cared about. Harder still for him to show it. Nevertheless, John reasoned that they'd had enough talk of Emiko's end and their focus needed to be on the battle.

"You got it," Bill chimed in before any further instructions could be given. Even in his voice there was something less than upbeat. It'd been a hard few months for all of them with Callan's capture, Darius' deployment, Bill's wound and Emiko's death, but here was a chance for them to right those wrongs and finally establish the Yaiba as more than just some fleeting threat. They would be the blade that cut the throat of the Scarlet Kingdom even if it took a lifetime.

"Roaming Company," John addressed, "all I need you to do is start some trouble. Attack from all remaining sides. Use your individual cells to divide the enemy forces. Keep them guessing about which direction you'll be coming from until they feel they have no choice but to scatter."

"Yessir," Cal cooed through the comms. He wasn't the primary leader of the Roaming Company, but he was enough of one to answer.

"Let's get started," John spoke with just a hint of that dragonic hum in his voice.

"Say less," Cal responded. He unleashed a fierce "Hiyah" as he plunged headfirst into battle, and with the sudden roar of over three hundred Insurrectionists, the Scarlet forces were thrown into chaos. Cal bounded into the city with repulsors ablaze and kyoketsu-shoge to grapple. His platoon of 30 followed suit, and emerged from the southwest in a flurry of bright orange light in the darkness of the early morning.

The Scarlet patrols opened fire on them, and though they managed to nail a few Yaiba warriors between the eyes, 22 of them still flew around the battlefield with their targets in sight. To the Reds, whose mobility was limited to grounded movements only, the Violet Shadows were exactly that, violet shadows that shimmered in the blur of their own movements.

Regardless of how fast they flipped and flung themselves across the multileveled terrain of Johnson City, Cal was able to estimate the count of rapidly firing enemies below. They numbered somewhere between thirty and forty, and though they held their ground with a hail of bullets, it was hardly a continuous stream. Cal chuckled, and his men were less than impressed. For all their "esteemed" training, the Reds lacked coordination. Any strategist against an enemy of equal or greater strength would arrange a firing squad in a staggered formation so that some may fire while others loaded their weapon and then switch the order to produce a continuous spray. These troops just fired aimlessly with no direction, all at once as if they hoped to strike their enemies with luck alone. There was a term to describe such terrible gunmen in the past, but the term had been lost to time. It started with the word "storm," though Cal could never understand why.

Only a couple of minutes had passed by the time that the first of the enemy troops realized that their weapon had run out of ammunition. Seconds later, the rest of them had come to the same conclusion. They scrambled to reload, but by then it was too late for them. Cal was the first to swoop in, and instantly plunged his kyoketsu-shoge into the chest of the target nearest him. The enemy began to scatter, and the Yaiba went on the hunt. Gunshots fired in the distance to the north, southeast, and northeast towards the center of town, but Cal was only able to enjoy the sounds of their plan coming together for a split second. The enemy at the end of his kyoketsu-shoge was alive enough to slash a pocketknife straight through the boy's left eye.

Cal screamed in pain as he pulled away from his victim-turned-attacker, and as the man stumbled towards him, the young neo-ninja thrust his other kyoketsu-shoge through the enemy's throat. He collapsed to the ground, and Cal bounded off in search for cover.

****

October 24th, 2084, 3:16 a.m.,

Devin Dross jumped into the fray as soon as he heard the first gunshots from the southwest area of the city. His platoon, like a stampeding herd of elephants, spread through the northernmost part of the city as the enemy attacked. With the full register of his

Hanzo Gear under his control, Dross blasted forth on the repulsors with his kyoketsu-shoge spread to either side. The enemies before him shot at him to no avail, but then fell silent as their heads rolled from their shoulders to the ground.

Five of his own men fell to the onslaught of bullets brought by the Red dogs, and as he rolled along the ground, he cast one of the chains so that the blade sliced through the legs of one of the assailants. The other noticed him, and before the concept of response time entered Devin's mind, he cast the other bladed chain directly through the lips of the other enemy. Another Red that he'd earlier dodged approached him from behind, and in a rare display of acrobatics, he used the repulsors to bound upward and tied his legs in a knot around the enemy's throat.

Seven more of his men fell lifeless to the ground as his latest victim started to fade. Three enemy soldiers to the front of him turned their guns on Dross, and gave no regard to the life of their comrade. *Typical,* Dross thought as he dismounted the neck of his victim and kicked him forward into the line of fire. *Scarlets don't care about anyone other than themselves.* He spun left along the ground to rapidly dodge the shots of the man on the left and whipped his kyoketsu-shoge through the attacker's neck. His spray, formerly steady and forward, now tilted upward as the Scarlet troop fell to the ground.

Devin's Reikiken burned through the stomach of the barely conscious man that previously served as his human shield. Dross ran for the next one in the lineup, the woman that held the center position before her comrade got taken out. There was emotion in those brown eyes of hers, anger and hatred that derived from more than just an ideological difference. Her rifle shook with her rage and she fired a scattered array of bullets. She managed to hit her target in the chest, but the ballistic resistance of the Hanzo Gear tunic saw that he was barely slowed at all in his advance. She screamed as she fired more, and her sudden vociferation spurred her remaining comrade to action.

Devin was forced to slam the titanium blades of his kyoketsu-shoge into the ground and blast into the air with his repulsors. He ran through the air as if on the ground, and only occasionally had to bury the edge of the chain-locked blades into the sides of buildings to keep from an unsavory descent. With their eyes on the airborne Dross, the Scarlet Troopers below missed the swift onslaught of two grounded and unencumbered Yaiba operatives. The neo-ninjas cut down the two that attacked their captain, then dispersed to tend to other hostiles in the area.

Dross, still running along the air, swooped down like a bird of prey on a cluster of enemy soldiers. With a flurry of blades and bright orange flashes he felled them one after another, and darted ahead to take on yet another.

Devin Dross was so busy carving a path to the center of the battlefield that he missed the sniper nestled comfortably on the roof of the dilapidated intermediate school. The shooter watched her target carefully as he, the strong blond man with a body that looked to be carved of marble, beat and burned and bladed his way through a host of her comrades on the ground. She followed him with her crosshairs, eyed him through the scope, but as she readied her shot she couldn't help but think that there was something about him that drew her in.

It could've been his looks, of course. He had a jawline as cut as the rest of his body, a milky complexion with cheeks red from the constant movement in battle, blond hair in needle-like strands, and so many other qualities that she dared not even acknowledge. The truth was, everything about his body teased her taste and threatened to pull her too far astray from the battle. He was the enemy, and it was her job as the ace sniper at this duty station to do what she could to eliminate every threat.

Still, though… he was so in control of his subordinates. She saw the fierce expression on his face as he barked orders, the way his perfect lips would lift into a cocky smirk as he fought on the ground, on his feet, and in the air. He was as powerful as a titan, but as graceful as a butterfly. His men numbered at eight, now, and even though they were hopelessly outnumbered by the Scarlet forces, they burned through them like a light on a fuse line. If she didn't do something about it, her side would lose.

She slapped her hands against her cheeks and took up the sniper rifle again. She followed her mark with the patience and cunning of a rattlesnake before the strike, but when she fired, she hit one of her own companions rather than his. There was confusion. The men and women that engaged each other on the remnants of the baseball diamond froze in combined shock and terror, but another shot fired on the Scarlet Troopers woke them from their stupor.

The Reds started to retreat, and as the strong captain's remaining troops gave chase to their scattered enemy, he himself sprinted towards the school. She hastily packed up her weapon and equipment when she placed his position, and retreated into the dark, unoccupied halls of the building. She couldn't be spotted by him or anyone, for that matter. She looked down at the uniform she wore, the scarlet hue as red as the blood of her former allies splattered in the dirt by her own bullets. She had betrayed everything she ever knew, everyone she'd ever known or loved, and for what? A pretty face with a knack for control? He wouldn't understand her at all, and she figured that the moment he saw the red of her uniform would be the moment she would meet her end.

The loud metal clang told her that he'd burst through the rusted door hinges and found his way inside. She could hear his footsteps, frantic to find her, and made the decision to run down the corridor and around the corner. It would take him a moment to find her, but a moment was all she needed to give him the slip. It didn't take her that long to come upon the back stairwell. The side door at the bottom of the steps was her way out. She ran down the stairs as quickly as she could, but at the bottom, with both hands on his bright orange weapon, was the man she'd hoped to avoid.

****

October 24th, 2084, 3:36 a.m.,

Zayvier Peters led his platoon to the rooftops of the Plymouth Ridge and Blue Ridge apartments. They were quiet, still, and keenly observant of their leaders. Zay wasn't the stealthy type. That much he knew, and the game that they'd played during the attack on the Yaiba base got him thinking that he should fix that. He managed to pull it off there, yes, but it wasn't good enough. His skills weren't good enough. After all, if they had been, Emiko Ishikawa would still be the head of the Yaiba and he wouldn't have to live with the shame of being a part of the team that let her down the most.

A chill permeated the air, and the approaching sound of enemy footsteps served as a warning to calm himself. Now wasn't the time for regret. It was the time to take action against the despicable human trash that invaded their home in the first place. He eyed the coming patrol, and noted the slight nervousness in their steps. They knew that their enemies lurked in wait for the opportune moment to strike, but had no way of telling which direction they would come from.

Zayvier patiently watched as they neared the center of the broken Plymouth Road. He lifted his hand, palm open to the street and eyes locked on his enemies. He closed his hand into a fist, and his group of thirty men and women pounced from the roofs and blasted their way to the road. Chains rattled as kyoketsu-shoge were deployed and hungrily hunted for the necks, faces, hearts, legs, and arms of their masters' prey. The chilled air rose to warmth with the ignition of thirty brilliantly orange Reikiken, the lights of which gave the impression that dawn was just on the horizon.

The Scarlets, however, could only see the flames of hell as its gates swiftly opened to consume them. There was hardly any time to respond to the attack, and before too long, Zayvier and his platoon closed the distance between them and gave them even less room to breathe. The Reds shot, their aim shaky from the fear, and while they did manage to end the lives of three of their Insurrectionist attackers, the other 27 swarmed them like a plague of locusts. Zayvier grappled between the trees and buildings, spurred upwards and onward by every blast of his repulsors, and it seemed that with every movement another head was claimed.

The leader of the patrol sounded the retreat, and the men and women who were left of their small force all scattered in different directions. Zayvier's men shouted victoriously, and with his own firesword lifted, he led them deeper into the city.

All around them they could see the remnants of scattered patrols and wayward soldiers in red uniforms, hopeful that an escape from the city would mean freedom from the surprise attacks of the Roaming Company. Not even once did it dawn on any of the Reds that their attackers didn't give chase, let alone the reason for it. Zayvier tapped into his comms unit.

"We done," he said with a wide smile as his troops surrounded him and visibly threatened the already frightened remnants of the Scarlet battalion. John laughed through the channel as if he'd heard the best joke ever told. It wasn't surprising to him. In fact, it was all according to plan. He knew that if they went head to head, regiment versus battalion, the Shadows could win but not without taking heavy casualties. It was much smarter, then, to play to the enemy's arrogance. They never assumed that they would be attacked so randomly, especially with their superior armaments and numbers, which meant that the simple fact that the Insurrection was that bold was enough to rattle them into disarray.

"Perfect. All that's left is for us to do is destroy their command center and wipe out their remaining forces. Roaming Company, reinforce the Northeast, Northwest, Eastern and Western Companies from the inside. Drive them towards checkpoints A through D." He closed the comms before his subordinates could offer a reply and turned his attention back to those what, as of now, marched by his side from the southern forest. "Let's get going. I want to make it back to the compound in time for my morning cup of tea."

****

October 24th, 2084, 4:00 a.m.,

John's forces halted behind him as he eyed the outer wall of the old university. The whole thing was practically in shambles, no doubt the handiwork of their Kabuto allies from months ago. By the looks of things, they hadn't fully rebuilt, but with the Prince out west and the Scourge with him, they assumed that Johnson City wouldn't be much of a major point of attack, especially now that their key points had already been damaged when the Helmets extracted Callan. That, however, was a major oversight on the part of the Scarlet Kingdom.

John strode forward with a confidence that was almost regal, as if the entirety of the city belonged to him and him alone. It was a show, of course, and it did what it was supposed to do. A squad of Scarlet Troopers emerged from the wall, weapons pointed at the fresh Director and ready to strike. John watched them for a while as they cautiously moved closer, and thought that it was hard to take them seriously when they moved in fear. The surprise attack worked. Now it was time for the final stage, to defeat the remainder of their forces and take Johnson City whole.

"Have you come to surrender, trash?" asked their leader, whose itchy finger tapped lightly against the trigger of his rifle. "Close in," he told his comrades before John could utter an answer, and they followed the command without question. He could feel all of their weapons trained on him, and while another warrior might feel unnerved by this predicament, John Hamlin was not only at ease, but relieved to receive such a warm reception.

He smirked at the captain and watched his eyes carefully. His heartbeat hastened and it was all he could do not to grin with childish delight. Just as lightning surges from heaven to strike the ground, so does the Rairyu strike a battlefield from the mountaintop. John was at home here, a man raised by conflict and molded in adversity, and as the Scarlet Troopers took up a formation not unlike that of the training program, he was prepared to vent every frustration he'd had since the night the Reds attacked.

The captain blinked, and that was all the invitation John needed to get started. His arms, rested at his sides, twitched only slightly as they deployed the titanium blades and extra-thick chains towards the ground. The captain opened his eyes only after John was airborne and the chains were retracted. The Lightning Dragon flipped backwards and used a well-timed burst of his repulsor boots to lunge for the group of ten Scarlet soldiers that stood at his back. A slash of his kyoketsu-shoge brought them, headless, to their knees.

He blasted his repulsors again to flip forward to his feet, and as his body rotated the chain attached to his arm guided its diamond-shaped blade towards another enemy. The sheer force of the rotation brought the blade up clean through his victim's central line, and as the body fell in two, the captain finally issued the order for his remaining troops to open fire. John, however, was unfazed by the sudden rain of bullets, and in fact more than welcomed the sudden crack of gunfire. After all, what was lightning without rain and thunder? He whipped his aura sword from his hip and instantly it came to life.

He spun low to the ground, out of the crosshairs of the initial spray, then bounded into the air with the assist from his Hanzo Gear. He crossed his legs and fired the repulsors as he extended a kyoketsu-shoge to the concrete below. It pulled him as he spiraled, and while the captain and his remaining men did what they could to get out of the way, the horizontal slash that flowed effortlessly through them hit with such a speed that their bodies crumbled from a combination of blunt force and fierce burns. The captain, now burned and grounded, still clung to his life and crawled across the concrete. He grunted as his body dragged against the loose gravel and rocks, but with the rattle of chains and the sudden swish of blade through bone, the struggle stopped.

John lifted a hand, and without a word his company followed him as he strolled through the front gate of the base. The sudden presence of a chocolate-toned man in black and purple attire with a bright orange sword started the unsuspecting guards to a scramble, but before they could take up their arms, John severed their heads at the jaw with his twin kyoketsu-shoge. He slashed them through the air to clear them of blood and retracted them before he resumed his leisurely stroll. He admired what the Reds had done with the run-down old school. What was at one point a heap of ruins now stood as something akin to a small city or a fortress of some kind. It would be his pleasure to tear it down around their heads. It was, after all, the least he could do to repay them for their "services."

Frantic footsteps of frightened foes filled John's ears from the distance, and in no time at all did their makers appear before him. They lined the walkway to the front of him, and to his rear more appeared. He chuckled as he tucked his hand behind his back, pulled his right leg to the rear and angled his blade slightly upward, though a bit closer to his chest. The tension was thick in the air, and with every second that passed his anger and excitement grew. The enemies yelled, and charged him now, but John was hardly one to back down.

He ran at them as well, and with a flurry of strikes he carved a new path amid the hail of bullets. Swift stab. Pivot. Upward swing. Slight pivot. His attacks flowed one into the next with a delicate grace the likes of which the red-clad enemies had only ever seen a handful of times. Downward slash. Wide spin and horizontal swing. Downward stab through the face of an unsuspecting enemy, and more rushed to his position from every corner. He smirked, as this was a far greater challenge than any training simulation that the technicians could generate. Reverse slice. Pivot to the rear and downward strike. The head of an oncoming foe crumbled under the weight. He started to sweat, but noticed that so did they.

The men in the Southern Company, those charged with protecting the Director and carrying out his every order, could only stand in the background and watch. It was amazing to see one of the Dragons in action, but even more incredible to see him bulldoze his way through an entire company of men with such control and poise.

Leg sweep. Diagonal cut. Reverse diagonal cut. John's onslaught continued, and with each swing the rain of bullets became more of a loose drizzle and the thunder behind it more of a dull roar. Stab to the front. Small flourish and adoption of reverse grip. Stab to the rear. Swift turn and stunning revolution. Downward slash. More and more enemies fell at his feet and the air adopted the putrid stench of burned flesh and salted sweat. He looked around and was surprised that none more than the thirty that stood around him remained.

"I'm a little disappointed," he said aloud as he bolted in an irregular pattern through the bullets and bodies. He took to the air once again and spiraled as he extended his kyoketsu-shoge. Three heads were severed from their shoulders as he ascended, and as he tilted forward, he drove his twin blades and the chains that held them through the torsos of another two. His repulsors rocketed him to the ground, but just as before he used another burst from them to flip forward and land upright. The second his feet touched the ground he became an infernal tornado.

He spun towards the nearest enemy and burned his firesword through his neck as he extended the bladed chain and cut the stomach of one farther off. The rotation continued and as he brought his sword through the midsection, he swiped the titanium diamond through the neck of a distant enemy. He pulled the kyoketsu-shoge back in before he thrashed it against the ground like a whip, and the sharp blade at its end cut clean through another adversary. Twenty remained. The Lightning Dragon, under fire, spun and flipped and dodged as best as he could to avoid serious injury. Every now and again the bullets would connect with his tunic and outer cloak, but they more often strayed from their target and hit friendlies in the area.

They fired on him still, their frantic shouts as loud as the thunder that echoed from their muzzles, but though they tried to keep their distance, they could see that their bullets did little to ruffle his ballistics-resistant clothing even if they did survive the distorting effects of the heat field around him. He approached, still at a sprint, though it was much lazier than it had been before when there were more of the Scarlets to keep his attention occupied. Before long, John was back on the attack.

Decapitation. Downward diagonal slash. Pivot and stab. Retract and pivot again with an upward swing. Spin the blade to generate momentum and downward strike to burn through a body. That was five more, and the remaining fifteen whispered prayers to the Dawn King to save them as they yet fought the Dragon before them. Wide spin and horizontal swing. Three more felled in an instant. Twelve remained. Spin of the blade over the head and decapitation. Reverse-grip stab. Retraction, spin into standard grip and reverse upward swing. Stab forward and kyoketsu-shoge extension to the rear. Downward swing then quick pivot to the rear and forward thrust. Seven down. Five more, just a little across the way.

They stood there, frozen at the sight of the pure monster before them. He was no man. No man could mow through an entire company of 250 men on his own strength. John smiled at them, and before their minds could catch up to their bodies, they ran from him. With a twitch of his arm, the chains rattled again. With a flick of his wrist, his enemies were decapitated.

Silence. There were no more enemies here. Everyone else had been deployed to meet the threat of the Roaming Company and likely either killed or steered to the main roads to be killed by now. John, covered in sweat, a little dirt and the blood of his enemies, turned to address his troops, who at this point discovered a newfound fear of the leader of the Seven Dragons.

"Alright, fan out. Destroy any enemy tech you uncover, salvage what you can from the food supply and weapons caches. Make sure you check for any trackers. We don't wanna tip our friends in New York off to the fact that we're stealing their weapons, do we?" He let out a deep, satisfied sigh. "I'll be looking for this 'Jr. Hall' that Callan told me about." Without another word, the congregation of Violet Shadows dispersed and in a matter of moments the silence was replaced by the sound of breaking glass and smashing plastic.

John took it all in as he strolled lightly down the walkway and across a broken slab of concrete with tufts of moss and grass sprouting up from its carcass. His plan had been a success and the city was now his. All before sunrise, too. It would take the Reds a while to mobilize their forces now that the Kabuto had scrambled their drone commands and destroyed their new secret weapons. That meant that there was time to fortify the entire stretch from the mountain to Johnson. He walked a few more feet, and when he noted the weathered and broken sign that read "Jr. Hall," he promptly entered.

There was an extravagant fragrance about the place mixed in with mold and sweat that told him that this was where the Prince was housed during his stay. It was a good sign, because where better to keep a command center than near a powerful figure such as he? He made his way through the old dorm and opened door after door. It didn't take him long to discover a room full of monitors and a projector. Jackpot. He entered the room, but a shift from behind him made him turn in time enough to catch the flailing arm of a rather round man who only barely managed to fit the red armor that girded his body.

John twisted behind his attacker, the man's arm still firmly in his grasp and with poorly relented force, drove the red-clad's face into the dirt. He placed a knee on the man's neck, but then thought back to his history lessons and moved his knee to the man's temple instead.

"Don't kill me," he begged through tears that dampened the dirty floor beneath his head. John chuckled as he twisted the man's arm.

"Kill you? Why would I do that? Someone has to go before the King and tell him what happened here, after all," he said. He pulled out his Reikiken and pressed his palm against the heat-syphon hard enough to activate its flashfire mode. The sword burned bright and hot in an instant, and with a look at his captive, John was able to see how intimidating it was for an outsider to see such a weapon up close. The fat man trembled with great terror as the temperature of the room rose. John, ever in the mood to have fun at another's expense, pulled his weapon hand back far enough to give the impression that he would drive it through the Red soldier's skull.

The soldier closed his eyes tightly, and John laughed as he pushed it forward into the projector table. The thing caught fire from the heat, and John moved away from the groveling coward on the ground to slash at the monitors. The control room was destroyed, and with Johnson City cleared, the mission was accomplished. He turned his attention back to the bear of a man that he'd taken down, and with a wordless glare, inspired him to hastily take his leave.

****

October 24th, 2084, 8:57 p.m.,

The battles of the main roads were lengthy, but not too much. Callan's Western Company finished first, followed by the Eastern, then the Northeast and Northwest Companies respectively. The rest of the day was spent remotely deliberating with the construction crew, planning for the Scarlet Kingdom's inevitable retaliation efforts, and more than anything else, going through the wares and goods left behind by the departed red-clads. It was only after they'd been at it for hours that they'd realized Devin Dross when he approached with a woman in red, handcuffs around her wrists.

"The hell is going on here," Zayvier said in a rare outburst. John looked up from Cal's side, hand still gently on the side of the boy's face that bore his bandaged injury, to see the dark skin, curves, black hair, and the distinct red uniform of the Scarlet army. He looked at Zay, who corrected himself instantly. "I'm sorry, Rairyu." John waved it off.

"No, no, you're absolutely right. Dross, the hell is going on here," John inquired sharply, eyes narrowed. The look on his face made Devin freeze, and even startled the captive by its sheer intensity. Though he hesitated, Dross brought her forward to meet the Director if out of nothing but respect for him as a person and a personal mentor.

"Sir, this sniper," *this envy of angels*, he thought as he spoke to the Director formally, "fired on her own comrades while I fought them. In the hours since our initial attack, she's given me no sign that she bears any hostility towards our people."

"What do you expect is gonna happen here, Dross," John asked, and folded his arms. Cal stirred in the background. Even though he'd been given a hasty dose of pain medication, it would take a lot more than that to ease the discomfort. Manny stood by him and held his hand to try and sooth him a little more. John returned his gaze to his subordinate.

“I have information about the Kingdom that might useful to you,” spoke the woman. John eyed her more closely, and though nervous, she continued. “All of their key bases. Their intel. Their communications networks. Their plans for the Wastes. I’ll give it all up willingly if you take me with you.” John’s ears perked up at the mention of the Wastes.

“Name,” he demanded, and the girl shook.

“Zahara Boyd,” she responded.

“You betrayed your comrades,” he said flatly, his piercing eyes just as intensely hot as the sword he brought to life in battle. “For what reason?” The woman hesitated for a moment. It was difficult for her to talk about her life back in the Kingdom. But she knew that if she didn’t say anything, her life would be forfeit right here and now.

“I’m dark-skinned. I might’ve been fighting with them for a time but I was never their comrade. I was a tool, plucked from a family bound by a military past and fine-tuned for war against people who share more in common with me than the ones I was raised around. The moment I thought to take the shot to kill your grunt here was the same moment I thought about finally being free,” she told him. There was no deceit in her eyes, nor was there anything shifty about her tone. Even still, John couldn’t base his decisions on pure sentiment with no rationality.

“Well you won’t be,” he told her. “Load her onto a transport. When we’re back at base, take her down to the detention level.”

“But—” she began to protest, but John raised his hand.

“You’ll have a chance to prove yourself when you give us your intel. If it turns out to be true and you’re not just telling us what we want to hear, we’ll grant you asylum with us and induct you into our ranks. Until then, please understand that I have to protect my people.” He walked away from her, and while Dross escorted her to the transport, John returned to his post by Cal's side.

Chapter Fifteen

October 24th, 2084, 10:15 p.m.,

The King drove his fist into the table before him, and the entire Court jumped in fear. The report had only come in a few moments ago, and while the sole survivor of the Johnson City encampment relayed the events, the King gave no indication of emotion. Now that the man had since ended his transmission, however, the King was loath to mask his indignation.

"The loss of Johnson City marks the second blatant attack on my Kingdom in the span of ten days," he grumbled, and ice filled the room.

"It appears, Sire," sniveled Lord Phineas Blackwell, "that these outcasts have forgotten their place."

"Appears," Marquis West mocked in a typical display of arrogance. "It simply is, Lord Blackwell. The lower factions have mistaken our kindness for weakness, and it's time to fire back."

"Do you presume to give your King orders, Marquis West?" The King's tone was rife with irritation, and his eyes dared the lesser nobleman to speak carelessly again. Instead, West shook his head like a frightened child.

"Never, Your Grace," he assured him quickly. The Marquis cleared his throat. "I merely meant to say that we cannot allow this brazen behavior to go without consequence."

"Yes, but how will we do that," Countess McBride asked in her signature timidity. She rarely spoke during these meetings, and seldom ever dealt with the nobility outside of them, so when she did, everyone listened. "I only meant that the drones are still offline. I haven't been able to get so much as a package, so coordinating an airstrike on the Yaiba is out of our reach."

"Yes, and the Helmets that took out our largest weapons depot haven't had a steady home since we tested our bomb last spring," Baron Stalks said bitterly as he glared at Prince Nash. He wasn't so bold as to call out the Prince in front of King Shane, but this retaliatory complication needed to be addressed regardless. Prince Nash cleared his throat nervously, and avoided eye contact with his father.

"The Kabuto attack on the Penn Armory and Research Facility was unfortunate, but just because we don't have air support on our side right now doesn't mean we're unable to fire back," the Prince said in an attempt to shift the focus from himself. "Our ground forces were more than sufficient to end the line of Ishikawa and it was they who discovered the location of the Yaiba base. What's stopping us from going back and tearing them apart?"

"The fact that they stormed and took an entire city with a single battalion of troops. They were outnumbered two to one and they still managed to destroy 3000 of our soldiers in a single day," Viscount Leyva supplied. His answer was unwelcome amongst the nobles, but it was the truth, and in times such as these, the truth was of the utmost importance.

"Ground troops would also take time to mobilize," said Marquis West. "A large fighting force was already dispatched with Prince James to survey and potentially engage with the Yoroi Alliance. Another force twice its size has been assigned to accompany the colonists in the Old Southern Wastes. We can't just uproot them when we're so close to occupying that region again. Control of the major eastern ports is essential if we want to cut off our enemies' supply lines!"

"Right your tone, Marquis," Phineas warned, and after a heated exchange of looks, the King's displeased expression caught West's eye and coerced him to silence.

"To think that if I'd headed up the extermination squad those years ago we wouldn't be dealing with this right now," King

Shane grumbled. Nash heard this complaint often throughout the years. His father the King always said that his biggest regret was underestimating the enemy right when they were on the brink of defeat by Scarlet hands, and that it was the cornered animal that attacks the fiercest. "What of the Scourge?"

"Along with Major Crawford's intelligence unit and the 602nd Infantry Battalion, the Scarlet Scourge is out in the Southwestern Territory observing the Yoroi Alliance," Stalks informed in his humblest of tones. "But surely there must be a division capable of handling a simple counterstrike."

"No," said the King with lifted hand. "We won't waste our time with retaliatory measures at the moment. The simple fact of the matter is that aside from the Scourge and the 602nd, our forces are woefully underprepared to engage the Yaiba in a head to head conflict."

"How would His Majesty propose we fix it," Viscount Leyva asked, a mix of eagerness and respectable fear in his voice.

"You tell me, Viscount," replied the King, much to everyone's surprise. King Shane bore a twinkle of satisfied humor in his eye as he turned his gaze to the now startled noble. "Your family has proven to be exceptional in getting me results."

****

November 4th, 2084, 8:07 p.m.,

In almost a month since leaving the Insurrection, the most that Bryan Piccio had managed to do was wander about the Midwest. During his first week alone, he reflected on the look left on Sharon's face, how angry and hurt and disappointed she was to have been foolish enough to marry such a weak man. After the third day of his sullen contemplations, he was attacked, hunted by a pack of wolves displaced by the Red occupation of Johnson City.

He slept in the trees from that point on, and thanked the heavens that he'd been smart enough to take his Hanzo Gear with him.

The second week he wandered northwest, but steered clear of most of the old cities. The Second Civil War was much worst than the first, and only a handful of Old American cities still stood. They were in shambles, and most of what was left of the population had abandoned them in favor of one of the Four Factions and the protection they offered, but every now and again you could find deserters and remnants in the Wastes left behind by the war. The Southeastern Wastes were the worst for this. Hurricanes and rogues of all kinds existed in those parts, but the land was valuable. More than the land, the ports were something that the Yaiba Insurrection craved. But none of that was any of his concern now. By the end of the first week he'd realized that he hated the way the Insurrection handled things. He hated their false benevolence, their manipulation of those who trusted them, their unhealthy need to dive into battle headlong under the false pretense of fighting for the freedom of all. But most of all, he hated that his family had, time and time again, fallen victim to the ideologies of those battle-crazed fools.

By the third week, he drifted back towards Johnson City, specifically to the area that Callan and the boys had reported as the Scarlet's base of operations in the old city. He sought the Prince, but there was no sign of him. After a careful amount of surveillance, he overheard a couple of lower-class soldiers talk about how Prince James and the Scarlet Scourge had moved out to the Southwestern Territory, and that was when he picked up to venture out there as well.

He snuck into the mess of an old motor pool and stole one of their transport vehicles, though not without being noticed. Still, by the time he'd been spotted it was already too late. He was on his way, shielded by the armor plates of the car and confident enough in his new security to smile at his shooters as they fired upon him. He broke the tracker as soon as he was far enough away from

Johnson City, and continued on for hundreds of miles before he had to stop. He refueled with a gas tank he'd found in the trunk, and ran over hypothetical conversations with his wife in his head. He did this to protect her. He left to make things right with their family. It was the best thing he could think to do, and she just couldn't see it.

Bryan got back into the car and drove off into the sunset. It wasn't until 2 this afternoon that he had to refuel again, but with his eyes on the gas gauge he knew that it wouldn't last forever. Worse, still, the gas tank he'd used earlier was the last that came with the transport and he was still a ways out from his destination. Wherever that was.

There was a loud bang as a massive burst launched the car into the air. The airbag deployed, but it did little to help Bryan after the jarring explosion from below. His head, back, knees, and left arm all throbbed with pain. His ears rang with a slight metallic tinge, and his eyes blurred in the darkness. It was colder now, partially because the fall gently migrated towards the winter, partly because the desert regions of the Southwest did little to retain heat in the absence of the sun. He could hear the rushed yet synchronized footsteps of soldiers, accompanied by the assorted clicks of their weapons and equipment.

Bryan crawled from the wreckage over the broken glass of the windows. His hands were cut and bleeding, as was his face, but thankfully his Hanzo Gear kept him from sustaining any more serious lacerations to his chest or abdomen. A heavy boot collided with his gut, and while it wasn't enough to deal much damage, it turned him over on his back. The face he saw when he looked up was enough to halt his breath and bring a tear to his eye. He reached up slowly, gingerly, determined to grace the face of his onlooker with a gentle touch before another soldier kicked his arm back to the dirt and drove the muzzle of his rifle into Bryan's face. He chuckled, though whether from renewed hope or wonton disbelief he had no idea. She screamed at the other soldier, and with lightning reflexes he pulled his gun away and drove the butt of it into the ground as a sign of extreme compliance.

Subordinates, Bryan mused as his consciousness began to fade. *I always knew my little girl was a boss...*

****

November 8th, 2084, 8:00 a.m.,

Class would start in roughly thirty minutes, and Darius was more excited than he'd been for a while. His first class was a difficult one, mostly because he had to shame his students before they could get through any significant material, but it was sometimes necessary to destroy a thing before creating something new. It felt like a waste of time before, but the results of his students proved otherwise.

Bobbi Brynarr, the woman with the honey-brown hair and matching eyes, was the one that surprised him the most. She was beautiful to him, her curvy body everything that a young man dreams about and her aloof yet wise personality proved to be beyond fascinating, but her feminine wiles and goofy charms misled him momentarily into believing that she didn't have a knack for combat. He was mistaken. It was only after class that he'd found out that she was something of a bare-knuckle boxing champion in the underground scene of the Yoroi, and he didn't know what was more impressive to him: the fact that she indulged in such a brutal sport with nothing to show for it, or that there was something in the Yoroi Alliance more underground than this.

Less surprising was the blond muscular man that Darius had attack him on day one. He was in his early twenties, so a couple years older than Darius himself. Realizing that made him marvel at how easy it was to forget his own youth when in charge of someone else's education. This man, Lex Ford was his name, managed to grow by leaps and bounds in such a short time despite his propensity for wide swinging arcs. He would be something if he ever took up the Tsuchiryu form.

Alongside him was Leroy Baptiste, the man with the black hair, dark eyes and distinguished beard, who made it surprisingly difficult to guess his next move. He performed the movements sloppily at first, but improved with each sparring match and every minute instructional note that Darius provided. His lack of expression in combat was a very valuable tool.

Those three students excelled with little problems, and in fact made Darius search the pools of his memory to give them something that would hold them over for a little while. Even below them, the others in the class were all determined to impress their new master, or at the very least defeat him in combat so as to earn the right to do as they pleased. That is, except for Tony Landry, the androgynous person with golden eyes and black hair, who struggled to master even the most basic of movements. They were a source of irritation for Darius, but at the very least they made things entertaining. Still, it was his job as a teacher to stifle the laughter and exhibit the utmost patience.

He checked the clock on the wall as his class started to filter in. As always, Bobbi was the first to arrive, followed by Leroy and Tony. Lex arrived shortly after, and while the others that filtered in one after another found their places on the floor, Darius noted the wry look on Bobbi's face.

"You seem a little eager to start, Ms. Brynarr," he said playfully, and looked around to see that most of his students had the same look. This was only their third week of training, but the atmosphere had shifted so much that he felt as though it'd been years since he arrived. "Okay, you all seem a little excitable today. What's going on?" The students laughed at the suspicion in his voice.

"What's the matter, Teach," Leroy all but taunted with his charming southern accent. "Sounds to me like you're a little nervous."

"He's just scared that we'd try to gang up on him again," Lex answered on Darius' behalf. The class laughed again, and Darius, too, offered a chuckle albeit a bit more terrified than those of his students. It was true that about a week and two days before, he walked into an ambush. His students beat him to class, hid amid the stone pillars in the dark of the training facility, and waited for just the right moment to pounce. Darius had only narrowly survived that encounter without a single hit and barely had a second to bring out his Reikiken before the others started to swing their swords. Luckily for the Rebel Dragon, his preferred method of combat was one of absolute defense, and enabled him to take on and take down at least twenty opponents at once.

"Please," Darius said as the laughter quieted. "You're at least five people short to pose a threat to me, and ten short at your current skill level."

"Then we'll just have to do something about that, won't we," Lex said with a slightly threatening grin.

"If that's your way of asking me to get started with the lesson, don't worry," Darius assured them with a charming smile. "I've got just the skill-builder for you. I need five groups of three."

"Hold up," Bobbi asked as the fourteen other students moved about the floor. Darius looked at her, a puzzled expression plastered about his face.

"What's up, Bobbi," he asked, "you look like you wanna ask something."

"Yeah, ummm…" she paused and looked around at the others. "Why are we doing this?"

"Well, I thought I'd give you a break from drilling the basics. You've all familiarized yourselves with the standard cadences and speed-drills from Hikariryu and after what I saw a few days ago, you all have a knack for teamwork and group exercises work really well for what I had planned for the next phase of your training." Darius spoke louder for the others to hear now. "Take a good look at the members of your groups. These same people will be…" He paused deliberately and surveyed the cocky grins and annoyed glares from each of his students. He could almost hear their minds come alive with the question of who their teams were fighting, "your enemies for this exercise. Right where you are, you're going to have a free-for-all style matchup. Three competitors, everyone for themselves."

The arrogant looks turned to pleading as they stared at their instructor. Part of them hoped that he had been joking, that he wasn't serious. Yes, attacking him as a group was a great show of their coordination and skill, but that saw them as a cohesive unit, not adversaries prone to in-fighting.

"This doesn't seem fair," Tony cried. Their voice was feminine, which gave Darius a start just the same as the one he had when they met. That aside, his face reflected seriousness now. "How do you expect us to be able to fend off two enemies at once when all we know are the basics?"

"It does seem a little harsh to 'reward us' with an exercise like this, Teach," Leroy stated with an air of uncertainty of how this was going to go.

"It might be," Darius admitted. It surprised him how easy it was for him to act like his father in these moments. But then, some things he just picked up from simple exposure to his dad. John hated being questioned when he gave a directive, and now Darius understood why. "Regardless of how harsh it is, it's the standard for everyone in the Violet Shadows to go through training like this."

"But why," Bobbi reiterated, her arms folded as though her patience was gradually lost by the second. "We were just learning how to do all these movement drills last week."

"How is a drill going to help you if you get surrounded by the enemy and you need to break up the sequences you've learned into more practical attacks and defenses," Darius snapped, obviously fed up with all the questions. He calmed himself. It wasn't right for him to yell at them. They were still new to this, after all, and the security of the Yoroi's outer defenses ensured them that they didn't have to even come in contact with battle if it wasn't their wish. It actually made him jealous how spoiled and privileged they were. "A battle against the Scarlet Kingdom is unpredictable. Sometimes you'll be one on one, but that's usually after a massive slugfest with your squad pitted against theirs. If you want to survive, you have to be able to switch between targets quickly, use the weapons at your disposal, and adapt practically without thinking. Running drills helps you get the basics of a fighting style. Sparring practice gives you the ability to use those skills freely." He stifled a chuckle. He sounded like his old teachers the more he taught his own students.

Bobbi looked around and joined the only group with two members. Leroy took up a squad with Tony and a young brunette woman named Christi, who graciously thanked him for lending them his strength. Lex and the stronger gentlemen in the class, DeShawn and Gael, formed their squad with more excitement than was expected. Darius thought it unusual that Lex, the most prolific complainer of the group, had little issue doing what he was told in this instance. Once everyone had found their groups, Darius gave them permission to begin.

It didn't take long for them to use their creativity, though it was at the expense of the form. Darius reminded them to make good technique as they fought, and occasionally took a moment to show them why certain things won't work in a real fight. He let them go again, and this time the group as a whole did a lot better.

They were grounded, their backs straight, shoulders square, eyes ever watchful of their two opponents. They figured out how to pivot and turn on their own, and paired it with a stagger of their footwork to occasionally confuse their opponents. It also made up for a speed deficiency that they'd noticed ages ago.

Tony, though, seemed to really shine in this exercise. They had fumbled with proper defense in the drills from before, and struggled to make good technique when attacking at a phantom opponent, but here, in practical application, it seemed as if they were a natural at the form. Darius was extremely impressed, and commended her audibly. The praise he offered struck home with the others, who instantly increased their efforts to be noticed by their master.

Coordination became a part of the experience, which made Darius happy.

"Good," he told them. "Everybody stop for a second. I've noticed that some of you are starting to really find your bearings for combat. Are we noticing anything in particular about this exercise?" Patrick, the younger man from Bobbi's group, raised his hand. "Yes?" He moved his bright orange hair out of his pale, freckled face and smiled.

"Sometimes the best thing to do is cut down the number of enemies you have to make the work easier on yourself," he answered, and Darius nodded with a smile of his own.

"Absolutely. If you're surrounded by more than one enemy and you need to take them both down, work with one to take out the other." Darius' statement clearly went over the heads of a good number of them, and he decided to take it from another angle. "Coordination on a battlefield hardly requires everyone in the fight to be friends. If everyone's gunning for you, lead their attacks towards their friendlies and when they take each other out of the equation it should be easier for you to handle what's left."

"Oh, I get it now," said Aaron Conrad, a young man with sharp features and a perpetual sly grin on his brown-goateed face. He ran a hand through his curly brown hair and half the ladies that heard his voice eyed him with a deep-seated thirst. "It's a 'by any means necessary' sorta game."

"Yes, exactly," Darius confirmed. "When you think about combat, the quickest way to get yourself killed is by letting your brain relax. Battle is a conversation and a dance. You won't get very far if you can't think of the right words or the right moves, so do whatever works in the moment. Be smart, and you'll do fine." He checked the clock on the wall again and tapped his foot anxiously against the stone floor. "It's time to go. Practice on your own, but instead of imagining you have one opponent, picture having at least two. Next time we'll up it to three groups of five so I can see how you handle it and if it's too tough, we'll go back to the inverse and practice there until you're ready." The students winced as if from pain at the mention of the hard training yet to come, but with satisfied smiles they all exited the training hall. The teacher breathed a sigh as he made for the door.

Darius couldn't help but applaud all of his teachers for making the job look so easy when it wasn't. He walked the rocky streets of the Alliance, past a number of brightly colored shop signs and dimly lit restaurants whose tantalizing aromas and soothing atmospheres caressed the senses and invited him in. For a moment he had to wonder if what he saw in the tall buildings and streams of shopping, service and entertainment was a portal to the past. He had heard stories from the older folks in the Insurrection about how the ruins of cities across the continent were once alive with noise and full to the brim with people young and old. It was like that here, carved into a great stone landmass and out of the sight of the Scarlet Kingdom.

It made him curious what it was like to live here fully, as one of the Yoroi and not as some outsider that they still treated like a social leper. He turned towards the crater car tracks and pushed past a cluster of Yoroi civilians who disregarded his presence and stood in the middle of the path. They complained, and one of the older women told him to go back to where he came from. He eyed her a moment and wondered how a civilized outcast like her learned to speak the same xenophobic drivel of the Scarlets, but ultimately decided the situation was beneath him and pressed on after a less-than-sincere apology.

Not even a full minute had passed before the woman erupted again with shouts of anger and accusations of stupidity. Darius looked behind him to notice that the latest to incur the wrath of the beastly lady was none other than his student, Tony. They smiled warmly at him as they approached, and while he returned the gesture, it was a cause for concern that any of his students would follow him this far away from the training facility.

"Mr. Hamlin," they called, slightly winded from an apparent run. The crowd of people in the area continued to bustle about, and routinely knocked shoulders with Darius as he stood motionless before his charge. "Mr. Hamlin, I needed to talk to you about today's training exercise."

"Hmm…" suspicion was replaced with the jovial attitude he'd commonly displayed in his instruction as he said, "I hope you're not trying to get a leg up on your classmates. Not that you'd need it after today. I never would've guessed that you could move like that." Tony clasped their hands together and looked away from Darius. It was clear to him that they had a crush on him, and he wondered if this was their way of testing the waters.

"I didn't either," they said with a femininity that wasn't present at all during the day's training. "Can we talk somewhere less crowded?" After another knock against his shoulders, Darius reluctantly agreed. "Follow me, I know just the place." Tony walked through the crowd to a larger square where the people who walked had room to breathe. There was a lot of noise, both from the people and the crater cars that moved in the distance between this portion of the Yoroi territory and the two others. "Come on,"

Tony said when they caught Darius ogling at every bright light and moving crater car. He didn't hear at first. Things were so loud here, totally unlike the typically quiet tunnels of the Yaiba Insurrection. It was almost as if he'd missed living life for as long as he'd been alive. Tony yelled again, and this time got his attention.

He sighed, disappointed that he couldn't stop for even a second of honest tourism. Even so, his student needed him, and it was his responsibility to help them however he could. It wasn't long before they'd led him down a dimly lit path, out of the view of the general public. As they walked, a sense of uneasiness swept the teacher. It was quieter here, which only made the silence that rose between them that much more uncomfortable. He noticed their curves, embellishments of the flesh that could only be described as female, though it was clear that their identity was something more fluid.

Regardless, Darius was attracted to them, the tender lips, the soft skin, the way her body bodied him with its very image and sway when they walked. But he was their teacher, and that was something to be honored. Even if they were close in age. Even if they could get away with it… He shook his head free of the cobwebs and asked his student, "What was it you wanted to talk to me about?"

Tony turned to face him, and with tears in their eyes, they told Darius "I'm sorry," before they buried a knife in his abdomen. Speechless, the Rebel Dragon looked down at the wound that now bled profusely, and cursed beneath his breath that he'd fallen victim to such a simple attack. He looked at Tony again, whose expression was full of sincere regret, and realized that their apparent lack of skill, their interest in him, their protests and questions in class for the last month, all of it was a ruse to learn where to strike and how. He had been played like the lute in his favorite fantasy novel, and all his attacker could say was, "I never wanted to do this. They made me!"

They were gone, and Darius was left in the dark alley friendless, foreign, and fading to black…

****

November 8th, 5:47 p.m.,

Nash reached out again, but there was still no answer. He was offended. The one time he decided to act like James was actually his little brother was the time where he was conveniently unavailable. He tried calling again. There was a faint crackle of fire in the background as the image of Prince James, colored blue by the projection, appeared before his elder brother like a ghost from the great beyond.

"It's about time you answer," Nash said without even a slight effort to disguise his irritation. "Do you have any idea how many times I've called you?"

"I lost count after 38," James said with a wry grin that incensed his brother all the more. "Honestly, if you're calling to mock my assignment, then you should end the call here—"

"Johnson City has been taken over," Nash interrupted with exasperated seriousness. He watched James sober. It was unusual to see him think so clearly when he had built a reputation as just another blithering idiot of a prince with no tactical sense whatsoever. The last few months, though, had proven that perception to be less than informed. Nash had to wonder if his brother was sleeping with the Scourge's leader for something more than just pleasure. James looked up from his thoughts, and the look in his eye was enough to cause his older brother to pop a finger on instinct. James raised his eyebrows, as he hadn't seen this nervous tic from his brother since their late teens. Under different circumstances, he might've teased him about it, but he was too focused.

"What did dad have to say about that?" James knew that he was forbidden to call his father anything other than King, but he didn't care. Shane O'Neill always treated James like he was no better than the outsiders, so James did everything he could to voice his disrespect for his father.

"For now it's hold your position," Nash told him, and watched as his little brother's face took on a childish look he'd not seen in ages. It was the same look that James took with every show of the King's neglect. "I'm sure he's just confident in you, James. As of right now there's nothing to fear, so stay on course."

"Yeah," James muttered. "Sure." There was a silence between them as awkward as anyone could imagine.

"So," Nash said with a hopeful expression, "about that other thing that you asked me about. You wanted me to find out what's up between Colonel Crawford and that Rouge fellow from the Yaiba?" James' eyes grew more stern at the mention of his name, and a bit more of his energy came back.

"What did you find?" He asked the question not with haste, but desperation. Serenity's attitude towards him was fine, but whenever the name of their former captive came up, her demeanor changed. At first he assumed that it was because of their failure in keeping him in custody, but it was deeper than that and he couldn't figure out why.

"Turns out that Callan Rouge is the son of a Scarlet citizen named Rosaline Kluger and a deserter, Carson Rouge," Nash informed him with the skill of a seasoned storyteller. James offered no reaction, so Nash rolled his eyes and continued. "According to our records, Carson had a fierce and bitter rivalry with Rosaline's brother, Lieutenant Owen Kluger. Actually, Carson met Rosaline after a fight with Owen at a promotion announcement. Carson beat him to Captain, and it seems like Owen just couldn't take it—"

"Is this story going anywhere or not," James asked impatiently. Nash folded his arms and gave his brother his most parental look, which prompted a swift apology.

"If you must know, yes, it is, but I can't just rush through telling it, now can I? Not when many Vothans died to bring us this information," Nash told him.

"Why *do* we say that, anyway," James inquired.

"Nobody knows. You gonna let me finish telling you what you wanna know or are you gonna keep asking questions?" James was quiet, and Nash continued. "A couple of years passed, and Carson left the Scarlet Kingdom abruptly. The only thing he left behind was his then-wife, who was charged with aiding and abetting a fugitive. The penalty, of course you know, is death." James whistled in surprise. He was caught off-guard by how romantic it was that Rosaline died to get her husband away from the harshness of the military. "If you think that's something, get this: Owen volunteered to perform her execution. He was quoted as saying that she deserved to die for having a deserter's baby."

"So Carson took Callan when he left," James determined.

"Right," Nash confirmed.

"But what does this all have to do with Serenity," James asked, and Nash smiled as wide as the Cheshire Cat.

"Looks like you're the dense one today. Carson and Owen ended up killing each other the night of the White Ruins Massacre because of Rosaline's execution. But what I haven't told you yet is that Owen left behind a daughter by the name of Serenity Kluger, but the records show that when he died her mother committed suicide. She was adopted by the only man to survive that mission: Alan Crawford. Long story short, little brother, you're caught up in the middle of some complicated family business…"

Chapter Sixteen

"Dad, look!" Jaden Piccio said as excitedly as a child. He pointed to a brilliant bird of dark brown body and bald white-feathered head and ran a bit closer to observe it. It was majestic, perched atop a slash pine with its eyes on the horizon. The orangish-yellow light of the rising sun washed the bird and the backdrop, and gave the young Jaden's eyes a more deeply pronounced glint. Bryan, who looked on, was stunned. His boy was alive, rosy-cheeked and excitable as ever. He couldn't breathe as those bright green eyes turned back to him and stared a fissure into his soul.

A warm, gentle, deeply familiar hand gripped Bryan's that sent shockwaves through his body. There, with her head on his shoulder, was Sharon, the undisputed love of his life, the woman who he'd known on every level, and then heartlessly abandoned under the pretense of doing what was best for their family. Her face, however, radiated a peace and happiness that admittedly he'd never seen. She could feel the gentle heat of her body as she gripped his arm and leaned into him like an excited schoolgirl whose crush asked to hold her hand. Wordlessly he lifted her face and stared into the mesmerizing pools of emerald shimmer. She smiled at him tenderly, as if this was the reflex that came with the sight of her husband, and he felt drawn to her like he always had.

"Dad!" That voice… it was enough to stop him in his tracks, to melt his heart and fry his brain and yet make him feel right all over again. He closed his eyes, his brow furrowed with a mixture of joy and sorrow, of anger and anguish, of peace and relief relayed in its every crease. He opened them again, and with extreme caution did he turn his head. The sight of his adopted daughter, of Lyla Ortiz, stunned him to the dropping of his jaw. "Your son's been messing with my things again! Tell him to keep out of my…" she trailed off as he rushed towards her with the sternest look on his face. "Dad?" He reached out his hand to touch her, because he couldn't believe that the young woman that stood before him, who twisted the curls of her brown velvet hair and watched him through chocolate eyes, could be real. He cupped her cheek in his hand, and felt the reality of her warm caramel skin. "Dad?" She asked it again, but the sound of her voice registered in his ears as naught more than a muffled jumble of letters. Overcome with emotion, he flung his arms around her, then looked at his wife and son with streams of tears down his face. In that moment, he thought life to be beyond perfect. In the next, he awoke.

The room was dark, but comfortable. His head throbbed and his body ached, but he had no idea why. He tried to remember, but the more he probed his mind for answers, the more Bryan saw of that dream. His heart sank. It was only a dream.

He remembered now. His wife hated him. His son was dead. He'd left the Insurrection with little more than a set of Hanzo Gear and the fullness of his own rage and sadness. He was on his way to find Prince James and the Scarlet Scourge when…

"You're awake," came the same soft alto that he'd heard in the dream. He looked up and saw before him the daughter he'd thought he'd lost all those years ago. She was just as he remembered her, albeit a lot more mature. She sat in the chair across the room, and by the unkempt state of her hair and the smears in her makeup he could tell that she'd been there by his side since she brought him here. "I'm glad. I was starting to think you weren't going to wake up."

"Lyla," he croaked. The sound of her name on his voice nearly brought her to tears as she rose from her chair and came to the bedside. "Your mother and I have been worried sick!" The sudden change in mood caught her by surprise, but made her crack a smile.

"You never lost hope that I was alive when I didn't come back from Gansu," she spoke in awe. She couldn't stifle the emotional rattle in her voice, nor did she want to. Until Bryan's expression grew serious.

"Why didn't you come back from Gansu?" He looked her over now, and noticed that she wore a blood-red battle suit with three golden stars on the collar. She was a general, somehow, and he knew instantly that it was a rank ill-gotten. "You joined the Scarlets." She looked away, as though she wouldn't be able to bear the shameful gaze her father must have cast her way, but he cupped her chin and brought her eyes back in line with his. He caressed her cheek with his thumb and gave her the fatherly smile that, until now, she hadn't even realized that she'd missed. "It's alright. You can tell me."

There was hesitation in her, but the stern look in her father's face made her speak, as if she were still the little girl that her real parents had thrown away. "I couldn't. The rest of the world doesn't live like we lived, Dad," she explained as her voice escalated. "People walk the streets of cities that have stood for thousands of years. A good portion of them are at peace with their own people, not divided like we are on Prevalence. Families see the sun on walks through the park, not as a reward for becoming a warrior." She thought back to a little girl who seemed so happy to be with parents so clearly hers. She thought she was over it, but how could she be? Her own parents abandoned her at the age of six to go live in the Southern Wastes. "So, I joined the Scarlet Kingdom as soon as we docked in Virginia."

"They must've treated you like dirt," Bryan said with a tinge of anger in his tone. The thought of someone even thinking about hurting his little girl was a source of rage for him, but to his astonishment she shrugged.

"They did at first. They tolerate us brown-skinned types but they don't really like us. Anyone darker than white is seen as a potential servant, or at least an interesting social experiment. I just happened to pass the test," she said as if the words meant nothing. She was more than content with where she was.

"What was the test you had to pass?" Bryan felt compelled to ask.

"Same as everyone else," Lyla told him with another shrug. "I had to prove to them that I could be useful. For a while that meant grunt work like cleaning the streets of the capitol, running errands for generals, you know, boring stuff. About three months in, I was assigned guard duty outside the King's chambers for a week straight." Bryan raised his eyebrows in surprise, just as she knew he would. There was a moment of silence between them as she savored the moment. It had been a long five years since she talked to him, five years since she saw his face contort with a range of emotions, and she couldn't help but enjoy every second of it.

"You guarded the King of the Reds?" was all he could think to ask, and her mouth split into a wide grin.

"And saved his life. The third night of my guard duty, a Kabuto assassin broke into the palace and tried to take him out. Sent the whole security detail into a frenzy trying to find him but I just barged into the King's personal chambers," Lyla explained as though it were no big deal. "I still have no idea how he got in there. But it didn't matter. After old man O'Neill gave me an earful and threatened to have me killed for treason or disrespecting the royal family or some pointless crap like that, the crook came in. After I shot him center-brow, the King changed his tune pretty quickly. Bumped me up to Lieutenant General and gave me special permissions to keep my Hanzo Gear and do anything else I please so long as I don't go killing the royals when they piss me off or anything."

"Lyla," Bryan's voice was stern, and the look on his face that he knew to be pensive registered with her as judgmental. It surprised her to hear him say, "I'm proud of you, kiddo." She hesitated.

"That's not exactly what I expected to hear you say," she admitted. "But thanks. Do you need anything?"

"Yeah," he said with a grin to ease his daughter's mind. "A few things. Let's start with where I am, though, and we can build from there.

"You're in a safe-house outside Harrisonburg—"

"'Harrisonburg?' We were in the Southwestern Territory before I blacked out," Bryan exclaimed the interruption, and was met with a nervously wry smile that brought out his daughter's inner girlishness.

"About that… you've been asleep for the last three days. Heading deeper into the Southwest Territory with you in tow didn't seem like a bright idea for you, me, or my subordinates, so we phoned it in and got you out." As she spoke Bryan shook his head, a look of utter disappointment and muted anger stapled to his face.

"You don't understand. I needed to talk to Prince James and the Scarlet Scourge," he all but shouted. "I needed to know if they were the ones responsible for…" he couldn't finish the sentence. Jaden's death was so much easier to admit in his dreams. There he didn't have to speak it, because it might not even be true. Jaden could live in his dreams. No fighting. No tears. No loss. But this was reality, where his son's body lay cold God only knows where, unrecovered by the people he claimed as family and spat upon by the enemies that took his life. His hands trembled at the thought, his heart and flesh burned from the anger, his eyes stung with the well of tears that sprang from his face to his clothes as though fleeing from the wrath that stewed within him. Lyla had no idea what was going on, and though she wanted to ask him questions, to uncover the source of her father's pain and be a comfort for him, she sat in silence and merely looked at him with her hand in his. A lot can change in five years. The man who so bravely took on the world up until the day she left now sat in tears opposite her. Bryan gripped her hand a little harder and said, "Jaden's dead."

The shock of those two words were enough to make a tear stream down Lyla's cheek as her body pulled its hand away from Bryan without a thought. She felt as if her brain was scrambled, and then a flood of memories with her little brother, the goofy kid that loved to mess with her stuff but loved her even more, assaulted her with every vivid recollection. She stammered and searched for the words. They wouldn't come. Lyla took a deep breath, relaxed herself, and then forced herself to meet her father's gaze.

"I'll address it with the King once we're back in the capitol. I'm sorry that he died. I'm sorry I wasn't there. If I had been," her voice cracked, and though she mouthed, she couldn't finish the thought that Bryan already knew she had.

"You did what you thought was best for you," he said as he pulled her closer to him and let her rest her head against him. She wept quietly, bitterly, and though it pained him to see, it was a relief to be around his daughter once again, and even more to be restored to the place of parent. "That's all we ever wanted for you kids. Unfortunately," his tone became colder, and though she couldn't see them, so did his eyes, "someone murdered your brother before he had a chance to and I intend to make it right." She looked up at him.

"What are you gonna do, Dad," she asked with tears in her eyes. He moved her hair out of her face, stroked her cheek with the back of his hand and smiled a genuine smile rooted in both joy and savagery.

"Don't worry, my girl," he said so sweetly that her heart melted. "I have a plan."

****

November 11th, 2084, 1:35 p.m.,

Johannes was an irritating man to question. Between him and Callan, Aria Black was unsure if there was a future left for her as an interrogator. Callan had been snide and condescending when she saw him last. He insulted everything from her character to her intelligence, but anything was better than Johannes Thornhill. He never spoke to her, never smiled, only breathed, and it was the most irritating thing in the universe. Aria wouldn't describe herself as a showy person, but she knew her worth, and in her mind, she was a queen if ever there was one. Her existence was to be celebrated, her name was to be known and respected, her personality was to be indulged in, and Thornhill refused to acknowledge her in the slightest.

Even though Aria hated this process, she had to go back into the brown camouflage tent to see him. She donned her finest perfume, put on her signature black lipstick, and brought out a black cocktail dress and heels that, while out of place in the desert, made her stand out as a bombshell of a woman. She was confident that this would crack him, since nothing else seemed to, and when she entered the tent, she did so with confidence.

Johannes eyed her, grunted, and then leaned his head back in the chair he was bound to. Bandages covered his arms and legs from where Aria stabbed him or cut him or burned him, and now she had the audacity to stand before him in a cocktail dress. He expected today's torture to be something particularly depraved.

"Good afternoon," she bade him. No response. "Do you know why I'm dressed like this?" There was, again, nothing that could be considered an answer. "You've been under my…care for a little over a month, now, and in all that time I've tortured you in as many ways as I know how." Silence. Aria sighed, exhausted of this game. "Still, you haven't even done as much as open your mouth in my presence. So, I give up." Johannes raised his brown eyebrows as he lifted his head again. Something felt off, and for some reason it made him nervous. "I don't try to make a habit of wasting my time, and trying to get you to give up information on your precious Alliance seems to be a lost cause. Please, stop me if I'm wrong," she prodded with a turn of her head in his direction, but his eyes were as cold and spiteful as ever. "I thought not. So, since I can't open you up, I was wondering if you wouldn't mind…opening me up instead?"

Johannes' eyes nearly doubled in size at the suggestion. He couldn't believe that someone would even say it like that, let alone someone that he knew beyond a shadow of a doubt to be an enemy. And even if he were to, it would be wrong. It would be twisted. It would go against everything he stood for and violate the trust that he had with his people, with the Yaiba Insurrection, and with *her*.

"No," he said flatly, the first word he'd spoken to her since his capture. Aria couldn't believe it, but shocking though it was, she retained a sultry demeanor as she strode closer to him. She knelt down before him, her upper body between his legs, her dark eyes locked on his shimmering green ones.

"Are you sure," she asked with a predatory smirk. "It must be lonely in here when I'm not around. A man as attractive as you must be used to getting any woman you want." She traced circles with her finger along his inner thigh, and though he tried to jerk away, the restraints that bound him to the spot prolonged his suffering. "A month dry isn't easy for anyone—"

"Please, stop," he grunted through clenched teeth. It took every ounce of discipline he had to keep his body from reacting to her touch.

"How come," she asked as playfully as a lover. "Your muscles are tensing. Your breaths are getting shorter and shorter." Her voice was little more than a whisper now as she rose to her feet and leaned in. Her face was centimeters from his, and the sweet smell of her perfume taunted him more. "I didn't want to torture you, you know. If it were my choice, I'd have found another way to make you open your mouth, if for no other reason than to scream my name."

"Enough," cried the captive emissary as he squirmed away from her. She took his lips with her own and savored the taste of him on her tongue.

"I don't think you mean that," she hummed and looked down at his lap. "I think you want to, but right now you're too hurt and tired to put any conviction behind it." She saw the fire behind his eyes start to dwindle, and knew that if she kept it up she might get somewhere.

"What do you know about me?" Johannes snapped, as aggravated as he was aroused. It was difficult for him to focus on anything besides her gentle face and soothing voice. Gradually he took in the way she smelled and even how she tasted. Her curves and caresses excited him even through the pain of his limbs, and while he wanted to get another taste, to work out all the aggression she had given him through a primal release of passionate hatred, the thought of *her* compelled him to get ahold of himself.

"I know you want me, but you're fighting it," she told him as she ran a finger down his chest. "I know that you think that there would be consequences to this, but there aren't—"

"But there are!" He shouted it before he realized it, and hated himself for it. "There's something—someone—that I can't risk." Aria leaned in and once again conjoined their lips.

"They never have to know," she said soothingly, but his reaction was irate.

"I already told you to stop!" To Aria it sounded more desperate than angry. She took a moment to gaze into his forest-colored eyes and found that they retained no trace of the fire he'd exhibited over the month. She smiled at him honestly as she leaned towards him. She placed her hand gently on the back of his head as she traced the edge of his ear with her tongue.

"What are you going to give me if I do?" Her expression was as conniving as a cat that'd cornered a mouse. She could feel his breath brush her shoulder. He was nervous, excited, giddy, and guilty, and she could taste it in every kiss she'd stolen from him. She pulled back a moment, and with excitement in her eyes he spoke to her all the secrets that he knew.

****

November 11th, 2084, 1:52 p.m.,

The door to the Prince's tent whipped open with a burst of cold air that grabbed everyone's attention. Aria hesitated a moment, caught off-guard by the meeting of the Scourge and Prince James.

"Sorry to interrupt," she said, her previous confidence suddenly nowhere to be found.

"Not at all," James replied with a smile. "Did you get him to talk?" There was just enough of a threat behind his voice to assure her that this was her final opportunity to impress.

"I did," she confirmed. "The suspicions of the higher-ups are confirmed to be fact. Yaiba and Yoroi have brokered an alliance, and the Kabuto Sanctuary is in on the whole thing too." The reception to the news was mixed. Trisha Kant looked as if she might cry while her sister Cecelia merely chuckled with excited expectation. Kerri shrugged as though she didn't care, and the Prince and his Colonel both radiated intensity that stirred the air like a storm.

"This isn't good," James muttered. "Three days ago, we received a transmission from Prince Nash that Johnson City has been taken by the Insurrection, which means that any reinforcements we may need will be delayed. The Kabuto Sanctuary has already turned to violence on top of their sabotage as we witnessed firsthand. Now we're in prime position for what could be the greatest pincer attack the modern world has ever seen."

"It gets worse," she told them, and this time the entire room became sober. "Thornhill said that there were talks of a shipment of Hanzo Gear being moved into the Yoroi Alliance. Knowing Emiko, they wouldn't just turn over their weapons without a reason, and even then, they'd have to make sure that their allies knew what they were doing with them."

"So you think they're sending them a teacher?" Serenity asked.

"Oh I hope they do," Cecelia practically sang. Nothing made her happier than the idea of combat, and the fact that they were sent on a scouting mission made her mind grow hungry for something more.

"We're assuming that they haven't already," Kerri, the brunette bombshell chimed in. "If they've already taken Johnson City from the battalion we left there, it's possible that we missed the deployment of Yoroi troops to go and help their new allies."

"But," squeaked Trisha as she nervously played in her blonde hair, "wouldn't we have picked up on that? I just don't think we'd miss a large force moving across Prevalence like that."

"You have a point," the Prince was forced to admit. He was silent for a while. Pensive. If what their captive said was true, then there wouldn't be a lot of options on the table for a tactical win. Their EMPs could only be deployed in a location far enough away from their own tech, but if the Yaiba found a way to take an entire city from a whole battalion of Red soldiers, then it was likely that they just rushed in when their mark's guard was at its lowest. "I really wish we had an idea of how large their army is. If we did, we might be able to flush them out and bring this battle to an even playing field."

"It doesn't help that they only send a handful of troops into the field at any point in time," Serenity added. "I don't like this. The person who controls information controls the outcome of the war, and we've been kept in the dark for way too long." James looked at her and noted her pitch-black hair and bright green eyes, the ferocity on a face so beautiful, the warm redness in her otherwise milky cheek. There was so much life to be lived with her, for her, by her, and it was in that moment that he made the decision to play it close to the vest. He thought of her being related to that Callan Rouge man, of how their fathers had died at war with one another, and thought that he could use that information to control the outcome of a very specific battle if the moment ever came around.

"Well," Cecelia shrugged as she looked from thoughtful face to thoughtful face, "since it sounds like you'll be thinking about our next move for a while, I'll just slip on out of here to take care of our little hostage friend—"

"Leave him alone," James ordered, and when she looked at him with immediate disgust, he returned with a challenging look that begged her to speak out of turn or disobey him in the slightest. "If it turns out that we can't regain our edge in this conflict, we'll need some bargaining chips to at least ensure that we can get behind enemy lines. I don't like the idea of stooping to the dirty tricks of those pacifistic Helmets, but I like the idea of losing a war against a ragtag bunch of rebel scum even less."

"Not a bad plan," came a voice completely unfamiliar to the Scourge or their leader. "In 1558, a group of ninja were hired by a certain feudal lord to burn down an enemy castle." Every eye in the tent turned to the speaker, a young woman as beautiful as Aphrodite and as brown as cinnamon. Her dark eyes traced the room with a muted excitement that made the members of the Scourge give pause. "So," the stranger continued, "the ninja stole a lantern with the family crest of their enemy and made enough exact copies to pass out for all their allies. When the night came for them to execute their mission, the ninja showed the lanterns at the front gate, and all 48 of them were allowed to walk through the front door. No fighting, no bloodshed, no raised alarms. After they got in, though, the castle was set ablaze, and in all the confusion, the 48 ninja disappeared into the night. The castle fell, the warlord's army tasted victory, and the ninja themselves moved on to something more worthy of their time."

"I'm sorry, who are you," Serenity inquired, clearly ready to start a fight. The young woman gave a smirk that begged the Colonel to bring it.

"Serafina Leyva," she said with a somewhat mocking salute. "I'm your new squad member."

****

November 11th, 2084, 3:11 p.m.,

Dre Hamlin stood at the door of the Director's office. All the memories of his time in service to the cause rushed back to him. The fight to protect the bunker in the White Ruins. The deaths of his friends on the battlefield. Everything that'd happened with his son.

It was hard for him to be here again, and harder still for him to realize that John had taken the reins as the Director of the Yaiba Insurrection. He never wanted his boy to be in this position. He never wanted his only child to risk his life so brazenly for a cause that never seems to have an end, and that was why he was here. He watched from the door as John talked to a young man with darker skin and black hair in medium-long dreads. He was strong, even among the Yaiba, and decked out in full Hanzo Gear. Dre imagined him to be a new graduate of the program.

John dismissed him, and the youth, in his haste, bumped into Dre upon his retreat. The old man almost fell over when the firm grip of the young warrior's hand saved him.

"Oh my god, I am so sorry," the young man exclaimed, and frantically dusted the legendary warrior off. "I got a new assignment and I got so excited that I stopped looking where I was going for a minute and…" he caught sight of the old man's face and had to do a double take. His lips parted in a childlike smile that reminded Dre of how John was when he was younger. "You're Dre Hamlin. Oh my god, you're Dre Hamlin! You're a big part of the reason why we even use the Hanzo Gear! It's an honor to meet you, sir! Oh, crap, now I feel even worse for knocking you over! Is there any way I can make it up to you?"

"Ryan," John called from his seat, "Get out." Ryan, the young man with more energy than Dre was expecting, left promptly and apologized for taking so much of the legendary rebel's time. When he was gone, John shifted focus to his father. "Can I help you?"

"I was just stopping in to see how you were doing," Dre told him, but John didn't buy it.

"I'm fine," he replied, unashamed to show the full register of his suspicion. He returned to his desk and started going over some papers and maps. "Or at least, as fine as a person preparing for a counterattack can be. The Battle of Johnson City was a success, and preparations to fortify our new territory have begun. Better still, I already sent word to our friends in New York that our forces now control their primary route west, and that they're isolated from their beloved Prince James."

"Seems like it's all going according to plan," Dre said, and though he was irritated, he did what he could to mask it.

"It should be. I selected the best for that mission," John retorted lovelessly.

"Like yourself," Dre challenged, and folded his arms. John looked up at him from the papers on his desk.

"Come again," John's tone issued a challenge of its own, and that was when Dre lost his patience.

"I heard about what you did in Johnson City," Dre said solemnly. John, unimpressed with the tone his father used, grunted to show his disapproval. "Heading into the command center and eliminating a company on your own? God in heaven, boy, do you know how reckless that was? After all that's happened to us, after what happened to Emiko, you'd think it was too soon to do something that insane."

"That's funny, because last I checked, I was the one calling the shots here," John shot back.

"You're right, kid, you're a leader! You have a responsibility to lead these people, which means you have to live for them, too—" Dre yelled, but the calm voice of his son cut him off.

"If we were gonna take Johnson City from the Reds, then our forces needed me on the front lines with them. It's not just about keeping the community together—"

"That's all it's ever been about. The Reds issue division, but we give unity. They sacrifice bodies, but we preserve life," Dre interjected. His tone was that of a man who had been saying the same thing so long he'd grown tired of it.

"And how are we supposed to succeed in that when the Kingdom moves however it wants to while we hide in a mountain except to get salvaged supplies? We need to put an end to this, and giving our forces a good example of our strength is as necessary for that as it is for getting everyone in the faction on our side." John had a fair point, but it still didn't excuse him for behaving like such a petulant child and putting on a performance for his soldiers. That was the kind of thing that serial killers would have done in the old days.

"You can't let the opinions of other people determine how you're gonna lead them, son," Dre said earnestly, and John raised his eyebrows in surprise.

"Oh, so now I'm your son," he said with a mocking smile. "I don't believe this. Up until mom died you didn't even want anything to do with me but now you're here, in my office, telling me how I should do things. Let me tell you something, 'Pops,' I do what's best for all of us, even if you're too blinded by your own problems to see it."

"I just didn't want—"

"I don't really care what you want, Dad. You never gave me that much courtesy so why should I extend it to you?" John's tone shifted from heated argument to arctic indifference. There was a silence between them now, their eyes locked and emotional.

"I know I didn't do right by you," Dre admitted. John opened his mouth to return fire, but Dre raised his hand in a placating gesture to quiet him once again. "I let my own issues get in the way of how it used to be between us. And you know, maybe you're right. Maybe I was using grief to bridge the gap but John," his tone was pleading, "You're all I have left."

John thoughtfully tongued his cheek as he lifted his head a bit to look down his nose. He spent a long time trying to push the happier memories with his father out of his head. He didn't care that the old man used to fall on him at random and tickle him just to hear his laugh. He didn't want to look back on how he would sneak him sweets behind his mother's back. He erased the sounds of his father's confessions of "I love you" on a daily basis. The only thing he cared to remember was how the man disowned him, berated him, made him feel like all of that was a lie. It was the only thing that kept him from going back and opening himself up for the disappointment again.

"No," he finally responded, "I'm not. There was a time where I would've been. But you gave that up when you kicked me out. Now if you'll excuse me, I have work to do." Dre shook his head in acceptance as he turned towards the exit.

"You know," he said as he stopped, "I had to learn to see you past what I experienced that night. I still don't like you being in this position, but for what it's worth, I'm still proud of you. I just don't want you to end up making the same mistake that Emiko did." He left, and John couldn't resist the urge to smile a little bit.

****

November 11th, 4:28 p.m.,

Devin Dross went down to Holding Level AA without company…or permission. But he had to see her again. Something about Zahara was as inviting to him as honey was to a bear. Maybe it was the fact that she saved him that he couldn't get out of his head, or maybe it was what she said when she met the Director. She just wanted to be treated fairly, and the first thing they did was throw her in prison. Of course, he understood where John was coming from. It was his responsibility to look after the residents of the Yaiba Insurrection, but he still felt that they could've shown Zahara more kindness than they had.

He made it through security without detection, and pat himself on the back for having the foresight to learn that particular set of skills. It'd be a while before the guards cycled back through, so he had time for a quick conversation.

"Hey," he whispered through the bars. She looked up, and her chocolatey eyes locked on him with a sharpness that made his fingers twitch. "You look bored."

"Really? Well you've got it all wrong, looking at the wall for hours on end is more entertaining than you might think," she retorted with a steady drip of sarcasm. "What brings you down here to my marvelous Wonderland?"

"I brought you something," he said, and tossed a rations package through to the other side. The rations packages were a share of all the food salvaged from the raid a few days ago, so it was better than the stuff she would be served down here by far.

"What's the catch?" Zahara asked as she moved a strand of her black hair behind her ear. Dross shook his head.

"No catch. I just wanna know that you're being taken care of down here," he told her, and in the moment her heart beat as fast as his did.

"Thanks," she said, and cracked a brief smile at him. Devin turned his head at the sound of heavy footsteps in the distance. He looked back at her with an almost pitiful look. Guess you better get going."

"I'm really sorry," he assured her. "I—"

"Just make sure you come back tomorrow," she teased. "Bring something to drink, and we'll call it a date." He smiled at her, and she at him.

"Sounds like a plan," he replied. She turned to look toward the direction of the footsteps, and when she went to look for Dross, he had vanished into the shadows of the prison.

Chapter Seventeen

November 11th, 2084, 5:15 p.m.,

The sun drifted lower, closer to the trees than it had been even five minutes ago. Bill was alone, and wanted nothing different for himself. He hadn't quite recovered from Emiko's death. She was more than a leader. She was his friend. She was the person who set him up with Bri and officiated their wedding. She would crack jokes on him when the other Dragons were gone. She was the person who recommended that he take the Dragon Trials in the first place. And he'd let her down.

For over a month he'd struggled with himself. Bri did all she could to comfort him, and inconsolable as he was, she never stopped. He honestly felt that he didn't deserve her, but resolved to do better so that maybe one day he could get there. The question was, how? How would he be worthy of someone else when he wasn't even sure he was worthy of his next breath? It wasn't just himself that he'd failed. When he failed to prevent Emiko's death, he robbed every Yaiba citizen of their leader, their protector, their shield against the ugliness of the outer world left in the wake of the Dawn King and his legions. He didn't think that he'd ever recover from the disappointment—

"Hey," came the familiar voice of his beloved younger brother. "This seat taken?" Bill chuckled for perhaps the first time in a month.

"I mean it's the top of a mountain, little brother. There aren't really any seats to have a dispute over in the first place." John sat down next to him and nudged him gently with his elbow.

"Still not feeling it, huh?" asked the Lightning Dragon. Bill just shrugged. He wasn't sure how to answer that question. There was so much in his life that he could be happy with. The beautiful wife that tirelessly labored to make him feel himself again. The little brother who, despite his new rise in position, still made time to check on those closest to him. The kids that he taught who showed him daily what strong warriors they'd become.

Regardless of how he felt about them, about the good that he could clearly see in his life, the answer was still, "No, not really." He hated even thinking the words, so when he said them, it made his stomach churn. There was a long stretch of silence before John sighed.

"You're not a failure, you know," John finally said, and placed a firm but comforting hand on his brother's shoulder. "Tragedy happens so that we become aware of how limited we are and work to restrict that limitation."

"But if I had been there—"

"You don't know what would've happened," John interrupted gently. "You could've been killed right along with Em. Sometimes things go sideways and we lose the people we love because of it. But tell me, Bill, how are you honoring Emiko's memory by losing yourself and giving up" The question was enough for Bill to turn his sullen eyes from the horizon to John.

"You make it sound so cut and dry," Bill said with narrowed eyes. "I'm not giving up, I just…" his voice trailed off, and his eyes returned to the sinking sun in the distance.

"What?" John asked patiently.

"I just don't know where to go from here," Bill admitted, and John's expression softened further. "I don't know how to recover from this. I'm open to suggestions."

"Well I'd suggest that you become the next Rairyu," John said blankly, which only made the shockwaves sent through Bill's body worse. John looked at his big brother to find his jaw now agape, his brow furrowed in deepest confusion, and his head tilted to the side.

"I—you—wha?" Bill stammered. He got to his feet. "I don't think you're thinking this through little brother—"

"I am," John assured him.

"Well I don't think I'm qualified for the position," Bill retorted, arms folded across his chest.

"You are," John told him with a chuckle as light as the breeze. There was a moment of silence as Bill eyed the new Director suspiciously.

"What brought this on?" His question bore a semblance of his normally upbeat yet quizzical nature, so John obliged him.

"If I'm being honest, my dad came to visit me and scold me about how reckless my actions were on the Johnson City Raid. He pointed out that if I'm both the Director and the Lightning Dragon that aids him, then I'm doing something far crazier than what Emiko did the night the Reds attacked. I need someone other than me to watch my back. Or at least take over if something happens to me," the Director explained. Bill's eyebrows lifted in further shock.

"I never thought I'd see the day that you and your dad agreed about something," Bill joked. It was the first time he'd done so in a month, and it made the smile that crossed John's lips a little more real.

"I know, right? It sucks, but since I'm the head honcho now, I no longer have the luxury of ignoring what the old man says. When he has a point, I unfortunately have to hear him out. But I will say this: he's not the only reason I'm thinking like this," John admitted.

"Oh?" Bill asked with one eyebrow raised this time.

"I think it's only fitting," John elaborated, "that if you're feeling guilty about what happened to Emiko, then you should do what you can to watch over me. It's nothing that you're not already used to, after all. Make up for whatever mistakes you believe you've made by serving as the new Rairyu." Bill hesitated, but the strength of John's gaze and his quiet determination did much to steel Bill's resolve. They shook hands.

"I guess I don't have a choice," Bill said, and with a pat to his big brother's back, John returned to the base in the mountain below.

****

November 15th, 2084, 2:37 p.m.,

Class was over, and Darius was relieved. His students had been able to tell when he showed up the day after the stabbing that he wasn't well. They never said as much out loud, but they went a little easier on him than they usually did. Darius, though, went a little harder on them. Just as he promised, he upped their grouping number from three to five and watched as they went at it. That had been his practice for the last week, and for that entire time it drove him to an anger that he couldn't quite stomach.

"Keep your distance," he remembered of the voice of the woman who patched him up. The image of her in his mind was stunning, to say the least. She was 5'3" with thick dark curly hair and mysterious dark eyes that trapped a person in the abyss of curiosity. "Your students probably aren't the only ones tasked to take you out, so stick to yourself if you can help it."

He ground his teeth every time he remembered her warning, because what was he supposed to do in this state? His wounds weren't completely healed yet so even carrying a Reikiken was dangerous. Sure, he had some room to fight with the kyoketsu-shoge, but where the Yoroi compound was spacious enough to allow freedom of movement, there were too many civilians scattered all over. One wrong move would end with him killing someone who, likely, needn't be killed. That alone was enough for him to do as he did presently and sit in the emptied training facility in full view of the door. He was a sitting duck, a revelation made all the more potent with the realization that he wasn't even able to make a hasty retreat here.

"Ever since Vargas went to broker a deal with the Yaiba, the Yoroi Council has been divided. Those in favor of the treaty welcome you here as an asset that could help free us from the Reds. The others see you as a threat that could get us all killed," she'd told him. He remembered the pain he'd felt when he'd tried to sit up. He crashed back to the bed.

"And what do you think," he'd asked her, even before he'd asked her name. He watched as she turned around to face him with fresh bandages in her hands. She applied them, and focused intently on the covered wound.

"I think that if you messed around and got stabbed like this, you must not be that much trouble to deal with," she said sharply, and laughed at her own joke.

It wasn't flattering, but it did give him a little bit of comfort. What contributed most to his newfound discomfort, though, was hardly the fact that a split faction within the Yoroi wanted him dead. It was that grieved look on Tony's face as they apologized for attacking him. He knew himself to be a fool for thinking compassionate thoughts towards his attacker but still, there was something about the deceiver that he was drawn to—

A knock at thc door jolted Darius from the depths of his thoughts. He groaned. He'd told her that there was no need to pick him up from work, but here she was. She opened the door, and with a hand on her hip she looked the Rebel Dragon over. He gathered his nerves and gingerly proceeded across the arena floor with his hands on the nearby earthen pillars for support.

"Enjoying the view," he asked, irritated at the humored look she sported. "The least you could do is help me move around, Ina." She watched him wobble about the floor and stumble over his own feet from time to time, but decided against any offer of further assistance.

"I'm already helping you enough by making sure you stay safe enough to teach," she shot back.

"Something I didn't ask you for in the first place," he reminded her, and she shrugged. She knew he appreciated it, even if he didn't want to admit it to her. Moreover, she knew why he wanted her to leave him alone. But she couldn't. Too much was at stake for her and she was not about to lose this kind of opportunity.

"But it suits you," she responded, not a trace of ulterior motive in her angelic voice. "How many wanted men get to say they have a volunteer bodyguard?" His eyes narrowed, but he knew she had a point.

"I guess," he uttered. She opened the door of the facility for him and he left through it. She locked the door and returned to his side in time enough to catch him before he fell. "You're not afraid of being seen in public with me?"

"Please," Ina replied. "I'm a teacher. If anyone here sees me with you they'll assume more that I'm trying to make you less of a stone-cold idiot." She laughed and he groaned. "I have a level of respect that cannot be challenged. It doesn't mean I have too much sway in the politics of this place, though. If I did, we wouldn't be fighting amongst ourselves while our enemies are gathering at our front door." She heaved a sigh and regained herself. She did what she could to remain rational and controlled, though it was her nature to be gripped by passion and spurred to move accordingly.

"You must be very devoted to the Alliance," Darius observed, but she shook her head as a wry grin pulled across her jaw.

"I'm devoted to my kids," she said with an air of correction. "I spend my day with little ones and teenagers alike, shaping them and caring for them in the hope that they would bring us all a better future. Infighting and invasions put those kids at risk." There was a seriousness to her voice now that made the dragonling's heart cry. "That's not something that I can just sit down and take."

"I think I understand," he told her comfortingly. He was still extremely new at teaching himself, and while his students had been averse to his tutelage at first, he now felt a bond with them that could only be described as rewarding and hopeful. Ina looked him over, this time more thoughtfully than she had when she picked him up, and figured that he told the truth. Something about him struck her as a true teacher, though nowhere near her level. "Is it crazy for me to want to know if Tony is okay?"

"Yes," Ina said without even the slightest hesitation. "She stabbed you in the abdomen."

"You mean 'they,'" Darius corrected to an eyebrow raise from his companion. "Tony identifies as a genderfluid individual, or so I'm told. And besides, they missed my vital organs."

"On purpose or by accident?" Ina was less than amused and her sudden shrewdness caught Darius at a disadvantage.

"I…" he hesitated an answer. "I think on purpose."

"Exactly, you *think*. Just like you thought that your students wouldn't be out to get you because you're their teacher," Ina chided. "That brings us back to my number one rule for you. Would you be so kind as to remind me of what that is again?"

"Ugh, 'don't trust anyone,' I know," Darius answered with all the zeal of a disinterested child. "That apply to you, too?" Ina got quiet for a moment as her reason presented itself at the forefront of her mind. She shrugged.

"Of course," she told him as if he should've already known what her answer might be. "Listen, people may like you, some might even love you, but the fact of the matter is that they're all after something in one way or another. I'm not saying put the idea of trust out of your head. Just do a better job of telling the ones who mean well from the ones who don't. Trust nobody, at least until they prove themselves worthy of your trust."

"I guess that makes sense," Darius decided aloud. The path they walked was different than his usual one had been in the month and change before. It was still noisy and full of life in the area surrounding the training hall, but after a left down a poorly-lit alley that gave Darius a slight tremble, Ina brought him through a few more turns, an open door and a steep incline that inevitably led him into the maintenance tunnels of the compound's Cluster B. "Where are you taking me?" The boy was out of breath, and while his bandages held firm, they also began to chafe from the sudden leak of his blood.

"You didn't think we were gonna take the main lines back to my place, did you," she asked with a chuckle. Darius' eyebrows lifted in surprise. "Don't even ask," Ina commanded just when his mouth opened in protest. "We're gonna take the maintenance line back to my place because I'm not the one marked for death. You're okay with surviving the night, yeah?" Darius reluctantly nodded in agreement. "Good. The crater cart should be just up ahead. You good to make it?"

"Yeah, I should be," Darius started, "but are you sure this is legal?" He was already in enough trouble as it was, and with every second that ticked by, Darius questioned even more whether he should tap frequency 22597 and bring the Violet Shadows to the front door of the Yoroi Alliance, or if he should fight on his own, without the help of his father or brother or friends. Ina chuckled again, which didn't help his decision-making process.

"It is if the maintenance director is your cousin. Don't worry about it, we're already approved for passage. I just hope you don't mind a little company on our short trip." This time Darius chuckled.

"If it means someone else is gonna be on the receiving end of your jokes, then I'm all for it," he told her. They came to a dark platform, damp with God knows what from the level above, and lit with only a single work light haphazardly settled near the edge. As Ina had said, the crater cart was in place, and a burly man with an ash-gray mustache on his golden-brown face stood beside it as though to usher them in. His blue coveralls harkened back to the images of Old American mechanics, and while his skin was hidden his warmth was on full display.

"Yo, Ina," said the maintenance man. "Been a while since you flew under the radar. I was beginning to think that you forgot about us, what with you being a big-time teacher and all that."

"Forget about you, Tanner?" She spread her arms and embraced him with a smile. "Never. It's just hard getting away from work these days with everything going on." Tanner looked at Darius, and while the young dragon thought he would be met with hostility, Tanner's demeanor didn't change at all.

"Hard times, and all that," he said gruffly, "but hopefully this one can give us the edge we need to come out on top."

"If he can stop making stupid decisions long enough, then he just might," Ina joked, and Darius grumbled.

"You're free to board. Gotta warn you, though, the crater cart's occupied with some pretty stiff figures," Tanner warned them. He leaned in and placed his hand to the side of his mouth to keep any onlookers from reading his lips. "Awful company, these ones."

"We'll manage, T," Ina assured him. The large crewman shrugged and allowed them entry into the cart. It was a single metal vessel with tinted windows and a pair of sliding doors. Ina entered first, gave a cordial but brief greeting to the other passengers, and then took her place in the nearest seat. Darius uttered a genuine thank-you as he moved past Tanner, but what he saw when he stepped into the cart was beyond his wildest nightmares.

There, directly across from his momentary caretaker sat a hooded man of stardust-gray eyes and blond hair, and beside him, the leader of the Scarlet Scourge herself.

****

November 15th, 2084, 3:33 p.m.,

Serenity recognized him immediately as one of the brats from the pharmacy. She instinctively moved for the pistol at her side, but the Prince grabbed her arm before she had the chance to draw it. She looked at him and he shook his head. She relaxed her arm, but her expression still sent waves of disgust and hatred through the cart.

"What are you doing here," Darius asked before he could stop himself. There was fear there, and Serenity reveled in it.

"You know them," Ina asked with a raised eyebrow. James, who couldn't help but observe the utter beauty of her features, donned a coy smile that only put the lady more on edge.

"Not face to face, no," admitted the Prince, "I'm a friend of his Uncle Callan, here on a diplomatic mission of sorts. I didn't know you'd be the one they sent." His voice trailed off with a degree of cunning that made it hard for Darius to do anything other than sweat. Serenity's face softened a bit, though not enough to make the other passengers more comfortable with the situation. Ina, of course, took notice.

"What's up with her," she asked, unconcerned about how abrasive the question might appear. Serenity cut Ina a look but quickly gave her best embarrassed smile.

"I hurt my back on the way to your base," she said in an almost girlish tone. The sheer sound of it was enough to coat Darius in curiosity, and when combined with the look on her face, it made Ina a little less apprehensive. "Sorry if it makes me look a little edgier than I am." The lie made her want to vomit. She knew the kind of fighter this kid was. She was the one who engaged him back in Johnson City the night the Scourge captured Callan Rouge, and if he was here, that meant that there was a good chance that the little vermin was the teacher sent by the Insurrection.

"So, how is your uncle, anyway," the Prince asked Darius. On the surface the question sounded sincere, but just beneath was a threatening resonance that seemingly went over Ina's head. "Last I saw him he wasn't doing too well."

"He's fine," Darius burst with frustration. "No thanks to you." The Prince's expression softened and he clasped his hands together.

"Yes, well," he began in a sympathetic tone, "unfortunately taking care of him was a lot harder than we imagined. That man is a lot more stubborn than I ever thought possible. I apologize for our inadequacy before." His eyes became hard as stone once again as he said, "I am glad to hear that he's doing better, though."

"And I'm happy that I got the chance to see you again," Serenity said with an air of delight. She seemed sweet, though from where Ina sat her expression was less than inviting. For the life of her, though, she couldn't figure out why. "The last time I saw you, you barely felt comfortable leaving your own base." Darius' muscles tensed at the mention of his home. "Of course I can only imagine that being raised in a hollowed out mountain would make the outside world seem a little scary," she continued, and watched him struggle to mask his discomfort. He didn't know how she knew what she knew but it didn't bode well for him or for the Yaiba Insurrection. His breaths grew shallower now as his mind raced with curiosity of the wellbeing of his family and friends. His wound leaked blood from the stress, and the metallic smell of it attracted Ina's attention. While she tended him, Serenity relished in the look of bloodlust that washed the boy's face. "But look at you now, all the way out here in Alliance territory. You must've gone through quite the transformation in the last few months."

"You have no idea," Darius said with the flash of a smile. Serenity raised an eyebrow, intrigued at the challenge in his tone. She couldn't tell at first if he was serious or just bluffing to put them on the defensive, but she looked to Ina and followed her eyes to the wound in his side. Instantly she relaxed.

"Now that it's come up," James spoke with an air of sophisticated curiosity, "you never did say what it was that brought you all this way." His eyes homed in on the wound in his side. "Hopefully nothing too dangerous."

"Nothing that you need to be worried about," Ina spoke up. She didn't know what those two were after, but she knew that it was a smart idea to keep whatever information they sought out of their hands. "He just got blindsided by some of our more unsavory types. Best be careful," she warned with a sudden darkness to her usually cheerful voice, "it's very easy to get yourself hurt around here." The tension in the air was enough to make the hairs on the back of Tanner's neck stand.

He couldn't imagine whatever insanity lay beneath those comments, nor did he really care to. He kept his eyes on the massive expanse before him as the cart moved on the railing with ease. It would take ten minutes more before Cluster A came into view, and those ten minutes couldn't pass fast enough. The four passengers in the crater car eyed each other with deep suspicion. Serenity felt her fingers twitch from an intense urge to grab her pistol while Darius, still dressed in his Hanzo Gear, thought about what kind of praise his father would lavish on him should he slit the enemy's throat with a kyoketsu-shoge.

"We're coming up on the Cluster now," Tanner shouted to the people in the back. "Prepare to get off when we pull into the maintenance tunnel." He wiped his brow, nervous and more than ready for the discomfort they brought to leave him.

"Where are you staying while you're here," Serenity asked the young dragon, whose eyes narrowed at the address. "I'd love to pay you a visit after we finish up our business."

"That would be lovely," Prince James said with faux excitement, partially as a means to cover up the increasingly devilish tone of his beloved. "Perhaps your friend would like to join us and show us some of the highlights of the Yoroi compound." He donned a smile, but no matter how warm and friendly it was, Ina knew better than to trust it.

"Sorry," Darius spoke up, "but I don't have much time on my hands." There was stillness on James' face, and a glimmer of anticipation in Serenity's eye.

"Pity," she said, her tone almost sultry. In the months since their first meeting, she was truly perturbed at the fact that they had managed to fight the Scourge and live. As much as she was there to protect James from the warrior cave-dwellers called Yoroi, she was just as eager to restore the reputation of her death squad should the opportunity arise.

"Don't worry," Darius said with a coy grin the likes of which would've made John proud. "I'll make sure that the next time we meet is really special." The car pulled to a stop in front of a platform as dank and dreary as the last. The tunnel on its other side emanated a rotten sort of smell that made every regal cell in Prince James' body convulse in disgust. Outwardly, though, he only wrinkled his nose.

"Until next time, then," said the Scarlet Prince, and without delay, he and the Scourge commander moved from the crater cart to their only and putrid exit. Darius waited until his enemies were out of sight and earshot before he breathed a heavy sigh and he sank into his seat.

"What was that all about," Ina asked, mildly irritated that he'd gone this long without explaining the situation already. "Who were those two? Because it's pretty clear that they're not friends of yours." Darius didn't answer right away. He was too caught up in thoughts of a burning Insurrection base and the potentially mangled bodies of people he'd known all his life. Still, he knew the value of that information and he didn't know why Ina was so determined to look after him.

"I'll tell you," he said, "but only if you tell me what you hope to gain from playing caretaker with me." She met his gaze with a sharp one of her own, but at the sight of his determined cool, she sighed.

"Fine. I'll tell you what you want to know, but only after we've gotten someplace safe." She nodded her head towards the previously occupied seats of their company and noted a small, roundish object no bigger than a thumbtack and almost perfectly blended with the metal seat. Darius fixed on it almost instantly, and with a nod they wordlessly left the crater cart behind.

****

November 15th, 2084, 5:24 p.m.,

Callan took a deep breath in his office at the Bluff City Outpost. It was refreshing for him to be back in the field after his capture, and life seemed a little bit sweeter now that he was in charge of this outpost. An entire regiment of 3,000 Yaiba troops plus a battalion of 1,000 Helmets were at his command, and it was their collective duty to warn of any mounting threats from the Northeast Territory. The thought made him giddy with expectation, because after the way the Insurrection repaid the Kingdom for their intrusion at the Roan Mountain Base, it was only a matter of time before the Reds sent their response.

A knock came at the door, and with a sigh, Callan stood and called, "Come in." With a speed that was markedly less formal than the ranking structure permitted, Ryan Morrisey burst through the door and presented himself before the Suiryu. Callan gave a stern look, but the expression of pure excitement on the rookie's face gave him reason to be concerned.

"Sir!" Ryan's zeal was palpable in his address. "Enemy forces are gathering to the northeast in the Holston Valley, just east of Bristol." Before he realized it, Callan adopted a devilishly crooked smirk and came to stand before the boy.

"That's exciting," he said succinctly. Ryan raised his eyebrows and smiled, but a stern expression from his commanding officer prompted him to settle his facial features in a more situation-appropriate manner.

"What are your orders?" Callan massaged his chin with his index and middle fingers as his eyes lit with a boyish joy that he rarely exhibited.

"Gather the troops and prepare to deploy. Utilize frequency 22566 to alert central command and request reinforcements. Speak with Agent Resnick and have him reach out to Senior Agent Kincaid about this as well. Somehow I don't think they'd like to be left out of our little welcoming party." Without anything else to relay, Callan dismissed him and returned to his desk. He swiveled the chair around to look out the window at the setting sun over the treetops. He tapped his foot nervously, but with more excitement than he imagined he'd ever felt before. For him, it was time for payback.

****

November 15th, 2084, 7:20 p.m.,

"…and then he crashed right into the training post!" She laughed at his story, and it was like music to his ears. Dross had found his way back to her every night since his first visit, and every night they shared food and stories about their lives outside the prison block. It was easier for him to maneuver around the depths of Holding Level AA, though he wasn't sure if it was because of the frequency of his visits or the reason behind it. The more he talked to Zahara, the more he found himself taken in by more than just her beauty.

She was artistic, and loved to paint and sculpt and work with her hands. She had ever since she was a little girl, and had it not been for her grandfather's prior service in the Old American military, that would've been the path she'd have selected for herself. Devin remembered the anger he felt when she first told him, and even now he couldn't believe that a society would force military service on someone just because of their family history. So he took it upon himself to tell her about all the hilarious things that happened in the Yaiba Insurrection, like how Manny Bautista would tell all the kids weird facts about life and get all their parents mad at him, or how Zayvier Peters misfired his kyoketsu-shoge during training and swung out of control and into one of the metal training pillars. His stories always made her laugh, and every time he did so she would tell him about her dreams and desires.

"What I would give to be a spectator for one of those training sessions," she mused with a happy sigh. Devin grinned at her through his rugged blond facial hair and it sent shockwaves through her body.

"You will," he assured her.

"Yeah, if I ever get out of here, that is." It was a bitter joke, but she laughed to show Dross that it was okay for him to do the same. Instead, he thought about a way to get her out and among the people faster.

"You said that the Reds have plans for the Southern Wastes, right?" She looked at him suspiciously, and at the bright-burning anger in her eye, he raised his hands in a placating gesture. "I'm only trying to help. The Director won't just let you out just because I asked nicely. He'll need information and if you have it to give, then you might want to do so ahead of your hearing with him." She hesitated, and slowly backed away from the bars of her cell. Dross looked wounded at the gesture. "Zahara, please. I'm sick of seeing you locked up like this. How am I supposed to sleep at night knowing that you're in jail for saving my life?" She looked into his deep brown eyes, and when she saw that they didn't waver, she reluctantly stepped back towards the cell bars. Footsteps sounded in the distance. Dross grappled up to the ceiling and held his position in total silence. Zahara feigned boredom on the bench in her cell and stared at the stone wall opposite her. The guards came to peer into her holding unit, and when she noticed them she waved. They grunted, but then returned to their patrols. As soon as they were out of earshot, Dross descended from the ceiling.

"The Kingdom knows about your deal with the Chinese to smuggle tungsten into Prevalence," she said in a hushed tone, lest she attract the patrolmen from before. "Even so, they don't want to go to war with China because the Insurrection poses too much of a threat…" As she spoke the intentions of the Scarlets, Dross went pale with the revelation. He left before she could finish, and apologized profusely as he went.

****

November 15th, 2084, 8:40 p.m.,

John was exhausted. His day was more than he'd bargained for, and filling the role of the Director was a challenge the likes of which he'd never seen. It was something to watch as the job was performed, but another animal entirely to fulfill the responsibilities he'd inherited. He gazed up at the ceiling of his office for a moment and silently asked Emiko how she'd managed to do it for so long without going crazy.

He closed his eyes, and the very second he did, the door to his office burst open. He sat up and turned a steel gaze to the intruder, prepared to chew them out for disturbing his peace, but it was Devin Dross, and he spoke up quickly.

"The Reds intend to cut off our supply lines, sir." There was an urgency in his tone, in his walk, in the gasps for air that he failed to mask that couldn't be ignored. John's expression grew grim.

"What?" he inquired with a dragonic hum in his voice.

"They're attacking our Hanzo Gear."

Chapter Eighteen

November 17th, 2084, 9:30 a.m.,

The tension in the air ran thick enough that those in the room thought they would suffocate. Their meeting was supposed to be a private one, but ever since Prince James and Colonel Crawford burst in, all eyes could do nothing but focus on the Scarlet leaders in their midst. There was no conversation, not even so much as a whimper filtered into the air to grace the ears of their guests.

Those guests, however, were more than accepting of the silence. Serenity, for one, felt more than at home in a strained and potentially dangerous environment, and was no stranger to interrupting a covert assembly of quiet conspirators in foreign lands. Prince James, while less experienced than his beloved Colonel, had an eye for opportunity, and this was as good an opportunity as any. A single glance around the room told me everything that he needed to know. Six men, eight women, two "other," though they leaned more towards the masculine side. All of them were exceptionally desperate, and desperate people always made the best pawns.

"Please," James urged in a charming manner that was unique to him, "don't stop on our account. You were just talking about how you might appease the Kingdom and salvage the ceasefire agreement, yes?" There was no answer, just a narrowing of eyes.

"What are you doing here," someone finally spoke up. Serenity looked in the way of the voice and immediately recognized its source as one of the Council members. He was an old, gray-haired man of pale skin and stark blue eyes that almost looked hollow when the lights hit them.

“Why, I just came to listen in,” James answered honestly. “See what all the fuss was about, as it were. From what I’ve heard, the dissent between the pro- and anti-rebellion factions in your land has become a serious issue that threatens to tear the Yoroi apart.”

“How do you—” the man started to ask, but the stardust-eyed Prince raised his hand to stop him as a humored grin slithered across his jaw.

“Come now, Francis,” he said, just as charmingly as ever, “you know that the Kingdom has eyes and ears everywhere.” He started walking around the room, and met the eyes of every man, woman and gender-neutral individual in his presence. The assorted skin tones did strike him as a fine work of art, and for a moment he wondered what it would be like to be in possession of this image more permanently. Getting back to business, he took a seat at the table and locked eyes with Francis again. “It’s a shame that the Thornhill boy went missing. That seems to be the thing that made everything worse.”

“Nobody outside of the Council and this congregation know of that,” Francis spat. “How is it that you’ve come into that kind of knowledge?” Serenity laughed as she moved over to stand by her beloved. None in the room would meet her gaze, and even Francis shifted nervously under it. She smirked as she placed a hand gently on James’ shoulder.

“We were the ones who took him in,” she said as if he should’ve already figured out the answer. “Imagine our surprise when poor Johannes was found in the custody of three Yaiba Insurrectionists. Now I know you’re not so reckless that you’d flaunt such an insult in broad daylight. Not after all the peace you’ve enjoyed courtesy of the Scarlet Kingdom.” Her voice became more threatening as she spoke, and all of the Anti-Rebellion faction started to sweat from the nerves.

"Of course not," came the voice of a younger woman. "We had nothing to do with that, Mistress." She bowed her head out of respect and her pristine light-brown hair draped as a curtain to hide the shame in her peach-colored face. "It was Pro-Rebellion, really it was!"

"Raise your head," James demanded coolly, and the room tensed again. "Your sniveling is embarrassing. And in any case, you are all Yoroi, regardless of your frivolous infighting, are you not?" There was silence. For all their planning to depose the longstanding order of the Alliance in favor of peace with the Kingdom, this is how the Reds saw them. "Tell me, how do you think my father the King will respond to such a blatant and egregious gesture of disrespect?"

"I—we—" there was an uproar of stammered responses now, as if they were children trying to shift the blame after being scolded by their parents. James held up his hand, and the room instantly fell silent.

"We didn't come here to exact punishment," he told them and watched them all decompress. "We came to offer you a chance to redeem yourselves."

"What are your demands," Francis asked, the speed of which made Prince James raise his eyebrows.

"A Scarlet defector sits on your Yoroi Council. We would like her returned to us, if not eliminated. Whichever path you decide on, the end result will be the return of one of your own," Serenity supplied. The hushed murmurs of the crowded room were enough to make her stifle a girlish smile.

"You can't mean…" Francis started, as if they couldn't possibly be using their own ambassador as a bargaining chip.

"Oh, but we do," Serenity filled him in, and the smile on her face told Francis and the others that she derived a great joy from doing so. "If you help us take care of that traitorous dog, we'll return Johannes Thornhill to you so that you can go back to plotting your takeover without the threat of internal war." There was such a great pause in the man amid the excited yet wary whispers of his comrades that the Prince figured him reluctant to accept the terms. Serenity, however, wasn't nearly as doubtful. In all her missions, in all her travels, in all her experience with the world outside New York, she'd learned to spot a man who was merely feigning uncertainty as a means of pressuring negotiations.

"We accept your terms," Francis finally said when he realized his ploy wouldn't work. "Felicity Wheeler will be brought to a location of your choosing within seven days on the promise that Johannes Thornhill will be returned alive." He stressed that last point, uncomfortable with the idea of giving such a loophole to the Scarlets, who at one point had sacrificed thousands of their own troops just for a chance to discover the Alliance's front door. The Prince smiled.

"Excellent," he all but cooed, and rose from his seat at the table. "My people will be in touch with you."

"And Francis," Serenity said to get his attention. When he looked up, she quickly whipped her pistol from its holster and fired a round in the forehead of the girl that had previously groveled apologetically before her. The young brunette woman fell dead with a thud against the floor. "Don't mess this up." With nothing more to be said, they left the Anti-Rebels to continue their meeting.

****

November 17th, 2084, 11:16 a.m.,

"How long do you think we can hold them off," Callan asked. He carefully watched the enemy draw their battle lines and march towards the Bluff City Outpost. Every now and then a bomb would go off, or a pitfall trap would be sprung. Even with all that, their ranks were adaptable and steady in their advance.

"Hard to say," Nick replied. They'd already held back the oncoming Scarlet assault force for two days without having to send in their troops, and while the traps set by the Kabuto saboteurs proved sufficient for the time being, both of them knew that it was only a matter of time before they ran out and had to fight. "I'd say that we have another day or so on the traps. Depending on the fighting capabilities of our troops, I'd wager another two or three at best, but we won't be able to hold them off forever."

"Agreed," Callan stated shrewdly. He thought for a moment and then arrived at something of a solution. "We'll arrange a joint infiltration detail to scout out the enemy's camp. When we have their report, you'll dispatch a stealth team to…even things out in the numbers department, if you catch my meaning."

"I like that plan," Nick said with a devious grin. "But wait, what happens when they retaliate?"

"Then we fight them on equal footing," Callan said quickly. "I have a plan for that, don't worry. Go along with it for now, and I promise you I won't disappoint."

****

November 17th, 12:22 p.m.,

"Is it true," John asked her. He'd spent two days thinking about what Dross told him, and for two days it was the most stressful aspect of this war. If it was true that the Wastes were the main focus of the Reds at this juncture, then all of the fighting done inland at the moment served as nothing more than a clever distraction. The Reds wanted control of the waters surrounding the continent. They wanted to hit the Yaiba where it hurt.

"I don't have any reason to lie to you, sir," Zahara answered without even the slightest hint of attitude. No, what had found its way into her tone was genuine fear, because she realized that any wrong answer could result in her execution. After all she risked just to be here, that was not an option. "The Scarlet Kingdom has been planning this move for months, and they plan to carry it out in the span of the next two weeks."

"Then we have to do what we can to deploy forces to that region," John thought aloud. He eyed the young ebony-skinned woman before him and the man that advocated her release. "Dross, what do you make of this woman? As both a warrior and as a person?" The question caught everyone off-guard, most of all John, but he needed an answer quickly.

"I—she's amazing," Dross stammered, then caught himself and reorganized his thoughts. "What I mean is, she shot around me from across an old park thing with impressive accuracy, and she risked her life just to come here."

"I see," John said after a moment. He stood up, which was an unusual course of action for a man in the Director's seat to take in the massive audience chamber on Conference Level D, and Zahara stood up as well. John, whose flesh still crawled at the idea of being the new Director, took a step towards her in a total breach of Insurrection formality and gave her a look that sent chills down her spine. "You were raised in an environment where you were constantly underestimated or looked down upon because your skin was darker than everyone else's. From what I'm told, you were forced to serve a government that didn't agree with your existence but never said as much out loud. You fought and scrapped for respect you never got, and no matter how hard you worked, you were never seen as much more than a tool."

A tear streaked down Zahara's cheek at the sound of a stranger reciting her past, and immediately she went on the defensive. "What's it to you?" John's face soured at the sudden display of attitude, but then broke into a smile of approval.

"I want to give you something that you don't seem to have had a lot of in your life," he told her, and the look of absolute suspicion made the reveal even sweeter for him. "I want to give you a choice. I know that you probably don't want to fight anymore, and if you don't, that's fine. The Violet Shadows have seen difficulties before and while it would be helpful if you joined us, we can manage. However, I want you to think of the other little black girls and young black boys and every other person of color trapped in a system that hates them. If any part of you wants to save them from the same kind of hell you grew up in, then join us. Help us put an end to it and together we can create a better future not just for them, but for us as well."

The sniper froze. It was the first time in her life that she'd heard such conviction in someone's voice about something so well-intended. She used to dream about someone saving kids like that, back when she was one of them. Somewhere along the way, she gave up that hope. She bought into the anti-foreigner propaganda that dictated that everyone outside the Kingdom was some kind of savage, and numbed herself to the dangerous simplicity of her work. But here, in this moment, she realized the truth, that she could be a part of something so necessary for people with similar struggles as the ones she had. In this moment, her faith in a brighter future was on the verge of restoration. In this moment, she only had one question to ask.

"What do you need me to do?" John smiled, and gently wiped the tears from her eyes as Dross breathed a sigh of relief in the background.

****

November 17th, 2084, 6:31 p.m.,

Darius was still stunned. For two days since he arrived at Ina's place, he couldn't bring himself to leave or get back to class. If he was honest with himself, every waking moment made him feel sicker, and every moment asleep was filled with dreams of Ina's lover, and the massacre that he must've witnessed. She told him more about the Yoroi political scene. The Pro- and Anti-Rebellion conflict started off as a simple disagreement, but after the Scarlet raid on the Midland Outpost, the slaughter of three Yaiba escorts and the kidnapping of an esteemed envoy from the Alliance, the governing body was split into two factions that threatened to tear the Yoroi apart.

As soon as she mentioned the whole thing, she knew that among the dead now was his cousin Jaden Piccio, who had greeted him the morning that he got the mission. It was months ago that all this happened, and to find out only two days ago made Darius fraught with grief. He was powerless to stop it, and more than anything kept out of the loop.

To make matters worse, he knew who the captive envoy was before Ina revealed his identity. What he didn't know was that Ina desperately sought a way to bring about his return. Her trips into the Clusters were covert missions, from what he could tell, a self-imposed directive to keep watch over the shady dealings of the Anti-Rebel leaders in the hopes that some clue would present itself as to Johannes' whereabouts. She figured that if they were in league with the Reds, then they would be her best chance at finding her.

He still struggled to comprehend his role in her schemes, even after he'd been told. Ina said that she needed him alive and recovered to help set things right inside the Alliance. She'd heard the stories of the White Ruins Miracle that his grandfather Dre took part in. She knew of the formidability of his father, the Lightning Dragon John Hamlin, and with his combined pedigree and knowledge of the Hanzo Gear, Ina believed that Darius was just the man to help lead the Yoroi back to a place of unity.

Darius, on the other hand, had no idea what that even looked like. It frustrated him that the Director promoted him on his leadership qualities in the first place, because to him he'd been nothing more than a scared child on that mission. Even in his teaching, he only did what he thought his father or his Uncle Bill would've done, and while he was tough on his students he knew it was just his best attempts to disguise his inexperience. He sank on the couch, seemingly crushed by the weight of his father and grandfather's combined greatness and Ina's delusion that he could somehow measure up to the family legacy. But would he? He couldn't help but feel like an imposter, a cheap imitation of his pops that could barely hold his Reikiken by comparison.

The thought of Jaden, lost in Midland, also gave him a fresh sea of doubts. His cousin was always more confident than he was, and a much more capable leader for the people that depended on him. But now here Darius was, trapped in a situation where he struggled to decide if he was going to push himself through the dangers of the Yoroi Alliance and get them ready for war as was his mission, or if he would succumb to them and die the scared little boy he saw himself as.

He looked down at the collar and connected mask of his Hanzo Gear. He thought about tapping the designated frequency and calling his father for support, but then cursed the thought. It occurred to him that that was his signature move, his go-to tactic. He always depended on his pops to bail him out of trouble, and when he was a boy that would've been acceptable but now? Now he was Hanran no Ryu, the Rebel Dragon of the Violet Shadows. Now he was a Master of the Insurrection and represented his home as a foreign dignitary as much as a teacher. How would it look if he called daddy to solve his problems after his leaders—his father—put their trust in him? He slammed his fist against the side table as his frustration reached its peak.

He couldn't afford to sit around like this anymore. He needed a strategy that would keep him alive and prevent him from sustaining any more wounds now that the one in his side was almost completely healed. The Anti-Rebels wanted him snuffed out, but that was only a part of a much larger problem. Darius knew that if he walked back into the training facility without a plan it would be dangerous. Even more so, going back to his government appointed dwelling seemed to be…unwise. Fortunately, Ina told him that he could stay here for as long as he wanted, but he knew that that would be more inconvenient than anything. He needed to be somewhere where nobody thought to look for him…

She came in, and when Darius smiled at her, Ina crossed her arms and made a face. "I don't know what that look is for, but I don't like it," she said, and while there was a hard edge to her voice, her face gave way to an almost charming smile. "You seem to be in a better mood than you were for the last couple of days."

"I just decided that it's time to do something with myself," he replied, and noticed that Ina left the door open. "What'd you do today?"

"Nothing out of the ordinary," she said with a shrug. "Got some intel on the Anti-Rebels. They've been scouting your dwelling for the last couple of days and, let's just say, your class has picked up some 'new students' that have rubbed your originals the wrong way."

"Didn't realize I'd be that much of a priority for the Anti-Rebellion big wigs," Darius joked, and realized that this was the first time he'd done so freely since John returned from scouting the Yoroi. As if on cue, a shadowy figure appeared in the doorway. There was a hood over his face, but the frame of his body was unmistakably that of the shrewd and imposing Ambassador Ezequiel Vargas. He entered the well-decorated room and observed the luminous trinkets and tasteful wall paintings that gave the otherwise dismal setup of Yoroi architecture a pop of color. Darius swallowed hard, nervous to see the man again for the first time since their arrival at the Grand Canyon, and watched in silent horror as the oftentimes distrustful Alliance leader closed and locked the door.

"You are," he started as he turned around, his face still as stern as ever, "the highest priority target for these Anti-Rebels." His accent flourished the sounds of disdain as their name crossed his lips. "It was because they were after you that we had you stabbed—"

"The hell?!" Ina shouted it before Darius had the chance, and while he thought to shrink, to stew on the sadness he felt for his student that did the deed and disappeared, he chose to respond with anger.

"That was you," he hummed in a dragonic way that mirrored, not mimicked, his father. "I could've died! Not to mention—" the thought of Tony's pained expression made him think about the damage done to their mind after that. "You know, you'd think that someone of your standing in this place would take a less reckless course of action!"

"Yes, well," Vargas hesitated. He wasn't overly fond of the Yaiba Insurrection, especially after their clashes in the past or the threatening demeanor of this boy's brutish father, but time did not permit him the luxury of withholding any vital information. "My standing," he continued, "is as much in jeopardy as your life, young Master. The only hope my people have of breaking free from this Scarlet Kingdom comes through you." There it was again, the burden of another's hope thrown at Darius. He would've made it a point to show his disgust if his face hadn't already been so gripped by rage.

"If the Anti-Rebels get their hands on you, though, all that's shot," Ina added. "Vargas looks like the weak leader that couldn't even keep you safe despite inviting you here, the Yoroi go on without any clear offensive training, and the status quo is maintained in the form of a big red stranglehold over our people."

"I know you probably don't understand the necessity of the methods I chose—" Vargas started, but was promptly interrupted.

“You wanted to create the illusion that I was taken out of the picture before your enemies could have the satisfaction,” Darius assumed. It was a shot in the dark, but judging from the look of surprise on Vargas’ face, he must’ve nailed it.

“I was on standby to make sure you recovered,” Ina admitted begrudgingly with a side-eyed look at Vargas who paid her no mind. “I brought you to my place to make sure that that wasn’t interrupted.”

“So then what now,” Darius asked with mild irritation in his tone. It was clear to him that Ina had no intentions of coming clean about her role in all this, but he knew that despite the clear deception it was all in an effort to spare his life so he let it slide.

“You rally your troops and get them ready for war,” Vargas said as though Darius should’ve already known the answer to his own question. “We will meet here in three days to discuss the intelligence that we have gathered. I trust you will be recovered by then?”

“I should be,” Darius told him warily. “What do you mean by ‘rally my troops?’ What troops do I have?” Vargas flashed a rare smile at the boy before he turned to walk towards the door.

“You didn’t think that your students were placed in your care by happenstance, did you?” And without another word, the Ambassador took his leave into the night.

****

November 17th, 2084, 9:20 p.m.,

Erik Kincaid made haste the moment he’d heard. He wasn’t one to be rushed, and preferred to take in the beauty of his surroundings, even when he was surrounded by the slopes and serpentine paths beneath Johnson City’s outskirts. Many of his operatives had moved aboveground with the Yaiba occupation of the city, and did what they could to help with its reconstruction and fortification while Kincaid and the other leaders remained underground. Progress was slow in establishing their base, but with the self-correcting virus the Helmets uploaded to the Kingdom Drone Network, they knew that the Scarlet Air Fleet wouldn't be taking off at any point in the near future, so they had the time to work in peace.

Now, though, a more pressing concern had made its way across the desert and into the audience chamber. When Erik arrived he noted himself the last of the Elders to do so, and with terse greetings to his fellow leaders he took his seat on the tatami mats that circled their roughly-designed holoprojector. The otherwise dark room, illuminated only barely by the faint orange tint of burning candle wicks, was suddenly engulfed in a flickering blue light.

"Ambassador Vargas," Mercutio Forza uttered with an air of surprise, his usually black hair and graying goatee cast in a uniform azure hue. "Good evening. I must admit that a late-night call from you is more than just a little surprising."

"The call is not without its reasons, good Mercutio," Vargas assured him in an almost thespian manner. Elder Forza rolled his eyes, and the Yoroi Ambassador curled the corner of his mouth into a minor smirk. "Jokes aside, the tension within our borders is escalating by the day. As much as it pains me to admit it, I fear that the measures we've taken to reunify our people in the Yoroi may not be enough." The tone of the meeting shifted to serious concern in all the Elders present.

"What's going on that's got you so shaken, Ezequiel," asked Elder Olivia Morton, a brunette woman of middle age and an indeterminable accent of Latinx origin. The smooth texture of her silky voice calmed the typically unmoved Alliance leader, and revealed to him that he had been exactly as she said.

"The Anti-Rebellion faction threatens civil war against the rest of us." Vargas hesitated, unsure if he should divulge sensitive information over a channel such as this, and to these outsiders, no less. But he was a desperate man, and involving the Yaiba Insurrection would only complicate matters further. "Two days ago, the leader of the Scarlet Scourge and her Prince James were seen…visiting the Clusters. This morning, the body of a suspected Anti-Rebellion leader was discovered in a building the enemy was seen leaving."

"But what does that have to do with your Anti-Rebellion problems," came the voice of Alberto de Jesus, a man of darker skin and curly hair that, like the others, adopted the ghostly cerulean gleam of the holoprojector. His face was as stern as Vargas' was usually, and while the Ambassador had always respected that about him in their dealings since last spring, it only exasperated him in this moment.

"They've already begun twisting the situation," Vargas almost shouted, then collected himself. "They're using it as propaganda, claiming that the freedom fighters among us will do whatever it takes to, and I quote, 'end the protection of the Scarlet Kingdom,' including kill our own people."

"It doesn't seem untrue at this point," Kincaid was forced to admit with a wary look in his blue-washed expression. Vargas lost it.

"Because we have been forced to this point by the true aggressors! Stripling! You weren't even alive when the Second Civil War broke out, but I watched the whole thing! The Scarlet Kingdom demonized the freedoms granted by the society they burned to ashes. They slandered and dehumanized all those who opposed them. Even now our founders and your ancestors are little more than rat-eating savages to them! Now you would spit in my face for trying to spare my people the same evils?" There was silence in the room. Vargas breathed heavily and teetered a bit before he forced his legs still.

“Nobody’s spitting in your face, Ezequiel,” Erik said firmly, though his eyes narrowed in irritation. “But if things continue to escalate, and they will, you won’t have much choice in the matter.”

“Indeed,” Vargas breathed heavily after a moment. “I have worked so hard for peace within my borders. An entire lifetime I have labored, for years I gave my best efforts to keep the Yoroi Alliance safe from outsiders, and now it threatens to fall to pieces from the inside.” He inhaled deeply, and this time breathed out with more control in his expression. Even in the grainy image of the projector, the stern Yoroi leader looked sad. Defeated. Inconsolable. “If you can manage to forgive me for my outburst, I would like to ask you for your help.”

Every Elder in the room fell silent, and their eyes showed what could only be described as a deep concern. Never before had Ezequiel Vargas asked for help, especially not from a foreign land. Never before had he risked looking weak to anyone inside the Alliance or outside of it. None of them could doubt that this was a difficult situation for him.

“Our forces are already stretched thin,” Forza was the first to speak. “The Scarlet Kingdom is at our door, and between the threat of violence at the Bluff City Outpost and the restoration effort in Johnson City, it’s safe to say that we have our hands full.”

“However,” Elder Morton spoke in her usual delicate manner, “if you could find a way to use them, we might be able to spare a small team of saboteurs and warriors to help you in this time.” She looked around the room, partially to seek agreement and partially to gauge Erik’s expression to see if she’d gotten ahead of herself. To her delight, the others nodded in approval.

“The Alliance would be grateful for any help you could spare us,” Ezequiel assured them with a gracious bow of his head. Kincaid sat quietly for a moment, fully aware that the rest of them waited for his input before adjourning the meeting. He marveled at how difficult times had become since the dawn of this new war, that they would make a proud man like this bow his head to those he once regarded as enemies.

"I will send you one of my personal guards. He's more than capable of evening the odds if that's what you're looking to do," Erik finally spoke. "He and his team will arrive in roughly three days. Please ensure that we have a map of the safe paths into your territory ahead of time. It'd be most unfortunate if anything were to happen to them on the way out West."

"Absolutely," Vargas agreed. The transmission ended, and all of the Elders felt the same strange sensation, as if the darkness around them waited for the slightest invitation to engulf all it saw.

****

November 17th, 2084, 11:00 p.m.,

Ryan Morrisey was new to this line of assault, but the more he committed to following the plan the more it appealed to him. From a tactical angle, of course. He was a strong-style user, and a prodigious user of the Tsuchiryu style even though he was new to the warfare scene. It was his typical strategy to run through enemies with interchangeable offense and defense, to smash and pierce and tear with little more than the firesword in his hands. But this method gave them an advantage, and he would do anything to cripple the advances of the Reds.

Hand over mouth to prevent the screaming and a swift slit to the throat. He must've put the Kabuto knife to work on a hundred or so Scarlet Troopers by now, and had yet to be caught by any of the patrolmen in the area. The Holston Valley was rife with trees and shrubbery, so the infiltration of the enemy camp was a simple matter, as was the continuance of their operation just under the noses of the trained and merciless Red soldiers.

The heavier machinery was targeted by some of Resnick's men, who placed charges set to go off after they were a decent ways away. They mentioned something about some special radio signal that kept the bombs from blowing too early, but Ryan wasn't concerned with that. All he wanted to do was show his worth in the field, and the five other Insurrectionists that skulked through the tents around him felt the same.

He waited a few seconds so the patrol outside his current tent could pass, then quickly darted through to the weapons cache. He stowed a few adhesive explosives and smaller guns on his person, and when he noticed the Kabuto bomb that was placed on the side of the bigger crate, he slipped under the back flap at the bottom of the tent. The muzzle of a gun met the side of his skull as soon as he sat up, but despite the chill of the metal pipe that dug through his locks and into his scalp, Ryan was more smug than anything. Something made him happy about dealing with an idiot who just didn't know.

"Hands where I can see 'em," the enemy soldier demanded, and with the smug expression still on his face, he raised his hands. The enemy briefly took his eyes away from his target to reach for the walkie-talkie at his hip. Ryan took it as an invitation to pull the gun away from his head. As the enemy jerked forward, clearly stunned by the strength and speed of his adversary, the cunning Insurrectionist slashed his throat seamlessly with the handheld blade and watched as the blood disguised itself with his victim's uniform.

"Charges are placed," came the voice of Tom Freeman, the shadow-skinned Kabuto leader of this operation. "Pack it in and head back to base." His voice was confident, and that was enough to make Ryan's lips peel with excitement as he hastily strode into the black thicket before him. As he rounded the Scarlet camp and met back up with his team, the sounds of blood-chilling screams rang out into the night, and the young Yaiba could almost taste the victory.

Chapter Nineteen

November 20th, 2084, 10:20 a.m.,

This was the moment that Bryan was waiting for. All his time in New York up until this point wasn't for naught though. Having a connection to the fastest-rising star in the Red military and direct bodyguard to the King proved to be more than a little beneficial. Lyla leaked him all their classified information, though with the permissions that she had as the King's favorite, it was unlikely that she would be punished for it.

In two days, he'd discovered that the Kingdom had discovered the Roan Compound shortly after he left, and during their invasion, Emiko died. He wasn't sure how to feel about the news. They'd grown up together, and up until his departure their relationship was a good one. But then his son got killed and all that went out the window. He also discovered that around the same time that he was brought to the capitol, the Yaiba retaliated by seizing Johnson City and exterminating all but a single soldier.

That much was impressive to him, and he noted the sheer tactical genius and equal brutality of the event to be nothing short of John's handiwork. He always knew that his old friend would make a great leader, but it threw a wrench in Bryan's plans to make the Yaiba suffer. He could only see it thriving under the leadership of the Lightning Dragon. It did mean that that was no longer his title, though, and there was one less Dragon to worry about should things come to a head. What he'd learned about the Kabuto Sanctuary's activities beyond what he already knew from their few encounters was still minimal, but he shrugged it off. It was only a matter of time before he was able to figure up countermeasures for them as well.

By the fifth day, Bryan's plans for this war started to come together. From the information that his daughter gave him, the Scarlet Kingdom failed to move past the joint Yaiba/Kabuto outpost in Bluff City. She mentioned something about how half their forces were wiped out in a single night when apparently nobody was looking. The commander put in charge of that operation was relieved of his duties and was executed in the public eye on the sixth day. He was able to see the people in the crowd through the television. At first it felt strange for him to be watching one at all, but that gave way to feelings of disgust at the raucous mob before him. They chanted and cheered for the immediate disposal of the former military leader. They praised the firing squad before they even lifted their rifles, and to Bryan, their wanton barbarism was beyond disgusting. Just another thing he would have to change down the road.

For the two days after the execution, Lyla informed him that he'd have an audience with the King and his Court and then drilled him relentlessly on the proper protocols in addressing royalty. He didn't care, and despite his best efforts, couldn't muster the will to do so. He saw no point in impressing some old man who didn't fully understand the scope of things. Nevertheless, he played along. It was too soon for him to act on his disdain for the way they ran things. He needed to gain their trust, and as much as he hated to use his daughter toward that end, he also knew that it was unavoidable with his limited list of contacts within the Kingdom's borders.

That was what today was for: using his daughter's position to earn a seat at the table for himself. Bryan looked between the panel of decently aged Court members, save for Prince Nash the Barbarian whom he'd met on the battlefield once or twice in his younger years and with whom he had the most tension. It gave him a rush, like the reawakening of his most primal sensibilities, to see one of his oldest foes in such good health. He had half a mind to rectify that problem when the King of the Reds entered.

When Bryan was a boy, he remembered his mother's sudden mental breakdown. She rejected him, despised him, abused him for what had been done to her and the uncertainty of whether he was a product of that. It wasn't until after she was gone and he was a man that he learned of the Raeford Raid. The King of the Reds led the assault on the Yaiba Insurrection's second pre-White Ruins base, and raped his mother right in front of her husband before he was ordered to be executed by a firing squad of the King's personal guard.

Now, here sat the same monster, practically within his reach. The beast of a man, so sculpted with muscle that he could be mistaken as a youth if not for the gray hair, locked his hard gray eyes onto Bryan, who flashed his teeth in a devilish smile.

"That's a peculiar smile," said the King, his voice thunderous, even in his calm. "Do you know why you're here?"

"Because your grace summoned me," Bryan responded quickly, but calmly. To refer to this rapist with honorifics was almost enough to make his eyes water, but he choked back the tears. "Was I to believe that there was another reason?"

"You are here," King Shane spoke pointedly, "because I haven't decided if it would be better to draft you into our service or to kill you in the public square." There was a long, excruciating moment of silence now. When the Red-Clad King saw the lack of expression on Bryan's face, his face became grim as he continued. "For years your little band of rebels has interfered with Kingdom business, but my son Nash tells me that you were the worst of them all. Why do you suppose he would say something like that?"

"It's because I had a habit of showing him how dimwitted he was whenever we met on the battlefield," Bryan said bluntly. He caught himself, and quickly added, "your grace." Nash slammed his fist against the handcrafted table.

"You dare speak of a prince so carelessly," he barked, but the simple twitch of his father's finger was enough to silence him like a frightened boy.

"My sons have never exhibited the tactical genius or martial fortitude that I'd envisioned for them," spoke the King, and Nash dropped his jaw in a mix of surprise and disgust, "but they are my sons, and if you speak of them in such a way again then my decision will have been made. Am I clear?"

"Abundantly, your grace," Bryan stammered. It was fake, of course. A single signal to his daughter and his Reikiken would be in his hands and the entire court would be dead before they could call for help. But killing everyone in earnest wouldn't be wise at this juncture. He needed them to grant him access to their facilities, and so it was in his best interests to woo them with his most charming qualities. "If I may, your grace, I would like to make a confession." Shane raised his eyebrow, but silently nodded. "I have spent a great deal of my life as an enemy of your Kingdom. I have gone to battle against your son, and have won against him and a long list of your best military officers for little more than fun." He hated this stiff tone, and for a moment he wondered if this was what John felt like when Emiko had had him play politics by her side. "But I was wrong to do so." That single utterance was enough to turn every head in the room.

"I don't buy it," Nash was the first to say. "You can see it in his face that he wants something." It took everything in Bryan's power to keep from rolling his eyes at the moronic Prince.

"I only will that the King spares my life so I can prove my use to him," he said with false humility. "It wasn't long ago that my son, Jaden, was killed in battle at the Yoroi's Midland Outpost. It's my understanding that your forces were the ones to raid it, and I applaud you for that."

"You would applaud us for an attack that resulted in the death of your child," Lord Blackwell said with a stern look on his already skeletal face.

"I have no love for the Yoroi, and have battled them almost as many times as I have battled the Prince," he admitted, and for that moment it felt good for him to tell the truth. "And it wasn't your intention to kill my son when you had no way of knowing to whom he belonged."

"Then who is it that you blame for his death," Marquis West asked as he fingered the stubble on his chin. His beady blue eyes were as ice to Bryan, but the Yaiba sellout was unbothered by their chill.

"Why the Insurrection, of course," Bryan remarked in a tone that suggested they knew better than to ask. "Emiko Ishikawa was a childhood friend of mine. We grew up together, played together as children, but none of that sentiment kept her from sending my son and countless others to their deaths over the years and for what? To fight a losing battle and live in a cave in the mountains? When Jaden died," his voice was darker now, and for a split second the King and all his court thought that his eyes lost a little bit of their light at the mention of the boy's name. Something caught in his throat, and after he cleared it, Bryan started over. "When Jaden died, I realized that I'd had enough of the losing side. I wanted to join the winners, and more than anything, I wanted to ensure that they kept that title as long as I was with them, if you catch my meaning."

"How can we be sure that what you say is the truth?" It was the timid Countess McBride that spoke. Bryan shifted his glare, suddenly venomous, to her, and she immediately understood. No parent would ever lie about a loss so great.

"I am the man known as Usagi no Kamikaze, the Rabbit of the Divine Wind. In addition to being a better warrior than most in the Yaiba ranks," *or your own*, he thought, "I was also one of their leading technological researchers and engineers. I know the ins and outs of the Hanzo Gear, and the clever little aura swords that you all are so afraid of." The room was stunned to silence, and despite how he felt inwardly, Bryan's smugness did not find its way to the surface. He patiently awaited the King's judgement. Even Nash sat quietly, unsure if he would want to pass up an opportunity like this just to satisfy his need for vengeance.

"We will…" King Shane started. His voice was little more than an exasperated grumble. "We will take this under advisement. You are dismissed."

****

November 20th, 2084, 12:44 p.m.,

The trip through the extensive minefield was more than challenging for the Kabuto agents, but not for the usual reasons. The Scarlet Prince, James O'Neill and the Scarlet Scourge with him, kept a watchful eye on the Yoroi Alliance from the outside, so entering through the front door was out of the question. With the assistance of their transports and the familiarity they had of the Alliance's territories in the Southwest, Levi Taylor and a team of six Kabuto men and women circumvented the main entrance and entered through the same secret pass that the Yaiba had used over a month before.

Levi's face remained stoic, but with every inch they gained on their objective his heart beat faster. It was his first mission as a team leader, and he felt that his first mission without Erik watching him closely needed to be commemorated by a successful execution of all of his duties. He knew that Erik was the way he was because he cared. Out of all of the Elders of the Kabuto, Erik was the one most attached to his people, and as irritating as Levi saw it, it was probably the most important factor in his drive for success.

His team was finally in range. Levi held up his fist at the edge of the canyon and tapped the frequency specified by their hosts. His agents, who guided the transports to a halt behind him, watched in astonishment as a loud metallic screech permeated the air. The sound stopped, and with a swift signal from Levi followed by his expedient return to his own transport, the Kabuto convoy was on its way.

****

November 20th, 2084, 1:26 p.m.,

Darius paced the floor of his new dwelling impatiently. It'd been three days since Vargas promised that he'd be able to resume his instruction, and he was more than eager to show his students that he was alright. It was only yesterday that the Ambassador and leader of the Pro-Rebel faction told him that there was a surprise in store for him as well, though since his last one stabbed him in the gut, he wasn't certain how eager he should be for any more, even if Ina did assure him that it was alright. He checked his watch again, and four minutes earlier than expected there was a knock at the door. He stood up to answer it, but immediately felt his heart drop when the door opened on its own. He grabbed his Reikiken and ignited it instantly, but breathed a sigh of relief when Ina emerged from the other side. She glared at him at first, but then allowed her jaw to unclench and a smile to take its place along its center.

"That how you're gonna start greeting all your guests," she asked him.

"I might," he said defensively, embarrassed. "Last time I tried to be nice around here I got shanked." Ina thought for a moment.

"Fair point," she conceded. "Speaking of that, Vargas is behind me with someone who claims to be acquainted with you."

"What?" Darius, for a moment, hoped that it was his dad, but knew that things wouldn't be that simple. Besides, he'd already made up his mind that he wouldn't call his father to bail him out; not this time.

"Yeah, now that I think about it, that might've been the surprise that Vargas said he'd have for you." Ina shrugged indifferently. "Oh, well." From behind her there entered a young man with brown hair, innocent green eyes, a milky complexion and, at first, a neutral expression on his face.

"Commander," he said as his face morphed to display a coy grin that almost looked out of place. "It's been a while."

"Levi," Darius said, stunned. Vargas entered the room and, with him, the startling chill of authority.

"So you do know each other," said the stoic Ambassador with what Darius thought was a hint of delight. It was weird to him but he didn't question it. "That will make this easier."

"What exactly is 'this,' if you don't mind my asking," the Rebel Dragon inquired. "We haven't gone over any plans aside from me staying in this cabin and training my students as previously discussed." He looked around at the cramped little shack built into the side of the Canyon and away from the Clusters. It was a place that could only be accessed through a tunnel network that had gone unused ever since the Insurrection bombed the main entryways and exits. It took five years to hollow out again, but by then there was no need for the Alliance to continue its use.

"We'll have time to get into the planning," Levi started hesitantly. He wasn't sure how to say what he needed to in any way that would be respectful of Darius and his feelings, but still he tried. "Look, this isn't easy to say, but there's something that you need to know." He took a deep breath and looked Darius in the eye with a sudden coldness to his innocent green orbs. "Almost two months ago, now, a group of Scarlet troops attacked the Insurrection compound in the Roan Mountain." Everyone in the room sobered, and could visibly see how Darius' heart dropped. Still there was more. "Emiko Ishikawa was among those killed in combat."

Darius was more than just a little shaken. Director Ishikawa was an aunt to him, and occasionally she came off as a second mother. Her last words to him rang through his head. *Represent us well.* A tear streamed down the dragonling's face, and though his body shook with a dark mixture of anger and sorrow, he steeled himself for what was to come.

"Who's leading the Yaiba now," Darius asked with a rattle in his voice that brought deeper concern from his allies.

"The new Director of the Insurrection is your father, John Hamlin," Levi informed him. There was a long pause, a stiff silence from the lot of them before Darius cleared his throat.

"Did you come alone?" Levi knew that the Rebel Dragon's question was directed at him, and for a moment the reptilian nature of Darius' voice made him feel pure terror.

"There are six others with me. They're running recon right now on the Clusters and trying to get a read on the Anti-Rebels. We should have everything we need to know about their hideouts, meeting locations, and plans within a week's time," he replied and Darius nodded.

"And what of that Scourge woman," Darius continued as his eyes drifted to Vargas. Even he was powerless before the ferocity of the young warrior. It was enough to make him question whether or not he was the same child he'd met before.

"Neither the Prince nor the Scourge have entered our territory in the last three days," he spat out quickly, then forced himself calm again. "Scans do show that a massive force is still lying in wait at our front door."

"Something is happening that I don't like," Darius murmured. "How massive of a force are we talking about, here?"

"At last check they numbered just over four thousand troops," Ina supplied, and Darius ran his hand over his dark curly hair.

"How many of them can the outer traps hold off," the Rebel Dragon inquired. The more he thought about the situation the more he realized just how many variables they needed to account for and how quickly they needed to do it.

"I would say about half of that number, a little more if they came from all sides," Vargas spoke warily. The four of them knew how unfavorable the situation was with just the Scourge at their door alone. Factoring in the internal threat of the Anti-Rebels only made things harder to predict since they weren't so open about their positions.

"Then it's settled," Darius spoke with a certainty that caught the others by surprise. "Ambassador, I'll be needing a meeting with the other leaders of the Pro-Rebellion Faction. Ina, bring me my students. Tony included. There's a lot I need to catch them up on and we're running out of time. Levi, if you don't mind, I need you to infiltrate the Scarlet camp and do your own thing. Sabotage their transports, seal off their weapons usage, jam their comms as much as you can with whatever tools the Yoroi can spare. We need to stall them for as long as we can if we have any chance of winning."

"Always quick on your feet," Levi said with his arms folded across his chest and a massive smile in place. Vargas' eyes went wide at his confidence, and Ina shifted her attention nervously from her boss, the newcomer, and the Hanzo Instructor that she assumed was so far out of his depth that he'd gone mad.

"You cannot be serious," spoke the Ambassador, careful to snuff out any light of hope that might shine through his eyes. "Do you think we can so brazenly engage such a large number of enemies?" Darius looked at him with the most arrogant smile that Vargas had ever seen.

"Absolutely," he said confidently. "The Yaiba have been doing it for years."

****

November 22nd, 2084, 3:43 p.m.,

The Scarlet Scourge patiently awaited the arrival of their Anti-Rebel "allies" and their precious cargo, and while they stewed in their own expectations they handled the labors of the camp as diligently as before. Serafina, however, groaned with agitation at the substantial lack of action.

"You know," she mused with a girlish tone that sent a chill down Aria's spine, "when I joined the Scourge, I was expecting a little more action."

"If you need more action," Aria retorted without skipping a beat, "then why don't you go talk to Cecelia about what to do about the rations? We've been out here for way longer than expected and food is starting to get scarce."

"Cecelia?" The intonation of the question radiated waves of disapproval. "You sure you picked the right person for that job? She comes off a little…brutish, don't you think?" Aria turned away from the fire she was trying to start to look Leyva over.

"Why are you here, Madame Leyva," asked Black, eyes squinted in a suspicious expression that made Serafina chortle.

"Ugh, no need to be so formal, Ms. Black," she said mockingly. "That 'Madame' stuff always got on my nerves. As for your question, do you mind getting more specific? Why am I alive? Why am I in Arizona? Why am I looking over your shoulder watching you fail to start a fire? I'm not entirely sure what you're asking me."

“Why did you join the Scourge,” Aria specified, a little more than agitated now. “More specifically, how did you join the Scourge without the Colonel’s approval?”

“King Shane owed me a favor,” the wily Leyva offered with a devilish smirk. Aria scoffed at the notion.

“You’re so full of crap,” she challenged, condescending as usual. “What could you have possibly done to make the King feel indebted to you?”

“Nothing major,” Serafina cooed with an indifferent shrug. Her eyes narrowed in a half-sultry, half-menacing way as she said, “I just killed Emiko Ishikawa of the Yaiba.” She waited for a moment and watched as Aria’s face twitched, clearly conflicted with emotion at the news of the former Director’s death. She couldn’t believe that Emiko would just…die. They trained together when they were kids, and while she was always sweet, Emiko always had an indominable fire at her core. This had to be some clever lie to get under Aria’s skin.

“You almost had me there,” Aria cracked a nervous smile. “You expect me to believe that someone like Emiko would lose to a nutjob like you?”

“Hey,” chided Leyva, “words hurt, you know? Besides, whether you believe it or not doesn’t matter. It happened, and I have the bodycam footage if you want to watch.” This time there was a discernable distress on Aria’s face that the Scourge’s newest member couldn’t help but savor. “Oh that’s right. You started off as one of *them*, didn’t you? What was it like growing up in the wilderness foraging for berries?”

“It wasn’t like that,” Aria snapped, furious that this glorified grunt had the nerve to talk down to her, but then she caught herself. What reason did she have to be defensive over the Insurrection now? “Not exactly, anyway.”

"So testy. It's almost as if you still identify with them." Serafina leaned in as the flustered Aria struggled to maintain her composure. "But that can't be true, can it, Ms. Black?"

"Not at all," Aria assured her more aggressively than she'd hoped. Serafina raised an eyebrow as a coy smile lined her jaw.

"Let's hope not. It'd be a shame if that got in the way of your duties…" The supposition that it could was enough to send Black over the edge.

"Here's some advice," Aria started in her sharp, calmly indignant tone, "instead of worrying about my job, why don't you go ask the Colonel what yours is around here since you're new?"

"Hey, you were the one who started the questioning, sweetheart. It's not my fault you don't like what I had to say," Serafina shrugged. "Here's some advice for you. Keep a tighter grip on those emotions. Let them run around too freely and you never know what might happen to you. Just girl to girl, you know." She walked away, and though Aria pretended not to care, the threat in Leyva's voice shook her to her very essence.

****

November 22, 2084, 7:42 p.m.,

Darkness took the Southwest Territory over an hour ago, and Serenity waited at the designated location between the Grand Canyon and the Scarlet base camp. Kyle watched from the distance with Ryan, the youngest, positioned out in the desert with his sniper rifle loaded and his body perfectly blended into the night. Two underlings of the Anti-Rebels marched toward their position, and all three siblings went on the defensive. It wasn't that they were so intimidating, and Kyle would've given Ryan the signal if he sensed anything dangerous through his surveillance equipment. No, none of them were able to put their finger on what it was that triggered this attitude from them. Perhaps it was the many battles they'd fought in the past, or the implications of this moment for them and their Prince. Regardless, history had proven to each of them that it was better this way.

"Got the target in sight," said Ryan Crawford with a boyish delight. "You want me to pick 'em off now?"

"Not yet," Kyle spoke through the comms. "Not until the Colonel confirms that it is the target." Ryan giggled at the way Kyle talked of their older sister.

"You know you don't have to call her that when it's just us, right," said the youngest. "I know she's scary but it's not like she'll do anything."

"Cut the chatter," Serenity demanded through clenched teeth. She was tempted to shake her head but resolved to remain stern. Her brothers baffled her, especially Ryan. He was such a smooth talker in briefings and could smooth over any debate in such a way that made the participants question what the fuss was all about. When it came to his siblings, however, he was still very much a child. Serenity fixed her eyes on the feminine figure behind the two Anti-Rebel grunts and smiled. "Good evening, Felicity. Looks like you've been doing well."

"Well, Serenity, what can I say? Life's a lot easier when people don't look down on you for being a woman," Felicity said. She was of pale skin, brown hair that looked black under the cover of night, and dark brown eyes that killed whatever lights hit them, and everything about her demeanor was that of a defeated woman saddened by a day of reckoning she knew was inevitable from the outset.

"As you can see," one of the grunts started as he stepped toward Serenity, "we have upheld our end of the ba—" a thunderous bang filled the air and in the same instant his brains coated the sands in a mix of red and gray. His body fell limp, and his companion could do little to squelch the shrill scream that bellowed from her gut.

"Sorry," Ryan apologized earnestly. "Finger slipped. Won't happen again." Serenity groaned out of frustration. She knew he was overzealous but a bloody mess like this was enough to cause unnecessary tension. One killing made a statement. Two bordered too much on either incompetence or blatant disregard of their supposed allies. She turned her focus back to the still-living grunt.

"You've done well. Tell Francis that we'll bring Mr. Thornhill to the specified location by tomorrow afternoon," she ordered as she turned to return to the Scarlet camp.

"B-but you…" the grunt mumbled as she twitched in place. The Scourge leader turned back to face her, an eyebrow raised at the audacity. "We—I mean I—can take him back with me now."

"And how do you expect to explain to the onlookers in your little home just how you came upon a confirmed captive of the Scarlet Kingdom?" Serenity narrowed her eyes as she spoke the question. The girl that stood across from her stammered as she thought.

"I just thought—" she started to explain, but was cut off by the methodical Red soldier.

"You thought that you, a member of the Anti-Rebel sentiment, could just walk into Yoroi Territory with a prisoner of war free and clear? Tell me, did you think about how it would make you look complicit in his capture or how it would undermine your entire efforts to bring the people to your side?" The girl offered no response, for how could she? Serenity Crawford was a master tactician, and if there was anyone with a bona fide method of creating or calming civil unrest, it was her. "Tomorrow afternoon. Be ready."

"Yes, ma'am," said the girl. She turned to hastily walk away, and once she was out of sight she sprinted back into the cavern from whence she crawled.

"Liquidate target," Serenity said into her earpiece, and before Felicity could think to run, her body fell to the desert floor, cold and lifeless.

****

November 22nd, 2084, 6:36 p.m.,

Levi arrived on his ShadowStalker just moments before the Crawford siblings headed out for their rendezvous, but they didn't notice. For him, he drove straight through their checkpoints on a speedy motorcycle-type transport, but for the Scarlet guards they only felt a strange yet sudden gust of wind whirl past them. He initially doubted the cloaking tech that the engineering team built into it, but seeing it in action gave him the edge he needed to slip behind enemy lines and carry out the mission that Darius had given him.

He stalked the grounds of the Scarlet camp with silent grace and weaved his body through their bustling crowd undetected. The transports were the easiest thing to find, and once he snaked his way through the seemingly never-ending flow of enemy troops, he got to work placing EMP devices and explosive charges over their machines and control panels. It wasn't enough to cause serious damage, but the repairs would take a while to complete, especially since the Prince's brigade was isolated from capitol reinforcements.

Once the bombs and devices were safely placed beyond the potential notice of their technicians, Levi found the part of the camp specifically reserved for the infantrymen. It was there, too, that he found the munitions and, despite his strong desire to steal a crate or two for the cause, continued his work of properly beautiful sabotage. The sheer volume of crates and weapons racks assured him that even with only a few thousand soldiers, the Kingdom's forces were more than ready for a lengthy battle. That alone was all the reason he needed to deploy charges here as well.

It was when he was on the way back to his ShadowStalker that his eyes happened upon Aria Black, headed into a tent and forbidding entry to a young Hispanic woman. Intrigued, he advanced on their location, careful to move slowly and avoid causing a stir. He inched closer, and as he did he could hear more of what was said inside. At first it was the muffled sound of Aria's voice alone, but Levi's ears perked up at the sound of an exasperated male.

"You really should be nicer to me," Aria scolded coldly, "since I'm the only reason you're alive right now."

"I'm alive," came the man, "because I told your Prince how to sneak into Alliance Territory unnoticed. It had nothing to do with you, hungry as you are to get your ego stroked."

"And who do you think keeps you from having a one-on-one chat with Cecelia," Black asked rhetorically. "Oh, that's right. I do. You know she'd sooner beat you bloody with her bare hands, don't you?"

"Huh," spoke the apparent captive, "and you keep me from meeting her? What a shame." Levi, transfixed by the moment, moved closer to get a clearer listen when he accidentally kicked the post of the tent. The young Hispanic woman swiftly turned her head and almost hit him in the eye with her long, curly hair. He took a step back, and as she stepped forward he walked around her as silently as he could. She reached out to grasp the air and found nothing.

As Levi backed away from the young woman's position the door to the tent opened.

"I'll be back in just a moment, Mr. Thornhill," spoke Aria Black, as she rushed forward and almost knocked into the effectively invisible Levi Taylor. He narrowly dodged and watched as Aria confronted the other woman. "What the hell was that noise?"

"I dunno," the other woman spoke. "I was just out here minding my own business and then I heard the pole knock." Aria surveyed the area, and though she found nothing, she could tell that something was off. "Have a team search the camp. Seems like we've been infiltrated." The words left her mouth at the exact moment that her eyes looked right through him. She entered the tent again, and just before the flap fluttered closed he could see the truth of a captured Johannes.

Chapter Twenty

November 23rd, 2084, 2:39 p.m.,

They infiltrated Cluster C in the same way that they had before, though this time Serenity and Prince James were accompanied by a clean and shaven Johannes Thornhill. He walked between them, the Prince at the head and Serenity at his back, and with every step he took he felt his life drain away. He wasn't concerned with the war, the Yaiba, or even the Scarlet Kingdom at large. No, what he was concerned with, however, was his beloved Ina, and the threat he'd led right to her doorstep.

They traversed the tunnels and met their contact, Tanner, the same as they did last time. The burly man in the worker's coveralls beamed at the group, and grew more excited still when Johannes was clear in his field of vision.

"Well ain't you a sight for sore eyes," he said with a mixture of relief and good spirits. "Johnny Boy! Been a while since anyone's seen you in these parts. You might wanna check in with your missus. Woman's been worried somethin' awful." Johannes gave a wry smile as he stepped forward to hug the crater cart driver.

"I will," he said out loud. "I guess I'll be in a little trouble when she sees me next. How've you been though? How are Marissa and the kids?" Tanner's ears perked up at the mention, and he slowly pulled back from the embrace.

"Oh, you know," he said nonchalantly, "just as lively as ever. But anyway, where am I taking you lovely folks today?"

"Cluster A, if you don't mind," Serenity breathed with no attempt to hide her scathing irritation. James looked at her, and she corrected herself. "Sorry, my back again."

"Cluster A it is. All aboard!" Tanner shouted, as though there were more passengers than the three of them. The Prince raised an eyebrow as a humored expression budded on his face, and Tanner, now embarrassed, scratched his head with a nervous smile. "Sorry, just something I picked up from my daddy." Without another word he led the way into the crater cart and took to the controls. In seconds they were off, and Johannes watched his escorts with due animosity.

Serenity smirked, totally unbothered by the captive, while the Prince just rolled his eyes. A tense silence persisted between them for roughly twenty minutes before Serenity tired of his idle gawking.

"Something on your mind, Mr. Thornhill?" She asked the question with such a flair that one might easily mistake her agitation for humor. "Don't be shy, you know you can talk to us about anything."

"I'm just curious to know what you think is gonna happen today," Johannes shrugged with surprisingly convincing indifference. "You two are—" he cleared his throat when the Prince's stardust gray eyes turned on him in a cautious glare. "You two are helping me get home, yeah, but have you thought about how you're gonna handle Ina?" James and Serenity looked at each other as if they were in the middle of some telepathic conversation.

"I don't think Ina will be anything to worry about," James said with an amused tone that sharply contrasted the grave expression on his face. In that moment, the charming Prince of the Reds revealed a lot to Johannes. He didn't like to be out of the loop. Twice now a strange woman had been mentioned, first in passing and now by name. He was beginning to question her significance, and the fact that he had questions at all was enough to anger him. Johannes saw an opportunity, and decidedly issued a knowing smile that he was sure would further incite the Prince.

“Then you don’t know my Ina,” said the emissary. “She’s a loving soul, yeah, but a bold one to put it lightly.”

“Oh yeah,” Tanner chimed in from the front of the crater cart, “she might be a teacher now, but Ina got her start as a guerilla fighter laying traps outside the Canyon. She was decommissioned for coming up with some of the most lethal trap combos to date. Higher-ups said she was bordering on inhumane.”

“She didn’t really take kindly to that, either,” Johannes admitted. “She loves her job now, don’t get me wrong, but I think she’s just waiting for an excuse to let out whatever pent up aggression is left over from her time in the military.” The simplicity of the exchange irked the Scarlet duo, because the sudden unpredictability of the situation meant that a certain degree of caution was necessary.

“Even so, we brought you back,” Serenity protested, then mentally scolded herself for even sounding afraid of another human being. She’d hoped that Johannes hadn’t noticed, but the young dignitary was aglow with humor.

“You would think that would mean something, wouldn’t you?” His expression was beyond smug, much to the chagrin of his two already hostile companions. “The first thing that Ina’s gonna ask you is why it took you so long to rescue me.” There was a moment of tense silence that made Tanner twitch a bit at the controls.

“How did you rescue him, anyway,” asked the burly crewman. The car slowed, which told its passengers that their destination was at hand. “Just seems to me that you would’ve brought him with you the last time you were here is all.” Prince James was about to fake an answer when the vehicle came to a halt at the same underground platform in Cluster A that they’d visited on their last excursion.

"It's a story for the ages," James assured him instead, "But we really must be going. I think we can all agree that Mr. Thornhill here has been away from his home for long enough."

"Yeah," Tanner reluctantly agreed. "You folks have a nice day." He watched carefully as James and Serenity escorted Johannes from the crater cart and onto the platform. He surveyed them as they hastily sped towards the outgoing tunnels that would inevitably lead them to the surface, and once they were out of sight and out of earshot, he picked up his comms unit. "Blazing Maiden, come in," he said with a sudden edge to his voice.

"What's up, Wagon Chief?" It was Ina, just as chipper as she always was when they spoke.

"You might wanna round up a crew and head to Cluster A. We might have ourselves a situation."

****

November 23rd, 2084, 3:57 p.m.,

It'd been a little less than a week since they started training. At her request, Zahara was granted access to the trainees most likely to graduate before month's end, and was given all the proper clearances to surprise them with firearm training. It was rigorous training that spanned the depth of gun safety and employment, from handguns and semiautomatic rifles to sniper rifles and RPGs. The class that she'd been instructing proved to be particularly gifted, and she made a mental note of the star players in this potential squad.

Orson Nucci, a tall muscular young man with fair skin, olive-green eyes and night-colored hair took to the M16 as though it were second nature. After three days of quality time with it, he'd figured out how to best optimize its single-fire and semi-auto features with minimal instruction from Zahara.

Drew McDowell, a dark-skinned man with deep-thinking brown eyes and black locks draped around his head, favored the Desert Eagle pistol and endeavored to use it with his off-hand while his main hand wielded a Reikiken. The first test run of that was only slightly less disastrous than it could've been, but heat-treating from the lab made McDowell's chosen firearm much more suited to his usual offensive tendencies.

Karina Velazquez was of a smaller frame than either of the other two, and was unable to do much with a standard sized Reikiken. She was, however, well-equipped for stealth operations and her brown sugar-colored eyes lit up at the first sight of her new M39 semi-automatic Enhanced Marksman Rifle. They came standard-issue for sniper training in the Kingdom, and with the way the Yaiba typically entered conflict, accurate shots were a necessity.

The other members of the class were adequate with the new weaponry so generously gifted by the Reds, but Zahara decided to test them one last time.

"On the line," she demanded, her voice hard as the stone floor of the gray-colored range, and the first five riflemen took their starting positions. She eyed the targets in the distance for a moment, partly to marvel at the speed at which the Director could have one assembled, but mostly to envision the men and women who, for all the years of her life, heaped abuse on her for no reason other than the color of her skin. Her brow wrinkled as she commanded, "Take aim!" The five designated gunmen raised the muzzles of their weapons, each pointed at a different target, each student firmly in control of their gun. Zahara minded their form, fixed the positioning of two of her students, and then when it was all to her liking, she raised a hand. Not a shot was fired, which proved to her that the neophyte gunmen had learned from their mistakes. She lowered her arm directly in front of her and, with the same degree of ferocity as before, ordered her troops in training to "Light 'em up."

Five shots hit five targets at varied degrees of proficiency, then again. Then again. Each of the M16s was equipped with a 30-round magazine well, and the five riflemen stayed in place until the last round. They adjusted their bodies in a windowpane formation to allow the next line to take aim, while their final shots were rocketed towards the distant targets. The first line fell back to reload while the second line took their places in full. Without a word from Zahara, they continued the volley of bullets until they, too, ran dry and were forced to make room for their replacements.

This process repeated until all four lines had had their fun and landed a shot to the targets. Zahara was proud, as were they all, after having come so far in only a week. It wasn't unnatural, to be fair. The standard time that any Scarlet Trooper trainee would train with the extensive firearms at their disposal was roughly a week. The constant disturbances to the Kingdom's peace ensured that, whether at the border of their territories or deep within the other regions, they would have plenty of opportunities to get comfortable with it. The Yaiba Insurrection, however, proved to be far less spineless at first than the neophyte Reds.

When the floor was quiet and all of the disposable ammunition had run out, Zahara paced before her group of trainees with her hands clasped behind her back. She weighed her thoughts, analyzed the proficiency of their shots, and occasionally glanced at the targets, much to her delight. She observed their faces as the eyes of every one of the young Shadows followed her methodical footsteps.

"Zahara-sensei," Karina asked. Zahara slightly turned her head towards her students as she lifted her eyebrow. The gesture made the young girl pause, but she continued to ask her question despite her fear. "How much longer are we supposed to train with the firearms?" Her tone was kind, though a bit timid, and Zahara had to catch herself before her glare of steel faded into something much softer.

"Actually, you're just about finished," said the intimidating sniper. "Listen up," she barked, and all of the surrounding trainees snapped to attention. She took a second to admire their intense obedience before she continued, "This week in your training was deemed necessary by the Director himself, and while you may think yourselves proficient enough with a gun now, neither he nor I are willing to believe that." A number of the students groaned, some looked heartbroken, and Orson and Drew protested in earnest. "Quiet," Zahara commanded, and instantly they were silenced. "As I was saying," her voice was slightly more menacing now, "neither I nor Director Hamlin will see you as proficient unless you demonstrate your skill when the stakes are a little bit higher than this." Puzzled, the group looked at each other, a rush of worried murmurs cast into the air. The corner of Zahara's mouth curled just barely into a smirk, but she capped it at that, lest her pupils see her as sadistic and patronizing.

"Excuse me, Sensei," Drew spoke delicately so as not to incite her to wrath. "Do you mean combat?" The thought had definitely crossed her mind, all things considered. The fact that they were solidly in the middle of a war made such thinking practical. But according to the Director, there was something else they needed to do before marching off into the fray.

"No," she replied flatly, "at least not yet. Director Hamlin and I agree that your individual skill is nothing without a willingness to pass it on. So, over the next two weeks, you will be educating the younger classes and passing on your newfound skills. After that, you lot will be joining me on a time-sensitive mission. Provided you're considered up for the task."

"Oh, we'll be more than ready," Orson assured her. She allowed her smirk to grow now. Orson was by far the cockiest of her students, but it was that surety of himself that made her believe that he would excel on the battlefield above the rest. She folded her arms and looked the lot of them over again.

"For your sake, I hope you are."

****

November 23rd, 2084, 7:17 p.m.,

John was exhausted. He didn't even feel like his usual trips to the training hall, which, for a moment, alarmed him beyond compare. As his time as Director crept towards two months, it was almost easy now to see just how Emiko had allowed her skills to diminish so. He mentally bit his tongue. It wasn't his place to criticize the martial skills of the old Director, especially since she was his friend.

He walked through the door of his home, frustrated with himself and with the job that had been left to him. Aaliyah happily rushed to meet him when she heard the door open, but when she caught a glimpse of his downtrodden demeanor, her expression sobered.

"Honey," she said soothingly, "what's wrong?" She took his hand in hers and tenderly stroked the back of it with her thumbs. John gave her a half-hearted smile, but it didn't last long. She pulled him close. "Hard day, huh? Tell me all about it." He took her sweetly by the shoulders and pulled her back just an inch so that he could see her face.

"You sure you wanna hear about it, love?" The quiver in his lip told her everything that she needed to know. He was at his limit, consumed by worry, anxiety, a crippling sense of urgency that he couldn't shake because he had to be strong for everyone in the Insurrection now. The misty look in his eyes told her that he wanted to scream or fight or curl underneath a blanket and hide from the world but he couldn't. He needed help, but he didn't know how to ask for it.

"Of course," she said with a slightly amused expression. "You forget, I'm here to help you when things get hard. Don't worry about overwhelming me or anything. I'm a big girl, and I can take it." He kissed her on her forehead before touching it with his own. He took a moment to calm down, and for a while the only sound between them was that of their breathing. He inhaled sharply, and their eyes met again. John opened his mouth, but then closed it. He didn't know where to begin, but even so, Aaliyah was patient with him.

She ran her hands along the length of his arms and smiled sweetly towards him as she said, "It's alright. Take your time." It was the show of her patient kindness that moved him to speak.

"There's just so much going on," John told her in a half-joking manner. She knew it was just his way of trying to keep from crying. "Scarlet forces are marching on Johnson City so I've had to send reinforcements to the Bluff Outpost to make sure that Callan can hold them back. The fortification of Johnson City is taking longer than expected because of the changing seasons and the limited amount of engineers between the Yaiba and the Kabuto."

"That really does sound like a lot," Aaliyah told him. To an outsider, it would seem as though she was at a loss for words, but John knew that her mind had already started to work on potential solutions.

"It's not even the tip of the iceberg," he told her as she tried to guide him to a seat in their living room. "Zahara, our newest recruit and provisional Master, says that we need to get to the Wastes as soon as possible, but the only way we can do that is by dismantling a Kingdom base in Jackson and I don't even know who I'd send along with her to make sure it all goes smoothly."

"Well you already know that Dross is out," Aaliyah muttered pensively. John looked up, a puzzled expression on his face.

"Dross? I think he's the perfect person to go with her since she already likes him," he protested, but Aaliyah shook her head.

"They're in love," she told him bluntly, and laughed at the shocked look on his face. "From what you told me they haven't realized it yet, but they are. You send those two on any mission together and it'll probably go sideways." He hesitated an answer, but ultimately realized that his lovely wife was correct.

"Well that decision got a lot harder," he muttered in the hopes that she couldn't hear. She did, but she knew that he was in a mood and didn't want to challenge it. As was her norm, Aaliyah only wanted to help John in the same way that he'd always helped her when her job became too much for her to handle. "Sorry," he said sincerely when he realized how much that must've hurt her. "I didn't mean—"

"I know, babe," she assured him with a sweet smile. He cleared his throat.

"Then there's everything happening in the Southwestern Territory. The Scarlet Scourge is still out there somewhere and despite their reputation for setting it off, their activity's been stalled for some time." John's muscles visibly tensed with the thought of his son being the next casualty of the Scarlet Death Squad. He worried more than he could even admit to himself, and the fear of losing his little one stayed with him the longer his dragonling was away. Aaliyah worried about the both of them. Darius because of the nature and conditions of his mission in the Yoroi territory, and John because nothing gave him quite as much joy as providing safety for his family. Now that Darius was gone, all due to the final spiteful act of Bryan Piccio, John felt as though he was useless, powerless to give his family what they needed. He felt as if he'd abandoned them, even though he and they all knew that it was the furthest thing from the truth.

"He's gonna be okay," Aaliyah told him as she massaged his shoulders. This time her tone wasn't sweet or understanding, but confident and unwavering. "That boy of ours has been a warrior from the moment he came into this world. He's strong and cunning, just like his pops. He also has his mother's compassion and analytical skills. Our son has the best of us both, and even though you were away for most of it, he got foundational combat training from the Seven Dragons. Nobody short of your level is going to be able to harm him that easily." She sat on the arm of the chair and ran her fingers through his low-cut curly hair.

"I know you're right, honey, I know that," John said, still frustrated beyond anything she could do, "but everything in me is screaming at me to show up and shield that kid from the world with my own body if need be. I already couldn't protect Cal in the field during the Johnson City Raid—"

"Honestly, given that boy's attitude that might just be for the best. He's been holed up in Kaneuji's workshop for days now, working away on some new project called the 'Kiringan' or something," Aaliyah told him, and with a shake of his head, John couldn't help but smile.

"That boy," he started, and Aaliyah chuckled, which drew his attention. "What?"

"They're not boys anymore," she said, as if he should be well aware of that fact by now. "They're young men, and both of them know what they signed on for when they decided to follow in your footsteps. Trust that you've prepared them well enough and let them live their lives. It's gonna suck, you're going to have moments where you watch them make mistakes and fall flat on their faces, but our boys are strong enough to get back up again and fight back twice as hard." John sighed as he sank in the chair and lifted his eyes to his beloved wife.

"This parenting thing sucks," he exhaled, which made Aaliyah laugh again. She leaned closer to him and kissed his cheek.

"Any chance you'll run away from it?" He smiled as he thought about his two sons, and just the simple fact that they existed was enough to produce a subconscious grin of fatherly pride.

"Not even a small one," he told her, and quietly wished for a chance to hug his kids along with the wife in his arms.

****

November 23rd, 2084, 7:17 p.m.,

Ever since Tanner made the call, Ina was more than a little on edge. Johannes was back, and just knowing that was overpowering to her. As soon as she told Darius, he started to throw together a plan. It amazed her how gifted he was at analyzing a situation and creating almost air-tight steps to handle it all. By 4 in the afternoon, Vargas, Leroy Baptiste, Bobbi Brynarr, Lex Ford, and even Tony Landry had all arrived at Darius' makeshift dwelling in the face of the Canyon. By 5, Levi and his team had returned from their final reconnaissance. According to his six subordinates, Johannes was being held in an inconspicuous location in the heart of Cluster A by the Anti-Rebels.

"I need a layout," Darius said pensively, and Levi smirked as his fingers snapped against the edge of his palm.

"Way ahead of you," he responded, and one of his subordinates came forward with a pocket-sized holoprojector. It flickered to life and cast a blue-hued image of the enemy base on the wall. "It's a pretty simple setup, unfortunately. There are only two main entrances. One here," he pointed to the north side of the building in the centermost position, and Ina's heart rampaged within her chest, "and another here," he said with a gesture to the west entrance.

"That is a challenge. To make things worse, it's at the center of the Cluster, so a full team of fighters at either entrance probably wouldn't be a good idea unless we wanted to send the civilians into a panic," Darius thought aloud. Ina was already ahead of the game when it came to panic. The building of discussion was not even a block away from the school where she worked. Terrorists had been nestled around the corner from her kids, and she'd had no idea in all this time.

"You also can't be in the field either, Teach," Leroy said with his usual calm. Darius flashed his student a look, as if to question where Leroy found the courage to tell him what he was and wasn't allowed to do. Leroy, slightly intimidated, hastily explained his reasoning, partly with the intent of begging his sensei's forgiveness for such an obvious breech of bounds. "You're not supposed to be alive right now, and it's best that the Anti-Rebels hold onto that lie for the time being. They feel emboldened, they have the hostage, and we can exploit that."

"How do you think we can exploit that," Darius asked from a place of genuine curiosity, and happily did Vargas chime in.

"These Anti-Rebels are desperate to win our people over to their side," he informed the group, his semi-thick, ambiguously South American accent on full display. "When they received news that you had been stabbed, the most radical among them were quick to claim the deed as their own handiwork."

"Oh, so if he comes back from the grave at the right time—" Bobbi came to life with the realization. "That makes sense!"

"We'd discredit them," started Lex, whose smile became slightly more devious at the thought. "Then the public opinion goes with us no matter what they try to do."

"Exactly," Vargas affirmed. Darius was more than reluctant to let his fledgling students handle the operation on their own, especially a reduced number of them. He looked around the room and exhaled sharply. Ina was the person that concerned him the most, because it was her loved one that dangled in the balance of life and death. He took a moment to consider all of the options, and while none of them were destined to be particularly good at this short notice, he arrived at one that was better than the rest. He looked at Ina again, and with a look of gratitude on his face he cleared his throat.

"Alright, here's what we need to do…" Darius' determination sent a wave of comfort through his friend and former host. After worrying about him for so long, Johannes was finally about to come home.

****

November 23rd, 2084, 10:00 p.m.,

Zayvier was hardly the kind of person to hold onto his negative emotions. In fact, his natural disposition was almost as upbeat as that of Bill Jerrick, his former Master. After almost two months, though, it was still difficult for him to shake the anguish he felt over not having the skill or timing to save Director Ishikawa. The time period of his suffering alone was enough for him to sink a little deeper into his depression, but when his old teacher sent word and asked to see him, he felt a little bit of his usual light return.

He walked the pathways of the Roan Compound in silence. He was alone, and with the dimmed lights and vacant grounds, he felt the strangest sense of unease creep into his mind. For a moment he thought that he was being watched, but quickly dismissed the idea since the shadows around him were scarce and often pierced by the dim lights. Even so, for the life of him he couldn't relax his guard, and he wasn't sure how much of that was related to his state of mind following the Roan Mountain Raid.

He turned a corner towards the designated meeting chamber, and tried to recall a time where the Conference Level was this dark. A chill dripped down the center of his spine, and though his destination was on the other side of the shadows, he was anything but eager to go through them. Zay took a deep breath as he stared into the darkness, and after a moment of self-motivation, he powered through.

Something wasn't right, though. The feeling that he had, that feeling of being watched, returned with a vengeance. Now, though, there were sounds in the background of shifting weight. Without warning a blade came down at his back. A hasty roll along the ground gave him the distance he needed to avoid a swift death, but just as he regained his stance another sword moved in for the kill. Peters blocked with the plate side of his kyoketsu-shoge and pushed into his opponent as he swept their leg.

Despite the close quarters, Zayvier could hardly see the faces of his attackers, and the darkness of the tunnel around him made him wary to move carelessly. The moment he shifted his focus from one of his assailants, the other (or others) would recede into the shadows from whence they came. Just as he heard another shift in the dark, he plunged his kyoketsu-shoge into the ceiling and pulled himself skyward. In a normal confrontation, this would've been a momentary fix, but in this particular scenario, the attackers wouldn't be able to do anything about it without first making a sacrifice of their secrecy. Or so Zay thought. A sword lodged itself in the ceiling, and while it failed to puncture him, it grazed his arm. Warmth slowly left it as blood dripped from the laceration, and just as yet another of the swords rocketed towards his position, he lunged for an opening in the distance.

It was a risky move, since he could do very little to defend himself in the air, but it was riskier still to remain stationary against multiple opponents. Moments before Zayvier hit the ground, one of his attackers stepped out from the shadows and took up a stance. The darkened figure swept in a horizontal motion, but with the click of his repulsor boots, Peters managed to alter his trajectory and vault over the blade. There, in the brief flash that his boots provided, he was able to make out five bodies spread out behind his latest attacker, two of them without their swords.

So that's it, he thought, and as his foot touched the ground he launched one of the diamond-shaped blades on his arms into the space above a distant door and leaped into the air again only narrowly before a second slash could connect. The power of his repulsors jetted him forward, away from his enemies and towards his destination. When he came within a proximity of the door, he fired his repulsors in the opposite direction and slowed himself down. His hand touched the handle, and with the sounding of a loud siren, the strikers hidden in the shadows vanished in an instant.

Zay heaved a sigh of relief, but was put on edge again when the door handle that curled within his palm made a clicking sound. He opened the large ornate chamber door, and where he thought there would be some elaborate trap, some endless array of warriors that he would have to fight through, some unfathomable challenge to put his imaginations to shame, there was nothing of the sort. Instead and much to his surprise, he entered the room to the sight of each of the Dragons positioned along the edge. All of them were outfitted in full Hanzo Gear. Their masks were on, their hoods draped almost sinisterly over their eyes, and the slick silver color of their kyoketsu-shoge met with a lustrous orange tint from their Reikikens' light. Overhead, just above their stations, Zayvier could vaguely make out the emblems of each Dragon. On the left were inscribed the kanji for Kage, Ki, and Hi. The right side bore the symbols for Tsuchi, Kaze, and Sui. In the center of them all was that of Rai. All but one of the positions, that of Tsuchi, was occupied by a Dragon, and before his mind could hazard a thought, the Rairyu slashed his burning sword to the ground.

"To the center," he commanded, and from the first moment he spoke, Zay knew it to be Bill. He obliged his sensei, and tried his best not to glance too long in the direction of the Tsuchiryu position. As he walked, so too did his former Master until they stood face to face. Despite the seriousness in Bill's tone, there was a smile behind his eyes as much as it was behind his mask. "Kneel," he ordered, and Peters knelt. His bright eyes quickly fixed on the Reikiken that turned his caramel flesh a vibrant orange. "State your name and rank."

"Zayvier Bernard Peters, Master of the Violet Shadows, Sensei," he said with utmost respect. Bill paced around him, and the methodical pacing of his steps made him nervous.

"Recite the code," the new Rairyu instructed.

"'Refine the mind through art, history, and culture, for it is impossible to live in a world one does not understand. Protect the weak, for it is the responsibility of the strong to do so. The community is a lifeline, and is only as well off as the least of its citizens. Live in peace with allies, rain terror on enemies. Lead fearlessly. Survive at all costs,'" Zay responded flawlessly and without hesitation. It wasn't his normal way of speaking, but in a situation like this, Zayvier knew it best to be as formal as possible. His eyes met the ground now, for he was far too antsy to meet his teacher's gaze.

"The three pillars of the Yaiba are…" Bill began and allowed his voice to trail off.

"Honesty, Battle, Liberation," Zay rattled off without a thought, something that did not go unnoticed by the Dragons in the room.

"Explain the pillar of honesty," spoke the teacher.

"Honesty with self, with one's surroundings, with one's circumstances, and with one's companions, honesty is essential if one is to defeat delusion."

"Describe the nature of the Battle," came Bill's voice again. It was perfectly neutral, no matter how proud he was of his old student.

"We Battle for the sake of honesty, against delusion and all its fruits that might manifest in the world, against tyranny in every possible place."

"And Liberation?" Bill inquired.

"Liberation is the end goal of the Yaiba. We do not fight solely for ourselves, but for the rights of all people to live without fear." Bill stood in silence now, his footsteps halted and his eyes solemnly locked onto his student. The other Dragons, who quietly watched the trial, lowered their blades to the metal-covered ground and instantly the entire room came to life with warm brilliance.

"You handled yourself well on your way here," Bill slowly started up again. "Your movements were efficient, despite being without your sword." He waited for a moment to see if Zayvier would respond, but when he didn't, the Master Dragon continued. "You led a platoon of the Violet Shadows during the Johnson City Raid. According to the reports filed by some of your men, you led them to victory without any more than three casualties. Well done, whi—"

"Thank you, Sensei," Zayvier said hastily, but quickly reprimanded himself for cutting the new Rairyu off.

"Which is why," Bill stated again with a cautionary emphasis, "we have unanimously decided to welcome you into our ranks. Rise up, Tsuchiryu, the Earth Dragon. Happy Thanksgiving, kid." Zayvier's eyes began to water as he stood before his teacher.

He met Bill's gaze, and with a wide smile that spoke of a childhood wish finally fulfilled, he stammered as he said, "Thank you, Sensei."

Chapter Twenty-One

November 24th, 2084, 12:00 p.m.,

Levi stumbled through the streets of Cluster A and watched the shocked expressions of the Yoroi citizens that passed him by. He didn't care in the slightest what they thought, and why should he? This was his time to enjoy himself, and their distaste for his awkward movements and his liquor-drenched clothing provided the kind of entertainment he wasn't likely to get in the Kabuto Sanctuary.

One particular gentleman that passed him simply tried to pretend that he wasn't there, and Levi took the opportunity to single him out to ask for directions.

"Hey," he grumbled as he scratched his belly and narrowed his eyes, but the man walked on. "Hey buddy! Ye-yeah, you with the schloppy, shtupid-lookin' hat!" His words slurred together and he adopted a momentary stutter. He yelled loud enough to attract the attention of the man, but also a good portion of those on the street. The man, once he realized his mistake, averted his gaze again much to the displeasure of the drunkard. "Whassamatter, puke pants? Shcared too many people will—" a hiccup cut him off abruptly, "—blind themselves off that baby vomit green you're wearing?" The previously frightened man now turned to glare at Levi out of intense anger, and the surrounding Yoroi visibly displayed their disgust. Levi paused for a moment and surveyed the onlooking crowd. "The hell are all o'you lookin' at? You got a problem with me tryna ask Puke Pants here for a good spot to eat?"

"Whoa, whoa, hey, let's not cause a scene," Bobbi said waving her hands as she dashed through the crowd. Tony and Leroy followed behind her, each with a concerned expression on their faces.

"Too late for that, it seems," Leroy muttered, and Tony jabbed him in the side with their elbow.

"Levi, it's alright, we're here to help," Tony offered through a pleading smile. Levi made a loud groaning noise and waved a hand in front of his face.

"Well I don'need any HeLp," he taunted as he staggered towards them. The crowd lingered, all intent to see how this situation would play out since day-drinking in the Yoroi had become scarce since the earliest days of the Alliance. Leroy pat him on the back.

"Alright, time to go, bud," he said with as much calm as he could. For him the situation was hilarious, and he wanted nothing more than to laugh, but he knew it wouldn't help.

"Get your damn hands off me," Levi shouted, and punched Leroy squarely in the jaw. The crowd, stunned by the reaction, came alive with murmurs of curiosity over what would happen to the poor man.

"Hey," Bobbi said as she drew nearer to Levi and forced herself to stomach the stench of alcohol on his breath. She took him by his hands, and for a moment, his heart pulsed with something that he'd not felt in so long that he struggled to identify it. "You said you wanted something to eat, yeah? How about we help you calm down and get you cleaned up, huh? Then we can go grab a bite?" Levi eyed her suspiciously.

"You's treatin' me like-a kid," he asked with more aggression than the onlookers thought she could handle, but with a shake of her head, his anger was assuaged.

"Not at all," Bobbi assured him, "I just want to make sure you get everything you need." Levi seemed to relax his guard as Leroy massaged his cheek.

"Alright then," he said happily, then slung an arm around Bobbi and Tony. "How soon are we—" Leroy punched him and seemingly knocked the drunkard out cold. The crowd was stunned, as were his two companions.

"What the hell was that for," Tony demanded as they stamped their foot against the street. Leroy shrugged.

"Payback," he said nonchalantly, as if it was to be expected. "You see how hard he hit me?"

"Well yeah," Bobbi chimed in, "but he's drunk—"

"Hey, he can't hold his liquor that's his own problem," Leroy interrupted. "If my momma taught me one thing, it was never to receive a gift from anyone you're not prepared to bless yourself. It's just good manners." Bobbi rolled her eyes.

"Well your manners just made this a lot more complicated," she spoke through clenched teeth. "Anybody got a place to set him down so we can let him sleep it off?" The crowd around them looked away, and pretended not to hear the question. "Fine. We'll take him over to those steps over there. That way when he comes to, he doesn't disrupt your precious peace again." Some people in the crowd glared at Bobbi for her passive-aggressive remark, but said nothing when she glared back in challenge. She and Tony, dainty as they were, painstakingly lugged Levi's body over to the steps of the target building on the west side.

"Alright," Levi said into his comms link as his head groggily bobbed from side to side, "we're in position. Next part's all yours."

****

November 24th, 2084, 12:37 p.m.,

"Copy that," Ina said in a hushed tone. The moment she heard the commotion outside, her meeting with the Yoroi Secretary of Education was adjourned. He advised her to get to a safe place, since the ruckus could've been some attempt by the ever-emboldened Anti-Rebels to undermine their efforts for self-sufficient life. She left his apartment, conveniently located in the same building as the Anti-Rebel hideout they were set to raid. Intel showed that there were only two entrances, and while Lex guarded the north entrance under the guise of her newly hired assistant, Levi's team covered the one on the west. The element of surprise was essential, and if they were to get anywhere in this operation, they couldn't be seen in association or even at the same entrance if it could be helped at all. If it was all to go according to Darius' expectations, then the moment they burst into the right place, the Anti-Rebels would go on the offensive in the hopes that they'd be able to escape and regroup. In many ways, this was their only decent shot at rescuing Johannes and squashing the conflict with the Anti-Rebels before anything serious happened.

Ina walked silently through the hallway and turned a corner. With every step she took her heart bashed harder and faster against her ribcage. She wondered if she would be able to complete the mission with the storm that raged within her, but then resolved that it wasn't a matter of "if." She needed to. That was the only option, because if she wasn't going to save the man she loved, who would?

"Resuming sweep," came the gruff voice of an Anti-Rebel security agent. The Kabuto, in their expert surveillance of the Clusters, found that a group of security personnel independent of the main military corps of the Yoroi Alliance frequently visited the location of the hideout in timed rotations. Avoiding them was ruled out altogether, as Darius assumed that their presence was indicative of the location of the base. There were, however, countermeasures to being detected so easily.

Ina pressed a finger underneath the folded collar of her brown knitted cardigan. She walked in the direction of the security agent's footsteps, and just as he turned his eyes on the space she occupied, she breezed past him completely unnoticed. Even Ina had to marvel at the Kabuto ShadowStalker technology. The bike could cloak anyone equipped with a sensory node to the point where their heat signature, audio output, and even their scent were erased nearly completely. She hardly thought that she'd be willing to give it back after this.

She moved around the man, who looked as dangerous as he sounded, and marked him with a microtag.

"Tony, time to get to work," she said, and then continued her investigation.

"I'm on my way," Tony said nervously into her comms unit, and steeled herself for her part of the job.

****

November 24th, 12:50 p.m.,

As soon as the words left their lips, a rather slender security guard emerged from the door behind them. Once she caught sight of Tony, Leroy and Bobbi huddled around a seemingly recovering Levi, her expression soured.

"Hey, you guys can't be here," she started, which drew the most pitiful looks from the three sober-minded spies. "This is a residential area for some of the most important people in the Alliance. Get lost!" The security guard's voice was deep for a woman of her figure, and though she frightened Tony and Bobbi a bit, Leroy did his best to stifle a laugh. The woman noticed, and her amber eyes narrowed on him with intense animosity.

"Not at all," Tony jumped in before Leroy's nonchalant attitude and smart mouth could make things worse. "It's just," their tone shifted to something more sympathetic, "we didn't plan to be squatting out here like this. Our friend had a little too much to drink and, if you don't mind," Tony said as they stepped a little closer to the guard and their voice adopted a sultry tone, "we could use a little…help?" There came an upward inflection at the end, and the playful curiosity in Tony's eyes made the woman blush and swallow hard as she stammered in a frantic search for something to say.

"Follow me," she said reluctantly. Tony whipped their head back to their comrades and flashed a smug expression before they switched back to their mark. The woman opened the door to the established hideout and, with Tony in tow, rounded a corner at the end of the hall and entered the apartment immediately to the left. It was quaint, unimpressive, and the perfect place to leave the guard unconscious and unassuming. The woman headed into the kitchen, and Tony followed. She reached into one of the cabinets for a glass and then began to fill it with water.

"Thank you so much," Tony said in their sweet, tantalizing voice as they ran their delicate hand across the nape of their mark's neck. "You really didn't have to help us, you know."

"Anything to get you lot out of here faster," the amber-eyed woman said, though her tone betrayed her. Tony could tell that she was flustered, excited, longing. They decided to let their hands trace the line from the guard's neck to her arms and listened to the sigh that exited her lips. Tony was nervous. Their heart beat with a ferocity unlike any they'd previously experienced, but they dared not let it show.

"Are you sure you want me gone so soon," Tony asked, and turned her gracious host to face them. They pressed their body against the woman, who was loath to object to the advance, and with their faces mere centimeters apart, Tony whispered, "I haven't even found a way to properly thank you yet." The amber-eyed woman traced the soft features of Tony's face with her eyes, and with a flippant gesture, took the spy's lips with her own.

Tony's hands gently caressed the security agent's coal-colored uniform, an act that was fully reciprocated. It was when Tony disengaged from the kiss that the node they'd planted on the woman's bare skin emitted a small electrical current. It wasn't enough to kill the guard, just incapacitate her for a while. Tony caught her, and hastily dragged her over to the couch in her small living room before they nervously left.

"I'm in," Tony said, and pressed the node on their own clothes. The ShadowStalker tech took the rest from there and shrouded them in mystique, the same as Ina. "Where are you?" Tony sounded calm, but their senses were on high alert. A few pairs of boots could be heard on the floor above, and the rhythmic thud of the footsteps only amplified the thud in their chest. Ina didn't respond, and that only exasperated Tony's feeling of dread as they assumed that the plan was about to unravel. They hastily walked through the building and came to the second floor, where Ina first said she would be.

After a few moments of scouring different apartments and carefully maneuvering around the inhabitants of the building, Tony caught sight of a few more of the guards as they headed for the stairs and began their ascent to the third floor. The third floor, Tony noted, was locked by a numeric pad. It was a good thing they'd found the guards when they did, otherwise that could've been another hurdle. This way, they could slip in undetected and therefore preserve their nerves.

Tony caught the door just before it closed behind the guards and infiltrated the third floor successfully. They couldn't help but think how weird it was that an entire floor in a residential area was locked up this tight. It was entirely too obvious for it to be a mistake.

"Tony," Ina whispered over the comms, "be careful of the third floor. Something doesn't feel right."

"You couldn't have said that before I got up here," Tony responded, more afraid than disrespectful.

"What do you see," Ina inquired, a slight edge in her tone to remind Tony who was in charge of the operation. After all, Ina was the one with the most to lose here.

"Guards are coming in and out of the hall. There are three rooms, two on either side, one at the far end." Tony did their best to focus, to refrain from an over indulgence in fear, and just before they could resume their report, the ShadowStalker cloak vanished. "That's…that's not good," was all they could say. Static masked the sound of Ina's voice on the other end, and two guards suddenly appeared on either side of Tony. "I'll have to call you back later."

"Right this way," one of the guards snarled and shoved them ahead to the central door.

"This is what you came for, isn't it?" said the other.

"Isn't it?" the first repeated with increased intensity.

"Isn't it?" the two guards shouted now, and pushed Tony hard on either shoulder. They stumbled forward, and when they looked back at their escorts they found two men, one light-skinned and one dark, both horribly marred in the face. Tony couldn't even muster the strength to scream at the hideous sight of them, but felt only pity.

"Keep moving," shouted the dark-skinned man, whom Tony recognized as the first voice that spoke to them previously. They refocused their attention to the path that lay before them, and watched as the door at the end of the hall creaked open. Inside, Tony could make out the image of a man with wavy—albeit disheveled—brown hair and fair skin bound to a chair at its center. Before Tony could stop in their tracks, another hard shove came from behind, this time strong enough to almost rocket them to the outer threshold of the door.

Tony caught themselves just before their face hit the ground, and with a clearer view of the captive, recognized him to be the man they were there to rescue. They scrambled over to him and frantically checked their comms link in a desperate attempt to reestablish a line with Ina or any of the others. But there was nothing. Tony was alone in this room save for an unconscious Johannes and the two brutes that forced her into this point. Tony turned to the door again, only to watch as the light-skinned man gradually closed it behind them, a sickening grin plastered to his jaw.

Tony quickly reached into the black pouch on their utility belt and brought out a kunai. They tossed it at the man's throat before he had time to react, and in the moment that he fell to the ground with his hand a mere inch from the blade in his neck, Tony rushed the door in an attempt to keep it open and fight for their escape. The fallen guard's companion, however, rushed the door from the other side and hastily shut and locked it in Tony's face. Tony beat on it with every ounce of rage that bubbled over from them at that point.

"Dammit!" was all Tony could think to shout as their captor laughed and walked away.

****

November 24th, 1:50 p.m.,

It'd been an hour since Tony went into the building. Levi, Bobbi and Leroy were forced to move from their spot at the western entrance and Lex vacated his position at the northern side of the building. Ina and Tony were trapped inside the building, with security stationed at the two exits. The third floor, on the other hand, was markedly vacant.

Ina had tried to use her comms the moment she lost contact with Tony, but the others on the outside were beyond her reach.

The third floor was a trap, and they walked right into it. What was worse, the plan they'd ironed out had changed significantly. This was no longer an in and out operation. It'd be a miracle if they could get out without spilling any blood, and with the numbers advantage on the side of the Anti-Rebels, things weren't looking good. Still, Ina wasn't about to leave this hideout without Johannes. She refused, with every fiber of her being, to lose him for a second time.

So she skulked in the shadows, the full extent of her malicious intent dispersed through her veins. The first thing she thought to do was simple. She needed to reestablish an exit.

****

November 24th, 1:50 p.m.,

Tony did nothing the first ten minutes they were locked in the room, save for swear and occasionally glance at the unconscious man across from them. The worst-case scenario had happened, despite their best efforts. They'd done everything right, so it didn't make sense that Darius' plan would fail. But it fell through, and now just Tony and Ina were left to pick up the pieces. Tony breathed a sigh, and wished that they could at least get a message to the outside to warn the others about the trap that was the third floor. Without that as an option, though, Tony had to come up with a different plan of action.

To start with, they felt it prudent to look for any indication of a way out. Unfortunately, that was a short search. The room was windowless, and the vent located just above the back wall was far too narrow for even a child to squeeze through. The only way in or out was through the door. The door that locked from the outside. In a moment of frustration and panic, Tony wondered who the hell built this place. They calmed themselves and moved on to the second thing in their own predetermined order.

They inched closer to Johannes and gingerly paced around him as they tested his reflexes through a series of probing movements. They waved their hands in front of his face, snapped their fingers, yelled in his ears, tousled his hair, but nothing Tony did spurred him awake. They checked his pulse, and sure enough he was alive. It occurred to them that perhaps they should check his eyes. They opened them up one at a time, and noted the traumatized shift. He'd been sedated, heavily enough to put him under but just enough to keep him from dying, which meant any kind of coordination between the two of them was beyond reach as well.

The more they thought about the situation the more it felt hopeless on all fronts. Johannes being drugged was expected, but they'd hoped that it would've been a little easier since the rest of this situation was as far south as it could get. The lock on the door clicked and Tony immediately went on the defensive. Someone was on the other side, though who it was they couldn't tell. What Tony did know was that this person was either incredibly brave for walking into this room after they were agitated to this degree, or remarkably stupid.

The door opened, and to Tony's surprise the person that entered was an old man of fair skin, gray hair and eyes bluer than a clear sky. They knew him, not as the Councilor that he'd been for as long as they were alive but as the kind, gentle old man that taught them to read and write, that showed them what it was to be a warrior, that encouraged them to live as they saw fit in spite of their circumstances, that they loved like their own grandfather. He was kind to them in a society that hardly tolerated. What was he doing here?

"Tony," Christophe Francis whispered in surprise the moment his eyes fell on the young intruder. His expression grew sorrowful. "Why are you here?" Tony cocked their head to the side, a mix of rage and sorrow in their face as they folded their arms over their chest.

"Why's that any of your business," Tony replied with more aggression than they'd ever shown. "Anyway, I could ask the same of you." Francis' eyebrows lifted, as if he was both surprised and offended that Tony would even ask.

"Is it so hard to believe that I would be in the area visiting a colleague," he offered, his tone slightly flustered. "I was told that Councilor Wheeler was a bit under the weather and that I could find her residence here. Now you tell me, how suspicious should I be of you since I found you here alone with an unconscious man?" Tony took a moment before they answered. This was the trap, to be found by an unsuspecting Councilor in a damnable position.

"I was locked in here," Tony told him. Tony had always known Councilor Francis to be an understanding man, even in the most difficult of situations, and chose to simply tell the truth. They weren't convinced he was as ignorant as he made himself out to be, but if there was any chance at getting out of this situation it was by playing to their shared history. Tony hated to be manipulative, but unfortunately there wasn't a whole lot of choice in this scenario. "My friend was drinking and caused a scene outside, so I came in to try and get him some help. Before long I was taken by some scary-looking men with scars on their faces and thrown in here." Christophe quietly surveyed his former pupil. Apparently, he surmised, Tony had forgotten that he could always tell their truths from their lies, and while they spoke with conviction, it was only half true.

"I get the sense," he began cautiously, and moved further into the room, "that you're not being 100% truthful with me, my dear. Come now. Tell me what really brought you here."

"I will if you will," Tony shot back, unable to contain the irritation and animosity in their tone.

"I suppose it *is* only fair," the elder finally conceded, and for a moment eyed the now half-conscious Johannes. "I am here to do what I have always done: what is best for the Alliance." Tony's expression became more wary.

"What do you mean by that," they asked with deep suspicion.

"Twenty-two years ago, just a short time before you were born, an agreement was reached between the Yoroi and the Scarlet Kingdom to end what could best be described as relentless bloodshed without cause. You see, in the days before the Flagstaff Ceasefire, the Scarlet Kingdom advanced on our territory. At first they didn't attack, but the sheer volume of their forces restricted our movements and our relations with the other factions. Our resources began to decline, and the people began to suffer."

"So you went to war," Tony supplied, and the old man nodded.

"Battle was not our first mind," he admitted, and paced the room now as he reminisced on what was clearly one of the more trying times of his life. "In fact, it was only after our attempt at an olive branch failed that we took up arms. Our Ambassador, you see, was murdered by the King of the Reds and his head was delivered to our front door." Tony gasped in shock, which prompted a sad smile from the Councilor. "It was a great blow to the Alliance, but we pulled through. Our forces collided with the Scarlets: guerilla warfare versus relentless assault. Hundreds of thousands of Red dogs died, but not without taking down a sizeable portion of our trapsmiths and warriors." His tone was pensive and mournful, his eyes fell to the floor at the memory, and despite the sincerity he projected, Tony gradually felt more discomfort. His pace was more descript than just "slow," it was methodical, as if something was to happen in the passing moments.

"What does any of this have to do with why you're here, Gramps," Tony uttered in the kind of even tone that spoke volumes of their skeptic concern. Francis, whose eyes lazily found their way to Johannes, smiled a fatherly smile that took Tony back in time to a simpler era in their life. Even still, the sheer familiarity was not enough to stave off the sharp uneasiness they felt. He could feel that, but it was beyond his ability to care. He looked up at them, and his fatherly smile grew just a bit wider, as if he was sure that they would see his side of things.

"Be patient, my dear," he told her. "I was just getting to that. The deaths of our fighters struck harder than the Scarlet Kingdom could've imagined. They weren't just troops, you see. They were parents. Some brothers, some sisters, all somebody's children, and all somebody's friend. They were people that, during the years of minor conflict, had graced the crater carts and Clusters of our home the same as we do today. So, when the Scarlets' manpower was on the decline and their advances on our home proved to be all for naught, our Council again approached the enemy, this time with an opportunistic proposal that would be known as the Flagstaff Compromise. For many years, it has been the only thing to keep us from suffering those kinds of losses again. Even a single soul lost to needless conflict is one too many."

"It sounds like you're committed to maintaining a false kind of peace," Tony delivered, much to his visible displeasure.

"A false kind of peace?" Christophe scoffed, blood vessels accented in his forehead and neck. "The peace I seek to maintain is the *only* peace the Yoroi have enjoyed for the last twenty-two years, and *that* is why I'm here. I'm curious, though, my dear. Do you happen to know why he's here?" Francis pointed to Johannes, an inquisitive eyebrow raised and his lips angled downward in an openly disapproving frown. Johannes stirred a bit at the sounds around him, and though his eyes opened for but a moment, he struggled to maintain his lucidity. "Mr. Thornhill was attacked on his way back from a meeting with the Yaiba Insurrection, an act that puts us in violation of the ceasefire agreement that we proposed. It is, no doubt, the result of Ambassador Vargas' rudimentary attempts to cast us into war again, as evidenced by the Yaiba filth he brought into our home."

“He was *not* filth,” Tony shot back more defensively than they’d intended, and Francis raised his eyebrows in surprise. The Tony he knew wouldn’t have been so eager to defend anyone, especially some outsider brought here for military work.

“Oh, but he was! Any threat to the safety of our people and the tranquility of our home is garbage, and like garbage they ought to be taken out,” Christophe responded. Tony’s expression darkened as the memory of stabbing their teacher pulled to the forefront of their mind at his implication, and with a boldness that sharply contrasted their typical disposition they stepped toward him.

“I’m sorry, I don’t think I understand your meaning. They should be taken out,” they asked with such a tremble that it scared the collected Councilor. He only showed his fear for a second, but when he looked beyond his former student at the groggily stirring man in the background, he solidified his resolve.

“Threats of that kind should be eliminated,” Francis said without hesitation, his eyes locked with his surrogate grandchild, “just as it was with the Yaiba intruder.” Tony was livid. As the person that was ordered to stab Darius before, it was an insult that the Anti-Rebels would take credit for Tony’s actions. Even more infuriating to them was the fact that they made light of the death of a stranger whose only purpose there was to give them authentic peace and a means of attaining it that minimized the casualties of a war already in motion. Their vision blurred from anger, their chest lifted and fell with heavy breathing augmented by a strange animosity, and on impulse, Tony reached into the pouch on their belt for the same dagger they’d used to wound Darius. Before Francis could formulate his next thought, the blade found its sheath in his abdomen.

“Tony, I—” was all he said, and then collapsed to the ground before them. Tony looked to Johannes, who now sat fully awake and shaken to the core from what he’d just seen.

****

November 24th, 2084, 2:58 p.m.,

The fifth body hit the floor, and Ina was almost out of breath. She needed some air, a change of scenery, a stiff drink, literally anything other than the sixth security agent that charged in her direction. She tossed a flash grenade to stun them, then jumped—legs first—at their head. She wrapped her legs around their neck and then twisted downward with enough momentum to sling them to the ground. She didn't know where she'd found the strength, but the time wasn't right to wonder such things. She withdrew a dagger from the pouch on her belt and drove it into the throat of the freshly downed enemy. She breathed a sigh of relief, as the hallway was empty…or at least it was until another cell of enemy agents appeared.

Ina slashed her knife through the air, dusted herself off, and cracked her neck as the assailants charged.

****

November 24th, 2084, 2:58 p.m.,

Tony tried their comms again as soon as they were off the third floor. A pile of bodies was left in their wake, and a groggy, confused and slightly frightened Johannes followed after them in his best attempt to dodge the downed security operatives.

"Come on," Tony called as they knifed through another agent. It was the most help they could give the emissary aside from clearing the path in the first place. They activated their comms unit as they kicked a security agent over the railing of the stairwell. The thud of the body against the tiles at the bottom made Johannes' stomach churn. "Ina, I've got him. It's time to pull out."

The words were uttered with such triumph that Ina nearly wept on the other end. There was a pause in their conversation, but Tony knew exactly what the news meant to her. They looked behind at the shaky Johannes, who clutched the rail for dear life. Two more security agents attempted to run up the stairs at Tony while two emerged from behind their charge. Tony, in a split second, reached into their pouch and tossed out two knives at the oncoming pair at the front, then another two at the ones that tried to seize Johannes. She ordered for him to retrieve the knives and stay close, and together they moved down to the first floor.

****

November 24th, 2084, 3:07 p.m.,

Ina heard the door from the stairwell click open and closed, and steeled herself for yet another round with the persistent guardsmen. She slid against the wall as she stood back to her feet, and turned expectantly in the direction of the sound. Footsteps approached somewhat frantically, but whereas Ina expected to be met with another horde, it was her allies that turned the corner with their backs to her.

She stood, stunned for a moment at the sight of the back of his blessed head, and stammered out a choked “Jo” when he turned his emerald gaze on her. She flushed red and rushed him, dagger still clutched tightly in her hand.

“Ina,” he almost sobbed, and then took her into his arms. They looked at each other for but a moment before their lips locked desperately, then passionately, then sweetly. The long three months they’d been apart had finally melted away, and everything that they’d wanted to say to each other was contained in the meeting of his lips with hers. “I thought I’d never see you again.”

The door burst open. A wave of angry security guards burst into the corridor and charged. Tony threw as many knives as they could from the pouches on their belt, and met a few enemies with a few sharp elbows and knees to sensitive areas before they finished them with their signature dagger. Johannes and Ina separated.

"Get out of here," she said as she placed the ShadowStalker node on his chest. He stood there and looked at her, then at Tony, who started to struggle with the still numerous enemies. "Go! I'm not going to lose you again!" Ina shoved him in the direction of the western entrance and dove into the battle with Tony. After they felled a particularly large enemy, Ina unleashed a flurry of rapid dagger strikes in all directions, so wild and furious that Tony had to disengage or else be cut to ribbons like their attackers. Ina saw amid the strikes and just as more filtered in that Johannes stood perfectly in awe of her. She rolled her eyes as a tear fell from them. "Tony, get him out of here. Call for help and take him back to the hideout."

"But—" Tony started to object, but Ina cut them off.

"Just do it! I've got this. After all," she said with a sadistic smirk that made the charge of enemies slow to a crawl, "I have to make them pay for what they've done to our family." As she dove straight for the horde, Tony took Johannes by the arm and led him towards the nearest exit.

A loud *bang* rippled through the air, like thunder on a vendetta. Tony told Johannes to press the stealth node and hide, and rushed back down their former path to offer assistance to Ina. What they found, however, was the body of their friend with a bullet hole in the forehead. No living enemies remained here, and Tony, now stricken with grief, returned to the area where Johannes had been. It was then that they heard him cry, that they saw him being carted off by a team of burly security officers, and that they realized that Ina, who only sought the safe return of her beloved, had just died for nothing.

Chapter Twenty-Two

December 7th, 2084, 11:47 p.m.,

An explosion rocked the landscape as one of the Yaiba speeders vanished in a cloud of smoke and debris. Zahara yelled through the comms, frantic to get her remaining troops behind their vehicles for cover as a scattered spatter of bullets emerged like miniature strikes of lightning from the distance. The pained screams of her soldiers filled her ears as an indeterminable number of them were gunned down almost instantly.

"Cover down," she yelled again, now more aggravated than anything. It was only their first leg of the journey and they'd driven right into an ambush. The Red patrols condensed in the Nantahala Forest between the Roan Mountain base and Chattanooga, no doubt an anticipatory measure to keep rebel presence away from the Southern Wastes. But they were in it now, and it didn't do Zahara any good to beat herself up for walking her troops into this trap. She checked her visor and saw that there were a few pressure sigs that resonated in the area. Anything over a 2,500 pounds flashed as a red dot on the visor. There were twelve of those in total, which meant that the Scarlets brought their Humvees, which told Zahara that her forces were outmatched at the moment when it came to supplies and ammunition. It also told her that if she was to take out the gunners that had them pinned down, all of that plus any spare weapons would be hers for the taking.

That, however, was easier said than done. Between their position and that of the Humvees were smaller dots that flashed a frosty blue. That, she learned, was synonymous with objects on the ground that weighed 50 pounds or less, and those dots were scattered all throughout the terrain. Zahara surmised that they were more of the kinds of mines that reduced that transport to a mound of twisted flesh and metal. She ground her teeth as her mind raced with potential solutions. Getting to the other side of this started to feel like an impossibility.

"Awaiting your orders, Master Boyd," came the voice of Drew McDowell over the comms. "What do you want us to do?" Zahara thought about it for a moment as she continued her observation of the geo-sensor signatures. Yellow lights, about twelve of them, flashed among the numerous blue dots on the map. Those were undoubtedly the enemy soldiers, though by no means all of them. They were a decoy, only there to lure the Yaiba into making sloppy mistakes.

"On my mark," Zahara started, and the team at her command perked up at the confidence in her voice. The section of 20 that she'd trained since her release from the Holding Level had blossomed into a full platoon of 55 trained gunmen, and they acted as the spearhead of this operation to make things easier on the battalion that followed. "Air Defense, get ready. The bulk of their firepower is hiding in the trees. T-Cell, there are mines scattered all over the place. Do what you can to trigger them. Spec-Ops, you're with me. I give the word, you open fire." The orders were concise, and though the troops had them, they were still pinned behind their transports by enemy fire. Some of them quietly questioned how long their machines would hold out against this onslaught, but then the ping of bullets against the reinforced steel coating of the transports stopped. This was the moment that they'd learned about in training, that moment where the Scarlet troops had to stop to reload. Zahara and all her trainees lit up with a smile as she told them, "Light 'em up."

Immediately the three teams that surrounded her executed their orders. Zahara, Karina, Drew and Orson quickly fired round after round in perfect unison at their enemies on the ground, all of whom struggled to replenish their own supply of ammo before they could be picked off. Unfortunately for them, it was not to be. As the shooters stationed in the trees ahead took aim on their Insurrectionist targets they heard the rattle of chains and the screams of their comrades in all directions. Shadows passed by their faces in one instance, and in the next their view of the terrain became a darkening spiral as their head rolled down from their shoulders.

With the way ahead cleared of enemies and the Air Defense members on their job, it created a freedom for the T-Cell operatives to search their transports for the Wavemakers they'd packed just for a time such as this. The Wavemakers, twenty-pound hexagonal rods fitted with a unique inlay of technology as generously crafted by the Engineering Corps, were driven into the ground and activated. After a moment or two, during which they gradually whirred to life, a massive quake was felt throughout the forest. Explosions followed, and just as the heat signature of their surroundings began to rise, the Wavemakers emitted a plant-safe fire-retardant foam to limit the damage the forest would sustain.

Once the first wave of mines was taken care of, the T-Cell got to work on the second and the process repeated as needed. Every so often, one of the heads or limbs or bodies of the tree-hidden Scarlets would fall and detonate a mine, but the bulk of the work was still left to the T-Cell to do.

Zahara watched on with pride, now from the comfort of her own transport, and reminisced to a few weeks prior when the lot of them were little more than grunts with the teamwork skills of a particularly introverted polar bear. Now they operated as a well-oiled machine. Still, she frowned. They handled themselves well enough in this small battle, but things would only become more dire down the road.

"Alright, let's get moving," she barked through the comms once the last of the fires was out. "We've got a schedule to keep."

****

December 8th, 2084, 2:14 a.m.,

Cal wiped his brow, and laughed as his hands started to shake from the excitement. Ever since his injury, he'd had this idea, and once he was well enough to get back to work, he did just that. So much of his intellect was poured into this one technological advancement, this one tool that was smaller in shape than anything the Engineering Corps had designed in the last decade, but with far more implications. It was the first piece of biotechnology that ever came out of a Yaiba mind, and with it in his hand, he knocked again on Anna Dominguez's door. He could hear the rustle of movement from the other side, and as his recent collaborator moved groggily to the door, Cal could feel a surge of adrenaline pump through his body. The lock clicked, and the door opened.

Dr. Dominguez, eyes blurry and half-open from exhaustion, vaguely caught sight of Cal despite her full efforts to see him. She rubbed her forehead and released a defeated sigh as she waved him aside and started down the corridor. Cal stood, perplexed for a moment, just to the side of her doorframe as he watched her walk down the hall. Anna, what with the lack of accompanying footsteps, turned to face the young man only just out of the dim light of the hall as she waved for him to follow.

"You didn't expect to get this done here, now, did ya," she asked with more energy than he'd expected. "Come on."

"Ooh, yes, ma'am," Cal said with his quiet excitement, and gently squeezed the sphere in his palm before he obliged her. She led him to the power-lift nearest their location and, once loaded, entered the command for the Medical Level I. The machine came to life, and though it did so loudly, such noise was not uncommon at all hours of the day and night. Yaiba operatives were dispatched on missions to fight or scavenge all the time, and so nobody at this point would have any cause to stir from their sleep because of a power-lift operating at this hour.

Dr. Dominguez quietly observed the young engineer, curious as to why he would be up at this time of morning anyway.

She knew that he was excited to get his prosthetic up and running, but she didn't know that it was enough to consume his sleep cycle. Of course, Cal was more interested in the technology of the Yaiba than anything else, save, perhaps, for testing it all out in the field. He was one of the few warriors who served a dual function within the Yaiba, and to many his very existence was a point of curiosity.

The power-lift stopped, and Cal was the first one to head down to the surgical bay. Dr. Dominguez followed behind him, though without all the energy and excitement that he had. When she'd finally caught up with him, she noted that he'd already removed the glass ball that stood in for his original eye. The empty socket would've been more than enough to startle one of the residents that she worked with routinely, but after working in the Insurrection's medical service for the last twenty-three years, she was used to the sight of much worse injuries.

Anna took a moment to put him under, and once she saw that he was unconscious from the anesthetic, she took the sphere from his hand and got to work. First, she sanitized it as best she could. It took only a moment, though her eyes lingered on the construction for a bit longer just so she could get a proper view of its design. She was impressed. Cal had spent the last few weeks asking about the optic nerves, prostheses, theoretical transplant methods for the human eye, and a lot of things that had never really seemed possible. When she confronted him about why he wanted to know about such things, he returned her question with one of his own, about what it would take to control technology with one's mind.

She could see that all of those questions found their answers in this little metal ball. Her thumb pressed lightly against the side of it, and a bright yellow light flashed to life as the object buzzed against her palm. She was taken off-guard, but regained her composure almost instantly. It wouldn't do for a woman of her degree of expertise to falter in a simple prosthesis fitting, and so she simply didn't.

She eased the ball towards the socket, and in awe watched as the myriad of metallic tendrils slithered from its back and into the dark hole in Cal's face. The light flickered, changed from yellow, to orange, then to blue, then purple, then green, all before it settled back on its original golden hue. The small orb's front twisted open like a camera lens as the tendrils gently pulled it into place. The honey-brown iris emerged around the yellow light that would've served as the pupil in a natural eye to create a deeply beautiful, deeply intimidating image.

"Well," Dr. Dominguez spoke to herself in total surprise, "would you look at that." She couldn't believe that the boy had made this thing work without a test. It was difficult enough for medical experts to fit a prosthesis to a person with 100% accuracy, and that was just on the simplistic designs. Here, Cal Richmond had created a multifaceted replacement for the eye he'd lost in battle, and managed to work in an AI program that allowed for it to do all the work she was prepared to do. That boy was a little more than a point of curiosity, she realized. He was a behemoth of innovative genius.

She wondered what other tricks he'd managed to pack into this little orb. It was a fleeting thought, one that she had as she moved for the door and let the sleeping technological giant lie.

****

December 8th, 2084, 9:45 a.m.,

Bryan Piccio stood before King Shane and his Court. It was less stressful this time, though not because he was so used to the King's perpetually disgruntled expression, and not because he was used to the squabbles and glares of disapproval from the rest of the Court members. Bryan listened to them as they debated for what seemed like the hundredth time about the Southern Wastes. Word had gotten to the Reds that the enemy, Bryan's old friends at the Yaiba Insurrection, had started their advance on Jackson only hours ago. The central point was that they didn't have the troops to spare.

Bryan held his tongue despite having what he felt was an obvious answer to their belabored problem. Just out of curiosity, he wanted to see if any of the spoiled nobles of the Scarlet Kingdom could figure it out for themselves. For a brief moment, Viscount Ronaldo Leyva met Bryan's gaze. The short man with elf-like ears quickly turned his attention back to the debate, and while his sudden reaction went unnoticed by most of the others at the semicircular table of the Court, it spoke volumes to the skeletal Lord Blackwell.

"Excuse me for my indecorum, Majesty," Blackwell said, the King now cut off in midsentence. Blackwell gestured to the man of brown hair and blue eyes, whose cheeks were colored as red as the garden roses and whose belly quaked from sheer joy at the political spectacle. "Is it absolutely necessary to have *him* here? If I may ask, what purpose does he even serve?" The King, whose face scrunched into a deeper kind of scowl that, in all truth, Bryan hadn't thought humanly possible, was more than just a little upset at the interruption, but surprisingly let it go.

"He does seem a bit too amused," King Shane conceded his crushing gray eyes narrowed on the foreigner. "Care to share what's got you quaking like that?"

"I'm sorry, Your Grace," Bryan assured him as he forced himself to stop laughing. "I was just thinking about how easy this issue is to solve." The room fell silent as all eyes turned to the audacious cur that dared laugh in their faces.

"By all means," started Marquis West, a familiar edge to his voice. "Enlighten us." It had been no secret that the increasing number of Court meetings had started to take its toll on the Marquis, but today he looked particularly bad. His beady blue eyes had grown slightly paler as dark bags lined the bottoms, and his chestnut brown hair had grown a little bit grayer. Bryan enjoyed the sight, and fancied that the more they went on like this, the closer they would all come to matching their insides with their outsides. Nevertheless, he shrugged.

"I can't," he told them casually, as if they had all been friends for years. "At least not without some way to get into the drone central control system."

"Not a chance," cried Baron Stalks, whose light caramel skin showed signs of reddening from his anger. His thick black mustache had gone without a trim and his usually tidy black hair was almost as frizzled as West's.

"The drone controls are highly sensitive," came the startlingly less sensitive voice of one Miranda McBride. She was slightly thinner than when he'd last seen her. Undoubtedly the stress of the Court had influenced her diet. "Anyone with access to them could just as easily abuse them the same way those Helmet bastards did a month ago." Bryan's eyes narrowed on them, now.

"I don't like what you're implying," he told them with a venom in his tone that made all but the King and his Prince shrink back. "But what seems better to you: having me in the system to undo the damage that's already been dealt, or letting you continue to bicker about how to solve a problem I already have the answer to?" The room fell quiet for a moment. The nobles, all of whom seemed so sure of themselves at all times suddenly tasted unequivocable doubt. Bryan could read it in each expression. Even the hardened face of the King of the Reds echoed the sentiment, and in the moment their eyes locked, Bryan raised his eyebrows as if to spur his decision along.

"Give him access to the Capitol Research Facility," King Shane ordered to the stunned looks of his son and Court. "I want him briefed on all the passcodes and protocols before lunch. Have Lieutenant General Ortiz and her soldiers stand watch over him. Wouldn't want him taking any liberties, after all."

"B-but, Your Majesty," Lord Blackwell nervously protested. Bryan took a great deal of pleasure at the shocked indignation that adorned such an aged face, and savored the unmistakable fear that replaced it when the King shot him a glare. "Yes, Your Majesty." He was defeated in an instant by the wordless expression of his lord. Blackwell, in turn, shot Bryan a look, and was disgusted to find that this outsider peasant had the nerve to meet his gaze with a cocky grin.

"Thank you, good people of the King's Court," Bryan said with a knowing smirk and an inelegant bow. He turned to take his leave, and with a careless wave of his hand, he said, "I promise you I won't disappoint."

****

December 8th, 2084, 3:15 p.m.,

Callan had only been back at the Bluff City Outpost for a week. He was surprised to get an emergency summons from the Director, even more surprised to find out that it was to add a name to the roster of Dragons, but it was a much needed break from the seemingly endless defense of the Johnson City base. The Reds had regrouped in the distance while he was away, and by the time Callan was back at his post, a fresh regiment of Scarlet Troopers had drawn up battle lines directly to the east of the outpost.

He was unconcerned, because while this showing was a strong one, he knew that the stealth attack led by that Kabuto kid Tom Freeman instilled the fear of God in the Red aggressors. Callan was so unconcerned, in fact, that every afternoon around this time he would take his afternoon tea and watch them from the window of his office. Until today. When Callan looked out the window, he noted that half of the enemy camp was abandoned while the half that stayed took up arms.

Callan bit his lower lip and it bled. He knew that they were up to something, but had been counting on their fear to delay whatever plan they'd hatched. He called for Nick Resnick and Ryan Morrisey, the two young attendants that had been placed by the Kabuto and Yaiba under his direction. They were capable, eager to get the hard part over with in one case and eager for a fight in the other. The way things looked, Callan was sure that a fight was imminent.

It took them a couple of minutes to reach his office, and as soon as they walked through the door Callan spewed a line of orders at them.

"Resnick, use the Kabuto comms relays to explain the situation to Johnson City. Ryan, position troops at the eastern- and westernmost walls of the outpost." Ryan's brow furrowed, and as he formed his lips to ask the question, "Why?" Callan cut him off with a lift of his hand. "Assuming they're attacking in two waves they'll try to distract us with the one we can see while the other circles to our blind spot. Station the Elite Guard at the northern and southern walls. Move. Quickly. They don't know that we know anything and for a limited time, that works to our advantage."

"Yes, sir," the two young warriors shouted in unison, and hurriedly left to move heaven and earth at Callan's order. He looked out the window again. He had a bad feeling about this.

****

December 8th, 2084, 3:45 p.m.,

Cecelia Kant watched the frantic scramble of the Yaiba and Kabuto forces. It impressed her how quickly they managed to throw this outpost together after they took Johnson City. Even more impressive was how they outfitted it with defenses, no doubt to spare it from a similar fate to what the Midland Outpost suffered months back. Even so, she relished the challenge. That was why she kept her Eastern Battalion utterly motionless, though they were more than poised to strike.

She enjoyed the thick waves of fear that emanated from the peasant scum on the other side of the Bluff City walls. She enjoyed their uncertainty, the cautious fidgeting of an enemy force trying their best to gauge the exact moment of attack. Cecelia didn't feel it yet. She wasn't yet full of their trepidation, but the moment was close. They might've known that the Scarlets were up to something. Hell, they might've even set up countermeasures. But one thing she knew they didn't suspect was the presence of a Scourge member.

Cecelia's face twisted into a sinister smile. It was almost time. Their fear was almost at its peak. She just had to drag it out for a little while longer, make them stew in their own insecurity just a bit more and then, and only then, would she strike.

"Um, Sis," came Trisha's voice through the radio. "I think we should get started soon." Cecelia rolled her eyes. She loved her sister. Trisha, in fact, was the only member of the Scarlet Scourge that she wouldn't throw in the way of enemy fire. But both her prudence and her sensitivity were more than a little annoying.

"Yeah, yeah, alright," Cecelia responded. Just once she wondered if her sister had the ability to take it easy and let loose. She often worried that Trisha would end up dying young if she didn't learn how to live a little. She shrugged slowly and relished in the multiple pops of her shoulders. The relief of tension was the perfect way to start a battle, and she lifted the radio back to her lips with a smile on her face as she told her troops, "Let's tear 'em to shreds!"

The Eastern Battalion lifted a war cry, and with ravenous delight marched on the outpost.

****

December 8th, 2084, 3:55 p.m.,

“Hostiles on the move!” Someone shouted it from the eastern wall, and at Callan’s command a battalion of his joint forces ran to meet them. The loud crack of gunfire permeated the atmosphere, and Kabuto bodies fell left and right. The Yaiba troops pressed on and did what they could to provide cover through the use of their Hanzo Gear, but the valley offered little in the way of closely grouped trees or buildings to grapple on. At most they were meat shields meant to catch the bullets of their enemies. Callan spat in disgust. The best strategy he could come up with was to lure them into Bluff City, but with the other half of their forces as of yet out of play, it wouldn’t be wise to restrict their own movements to such a degree. They were firmly in the hands of their enemies, and it would take a miracle for them to escape with even half their forces intact.

The Yaiba managed to shield the Kabuto just long enough to bring the cunning Helmets to their foes, but the moment the union of Helmet and Blade got close enough to the enemy’s front line, the Reds broke formation and spread out in smaller platoons.

“Suiryu, sir,” came one of Callan’s lieutenants from the battlefield to the east of the outpost. “The enemy is splitting up, what do you want us to do?” The question gnawed at the Water Dragon the moment it was asked, because in all truth it was a question he’d already asked himself. Everything about this spelled disadvantage. The traps that kept their enemies at bay were either triggered or disabled ages ago. The valley was flat and open. Enemy technology was at a minimum so the Kabuto saboteurs were little more than rocks in the pockets of a drowning man and now—*now*—the Reds sought a divide and conquer scenario.

“All Kabuto agents move to the center of the formation,” Callan ordered urgently, though something in the back of his mind urged him against it. “Violet Shadows, grant cover to our allies. Use the kyoketsu-shoge to carve your way through the enemy as much as you can.”

"Yes, sir," came their roar from the distance. They got to work immediately. Positions shifted, chains rattled in all directions, and at least fifty of the enemy troops fell to the ground from the sudden change of tactics. *That ought to hold them for a while,* Callan thought, but then came the sound of an explosion to the southern wall. The Elite Guard stationed there were wiped out instantly, and three dozen more Yaiba and Kabuto men and women met their end in the chaos that followed.

A wave of Scarlet troops—undoubtedly the missing battalion—swarmed the Bluff City outpost and, before a single one of their number felt defeat, ran through dozens more of the resistance members. Callan pressed through the city, desperate to save as many as he could. Everywhere the shouts of his comrades and the pained cries of the dying could be heard. Smoke billowed through the air, as dark as the feeling in his heart.

Callan's Reikiken came to life, and before long he used the combined efforts of his kyoketsu-shoge and repulsors to grapple and glide through the city. It wasn't long before he saw a swarm of them, those damned Scarlets in their blood-red uniforms. The soldiers of the outpost fought as best they could, but they were caught by surprise and it showed in their movements. Callan's ears twitched. Was… was that laughter he heard? The Reds *laughed* at the wanton death measured out by their hands.

Enraged, Callan dropped from above as soundlessly as a leaf descendant of a tree. He flipped forward so that his boots landed on the face of one of the aggressors. He ignited his repulsors and savored the sound of the man's scream. His feet hit the ground as the other enemies in the great red cluster stared at their comrade and his enflamed face. Callan spun his firesword and pointed it straight ahead, the tip of his blade angled downward in a hand lifted high above his head. His empty hand, bare except for the kyoketsu-shoge at its back, extended forward as if to invite his opponents to make a move. An unsuspecting and foul-tempered Scarlet Trooper lifted his rifle at Callan's face, but when he went to fire, he found that the Water Dragon had already clipped him at the arms. He screamed, and a look of serenity washed over Callan's face as his enemies shouted for each other to keep their distance.

They all moved away from him, but he didn't care. It was poor form indeed for Callan Rouge, resident master of the Suiryu form of combat, to be concerned for what his opponents did. He focused his mind on his blade, and as the adversaries around him rooted themselves and opened fire, the sounds of their rounds resounded in his ears as ocean waves that crashed against jagged rocks.

Truthfully, that was the sound he always heard when he was serious. It was as though the tension of a battle unnerved him so that he had to find a peace that, in that moment, did not exist. His peace was oceanic, steeped in waters so deep that no man could explore, an endless flow of mystified tranquility that overshadowed the prolific gore of a warzone. In this moment, just as in training so many years ago, just as in all the battles he'd fought up until now, he simply moved with his sword as his guide. It spun at his side, above his head, behind his back only inches from the hooded cloak that was as much a part of his Hanzo Gear as the weapons and repulsors.

He swept in the occasional wide arc, felt the muted impact of his bladc against some object, but now his eyes were closed and his only focus was the delicate dance of defensive flow that he dared treat his enemies to. The outside world, amid this euphoric experience, this display of martial prowess shrouded in elegance, was little more than a reef drowned in the deep. Callan's flow slowed, the sound of metal against metal erased by the waves in his ears. The enemies screamed as his feet tread the ground like a child's tread the beach, but he heard nothing but water all around him.

The mist of bullets thickened, and while the natural flow between his movements was enough to push the spray to any given side of him, still a few pellets met with his cloak. It stung at first, but he tapped into greater focus. There. He exhaled as his Reikiken danced in his arms with more intensity. It was a feeling, a song, the sweeping sensations of love and passion, of hate and disgust, intertwined in every stroke of his wrist and every gentle placement of his feet.

It wasn't long before the bullets slowed, though whether from a lack of gunmen or the water in his ears Callan couldn't tell. Something felt—

An explosion sounded in the distance, and a panicked shriek over the comms pulled him out of his battle meditation. He looked in the direction of the eastern battle, and instantly Callan knew what had happened—and what he had done. He took a single step in that direction, blood and mangled bodies at his boots from all directions, but another detonation not far from his position swept him into the rubble of a nearby building. His body rippled with pain from the impact, but he returned to his feet regardless. His left arm felt heavy, but he could still move it. Blood from a cut on his forehead dripped down into his eye. He chuckled. Not the first time that that's ever happened and it probably wouldn't be the last. His vision blurred from the blood and the impact, and he gave himself a moment to stabilize. The heat from his Reikiken stung his many newfound scrapes and lacerations, but those were of little consequence to him.

It hurt to stand, hurt to move, hurt to breathe, and yet he insisted on all three. His subordinates fought and died all around him, and he would not be the kind of leader to let them die in vain. He took a step forward, and when he saw that he could move without the threat of falling over again, he pressed onward.

"Um," came a nervous voice from a little ways away. It was girlish, and absolutely the opposite of anything that could have been considered authoritative. "Stop right there!" Callan focused his gaze in the direction of the order and saw the slender woman with vivacious blonde hair and hypnotic emerald eyes. She wore a form-fitting red uniform and carried a rifle in her hands that she aimed squarely at his face. He paused for a moment as he surveyed the delicate features of her alabaster face, and while it might instill some form of pleasure in someone else, it invoked the darkest rage in Callan Rouge.

He stepped forward, and the moment his foot met the ground the woman shot. He pulled his Reikiken up in a diagonal in front of his face and the bullet ricocheted away.

"You're one of the Scourge, aren't you?" There was silence after he asked the question and the girl visibly shook from her nerves.

"Callan…Rouge," she stammered the name, gripped with fear born of her recognition. He was the captive that had escaped, the Water Dragon of the Violet Shadows, and—if he had anything to say about it—the agent of her destruction. She fired off round after round with expert precision, but each bullet dislodged from her weapon was swatted away like a gnat as the furious Dragon charged in. The beautiful blonde woman did what she could to establish distance, and knew that it was only because of the bomb's doing that his mobility was fractured. Even still, he moved with such speed and accuracy that it was a terror for her to watch. It was bad enough that he'd massacred her whole battalion without so much as a truly offensive blow, but to see him back up on his feet after taking a blast to the back was nightmarish.

She rattled off round after round, and did what she could to root herself to steady her aim. Like it mattered. Every so often a bullet would connect with her opponent, but the heatwave provided by the Reikiken ruined their trajectory and made them easy for him to deflect. This time, though, his wrist flicked in a different manner and a bullet was knocked back where it came from. She hit the dirt with barely enough time to dodge the returned projectile, and when she looked back at her opponent, a sinister grin slithered across his face.

“That was pretty cool,” he said, his voice low and borderline inhuman. “That’s the first time that trick actually worked. Shame it didn’t hit anything though. Guess I’ll have to try again.” He grinned wider when the Scourge member shuddered, and lunged for her position with an animosity he’d never exhibited before. It was out of character, but what else was he to feel? He hated the Scourge for the condition they’d kept him in when he was their captive. He hated them for their taunts, their tortures, their refusal to treat him like a person, and everyday since they took him back to their base he was reminded of it all through a plethora of minuscule sights and sounds. This was the moment that he’d waited months for. This was the moment that he would finally have his revenge and let them know what it was to go up against one of the Yaiba Insurrection’s Seven Dragons.

The blonde woman took a knee and lifted the muzzle of her gun once more. This time, though, she held it sideways. Callan noticed a secondary muzzle, much wider and shorter than the primary funnel of the gun. A grenade launcher. She smirked, a sign of relief more than arrogance, and pulled the trigger. There was a click, and a small black orb emerged from the end of it. The grenade flew a couple of feet, and for a moment the blonde woman felt a sense of pride, as though the battle had finally reached its end. She couldn’t wait to tell her big sister about what she’d done.

Chains rattled, and before the woman knew what happened, the orb returned to her in two halves.

“Wha—” was the last thing she said before it detonated, and she sprayed in a fountain of pink and red about the ground. Callan took a moment to catch his breath, to fall on the ground and rest his aching body. More gunfire and shouting echoed through the air from the east. His men hadn’t gone down so easily, and he was thankful for that.

Wheels approached. Callan, on edge again, quickly rose to his feet and reignited his Reikiken when he realized that it was a Yaiba transport piloted by his subordinate, Ryan Morrisey.

"Time to go, boss," the young Insurrectionist urged. "We can't have you dying on us." Callan sighed. It was all he could do. He wasn't in any condition to fight off the rest of the enemy regiment, and with more than two thirds of their fighting force—maybe more—dead, it would be suicide to stick around. The outpost had fallen, and Johnson City was fair game.

"All forces fall back to Johnson City," he ordered through clenched teeth as he entered the transport and sped away. "We lost."

****

December 8th, 2084, 6:17 p.m.,

Cecelia Kant paced the floor of what once was Callan's office, more nervous than she'd been in a very long time. Her forces had achieved a victory. Sure, the Scarlet casualties were a little higher than she would've liked, but they would always be able to supply more bodies to the cause. A win was a win. Except, of course, when it wasn't.

She'd deployed her remaining forces to scour the area for her sister Trisha, who had gone radio silent after the last two explosions within the city walls. She hadn't been seen for hours, and Cecelia couldn't bear the implications. A knock came at the door, and she brutishly opened it.

"Many pardons, Ms. Kant," said the grunt nervously. He extended his arms to reveal a cylindrical object wrapped in red cloth. Cecelia, eyes widened with shock and disgust, snatched the object from the man's hands and opened the cloth. She saw the charred, disembodied hand of her beloved sister.

Chapter Twenty-Three

December 11th, 2084, 12:04 p.m.,

"Ballistic Formation Beta!" Zahara's voice clapped through the air like thunder, and without question her soldiers obeyed. She took the centermost position and her gunmen crowded around her, each one faced to a different direction. As the enemy gunfire blasted through the air the swordsmen of their number wrapped around the cluster of shooters with their backs to the trees and their arms spread so that their cloaks would form a defensive shield around their allies. The gunners lined up their shots on the shoulders of their protectors, each one with their eyes on their aggressors' positions. Zahara donned a muted grin as she called out to her soldiers, "Fire!"

Shots burst forth from either side. People screamed and died, though more on the Scarlet side of things than the Yaiba. It was an impressive trap that they'd walked into. Two days had passed since their last battle against the Reds, but the area was still dense with enemy patrols and moving recklessly would likely get them all killed. Zahara did what she could to coordinate with the Kiryu, Raven Shadid, and together they mapped out the best course of action. They both knew that leading the Shadows through the Wastes would likely be met with opposition at some point, and of course it came in spades.

When the Reds realized in that second frontal assault two days prior that they couldn't take the Yaiba with those tactics, they decided to lie in wait until the opportunity to ambush came along. It did, but unfortunately for them they had to square off against Zahara's wits, and she'd trained her students exceptionally well for such a time as this. The blasts of gunfire still resounded through the woods. Two of her gunmen fell dead on the ground, but the Scarlets suffered greater casualties. Those that remained sought to flee, but were unaware that they'd been surrounded by Raven's men during their firefight. They ran right into them, and were mowed down like startled deer by the ravenous Shadows spread throughout the treetops. In no time at all the final scream was heard, the gunfire ceased, and Raven stood side by side with Zahara.

"You really are something else," the Kiryu complimented. Raven wasn't sure what to make of the Red Traitor upon her release from the holding cell. It wasn't that Raven had a hard time with trust. In fact, she was one of the quickest to trust in all the Yaiba Insurrection. Still, it didn't mean that she was a fool. Anyone would assume that a traitor in war would only be out for themselves, and that was what she thought of Zahara. That is, until Zahara proved her merit by her command of her platoon. Even though their number fell from 55 to 41, they were still a well-oiled machine and made the work quicker for the Dragon's forces. It almost felt like a vacation compared to some of the other operations Raven had been a part of in her earlier years. "I can't remember the last time things moved this fast."

"Thanks, though I haven't really contributed much to the op," Zahara shrugged with a wry, girlish smile. This experience was so unusual to her. She was a dark-skinned woman with long curly hair. Her past was adorned with so many instances of overt discrimination and derision that at this point she'd thought it was how things were supposed to be. Even though Raven was clearly not all white, the only identifier of another ethnicity was her hair and even then, it wasn't something the Reds would've paid too much attention to. Yet despite her tone and her position of power within the ranks of the Insurrection's Violet Shadows, she treated Zahara like an equal. Like a friend.

"You're joking," Raven joked with an incredulous chuckle. "You brought us your intel. Knowledge is control in times of war, and you coming to our side and giving us as much as we need might just be enough to finally push the Reds on the defensive." Raven placed a hand on Zahara's shoulder as the ballistic platoon and Zahara's company returned to formation and marched at the subtle orders of the women in charge. "Just by showing us the way to the Jackson compound you're doing so much for our cause, not just the operation."

"Let's just hope that it amounts to something," Zahara said, and took to the rear of her platoon with wary diligence.

****

December 11th, 2084, 12:52 p.m.,

Serafina Leyva jolted as Prince James slammed his fist down hard on the table before him. The news had gotten back to him that not only had their primary contact in the Yoroi Alliance been killed, but so had one of the two members of the Scourge dispatched to provide reinforcements to the Bluff City regiment. Serenity glanced at him, and through her usual expression of cold indifference, just for a moment, Serafina could see concern in the Colonel's face. Serafina's brow lifted, but she decided to leave it alone for the moment.

"What do we do now," Aria Black asked over the awkward silence. Prince James looked up at her, then back at his fist, slightly bruised from the prior impact. He didn't know. He'd pleaded with his father to return to the capitol through his brother Nash, but the King of the Reds saw this as an opportunity to teach his more aloof son to be a warrior and stand on his own two feet. The problem that James saw in that plan was their limited number of resources and personnel. Standing between the Scarlet Kingdom and the Yoroi Alliance was rocky at best, left up in the air by the ongoing conflict between the Pro-Rebellion and Anti-Rebellion factions that split the group. To make matters worse, the Yaiba Insurrection backed the Pro-Rebel side, so James guessed that it was only a matter of time before their alliance with the Yoroi dissolved entirely. Unless…

"Leyva, Waldheim," the Prince called, and the two of them snapped to attention. "Take the secret passage into the Yoroi Clusters and find the Anti-Rebel camp. See if there's any way that we can salvage this situation. Black," his head turned to the nervous Scourge manipulator as he spoke the name, "you're to rendezvous with Kant outside of Johnson City. Monitor the Yaiba's movements and report back to me daily." The remaining members of the Scarlet Scourge voiced their acceptance of their missions and departed promptly. At their leave, Serenity cupped James' chin and brought his lips to hers. It'd been so long since they had a moment together, so long since the last time they could be intimate, and so she lingered. She released him, satisfied for the moment at the taste of him.

"I needed that," she said, and her cold visage softened to the warm look of a lover. "Are you sure that splitting up the Scourge is a good idea? It isn't the first time that my members have gone on solo missions or carried out operations in smaller teams, but things seem a little… uncertain right now."

"It's fine," James assured her, but the tone that carried those words spoke to the opposite. "My father just means to teach a lesson, is all."

"Yes, but at what cost," Serenity asked. There was genuine concern in her voice. She was a tactician, and certainly more of one than the Prince though his abilities in the last few months certainly impressed her. Still, she knew a losing situation when she saw one, and in those moments, the division of their prime fighting force was less than ideal.

"My father tends to think of what's best for the Kingdom—" James started, prepared to give one of his usual charismatic political speeches. A sharp look from the love of his life—no—from the leader of the Scarlet Scourge quickly put an end to that.

"What about what's best for his son," she challenged. He let out a pained sigh as he truly considered that question. For as long as Prince James could remember, his father always favored his older brother. Nash was dimwitted, impulsive, overcompensating, and selfish beyond compare, but he was the firstborn. The crown prince. Everything that his father had would one day belong to Nash, which meant it was always James' place to be overlooked.

He wanted more than that. That was why he arranged to be in the field with the Crawford siblings, each a specialist in their field and each more than capable of masking any mishaps that he walked them into. It seemed, though, that his efforts to prove himself worthy of his father's love only reassured the old man that James was worthless.

He rubbed his forehead as he closed his eyes. Their conditions were subject to change at any moment and it was abundantly clear that his father had no intentions of sending help. James smiled. At least Nash had tried to be helpful these last couple of months. It was more than James ever expected of him, honestly. He looked back at Serenity.

"I couldn't tell you," he said frankly. "I have a few bargaining chips that could buy us safe passage into one of the other territories if we need it—"

"Wait, what are you suggesting?" Serenity's voice shook for what he believed to be the first time in his hearing. She eyed him quizzically, and when his face never left that pensive yet determined look she shook her head. "No. No, what you're suggesting is insane, James."

"It's plausible is what it is," he rebutted. He stood up from his chair and took Serenity by her hands. They were oddly delicate for a woman so hardened by war. "I've wanted to run away with you ever since I first saw you. These last few months, with us being together constantly but unable to be together, it's only made me want that even more." Serenity pulled back. Everything James said ran contrary to who she was as a person. Her birth father died fighting for the Kingdom. Her adopted father was a Scarlet war hero. Her brothers were only just tents away, all fighting for the same cause and James, the Prince of the Scarlet Kingdom, just suggested they abandon everything because things were a little shaky.

"I understand," she said slowly, "I really do. But you know I can't just drop everything and leave—"

"Even if my father tries to snuff us out," James interrupted. His eyes were hard now, like Serenity had never seen. This ordeal, being out in the field with the Scourge and the Infantry and Intelligence Corps, it changed him. And it was attractive to her. She took a deep breath.

"You're forgetting that I'm at risk of death just for being in love with you," she reminded him. He didn't have anything to say to that, and his eyes softened again as she continued. "I have a duty to the Kingdom. To your family. I swore to forsake my wants and needs in the service to His Majesty the King, just like my fathers and brothers did. It's not something I can just walk away from."

"Not even to save your own life," he asked, tears visible in his eyes. Serenity could tell that he wanted so badly to save her, that if nothing else went right he at least wanted that much to go off without a hitch, but she couldn't give him that. One thought about what the Kingdom would do to her brothers if she left was enough to convince her of that.

"I can't." Serenity had to catch herself. She was on the verge of tears, and she never wanted James to see her cry. She closed her eyes and steadied herself. "And we shouldn't even be talking about this. Let's just…" she paused, as for a brief moment she allowed herself to indulge the possibility of putting all of this behind her. She came back to her senses almost immediately. "Let's just forget we ever had this conversation." She left the tent in such a hurry that she knocked into a Scarlet Trooper, whom she then punched squarely in the gut. "Watch where you're going,

Trooper," she demanded, and stormed off to go mind her own business.

What she missed, however, was Serafina Leyva just to the side of the Prince's tent, quietly entertained by every word.

****

December 11th, 2084, 3:15 p.m.,

Three days had passed since the Bluff City outpost fell, but they'd bought all the time they needed to secure defenses from Johnson City to the Roan Mountain Compound. A wave of Scarlet Troopers attempted to breach the city, but the EMPs and long-range weaponry commandeered from their own stocks ensured their failure. Callan was relieved. The Scarlets had kept the other territories on the brink of destruction not just because of superior numbers, but superior firepower. The combined efforts of this alliance, though, proved to be beneficial in all the right ways. The Yoroi, however, were still absent.

It didn't matter, at least not right now. Erik Kincaid and his men had disabled the war drones of the Scarlet Kingdom, and with as many casualties as the Reds suffered at Bluff City, it would be harder for them to move against the Yaiba as freely without them. Callan thought about the presence of that Scourge member he'd fought. The last he'd heard, intel put them further west, just outside of the Grand Canyon. If they were moving around the map to offer assistance to much broader forces, then it probably meant that the war was going in the Insurrection's favor.

Still, Callan couldn't help but wonder how long that advantage would last. If the Reds could get their drones back up or secure more lands within the Southern Wastes, then it would be disastrous for the resistance forces. Lord forbid both of those things happen.

"Hey Callan," a familiar voice reached his hears and he turned with excitement. Shonda approached him at the heart of a moderately refurbished Johnson City. She was out for a stroll with her girls. Hope, the older daughter, happily swung her mother's hands in a hyperactive sort of way. She had her hair tied up in an adorable little puff at the back of her head and wore a nice pair of dark blue jeans and a tan sweater over a bright yellow shirt. Aya, the younger, hid behind Shonda's leg and watched Callan as though he were her mortal enemy. She always made him laugh.

"Shonda," he replied with a smile, "what brings you down this way?"

"Oh, you know, work as always. John had me and Ezekiel stationed here to give backup to the outpost. Sorry we couldn't, by the way," she said somewhat sheepishly. Callan stood stunned at that. Shonda was such a monster on the battlefield that it was sometimes hard to believe that she was a normal woman too. Callan had to guess that being around her girls brought out the best in her, and the idea of that made him smile.

"Oh no, it wasn't your fault," he reassured her. "I let my guard down and the Reds took advantage of that. I fought one of the Scarlet Scourge." The very mention of the name pumped Shonda up and for just a moment the monster emerged.

"The Scourge is here?" The way she asked the question was peaceful enough that her young daughters would remain oblivious, but Callan could see the animosity blossom.

"In part, at the very least. I've already sent word back to John about it. We may have lost the outpost, but we did what we needed to. The city and the mountain are armed and ready for any surprises the Reds have in store for us." There was a smugness in his tone as he said it, and Shonda smiled a devious smile. Frantic footsteps approached, and with the turn of their heads, the Dragons noted the presence of Esau Tillman, stoic as always.

"Master Rouge," he started with due respect of the Yaiba titles, "Senior Agent Kincaid has requested your presence."

"Apparently duty calls," Callan said to Shonda, then turned his attention back to Agent Tillman. "Any idea why the urgent summons?"

"I don't have the details," he admitted, "just that Director Hamlin has a new assignment for you." Callan took a moment to consider. He nodded, and Esau led the way.

****

December 11th, 2084, 3:41 p.m.,

Esau and Callan entered the Hall of Elders, and while Esau's face rarely showed emotion, he couldn't hide the frown he'd adopted at the thought. These were Sanctuary tunnels, spread throughout the entire continent for their use alone, and never once had an outsider breeched these hallowed grounds. They were the insurance policy of the Helmets, and the sole reason they'd been able to survive for as long as they had since the Second Civil War. Now, though, the secret was exposed, and actually had been since the initial plan to sabotage the Kingdom Drone Network. It was almost more than he could bear.

"You're dismissed, Agent Tillman," Erik Kincaid spoke upon their immediate entry. The frown on the young agent's face deepened, but he left without a word. Callan looked around at the Kabuto leaders, all seated on the tatami mats that surrounded the holoprojector, alive with azure light and a crackle that attested to the poor reception that one would have beneath the earth. The Elders of the Kabuto Sanctuary, with the sole exception of Senior Agent Kincaid, all looked on the Dragon with unabashed indignation, as though his mere presence in the chamber was an affront to their station. "Welcome, Master Rouge. Under different circumstances I'd introduce you to everyone present, but unfortunately we don't have any time for that."

"What's going on," Callan asked frankly. He was laid back in a sort of intense way that left all who knew him unaware of what response he might give. He was fun, but serious. Personable, yet distant. It was his nature to be driven and contradictory, and this moment proved to be no different.

"I think it's best that Director Hamlin explain it," Erik said gingerly, and with a series of commands inputted into his cuff, the shape of his longtime friend and brother in arms materialized. So to speak.

"Suiryu," John said, his face stoic to the Elders but grim and angry to the Water Dragon that knew him, "frequency 22597 has been accessed." Callan's eyes went wide at the mention, then narrowed. It was the frequency they'd used to communicate when John was on his black ops mission to the Yoroi territory. The only reason it would be accessed at this point was if Darius was in trouble.

"Understood, Director," Callan assured him, which left the Kabuto elites in confusion. "I'll head out immediately." Callan's voice became sharper as the anger set in. It wasn't that he was angry for the boy getting himself into trouble again. It was the simple fact that there was someone, somewhere, who had the audacity to raise a finger to his beloved nephew and that he couldn't abide.

"I've assigned a team to accompany you. They should arrive in Johnson City within the hour so when they make contact, you have my orders to move out," John assured him. Callan nodded in understanding, and the transmission ended. For a moment Callan stood and, with eyes that shifted nervously between the faces of Kincaid's colleagues, smiled awkwardly at them. He wordlessly left the room, and tread back down the path that Esau had brought him on.

****

December 11th, 2084, 5:27 p.m.,

Manny loved Atlanta. It was a far cry from what it once was, there was no denying that. The city once rich with black history and innovation, that teemed with life at every corner and boasted some of the best food, music and entertainment, now stood desolate and empty, save for Scarlet Troopers and the people they oppressed. Where the lights once shined brightly, now there was only darkness. Where the sounds of cars and conversation echoed through the distance, now there was silence, save for the occasional gunshot or Red transport. It was morbid in the worst way, and Manny hated that.

What he loved, though, was that even in this desolate state, Atlanta boasted great spires and high rooftops, all great accessories to his particular brand of mischief. If he happened to save a few of the Waste-Raiders as well, then his fortunes doubled. With his son Lukas by his side, they tripled. Lukas, ever the optimist, had a taste for the morbid just like his father, and was a quick study when it came to crafting mischief of his own.

"Okay, guys," he said cheerily into the comms network, "we're about to play a game!" The way he stressed the word "game" made his subordinates feel a deep degree of concern, but Lukas felt otherworldly delight. "It's called Extreme One-Word Story, and before I explain the rules does anybody know how a One-Word Story works?"

"Isn't that where you go around a circle and everyone says one word and you try to build a story out of it," asked one of the young ladies in his battalion. It was a smaller cluster, since three of the Dragons, Manny included, were dispatched to different subregions of the Southern Wastes to hit some of the major targets from Zahara Boyd's intel. The idea was to establish a secure route through the Wastes to the nearest accessible port for the ship from Gansu.

"Good job," Manny laughed. It was wily and brilliant, a testament to who he was as a person. "So the extreme version of the game would work the same way, except," he gave a faintly dramatic pause, then continued, "you have to give a word if you take out an enemy. How many of us are there?"

"Three hundred, Master Bautista," came another young man under his command. Manny smiled as the gears in his head started to turn.

"Okay so are we gonna split four ways or eight?" His question was asked frankly, the raspy tenor of his voice somehow a comfort to his subordinates.

"I think eight," came Lukas' voice, almost a perfect match for his father's. Manny didn't know if he would ever get used to hearing his mini-me on the other end of the comms, but the fact that the boy had the same thought as his old man made the Kazeryu smile. "Gives us a chance to cover a wider area and find more enemies." *Of course,* Manny thought. His son would want the game to go on as long as possible.

"Then eight ways it is," Manny confirmed. "On your mark," his troops could hear the childish excitement in his voice. They were stationed around the Bank of Am plaza, eager to go. "Get set," Manny continued, and a manic surge of energy hit him as he could feel the suspense of his subordinates, some excited to get going and others terrified beyond belief. "Go." And that was it. No direction given, no further insight, just a flurry of black and violet and orange that danced in the dying daylight.

As his soldiers scattered to their preferred directions, Manny looked at his son, who sat near him at the summit of the mountainous skyscraper. Lukas admired his father. To the Yaiba he always came off as the chaotic good sort. His methods for battle were…unconventional, and usually amounted to little more than ill-advised antics in the minds of everyone else. He was effective, though, and boasted the lowest casualty or capture rate of any of the Seven Dragons. It was because of that that he was largely left to his own devices.

To his enemies, at least from what Lukas understood, his father the Wind Dragon was a chaotic evil, a malicious gale that not only rocked the boat, but sank the ships of the Scarlet Kingdom. To Lukas, though, Manny was just chaotic in all the best ways. His unorthodoxy confused allies and enemies, and afforded his troops to think on their own to get out of a difficult situation rather than rely on the sometimes questionable decisions of their leadership. He was a man aware of his own flaws, and so he trusted his soldiers to do what was right in the moment.

"Ready to go?" Manny asked the question with a bright smile that contrasted the still-encroaching darkness.

"Sure thing, pops," Lukas replied in his usual chipper tone, though that was accented by the subtle ring of admiration. The Wind Dragon jumped, as did his dragonling, and as they plummeted towards the nearby rooftop of an abandoned hospital, both came alive with the rush of the wind. Something about it was addictive. The adrenaline? No, it wasn't something so chemical. Lukas would've thought the bond between him and his father, but that wasn't it either. Even on missions where Manny wasn't present he felt himself come alive with every boost of the repulsors and swing of the heat-treated chain. It was deeper than that, as if his very soul was somehow bonded to the air, be it a gentle breeze or raucous tempest, and now they would both become the latter.

The hospital roof approached quickly, and wordlessly, in unison, Manny and Lukas flipped so that the soles of their feet faced the concrete slab. The repulsors activated, and their rapid descent became a controlled drift. The two Shadows extended their kyoketsu-shoge and anchored them into the roof. By the time their boots hit the cement, enemies swarmed from the stairwell door across from the rundown helipad. Before Manny could even ask which of them was to go first, Lukas drove a kyoketsu-shoge into the neck of the first enemy to step towards them.

"I guess the first word's yours, kid," Manny told him. The enemy troops, who numbered at twelve, opened fire. Manny turned his back to them and spread his arms so that his cloak and body would serve as a shield for his son.

"The," was all he said, and so the first word of the story was uttered through the comms.

"Reds," came another of the soldiers from a distant location. Another enemy had fallen.

"Were," sang a feminine voice through the comms. Manny beamed as bright as the moon that slowly took her place over the city. His soldiers enjoyed this. The game more so than the act of violence. That was, after all, why Manny suggested they play. It was morbid, but it was a good way to get the job done and provide an alternative focus to lessen any trauma that might accompany their present ordeal.

"Clumsy," grunted another man, and then an engine revved in the background. Apparently he had commandeered an enemy transport for the fun of it. "They…" he continued with the disposal of another enemy, "were…" there, another one felled, "classist."

"And," someone else contributed. It was less lively than the last guy, but also somehow lighter, like the air. That alone was enough to make Manny suspend his position as a shield and dive into the crowd of enemies, Reikiken poised to tear through flesh. When he landed at the center of their small congregation, they looked confused. The Wind Dragon pointed the tip of his blade back towards his son, and the hilt of his weapon was seemingly aimed at his opponents. The potential aggressors raised their guns to him, and Lukas in the background stood with a delighted smile across his mouth.

"Any last words," asked the apparent second in command. Manny rolled his eyes as he reached for the second Reikiken at his waist.

"What is it with you overconfident types and falling on clichés," he asked as the second blade came to life in the palm of his hand. Without so much as a moment's hesitation, he twisted his initial weapon hand and connected the ends of the two tungsten swords, and the intensity of the heat was enough to make even the Insurrectionist General sweat. "Oh wow," Manny said, pleasantly surprised. "This is intense. I'll have to remember to thank Kaneuji for this upgrade. Now, let's rewrite this story," he told the terrified Troopers that surrounded him.

The enemies opened fire, but the Hanzo Gear and firestaff served as more than enough of a barrier. The wave of heat that emanated from the new weapon threw the flight path of the bullets off, and the doubled blade deflected a great deal of them to all sides. Manny struck the enemy before him with one end, and the other burned through an enemy to his rear. Two down.

"Egregious," he offered, in an effort to continue the game he'd proposed. He took a wide swing as he spun the staff and stepped forward to adjust his stance. Four more enemies fell to the ground with a thud. "Why not make them scream" he continued, determined to wrap this up quickly and move on.

"'My'" came the voice of another soldier from somewhere in the city. Manny couldn't hold back his toothy grin. They were catching up.

"'Cabbagetown,'" screamed another of the Violet Shadows. Manny and Lukas laughed as the elder between them stabbed forward through one of his enemies and instantly reversed the motion to burn a hole through a second.

"And run," Manny added. The Scarlet Trooper behind the Dragon dropped his gun and pulled out a knife. While Manny eyed the enemy soldier's remaining comrades, he crept in with his weapon hand lifted. Lukas, like a falcon whose wings were carried by a divine wind, propelled himself through the air on his repulsors and cleared the helipad in a single bound. His Reikiken aimed forward, he struck the chest of the would-be assassin and rolled along the ground from the momentum.

"Like," Lukas said into the comms with a smile as audacious as his father's.

"Crazed," came a woman from the other end. Manny slashed down with his Reikinobo, but unlike before he only managed to take down one enemy.

"Baboons," was the cleanest word that came to mind. He made it a point to always appear respectable in front of his troops and his child, though he had to admit that he was often tempted to drop any pretense of decorum. He slashed through the last enemy to his left while Lukas took down the final foe.

"Let's," spoke the elder operative, and he ran to the southern edge of the hospital roof.

Lukas ran after his father as he spoke into the comms, "go."

****

December 11th, 2084, 9:00 p.m.,

Bryan was happier than he'd been in months. Since the moment they turned him loose in the New York research facility, he'd been on a computer with his eyes widened at the abundance of information suddenly at his fingertips. Weapon designs, future projects, resources at the lab's disposal, and the deepest inner workings of the whole Scarlet society were his to observe, enact and command. It made him fell…powerful.

There was a brief moment where he thought to relay the sum of this information to his former allies at the Yaiba Insurrection. The Reds were awful. He knew that much, even though they placed him in the lap of luxury at his daughter's request. But they were a means to an end, and while they were part of the reason that his son no longer walked amongst the living, the Insurrection played a part all the same.

For the time being, he would insert a few design ideas of his own. Liquid nitrogen bombs that would work wonders against the heat-fields of the Reikiken. A lighter version of the fireswords that made the Yaiba such a threat. They were more brittle, sure, but the speed they would offer would be more than enough to even the playing field against his old friends.

Bryan's greatest source of entertainment and pleasure, though, was the Kingdom Drone Network. The virus that the Helmets uploaded to it was a thing of beauty. For every counter Bryan could think of, the virus would repair itself. He was locked in a deadlocked battle with the tech for the last three days, but he'd discovered a subtlety in the infrastructure of the Network that he could exploit. The virus was designed to incapacitate the main Network and render the deployment and weaponry functions of the drones inaccessible, but it paid no mind to the subroutine that allowed for updates. So Bryan began to patch the system with the same meticulous algorithm that provided security to the Yaiba communications networks. It was something that helped keep their channels private when they'd fought against the Kabuto a few decades back, and by the looks of things, it had already begun to work its magic.

A few more days, and the Reds should have their precious air support back. Bryan chuckled as he input command after command. There was one small thing he needed to do. He knew that the nobility couldn't be trusted. Once they got what they needed out of him, they would likely try to kill him. He needed a failsafe, something of a preemptive strike against the Crown so that his life was spared and his vengeance was secured.

He looked up at the ceiling of the facility. His vision blurred for a moment from the sudden lack of the computer screen before him. All he could see were rings of light and shadow spread over the bespectacled tiles. The rings grew more intense for a moment and then just…faded away. Suddenly, he had an idea.

Chapter Twenty-Four

December 15th, 2084, 1:09 a.m.,

Her lungs burned, and every inch of her tinged with pain. The sting of the cold bit at her with every step, but still she ran through the forests that surrounded the main roads. Though the Red uniform covered the sum of her flesh below her neck, her body was bruised all over and cuts and scrapes adorned her otherwise beautiful face. *Almost there*, she thought as she panted like an overheated dog. Her leg snagged on an exposed tree root and though she stumbled, she caught herself and pressed on.

Jackson wasn't too far away. If she could just make it to Flowood then—

A gunshot cracked through the air. They'd caught up to her just that fast. But it didn't matter. Zahara knew more than enough to get through dangerous territory like this and she'd never be caught or killed so easily. Not by those filthy Insurrectionists. Thunder roared, or maybe it was another burst from a rifle. She darted left, just in case. It was closer to the main road, so hopefully her pursuers would fall for the feint and pass her by. She glanced behind her as she ran and heard the shuffle and stomp of boots in the distance. Their gunners stopped firing. Apparently, the trick worked.

She receded back into the thicket of trees and propped up next to one. The moment her legs came to a stop they buckled, but she was proud of herself. She'd run for miles, outwitted the Yaiba, and was only a couple of hours outside of the Jackson base on foot. If only there was a—

"You," came a hostile male voice from a few feet away. Zahara looked up and smiled with relief. "What do you think you're doing out here?" His teammates emerged from the surrounding foliage, all of them with rifles trained on her.

"It's about time a patrol found me," she said with enough irritation to give the entire group pause. "Why is there a massive gap in the middle of your defensive perimeter?" The head Trooper's eyes narrowed on her as his finger slowly inched toward his trigger. "You can relax, numbskull, I'm not an enemy."

"How can I be so sure," he asked back. It took her a moment for the meaning of the question to register. She'd spent so much time in the Roan Compound that she'd become too used to the idea that her skin tone was a non-issue. To the Reds, though, it was often the only one, even if most of them would never admit it out loud.

"I'm sorry, I was momentarily stunned by your total lack of competency, soldier, but maybe I'll make it easier on you. My name is Captain Zahara Boyd, SKA designation 06529-002," she rattled off with express irritation. The soldiers that surrounded her all shared the same stunned expression as she gingerly got back to her feet. "Now that you apparently know who I am, why don't you get to answering my question. Since you seem to be a little slow, I'll ask it again: Why is there a massive gap in the middle of your defensive perimeter?" The leading soldier began to stammer, to which Zahara held up her hand. "Ma'am, Trooper what?" The Trooper swallowed, hard, and momentarily glared at Zahara. She raised her eyebrows as if to challenge him to do something, but she knew he wouldn't. Lifting a hand to a superior officer was grounds for the guillotine in the capitol and she would gladly send him there. He snapped to attention and wiped the look of anguish from his face.

"Ma'am, Trooper Sanchez reports," he almost growled. Zahara nodded, and Sanchez snapped to parade rest with his hands overlapped behind his back. "The perimeter was fine until a few days ago when we lost contact with a couple of our patrols. The Commander sent a few of our patrol squads to investigate the disappearances. Those squads haven't come back either." Zahara's body tensed as he spoke and her eyes went wide with a mixture of panic and indignation.

"You mean there aren't any more of you who could defend this sector," she demanded, and bashed the bottom of her fist against the tree. The entire squad jumped.

"No, ma'am," said Trooper Sanchez, an air of nervousness now so very clear in his voice. "Conflicts have been popping up all over Providence faster than the higher ups can account for. A lot of those are still going on and with our forces spread so thin already, it's…" he didn't know how to finish, and she didn't want him to.

"I need to get to the Jackson base," she said with a sense of urgency that was, unsurprisingly, lost on the whole group. "Immediately," she told them in such a way that conveyed that they should've already begun their return. "I'm assuming you have some sort of transport nearby?"

"Yes, ma'am," Sanchez supplied, still clearly on edge from the news. "Right this way." One of the subordinate troops took Zahara on their shoulders as Sanchez led the way back to their transport, and with every step the patrol took, Zahara resisted the urge to smile.

****

December 15th, 2084, 2:27 a.m.,

The entire city of Jackson was a fortress of the Reds, three rings separated by walls and populated by a mix of the Scarlet forces and the Waste-Raiders that they oppressed. A massive storm from the previous week had breached the outer wall near the southern stretch of State Street in Le Fleur Bluff, and now, only days later, the Yaiba Insurrection's Violet Shadows stormed the opening. It didn't take the higher ups long to order that the gates of the second wall be closed immediately with gunmen posted at any break in the walls.

Bullets rained from both sides, all fired from Kingdom weapons. Reikiken whipped through the air in an elegant array of movements designed for deflection and decimation alike. Chains rattled through the deep howls of the wind to ghostly effect. Raven Shadid watched from the background as her company and the ballistic platoon did their worst to lay waste their enemies. She was never drawn to combat, and despite her eagerness to participate in the Battle of Johnson City, she never enjoyed it. However, she was drawn to help those in need, and the Southern Wastes were full of sick, oppressed, underprivileged people who were left to rot along with the conditions of their city.

The Scarlet Troopers fired into the expanse beyond the second gate with no regard to the Waste-Raiders that lived there. The only objective of the Reds was to eliminate any threat to their precious power. They were, after all, the last of a dying breed, the remnants of the once-great White Supremacists that for centuries gripped the land with an iron fist and a fluid wallet. Raven watched as stray bullets veered off in a myriad of ways. People and their families were in danger, and all because the Yaiba had barged in recklessly.

The Insurrectionists swung and repulsed in a number of different angles so that they would take the bullets, not the civilians. The noncombatants took shelter and, for the moment at least, gave up their pursuits of whatever was on the other side of that wall. It was enough to give Raven a brief moment of solace while she wondered just what the hell Zahara had been thinking when she came up with this ridiculous plan. The gates opened, and a company of gunners emerged from the other side of the second wall, each one an addition to the madness of the moment.

The company of Insurrectionists was caught between the protection of the weak and the dispatching of the oppressors that their usual expertise in combat was largely diminished. Raven, who would typically pride herself on her casual demeanor even in the thickest trouble, sighed out of aggravation.

“Concentrate your efforts on the civilians,” she ordered through the comms. “Deactivate your Reikiken and focus on rescue and retreat for now.”

“What’ll you do, Master Shadid,” asked Orson Nucci, one of Zahara’s top three pupils. She didn’t much care for his excited tone, but something in it let her know that he understood the severity of the situation and the necessity of her order so she let it slide. Raven Shadid, the Kiryu, ignited her aura sword as her eyes became a bit darker.

“I’ll draw their attention,” she replied, and without another word her feet hit the battlefield.

****

December 15th, 2084, 2:44 a.m.,

“Commander,” Sanchez called as they entered the command room. Zahara was caught off-guard by the obvious lack of decorum, and noted that it must’ve just been his personality. “There’s someone who wishes to speak with you.” There across the room stood a woman with silver hair down to her lower back, sharp blue eyes amid her otherwise delicate features, with all the poise of a Greek goddess. She surveyed the map projection, determined to optimize defenses and delay the Yaiba’s entry for as long as she could. All around her a number of men and women checked their devices, monitored the terrain to the finest shift of an abandoned car, all with the hope of ascertaining the threat level. The Commander sighed as the seconds ticked by.

“Then speak,” she demanded, eyes still focused on the map of the battlefield. The outer wall that circumvented the whole of the old city suddenly flashed in red, which signified its loss and the loss of the territory that it was supposed to guard. "I have more than enough on my plate as it is without such an egregious waste of my time—"

"The Insurrectionists have arrived at your door," Zahara spoke, as ordered, and the woman at the holoprojector laughed in disappointment.

"Tell me that you didn't come into my command center just to relay intel I've already got," she warned, and for a moment Zahara's blood ran cold. *Mental note, kill her first*, she told herself.

"No, ma'am," the cunning Boyd assured her with a sense of urgency. "The enemy force is led by Raven Shadid, known amongst the rebel scum as the Kiryu, one of the Seven Dragons of the Violet Shadows." The mention of one of the Dragons shifted every eye in the room, and finally the Commander looked up from the holoprojector. "I didn't get a good look at their number but I'll bet they're not numbered any less than a battalion of about 300 or so." The Commander was more than suspicious, and now carefully inspected Zahara in all her scrapes and bruises.

"And how, exactly, did you come into this kind of information," she asked with eyes like a rattlesnake ready to strike. Her tone was just as serpentine, somewhere between amused and darkly calloused. The sum of this woman's personality made Zahara, a trained soldier and expert markswoman, feel like a desert mouse just within reach of the viper's strike.

"I was the only one to survive the Battle of Johnson City," she clarified. Her voice shook with the words, though not from any performance she had prepared before she made it this far. It was from a genuine sense of unrest. "The enemy discovered my position and took me captive. They were about to execute me before I told them about Jackson."

"So you were the one that brought them here," the Commander's voice became more enlightened, and adopted the subtle venom of disgust.

"I led them to the forests to be attacked by Scarlet Troopers," Zahara retorted with just the right amount of feigned offense at the Commander's (unmistakably correct) insinuation. "By the time the smoke cleared I was already on the run. I tried to make it here before they could, but unfortunately your men saw fit to practically interrogate me before I could. Had they just brought me right away we could've worked out a strategy against them. Maybe even saved some of our men from a fiery death." The Commander shot Sanchez an almost starved glare, and Sanchez felt a little piece of himself die. She looked back at the projection, and again she sighed, though this time as a sign of relent rather than roused suspicion.

"I won't lie to you," the Commander started, a reptilian hum to her voice, "I'm not entirely sure we should keep you alive." Zahara's heart leapt into her chest as the Commander sauntered slowly, methodically toward her. "After all, you brought our enemy to our doorstep, and whether or not that was an intentional move is wholly irrelevant." The Commander stepped around the shaken sniper as she looked her over. Zahara shivered at the Commander's touch as she gently swiped a finger along the length of the Captain's shoulders, surveyed the grime that it had picked up, and then wiped it on her nearby subordinate. "Still, you've brought me more information than the sum of my greatest Troopers, and that deserves a reward." She gave a pause to smirk as Zahara let out a barely audible sigh of relief. "I'll make you a deal. If you can continue to make yourself useful, I'll continue to let you live."

"How can I be of service, Commander… I'm sorry, what was your name again," Zahara asked with an air of wariness, determined to only speak what would be beneficial to the mission at hand.

"Nathaira Connors," she supplied in a tone so condescending and terrifying that Zahara stood stunned for a moment longer. "So," Commander Connors started when the silence encroached upon the realm of awkward, “care to provide a solution to the problem you created?” She gestured to the floor, and Zahara looked out into the sea of eyes, all pointed at her for some semblance of direction.

“W-well,” she started, then immediately steeled herself. Now was not the time to be hesitant. There was no more crucial a moment than this for her to maintain her composure. “Have we had any contact with the capitol?”

“Yes, ma’am,” one of the troops, a shy-looking redheaded man, responded. “Reinforcements will be on the way at the first opportunity, but all over the map our forces—”

“Are spread thin. So I’ve heard,” Zahara remarked as she stepped down into the control room and to the holoprojector. She keyed in her designation code and enlarged the map to show the fortress-city’s defenses. She took a moment to account for every power generator, every energy node, all entrances and exits, and, as they came, reports of damage to the walls from across the base.

“What have you got for us,” Commander Connors’ tone threatened oh so casually from where Zahara had left her.

“If the capitol can’t send support right away then we’ll have to stall the Insurrectionists for however long it takes for our reinforcements to arrive,” Captain Boyd explained as all the Troopers in the command center watched her carefully. “These generators; what purpose do they serve right now?”

“Standard functions,” came another one of the Troopers, a dark-skinned female who, in the presence of this many overseers of alabaster complexion, instantly regretted the decision to speak up. “Defensive arrays are powered by the auxiliary generators—”

“Do the primary generators yield more power?” Zahara was frantic as she tapped the keys on the holoprojector console. The ebony-skinned Trooper from before glanced at the Commander, who gave her a nod of approval.

"Yes, ma'am, the auxiliary generators are for emergency operations, just in case the primary ones are knocked out." Zahara thought about that for a moment as she scanned the schematics before her. The nodes atop the walls were clearly designed to create some sort of energy field, no doubt a defense against the potential of enemy aircraft. She surveyed the layout of the walls, and, by now, the positions of the Reds and Shadows just off of the old Highway 80.

"The energy field that those nodes project," Zahara started again, still as urgently as before, "I need the range and function. What can we do with it?"

"That," Nathaira offered in response, "is something you'll have to figure out on your own. Nobody's used that system since the Second Civil War when this region first became the Southern Wastes." Zahara's fingers danced rapidly about the terminal as she tossed her hair behind her.

"Here goes nothing," she said, and tapped the final key.

****

December 15th, 2084, 2:44 a.m.,

The emergence of the Kiryu alone was enough to make the enemy wary. Though her presence did little to stop the hail of bullets that raged in her direction, it was enough to cause a decline in the accuracy of their aim. Raven turned her back to the shooters to allow the shield of her cloak to take on whatever bullets found their way to her back. It stung, but there were worse pains to be felt. For the moment, this was all she could do to protect the innocents that her own troops worked so hard to evacuate.

"Master Shadid," Drew McDowell said calmly over the comms, "the civilians in your area have been moved to the other side of the outer wall."

"Excellent," Raven replied as a relieved smirk graced her lips. "Continue to evacuate as many non-combatants as you can. This is bound to get a lot worse before it gets better."

"Yes, ma'am," Drew assured her, and then as soon as the comms fell silent, Raven bounded into the air with the help of her Hanzo Gear. She flipped backwards as she descended to the earth once again, Reikiken extended right for the chest of one of her assailants. The greater ranks of the Scarlet assault team couldn't believe the inhuman distance covered by such a single, elegant jump. Raven used the repulsors to lessen the impact of her legs on the ground and, as she burned through the man's body, spun rapidly through the air to take out the nearest enemy with a horizontal swing.

The gunfire that encircled the Wood Dragon became even more erratic, and though it was meant to stop her movements, it only ensured that the dark-haired woman moved as elegantly as a leaf carried by the wind. She followed the momentum from her horizontal swing and seared through the legs of yet another adversary. She crouched now, but only for a moment, as she vaulted in a back handspring with her blade extended into the face of an oncoming Scarlet.

From their view, she appeared as wild swings of orange light surrounded by an ever-changing shift in the shadows. She was the shade and the leaf, unmovable to them but swaying with the changing of the breeze. This, they realized, was the power of a Dragon. The moment Raven's legs hit the ground she swung her blade through the abdomen of another foe and allowed it to change her direction before she jumped and stabbed through the throat of yet one more. Three Red assailants charged her, electrified batons at the ready, but Raven jumped away from them with only her Reikiken extended in her wake. Their legs were burned from their bodies, and as they crumpled to the ground amid their screams of agony, Raven shifted the flow of her combat with the reversing of her grip.

She dove through the air, her reverse-gripped blade extended for a strike, and as her body rapidly twisted midflight, her weapon elegantly returned to its original grip to cut down another enemy. She stepped forward and slashed through the air, then jumped at another Scarlet Trooper. The Trooper lifted their rifle in the desperate hope that they could somehow defend their head, only to find that Raven had bisected them at the waist.

"Retreat!" The shouts of the remaining Scarlet Troopers to return to the other side of the second wall resounded, and as the gates opened up again, Raven saw this as a fortuitous opportunity.

"All personnel to me," she said into the comms with a sense of urgency that was, at least in the hearing of her troops, unusual for her. "The gates are opened. If we hurry, we might just be able to force our way in—" The gates started to close again. Raven rushed for the opening, her kyoketsu-shoge and repulsor boots put to full use, but she arrived too late to find a way through. She beat her fist against the giant steel door that blocked her path and cursed under her breath. "Belay that order," she told her troops, then all of a sudden, everything went dark.

****

December 15th, 2084, 3:37 a.m.,

Within moments every light scattered throughout the Jackson Fortress came back online and the faint hum of the auxiliary reactors filled the silence in the background. Every eye in the command center shifted to Zahara, who wiped her brow and breathed out in deepened relief.

"What's happening," someone asked, "why did we go dark?"

"I enacted the energy field and expanded its reach to just beyond the outer wall," Zahara explained, to which the eyes of the Commander narrowed.

"And what does that mean, exactly?" Nathaira and Zahara locked eyes for a moment, but the latter quickly looked away. Just that fast, she'd forgotten how cold this woman really was.

"The walls have become impossible to scale, meaning the Insurrection can't come any closer to our position," the Captain spoke. "The caveat is, unless the gates are opened, we can't get to them either."

"Wait a second," Commander Connors demanded with an air of unsettled realization. "what did you mean you expanded the reach of the field to just beyond the outer wall? Does that mean…" Nathaira didn't want to even acknowledge the possibility, but Zahara's expression confirmed it. They were trapped under an electrified dome with their worst enemies and with an insufficient number of bodies to throw at them. But… Commander Connors quickly regained her composure as she narrowed her focus on Zahara. "I suppose that was the correct move. Well done, Captain."

"Thank you, Commander," Captain Boyd responded with a faint smile. The Commander's gaze shifted around the room to her subordinates, all of whom grew increasingly nervous by the sheer power of her notice.

"Sanchez," she called, and the man in the doorway stiffened. "Escort our guest to the Officers' Quarters, would you?" Sanchez clenched his fist, but calmed himself before he said or did anything that would cost him his life.

"Yes, ma'am," he replied, and led the way back into the hall.

****

December 15th, 2084, 5:20 a.m.,

Bryan Piccio was almost done with the side project that held his attention for the last few days. Sure, it might've delayed the restoration of the KDN to full operational status, but the King and his Court had waited months for the drones to return to their command. What was a few more days? It was, after all, an intricate and delicate job. Not nearly, though, as the seven control rings that linked directly into the network. Each one had been designed specifically for the Court members, and Bryan had been so kind as to make one for the King as well.

They just needed to undergo one final change, one more little tweak before he could turn back to his work on the Drone Network. It was a stroke of genius to even craft these little trinkets. They would serve as a way for the Scarlet upper echelon to maintain control of their confounded devices, at least for a while longer and under the direct control of the royals. However, given that they were Bryan's creation, it ensured that there would be nobody else in the whole Scarlet Kingdom with the technological knowledge and skills needed to repair or adjust them should anything happen.

He soldered the last ring shut, all the tech inside of it tightly secured and fully functional. Now all he needed to do was dip them in gold and make them fashionable for the entitled pigs that were the nobility. He paused a moment, and in the midst of that great feeling of triumph remembered the gentle spirit that was his lost son. The sense of grief at Jaden's death was still just as palpable to him now as it had been when he first decided to leave the Yaiba Insurrection. Jaden deserved better than what he got, and it was almost time to repay everyone involved in his death.

"Dad?" It was Lyla's voice. While he stewed on his worst emotions, she'd managed to get into his little corner of the Capitol Research Facility without his notice. She entered his lab and the door shut behind her. "You're still here?" She inhaled, and the smell of musk and desperation filled her nostrils. She wasn't pleased. "When was the last time you took a break?"

"It's been a few days," he admitted sheepishly, and raised his hands in a placating gesture at the sight of her shocked expression. "I'm almost done," he told her. She warned him with her eyes and he couldn't help but smile. "I promise. Everything's almost ready."

****

December 15th, 2084, 7:00 a.m.,

John was already over it, but the decision to have both Vanessa Duncan and his father in the same room at the same time. Vanessa, a dark-skinned woman with bounce in her hair and ferocity in her eyes, flashed him a look that begged him to correct his father. John reciprocated it with a look of his own. Dre Hamlin was unbothered to the utmost. He knew this new generation of Dragons to be soft, or at least softer than his generation had been. The only exception to that was his son. Still, him saying that out loud did nothing to aid him in his objective of continued retirement. John wouldn't budge on his decisions, and Dre supposed it was a little much to think that he could appeal to any soft side of the boy.

"Regardless of what you want," John told them both, "what *I* want is for the two of you to work together. Assemble a team to man the command center on Level X. Feed our troops in the field tactical movements and intel based on the geo-sensor readings in their respective areas if possible."

"Are you sure that this pairing is wise," Vanessa asked, which drew an instant glare from the former Rairyu.

"You question my wisdom?" The way he spoke emanated power in the form of a reptilian hum that typically only showed itself on the battlefield.

"It's not that," she quickly corrected herself. Vanessa wasn't afraid of John. In fact, they were close friends before his ascension to the role of Director of the Yaiba Insurrection. Still, she needed this assignment to go away, and thought it better to try to placate him. "It's just that Master Dre and I don't really care for each other too much."

"Join the club," John told her, almost dismissively. "The old man's a jerk to most everybody. The only person that liked him was my mother. But you two aren't here because you like each other. The war has already taken some distressing turns in the early going. The Yoroi have yet to engage with the Scarlets because of infighting, Bluff City has fallen and the Reds are attacking Johnson City. We've dispatched a few light battalions to the Southern Wastes to clear a path to the eastern shoreline and expand our territory as well, but that endeavor is shaky at best."

"Even so, I don't think—" Vanessa started, but a sharp look from the Director cut her off. Dre sat silently in his seat in the Director's office as he took everything in.

"It's because of the unpredictability of this conflict that I'll be taking to the battlefield myself," John continued, and both the senior warrior and the Kageryu shouted their worry and disapproval. "Noted," John said once their indistinguishable clamor came to rest in silence once again, "but no argument that you could make would change my mind. I can't allow for my men and women to take the front lines while I sit here and deliver orders. That said, Vanessa, you'll be my proxy. Administer orders and deploy soldiers as you deem necessary."

"This is insane," Dre grumbled. "No Director since the foundation of the Yaiba Insurrection has taken to the battlefield themselves. You are to be protected."

"How did our protection work out for Emiko?" Nobody spoke a reply. Nobody dared to. More than two months after her passing and the mere mention of her name was still painful for the whole faction. "Emiko was the type of Director better suited for straight politics and survival tactics. While we were in survival mode, that was fine, but we're at war now."

"John—" Dre started, but John lifted his hand.

"My responsibility is to not only lead the Yaiba during this time, but to lead it to victory. Being that I'm one of the strongest fighters we've ever produced, I don't think it's unreasonable for me to lead from the front lines," he explained. "Now if you'll excuse me, I have a mission of my own to attend to."

****

December 15th, 2084, 9:19 a.m.,

Cal breathed out calmly as he felt the chill of winter against his skin. His eyes were closed. He wasn't sure how it would feel to test out his "new equipment" yet, since the only thing he'd looked at for the last two weeks was the wall of his home and Dr. Dominguez. It felt good for him to be outside again, Reikiken in hand, outfitted in full Hanzo Gear. Slowly he opened his eyes.

He stood just at the foot of the Roan Mountain, though a little ways off from the main road that ran to Johnson City. It wouldn't do well for the rest of the Insurrection to know about his little invention before it was time. The sun shined brightly through the branches of the trees. Cal focused more on what he saw from his now mechanical left-eye.

"All images clear," he muttered. "Yessir!" He could barely contain his excitement, and at his own exclamation he did his best to gather himself. "Play it cool, man. Play it cool. Lemme see some thermal vision," he told himself, and the Kiringan instantly shifted visual input modes. "Nice, nice," Cal said to himself as the birds in the sky, soldiers on their transports, and even the engines of those vehicles all lit up orange in his field of vision. "Scope mode," he thought aloud, and the visibility returned to normal. "Two miles," he inquired, not really sure if it would work. The camera within the eye zoomed in and focused on a distant mark that he had Dr. Dominguez set up a few days ago. It turned out to be a wooden post with a note on it that said, "Don't hurt yourself, kid." He laughed, and gave the order for another two miles. There was no mark this time. This time, Cal just wanted to see what was in the distance. Deer grazed, a couple of rabbits scampered through the brush, and a bear roamed towards a greater distance than he desired to test at the moment. "Beautiful," Cal cooed, then commanded the Kiringan again, "Return to local mode." The camera zoomed out, and Cal couldn't have been happier with the experiment. Distance and visibility tests were successful. Now he just needed to test its combat applications. If that went well, he'd approach the Director with it.

The witty engineer rubbed his hands together smugly as a generous smile washed over his face. If Cal was honest, he half expected the Kiringan to explode in the socket. He was glad it didn't. He was so pleased with his new invention, in fact, that he decided to toy with what features he could on his way back to the compound.

"Thermal vision," he said as he turned back to the path up to the compound entrance. He flashed a smile as he caught the heat sigs of his comrades on the main road. Then he noticed something strange. A woman in full Hanzo Gear ran—on foot—up the side of the road, but when Cal focused in with his natural eye, nothing was there. "Huh. That's interesting."

Chapter Twenty-Five

December 15th, 2084, 9:45 a.m.,

Despite her initial reservation, Aria Black eventually came to embrace her orders to infiltrate the mountain base of her old comrades. None of them would be too happy to see her, and she knew that if she showed her face she'd be killed on sight. That was the penalty for a betrayal as deep as hers had been. Even so, she longed to see what it was like now, how the Insurrection had moved forward without her. How John had moved forward without her.

She remembered a time where he loved her dearly. She'd never felt anything quite like it since, and a part of her needed to know if he still felt what it was to need her. She never really saw much of a future with him, she had to admit, but even the ghost of passions once shared between them would give warmth to her body so often left in the cold of the Scarlet Kingdom. Then she mocked herself for such a pathetic whim. She lived in the lap of luxury in the capitol, not in some remodeled cave like some kind of sophisticated bat. Aria told herself that she didn't need a kind of love that took her back instead of drove her forward.

In any case, she thought him to be a liar. Not really, of course. But when she'd traded him in on a whim, he had the nerve to tell others about it. He said she'd lied, led him on and cheated, then flaunted her new beau when John would no longer willingly obey her. All of that was true; she had always done what she could to control him and punish him in great or small ways whenever he stepped out of line. She couldn't be mad at the truth. She could, however, be mad at the fact that it ruined her reputation within the organization.

Not that that mattered. Aria was always determined to leave at her earliest convenience, and when her friends turned against her for something that was simply her nature, she decided that there was no finer time to get out of dodge than that. At first, Aria sought to salvage her reputation through vehement denial of everything she'd put John through, but it never worked. That was the problem with intimate communities, the truth is seen a lot clearer than any lie. When that didn't work, she waited for a mission, ironically one with her new boyfriend, Tom, positioned right at her side to make her move. Right in the face of the Scarlet Troopers they were intended to fight, she slaughtered them all without remorse and started with the very man she thought she traded up to.

She skulked through the shadows of the tunnels burrowed into the Roan Mountain, surprised by everything from the power-lifts to the sheer organizational integrity of the Insurrection itself. Emiko Ishikawa had done a lot for the group. It hurt Aria to know that she was gone, even if they were at odds for the last decade and some change. But she put that out of her mind for now as she toyed with the controls of the lift. She needed to get to the Conference Level, which intel from the raid told her was on Level D. After a moment of button-mashing and strange noises, the power-lift began its descent into the bowels of enemy territory.

Her heart beat wildly as the machine slowly ticked down. Her mission was to secure an audience between the Director and the Prince, but Aria had no idea who the new Director was. It was enough to put a serious wrench in things. Usually she would rely on her wits and manipulative ability to accomplish any assignment. It was her unique ways of getting people to talk that warranted her place on the Scarlet Scourge in the first place. But how does one prepare for an enemy they know nothing about?

The power-lift halted abruptly enough to make Aria's blood pump with greater ferocity than before. She peered at a nearby sign that marked the name of the level. Training Level C. Aria swallowed hard. This was the origin point for every wretched warrior that filled the ranks of the Violet Shadows. She knew that her mission was one of stealth and diplomacy, but a sudden desire to bomb the place overtook her.

"Alright," came a voice so sickeningly sweet to her ears that it stopped her in her tracks. "Time to go visit John." Aria's eyebrow lifted, and she couldn't help but smile a dangerous smile. The woman emerged from the control panel off to the side and took her place on the platform. She was slightly taller than Aria, and boasted a soothing latte-shaded complexion perfectly accented by her dark hair and milk-chocolate eyes. Her body looked dainty, but the fact that she so casually tucked a Reikiken into a holster at her side proved that she was much stronger than she let on. Suddenly it clicked. Aria recognized her now, the girl that was a year behind them in training. What was her name? Alyssa? No, that wasn't right. Aaliyah; that was it. She always did have a crush on John, even when Aria counted herself among their number.

It was funny how things never seemed to change. Still, if it got her anywhere near John, she would take it. She might not be able to work the new Director, but playing with John's emotions was always something of a pastime for her. She watched Aaliyah closely as she evened out her breath. She couldn't reveal even the slightest hint of her presence yet, especially if her enemy was outfitted in Hanzo Gear. Any kind of conflict before the proper time would only ruin her chances of mission success. Aria looked down at her own aura sword and repulsor boots. They were all she retained from her Hanzo Gear, and for all that she found good and decent she hoped that she wouldn't have to use them.

****

December 15th, 2084, 9:50 a.m.,

"They a little too smart," Cal muttered out of frustration. Not only was there some rogue agent inside the compound, but the comms were jammed. Something was about to happen, but it was beyond his ability to report on now.

“I was wondering how long it’d take you to realize that your comms weren’t coming back online,” came an overly assertive yet strikingly familiar female voice from the trees behind him. He turned around and saw her, that brutish woman that sacrificed a comrade the last time they fought. The voluptuous blonde from the Scarlet Scourge. “You look a little sad. Do you need some help, little boy?”

“Hey, man,” Cal started in a warning tone. “I don’t think you’re supposed to be here.”

“And what if I’m not,” Cecelia challenged, arms spread and ready for conflict as she stalked forward like a mad lioness. The look in her eye was somehow even more deranged than the last time they’d clashed. So the rumors were true. The Scourge’s roster was short another name. “You gonna make me leave?” The tone was provocative, delighted at the possibility of combat and wishful that he was as well.

“I mean…” Cal shrugged, and his new eye came alive at the center with a mysterious green light. “If you want the smoke…” He couldn’t even pretend to be disappointed. The only thing he hadn’t been able to test was the battle compatibility of his Kiringan, and without a way to reach the rest of the Insurrection, he’d probably never get another chance like this. Cecelia reached into the cargo pockets on her scarlet pants and pulled out a pair of gloves. Cal flashed a puzzled but cautious look. He’d expected a rifle, but apparently she intended to settle this with her fists alone.

“Gimme your best shot, then,” she goaded, “little boy.” Cal’s eyebrows raised as his usually sunny disposition descended into something much darker.

“What,” he uttered in a manner that was still borderline comical, but something about him changed. He walked up to meet her, his Reikiken still sheathed at his side and his kyoketsu-shoge still wound tightly in the gauntlets on his wrists. He reasoned that if she was determined to fight hand to hand, he would meet her challenge.

****

December 15th, 2084, 10:00 a.m.,

Aaliyah arrived on Conference Level D, and as she exited the platform of the power-lift, she all but skipped down the corridor to her husband's office. She was overjoyed that he'd allowed her to complete her training with the Hanzo Gear, and while she knew it was because he didn't want anything to happen to her in the event of another attack, she chose not to focus on that. She only ever wanted to give John the same amount of support that he gave her. That he gave all of them, if she was honest with herself.

She was more than a little aware that her husband had given his all to support their way of life and ensure their safety long before he was ever the Director. At least by joining the ranks of the Shadows she could ease his load just a little bit. She recognized him as a gift from God, just the kind of curse-breaker that she needed to help her live in such a harsh, cruel world. There's no way she would let him carry everything on his own.

Aaliyah turned the corner toward his office, and instantly felt that something was off. She turned her head to check the hall behind her, but there was nobody there. Or at least, nobody that she could see. She'd heard about the cloaking tech that the Kabuto worked with. She knew that John trusted them, and so far the Helmets haven't given any indication that they might betray the Insurrection, but that didn't mean that their technology was exclusively theirs. The last few decades demonstrated that the Reds weren't above stealing an idea if not the technology itself. She paused for a moment to survey her surroundings, but when nothing struck her as out of the ordinary, she cautiously continued to see her husband.

She paused before she entered the office and recouped her angelic smile, and instantly her heart came alive with the desire to be near him. She walked in, no hesitation, and did what she could to put her unease out of her mind.

"Well, well," she started as the smile on her face became more genuine, "what do we have here?" John looked up from the papers on his desk and smiled back. He was genuinely glad to see her.

"A very tired Director," he admitted, but stood up as she approached his desk and pulled her into a tight hug.

"I think I can help with that," Aaliyah tempted in her soft, sultry voice as she stared lovingly into his eyes. She tilted her head up and met his lips with hers. She was an angel to him, and every reinforcement of that kiss was a bridge built between heaven and earth. She pulled away slightly, so that his forehead came to rest on her own.

"Look at that," he said just as lowly as she had spoken a moment ago, "I'm just filled with energy." She rubbed his arms, strong from training and battle. They'd always made her feel so safe.

"Did you get a look at Cal's new eye," she couldn't help but ask. It was a random thought, but the image of the Kiringan was so jarring to her that she had to call attention to it, even in passing. Mostly, though, it was her way of not talking about Darius.

"I think it looks cool," John told her with a wry smile. He was seriously impressed with the way that kid's brain worked. "I wonder what kinds of toys he's got built into that thing. I don't know if I'm more excited to see that, or see Darius' reaction to it." He realized immediately that he'd stuck his foot in his mouth. His wife adopted that pained expression that he couldn't bear to see, and he immediately moved to set things right. "He'll be fine, love.

Callan's team is working on infiltrating the Yoroi compound as we speak. They'll get to him, and ensure he's safe."

"I hope you're right," Aaliyah replied, her voice stern. "I know I sympathized for Bryan when he lost his son, but that doesn't mean I want to lose ours."

"If that's the case," came the condescending timbre of Aria Black as her cloaking device deactivated, "then why don't we all just have a little chat?"

****

December 15th, 2084, 10:00 a.m.,

Cecelia Kant moved like a rabid beast, hard and fast, but Cal was always a step ahead of her. She punched at his face, but he ducked. She tried to knee him in his face, but he blocked. She tried to bring her elbow down on the back of his head, but he rolled off to the side and took a crouched position. The young Shadow was happy that he'd installed the predictive combat view. It calculated the moves his enemy made based on what moves had already been displayed, and from there it was just a matter of what Cal could do to respond.

Before he had time to jump back at her in his typically high-octane Kiryu style, Cecelia had already taken flight towards him, her fist poised high in the air for an undoubtedly debilitating blow. Cal narrowly dodged backward just in time enough to see the ground give under the weight of her fist. Dust blanketed the battlefield. Cal closed his natural eye, but the Kiringan remained sharp as ever.

"Thermal vision," he muttered, then watched as the deadly Scourge brawler ran circles through the dust cloud. Once behind him, Cecelia tossed a hand grenade at the boy, but was astonished when he turned to face her and pushed the kyoketsu-shoge blade on the back of his wrist in an upward motion. The grenade was launched into the air, and the shockwave from the explosion took them both to the ground. *Since when can she do that,* he wondered as his mind finally processed how she'd broken the frigging *earth.* It didn't matter. He had to admit that she was good, but he wasn't impressed.

He pushed back to his feet, despite the fact that his ears still rang from the detonation, and found that his adversary already regained her legs. She had a half-cocked smile, as though she really enjoyed a challenge totally unexpected. She said something, but Cal couldn't hear it over the ringing.

"What?" he shouted it, and to his humor so did Cecelia. "I can't hear you! There's—no, my ears are ringing!" Kant rolled her eyes and sprinted for him again, that deranged smile still on her face. She faked him out with a swift jab and got him in the side with a solid kick that sent Cal straight across the battlefield. As soon as he hit the ground, she was on top of him again, fist raised and ready to collide with his flesh.

Cal kipped up to his feet to dodge, but the shockwave of her fist against the ground made him wobble. She punched at him again as he pushed off a nearby tree and rolled along the ground beside her. He sprang back to his feet, and to his relief the ring in his ears quieted down so that he could at last make out the sounds around him. He watched her fist burst through the side of the tree, and the sudden lack of a stable trunk brought it down in an inelegant bow.

****

December 15th, 2084, 10:05 a.m.,

John was frozen in place, petrified by the feelings of rage that mingled with the ghost of the trauma that woman caused him. He cursed himself under his breath. He thought he was over this, but the sensation he felt in that moment was akin to what a child might feel if the monster they dreamed of suddenly appeared over them in their bed. The Scourge member smiled cheerfully, as if all of what had happened between them was naught more than a figment of John's imagination. It had already begun. John dropped to his chair, hardly able to come to a rational response to her appearance, while Aaliyah stepped around to the front of the desk.

"It's been a long time, John," Aria spoke in a wistful, almost sultry tone. She stared dead at Aaliyah with no expression, as if John's wife weren't even there. "You look good." John didn't answer. He narrowed his eyes and carefully considered how best to go about this.

"What are you here for, Black," Aaliyah snarled. Clearly Aria's audacity was felt throughout the room. Finally she focused on the woman who, in Aria's mind, occupied a space that once could have been hers.

"I'm here to take your husband from you," Aria responded in a carefree tone that prompted Aaliyah to take up and ignite her Reikiken.

"You might wanna explain what you mean by that," suggested the wife, who bared her fangs as would befit a Dragoness.

"Ooh, feisty," Aria cooed, and reached for her own firesword. She tucked one hand behind her back and angled the tip of its blade at Aaliyah's head as it donned a bright orange hue. Aaliyah extended her free hand as she swung her own weapon into a fixed position over her head, blade firmly angled down at her enemy's eyes. "Since you've got so much energy, why don't you try and make me talk?"

John still sat with his hands on his lap and his eyes on the desk. This was too much for him, and while he wanted deeply to dissuade his wife from fighting in his office, he couldn't muster the courage to even speak. It didn't seem all that long ago that they were trainees, stuck in sparring matches on the floor of Level C. He knew what this moment meant for Aaliyah, but he also knew that back then, she couldn't even touch Aria without permission.

"Huh. I guess you find it tough to talk to someone without a penis, don't you?" Aaliyah's remark left Aria stunned, jaw agape and eyebrows lifted from a mix of shock and disgust. "Makes sense, since you were always so busy eyeballing the guys during their sparring matches." She flashed a devilish grin as Aria lunged forward, but with expert skill and timing, Aaliyah brushed the thrust off to the side. Aria simply used the parry as fuel for a shoulder strike, but Aaliyah blocked it effortlessly with a flick of the wrist and a step towards the traitor.

Aria jumped away with an attempted blow to Aaliyah's head, but in a motion as mundane as a taken breath, the Dragoness deflected the shot to the side. Aria couldn't believe what she'd seen. The last time they squared off, the thrust alone was enough to breach Aaliyah's defenses and put her on her back but now she was… Aria adopted an unexpected grin.

"Looks like someone's been practicing," she taunted. "But do you really think it'll be enough?"

"Judging by the way you just ran from me, I won't even get the chance to show you just how outclassed you are," Aaliyah shot back. Aria dove in again, her swings light and fast, all with the intent of pushing the Director's wife back, yet all deflected with grace and fluidity. Aria's face couldn't contain the astonishment, while her adversary boasted no such emotion.

Aaliyah pulled her head back as her blade guided Aria's along its path and avoided decapitation in the process. The sideways swing that the Scourge member failed to connect with swiftly gave way to a downward attack at Aaliyah's knees. The Dragoness lifted her leg as she pushed the enemy blade through again, and when she once again planted her foot, she swung her aura sword down on Aria's head. The unwelcome intruder parried the strike and disconnected from her foe, again deeply confused by what she witnessed.

"Your moves aren't as sharp as they used to be," Aaliyah taunted, though it wasn't untrue. "Apparently spending all those years being pampered by the Reds has made you soft." Aria seethed with anger, more at the idea that she'd been pampered than she was at Aaliyah assessing her combat savvy. "Now what were you saying about coming to take my husband?"

"I'm sorry, did I miss the part where you beat me or…?" Aria always became sarcastic when her weaknesses were prodded. She knew she was out of practice, but she hadn't accounted for Aaliyah to come this far along. Last she'd heard, her opponent had traded in the warrior's path for that of the educator. Thinking about it made Aria's skin crawl. "How the hell did someone as lowly as you manage to even withstand my first stab?"

"You're still just as self-important and condescending as ever," Aaliyah sighed with an air of humor. "You'd think you'd have gotten over yourself by now. I mean, you traded the idea of freedom just to be the King's lapdog. You probably can't get a man because in the Kingdom they don't view melanin as a symbol of beauty. That, and all you ever seem to do is try to control everyone else." Aria was offended that this little girl who couldn't even hold her sword right in training would even think to say something like that…or that she would be 100% accurate.

"How dare you talk to me like that," Aria yelled, and a flood of horrible memories swam to the surface of John's mind.

"Easy," Aaliyah replied, "you're a loser. It's all you've ever been. You're always trying to get people to believe that you're amazing and, for a time I guess you were, but deep down you know how pathetic you really are. You run away from commitment because you're afraid to show other people how weak and spineless you really are, but little did you know, we all see it. Huh. That must be why you're here to try and take my man, right?

You were hoping to rekindle some kind of spark from your abusive relationship with my husband?" Aria had heard enough. She swung her Reikiken wildly at Aaliyah's shoulder, then the leg when the first move was blocked. The second move was parried through, so with a minimal twirl of her wrist and a lot more wind-up, Aria brought the sword down as if to cleave through Aaliyah's head.

"You don't know what you're talking about," she snarled, now hunched over Aaliyah, who leaned with one hand firmly on John's desk. She could tell that her enemy pushed against her with all her strength, but it was still futile. Aaliyah locked eyes with Aria, then with a taunting smirk, turned her head away.

"Hey, John," she whispered, even as the sparks from the two fireswords cracked about the floor. He looked up to see his beautiful wife, who exerted no effort in what seemed to be a very real battle. She smiled at him, and with the understanding that she simply could, she kissed him as passionately as she would've had they been alone. The room boiled along with Aria's blood. John was awake now, and unaffected by his former interest's presence. He smiled at his beloved wife, then laughed to himself as she kicked her attacker away. All it took was Aaliyah to make him whole again, something he was loath to allow himself to forget.

By the time his eyes refocused on the battle in his office, Aria had burn marks on both her arms, her legs, and her abdomen. Aaliyah stood over her, Reikiken pointed at her enemy's face, and smiled with the deepest satisfaction.

"So let's try this again," she cooed, and watched with joy as Aria's eyes burned with hatred and spite.

****

December 15th, 2084, 10:05 a.m.,

"Who designed those things," Cal said as he dodged another crater-making punch. It was clear that there was nothing ordinary about his opponent, and when paired with those gloves, gloves that the Kiringan had assessed for a strange energy signature, it was as bad as it could've gotten…under normal circumstances, at least.

"Some of the best engineers on our side," Cecelia volunteered, happy to oblige since this whole ordeal had turned into a lot of fun. She knew it was just an escape, that she was running from facing…*that*, but she didn't care. Battle eased her mind, until it suddenly didn't. "I—I had them made as a gift…" her voice trailed off as her expression went dark, and her movements became more erratic and dangerous.

"Oh nah," Cal whispered under his breath as he narrowly dodged and jumped to the branch of a nearby tree. He turned his attention to her and spoke openly. "You know I'd love to get the design specs for those gauntlets—"

"Not a chance!" Cecelia snapped, and punched the middle out of the tree to bring Cal back to earth. The combat engineer took to the air instead, and brought his Reikiken down for a Falling Leaf. To his surprise, however, the force of his firesword was met with the overwhelming power of the Scourge member's blast gauntlets. The shockwave from the impact was enough to send Cal across the broken ground and shatter his aura sword like glass. Cecelia, calmer now, more methodical than Cal would've thought her capable, stood there for a moment. Her eyes seemed glassed over now, hazy with whatever thoughts blinded her to the present. "What will you do now," she asked, though she'd already assumed his despair. Then, at the moment that she expected him to break down in tears, Cal brandished a cheerful smile instead.

"I thought you'd never ask," he cooed, to no response from his brutish opponent.

****

December 15th, 2084, 10:13 a.m.,

Sora Kaneuji was in the middle of his morning tea when the alarm in the lab went off, and when the sound reached his ears, he spilled the cup in his excitement. He sprinted from his office and looked out over the workshop, first at the gaggle of engineers that exchanged confused glances, then at the eight pods that lined the western wall. One by one they emitted a loud burst, and Sora raced down the stairs to the ground floor to watch up close. He placed his hand on the final pod just as its contents were launched from the mountain and into the air.

"Oh, good God," Kaneuji squealed with delight as the last few vibrations from the pod pulsed through his hand. "He actually used them!"

"Used what," asked one of his subordinate engineers. Kaneuji spun rapidly and happily sped towards the young man.

"We call them the Lightbeams," the head engineer informed him as he took his hands in his own, a gesture that the young scientist found a little more than uncomfortable. "Apparently our young Cal has gotten quite serious."

****

December 15th, 2084, 10:16 a.m.,

Cecelia burst through a boulder, this time only a second away from Cal's face as he barely got out of dodge. As her body turned from the powerful punch, she lifted her leg and used the force her torso generated to kick at Cal's chest. It was all he could do to block with the blade of his kyoketsu-shoge, but his hand behind it stung. She punched again, this time at his sternum, but he ducked the enemy soldier's attack and crouched at her feet. By the time she noticed and lifted her arm for another attempted assault,

Cal threw his upper body backwards just as he kicked up from the ground. His feet brushed her chin, and as he landed he was proud of himself.

"Yessir," he said, elated that that trick actually worked. "Your boy got the hands!" Cecelia stumbled backwards, but it didn't take her long to plant herself firmly. She wiped her mouth and noted a fresh scarlet liquid on the back of her hand. She looked up at Cal, pure animosity in her gaze.

"You made me bleed my own blood," she screamed, and just as she ran at him again, she was taken off her feet by a golden flash. Her body skidded along the ground and then rolled to a stop, and though her uniform now boasted a deeper shade of red in a couple of spots, she got back up as if it was just a love tap. "You're gonna pay for that," she told him. She took off towards him again, this time more prepared than the last time. The golden flash reemerged in her periphery, but as it came she planted her weight and punched, hard, with her blast gauntlets. Its body, a bright white with luminous golden accents, burst apart and fell to the ground. Cal's jaw dropped. He remembered the process of building that android, and worse, the trouble of syncing it with the Kiringan's frequency so he could control it wirelessly. His brow furrowed as he looked back at the machine, then at the enemy, then at the machine again, and back.

"Whoa, whoa, whoa, whoa, whoa, whoa there partner," he said as he waved his hands. Cecelia just stared at him, that same unconcerned stare that she'd adopted since she remembered why she had those gloves. "Can't just go around breaking people's stuff. You have any idea how hard it was to build that guy?"

"Who cares," Cecelia uttered as she stretched her blast gauntlet-clad hand forward. "You're about to be next." There was a bright flash as soon as the words left her lips, followed by a *swish* and a feminine scream that she'd recognized to be her own. Her hand was gone, and with a loud crash that rippled through the forest and mountain base deeper than the blast gauntlets could ever, she saw seven more of those metallic humanoid creations in a triangular formation around her opponent.

"Kant," shouted another's voice, one Cal hadn't heard since that scavenging mission. "The message has been delivered. It's time for us to go." The other woman, who Cal couldn't see through the Lightbeam formation, took to the woods and initiated cloaking tech as she did so. Cecelia glowered at Cal and his mechanical troops and growled with the frustrating knowledge that this would be the second time he'd survive a brush with the Scourge.

"This isn't over," Cecelia snarled as Cal stepped out from the formation. He was so smug, so nonchalant, and shrugged in a manner that conveyed both.

"I mean, I got the fire if you want the smoke," he told her with a certainty that mocked everything she stood for. She grumbled profanities as she activated her own cloaking and disappeared into the shadows of the trees.

****

December 15th, 2084, 11:00 a.m.,

Things had died down in the compound once Aria was gone, and John had gone with Aaliyah to their home. She was less than thrilled.

"I can't believe you're going," Aaliyah griped with her arms crossed as John gathered his mission equipment. He couldn't help but be excited about it. He'd thought that his days of mission execution were behind him now that he was the Director, but it was a stroke of genius to make Vanessa and his father Dre the acting interim Directors so that his movements could be a little closer to what they were as the Rairyu. Still, he needed to help his wife understand.

"Callan and his group are already in the area, and the comms channels are open. If I need any help I can signal for the others to come and give it," he told her in his most reassuring of tones. She didn't buy it, so he opted to sweeten the deal. "Besides, while I'm out that way, I can check on Darius. Maybe even bring him home if he needs it." Aaliyah couldn't believe him, though her ears did perk up at that last remark.

"As sweet as that sounds," she told him evenly, "your evil ex-girlfriend just broke into our home to tell you that the Prince of the Scarlet Kingdom wants an audience with you. This just doesn't feel right to me." Her flesh began to crawl and she shivered from the displeasure. "All I'm saying is, what if this is a trap? You and I both know that Aria loves to mess with people's minds, and she's been at odds with the Insurrection for years just because you wouldn't put up with her bull—"

"I hear you, angel," John assured her. He walked up to her, put his pack at her feet and scooped her into his arms. "She's a trash human being. That point has been well-established, but so has the one that says I can handle whatever *any* of the factions throw at me." He kissed her cheek, and she smiled against her will. "Fighting aside, this might be a chance for us to talk things out peacefully. If nothing else, we could get the Prince to pull his forces away from the Yoroi territory."

"You really think they'd go for cordial negotiations," Aaliyah asked, one eyebrow raised.

"Oh, not at all. I'm a black man, after all. Worse, I'm the black man that they know killed almost three hundred of their soldiers. But I don't know," he thought for a moment as he looked down at her beautiful black hair and stroked her soft, smooth skin. "I get the feeling that Prince James is a little different from his father and brother." He gave her another kiss, this time on the lips, and picked up his pack. "I won't be gone long. I promise." Without waiting for a reply, he was off.

Chapter Twenty-Six

December 17th, 2084, 2:15 p.m.,

Dark smoke filled the air around the Clusters. The once polished buildings and bright lights had become covered in explosive residue if they weren't chipped or shattered, and the once lively hubs of daily life had been emptied for weeks now.

Another explosion in the distance rattled the rocky foundations, and more smoke contributed to the darkness of the former haven within the canyon. Bobbi bit her lower lip anxiously and angrily. The Anti-Rebels had escalated the conflict to a miniature civil war within the Yoroi Alliance, and the civilians that once occupied the bulk of the Clusters were forced deeper underground. A bottle whizzed past her head and collided with the broken wall near her. She looked back down the path from which the object came and saw a little boy, his face covered with soot and his eyes filled with tears. Bobbi wondered who this conflict had torn from him. A father? His mother? A sibling perhaps? Or perhaps he was simply disgusted with the Pro-Rebellion just like the rest of the Yoroi had become.

She heard rummaging in the surrounding debris, so she flexed at the kid to scare him back into hiding. She hated that she had to, but Bobbi knew that it was either that or let him find out the truth about his so-called Anti-Rebel Protectors. The opposition, clad in the same charcoal color as the covert security force, emerged with weapons in hand. They shot at her, but Bobbi had long since abandoned her clumsiness and learned to trust her training. She pushed up with the repulsor boots, her cloak wrapped around her like a shroud of shadows, and plunged her kyoketsu-shoge into the ground near her attackers. She grappled to what remained of a nearby rooftop, then fell upon the four hostiles with her Reikiken hot. They fell one after another, and before the last of their bodies could hit the ground Bobbi had taken to the rooftops again. She looked out over the broken buildings and piles of rubble that now characterized Cluster B. She was disgusted. *How long is this gonna last*, she demanded of herself, and sprinted off to regroup with her allies.

"Just a few more left," came Lex's slightly exasperated voice over the comms. "This Cluster's almost ours for the taking."

"Great," Leroy responded. "Then we can all go home."

"Not yet," Tony reminded them all. "We have to disarm the rest of the traps in the area and salvage as much food as we can." Shouts and gunfire could be heard over the comms. Apparently Tony had encountered another group of Anti-Rebels. Bobbi stopped at the edge of the rooftop, a massive screen cracked at the bottom corner in her face. She clenched her fist, and as another group of enemies ran beneath her, she dropped from the rooftop and slashed them all ferociously with her Reikiken. When she'd first selected the Hiryu style of combat, she wasn't sure it was the right move. It was brutal and fast, wide-swinging and ferocious. The more she saw of war and the atrocities committed therein, the less she questioned that decision. If anything, it gave her a means of venting her anger the way she needed to, and she graciously thanked her enemies for giving her a chance at restored tranquility. They probably didn't see it that way, but what did that matter?

"My area's clear," Bobbi told them. "Guess I'll start disarming the traps so we can get out of here faster."

"You're a saint," Leroy told her in a breath of relief. "Try not to take too long." Bobbi snorted.

"*You* try not to take too long gathering up the food." A flash of light came from the eastern quadrant of the Cluster, followed by a shrill scream through the comms. "By the looks of it you're pretty behind already."

"I am not," Leroy protested, and something about his tone struck Bobbi as boyish. "None of that was even on my end."

"Well it wasn't on mine," Tony verified.

"Mine either," Lex added slyly.

"Okay fine, it was on mine, but that doesn't mean I'm falling behind. I'm just…" Leroy trailed off. It was difficult for him to explain what he felt. Friends that he'd known since he was a kid and family members that he used to respect more than anything in the world had joined the opposition in just the month since Ina…He was shaken, and every time he had to cut one of those Anti-Rebels down he wondered who they were. He couldn't figure out how to say that to his comrades, and didn't want to run the risk of being ridiculed because of his conscience.

"We're all thrown by this," Bobbi reassured him. "People I never thought capable of violence pointed guns at me and tried to kill me. They bought into the lie and they're not going to be convinced of the truth so easily." Bobbi carefully used the visor in her hooded cloak to scan for anomalies in Cluster B's foundation. A poorly constructed wire-trap lay just before her. She whipped her kyoketsu-shoge through the air and severed the bond that held the trap dormant, and watched as an array of kitchen knives rocketed into a distant wall.

"I don't understand why Teach still wants to lay low," Leroy all but whined. Bobbi couldn't blame him. Just a few hours before the mission began, she'd let herself cry in a corner, out of sight of everyone else. "If he just showed up then—"

"It's not that simple," Tony interrupted. They'd thought about it more than the rest of their team. "There's too much going on in the Alliance right now. The whole faction is on the verge of collapse. If he were to come out into the open right now, it wouldn't make the splash that we'd need to turn things in our favor." Bobbi nodded in agreement, though her teammates couldn't see it.

“It’s more than that,” Lex added. “We still don’t know where they’re keeping Johannes. If we play our trump card now, the Anti-Rebels might panic and they might kill him.”

“No doubt they’d put some kind of dramatic flair on it,” Bobbi grumbled into the comms. “Make it a public execution like in the Rise of the Reds.” It was when she rolled her eyes that she caught sight of something strange just a few feet away. It was…cloth? Not exactly a rag, but something stripped from a formal garment seemed caught on the broken post of a damaged kiosk. It was brightly colored, not quite as bold as something that Vargas might wear, but still something worthy of an emissary…

“I mean, it makes sense,” Leroy said, which snapped Bobbi from her fixation and prompted her to snatch the cloth. It was hard for Leroy to accept the rationale but there was no other choice. If anything, it did make him more motivated. “Let’s find him as quickly as we can, then.”

****

December 17th, 2084, 3:08 p.m.,

Johannes trembled as he carried the tray into the spacious seating area. The usual gray hue of the room was somehow darkened in the dim light. He set the tray down, and with a smile the lovely Scarlet soldier—Serafina was her name—took the cup before her. The Scarlet visitors had requested tea, and Johannes was more than happy to oblige if it meant that he could get away from the oppressive nature of Katarina Estevez. Since the death of Christophe Francis, the Anti-Rebels had been run by his second-in-command, Katarina. She was nowhere near as merciful or patient as her predecessor. The very week the old man died, Katarina published the footage taken from his encounter with Johannes and Tony, carefully edited to only show what happened after he entered the room.

Francis was a beloved member of the Council, so his death at Tony's hands was more than enough to take the passing tension between the Pro- and Anti-Rebels down the path of violence. Not that that would've taken much in the first place. No, the real reason Estevez released the video was to turn the public against her opposition, to paint this conflict as a longstanding machination of the Pro-Rebellion, and to ensure that her Red masters would be appeased.

Katarina smiled at Serafina, as if she looked upon a long-lost sister, and then took a cup of warm tea from the tray herself. Kerri Waldheim, the stoic brunette with twin pistols at her hip, offered little more than a twitch of the corner of her mouth as she took her cup and strode to the window. The horizon was all smoke and fire, but the closer they got to the Anti-Rebel base, the cleaner things appeared.

"That will be all, Mr. Thornhill," Estevez spoke sweetly, but commanded nonetheless. Johannes left the room and returned to the kitchen to make himself look busy, but listened to the conversation. "How do you like it?"

"Mm, the flavor of this tea is remarkable," Serafina iterated with an air of surprise. "I didn't think that barbarians could produce anything this exquisite." The newest Scourge member watched the new loyalist leader closely, but marveled at the total lack of expression on her face. Katarina was, no doubt, deeply offended by Serafina's remark, but refused to show it. This was her opportunity to restore the peace of the Yoroi Alliance and seize power in the process.

"I think you'll find that there are many things in the Yoroi Alliance that would please you, Lady Leyva." Katarina noted the pleasure Serafina derived from her noble address.

"And what of this little spat between your people," Serafina questioned in such a way that chilled the room. Katarina resisted the urge to swallow. "Surely you don't intend to let things devolve any further."

"Certainly not," Katarina spoke evenly, her eyes steeled as much as they could be. Johannes, from around the corner, knew that she was just as uncertain as anyone else. "The more the Pro-Rebels fight, the more they strike fear in the hearts of the commonfolk. We're in control of the narrative, and that only gets clearer when you look at the footage we have on hand." Katarina snapped, and a holoprojector built into the roof replayed the conversation between Tony and Francis. Serafina's eyes went wide with delight.

"And how did you manage to come by this," the ambitious Scourge member inquired. Katarina relaxed a little, though not visibly, and gently tucked her dark brown hair behind her ear.

"We set a trap," was all she said, which prompted Serafina to raise an eyebrow. "As you can see, it was a successful one."

"I wonder about that," Lady Leyva mused, and just like that, all the fear and anxiety that Katarina had thought laid to rest had resurrected in an instant.

"I'm afraid I don't understand what you mean—"

"She means," Kerri finally spoke with a tinge of irritation and eyes still fixed on the Cluster beyond the window, "'have you bothered to pay any attention to how the battles are going?'"

"Undoubtedly in our favor, Lady Waldheim," Estevez replied incredulously. "Our guerilla tactics are as effective as ever, and the traps we've strewn around the Clusters—"

"Are only so useful against an enemy that understands your tactics in explicit detail," Serafina cut her off. "Correct me if I'm wrong, but how many of those traps have misfired since your little conflict broke out?"

"Almost half, but these things happen." Katarina's anxiety escalated, and a bead of sweat formed on her brow.

"But for the Yoroi? For a faction that has boasted nigh impregnable defenses for the last 64 years? I find that hard to believe. Come to think of it," Serafina's tone became colder, more political and unnerving all at once, "wasn't the Yaiba Insurrection supposed to send a shipment of Hanzo Gear to the Yoroi?" Katarina detested this. What was supposed to be her moment to curry favor had backfired and transformed into an interrogation. She could feel control of the situation ebb away from her with every second she sat there. Johannes, in the kitchen, enjoyed it.

"Along with a teacher, yes," Estevez remarked with an air of irritation that fed Serafina's pleasure. "But as you heard in the recording, we eliminated the Insurrection's representative. Without him the opposition poses no threat—"

"Then I assume you also eliminated their access to Hanzo Gear. You did have the foresight to do at least that much, didn't you, Ms. Estevez?" The Lady Leyva's tone was as condescending as a noble's ought to be, and when Katarina declined to comment, Serafina knew that this was hopeless. "So to summarize, you've neglected to detect the Kabuto agents at work in your territory, underestimated your greatest threat, and you've failed to restrict their access to the only weapon outside of the Scarlet Kingdom that can make things exceedingly difficult for you."

"Your incompetence is astounding," Kerri said, her gaze still fixed on the smoky distance.

"Unfortunately, I have to agree," Serafina sighed as she set her cup down on the tray and stood from her seat. "I suppose we'll take our leave, then."

"You'll hear back from us later," Kerri added in an icy tone. "Provided we get orders to help you fix your mistakes." And with nothing left to be said, the Scourge emissaries left.

Katarina exhaled a breath of relief and nearly collapsed. Her body shook involuntarily, and as the moments passed, she became more and more irritated with her failure to impress. Johannes reemerged from the kitchen to take the tray, and on sight he was met with a kick to the groin and a teapot over his head. He started to fade, and the last sound he heard was the aggravated scream of his mistress.

****

December 17th, 2084, 4:40 p.m.,

Bill was, for the first time since Emiko's death, truly excited. He was the Rairyu now, and his first order of business with his new title was to break the blockade that ran from north to south in what used to be known as North Carolina. The weakest point of the blockade, or at least the point in the long line of Scarlet military operations that afforded the most chance of a clean break, was in Greensboro, so that was where Bill directed his troops.

The new Lightning Dragon kept his eye on the setting sun as he and his legion of 9,000 troops approached the key city via Yaiba transport and Kabuto ShadowStalker. They were still about twenty minutes out, and in that exact amount of time the last lights of the evening sky would fade.

"Everybody clear on the plan," Bill asked. He was glad that his face was covered by the shadow of his hood so the others wouldn't see him smile.

"Yes, sir," they all shouted. Bill loved that. Being in charge of so many people at once was a new experience for him, but he could definitely get used to being covered on all sides.

"Alright, guys and gals," he cooed into the comms as he activated the ShadowStalker cloaking device. "Let's hit it."

"Aye, aye, Captain," Devon Dross grunted in approval as he did the same. The two of them sped off into the distance towards the city while the rest of the legion split up.

"I can't help but feel as if you guys are taking this way too lightly," groaned Esau Tillman as he activated his own cloaking tech and sped after Bill and Dross.

"Admit it, Till. We make life more fun," Bill replied. Esau said nothing in reply, but couldn't help the slight smile that ticked up to one side of his mouth. Bill gave a gleeful war cry as he headed into the heart of the city. The other transports, both visible and invisible, scattered along the 40, the 73 and the 85 in predetermined formations and waves. It wasn't long before they saw enemy troops, tanks and transports of their own in the distance.

Tillman sighed as his eyebrow twitched in a mix of irritation and dread as he said, "Yep. More fun, alright."

****

"Sir, our sensors are detecting multiple transports rushing our blockade," said one of the techs as he stared into the nearest monitor. "That's...odd..." The sudden drift of the young man's voice stirred Prince Nash more than the report.

"What is it," he asked, more thoughtful than any of these had ever heard him. It didn't come as a surprise for them, though. Nash was a decorated warrior prince among the Reds, a prodigy, even. He'd been winning battles against the Yaiba Insurrection since he was 17, and was the sole reason that the Kabuto Sanctuary hadn't been heard from in over a year until they found help. Even in the most unpredictable of circumstances, he managed to turn the situation in his own favor. Knowing all this, the young tech did not hesitate to tell him.

"The number of enemy vehicles is in flux. First they appeared as no more than 40, but every couple of seconds that number changes to 400 or more—"

"It's those damned ShadowStalkers," Nash interrupted with a heavy sigh. He rose from his throne and stepped off the dais as he moved to peruse the monitor. He noted their movement, their various formations and how they diverged. "Deploy our auxiliary forces to I-40 and I-73. Run counter to their formations and steer them inward towards the center of the city."

"Sir," called the left side of the command center. Without delay they relayed the order and the clusters of Troopers and the vehicles at their command made for the outer and innermost highways.

"Have our central force concentrate around Greene Street and Washington," Nash continued. His calm dismissal of his enemies as naught more than an annoyance boosted morale, and each of his subordinates smiled as they got to work. "Brace yourselves. This might just be the most grueling battle you've ever seen."

****

"Heads up, boss," Dross spoke through the comms. "We have incoming."

"I see them," Bill assured him, though it was hard for him to keep the excitement out of his voice now. "Huh."

"What," Esau asked as he adjusted the screen of his ShadowStalker, but then he saw it. "They're spreading after the other formations."

"Do you think they're onto us?" It was Dross who asked the question. Bill took a moment to analyze the enemy movements. Some of the cloaked vehicles had already gone down with the ones that were plain to see. It could've been sheer luck. There was no real indication as to whether the enemy had targeted them specifically so he couldn't be sure, but he was determined in any case.

"Can't be sure," he admitted aloud, which did nothing to ease the tension that his subordinates felt, "but it looks like they're trying to steer us central."

"It's crazy to think how fast they came up with a counterplan," Esau muttered, which triggered a laugh from Bill.

"Is that what you think they did?" The way he asked the question caught everyone who listened off guard. "All units, follow the Reds' directive and head to the center of town. Defend yourselves at all costs. Remember to make it look good."

"Sir," they called back to the Dragon, and his smile grew wider.

"Mr. Tillman," Bill addressed in his most bourgeois tone of voice. Esau couldn't help but think that Bill thought all of this was just some elaborate game. He wasn't wrong. "The ShadowStalkers are outfitted with what kinds of tech, exactly?" The question caught Esau off-guard more than the off-putting sense of joy that Bill derived from this line of work.

"The cloaking feature is linked to a biometrics interface and optics system that allows the bike to track your movements. It's worth noting that your body is only cloaked in this mode while it's connected to the bike. If you disconnect, you'll be visible to any enemies in the area," Esau explained.

"I can still control it remotely, right," Bill asked. His jaw split in a hopeful grin when Esau let out a nervous huff.

"Yeah," he started reluctantly. "There's an AI built in capable of adapting to the battle flow of the user. We call her ARTEMIS. What do you have planned, Master Jerrick?" Dross was the one to chuckle through the headset.

"Oh, I can think of a few clever ideas," he said. Bill cracked his knuckles and his neck, then pulled out his Reikiken.

"Don't you worry about that, my friend. Just keep heading towards the center like I said. I'm about to clear us a path straight to Yorktown. Once we get there, you do what you can to help the other formations. I'll handle whatever trap they have set for us." Bill shifted focus. The sound of the enemies' engines was closer than it had been before. The highway was about to run out, and pretty soon Bill, Esau and Dross would have to go their separate ways for the time being. Still he was happy. "Hey ARTEMIS, you ready to have some fun?"

"As ready as I can be, sir," ARTEMIS replied with a feminine and vaguely British accent. Bill's expression was one of pleasant surprise.

"Alright, then," he told her excitedly. "Whenever I disconnect from you, track the movement of my open hand. However I move it, you move. Got it?"

"I believe so, yes," ARTEMIS replied. Bill chuckled as his adrenaline pumped aggressively through his veins. He stood on the back of his ride, still invisible for the moment, and watched as his enemies came into view.

****

Two Scarlet Cyclist formations rushed down Friendly Avenue with all the zeal that came from having a leader like Prince Nash. They couldn't hear their enemies. Apparently the ShadowStalkers cancelled noise and erased any thermal signatures, but despite going in blind, the confidence of the Scarlets was at an all-time high. Until they saw him.

In the distance, a single man garbed in a purple shirt, black trousers and a black hooded cloak appeared like a phantom in the dying lights of the sun. Before the Reds could train their weapons on him, his body disappeared, only to reappear in midair just a few feet closer. A few of them fired off rounds, but there was no way to tell if the bullets met their target. A moment later, the Phantom reemerged in the air, chains at his sides as he barreled towards them.

He struck one of the captains in his chest with the diamond-shaped blade that guided the chains and blasted forward with a kick of his boots. The Phantom dislodged the extended blade, and the rattle of the metallic links broke through the confidence of the Red riders. They tasted a fear unlike any they'd ever known, and broke their formation only after a bright orange light burst through the bodies and bikes of another three riders. The fifteen that remained did what they could to limit his mobility, but as soon as they'd gathered their wits about them, he was gone once again.

The engines halted, the Reds too afraid to press onward with this menace disguised among them. The remaining captain disembarked his machine, pulled his pistol from its holster at its hip and waited. They all did.

"What's happening," one of his subordinates asked at the front of the circle. The captain, who could offer no response, slowly moved to the center of the new formation. The wind howled fiercely through the trees and debris that filled this part of the old college town, and the full register of the surviving Troopers shivered with unease. The sudden stillness that matched the encroaching darkness escalated the terror in the Reds as they surveyed their surroundings, each one left to wonder which of them would be next. Then, the captain's blood chilled.

"You tell me," snickered the Phantom as he reappeared at the center of the circle. He was a mere hair's breadth away from the captain, who stumbled back in terror and disgust. The Phantom slashed the infernal chains through the air and as the blades hit the ground, so too did the bisected bodies of his victims.

"Open fire!" The captain shouted it as he scrambled away from the alabaster Phantom shrouded in the dark. The ghostly figure smiled through a semi-thick brown beard as he leapt forward, aura sword at the ready, and got to work. He blazed through the rifle muzzle of the Trooper just in front of him before he cleaved through her abdomen. Her body hadn't even fallen to the ground when he adjusted his position, spun his weapon to rest comfortably in both hands and pointed at his next enemy. He thrust forward through their gun and their chest alike, but it wasn't until this specter raised his weapon to the captain that the remaining eleven in the circle followed the command of their officer.

The Phantom slammed his ghostly chains into the ground and blasted himself into the air with his boots once the bullets began to fly. He landed squarely in the center of the formation and, with one arm raised and one hand open, readily revolved as if to welcome the rain of enemy fire. The Troopers marveled as some invisible field rejected the course of their bullets as soon as they took flight. The Phantom, an enormous smile planted on his jaw, caught sight of the terrified captain out of the corner of his eye.

"This is Captain Nicodemus Iannuzzi," he shouted over the gunfire into his wrist-comm. The Phantom's smile grew with more delight, as the sounds Captain Iannuzzi made were frantic, words oversaturated with cold fear. *Well, that's kinda sad*, thought the ghost. "We need immediate backup to the corner of Edgeworth and Friendly Ave. I don't know how much longer we can hold out."

The gunfire raged despite the shield, and the Phantom leaped into the air once again with his open hand extended just in front of him. Before his feet could grace the ground again, he vanished as if he had never been there in the first place. The gunfire stopped, and instantly the eleven Reds that remained questioned their sanity. Obviously their enemy was Yaiba, but unlike any other Yaiba they'd ever seen or heard about. All of them couldn't help but wonder how they were ever meant to fight something like this.

****

"Having fun over there," Dross asked his teacher through disappointment and jealousy. He and Esau had long dispatched throughout the city to help strike down a few Scarlet Cyclists themselves. The bigger caravans they'd brought along had survived, though not without a few casualties along the way. Bill laughed at the question.

"You know I am," he replied to his student matter-of-factly, and the warmth in his voice made Dross smile even though he did what he could to resist the urge. "Do me a favor?" Dross took a moment to consider how he should answer. He loved his teacher, but he was a little bit petty when he was left out of the fun.

"I guess," Dross replied. "What's up?"

"You and Esau split up the ranks a bit. The Captain here has called for reinforcements to my position." Bill sounded excited, as if everything was going according to plan.

"Wait," Esau interrupted, "does that mean we don't head to the center of town like you told us to?"

"Oh, no," Bill answered, a hint of delighted deviance in his voice. "On the contrary, my friend. You guys are just going to surround the enemy that surrounds me. Once they come out of hiding and reveal their full hand, we'll cut them down and hit the road in time enough to make it to Yorktown by breakfast at the latest." There was such a surety in his voice that even Esau was put at ease. That was, of course, the defining feature of Bill's personality. He could make anyone feel calm and in control, regardless of if they were a friend or foe. His knack for people was the very thing that made him a phenomenal leader on the battlefield. He would fight to include his allies in his victories, make them feel hopeful and happy and accepted in every moment that lead up to them. For his enemies, however, he would lure them into a false sense of security, just as he'd done with the Reds the moment he led his troops into the city.

"We'll do what we can," Esau replied with a huff. He was thoroughly impressed. For all of Bill's lackadaisical charm, he was a master tactician.

"That's all I ask," Bill said, and with another jump, he reentered the fray.

****

The Phantom reemerged above the crowd and once again warranted the blitz of gunfire from his surrounding enemies. His feet blasted in two divergent directions as his chains rattled forth again. The blade that led them lodged into the ground and pulled the human spiral to the densest edge of the enemy circle. He flipped forward, landed hard, and swiped through the weapon and torso of the nearest enemy. They screamed while they fell apart, and the ghostly warrior quickly brought his blade back through an adversary in the opposite direction.

He stamped the ground as his body spun around to face a third potential victim. His torso angled forward, his hands on the hilt of his bright orange blade and arms dropped just in front of his leg like a beast poised to pounce. They stared each other down, but when the Phantom feigned a lunge, the Scarlet Trooper rolled along the ground and took a kneeling position. He aimed his weapon, but a swift slash of the rattling chains split the gun in two. The Trooper, undeterred by his fear, drew a dagger from his hip.

The Phantom smiled wide as he spread his arms through the gunfire. "You ever hear the expression, 'Your arm's too short to box with God,' kid?" The Trooper ran at him to answer, blade brandished and brow beaded with sweat from the sweltering heat of the aura sword. The Phantom sighed as he extended his open hand, and the courageous trooper met an invisible force that barreled into his sternum at bone-crushing speed. “I’ll take that as a ‘no.’” The Phantom whipped with his bladed chains set free through the air, and sliced through the head of one of the shooters. He retracted the coil as he launched himself through the air. Seven more enemies remained, three of whom dropped their guns in terror and ran. The Phantom seemed content to let them cling to their wretched lives for a while longer.

Instead, he turned his attention to the four that closed in around him. Now he was purely visible, and dead in the center of what was left of their formation. It thrilled him to the core to see Captain Iannuzzi up close. He was a short man, pale skin with green eyes and jet-black hair. He was round in the middle, but the state of his arms told the story that he might’ve been muscular at one point in time. These, however, were not the features that the Phantom delighted in. It was the fear in the man’s eye, the way his hand trembled even as it pointed a pistol right between his eyes.

“You know you should lighten up,” joked the ghostly figure. He could hear the faint whirr of engine motors in the distance on all sides. Allies and enemies alike, he knew. The corner of his mouth pulled into a sly smirk. His body straightened, hands and the firesword they held lifted high above his head. “All that frowning isn’t good for you. It’ll give you wrinkles.”

“Fire,” shouted the terrified Captain, and as soon as the words left his lips, the Phantom sharply jerked the blade down and back to his rearmost enemy. They fell limp just as the specter whipped his sword through their body and into the skull of the left. He spun it from side to side and blocked an oncoming bullet—a rare occurrence—just as Scarlet tanks and Yaiba caravans emerged from multiple directions. He swung in a wide arc that narrowly missed the captain, but folded the last of his subordinates with the sheer power of the blow. By the time the Phantom returned his attention to Captain Iannuzzi, they were surrounded in full.

The Scarlet Kingdom and the Yaiba Insurrection stared each other down, and suddenly the Captain put aside his fear.

There it is, the Phantom thought, *he's all smug now.* Iannuzzi took a moment to catch his breath before he spoke, "You don't really mean to keep fighting, do you? I mean, even you have to realize how hopeless this situation is." The Phantom—Bill Jerrick—smiled from ear to ear.

"The objective was never to fight you, Cap," Bill replied, and Captain Iannuzzi's face twisted with the resurgence of fear. "I just needed all your able forces to come out into the open. Code 1783, initiate." A brilliant blue flash emanated from the Yaiba caravan. The Scarlets were blinded, thrown into confusion by the noiseless explosion of light around them. Then there was the sound of vehicles on the move. It was Bill that the noticed last, and when the Captain came forward in his anger, the phantomlike Rairyu shrugged coyly as he slowly walked in reverse. "Electromagnetic pulses! You'd think you'd have some kind of shield against that sort of thing by now since you use it all the time." The Captain shook as he watched their enemies casually glide through their blockade. "Think of it this way, Nicky-boy…Nick…Nico…whatever your friends call you. You'll always remember this as the day where you *almost* kept me from getting what I want. Ciao." Bill shot him a mock salute and, as he jumped onto his ShadowStalker, laughed at the pained scream the Captain lifted to the sky.

Chapter Twenty-Seven

December 20th, 2084, 6:30 a.m.,

Zahara had been confined to her quarters since she helped the Reds fortify the Jackson base. She knew that it wouldn't be easy to earn Nathaira's trust, and that was what she counted on. She made it look like she bought the Reds time, which in turn gave the Insurrectionists just two walls away the chance to do some recon and figure out a way to get around the base's more threatening defenses. They were locked in a stalemate, and one that served the Yaiba more than Kingdom Scarlet.

Still, almost a week of inaction had driven Zahara up a wall. She was let out only to utilize the latrine, and was given company only when soldiers on meal detail brought her something to eat. Every second was a reminder why she'd defected. To them she was an animal, some dark-skinned creature best kept in the service of those with fairer complexions. The idea made her want to gag, but she held it together. Or as much as she could have as the base began to stir.

Captain Boyd sat in the armchair that rested just a few feet from the door and listened to the urgency in the steps of the troops without her walls. She missed that level of false freedom. She'd always known that as long as she was in service to the Kingdom she would never be free, but for crying out loud, at least she could go to the bathroom by herself. She quickly shook her dissatisfaction from her mind. She needed to focus, because now was the most crucial part of the mission.

She carefully listened to the idle chatter, the bustle of the royal warriors so determined to defend their way of life to the last. It would've been admirable, Zahara figured, if their way of life wasn't so disproportionately in favor of white skin and ill-gotten gains. It didn't matter. Not right then anyway. She listened harder. Something had happened that made the soldiers frantic. Not noticeably so, and had one of the other Violet Shadows been named to handle this part of the mission, they might've missed it. But Zahara was Scarlet first. She knew what a normal day in the life of a Trooper looked like and this was not it.

The door opened. Nurse Charlie-Jack Thompson strode in with the meal cart that Zahara had come to so look forward to. He struck her as a little weird, like some alternate universe example of what a real human would act like, but he was pleasant enough company. Not like the rest of the people that currently held her captive. He smiled at her, and she smiled back. Then she frowned.

"You doing alright, Charlie," Zahara asked. "You're looking a little paler than usual. Kinda scruffy, too, if you don't mind me saying." The nurse sighed.

"It's been a pretty tough morning, but I can't complain too much," he assured her, then made his best effort to mask the unease behind his eyes as he smiled. "It's nothing you need to worry about. I brought you some pancakes. I figured since you don't have to pass a PT test anytime soon you might as well enjoy life a little bit." Zahara returned his smile, which changed to a shocked expression as someone sprinted through the halls in a red and white blur.

"Doesn't sound like too much 'nothing' is going on out there," she joked. "You still wanna claim that lie or you wanna tell me what's going on?" Their eyes met, his stern, hers sharp. He eventually adopted a pleading look, which told her that he wasn't as strong-willed as he thought he was. "Charlie," she said in warning, and he huffed like she imagined a disappointed child might. He closed the door, finally, and began to set the table with her food.

"Those Insurrection guys are moving around the outer territory," he said with a sniffle. Suddenly, Zahara was wary of any food he set in front of her and watched to see if he repeated it. He hadn't. "Until recently we've been able to track their movements." This caught Zahara's attention, and her eyes narrowed.

"How recent are we talking," she asked. Her voice was the perfect mix of authoritative and calm, which expertly masked how giddy she felt at the idea that their little siege would continue.

"Trackers went dead yesterday morning," Charlie confirmed as he cut a small cube of butter, placed it at the top of the stack of pancakes and drizzled syrup all over the plate. "You didn't hear that from me, though. Orange juice?" He held up a huge pitcher in one hand and a glass in the other.

"Sure, thanks. So all this chaos because the trackers went dead? Doesn't seem like it would be worth that much stress." Zahara's brow furrowed to feign deep thought. "Unless the Yaiba were in the middle of doing something potentially dangerous…" her voice trailed off, and Charlie refused to meet her gaze as he poured the orange juice. She smiled anyway. "Thanks for the information, Charlie. If you don't mind, could you tell the Commander that I want to speak to her?" He snorted a laugh.

"Oh sure, because she'd really take a request from the only combat medic who specializes in veterinary medicine." His tone dripped with sarcasm, and she smiled. "I'll see what I can do, but don't hold your breath, babe."

"Don't call me babe," she said in a sickeningly sweet to the point of being threatening sort of tone. He nervously fled the room and she laughed. "And now," she dragged the knife through her pancakes with effortless motion. She took a bite and let a small delighted moan escape her throat. "Now we wait."

****

December 20th, 2084, 8:22 a.m.,

The pair of Scarlet Troopers screamed. The Reikibo, that beautiful staff made of two Reikiken, stabbed one and sliced through the other, much to the enjoyment of Manny and Lukas. It wasn't that they enjoyed the taking of life. That was always tragic, and not just to them, but to every Insurrectionist that ever had to do it. They did, however, marvel at the sheer efficiency of their weaponry. The Reikibo was a relatively new concept, only dating back to the intermittent battles from the last twenty years. Only a handful of people had managed to master the form, but due to Emiko's order against modded Hanzo Gear, the production of Reikibo staves was halted. Since her death…

Manny refused to think about that, because no matter what might've changed in the aftermath, her loss was a wound to the Yaiba that would never heal.

"Hey, uh, dad," Lukas started with uncertainty as he looked around. Manny turned to face him and cleverly masked the discomfort he'd brought on himself under the pretense of good humor.

"What's up," he asked with a warm smile. He sensed the air of nervousness around his son, yet it hadn't yet passed.

"Have you noticed that the Red patrols are a lot lighter today?" Manny's eyes narrowed as he took the time to survey the terrain. It was true that since their arrival five days ago they'd managed to clear out a good portion of the enemy population in the area. The local Waste-Raiders, those remnants of old Southern life left to rot in the aftermath of the Second Civil War, proved grateful to the Yaiba for helping them get their freedom back. Even so, the intel Zahara had supplied projected more activity than what they'd seen.

"Now that you mention it, it is a little weird." The Kazeryu changed the frequency on his comms. "I need a favor."

"What's going on," came a shockingly feminine voice from the other end. Manny's eyes glanced in the way of his earpiece.

"Vanessa? I thought this was the frequency for the command center," he said briskly. Manny and Vanessa had a rather tumultuous relationship. She found him to be shifty, he found her pretentious. Despite their feelings, though, they'd always managed to put them aside for the better of the mission.

"It is," Vanessa replied. "John put me in charge of the command center. Well—me and Mr. Hamlin."

"Uncle Dre is there too?" The sudden explosive excitement in his tone gave Lukas an idea of what his father must have been like as a kid, which made him smile through his unease.

"Yeah, kid," Dre assured him. "I'm here. What do you need?" The question sobered Manny again, and as his eyes narrowed on the distant buildings, Lukas could see why his old man was to be feared.

"Something doesn't feel right out here. Can you run a scan of the whole city? We're looking for high concentrations of enemy forces, if you can find them." Dre chortled.

"What's the matter, not enough fight out there in the field?" Dre, who had always opposed his son's participation in military operations, felt no different with Manny. Even so, Manny wasn't his son, so the most he could do about the discomfort he felt at his former teammate's kid throwing his life away was laugh it off as much as he could.

"Plenty of fight, Uncle Dre. Just not as much as the intel suggested," Manny confessed. There was a pause that radiated tension.

"You don't think that Boyd woman lied to us, do you?" Vanessa asked. Manny thought about it for a moment but shook his head as if she could see him.

"Nah," he said, "she doesn't have anything to gain by lying to us about something so malleable as enemy movement."

“So then what are we looking for?” Manny could hear the agitation in her tone as she asked the question. He rolled his eyes, but before he could answer her question, she’d already scanned the city and cross-referenced what she saw with the recorded intel that Zahara had given them. “Hold on a minute.” There was typing on the other end of the comms. “It looks like the Reds are retreating.”

“Well yeah, we can see that from where we’re standing,” Manny replied, slightly more than just annoyed. “We’ve been killing them for days, so it makes sense that they’d want to get out of dodge.” His anger was subtle, and only those who had known him for a long time would be able to tell what he meant by the slight shift in his tone and the sudden use of disparaging sarcasm.

“No, kid,” Dre interjected before Vanessa could go off. “The droves of Scarlet Troopers at the edge of town—the ones that should be sweeping the city to engage with you—are on the retreat.” There was a moment of silence between all three of them, and Lukas in the background watched his father stiffen from behind.

“I have a bad feeling about this,” Manny said, and kept his eyes on the horizon.

****

December 20th, 2084, 9:00 a.m.,

More bombs echoed in the distance, a sound that made all of the Pro-Rebellion faction flinch with discomfort. They needed to wrap this up fast—Darius knew that—but without Johannes back where he belonged, there was no guarantee that a speedy solution to the Yoroi Conflict was plausible. If Darius revealed himself too soon, it might endanger their friend the emissary and any shot they might’ve had of creating a clear picture of who the loyalists actually were.

They needed to get him back, but their searches had turned up nothing. Darius' eyes narrowed on the ornate piece of blue and gold cloth before him.

"You found this in Cluster B?" Darius asked the question without looking at Bobbi, and his tone was less hospitable than she'd known it to be in the past. Ina's death shook him more than he'd expected it to, but how else was he supposed to act when the person who saved his life died so soon? He blamed himself for putting her in danger. He blamed himself for taking her away from Johannes. He swore that he would make it right.

"Uh, yeah," Bobbi told him nervously, then swallowed and found her focus. "I found it after I tripped one of those faulty civilian traps."

"And you're sure it's his," Levi asked, his eyes narrowed.

"Oh, it's his, alright," Leroy chimed in. He had his arms folded across his chest and comfortably leaned a shoulder against a nearby doorframe. "Anyone around here could tell you that much."

"Yeah all those guys with the diplomatic jobs wear a lot of fancy stuff," Lex added. "It tends to be pretty expensive though. Can't imagine that he'd allow someone to damage his clothes, frugal as he is."

"Just say he's cheap man," Tony told him, their face twisted in visible annoyance. "But you're right."

"What are the odds that he's leaving fragments for us to find?" Darius wasn't certain that the scrap that sat in front of him was enough evidence of anything like that. There was no way to even tell that it was his, but without anything else pointing in Johannes' direction, they all felt desperate.

"They're slim," Bobbi was forced to admit. "Lex and Tony are right, he's too cheap to let his nicest clothes get shredded this badly, but it's not like we have any other leads right now."

"Do we at least know where they're hiding out?" Levi asked. "I mean, that knowledge would certainly come in handy." The whole room sighed heavily, which answered the question with more than just a slight flair of hostility.

"We're doing all we can," Tony assured him with an edge to their tone.

"And what does that look like, exactly?" Levi's distaste for Tony's aggressive address created one of his own. He felt he was justified in asking, since espionage and sabotage were the cornerstone skillset of the Kabuto Sanctuary. Tony didn't agree.

"We're out there scouring that damned war zone just like you are," Tony spat, "risking our lives for the life of our friend and to preserve our way of life. Or what's left of it, anyway. Do you know how many times we've had to kill someone we love?"

"Do you know how many times you could've avoided those kinds of conflicts if you'd just stuck to the shadows for a few days and observed?" Levi's response was logical, and Darius could see the value in his opinion. That perspective, however, wasn't shared among the other Pro-Rebellion leaders.

"Oh, so do you know where they're keeping him now?" It was Bobbi who bit back this time, arms folded across her chest and eyes alive with a rage that was so unlike her. "Tell us, then." Levi glared at her, but offered no response. His breaths grew shorter, his hands curled into fists, but he couldn't find the words to speak. Bobbi raised her eyebrows in annoyed expectation. "You obviously know so much about tracking and spying, Levi, so tell us what the hell we ought to be doing, dammit!" She hadn't meant to yell. She was the aloof, carefree, cool-headed member of their leadership, so when her voice raised everyone within earshot flinched in as much shock as discomfort.

A knock came at the door. Everyone froze and all conversations ceased. A single thought passed through each of their minds: *Nobody should know that we're here*. Darius stood from his seat on the raggedy couch and carefully pushed past his comrades to the door. Every step he took escalated the sudden fear and anxiety that the team felt. He reached out for the doorknob, then paused to look back at his now silent teammates. He slowly opened the door, and relief washed over him at the sight of the three men in the doorway.

"Hey kids," Callan said with more joy on his face than Darius had ever seen. Ryan Morrisey stood at his back and eagerly darted his eyes back and forth over the Yoroi's damaged Clusters. Tom Freeman, of the Kabuto Sanctuary, smiled coolly at the others in the room. "I think I might have an answer to your question."

****

December 20th, 2084, 11:17 a.m.,

"And you're certain this is a good idea," Erik Kincaid asked as they drove through the desert on their transports. It took a considerable effort to navigate the wasteland around the Grand Canyon since the Yoroi had their blasted traps everywhere. Even though Kincaid knew where most of them were, it only took a moment's negligence to spell his doom. Not something he was overly comfortable with.

"Not even a little," John had to admit. There had only ever been one attempted olive branch between Kingdom Scarlet and the Yaiba Insurrection. To say that it ended in bloodshed would be an understatement. "History has proven that they can't be trusted, but if there's a chance we could learn something from them or tip the balance of this war into our favor then we have to take it."

"As logical as that sounds," Kincaid replied with a more measured manner of speech, "I can't help but feel as though you might be letting your nerves get the better of you. The war is already going the way we want it to. Every battle pushes the Scarlets to their limit."

"Yeah, but we been takin' some heavy losses, too, man," Zayvier told him. His palms were wet with sweat and it took everything in him not to spin out of control on his transport out of sheer nerves. He was the Tsuchiryu now, successor to his sensei, Bill Jerrick, and this was his first mission as such. It was a lot to take in. "We might be winnin' but at what cost?"

"That aside, we're only doing as well as we are because you took down their Drone Network, Erik, and it's not like it'll stay down forever." John told him.

"I mean, we been fortunate that it's been down for as long as it has," Zay commented. He shuddered at the thought of having to contend with gunfire on the ground and airstrikes from above. The Hanzo Gear could handle a lot, but there was no way it could go toe to toe with a plane.

"Exactly my point," John told them both. "While the situation is still under our control, we need to cover as much ground as possible, learn as much as we can. We don't know how long we have before their precious system comes back online. If it does while we're unprepared, even slightly, then I'm afraid that all the work we've put in up until now might've been for naught."

"Well," Kincaid said as the edge of the base of the Scarlet Prince came into view, "let's just hope this opportunity doesn't go to waste."

****

December 20th, 2084, 11:17 a.m.,

The Scarlet Scourge was worse off than they'd ever been in the days since Serenity took charge. Cecelia lost her hand only days after her sister Trisha had died. Amelia Kluger had been dead for months, killed at the hands of one of those junior Violet Shadows back in Johnson City. Even Aria Black wasn't without her fair share of bumps and bruises from her infiltration of the Roan Mountain base. It aggravated the typically unflappable Colonel Crawford, and it had gotten to the point that she could no longer hide it.

The only two members of the thinned down Scourge fit to defend the Prince were Kerri Waldheim and that chaotic fox Serafina Leyva. If it were up to Serenity, she'd keep Leyva under strict surveillance, but they neither had the time nor the manpower when the new Director of the Yaiba Insurrection was to arrive at any moment. Besides, it was better to have her front and center for the day's planned festivities anyway.

Serenity tapped her foot against the floor of her tent, hands clasped in front of her face and brow furrowed. She still couldn't bring herself to be overly optimistic that this meeting would work out. She'd heard the stories in her earlier years as a Scarlet Trooper, the ones about how Director Isao Ishikawa, Emiko's father, killed the former King in cold blood. She thought of James, who was a bargaining chip in the best-case scenario and wholly expendable in the worst.

Nothing about their present situation was ideal, and as if to make matters worse, the chill of Leyva's evil manifested in the Scourge Leader's tent.

"My, my," Serafina started in a delighted cadence of voice, "you've seen better days, Colonel Crawford."

"What do you want?" Serenity's aggravation showed, and for once she was too exhausted to care. When their eyes met, the Colonel noted a sparkle of mischief behind those dark brown eyes. Serafina did nothing to hide it as she paced toward her leader.

"I just wanted to check on you," she offered. They both knew the lie in those words.

"I'm fine," Serenity snapped, "and you can leave." Serafina pressed her collarbone in mock surprise.

"I'm sorry, Colonel, I was just trying to help…" she turned to leave, but then whipped back around and approached Serenity again, this time with more ferocity and ambition in those eyes than the Scourge Leader had ever noted in a troop before. "But let me just say that I'll do whatever I can to make sure that Prince James is safe during this meeting."

That caught Serenity by surprise. With narrowed eyes and the unfolding of her hands she said, "Come again?"

"The meeting with the new Yaiba Director," the Lady Leyva clarified, and couldn't resist the smirk that pulled at the corners of her mouth. "Black says he was the same Lightning Dragon that slaughtered over two-hundred of our men on his own strength." Serenity's face grew sterner than it already was before. This was apparently Leyva's intention, as she smiled with the sudden severity of her commander. "No," she said in response, "I don't think I'd want him anywhere near the Prince either if I had such an…*amicable* working relationship with him." With the simple utterance of that statement, Serenity finally understood the ambition in Serafina's eyes, the whimsy in her tone, the way she always strutted around the camp as though she was superior to everyone else, and why wouldn't she do that? She knew the secret that the Prince and the Colonel had worked so hard to hide from the upper echelon. "But you don't have to worry," Serafina said on her way out. "I would never allow anything to happen to him." *Just you.* The implication was clear, and for the first time in discernable years, Serenity Crawford, Colonel in the Scarlet Kingdom military and leader of the Scarlet Scourge, felt fear for her life.

****

December 20th, 2084, 11:30 a.m.,

Prince James stood on the edge of camp surrounded by a detail of four Troopers, and patiently watched as his guests pulled their transports to a stop. There were only three of them, one of whom had been reported to have slaughtered two hundred Troopers. Erik Kincaid was easily recognized by the Red Prince, as they had seen each other in negotiations in the past. The fact that he and the Kabuto had joined up with the Yaiba Insurrection was a testament to Prince Nash's failures as a tactician.

The man to the far left, smooth caramel in his complexion, bore emerald eyes that pierced James' soul. He wore a distinctive look of disgust that matched the wintry chill in the air. James felt afraid of him, even surrounded by the detail of Scarlet Troopers.

The man in the center of their delegation stood tall, was lean but muscular, with trimmed curly hair, milk chocolate skin, and deep brown eyes that told countless stories of hard battles and sweet victories. The poise with which he carried himself, the authoritative presence of him, the surety of his own safety lavished on the sharp features of his face and the hand gently at rest atop the stowed but dormant Reikiken at his side told James that this was *that* man. This was the Yaiba's new Director, the former Rairyu with such a storied past that he was a legend even amongst Kingdom citizens.

"Welcome," James spoke with a humble bow. "I must say I'm overjoyed that you decided to accept my offer, Director Hamlin."

"Make no mistake, Prince," John spoke with his distinct reptilian hum, "I'm only here out of curiosity, and to warn you never to send that traitorous dog Aria Black into my presence again." James raised his hands in a placating gesture.

"My apologies for the underhanded tactic, but the matter is urgent," James clarified. He was proud of himself for the fact that his voice didn't rattle in the slightest. The fear that almost paralyzed him somehow hadn't manifested, and as he allowed his confidence to grow, he said, "Please, follow me this way." John, Zayvier and Erik followed the Prince and his men back into the camp, where every other Scarlet Trooper watched them closely.

"Doesn't look like they're too happy to see us," Kincaid muttered, his reservations about the situation firmly back in place.

"That don't matter," Zayvier told him. "We didn't come here to make them happy. Let 'em try somethin' if they wanna."

"Both of you calm down," John commanded, and the chatter ceased. They could hear the focus in his voice, a sharp determination that could easily be transfigured into pristine and thunderous animosity. Neither of them wanted to be on the receiving end of it, but they were more than ready to watch it turn on the Scarlets.

Prince James led the three visitors to the centermost tent that served as a makeshift briefing site. Therein stood Serenity Crawford and Serafina Leyva, who stood with perfect military bearing off to the side. The hand that John kept on his weapon tensed for just a moment. His prior brushes with the Scarlet Scourge in the years before his ascension proved to be more volatile and demanding than most of the other battles he faced. The sight of Serenity was enough to trigger a response, but he resisted the urge to cleave her in two as he took a seat at the table. There was a pause as the Scourge members eyed him disrespectfully, as if John showed the utmost contempt for their people and customs by taking the spot at the head of the table and sitting before the Prince offered him permission to do so.

Zayvier and Erik followed his lead reluctantly. They could feel the tension in the air rise higher and higher, but they knew the man they accompanied, and knew that even the universally feared Scarlet Scourge would be foolish to try and contradict him. Prince James took a seat at the opposite end of the table, and suddenly the tension eased.

"Well?" John's question came out as abrasively as he intended, and caused a nervous twitch in the entire room. It was clear that the Reds had no idea how to handle him, and it pleased him to understand this. "Why am I here?"

"Yes," said the Prince with due caution, "I'll get straight to the point. I want to propose an end to all this fighting." The Scourge Leader and her subordinate both gawked at him.

"You gotta be joking," Zay chided in disbelief. "If that was the case then y'all would've left us alone. The Second Civil War wouldn't have happened. Emiko Ishikawa would still be alive! Man, this some bullshi—"

"Master Peters!" John raised his voice and cut off his indignant bodyguard. Zayvier shot John a look, who returned it with a sense of daring so strong that Zayvier immediately took a knee and bowed his head. "You will let him finish without any interruption. Am I clear?"

"Yes, Master Hamlin," Zay spoke through gritted teeth that expressed more anger than apology.

"Please, continue, Prince James," John invited, which visibly angered Serenity though she dared not move.

"I understand your friend's anger. It's warranted. The Kingdom has done so many unspeakable things in the name of reestablishing order and your respective peoples have a right to hate us," he admitted. "I also understand how bold it is of me to ask for peace when my father and our soldiers have made multiple attempts on your lives, but I have to ask you, how much longer will this go on? Will we find common ground to stand on, or will we continue to destroy each other until there's nothing left for your children to inherit?" John's jaw tightened at the mention of his kids, a change that the Prince noticed immediately. "That's your son in the Yoroi Alliance, isn't it? He's strong; no doubt he gets that from you. But surely you've wondered what life would've been like if your son could've just been a kid."

"Enough," John demanded with the slam of his fist against the hard steel table. The Troopers that surrounded the Prince pulled their guns and pointed their muzzles at him. Zayvier pulled out his Reikiken and Erik drew his sword from the sheath on his back. The

Yaiba Director slightly raised his hand, which calmed his comrades almost instantly. The Prince nodded to Serenity, who ordered the Scarlet soldiers to stand down as well. John spoke plainly. “Make your point and let’s be done with this.”

“What I want is simple,” the Prince assured him as an embellished hush fell upon the soldiers and diplomats. “I want you to kidnap the Scarlet Scourge’s leader.” After those words were spoken, the once lively makeshift meeting hall became a soundless void of confusion.

“What,” came the slightly jolted voice of Serenity Crawford, her bright green eyes suddenly sapped of their strength and full of tears. John looked to her, totally devoid of emotion, then back to the Prince.

“Well, Prince James, at first you had my curiosity, but now you have my attention,” John told him. “Why would you willingly sell out one of your own? And more to the point, why do you assume that we wouldn’t kill everyone here and take you as our hostage instead?” Serenity’s heart pounded in her chest as the enemy leader spoke the words with such audacious certainty and unnerving calm. James merely chuckled.

“Serenity has proven to be an invaluable member of our military community,” James supplied. “So much so that whatever decision she makes is automatically defended by the King himself. If you take her, you will have stolen from the Scarlet Kingdom the very image of military excellence and the example of what all our citizens should strive to be. I, on the other hand, am only my father’s *second* son. I’m worth less to him than the dirt *you* stand on, and no amount of threats or torture to me would ever make him adhere to even one of your demands—”

“No deal,” John shot, much to the surprise of his host. “You expect me to believe that you’d just give me someone of such great importance? To what end?”

"The assassination of the King of the Reds," James responded flatly. "You take Serenity and the military will be thrown into chaos. The Scarlet Scourge won't be able to function. My father will go out of his way to bring her back and restore order, and while he's distracted with negotiations with you, I'll deal the finishing blow and take the throne for myself."

"I fail to see how your overly idealistic plan is beneficial to my people," John said without skipping a beat. His eyes narrowed on the Prince, and with Serenity and the other Troopers too stunned to notice, nobody checked him on his blatant disregard for royalty.

"If you help me take the throne in Kingdom Scarlet, I'll cease all hostility towards the Yaiba Insurrection, Kabuto Sanctuary, and the Yoroi Alliance. You'll be able to live a normal life with your families, totally safe from the oppressive hand of King Shane. In the case of Callan Rouge, you might even restore to him what little family he has left." John tilted his head back in dangerous curiosity.

"What do you mean," he asked. In response, James only looked over to his beloved Scourge leader. When John followed his glance, he couldn't help but say, "No way."

"I can have the records pulled for you if you want," James offered, "but time is of the essence and I have need of an answer immediately. If you want to know the truth, you'll help me kill my father." Before John could part his lips to answer, a grainy blue projection took to the center of the room. The man whose image emerged from Serafina's lapel wore an ornate crown over his obviously gray hair, and his soul-crushing eyes found his son at the other end of the table.

"You miserable little wretch," spat King Shane O'Neill with a look of unfathomable loathing. "I give you the freedom to roam as you will, even overlooked your illegal affair with the Crawford girl, and you repay me by planning my assassination?"

The King paused, a dare for his son to speak out of turn. The fear had taken its hold, though, and the wayward Prince kept silent. "Since death is what you crave, I shall see to it that you have it. Troopers," the King said coolly, and the soldiers in the tent raised their weapons and pointed them at James, "do away with the traitorous former prince, would you?" The transmission faded out, but just before it did, James was almost certain that he saw his father…smile.

Chapter Twenty-Eight

December 20th, 2084, 12:17 p.m.,

Tension shot through the air like a bolt of lightning. Serafina was the first to move, and stood between the former protection detail and the now former Prince. Serenity was stunned to say the least.

"Everyone calm down," Serafina ordered, her voice dire and serious rather than drenched in playfulness as always. Her arms spread to either side as if to serve as a shield, but then a knife slipped out from her sleeve as a demonic smile slithered across her lips. "This kill is *mine*!" Just as she turned to literally stab James in the back, Serenity drew her pistol and shot the knife out of the Lady Leyva's hand. Two of the four other troopers in the room trained their rifles on Serenity, but never fired a bullet. John snapped his fingers, and the rattle of Zayvier's chains filled the room instantly. Hearts were pierced, bodies fell, and the two femme fatales of the Scarlet Scourge stared each other down with equal animosity.

"What ever happened to not letting anything happen to the Prince," Serenity asked with gun in hand, carefully aimed at the face of her adversary.

"He has to actually *be* a prince in order for that to apply," Serafina answered with a shrug. "Can't blame me for the situation changing."

"I always knew you were full of crap," Serenity laughed, her eyes sharp as ever. "James, come over here with me." James moved to stand up, but a firm hand on his shoulder made him rest in his seat again.

"Can't let you have him," Serafina said with a faux wince. "You heard the boss, didn't you? James dies. Today."

"How much you wanna bet that he doesn't?" Her voice was enough to raise John's eyebrows in both surprise and pleasure. It was no shock to him that the Scarlet Kingdom would disregard the importance of any one soldier, but he'd thought the same thing that James had. It had always been his assumption that Serenity was far too valuable to lose, an icon to a military state that never ran short of any enemies. She was a titan among their ranks, but he supposed it was a titan's destiny to fall before false gods.

John stood from the table, and with his bodyguards in tow, he turned to leave. James noticed this and became frantic.

"Wait, Master Hamlin," called the former Prince, Lady Leyva's hand still clenched tightly on his shoulder. John and his band stopped. He turned his head to see the desperate James, weak and abandoned like so many of the Scarlet Troops on the front lines.

"You've lost your negotiating power," John started, tone rife with indifference. "I would imagine that this brings our meeting to a close." Kincaid and Peters looked to him nervously. This cold demeanor of his was unlike anything they'd ever seen in him.

"I have information," James blurted out, and John turned to face him fully now. "Everything the Scarlet Kingdom has planned, the full measure of their military tactics and societal norms, everything that could help you overthrow them! Just please…help me." There was sadness mingled amidst the fear in his voice, and John couldn't help but draw his sword.

"I suppose," the Director said with a smirk, "but I'll warn you now, if you get in my way I won't be held responsible for any injuries you suffer."

"Deal," James said, and dropped to the floor. In an instant John covered the distance between his side of the tent and where Serafina stood, his weapon hand lifted for a straight stab to her face. The Scourge aggressor ducked just in time, and with his shoulder now free of Serafina's hand, James dove beneath the table. The two remaining members of the Prince's protection detail aimed their rifles at John while Serafina did what she could to hold him in place, but before they could pull their fingers to the trigger, Serenity lodged a bullet in both of their skulls.

The crack of the gunfire in the tent raised alarm with the Scarlet Troopers that walked the grounds outside, and as they made their way to the munitions undoubtedly spread all over the camp, Kincaid pressed a series of controls on his wrist. Bombs went off, and all the tech in the camp was disarmed. Screams and cries of pain echoed from all directions, and it was in that moment that Kincaid knew Levi had done his job well.

"What was that," Zay said over the rattle of his chains as he dispatched an unfortunate Trooper that dared enter the tent.

"A little present we left the Reds a while back," Erik responded with a smile as he tossed a dagger into the heart of another advancing soldier. "I was beginning to think I'd never get a chance to do that."

"You crazy," Zay replied, and couldn't help the smile that lined his jaw.

John ripped through the top of the tent when he jumped into the air with added force from the repulsors in his boots for extra height. Serafina, who at first sought to restrain him, now clung to him for dear life. She still managed to fall to her back, though, when John lodged the blade of his kyoketsu-shoge into the top of the tent post. The impact of Serafina against the hard ground below was horrible enough to shock everyone in the tent, but Serenity was the first to get over it. She punted her adversary in the skull, and just as she turned to face her former Prince, the door to the tent opened.

"Sis! Enemy bombs are going off all over the camp! We have to get what's left of our forces out of here before they—" The loud sound of Ryan's voice in the air alarmed Serenity, who now stood poised to shoot Serafina in the back of the head. Confusion registered on his face, then fear as he took the time to observe the scene. Two Yaiba, a Kabuto, and his beloved older sister stood over a mess of Scarlet Troopers and a Scourge member, ready to cut her life short just like the others. He couldn't help but ask, "What's going on?" despite the fact that it was so very apparent. John, Zayvier, and Erik were frozen in place, all eyes locked onto Serenity's youngest brother.

There was pain in his voice that Serenity hadn't heard since he was a child. It was almost too much for her. She did what she could to steel herself, shook the pistol in her hand at the unconscious intruder to her Scarlet Scourge as if to will it to fire, because she knew that if she didn't, then everything she worked for would fall into this psychopath's lap and turned against her.

"Ryan," was all she could say as her eyes met his. The second she turned to face him he turned his gun on her, the threat behind it more than the others could possibly fathom. "It's not what you—"

"You're protecting James," he cut her off at the pass. He was childish most of the time—very much so, in fact—but his eyes were sniper-sharp. "After the King ordered his execution!"

"Ryan, there's been a misunderstanding," she pleaded, but the infantryman shook his head and flexed his weapon hand.

"Don't," he demanded, the muzzle of the gun still trained on his sister. "How could you do this?" Ryan didn't want to believe that she could've even thought to turn traitor, but he knew that there was no thought involved here. "Did you really…with the Prince?" Serenity looked away, and Ryan made a disgusted noise that brought her narrowed gaze back to him. "Pathetic."

"You don't get to judge me, Ryan," she snapped, "nobody does!"

"Oh yeah? Why's that?" His anger escalated, but he still wondered if she forgot that he pointed a gun to her chest.

"Before you were even able to walk I was training, giving everything I had to the cause of restoring order! *I* was the one who enhanced our father's legacy and set the tone for you and Kyle! I was the one who overcame every barrier set before women in our Kingdom to achieve ultimate success and pave the way for all the ladies of the Scourge, even this filth under my boot. I am *incredible*, and you have the nerve to judge me for siding with the only man that brought me happiness in a storm of blood and war?" Ryan's expression softened, and the disappointment that he felt with himself for being blinded to the pressures his sister must have faced. "I wouldn't expect you to understand what it feels like to be loved in spite of the blood you've shed rather than because of it."

"I—" he couldn't form a response, not to her words, not to the look of unprecedented misery in her face. *When had her eyes grown so sad,* he questioned internally, *and how have I not noticed for so long?* He lowered his gun to the surprise of everyone in the room. "Get out."

"What?" Serenity asked almost as abruptly as Ryan had ordered.

"You escaped, along with the Prince and the enemy leaders. I arrived too late to stop you," he spoke at little more than a whisper. He knew that Kyle and a substantial portion of the intel unit was at the edge of the Yoroi Alliance's outer border. They were in the clear as long as they avoided them. John approached Ryan, an action that was received with the greatest fear. After a moment and a stern look, John passed him by, and Ryan couldn't resist the urge to exhale in relief. Kincaid and Zayvier passed through the tent's entrance after the Director, each with certifiable indifference. Serenity, who now realized what had just happened, approached her little brother. She placed a comforting hand on his shoulder, and to her look of gratefulness he looked away pointedly. She kissed his cheek.

"Thank you, little brother," she said, a tremble of emotion behind her voice for the first time since they'd been children. "I'll never forget this." She wanted to say that she'd be back for him, to tell him that she had other family that she'd never known before but wanted to, but couldn't tell him any more than she had.

"Hurry up and get out," he yelled at her. He tried to sound menacing, tried to hide the anguish and establish distance between them, but he failed and they both knew it. "If you come back—"

"I know," she told him, solemn sorrow in her voice as she acknowledged the horror of the unspoken truth. "All I can say is, it might not work out how you expect. Until then, Ryan." Then she was gone, and the little brother she left behind felt so alone for the first time.

****

December 20th, 2084, 3:19 p.m.,

"You managed to gather all that information in just a couple of days?" Darius was more than just a little surprised, but he was talking to his Uncle Callan. Callan Rouge had, at one point, been in the same black ops unit as his father John, and while he took a slightly less adventurous path after they ascended to the Dragons, he was still an expert at gathering intel.

"That's what happens when you're not running for your life," Callan jabbed, and Darius smiled as if none of the horrors of the last month had happened. "We know that they've been moving from place to place, stoking the flames of violence as they go. Their only source of leverage, though, seems to come from having Johannes in their custody. So now that we have the location, we have to come up with a plan," he explained with a toothy grin.

"Mmm," Darius started nervously, "judging by that look on your face, I'd say you already have one."

"You've guessed correctly, my incredible nephew," Callan answered in a tone that almost made him sound like Darius' Uncle Bill. He knew that nothing good ever came from him acting like that, especially when they were together.

"Well go on," Darius told him, "tell me." Callan paused as he surveyed the already empty room in the makeshift hideout and then smiled wider.

"We're gonna surrender," he said, and left his nephew completely stunned. "Get ready, kid. The plan goes live in three days."

****

December 20th, 2084, 4:00 p.m.,

Prince Nash quaked as he knelt before the Court. The neutral glances of the nobility only highlighted the King's anger as he slammed his fist against the semicircular table before him. The Atlanta troops had been withdrawn, an order that had been issued using Nash's virtual designation and behind King Shane's back. The Jackson base was thrown into chaos because of a similar evacuation order. Now, after news of the Prince's failures with the blockade and his brother's schemes of assassination, the King had had enough.

"If I wasn't so far along in years I'd have you executed along with that cowardly brother of yours," King Shane threatened. Nash trembled before his father all the more, though he resisted the urge to sigh in relief at his apparent immunity.

"Yes, Father," Nash replied with his head down. That was the trick. The easiest way to assuage the King's anger was to simply agree with him, even if what he said bore no need of agreement at all. "Yes" was something that the old man liked to hear, and wisdom dictated that one must say it as often as opportunity presents.

"Pardon the intrusion, Your Grace," said Bryan Piccio from the chamber doors. He was smug, despite the fact that Lyla Ortiz watched him closely from the background. Nobody had heard the doors open or close amid the King's fury at his son. "*I* was the one who delivered the evac orders." This audacious confession sparked intrigue and astonishment in the eyes of the Court, and a brief look of indignation gave way as gratitude washed over Prince Nash's countenance.

"You overstep your bounds," the King snapped, his decrepit finger aimed at Bryan's head.

"Perhaps," Bryan replied, "but seeing as how your drones are up and running again and our enemies becoming bolder, I thought it best to move our forces out of the way and quickly take control after the bombardment." The King of the Reds, along with the rest of his Court, were taken entirely aback by that revelation, something that Bryan took great pleasure in.

"This pleases me," said the King. "You have done outstanding work." Bryan smiled an almost fiendish smile.

"I know," he assured him. "If I may, I've taken the liberty of retooling the entire system so that it can't be hacked as easily from the outside."

"And how have you done that," Lord Blackwell asked, his entire demeanor rife with (admittedly) well-deserved skepticism. Bryan, in total calm, merely glanced in his direction and then returned focus to King Shane.

"I was hoping one of you would ask that." He snapped his fingers, and Lyla Ortiz stepped forward with a small metal box in her hands. "As a near-insurmountable security measure, I've coded these seven to correspond with your biometrics upon the moment you touch them. Once you place them on your fingers, the KDN will go live for military purposes again, and you'll be able to overwhelm the enemy from both the ground and sky." Bryan nodded to Lyla, and she began to dole out the rings to each of the seven members of the Court, including the previously shamed Prince Nash.

"I would think that the King would be more than enough for the system to run," King Shane grumbled. Bryan smiled, though inwardly he wished the old man would just drop dead. It was the nature of the Scarlets to be selfish. They were, after all, derived from a generation of people who were driven solely by self-preservation to the point that they destroyed their own country out of fear. Bryan could tell now exactly what that fear was. It wasn't the notions of communism or liberal thought like the history books had taught him. Here, in the moment of his tech's debut, he found that the root of Scarlet fear was that someone out there with a much bigger brain would steal away their control.

"In the past, that might've been the case, Your Grace, but a solo entry point was the whole reason the system was shut down for so long anyway. The more walls we put up, the harder it'll be for our enemies to take advantage of us again," Bryan explained, though that particular choice of words had proven false in the days of the Dawn King. Nevertheless, the nobles bought into it.

"Very well," Shane said after a moment and rubbed his chin. "We will test your trinkets on Christmas Day. I can think of no finer gift to the rebel scum than wanton destruction." He waved a hand dismissively, though his face was giddy with the possibilities. Bryan bowed his head before the King, but when he turned toward the door, his smile darkened with anticipation. *Neither,* he thought, *can I.*

****

December 21st, 2084, 10:32 a.m.,

Bill and his forces wasted no time upon their arrival to Yorktown. They split up to dispatch the enemy forces there, and once that had been handled they quickly regrouped and established a perimeter. They'd expected the enemy forces that made up the blockade in and around Greensboro to follow them to their destination and storm their shoddy base, but when they didn't, Bill gave the order just a few hours ago, to begin the fortification process.

His soldiers worked diligently under Dross' and Esau's direction, and he awaited Dr. Masamune's arrival at the very docks where he'd taken a bullet to the shoulder just a few months prior. It startled him how little that moment affected him. He could remember a time where he would scream uncontrollably at his injuries and would almost faint at the thought of them, but now Bill surmised that he was too used to life on the battlefield.

Before long, the small container ship with the initials "TSC" branded on the gray metal hull emerged from the distance. Bill wanted to take pleasure in Dr. Masamune's return, especially since it was semi-permanent, but something in the stillness of the air wouldn't let him. It felt too much like the calm darkness before a hurricane, and even his adoptive father's presence wasn't enough to put his mind at ease. He was on guard, and he knew even before the old man could get off the ship that he would likely have something to say about it. He cursed under his breath as he blamed the Scarlets for all this tension. It was always their fault. They never cared about anything other than themselves, and it made Bill mad enough to—"

"That's an awfully intense look," came the amicable call of Kazuya Masamune. His face sobered as he walked off the deck and onto the dock. "You didn't forget to pack extra underwear again, did you? You think you would've learned after that fiasco in 2066 when you had to wash your only pair in the river, stark naked in front of your whole squad. It was the talk of the whole Insurrection for weeks." Bill's cheeks flushed in embarrassment at the memory and quickly waved his hand.

"It's nothing like that," Bill said more assertively than he'd intended. A stern look from Masamune reminded him of whom he stood before, and the new Rairyu, still very much a boy before the elderly scientist, quickly righted his tone. "A lot of things are happening right now. The Reds are suddenly harder to read than before. They're trying to cut off our access to major waterways in the gulf and on the coast so we can't get more supplies for the Reikiken."

"Well it's wasted effort, to say the least," Masamune informed him. Bill's gut twisted into a knot.

"What do you mean?"

"Bryan defected from the Yaiba, right? Somehow the higher-ups of the Chinese Trade Union caught wind of it. They expelled me from the country just as I finished overseeing the loading process of what's now our last shipment of supplies from Gansu." Kazuya's explanation made little sense. Bill thought that relations between the Chinese and the Insurrection were on the positive end of the spectrum.

"How could this happen?" Every implication that resulted from the Doctor's elaboration culminated in Bill's singular question. Despite his indignant tone, he was more worried than he was angry. Masamune let out an exasperated chuckle.

"From what they told me, the Insurrection's lack of unity and senseless squabbling amongst ourselves is adopting too much of an Old American trait. By that alone they moved to terminate our existing agreement." That feeling of unease that Bill experienced before had grown tenfold now, and in greatest haste he ran into Yorktown to find Esau. *We have to alert the troops,* he thought, *time is of the essence.*

****

December 21st, 2084, 12:17 p.m.,

The panic in the Jackson base had grown since the day prior, and Zahara couldn't help but smile. She knew, of course, that the reason for the present scramble was due to the explosion that rocked the foundations of the whole city just an hour before. No doubt Raven and her troops had used their time wisely and gathered enemy munitions as planned. If Zahara guessed correctly, then that meant there would be a pair of Troopers sent to escort her back to the command center. A knock at the door proved her right, and though she wanted to smile wider, she resisted the urge.

Zahara got up from her bed and opened the door. The gentlemen that greeted her seemed stiff, but more out of fear than proper military disposition. Wordlessly they led her back to the command center where Commander Nathaira Connors sat in front of a dozen monitors. Each one showed a different sector outside the second wall and periodically shifted angles for alternative views. Raven Shadid and her troops, however, were shielded from sight.

"You rang," questioned Captain Boyd, an air of displeasure in her voice. "I was in the middle of my daily routine of staring at the ceiling until I drifted off to sleep."

"Now is not the time for your witticisms, Captain Boyd," said the Commander sternly. She arose from her chair and turned to properly face her guest. "It would appear that in my men's haste to get through the second wall, nobody thought to secure the outlying weapons caches." She shot a glance to Sanchez, as if somehow the entire thing was his fault. Zahara suppressed a smirk when his body tightened with fear. "The enemy has attempted to use our own munitions against us. No doubt you felt that quake in the earth?"

"I did, though I wasn't entirely sure what it was," Zahara lied. "That doesn't answer the question as to why you've brought me here, though."

"I've brought you here to make a deal," Nathaira answered with just the right amount of inflection to her voice that made the proposal interesting. Zahara frowned.

"What kind of deal?" Her voice echoed a false wariness that made the corner of the Commander's mouth turn upward slightly. This was the moment that she'd been waiting for, the moment that she could finally turn the tables.

"As it stands, we've been given the order to evacuate the Jackson base, but as long as there are enemies within our walls in possession of our weapons, I'm afraid we are unable to complete the order. If I may be so candid with you, my intention was to leave you here for the Yaiba scum to do with as they pleased."

"And here I was thinking we were almost like sisters," Zahara joked, which brought a disturbingly genteel smile to Nathaira's face.

"I had my sister executed," she said unblinkingly. "In any case, you would probably have considered the same thing were you in my position and I in yours."

Zahara considered it for a moment, her face bound in a thoughtful look, and then said, "Probably." Nathaira smiled even wider, twisted yet sincere, as she recognized Zahara's honesty.

"Sisterhood I cannot promise you," Nathaira continued, and now paced around the Captain like a serpent encircling its prey. "What I can, however, is your freedom along with a testimony of your honorable service to the Crown in warfare." Zahara's eyes narrowed. It sounded too good to be true, and she knew that it was. Not that it mattered. Her job was to remain detached from the Kingdom without giving any indication that she'd traded sides. She was determined to do just that.

“In exchange for what?” Zahara asked, though she already knew exactly what Nathaira wanted. When the Commander didn’t answer, her assumption was confirmed. “You want me to clear a path through the enemy, don’t you?” Nathaira smiled warmly, as though she was relieved that Zahara wasn’t as incompetent as Sanchez always proved to be.

“Indeed, I do,” the Commander confirmed. “According to your service records, you’re a sniper second only to Sergeant Alan Crawford, the adoptive father of Colonel Serenity Crawford of the Scarlet Scourge. You have an outstanding battle record for one as young as you are, having turned the tables more than three times from what appeared to be certain defeat. Even taking into consideration your capture at Johnson City, you’re a better gift than we could’ve asked for under these circumstances.”

“Careful,” Zahara cautioned, “it almost sounds like you’re glad you kept me alive.” Nathaira cleared her throat as her methodical pacing met a subconscious stagger.

“That remains to be seen,” she assured her guest. “I’m prepared to give you command of over half the personnel we have left, as well as your pick of what weapons we have on hand. Provided that you agree to assist us in our escape, that is.”

“Well, when you put it in those terms, how can I refuse?” Zahara allowed a toothy grin to take its place as the two women shook hands. Everything had finally fallen into place.

****

December 21st, 2084, 2:44 p.m.,

The former Prince James sank against the stone wall of the hidden entrance as the Director and his accompaniment passed him by. Serenity sat with him and beckoned the others to wait. They begrudgingly obliged. It’d only been a day since they were forced to flee their former life. An effort to restore peace and balance to the Kingdom and the other Territories proved to be more volatile than he'd ever imagined, and where he once had power and resources at his disposal, now he was a traitor and a fugitive.

He didn't even get a chance to say goodbye to Nash. Not that Nash would've thought him a priority or anything. What was worse was that he'd dragged Serenity into it all. He looked at her, and she looked away. She was mad at him for trying to gift her to an enemy force-turned-reluctant ally. He knew she would be even before he made the proposal, but now he needed her more than ever before and she wouldn't speak to him. Wouldn't look at him.

"Serenity, I—"

"We need a plan of action," Serenity interrupted as she addressed the Yaiba and Kabuto leaders. "The…" she trailed off for a moment as she took time to process that her former allies were now her enemies, including her Scarlet Scourge. She righted herself. "The enemy has plans to bring the Yoroi Alliance back under its heel to thwart your war effort. Since it's the only place on the continent that they can't just bully as they please, I suggest we start there." John's eyebrows raised in shock.

"I assume that you have a plan," he asked warily. It still felt weird to him—to all of them, really—to work together on anything beyond mutual destruction, but times being what they were, it was more important to band together against the seemingly endless stream of Scarlet Kingdom resources and troops than to kill each other off. For now, at least. Serenity smiled a sarcastic smile.

"Oh of course not," she told her former enemy, against whom she still bore a tightly-bound grudge, "I'm just in the habit of spouting off at the mouth."

"Serenity won her success in the Kingdom by being overprepared for every battle," James informed them, though it was wholly unnecessary given the tumultuous history of those present. "She wouldn't have said anything if she didn't have a plan."

"I don't need your validation, James," Serenity snapped. John, Zayvier and Erik exchanged a look. Zayvier pursed his lips and widened his eyes in a look that voiced his disinclination to get involved. Erik merely smiled at the sudden burst of anger and relished in the awkwardness of the moment. John's face remained unchanged. "But," she said with an instant change of tone and refocus on the former Rairyu, "before everything I worked for turned to ash, I had Leyva and Waldheim infiltrate the Anti-Rebel base within the Alliance."

"Why not just call them loyalists," Erik asked. John shot him a look, and Kincaid raised his hands placatively.

"It's what they've chosen to call themselves, sadly," Serenity answered. "The conflict between the Pro- and Anti-Rebellion factions has escalated to a miniature civil war, and right now the Red loyalist group has the high ground."

"We know," Zay told her. He had no patience for redundancy of information, and had less patience for a Scarlet—even a former one—even pretending to call the shots.

"Did you know that the reason they seem so untouchable is that they have your friend Johannes in captivity?" Serenity's question stunned the Earth Dragon to silence. "What's more, they claim to have killed your little dragonling," she said with a nod to John. His eyes enlarged as his brow furrowed, and for a moment he looked as terrifying as a king in anger. "When one of the Pro-Rebels killed one of the loyalist leaders, it only helped the Anti-Rebels turn public opinion against them."

John's fingers twitched, and his comrades flinched. None of them had seen what had happened on the day of the Johnson City raid, but they all knew. They could feel his murderous intent stiffen the air, and it caught nobody by surprise when he asked, "Where are they?"

"I can't tell you that," Serenity told him sternly. "We all know what kind of fighters the Yoroi are, and while they'll be vulnerable over time, we can't just barge in through the front door and expect everything to turn out fine. Not to mention, you'll probably be more of a liability than a help since you're clearly not in control of your emotions right now." John didn't know what to make of her comment. On one hand, he wasn't so used to anyone besides Aaliyah reading him, and nobody told him what to do aside from the late Emiko Ishikawa. On the other hand, there was a gentleness to her voice that radiated understanding. It almost soothed him, and probably would have had she not been possibly his greatest enemy until the day prior. "We'll take some time before we make our move. Hopefully you'll calm down by then and we can move forward with the plan."

"I—" John was the one who thought to protest this time. But she was right. He wouldn't do anything but fall prey to one of those infamous Yoroi traps, and while he figured he could probably kill a few enemies on the way to his demise, a single thought of Aaliyah's face warped by grief slapped him back to reality. "I suppose we've no choice. We'll wait. But in the meantime, you should enlighten us to your plan."

"Well, then," Serenity spoke with awkward surprise. She dusted off the legs of her battle suit and shifted to lean against the nearby wall. "To begin with, I have two…"

Chapter Twenty-Nine

December 23rd, 2084, 12:00 p.m.,

"Don't move!" The alarmed tenor ripped through the air, and soon every available Anti-Rebel gun in Cluster C turned on the intruders. They numbered fifteen, and of the lot only one of them stood out as truly terrible. They were androgynous, with short black hair, soft features, and golden eyes that seemed to glow with the dim lanterns that illuminated the path. Tony Landry, the one who had murdered Councilor Francis for all to see, now stood before all those that wanted them dead.

"We're here to surrender," called the tall black-haired man to Tony's right. His aggressive tone and muscular body poised to attack at any moment said otherwise. A number of the enemy guards, clad in that awful charcoal and veritably indistinguishable from one another, moved in while the loud one from before spoke into his wrist-comm.

"Ma'am," said the guard, eyes locked with the haunting orbs in Tony's head, "we have a situation…"

****

December 23rd, 2084, 12:00 p.m.,

Callan watched with a calculated smile from against the western side of the building. This hideout was easier to get into than the last. It was one of the fancier mansions of the Yoroi Alliance, and, while heavily guarded, was not without its cracks in the wall. Tony, Bobbi, and Leroy had been the perfect distraction. Their near constant battles against the Anti-Rebels in the last month or so had earned them a sense of notoriety, something that Callan could exploit with masterful skill.

He signed three tactical signals, and his group immediately dispersed. The saboteurs, Tom Freeman and Lex Ford, used the ShadowStalker cloaking tech to plant detonators around the outer perimeter without detection. Demolitions was the only job that Lex wanted to do on this mission, so Callan obliged. Meanwhile, the Water Dragon infiltrated the mansion via a nearby window. His sharp featured face, with piercingly bright blue eyes offset perfectly by his dark brown hair, proved as impervious to the mundane gray color of the Anti-Rebel garb as the others that wore it.

"I'm in," he whispered into his comms unit. "Activating body cam and beginning area sweep."

"Roger that," Darius said from a nearby building just outside the estate's border. "Ready to move on your signal." He frowned when Callan chuckled into the comms. It was a reminder that he was not to move at all, and was only there to be the figurehead that would hopefully undo the damage of the conflict. He hated feeling like such an afterthought.

"So," Tony asked loudly, with their comms active, "what will you do with us now that we're here?" The question was for Callan and Darius as much as it was for the Anti-Rebels that cuffed their patrol and stripped them of their weapons. They didn't know Callan, and only tried to trust him because they knew it's what Darius wanted. How could they refuse him after they stabbed him? And even now, amid the guilt, Tony felt something…more for him. He was kind, but determined. Sharp, but easygoing. Above all else, he proved to be more reliable than they thought he would be, and they felt as if they owed it to him to try to be as reliable in return.

"Just go with it for now," Darius told them. They proceeded wordlessly as the guards led them into the building, and patiently awaited their next steps.

****

December 23rd, 2084, 12:10 p.m.,

Serenity sat perfectly calm with the slightest hint of a smile at the edges of her mouth as Katarina Estevez squirmed uncomfortably in her seat. James paced the room to eyed her décor choices and the trinkets that adorned the shelves where books might go in an intelligent person's home. He regarded them with a special kind of agitated dismissal. Katarina had been silent since she let them in, and now, under the watchful eyes of the legendary Scourge leader, she couldn't quite find the words to say.

"I'm going to assume," Serenity started, the humor in her voice a further cause for concern, "that you would like to know why we're here."

"Yes, ma'am," said Estevez a bit too quickly. Serenity raised an eyebrow, and Katarina righted herself. "I mean, if it would please you to enlighten me." James, who looked out the window at the rocky space above Cluster C, smiled in weak amusement.

"Your incompetence, to be blunt," the Prince explained bluntly, which drew the unmistakable ire of the Anti-Rebel leader.

"Beg pardon, Your Highness," she asked with an edge to her voice that made Serenity's eyes narrow with more than just a little murderous intent. Indeed, she showed no sign that she was still furious with him.

"Do you really want me to rehash what Leyva and Waldheim told us about you?" It hurt her even to say those names. It felt wrong to invoke the station that she sacrificed for her lover, and appeal to the names of subordinates that no longer answered to her. But they needed this to go well, so that the favor of the Insurrection would be secured. "You've started a battle you had no ability to end. Do you even know how many people here were trained to use the Hanzo Gear that was sent over by the Yaiba Insurrection?"

"Fifteen," Estevez answered confidently, much to the irritation of the Colonel and the Prince. She was so desperate for their praise, for their approval. Serenity couldn't help but think it was shameful. Disgusting.

"And how many Pro-Rebels did you take into custody when they arrived at your doorstep?" It was the Prince that asked the question now, his tone bored with the whole ordeal, as if Ms. Estevez had missed something of great importance right in front of her face. She paused for a moment before realization gradually took her.

"Fifteen…" Katarina muttered.

"Exactly. In my experience, an enemy force that's taken few or no casualties wouldn't show up to surrender like this unless they felt they had the upper hand. Now think for a moment," Serenity bade her coldly, her voice rife with condescension. "What do you have here that would interest your enemies?"

It didn't take Katarina long to figure out the only target they would come for. "Thornhill," she uttered stiffly. Her heartbeat was out of control, and in that instant she feared for her life.

"Take us to him immediately," Prince James ordered with more calm than she had ever heard anyone speak. "You'll release him to my custody."

****

December 23rd, 2084, 12:27 p.m.,

It didn't take long for Callan to catch up with the detail that held his comrades captive. The guards still tightly gripped the gear they'd stripped from the fresh prisoners, which prompted the covert Dragon to change his course. He passed them in the hall, and with a nod, gave them the signal. Tony, Bobbi and Leroy exchanged looks with the subtlest of smiles. The guards that marched them led their patrol to a spacious but stripped room with low-quality furnishings and iron bars where the door should've been.

"In," demanded their leader as he activated a switch that raised the bars. The Pro-Rebellion operatives entered without question, which inspired suspicion from their captors. Once the last of the rebellion proponents crossed the threshold of the makeshift prison, the bars slammed back down with a heavy metallic clang. Tony stepped forward, which caught the attention of the guards.

They stared at them for a moment, but then Tony said, "Code 1642 engage." Before the guards could react, Shock Pads came alive and ran a strong enough electric current through them that the man nearest the door accidentally activated the switch again as he fell to the ground. "Well, that was easy. Come on, we gotta get moving." They took up their gear, and happily put it to good use as more guards revealed themselves.

****

December 23rd, 2084, 12:43 p.m.,

Serenity and James emerged from the room with Johannes in tow. He was reluctant to trust Red nobility and the leader of the Scarlet Scourge, but his treatment with the Scarlets was far less abusive than with their loyalists. It was when they turned from the door that they spotted him. He stood tall above a number of bodies that writhed on the floor. He hadn't needed his Hanzo Gear to deal with them, and the realization filled Johannes with greater admiration, and the others with a greater sense of dread. Johannes and the former Reds could only see his back, but they wondered if he simply admired his work, or if he contemplated their demise to make his escape easier.

“Callan,” Johannes said aloud, which garnered the attention of the Suiryu. Serenity’s heart pumped hard as she wrestled with a range of emotions that she was ill-prepared to handle. James placed a hand back as if to guard Johannes. Callen turned, and when his eyes shifted between those of the people who had held him captive only a few months prior, his typically unflappable face grew grave with animosity.

“Now what are you doing here,” he asked, but offered no opportunity for them to answer. He pulled a knife from a sheath at its back and lunged forward just as Serenity sprinted to meet him. She blocked his initial slash with the muzzle of her freshly drawn pistol and kicked him in the gut. Callan rolled backwards and only narrowly dodged the two shots she fired. Estevez emerged from Johannes’ room, shocked to see a man in the charcoal uniform of her soldiers engaged with the leader of the Scourge.

“Don’t just stand there, get out of here!” Serenity’s order took a moment to register, but James and Katarina took Johannes and ran.

“Tony,” Callan called through the comms unit, “they’re heading down the south corridor. Head them off before they can escape and don’t kill anyone! We need to take them alive.”

“Understood,” came the reply. Callan stood for a moment, frozen by the shaft of Serenity’s pistol. His mind searched a myriad of possibilities as to how he could get around it, how he could close the distance, how he could take it from her, and how he could end her once and for all. Then she lowered the gun and let out an exasperated sigh.

“I’m not surprised to see you here,” Serenity started, “but it complicates things a little.” Callan threw his knife at her head, but she dodged it just before she lost her eye. They closed in on each other and traded blows. Callan punched, but the former Scourge leader brushed his fist off to the side and caught him in the gut with a nasty knee. He, in turn, caught the back of her neck as he stumbled back and dragged her to the ground. She flipped over, her lungs emptied of air from the impact. Callan mounted her, fists raised to beat her face in, but he didn't get the chance. She kicked him in the back of his head and when he fell forward, she slid out from under him. She applied a stiff chokehold. "I'm not your enemy," she told him, deeply annoyed.

"As if I'd believe that," he coughed, and she wrenched her arms hard against his neck. He fell back against her, and she wrapped her legs around his waist for greater control.

"I'm not! If I guessed right, I'm here to save Mr. Thornhill, same as you." His eyes went wide, though whether from understanding or aggravation Serenity couldn't tell. "Look, I'm gonna let you go, and when I do, we're gonna talk like civilized adults. Understand?" Callan nodded, and when she kicked him away from her he gasped for air with his hands around his throat.

****

December 23rd, 2084, 1:02 p.m.,

James and Katarina stared down the hall at the mob of rebels at the other end. Bobbi was the one who stepped forward, and James stepped back to shield Johannes.

"Um, hi," Bobbi said in her usual thoughtful tone. It was the first time she'd sounded like herself in what seemed like so long. She looked to her ear. A transmission came through to her comms, apparently. "Understood." Bobbi turned her attention back to the three in front of her. "Um, yeah. I'm gonna need Johannes Thornhill to come with me."

Katarina placed her hands on her hips, an incredulous expression plastered on her face as she attempted to restore the regality that she'd always believed she'd had. "Under whose authority?"

"Mine," James said from behind her. The sudden utterance from her presumed ally startled her, but when she turned to look at him, all she could see was the dark mouth of a handgun in her face. "Go on, Johannes. They'll get you to safety." Johannes blinked, stunned that his one-time kidnappers actually came to save him, but then he moved along the wall furthest from Katarina and hurried to his friends.

"Guards!" Estevez shouted so loudly that James thought his eardrums would burst. Nobody came. She grew frantic, terrified by the fact that she was surrounded by enemies with none to save her. "Guards!"

"Lady, we either knocked them out or killed 'em," Leroy called to her. He was beyond annoyed at the shrill sound of her voice, and the fact that she didn't get the hint the first time she went unanswered didn't help. "Please, shut up." It was more a demand than a request.

"What is the meaning of this," Estevez snarled at James, who let his amusement show as a response.

"Turns out that daddy doesn't love me," he shrugged. "I'm helping the Yaiba take him down as my revenge play." Tony, Leroy and Bobbi, along with several others from the Pro-Rebellion group, rolled their eyes at him. Of course, he would make light of an entire war. Of course, he would undermine the suffering brought on by his family and reduce it to the pettiness of a father and son duo with more money and influence than they deserved. Such was the nature of the privileged.

"You're a…" Estevez swallowed hard in utter disbelief at the hard reality thrust in her face. "You're a traitor?" It was then that she realized that she'd been tricked into showing her enemies where her hostage was held. She'd practically gift-wrapped him for them, and sacrificed her winning hand to maintain favor with foreign officials who had lost all their influence. She'd never felt like such a fool.

"*E você está preso,*" came the raspy voice of Ambassador Ezequiel Vargas as he stepped through the crowded hallway "*minha querida*". The way his wood-brown dress shoes clicked against the white-tiled floor amplified the despair she felt when she registered his Portuguese: *And you are under arrest, my dear*. "You have incited violence in our home, sacrificed the lives of our people for your own selfish gain." His anger grew as he spoke the injustices perpetrated and watched with unsympathetic eyes as she fell to her knees. "You have conspired to kill Alliance governing officials, and jeopardized our entire way of life, our *safety*, Katarina! You will be dealt with according to your crimes."

"I haven't lost yet," Katarina growled. She lifted her wrist-comm to her mouth. "All units in Cluster C, converge on the mansion from all sides. Nobody escapes! Kill everything that moves!"

"Yes ma'am!" the sheer number of voices that replied almost knocked out the frequency. Katarina laughed maniacally, as if her victory was secured. She glowered at Vargas, who stood so sure of himself in the emerald suit that matched his eyes, and waited for his fear to surface. Then, a series of explosions roared in the distance that stunned her to silence.

"What's that sound," James asked, and Vargas smiled. The perimeter bombs had been triggered, and the strength of Katarina's forces dropped by the second.

"The sound of Katarina losing," he replied, eyes locked with hers as she exploded with indignant rage. "Take her." Leroy stepped forward and applied the cuffs, and Katarina was helpless to do more than listen to her ambitions get blown to smithereens.

****

December 24th, 2084, 10:30 a.m.,

The rumble of the tripped explosives had long ceased, and the remaining leaders of the Anti-Rebels had gone into hiding. Every civilian in the Alliance had seen Katarina's defeat. The visors of the Hanzo Gear broadcasted the entire mission to every working monitor in the Yoroi territory, courtesy of the Kabuto agents and their tech wizardry. Johannes, who was covered in bruises and torn clothing, was shown to all as well. The public didn't take kindly to the prolonged abuse of one of their most beloved public figures.

Johannes spoke to the people of the horrors he faced, how he was locked away and drugged by Councilor Francis, beaten into servitude by Katarina and her guards, used as bait for the trap that killed his beloved Ina. Vargas and Bobbi, who translated his sentiments into Portuguese and Spanish respectively, consoled him when his voice broke and he along with it. He took a moment, then continued his address to the citizens.

"The people who helped me were motivated to do so out of what was best for us all," Johannes spoke evenly now, more than prepared to do what came next. He caught sight of Director Hamlin in the crowd, a pained look on his face as he stood among the people and listened. Johannes wondered how long he'd been in the territory, but the anguish in his eyes told the envoy that the lie of Darius' death had made its way to his ears. "These brave men, women, and others risked everything for our way of life. Where the Anti-Rebels sought our bondage to Kingdom Scarlet, our friends here have secured our freedom. Where our enemies have lied to our faces, our rescuers risked everything to expose every falsehood…except one."

Vargas and Bobbi smiled at the insinuation, and stepped aside so as not to hog the spotlight. Johannes cleared his throat as he took in the uniqueness of the moment. "Exactly one month ago, you were all led to believe that the Anti-Rebels had murdered the envoy from the Yaiba Insurrection, and that without his knowledge of the Hanzo Gear there was no hope in breaking free of the

Kingdom's hold. Well…" Johannes trailed off, and with a wide gesture at the curtain behind him he revealed a rather tall but thin figure in a violet shirt shrouded in a black hooded cloak and armed to the teeth with chains and sword. He stepped forward, and as the crowd murmured their unease, the Director among civilians shed a tear as a relieved smile came over his face. "I can assure you that he is very much alive."

"Uh…" the sensation of public speech was new to Darius, but he decided that he would not falter. He took a deep breath, then continued, "I was sent here by former Insurrection Director Emiko Ishikawa to foster trust between our homes through the sharing of our tactics and the rescue of your representative. I know that a lot of you must've regarded my presence here as a threat to a peace you've fought to maintain. I get it. Outsiders can seldom be trusted. But here Johannes stands, safer than he's been since the Midland outpost, and not because of a lone Insurrectionist sent to cover up the mistakes of his superiors. Johannes stands free because a group of Yoroi trusted the training I offered, if not me directly. He's free because of the espionage skills of the Kabuto Sanctuary, who worked hand in hand with me to boost the effectiveness of all my strategies. The Clusters are safe again, not because of any one of us, but because all of us in some part came together to stand against the oppression of the Kingdom and those that sympathize with them."

Darius spoke with more fervor, and the people in the crowd, already moved to emotionality from Johannes' testimony, cheered him on. Callan, who stood in the background and watched the whole thing, smiled at his nephew with a twinkle in his icy blue eyes. "If the proposed alliance worried you, in any great or small measure," Darius continued, "if for a second you thought your freedom would be taken from you, or that the Reds would punish you for spitting out the bit in your mouth, then I ask you to look at what was accomplished with only a few of us working together. Thank you."

The minute he finished his speech, he turned from the crowd to a massive pop of cheers from all over. His team, his friends, and his uncle all offered him their warmest expressions, but then the rattle of chains from the crowd caught everyone by surprise. A figure in the same attire as Darius had appeared on the platform in an instant. The cheers instantly gave way to a sea of shocked gasped and murmurs. Darius turned, and at the sight of the man his eyes welled with tears. John took a step forward, then paused to get a better look at his son. Darius ran to him and wrapped his arms around his father. John returned the gesture, and for a moment the world melted away as relief took hold.

For the first time since his arrival, Darius felt truly safe again. His fingers curled against the cloth of John's Hanzo Gear, and for a moment the Director was reminded of the little boy that Darius had been once upon a time. He pulled away for a moment, placed his hands on his son's shoulders, and with the widest smile told him, "I'm so proud of you, my boy."

Darius cried, and John held him tight as he led him off the stage.

****

December 24th, 11:13 a.m.,

"I need more ammo," Zahara roared to whomever could hear her. The Scarlet Troopers around her scrambled to meet her demands, all while they shot volley after volley at the Shadows below in the hope that another convoy could make their escape. "Commander, with all due respect, you really shouldn't be up here for this."

"Nonsense," Nathaira called back as Zahara reloaded and fired more rounds into the city below. "I will see this through to the end and *then* take my leave, Captain Boyd." Zahara rolled her eyes, grabbed a nearby rifle and tossed it to Commander Connors.

"If you're gonna be up here, then make yourself useful and try to keep the enemy away from our ground Troopers." Nathaira was not accustomed to taking orders at her base, but since Prince Nash's evacuation order deigned that the base was no longer hers to command, she excused the impropriety.

Zahara fired shots at the Shadows, or at least pretended to. She nailed a few of them in their cloaks to knock them back, but she knew it wasn't enough to kill them from this distance. The Scarlet Troopers on the other hand…well, more than once they'd gotten in her way, and more than once she'd pretended to lose her temper about it.

"Anybody got eyes on the enemy leader," someone asked through the Red comm channel. A series of negatives came through amid the screams of the freshly killed.

"Well find her," Zahara ordered through a hiss of impatience that sent a tingle down Nathaira's spine. "She's more dangerous than all the rest combined. The sooner we take her down, the sooner we can proceed with a full-scale evac to the capitol." It did puzzle her, though, how Raven had managed to disappear into the chaos of the battle. The Light Dragon was so good at it that for a moment, Zahara had to wonder if she'd abandoned the plan and her men along with it. Then, an explosion rocked the wall from the opposite side. "What was that?"

"Bombs detonated off the eastern wall! Two mass transports and three tanks were destroyed," called a hysterical Trooper from the other end. Zahara bit her lower lip, and Nathaira looked at her with a reasonable degree of worry, an emotion that the Captain might've assumed to have been entirely alien to her. Zahara took a moment to consider Raven's genius. *So that's what you were up to yesterday when the shields were down,* she thought. She worked hard to suppress the smile that bubbled up inside of her.

"Are there any more traps?" Zahara finally called back as she shot at another of the Violet Shadows that glided a little too close to the gate. They did better this time than they had on entry. The way they employed their kyoketsu-shoge and repulsor boots to change directions on a dime made it truly difficult to hurt them, and the fact that there was so much cover from the broken buildings only assisted them in their fight. The ground Troopers, however, were still woefully incompetent enough to fall for their enemy's every trap, and were occasionally picked off by more guns than just the one Zahara put to use at the moment.

"Can't confirm, Captain," said the Trooper. The Captain huffed in exasperation and turned to Nathaira.

"The enemy is likely trying to get us to split our forces. We can either send some of our remaining Troopers to investigate the eastern wall for traps, or we could focus our efforts on—" There, in the distance, Raven Shadid ran across the metal rooftop of a run-down warehouse. "All Troopers fall back and concentrate fire on at the top of—" as soon as Zahara issued the order, Raven dove through the air and rocketed behind their formation. She landed gracefully, and split the backs of three Scarlet Troopers with a swift revolving slash from her Reikiken. Her movements, just as erratic as ever, got the better of so many of the Scarlet Troopers that it didn't make any sense to keep barking orders. Zahara aimed her rifle carefully, then fired on Raven to no discernable effect. "Last chance, Commander," she said without looking at Nathaira. "You might want to head to the nearest transport and get out of dodge while you can."

Nathaira failed to respond. She was captivated by the elegance of the enemy leader's brutality, enamored by the screams of her fallen subordinates to the point that she almost forgot to shoot. The mad array of slashes and stabs that seemingly came out of nowhere proved to be the most excitement that Nathaira had ever experienced. She fired round after round, and was even more impressed when the enemy dodged, endured or deflected each one.

Raven was determined to reach the wall despite the hail of bullets. She left her troops to contend with the Scarlets on the ground while she went straight for the head of the snake. A grenade detonated not far from her position and knocked her back a few feet. She rolled along the ground, but with the shock-absorbent nature of her cloak and combat gear she took to her feet in a matter of minutes. Bullets continued to rain down from the wall in thunderous waves, and when she stood back up she was swarmed by a fresh Scarlet patrol.

"I don't have time for this," Raven grumbled. She lunged for the nearest enemy soldier and ran him through, then swung her Reikiken through his side and bisected the troop that stood a little too close to their position. She shot the diamond-shaped titanium blade of her kyoketsu-shoge across the circle and into the forehead of another victim as she cut vertically through another enemy that rushed to meet her. Yet fired a single shot, but that shot was deflected by her blade. She spun with the momentum, the kyoketsu-shoge still extended, and reversed the grip of her aura sword in her lifted hand as the heads of several other enemies rolled down to the ground. When Raven's body came to a stop, the firesword at her command had already burned a hole through her last victim, and before long she continued her sprint for the wall.

None on the ground even dared oppose her now, but those on the wall persisted in their volley of bullets. Raven, however, was unfazed. She ran as fast as she could manage, then jumped with her kyoketsu-shoge extended forward. Once the titanium blades lodged into the concrete wall, the Light Dragon activated her repulsors and disappeared from the enemy's line of sight in an instant.

"She's on the wall," Zahara shouted. She knew how fast the Hanzo Gear could take a person. It wouldn't take Raven too much longer to reach their position. The others that lined the top of the structure must have realized the same thing, because they already started to scramble for the transports on the inside.

"Cowards," Nathaira yelled after them, but the sudden escalation of heat made her realize that they had been right to flee. She dropped the rifle in her hands as the wily Dragon gripped her arm hard.

"Commander!" The word escaped Zahara's lips before she knew to stop them as she watched the Reikiken flash in front of Nathaira's face. Raven held it only a few inches from her hostage, and stared with a smile back at her opponent.

"You thought you could get away," Raven said, her tone more vicious than Zahara ever thought possible for her. It was enough to make her wonder if Raven forgot that this was all just an elaborate ruse.

"I *did* get away," Zahara corrected. She dropped the rifle and pulled the pistol from her hip. Raven was impressed that the Scarlet pretender had trained it on her forehead before the rifle hit the ground. "And I'm not going back."

"Drop it," Raven demanded through clenched teeth, "or I burn out your Commander's eyes."

"As if I'd let you," Commander Connors interrupted. Both Dragon and deceiver were surprised by this, even more surprised by the hidden knife that only just made itself known to Raven's belly. The Kiryu screamed as she pushed Nathaira forward towards Zahara, who saw the opportunity and lodged a bullet in the back of the Commander's head.

"Oh no," Zahara exclaimed frantically as Karina Velazquez and Drew McDowell arrived at the top of the wall. "No, no, no, no, no, no, no, no! Raven!" The display of emotion caught the two students off-guard.

"You're really…" Raven started, but the pain in her gut made her inhale sharply. She continued. "You're really something else."

"We need to get a medic over here now," Zahara all but yelled at her students, which made them take a step back as they watched their teacher grasp the fallen Dragon by the hand. Every breath that Raven took was shallow, but despite that, the blood pulsed through her fingers. Zahara, for the first time, felt uneasy by the sight of it.

"Sensei, what happened," Drew McDowell, the more collected of her present students asked, though it took him little time to assess the situation for himself. The body of the enemy Commander was not that far away from the bleeding Light Dragon. The blood flowed slowly towards the edge of the wall. "Sensei," Drew started again, softer this time, "the medics are all the way back at the entrance to the middle gate. They wouldn't make it in time." He watched her brow furrow in frustration and helplessness, but he wasn't sure what he could say that would make her feel better. The others in what remained of their platoon finished off the stragglers while the last of the enemy transports rolled out. Some of the traps that the Shadows had planted the day prior.

"It's alright," Raven assured her. "We all have to die sometime."

"Master Shadid," Karina spoke through tears in her eyes, "please don't talk like that. You're gonna be—"

"Don't you dare treat me like a child," Raven ordered. "The enemy knew where to stab me to cause internal bleeding." She paused to catch her breath, then continued. "I'm not gonna last for too much longer." She turned her focus back to Zahara, who sat shocked with her hands wrapped around Raven's. "Have them report back to John. Make sure he knows what happened. You won't stay a free woman otherwise and they can't afford to lose you."

Zahara met the eyes of her two students, and with a nod they made the call through their comms. She looked at Raven again, who only smiled as she squeezed Zahara's hand. "I don't know what to do," she said. A tear fell from the Light Dragon's eye.

"Can you…stay with me?" It was getting harder for Raven to talk, but the fear in her voice was clear enough.

"Yeah," Zahara replied, "I'll stay."

Wordlessly she knelt beside her, until the lights of the Dragon had gone out.

Chapter Thirty

December 25th, 2084, 5:45 a.m.,

The silver tiles and sterile white walls of the research facility's conference room glowed intensely. The various monitors switched on, and immediately brought up the live video feeds of a number of different locales. The room itself had been freshly cleaned only an hour prior.

Lyla Ortiz watched her father pace about the room for the umpteenth time. He was excited, almost to a manic degree, as he checked each monitor, tweaked the settings on his neural transmission band, and finally paced in eager anticipation for the arrival of his esteemed guests. She knew that he'd done everything that he could to get the KDN back up and running, but found that she questioned if it was really that big a deal.

The way she saw it, all Bryan had to do was the bare minimum, like what she had done with the assassin that tried to take out the King. He'd be rewarded with status and power beyond his wildest dreams.

She knew her father better than that, though. He was a man of principle, one who had no interest in clout. So what was he up to? Something didn't feel right about this, but with no other option on the table, she was forced to sit back and watch.

****

December 25th, 2084, 7:00 a.m.,

"Good morning, everyone," Bryan Piccio greeted with a smile. None of the nobles of the King's Court greeted him. Baron Arthur Stalks stared down his caramel-colored nose at him. Lord Phineas Blackwell twisted the thin fleshy flaps that passed as his lips with disgust. Bryan secretly supposed that if he'd been so pale and decrepit, he might've been just as hateful. Marquis Harold West sat perfectly still, his beady blue eyes perfectly fixed on Bryan with an undertone of harsh judgment. Viscount Leyva and Countess McBride were both excited, as neither typically got to attend the spectacular technological reveals that this particular conference room was known for.

"Can we just get on with this, please," Prince Nash asked, as if there was some more pressing matter for him to attend to. After the severe tongue-lashing he'd received days ago from his father, Bryan could only assume that it ran something along the lines of restoring his reputation. Not that he'd ever had much of one from where Bryan stood. "It's not like we've anything new to see here, anyway."

"I assure you," Bryan spoke again with a delighted smile plastered to his face, "that the lady and gentlemen of the Court will be most pleased with the morning's events." Bryan clasped his hands together as his eyes brightened and locked with those piercing grays of the perpetually disgruntled King.

"We had better be," grumbled King Shane, no doubt angry that he'd been dragged out of bed for this. "For your sakes." In that moment where both he and his daughter were threatened by the King, Bryan saw the ghostly glimmer of Jaden in the corner. He smiled wider.

"You will notice," he started with the dramatic flair of an expert showman, "that behind me are six screens, each with a different location in view. These locations, Atlanta, the Roan Mountain, Johnson City, the Grand Canyon, the Jackson Base, and Yorktown…" he paced the room and pointed to each monitor, "are all either under attack or occupied by the Yaiba Insurrection."

"We know," Marquis West interrupted with folded arms and rolling eyes. "Nice to see that you've made expert use of the all-system access you've been granted." Jaden's ghostly form, now full of bullets and covered with blood, ran in front of the Marquis. Bryan laughed.

"I'm glad you're able to see it," he replied. Lyla's ears perked up at the subtle tinge of venom in her father's voice as he said it, but fortunately the nobles chose to overlook it. "But that's not the only spectacle I've got in store for you today. If you would all take out the rings I gave you and put them on your fingers..." The nobles of the Court did as they were asked, and while Bryan continued on in his theatrical antics, it increasingly disturbed the guests. He walked over to the table on the far left of the monitors and applied the neural transmission band. "Alright, the system is coming online...now."

"Wonderful," breathed Nash as he got up from his seat. He was more than just a little annoyed with all of this. "Now if that will be all—"

"Ah, but don't you want to stay for the test run?" Bryan's hypnotic blue eyes pierced through Nash's dismissive attitude and chilled the blood in his veins. He sat back down, which seemed to please Bryan.

"Test run," Countess McBride asked with a look of concern about her plump face. Bryan's eyes lit with wonder as Jaden's ghost whispered profanities in her ear.

"I'm glad you asked! There's a reason I picked these locations to show you, and it isn't for their visible appeal," he joked, to the continued discomfort of the nobles and his daughter. Lyla had never seen him act like this before, and that feeling of trouble that she'd had earlier now doubled. "Now before, the drones on the KDN would've caused some collateral damage, sure, but they weren't particularly effective at putting a stop to the Insurrection's goals. Until now. While I had access to your systems, I made some alterations to the drones to make them sleeker, more precise. Deadlier, you might say."

"Your responsibility," Lord Blackwell started as coldly as the corpse Bryan knew he pretended to be when nobody else was around, "was to get the system back online."

"True," Bryan admitted with a sheepishly boyish charm, "but then I thought, 'how can I prove to you that I can be trusted? How do I make the most out of this opportunity?' That's when I thought of it."

"Thought of what," King Shane grumbled. Bryan's crazed smile grew wider.

"Please, pick a location, Your Grace," the mad rabbit almost sang. The neural transmission band that he'd integrated with the smart tech all around him picked up on his thoughts. The cameras at every corner of the conference room zoomed in on the King, and stored all sights and sounds to a special pocket of the network that Bryan had made for his personal use at a later time.

"There," the King answered, steeled as always in his every expression, "Yorktown. I'm interested to see if you can right the mistakes of my incompetent eldest son."

"Ah, an excellent choice!" Bryan said as he watched Nash's expression sour. He let out a devilish chuckle. "Not without its emotional value, either, it seems. As you wish, sir! Everyone, if you would be so kind as to turn your attention to the second middle screen…"

****

December 25th, 2084, 7:20 a.m.,

"Any news?" Vanessa Duncan asked the question with so much worry that it triggered Bill's most comforting smile.

"Nothing yet," he told her. "You don't have to worry, you know. We haven't encountered a Red patrol in days."

“That’s exactly why you should be worried,” Dre Hamlin growled from the holo-projection. “Back in my time, if the ground troops pulled out, an air raid was right around the corner.”

“Not likely with Kingdom drones grounded indefinitely,” Bill grumbled under his breath. It amazed Dre how he could still be such a child sometimes. Before the elder could hazard a response, a series of raucous explosions rattled the ground at the edge of town. The hum of the drones’ electrical engines permeated the morning air, and only barely managed to overshadow the screams of Bill’s men. He looked between the blue projections of his uncle and his friend, and before they could tell him anything about the situation, Bill rushed from the command center out onto the street.

His troops scrambled as the drones dropped a stream of bombs atop the city. Fire and ice worked in tandem to destroy Yorktown. Those foolish Shadows that tried to destroy the oncoming bombs were met with sprays of liquid nitrogen and fiery explosions. Those that ran couldn’t run fast enough.

Bill watched the carnage, could feel the blood drain from his face, but the sight of old Dr. Masamune working to get the others to safety brought him back to reality. The bombs were getting closer to Masamune, so Bill bolted through the crowd of oncoming allies, blasted into the air with his repulsors and frantically grappled from building to building.

Another payload dropped, closer still to the only man that Bill knew to be his father. Tears welled up in his eyes as it became clear that he wouldn’t make it in time. He pushed himself harder, flew through the city faster, just to increase the chance that Kazuya would survive. *I can’t let him die,* Bill thought over and over again. It wasn’t a matter of strategy, it wasn’t because of his technological contributions. It was because of a childish need to have his dad there.

Masamune looked up in time enough to see Bill draw close. For a moment, it looked as if Bill would succeed, and Kazuya smiled a warm, proud smile. Just as Bill began his descent just a few yards away, a bomb fell upon the Doctor.

"No!" Bill yelled it when everything went bright. The blast knocked him back through the air in a spiral, and every moment he'd shared with Masamune burst to the forefront of his mind. *Seven years*, he thought, *wasted...* The tears fell from his eyes. He was blasted through a sturdy brick wall. The world around him went cold and black.

****

December 25th, 2084, 7:40 a.m.,

The camera of a low-flying drone displayed the image of Bill's motionless body on the floor of an abandoned church. Bryan's heart sank for a moment when he saw his old friend, but hardened when he remembered the indifference with which his "friends" disregarded the death of his son. Jaden's ghost stood beside him now, a sweet smile of approval engraved on his face, and Bryan took it in stride as the ultimate validation.

The room had been silent for the last five minutes as the nobles processed what had just happened. Whatever their opinions had been before the show began, there was now no denial of Bryan's results, or his genius.

"As you can see," Bryan said with his performer's flair, "my modifications can do a lot more than blow up a couple of buildings. The bloody man in the fetal position there is Bill Jerrick, one of the Seven Dragons of the Violet Shadows. I just made quicker work of him than your Princes could make of one of the average troops."

"Indeed," uttered the King. He was more delighted than skeptical now, as he saw that getting out of bed for this was well worth it. "You have done better than my idiot sons ever could."

"Are we in need of further demonstration, Your Grace?" Bryan asked, though he used the transmission band to give his orders to the legions of Kingdom drones. Within a matter of hours, the other targets would likely be reduced to ash if he had his way, and he would be able to watch his vengeance unfold in real time.

"That will not be necessary," King Shane spoke. "Proceed with the attacks and monitor them closely. I will summon you to the Court later in the evening."

"As you wish, Your Grace," Bryan accepted, and once the nobles of the King's Court left the facility, he flashed a malicious grin at the screens before him.

****

December 25th, 2084, 9:12 a.m.,

Gunfire rained down over Atlanta as smoke and flames reached for the heavens. The geo-sensors in that region had all been disrupted by the tremors from the bombs, and with their signals jammed by the drones up above, there was no way to get in touch with the command center on Level X. The Waste Raiders screamed as they scrambled for every building and bunker they could find, and while some were fortunate to escape destruction, it wasn't common.

Lukas followed closely after his father Manny, both of them desperate to keep their optimism alive. Maybe this wouldn't last long. Maybe their troops would escape. Maybe the Kingdom just wanted to make a statement and scare off the Insurrection. Sudden screams that were silenced just as quickly proved them wrong. The thunderous crack of enemy guns only gave way to the terrible rumble of the bombs they dropped.

That indifferent electrical hum of the drones overhead drove Manny into a rage. They threatened his son without expression, without any sound except for the mechanical whirring that suggested this was simply their work. No doubt it was to echo the sentiment of the twisted Scarlet dog that gave their orders.

"Go on ahead, son," Manny commanded. At first Lukas couldn't formulate a response. He stared at his father's back as they propelled through the city ruins on their Hanzo Gear's strength. "I won't repeat myself, Lukas." His tone was stern, protective to the point of frustration. They both knew that there was little Manny could do in the face of the KDN, but if it meant buying his son a few extra minutes to get to safety, he'd try anyway.

"Pops, I—" The way Lukas' voice cracked as he started to speak was as a knife to Manny's heart.

"Go!" Lukas did what he could, and blasted past his father on the force of his boots and the pull of his chains. Once he'd gotten far enough away, he couldn't resist the urge to turn back, despite the fact that he knew better. The Wind Dragon ran left toward the Bank of Am and scaled it with a few quick blasts of his repulsors. He jumped off the side and onto the back of a low-flying drone. Manny pulled out his Reikiken, but the sudden rise in temperature attracted the surrounding drones. Five of them aimed for his position, and before the Kazeryu could get out of the way, they collided with him in a fiery mass of metal and flesh.

Lukas watched the wreckage fall from the sky. He heard a scream rip through the air, and only after he had to take a breath did he realize it came from him. He wanted to drop to his knees, wanted to mourn the loss of his father, but the echo of his last order rang through his mind. *Go,* his father had urged him, and for now that was all he allowed himself to focus on.

****

December 25th, 2084, 11:23 a.m.,

The sky went dark with the shadows of the drone armada. Shonda stood atop the outer wall of the city and barked orders at all the men, women and children below. The bombs hadn't dropped yet and the signals weren't jammed, so she coordinated with the Elders of the Kabuto to open their tunnels. But before long, the thunder of the bombs erupted through the city. Shonda was lucky enough to avoid most of the blast when the walls began to fall, and maneuvered her Hanzo Gear to get to a vantage point.

She knew that her options were limited, especially as more bombs fell on the scared and screaming. Still, she was the Fire Dragon and it was her job to do what she could to ensure that the last of them made it to shelter. She threw her kyoketsu-shoge into the air and lodged it into the hull of one of the metal drones. She grappled up, Reikiken already drawn. With a violent slash, she cut through the drone. The others that flew alongside it started to converge on her position, but with a kick of her repulsors and a circular slash of her titanium blades, she managed to cut through about three or four before she grappled onto a fifth.

She drove her aura sword into the nose end of the drone, and as another flock headed her way, she dove downward just before the collision. She glanced back up to see the drones' flight pattern uninterrupted. It didn't matter. The evacuation was just about done, and all she needed to do now was get to shelter herself.

The Hiryu tossed her chains towards the top of a nearby building and used them to guide her descent, then flipped forward so that her repulsors could cushion the flow. The second her feet landed on the rooftop, a bomb dropped just inches away, and with a helpless cry, Shonda and the building were no more.

****

December 25th, 2084, 11:49 a.m.,

“Absolutely not,” Vanessa Duncan said with steel behind her dark brown eyes. “It’s bad enough that I’ve lost contact with our garrisons in the Southern Wastes. Now you’re telling me you wanna go out there and fight against the Kingdom’s drones? Not a chance.” The entire mountain quaked from the impact of the exterior assault. Vanessa was angry, sad, worried, and a plethora of other emotions, none of which were assuaged by the present conversation.

“Look man,” Cal told her, which made the Shadow Dragon raise her eyebrow in challenge. Cal refused to back down. “I understand how bad this is, but you gotta trust me when I tell you I’m the only one who can beat them.”

“No,” Dre interjected, arms folded across his chest and head tilted to the side, “we don’t. You gotta listen to orders when they’re given, Cal.” Cal shot him a look.

“Even if those orders are gonna get us all killed? The mountain won’t hold up too much longer unless we do something. It can’t!” Cal saw that he was getting too worked up. He took a deep breath and calmed himself before he continued to address his adoptive grandfather and his superior officer. “The Lightbeams and I can handle this.” Vanessa met his eyes. She wanted so badly to believe him, but he was still young. He didn’t have the battle experience that she did, and if anything happened to him while John was away, there’s no way she wouldn’t have to deal with a furious Director later down the road. She shook her head, and Cal’s heart sank.

“No,” she said abrasively, and waved her hand as if to signal the dismissal of the subject. “You’re not going out there.”

“Oh, I am,” Cal retorted, “just against your orders. But hey, I’ll make sure to tell my pops this was your idea when I win.” He was quick to leave, while his courage still burned bright and before Vanessa or Dre could talk some sense into him.

****

December 25th, 2084, 12:04 p.m.,

John and his squad were almost home when the drones came into view. The Roan Mountain base was under fire. Smoke came up from the direction of Johnson City. Now the drones moved westward, with their presumed target being the Yoroi Alliance. Vanessa had told him that they'd run into trouble from the Reds. How foolish it was of him to just assume that they could handle it in some previously rehearsed formation. There was no way for him to tell how much damage had already been done.

The Director sped through the open terrain and narrowly evaded the bombs as they descended from the aircraft above. Callan and Zayvier followed suit on their transports, and skillfully escaped explosion after explosion as they chased after their leader. Serenity had about as much fortune, though a sudden stream of bullets made it infinitely harder to do so. James clutching her waist for dear life did nothing to help matters either. Ryan Morrisey cheered loudly from a sense of misplaced excitement as Tom Freeman guided their ShadowStalker through the increasingly rugged terrain. Erik, who brought up the rear of the formation, thought it was charming.

More gunfire. More bombs. The path they drove became less and less direct as the drones that watched them sought their destruction with vigorous determination. John could see the fire rain down on the mountain, could hear the rumble of the terrain on all sides as he drew nearer by the second, and his heart nearly burst from his chest as a result. Aaliyah's face shone fresh and brightly at the forefront of his mind. He needed, more than his own survival, more than the survival of his comrades, to know that his wife was alright. The lot of them had only just made it to the base of the mountain when John saw them: eight humanoid figures exploding from the summit of the mountain.

****

December 25th, 2084, 12:07 p.m.,

Cal knew that he only had a short amount of time if he was going to make this work. He had already switched his Kiringan to battle mode and summoned the Lightbeams for protection.

"Alright," he muttered to himself, "lets see what we got here. Thermal vision," he commanded the eye, but it was no use. The increased heat of the air around the mountain skewed the imaging and made it impossible to see what was happening. He groaned. "Link to Lightbeams, then," he said, and in the next second his left eye split the view into eight parts and took in the sights offered by his machines.

Almost immediately the drones started shooting at the Lightbeams. Cal took a second to pat himself on the back for installing neural receptors in each of their bodies before he proceeded to command them through the air. Each Lightbeam was equipped with a single high-focused repulsor in one hand for cutting through metal, two kyoketsu-shoge chains at the wrists, compact super-electromagnets, and a number of other toys that would make this a test like none other.

He compelled one of the Lightbeams to slice through the hull of one of the aircraft with its repulsor beam while another would meet it at ground level. Four others maintained a defensive perimeter at four points around the rest of the formation, and used their super-electromagnets to divert the flight paths of the enemy bullets. The two that remained alternated between their high-powered repulsors and kyoketsu-shoge to dispatch the oncoming drones.

"Register as Lightbeam Aerial Attack Formation Alpha," Cal shouted as his head began to throb from the split focus. The edges of his left eye lit green to confirm the order. "Maintain Formation Alpha." Green again. He mentally took command of the first two Lightbeams and had them carefully take the downed drone apart. There had to be something he could use and— "There you are," he sang. A small red node at the heart of the machine told him all he needed to know. The drones of the KDN operated on several different networks all operated by a central processing drone. Take out the CPD, you take out every drone it was connected to. "But how many of them are there," Cal wondered aloud. He shook his head. No sense worrying about that now.

"Lightbeams, switch to EMP mode," Cal ordered as the idea came alive in his mind. "Tune to a 40-mile radius." The edges of his left eye lit green again, and the heads of the Lightbeams split open to reveal thick antenna with bright blue lights at the top. They hummed for a moment as more oncoming drones did what they could to fill the vacated airspace that the Lightbeams had created.

All of a sudden, the bright blue lights flashed green, and one by one the drones started to fall from the sky. Cal hastily retreated to the mouth of the mountain base's opening, and with a smug look he watched as his handiwork took effect for miles around. "Merry Christmas," he said with a boyish laugh, and made his way back to the Tactical Level to get chewed out.

****

December 25th, 2084, 6:00 p.m.,

Bryan expected to be summoned to the Court's audience chamber, as had been the case all the times before. This time, however, he was summoned to the palace banquet hall to enjoy an evening meal with the King, Prince Nash, and the other members of the Court.

The servants ushered him in, and he was met with smiles from all the nobles sans the Prince. He smiled back, a twinge of darkness in their eyes that was fortunately mistaken for playfulness.

"This is a surprise," Bryan told the King with feigned humility. "What have I done to deserve such an honor as to dine with the King?" *This is the least you owe me, you arrogant bastard,* he thought. His heart thrashed about in his chest, but his face never showed it.

"You've brought pride back to my heart for the first time in years," said the King with a hearty laugh. The comment made Nash flush red with anger. "I haven't seen our enemies so out of sorts since the days I took to the battlefield personally, and that deserves a reward." Bryan raised an eyebrow, as King Shane demonstrated an uncharacteristic show of personality.

"And for your services, that reward is that you get to live," Nash spoke, motivated by his disdain and his fear of replacement. The time had long passed since he believed his father above such things. After all, his only brother was now on the run for conspiring against the Crown. King Shane slammed his hand against the table in anger.

"You dare speak for me, boy?" The room fell quiet, and Nash stiffened under his father's enraged gaze. "You presume to know the thoughts of your King?"

"No, fath—"

"Did I give you permission to speak?" The King's aggression was unparalleled, a much more fitting display as far as Bryan was concerned. "You, the loyal embarrassment to my family line? Dawn King's Daughter, how did I end up with two complete failures as my heirs? If it were possible…" The King looked over to Bryan, then back at Prince Nash. He then smiled back at Bryan and waved him closer. The wily rabbit moved closer, his puzzled smirk still firmly in place. "As I was saying before the boy interrupted me, I am in need of a new heir, one truly befitting of my legacy and all that I've done. Now I am in your debt for the rendering of your services. If I were to name you as this new heir to the throne…"

"Then I would graciously accept," Bryan answered with a humble bow. The King clapped him on the shoulder as he extended his hand to shake. Bryan looked down and noticed that King Shane still wore the ring he'd given him. He gladly shook with the kind of pain-inducing pressure that a warrior like Shane might expect of a man. The ring punctured his skin, and the injection was complete.

"Then I believe congratulations are in order," said the King. The others of the court stood to shake Bryan's hand, and to his delight, they all still wore their rings. It must've brought them great pleasure to boast of such triumph in such a fashionable way. That was, of course, the plan all along. Now, as they shook his hand and allowed him the freedom to press the ring into their flesh, they sealed their fate. The only one that didn't get a chance to shake his hand was Nash, who had stormed out of the room. Bryan mentally shrugged, as the failure of a Prince could be dealt with later if he proved to be worth the effort. Even if he didn't, Bryan had never liked him, so it might just happen anyway…

"Now," said the King, a massive smile plastered to his face, "we eat."

Bryan thought it so strange how the atmosphere had changed. Just a few hours prior, everyone in this room hated him. The King had threatened his life on several occasions. But now, because of his careful manipulation of Nash's failures juxtaposed with his own technological and tactical genius, Bryan had ascended to a position he'd never believed possible. So yes, he ate plenty and yes, he smiled and laughed with the nobles of the Court. For this would likely be the last time he saw them alive…

****

December 27th, 2084, 5:22 a.m.,

Bryan sat in the chair across from the King's bed. He'd been roused from his sleep just an before and summoned to the monarch's side by his daughter, who had noticed that the King's health had begun to fail him since the Christmas festivities. Bryan heard from the physicians by the door that he'd been throwing up, that his body was sore and he wasn't quite himself. For what they knew, any number of things could be wrong with him and there was no telling if they'd be able to save him. It took everything Bryan had not to smile.

"What's happened," asked the new heir to the throne. His brow furrowed in mock concern as the pale blue ghost of his son Jaden played in the King's hair.

"I…" the King wheezed, and then took a moment to adjust to the wave of nausea. "I don't know. I think I've been—"

"Poisoned?" Bryan finished the thought, which drew a deeply worried glare from the King of the Reds. Bryan could no longer resist the urge to smile. He looked up at the guards, his daughter among them, and told them, "Give us the room." They did, for how could they disobey? He was the heir, and with the King on his deathbed, it was Bryan's word that was absolute. The door closed behind them, and Bryan got up to pace around the predictably scarlet-colored room. The furniture had gold accents, and the coffee table not far from where he sat bore a deep brown that really tied the room together. "You know, ricin is very hard to detect," the darkened rabbit started up again. "That is, if you don't know you've been exposed to it."

"What have you done to me," the King demanded against his weakened physique. The complete and utter joy in Bryan's eyes terrified him.

"See, that's the problem with you people. You, Emiko, John, Kincaid, your nobles, you all think that the rest of us have to play your little game because you have such lofty titles. You build your kingdoms on the backs of people like me, who only want to live out my days with the right to choose what's right for me. You set the bricks of your palaces with the blood of people like my son Jaden, whom you send out to die for your half-baked causes and your shameless propaganda. So I took your game and I changed the rules. I earned your trust, improved your systems to slaughter people I've loved for my whole life and you, *you,* Your Grace, gave me something I never thought I'd get my hands on. You gave me power. An entire kingdom with the military means to bring all of Providence to heel. So thank you for being so damn easy to manipulate."

"Your son…" there was an irate upward inflection amid the coughing. "You chose to end *my* life to avenge your dead brat?"

"What the hell is your life to me? Huh? You miserable sack of white supremacist sh—" Bryan raised his hand to strike the King, but calmed himself when the ghost of Jaden looked on him disapprovingly. "You took my world from me. You, your damned nobles, the Insurrection, the Alliance, the Kabuto, you *all* took everything that was important to me and burned it to ash right in front of my face. So now I'm taking everything from you. Now I'm gonna see to it that every single one of you pays for my son's death. And I'm starting with you and your nobles."

King Shane coughed violently for a while, his eyes locked on Bryan the entire time. Vomit soon took its place and shut his soul-crushing gray orbs. When it stopped, however, his eyes did not open. A few moments later, his breathing grew shallow, and eventually came to a permanent rest. Now all that was once Shane's belonged to Bryan.

"Time to start round two," the new King mumbled, then walked into the hall to alert the guards.

Appendix 1
GLOSSARY

- **Hanran no Ryu:** "Rebel Dragon." The Master Name given to Darius Hamlin.
- **Hanzo Gear:** Named for Hattori Hanzo, the legendary shinobi that saved the life of Ieyasu Tokugawa from Mitsuhide Akechi following the fall of Nobunaga Oda, the Hanzo Gear is composed of a hooded cloak filled with a shock-absorbent gel to resist bullets, a menpo mask that covers the lower half of the face and connects to a visor that displays necessary information, and a pair of kyoketsu-shoge. Standard-issue Hanzo Gear also includes a pair of repulsor boots that allow the user to cover greater distances, jump higher, change directions in mid-flight, and soften landings. The cornerstone of the Hanzo Gear, however, is the Reikiken.
- **Hiryu:** "Fire Dragon." One of the Seven Dragons of the Violet Shadows. The name is given to a dedicated master of the Hiryu Form.
    - Practitioners of the Form tend to be wild, but controlled. Their movements are ferocious, brisk, and powerful to end the fight as quickly as possible.
- **Kabuto Sanctuary:** One of the Four Factions of Prevalence. Pacifistic in nature, the Kabuto Sanctuary specializes in demolitions, espionage and sabotage. They philosophize that no fighting needs to be done if the enemy's equipment falls apart.
- **Kageryu:** "Shadow Dragon." One of the Seven Dragons of the Violet Shadows. The name is given to a dedicated master of the Kageryu Form.
    - Practitioners of the Kageryu Form prioritize disarmament of their opponents, wide swings and fighting in close quarters.

- **Kazeryu:** "Wind Dragon." One of the Seven Dragons of the Violet Shadows. The name is given to a dedicated master of the Kazeryu Form.
    - Practitioners of the Form prioritize a balanced approach to combat and can make use of a single Reikiken or, more famously, a staff made up of the two. The inspiration for the staff was taken from an old movie from the 1990s.
- **Kiringan**: "Monster's Eye/Kirin's Eye." A piece of advanced biotechnology that syncs with the user's optic receptors and functions like a human eye, albeit with added features.
- **Kiryu:** "Tree/Wood Dragon." One of the Seven Dragons of the Violet Shadows. The name is given to a dedicated master of the Kiryu Form.
    - Practitioners of the Form take a more acrobatic approach to fighting, a trait that is greatly accented by the mobility of the Hanzo Gear. Their movements are forceful, aggressive and precise.
- **Kyoketsu-shoge:** Long chains with blades attached to the ends. The Yaiba Insurrection versions of the kyoketsu-shoge are heat-treated to resist the high temperatures of the Reikiken and diamond-shaped titanium blades strong enough to resist gunfire. They can be (and often are) used as grappling hooks.
- **Rairyu:** "Lightning Dragon." One of the Seven Dragons of the Violet Shadows. The name is given to a dedicated master of the Rairyu Form and exceptional leader among their peers.
    - Practitioners of the Form prioritize body economy, speed over power, and extreme precision. Rairyu users are noted for their elegant combat style, fluid blade work, and one-handed style.
- **Reikibo:** A staff made of two Reikiken conjoined at the hilt.

- **Reikiken:** "Aura Sword." Named for the heatwave that radiates from the blade, the Reikiken is the signature weapon of the Yaiba Insurrection. Thermal amplifiers in the hilt transfer heat from the user's hand through to the blade at much greater temperatures, which grants the weapon the ability to burn or melt through most substances with ease.
- **Sasori:** The Grandmaster of the Legendary Founders, Sasori-sensei was solely responsible for imparting the samurai and shinobi wisdom from which the Yaiba, Yoroi and Kabuto blossomed. It is because of him that there is still a chance for freedom.
- **Scarlet Kingdom (Kingdom Scarlet):** One of the Four Factions of Prevalence. The reorganization of the United States after the fall of its democracy that seeks to bring the other factions on the continent under subjugation. Rarely sees people of color as worthy of recognition on merit alone.
    - **Scarlet Scourge:** An all-female death squad of seven members, the Scarlet Scourge has gained a reputation in the Kingdom for being able to pull off missions that the general forces cannot. They are brutal, merciless, and determined to maintain the station that they have gained for themselves. AVOID AT ALL COSTS.
- **Sensei:** "The one who has gone before." Sensei is a term used by the Yaiba, Yoroi and Kabuto in reference to anyone of superior rank, though not because of the rank alone. To be called "sensei" is to be acknowledged by one's subordinates as being wise as much as strong, and capable of leading one's students down the proper path. It is often interchanged with Master, Elder, or Agent, depending on which of the Factions one finds themselves in.

- **<u>Suiryu:</u>** "Water Dragon." One of the Seven Dragons of the Violet Shadows. The name is given to a dedicated master of the Suiryu Form.
    - Practitioners of the Form are noted for their purely defensive movements. They prioritize fluidity, timing, protection, body economy, and have an uncanny propensity to transform their defensive flourishes into subtle but devastating attacks.
- **<u>Tetsuryu:</u>** "Metal Dragon." A nickname formerly given to the newest members of the Violet Shadows that has been jokingly reassigned to Cal Richmond due to his affinity for technological developments.
- **<u>Tsuchiryu:</u>** "Earth Dragon." One of the Seven Dragons of the Violet Shadows. The name is dedicated to a master of the Tsuchiryu Form.
    - Practitioners of the Form are noted for their grounded stance, wide swings, and stunning movements that fluctuate between speed and power. These fighter intend to press the attack regardless of circumstance.
- **<u>Usagi no Kamikaze:</u>** "Rabbit of the Divine Wind." The Master Name given to Bryan Piccio for his unorthodox fighting style totally dependent on coordinating his kyoketsu-shoge and repulsor boots to fast-paced and deadly results.
- **<u>Yaiba Insurrection:</u>** One of the Four Factions of Prevalence. The Yaiba Insurrection was the first of the factions to put the Scarlet Kingdom on the defensive through purely offensive means. Their victory at the White Ruins Miracle changed the perspectives of the other faction leaders, and established their Violet Shadows as a military force to be reckoned with.
    - **<u>Violet Shadows:</u>** The general military forces of the Yaiba Insurrection, named for the black and purple of their uniforms. The glow of the Reikiken often skews visibility of them, so they look like shades to

enemies. Like the Yoroi Alliance and Kabuto Sanctuary, the Insurrection derives their military training from the Legendary Founders' samurai and military experience. When paired with their technological innovations, the Shadows prove to be more than a threat for those ignorant enough to challenge them.

- **Yoroi Alliance:** One of the Four Factions of Prevalence. Known for guerilla warfare and demolitions, the Yoroi Alliance has a stellar reputation for their trap mastery and impregnability. They are a very private, secluded faction that is extremely wary of outsiders.